"Parker Hudson scores again a picture of the demonic influence that is trying to take over our individual lives and our nation. Parker's storytelling creates a visual imprint that will pull at your emotions, and you will not put the book down. I highly recommend *Nation On The Edge* to anyone who loves thrillers and political intrigue."

Scot Sinnen

"I found *Nation on the Edge* to be exciting, riveting, educational, timely and filled with hope. I could not put it down and read it straight through. I loved the powerful ending."

Janis Chapman

"Parker's done it again! He's captured the essence of spiritual warfare in a way that doesn't cause the reader to cower in fright at the weapons of the enemy, but leaves you feeling emboldened and confident in the power of prayer and its conquering strength. You will be encouraged to pray without ceasing for your loved ones, your friends, strangers and those who govern us, as the war for our souls unfolds."

Carla Smith

"As one searches to understand the events unfolding in our culture, *Nation On The Edge* gives an excellent explanation of the unseen spiritual forces shaping our society through those whom they have deceived, as the battle rages for the heart and mind of every individual."

Stan Carder

"Hudson gives a clear picture of the spiritual powers, both darkness and light, that influence our human behavior and action. This is a 'must read' because it speaks of where we are as a nation today, and the Gospel preaching church must become a voice of Truth, leading to transformation and revival."

Bill Honaker

"In Parker Hudson's *Nation on the Edge,* a fictional but astonishingly realistic and timely story set mostly in modern-day Washington, the reader observes the inner relationships of agencies, companies and the media that can work for or against our freedoms. The description of heavenly angels and fallen demons battling in the spiritual realm for the very souls of these various players, as well as a remnant of Christians holding to and speaking Truth in the nation's capital, make for increasing tension until the very end."

Zanese Duncan

"The characters, events and dialogue not only taught me important lessons but also gave me example after example how to live a kinder and gentler Christian life, while still speaking and sharing the Gospel message with love and patience."

Kathy Paparelli

"*Nation On the Edge* deals with our country, our culture, spiritual warfare, and the effort to preserve America's Godly founding principles. It portrays good and evil in a gripping and realistic way that will not let you put it down. The book is extremely well written and pulls you into the world behind the world. Simply a must read in today's times."

Currell Berry

"The plot of *Nation on Edge* is eerily realistic and plausible in today's crazy world around Washington. Evil is around every corner, but true Christian goodness also abounds. Parker is a great storyteller, and this is his best book."

Bick Cardwell

"*Nation On The Edge* connects dots that I frankly had never considered."

Bo Jackson

# NATION ON THE EDGE

---

1. *http://www.parkerhudson.com/*

Dedicated to every American who will, with grace and civility, stand firm and uphold God's Truths against the manifold lies of the Deceiver.

# Nuremberg, Germany
# Wednesday, October 16th
# 1946

The three gallows stood ready in the dark and dusty gymnasium at the Nuremberg jail compound. Shortly after 1 a.m. former Foreign Minister Joachim von Ribbentrop entered the building as if in a trance and slowly mounted the thirteen steps to the platform. He was met by U.S. Master Sergeant John Woods, his executioner.

The official witnesses in the gym stood and took off their hats, a priest prayed, the noose was tightened, and Ribbentrop began to utter his last words about world peace. No human could see the hundreds of spiritual participants above him, filling the room to the rafters.

Proklor, one of Satan's key princes, hovered there effortlessly, suspended by spiritual forces just above the solemn gathering, surrounded by the leaders of his personal army. His large size and the gruesome scars from the Great Heavenly War on his face and hands proclaimed that Proklor was a fallen angel of great standing. Only Temno, his adjutant for two millennia, and a few trusted generals, dared to get close. The other demons circled discreetly around their leader, attracted by the great spectacle about to begin beneath them. And they could see that they were safe. Their spiritual eyes revealed almost no vectors of spiritual light, since the few answered prayers that did arrive from heaven that night were sucked down into the dark vortex which the demons created.

Like all demons, Proklor's army succeeded best when they adopted the dress, habits and speech of the targets they studied and whispered to. So they were dressed mostly in the clothes and uniforms found in Europe at the end of World War II. "It's been a great run," Temno said to the Prince, as Sergeant Woods placed the black hood over Ribbentrop's head.

"Yes, yes, it has. Who would have thought?—What, less than ten years ago—that we would accomplish so much? He—Ribbentrop—was living well in London as Hitler's Ambassador. Now this. How far he has fallen. Bespor, go and speak to him. Then be ready."

Bespor, one of the generals in the front row, broke off and stood invisibly next to the former Nazi government official, whispering in his ear. "You've been terribly betrayed! You are the victim of weaklings who don't know the truth. This is so unfair."

Another demonic general, Legat, leaned closer to Proklor. "I hear it's 50 million killed in Europe alone. And 6 million Jews! See what that does for starting a new Israel. All under your leadership, my lord."

Proklor nodded. "It's amazing what these people will do when we lie to them. Just the Corporal and a few of his friends to start with. Amazing. So many people believed what we told them. And acted! So here we are, full circle. These ten were some of the best. It's a shame it has to end."

The trapdoor sprang open and Ribbentrop dropped. The rope snapped tight.

Bespor floated down to the curtained area below the platform and emerged a few moments later holding the dead leader's startled and struggling soul, the terror on his face clearly visible to the spiritual assembly. The demons cheered and laughed. Ribbentrop, looking up into their faces, gasped, as the reality of eternity hit him full force. Bespor handed him to a lesser demon, who led the unbelieving Foreign Minister off to hear his fate at the Judgment Seat.

As Ribbentrop's body still swung on the rope, Field Marshal General Wilhelm Keitel, in a well pressed uniform with gleaming boots, briskly walked up the second scaffold. In under two hours that morning the ten men found guilty at the Nuremberg Major War Crimes Trial were executed by Sergeant Woods; Proklor and his horde watched and remembered each one.

When the last of the ten, Arthur Seyss-Inquart, the former Commissioner for the Netherlands, was pronounced dead, the witnesses began to leave the hall. The demons overhead, used to taking orders, turned toward Proklor.

Just then they felt a spiritual cleaving beneath them and heard the sound of an approaching tempest. The spiritual darkness under them began to swirl, and several terrible princes—Proklor's equal or worse—emerged from the pit and moved the lesser spirits back.

With a loud thunderclap the Prince of Lies himself rose and took his place in the middle of the gathering; Proklor was directly in front of him, trying not to tremble.

Satan addressed his assembled army with a sound like the killing wind of a hundred hurricanes. "Well done, Proklor. Well done, all of you. Now we need your skills in a new place—America. Our forces have not done well there—the Light shines even brighter, and they follow Him. The Soviet Union and China will be important, but they are already dark, and ready. America is our last challenge, and I have chosen you to subdue it. When we control America, we will control the world, and the Light will be extinguished."

The demons' eyes reflected a thousand bolts of spiritual lightning, diverting their gaze from their master, so close. Their crowding reflected, echoed and amplified the piercing sound like a thousand claps of thunder.

"Take your veteran army there and lie to them, as you did here. You, Prince Proklor, will be in charge. You will replace Pitka, who has not had a new idea since slavery, and is finished. You will have free rein.

"But they are different. You must be more subtle. They must not worship or revere us—at least not these next generations. Instead, they must worship and revere *themselves*! They must think that we don't exist—that nothing spiritual is real or important. They will then trust in their own might, not His. When you succeed, they will forget Him.

"They will tear their nation apart, all on their own. We will watch. They will kill their children. Kill their old people. Kill themselves. Lust after each other. Do whatever they want until they destroy themselves. Two generations, at most three. They will be led like lambs to slaughter."

He paused, then turned slowly as he spoke to all of Proklor's forces. "Your mission there is once again to destroy the truth with your lies. Now go. We will await your success!"

As the assembled demonic army watched, there was a huge, terrifying roar, like the combined screams of a million tortured souls, and Satan descended again beneath the scaffolds.

No one living in Washington on the following Sunday morning realized what was happening; the dark and dreadful storm clouds gathering over the Mall between the Capitol and the Washington Monument were invisible to human eyes. The demonic shapes massed into a brooding, living tempest of malice and death, every demon hating the Name and outraged that any human would escape their own fate.

Up and down they swirled and hissed, increasing in numbers and in the intensity of their writhing until the dark mass resembled a monstrous spiritual thunderhead, poised over the U.S. capital on the banks of the Potomac River.

Their leaders, Prince Proklor and his key generals, had chosen Sunday morning and this place for their unprecedented rendezvous because few angels would be in the city, and they could control the spiritual battlefield with their huge numbers.

"You are here to lie to them and their children with voices of 'human reason,' progress and emotion, until they no longer hear or know the truth.

"You have your assignments. Many of you will deploy to other cities as street leaders and sector leaders, to destroy families. Some of you will infuse their new television, and their movies. Their teachers' colleges are the key to upending their education system. Most of you will stay right here, the seat of power, to mislead their leadership, and through them, the nation. Let us begin."

With a shattering clap of thunder the invisible storm cloud spun outward, ever widening its diameter, until it covered the entire city. Then many of the demons began leaving, thousands heading out for their assigned locations across the nation: universities, newspapers, seminaries, courts, Hollywood, school boards. When only those demons assigned to remain in Washington were left in the cloud, the storm spun inward again, converging on their leader. Proklor rose high above the Mall, and his demons scattered to their assignments across the city.

A large contingent filled the Capitol, turning the area under the dome into an invisible broiling, sulfurous mass, awaiting the return of the lawmakers on Monday, eager to plant their voices of deception that God was no longer important. Many took up posts in the White House, warning each other about the angels which might show up when the simpleton president actually prayed. All across the city they went, fanning out into every agency and every office.

Many of the most senior demons descended on the Supreme Court, turning the marble building dark with their presence. They knew that if only a handful of these men, unaccountable to anyone, believed their lies, then the nation would be diverted to a course which their Master assured them meant certain destruction for these detestable people.

It would be Evil's greatest victory, and the Earth's darkest hour.

# 1

*It yet remains a problem to be solved in human affairs, whether any free government can be permanent, where the public worship of God, and the support of religion, constitute no part of the policy or duty of the state in any assignable shape. The future experience of Christendom, and chiefly of the American states, must settle this problem.*

Joseph Story

## Washington, D.C.

## The Near Future

Friday, September 11

"How would you destroy America?" President Alexander Rhodes asked the group seated around the conference table in the Roosevelt Room at the White House that Friday morning.

Tom Sullivan sat next to his boss, Olivia Haas, the Head of Cyber Security, at the end of the table.

Turning to the Vice President, the Secretary of Defense, and the Chairman of the Joint Chiefs in the chairs nearest him, the president added, "I'm sure we all agree that Climate Change is the greatest long-term threat, and we've been battling that since we took office. But I promised the Speaker we'd do a full assessment. Today is the anniversary of 9/11, and she and I are flying to the NATO meeting in Prague this weekend, so I want to review our progress with her.

"Tell your teams to consider that question with no preconceptions. How would *you* hobble, or do the greatest damage to, our nation? In two weeks we'll meet at Camp David to consider what you've come up with. Then we'll work together to find solutions—across disciplines and across the aisle. Hopefully she and the other more conservative members of Congress will help, and be satisfied."

Peter Sloane, a retired Admiral and former Deputy Director of the CIA, now the president's National Security Advisor, addressed them from his chair across the table, "Put your best people on this. It's clear with today's technology there are many ways to disrupt, or even bring down, our nation, and we need your combined expertise to focus on them."

The president rose. "So if anyone has any questions, talk to Peter, and he'll coordinate the presentations. Think out of the box. If you'll excuse me, we're flying up to New York for the 9/11 Remembrance and then to Prague tomorrow night, and we've got a few things to do. Thank you."

As the meeting broke up, Olivia Haas, writing a note, turned to Tom and said quietly, "You'll head our team. Besides already handling a lot of threats, you're our COG officer, and your experience in banking should give you a leg up. Bring in whomever you want, inside or out, and let's give our colleagues a compelling list of how the nation could be wounded."

Tom, nine years beyond a Masters Degree in Computer Science from Oxford as a Huff Scholar, nodded. "I'll give our team a heads up, and we'll begin right away."

"Good. I'll be flying with the president, the First Lady, and the Speaker to the NATO Summit. Hopefully our allies will agree to the tighter protocols we've proposed to stop the hacking into government databases." She smiled and stood. "But of course you wrote them."

He nodded and turned to leave. "Travel safe. We'll prioritize a grid with the threats, solutions, and responsible agencies."

"I know, as usual, you'll be all-in. Be ready to brief us on Wednesday."

As Tom walked down the hall, he ran into President Rhodes and Vice President Evan Carpenter, walking with their aides.

"Tom, how are you?"

"Fine, Mr. President. Good meeting."

"The conservatives are always worried about us being attacked, but I guess we don't want to be blindsided. By the way, how's your Mom?"

"She's fine, sir. She's on several boards now, trying to improve healthcare delivery in Africa and Asia."

President Rhodes smiled. "Good. Janet was a solid Congresswoman, even if a bit too far to the right with her policies. But a lot of common sense and heart. I'm glad you take after her."

"I'm not sure about that, but thank you."

Vice President Carpenter smiled. "We were in Congress together for four years, starting with President Harrison, and much of what we passed in those days as bipartisan wins was thanks to her persuasive powers."

"I certainly understand those."

The president added, "Would you like to come with us to Prague? See the NATO Summit up close?"

"Thank you, Mr. President. Olivia'll be there, and she put me in charge of coming up with our group's input for the Camp David meeting. So I better stay here."

"OK. I know you'll keep us on track. You're a thorough guy. Give us your thoughtful input on threats—current and long term. Maybe NATO next year." As he started to move on, he added, "Please tell your Mom and Dad hello for us."

"Yes sir, I will."

Tom walked through the tunnel to his office in the Eisenhower Executive Office Building, checking his cell phone. As he was answering a text, his phone vibrated.

"Jenny, what's up out in the real world?"

"Here in Lower Manhattan it's OK. How's my favorite public servant?"

"Wishing you were here so we could pick up where we left off."

"That *was* a pretty amazing weekend. And that's, like, why I'm calling. The bank is sending me to D.C. in a couple of weeks for a conference on 'Supporting Women of All Genders'. I hope you'll be around."

"Of course. But I just got an assignment that could be really important. And how many genders of women are there?"

"I thought all your assignments were important," she teased. "But what's that got to do with my conference? And I have no idea about the conference. I just know I was pretty proud to get this one-gender woman thing through the Naval Academy."

"Let me be clear that I'm all in favor of your gender. And you know how I am when I get focused."

"Yeah. Focus with a capital F. No loose ends."

"Yes. Anyway, this one's huge, and right now all the ends are loose."

"Busy, busy. And when are you running for president?"

He smiled as he flashed his ID for the uniformed guard at the entrance to his area. "I don't think I'm old enough. Maybe one day. Though I'd have to learn to put up with all the bull and the constant loose ends. And they tell me I'm great with plans but not so good with people."

"You were pretty good with me."

"Mmm. That's different. A skill. I probably focused on your gender details. In fact, I'm sure I did."

"I think it's a natural talent I should help tease out—if you can find time in your busy schedule."

He stopped outside his team's unmarked door in the hallway, remembering Jenny's athletic torso partially covered by a sheet when she visited him a month ago. "OK. Come on. It'll be good. But right now I gotta tell my guys that their weekend just got very busy."


Callie Sawyer's Persian American roots were evident in her jet black hair, dark blue eyes, and extra height. A few male heads turned as Callie entered the bistro off K Street, looking for her lunch appointment, Emily Schofield, an African American of similar height who was standing near the Order sign and working on her smartphone. Emily glanced up, waved, and finished her text.

The two women, Emily a little older at thirty, both dressed conservatively like the other young professionals filling the restaurant, smiled and shook hands.

"Try the Polynesian Chicken Wrap," Emily suggested as they turned to get in line.

"Thanks. My first time." Callie adjusted the shoulder strap on her large journalist's bag as she reached for a tray. A few minutes later they settled into a back corner table with their sandwiches and iced tea.

"I'm really glad you can join us tomorrow night," Emily said, putting sweetener in her tea. "Seth's birthday parties are awesome."

"My sitter can stay late with Grace, so I should be all set. You've known Seth a while?"

"He, two other guys and I were apartment mates when we first came to DC eight years ago. We all do different stuff now, but they're, like, great guys, and we've stayed close. My husband does the parkruns with them."

Callie cut her wrap. "So Seth's a producer with The News Network. What about the other two?"

"Clayton Hunt is at The Pentagon for Homeland Security. When we first met, he had the apartment; he's in the Marines. He chases really bad guys. He's a little older—married to Andrea; she administers the Trusted Traveler program at Homeland. They say he looks for bad guys and she looks for good guys. They're expecting." She smiled. "Who I really want you to meet is Tom Sullivan."

Callie's next bite stopped in mid-air. "And why is that?"

"Because I think you two will hit it off. He's Number Two in Cybersecurity at the White House. Very smart. Tall, like you. He can be a little intense. He likes rules and order in his life, but he's also a lot of fun. When you and I met a month ago, I thought of him and you."

"Actually, I think I know who he is. It's a long story, but my landlord, who's also my best friend and mentor, worked with my father in real estate in Atlanta. She knows Tom's family from a long time ago, and I think she suggested we get together when I first moved here. But we never did. And he doesn't have a girlfriend?"

"He runs through them pretty quickly. But if anyone can slow him down, I think it's you."

"Wait 'til he finds out I've got an eight-year-old daughter and a crazy job myself. Those don't exactly add to the order in one's life."

"We'll see. Anyway, we're meeting at Seth's at six. Seth always insists on grilling."

"OK. Thanks for asking me." Callie took a sip of tea. "Now, back to our subject du jour. What does Senator Bradshaw think about limiting genetic research?"

"Is this on the record, or for background?"

Callie smiled and leaned forward. "You're his staff's Communications Director. Which do you prefer?"

"And you run a journal on genetic research, so I better be accurate. Let's go for background now, and we can be on the record later."

"OK, good. Now that the Summer Recess is over and there are reports of human-animal gene splicing in China to create a chimera, will Senator Bradshaw co-sponsor legislation to prohibit the same thing here?"

Emily thought for a moment. "Maybe. But it's complicated in an election year. Many of our supporters are excited about the possibility to skip some of Evolution's steps and go right to a better outcome."

"Really? How would you know you'd done that, since Evolution is supposed to be random?"

"Well, I'm not sure. That's why I need to do some checking."

"Fair enough. Just let me know."


Balzor invisibly circled, watched and listened to their conversation. Like most gathering spots in the nation's capital, the restaurant was filled with demons, shadowing their charges, and the spiritual darkness was almost complete. Balzor was the most senior fallen angel present, and the others moved aside as he focused on Emily.

Balzor had been in the third row at the Nuremberg gathering in 1946. During the war he had volunteered for duty overseeing the gas chambers at Treblinka—in just three months he had streamlined the Nazis' mass killing system with incredible efficiency, but his specialty had been in convincing "regular" Germans, and particularly the leaders of the Lutheran Church, that the Fuhrer's changes were reasonable and patriotic, so they should not question them. Since arriving in America he had been a sector leader in several cities.

After a debacle twenty years earlier in which he was wrongly blamed when prayers and the ineptness of his subordinates had saved Tom Sullivan's father from the dark future he deserved, Balzor had feared being sent to the Abyss, and had in fact been demoted to a village near

Moscow. But with the explosion of the world's population and the increased pressure on the fixed number of fallen angels to produce results, he had won a reprieve a year later and been sent to Washington.

For the last three years he had been assigned by Bespor to lead the team in the Senate, focusing on Senator Henry Bradshaw, the senior Senator from California, for whom Emily Schofield worked as Communications Director. Bradshaw was a leader in the progressive party that narrowly held the majority in the Senate for President Rhodes; the more conservative party controlled the House, led by Speaker Rebecca Gordon.

Beyond his political views, Senator Bradshaw was actually one of the dark forces' greatest long-term successes, involving decades of work to harden his heart against anything spiritual. Building on this general foundation of questioning anything to do with God, Balzor's three years of reinforcing the lying voices deep inside the politician meant Bradshaw's exaggerated feelings of *Pride, Control* and *Superiority* were virtually permanent, and therefore they controlled his actions even when no demon was present to whisper to him.

The rigidity of the senator's spiritual heart meant that the usual ways God's truth could transform a person—through believers' prayers diminishing the demons' internally planted voices, or through believers speaking God's truth—would have little impact.

Balzor was quite proud of their accomplishments with Senator Bradshaw, along with about thirty other senators of both parties—Washington was awash in the voices of *Self-Congratulation* and *Pride*. He didn't worry much about losing any of this group to the Light—they rejected Him as irrelevant, almost as completely as Balzor hated Him. And he and his fellow demons were always looking for ways to expand this key group, including the senators' senior staff members, like Emily Schofield, who was almost theirs herself.

Given his seniority, Senator Bradshaw was elected by his peers to be the President Pro Tem of the Senate, with significant help from Balzor and his counterparts in other senators' offices. Bradshaw was therefore the Senate's ceremonial presiding officer whenever the Vice President,

Evan Carpenter, was not in attendance. Balzor loved to hover next to him in the chamber, whispering lies and encouragements.

Balzor studied Senator Bradshaw and his staff every day, and he routinely planted or reinforced thoughts and images in their minds, including Emily's. He had followed Emily to her lunch meeting because Callie Sawyer was a known believer—every spiritual being in the café could see the bright light shining in her—one of only three there that day. So he hated any possibility of Callie interrupting Emily's steady progress to a full secular rejection of anything spiritual. At this point, after a childhood in and out of the church, Emily was quite comfortable as a typical skeptic of her generation—right where Balzor wanted her—with no faith at all and no spiritual light. The hardening process was well underway.

But when Emily mentioned Tom Sullivan to Callie, it deeply concerned Balzor. Like all demons, Balzor hated every human. But Balzor especially hated Richard Sullivan, Tom's father, for the events of twenty years earlier. Richard had then infected his wife and children with his faith. A disaster. So anything that harmed or sidelined Richard Sullivan, Janet or their children was of great interest to Balzor.

He had therefore been interested when Tom wound up in D.C. Though the White House staff was not Balzor's direct responsibility—they were Nepravel's—Balzor kept up with Tom through Tom's eight-year friendship with Emily. At their nightly meetings, Balzor regularly asked Nepravel about Tom and offered advice on how to keep the tiny spiritual light, which sometimes flickered inside the young man, virtually out, dimmed by peer pressure, pride, temptations, and success at nearly everything Tom had tried since high school.

But tonight he would have to warn Nepravel that Tom Sullivan was about to meet a strong believer in Callie Sawyer that weekend. Nepravel needed to reinforce the young man's skepticism with the right lying voices.

As the two women discussed human cloning in the restaurant, Balzor wondered whether a human clone would have a soul. He'd have to ask Bespor at one of their nightly meetings.

Neither Balzor nor any other demons had been present at the White House meeting on security that morning. Despite the president's private agnosticism, he remained a member of a mainline denomination, and the spiritual blaze from the constant prayers for him and his staff during the day made it nearly impossible for a demon, even a prince like Proklor, to remain there for long. But reports from demons in the darker, more friendly staff offices around the city were filtering in, and Balzor imagined that Prince Proklor would be livid about the president's call today to look more deeply into particular threats. He knew he would find out that night.

Senator Bradshaw was not returning to San Francisco that weekend, since his Senate seat was not being contested in the upcoming midterm elections, but instead had a series of planning meetings set up with other Progressive members of his party, including three dinners at his Georgetown row house.

That Friday afternoon he was in his office finishing a video call with Andrew Boswell, the CEO of Juggle, the California-based, incredibly successful search engine. Over the past two decades the senator's career and Juggle had grown together, with Boswell funding every election and every cause in which Senator Bradshaw had an interest, and the senator returning the favor with legislation which ensured that Juggle would not face any difficult regulations or government intervention. Juggle, and its peers in the California high-tech/large donor category, headed up the one industry in which Senator Bradshaw was an ardent supporter of a very free market.

Drew Boswell had also helped two of Senator Bradshaw's three grown children land high paying Board seats with several companies at home and abroad, supporting the family income. He was almost part of the family.

And, by coincidence, the head of Juggle's lobbying efforts, Logan Schofield, was Emily's husband.

"Thank you, Drew, thank you," the Senator said to Boswell from behind his large desk, as he heard a knock on his office door. "It's wonderful that your trade group will be supporting so many of my colleagues in their re-elections this fall. I'll be sure to have the right person at party headquarters contact your staff on Monday. And we won't forget your help."

Emily opened the door and looked in. He waved her forward. "Yes, have a great weekend. And thank you again. Say hello to Sally." He ended the call and smiled, making a note on the pad in front of him.

His last office meeting that Friday afternoon was with Seth Cohen, a young producer with The News Network. Despite their age difference, the two men shared many policy priorities, and Seth had asked through his friend Emily to meet in the Senator's office in preparation for a series he was working on about The Silent Progressive Majority.

Bradshaw rose from his large antique desk and smiled when Emily and Seth entered. Unseen to them, Balzor stood just behind the Senator and nodded to Obman, assigned to The News Network, as he came in with the young producer. Balzor and Obman went back millennia together—Obman's reputation dated from his singular work with Potiphar's wife. Balzor said to Obman, "We need these three working together."

"Seth, Emily tells me you're celebrating a birthday," Bradshaw said, as he walked around the desk to shake the younger man's hand and to point him toward a small conference table.

"Yes, sir," he replied, taking the seat offered as the senior Senator sat across from them. "Thirty-four. Some friends, including Emily, are coming over tomorrow to grill out with us."

"I was thirty-three over half my life ago. Now we have two daughters in their thirties, and our son is forty. Well done. Hang in there, and maybe you'll again see rational politics and reasonable policies before you reach my age."

Reacting to his words, Obman turned up Seth's internal voice of *Disdain*. "I hope so, and that's what our next series is about. We hope you'll be one of the on-camera advocates for President Rhodes' progressive policies to undo so many years of 'Christian conservatives' in the White House."

"Yes, of course. It's been a battle these two years since Rhodes was elected, with a split Congress. The upcoming midterms are the key to making real progress."

"We hope to give him—and you in the Congress—a serious boost with our series on The Silent Progressive Majority."

"I like your approach. I can remember when President Nixon started using that phrase about the Silent Majority, and I agree. Thanks to decades of hard work in schools, corporations, the media and politics, there's now a majority who think the dismantling of government programs has gone too far, really hurting people. Everyone benefits when people are better educated and have more money in their pockets to spend. The government can provide both, and should. And, of course, level the playing field— we have to continue to push back against White Privilege, Gender Privilege, and the whole range of Social Injustices. Diversity, Equity, Inclusion are key."

Balzor whispered to Emily, "And Belonging."

Seth nodded and Emily said, "And Belonging."

"Exactly", Seth added. "That's why we plan an entire segment on your new Guaranteed Income proposal, which appears to be gaining support."

Balzor played the Senator's voice of *Superior Wisdom*. "I've been battling over these issues all my life. If we give everyone living in America a great education, pay every adult a living wage, whether they can find work or not, and provide universal health care, including of course paying for women's reproductive rights across the nation, many of our biggest troubles will be solved overnight. And there will be much more social equity."

"We plan to make that case in the series, Senator. It will have a documentary format which should work well for the upcoming elections. And that's why we'd like you to be one of the main participants. Can we compare notes with Emily and your staff to be sure that our facts and conclusions are in sync with yours?"

Bradshaw smiled. "Of course. When we work together we can accomplish so much. The Guaranteed Income is a key policy idea whose time has come. Even some of my conservative colleagues like it because of its efficiency. Emily, will there be any problem coordinating between Seth and our team?"

"No. It seems like a natural. We have a lot of data from friendly think tanks that we can share."

Seth smiled. "Thank you. We at The Network obviously believe in these policies, and in your leadership."

"Thank you, Seth," Bradshaw said as he placed both hands on the table. "Is there anything else?"

"Not today, sir. Just wanted your OK to proceed."

"Yes. For sure. Now you better get ready for your birthday party."

Seth glanced at his watch and smiled. "You're right. I'll swing by DCNet and then head out. Thank you."

"Thank you for the strong support at The Network. It means a lot."

As the men shook hands Balzor nodded to Obman and said, "Good work. We'll reinforce those ideas over the weekend."

Obman nodded as he and Seth left Bradshaw's office.

Returning to his desk, the Senator paused in front of a picture showing him serving meals at a Homeless Shelter. Balzor moved up next to him, and the Senator had a thought. "Emily, remember that summer when you helped me campaign while you were still in school?"

Their eyes met. "How could I forget?"

"Yes." He paused. "Well, nothing has changed. America is a very unfair place. White Privilege still keeps people down. The nation needs leaders like us to push back against their oppressors. With a big win in two months our policies will deliver for them. Those people simply can't make it in this ever-more-complicated world unless people like us step up and bring in the resources of the federal government to help them."

"I know. And hopefully we'll get the chance to make that difference after we win back the House in the midterms."


Clayton Hunt was a newly minted major in the Marines, part of the high-level Threat Identification Group at the Pentagon. Admirals, generals and their counterparts helped Homeland Security create policies and broad guidelines, but Hunt's group of fifteen "grunts," as they referred to themselves, were where the rubber met the runway, beach or road, as the case may be.

Hunt's responsibility at the TIG, along with his Navy and Coast Guard colleagues, was to monitor, assess and report on all issues related to ocean-borne threats, including everything from inspecting containers coming into ports to monitoring the positions of Russian and Chinese missile-carrying submarines. As a young Marine officer, Hunt already had a distinguished record, including two combat tours in Afghanistan as well as sorting out logistics problems at the port of Long Beach.

The senior Army member at the TIG, Major Ahmad Rashid, had an equally challenging task: Weapons of Mass Destruction. His role required him to coordinate with colleagues in many branches of the government to track the known warheads in difficult places like Pakistan and India, not to mention North Korea, as well as to keep up on the latest developments with dirty bombs. As young lieutenants he and Clayton Hunt had served together during their first deployments to Afghanistan, when Rashid had been embedded as a Green Beret with Hunt's Marine unit.

Housed in the Pentagon, earlier that afternoon the TIG had received instructions based on their online White House meeting with the president and his key security advisors. They were already formulating a first draft of prioritized threats from the military perspective for senior staff to review the following week.

As their meeting concluded, Clayton closed his laptop and turned to Ahmad, who was sitting next to him around the long table. "It's hard to prioritize a dirty bomb in a cargo container vs. simultaneous Stinger Missile strikes on airliners across the nation."

Rashid nodded as he withdrew the encrypting device from his laptop's USB port. "Either would mean immediate mayhem. Like 9/11, only on steroids."

"And then there are the other nineteen threats we reviewed and expanded just this afternoon."

"I'm glad you'll be presenting the priorities to senior staff, not me. They all look pretty terrible."

Clayton stored his laptop in his briefcase. "Thanks a lot."

The major smiled, then shook his head as he rose. "When you look at this list, or just think about it, you wonder how we've escaped one of these scenarios."

"Most would say we've just been lucky. You know me well enough to know Who I think is responsible."

"Hmm. Like on our patrols."

"Right. But on a much larger scale."

"Perhaps. But don't forget to take a break this weekend from evaluating possible attacks on the nation and find time to finish your DEI homework for Monday."

Clayton paused and looked at his friend. "You mean how you, the poor Muslim, have been systemically discriminated against in the Army?"

Rashid smiled. "And everywhere else, don't forget."

"Why don't you tell our instructor that this is all a load of crap?"

"Because I want to make Colonel one day and don't want to be reported. By the way, I meant to ask you, how's Andrea?"

"For a first-time mom-to-be, she's doing great. Six weeks to go. Nesting like crazy. And your two?"

"Growing like weeds. Let me know if you ever want to practice babysitting two boys."

Hunt smiled. "I'm good. Give Mariam our best, and have a great weekend."

"Thanks. You, too. Back to the threats on Monday."


Late that Friday night the president and First Lady were preparing for bed in the White House residence after their trip to New York and an evening spent with briefing books for the NATO meeting in Prague.

Out in the West Wing, the Oval Office was empty and dark, except for the glow of security lighting. Or so it would seem to human eyes.

But actually Prince Proklor was starting his nightly briefing with Temno, Bespor, Legat and his other key generals. They had been meeting in the Oval Office at night since the early 50s. Proklor loved the irony and the sense of power. Tonight another level of leadership had been called in—thirty in all—which was why Balzor and Obman were standing against the wall as Proklor nodded to Temno, who began as he usually did every night.

"Yesterday there were 2,525 divorces and 2,683 abortions. Both are up from the day before, and from a year ago." He looked back at the prince.

Proklor nodded. "Thank you. Most of you were with us in Germany, and all of you have helped sow our seeds here." He paused and looked around at the faces of those who, with him, had defied God, obeyed their commander, and reached for more, all those millennia ago. "Now, like we did there, it is time for the harvest."

There was a general stir as Proklor's words sank in.

Through the Oval Office windows they could see the occasional glow from answered prayer vectors landing in the second floor Residence, like distant lightning. But no one took notice.

"You all remember Kristallnacht, how it changed the course of German history. Tomorrow will be America's Kristallnacht! Our usually pliable President Rhodes with his unexpected inquiry today has caused us to move up the date. A little more splintering and hate would be good, but I know you are ready. Do any of you need more time to prepare your targets for our assault?"

There was silence, as every demon focused on their leader's dark face. He nodded to Temno, who told the other leaders, "Good. Starting tonight admonish your forces to unleash the mayhem we've so carefully prepared. Increase the confusion. Incite anarchy. Group against group. It's time to undo this 'Godly nation'!"

Proklor smiled. "Imagine a world without America, consumed by division and anarchy. No strong voices. No one carrying on about integrity, faith, freedom, believing in Him, or about any truth at all. Everyone segregated into permanent warring groups that we control. We are almost there.

"And without America, no one will bother my fellow Princes in China, Russia or Iran, where our rule is nearly complete, and believers cower. The whole world is almost ours, waiting for the fall of this one cursed nation.

"By employing their new Artificial Intelligence technology, they believe almost every lie they see and hear. Now is the time. Each of them will believe only his own tribe's truth, as we have taught them, and the anarchy will destroy them. It is our time!"

Proklor looked around. Some nervous stirring, but silence.

"Then go. You have your assignments. You know what to do."

# 2

*Only a virtuous people are capable of freedom. As nations become corrupt and vicious, they have more need of masters.*

Benjamin Franklin

Saturday, September 12

Tom Sullivan earned enough to afford a modest row house in the historic Capitol Hill area of Washington. Most of the two- and three-story homes on his tree-lined street east of the Capitol enjoyed shade from a couple of their own trees along the sidewalk, as well as a small fenced-in backyard. Tom's was just big enough for Beau, his Black Labrador Retriever, whom Tom had raised from a puppy over the last three years.

Many of Tom's friends around the city were now married, or had live-in partners. Like his peers of both genders, or of all genders as he now was careful to say, he was incredibly busy with his job, and the casual hook-up mentality of most women in his generation suited him perfectly. In fact, weekend gatherings seemed to produce a never-ending stream of intelligent, good-looking, hard-driving women, and one place they seemed to enjoy driving was to his bed, with no regrets the next morning. He sometimes wondered how he could be so lucky to live in a time and a place where casual sex was almost universally pursued. And with no consequences. What a town! What a great time to be young, successful, woke, and male.

Success had come naturally for Tom, from his undergraduate academic achievements to his graduate degree to his great jobs to bedding the best and the brightest young women.

At home he kept everything in its proper place. There was not even the most basic feminine touch, except right after a visit by his mother or older sister, Susan, who was married with two children.

That warm, blue-sky Saturday morning he'd participated in the Fletcher's Cove parkrun with several friends, including Emily Schofield's husband, Logan. When Emily drove them home after the run, she mentioned to Tom that she wanted to introduce him to someone at Seth's party that night.

Then breakfast of yogurt and berries. After a shower, he was sitting at the country-style table in his kitchen, Beau at his feet, looking out at the still-greenish leaves clinging to the trees in his backyard, and writing notes on a legal pad about the president's threat request. He also kept one eye on his email, as his staff added their input for the spreadsheet they were preparing for Olivia Haas. Tom prided himself on approaching any issue or challenge with logic and reason. That combination had always worked well for him. So he'd directed his three-person staff to first brainstorm on every non-military broad area of potential cyber-concern—financial institutions, communications, healthcare, energy, the grid, water, manufacturing, transportation, etc.—and only then to start writing specific threats and counters. He wanted his group's list to be the most comprehensive of any list presented at Camp David.

Everyone kidded him about his legal pads, and, even more so, the small paper notebook in which he kept his daily schedule and To Do list. He called it his L-Pad. His staff took notes and wrote drafts on their tablets, laptops, phones—anything digital. Tom preferred to draft and plan on paper. Maybe it was genetic, from his lawyer-father. Maybe it was because he liked to consider all options before making difficult decisions, and he could see them on a written pad. Maybe it was because he knew so much about hacking and figured that ink on a page was not visible, at least not yet, to the wrong eyes.

Actually eyes were there. Nepravel made a quick pass through Tom's home looking for anything out of place. He noted that this Saturday morning Tom was alone, and he knew that both of them would do their best to provide some Sunday morning companionship. Assigned by Bespor, Proklor's general over D.C., to influence the young staffers in the White House, Nepravel had learned on weekends to visit Tom later in the morning, after his mother and father, Janet and Richard, had finished their quiet time praying for him.

Nepravel, like Balzor, hated Tom's parents more than he hated most humans. Two decades ago, after Richard Sullivan unexpectedly became a believer, it had been Nepravel's responsibility to keep him quiet and

NATION ON THE EDGE 29

ineffective, as they always tried to do with new believers. He and Zloy had almost succeeded in having him killed, but constant prayers and meddling believers had ruined their plans. Now the father was a business leader known for this faith. That debacle had almost cost Nepravel his stay on Earth, and he hated the man.

And in those days his son, Tom, as a teenager, had made a profession of faith in Jesus. But Tom had then been pulled from the truth by several venerated professors in college, his peers, his early successes, and the internal voices planted by the demons who followed him. Thanks to them, Tom now believed that if God even existed at all, it would be making Him small indeed to think that He would only provide one way to know Him. Tom, with Nepravel's help, could not imagine that God would be that small. So the Holy Spirit, burning brightly in Tom twenty years ago, was now quenched to the point of near-elimination.

For that reason, now that Nepravel was in D.C. and assigned to the White House, he took very seriously his responsibility to keep Tom self-assured and full of himself. Nepravel kept the voices of *Intellect* and *Reason* spinning in Tom, who seemed to enjoy their message of "Do your own thing." So Nepravel didn't worry much about the very small spiritual light which he could see flickering now and then inside Tom, because it was almost completely out.

Since D.C. and its suburbs largely belonged to the Prince of Darkness, it was rare these days, but occasionally a single angel would follow a lighted vector of prayer and surprise an unsuspecting demon. Nepravel hated being confronted by a "pretty boy," as they called the angels who had been too timid to rebel—and he always had to assume that one might show up when Tom's parents were praying for him. So, since Nepravel had been warned by Balzor about how Callie Sawyer might meet Tom that night, he took some extra time with Tom that morning, but kept one eye out for a roaming angel.

He reloaded the internal voices reminding Tom how important his job was, how his own intellect and success had earned his position, and how attractive women in D.C. were drawn like moths to a flame to a man working in the White House, particularly one who was young, on the way up, and had a boisterous Black Labrador Retriever.

On the page in his L-pad Tom had started a list. He knew that a few governments and several terrorist groups wanted to attack the U.S.—some physically, and some through cyber means—to steal technology, secrets and personal data. Theft of any kind—taking something you hadn't earned yourself—bothered Tom.

What bothered him even more was that most Americans believed their government was already protecting them. Tom knew that full protection from well-known threats, not to mention the many new ones his colleagues might now identify, was almost impossible, particularly if two or more hits were mounted simultaneously. His team might get lucky—they had in the past—or they might not. But he hated luck. He much preferred to define a problem precisely and then deliver the right response to control the outcome. He felt a tremendous responsibility in his White House position to counter every cyber threat. And he didn't like to think about what would happen if the bad stuff really hit the fan. But he had to. And prepare for it. That was his job.

So he was glad that liberal, but middle-of-the-road, "decent" President Rhodes had finally pivoted from almost two years of simply undoing his predecessor's conservative domestic policies and was now at least partially focused on out-of-the-box thinking about threats, even if he mostly concentrated on the always-reliable issue of Climate Change. But he worried that the terrorists were doing the same, and not just about carbon dioxide. He looked forward to perfecting his draft with his team on Monday, then presenting a well-organized report when Olivia returned on Wednesday.

That Saturday afternoon he had promised Seth Cohen that he would help with the preparations for the birthday party. The two had known each other at their ivy league school. After each earned a graduate degree, they had lived together with two others, Emily and Clayton, in a large apartment when they first moved to D.C. Each considered the other to be a very close friend: Seth more a policy expert at The Network, and Tom focused on keeping everyone safe and secure at the White House.

So Tom changed into jeans and a well-cut shirt, grabbed the special bottle of bourbon he had chosen for his present, and walked the four blocks to Seth's row house with Beau. Sadly he had no female companion, since, unfortunately, Jenny was stuck in New York. He'd had a great time with another young woman, Erin MacNeil, a cybersecurity specialist, at the beach in August, and he wished she weren't traveling to the west coast this weekend for her job at the Information Initiative. He'd have to go to Seth's with only Beau, but Emily had mentioned someone she wanted him to meet, so maybe it would still be a great Saturday night, as Beau was usually a pretty effective chick magnet.

Most of Capitol Hill's row houses, though all different, shared a common floor-plan. What made Seth's special was the large fenced-in backyard with a couple of mature maples at the far end, perfect for a gathering of friends, and for Beau, who was always welcome to visit.

Seth lived with Natalie Ellis, who had moved in six months earlier. Natalie worked on the Follow The Money Team at the Treasury Department, but she was temporarily assigned to the Drug Enforcement Agency, and she traveled quite a bit.

Beau, Tom, Seth and the backyard were the natural foundation for a close fraternity of tennis ball throwers that included Clayton Hunt and other regulars. Beau would have lost weight except for the many grilled leftovers passed his way whenever he visited.

Tom knocked once. Seth opened the door.

"Happy Birthday." Tom handed his friend the bourbon, as Beau ran inside to find a ball.

Seth smiled. "Come in. And thank you. You can help Natalie with the tables out back while I administer the dry rub."

"Sure. Hi, Natalie."

Natalie stood from the sofa and they hugged; she had on a colorful but informal party dress. "How's everything at the Big House?"

"Crazy, as usual. And the state of the Treasury?"

Natalie glanced at her open laptop. "The drug lords don't know it's Seth's birthday and that I'm supposed to be, like, hosting. They keep doing stuff that I have to comment on."

He nodded. Tom knew that one of Natalie's roles at Treasury was to track funds moving between suspect people and entities both domestically as well as to and from places like Iran and China, which were now also dealing in drugs—hence her posting to DEA. But they never talked about specific cases. "I understand. Point me to the tables that need arranging and do what you have to do."

An hour later Natalie had finally helped solve the mini-emergency and was working in the kitchen on the hors d'oeuvres. The ribs and chicken were slow cooking on two grills. Tom and Seth took a break and sat on the back patio, tossing balls to Beau and sampling the bourbon.

As a result of Nepravel's work that morning, Tom began by asking, "Are those two cute producers from Florida coming tonight?"

"I think so. One may be with somebody."

"Where there's a will..."

Seth returned his smile but changed the subject. "What does the president expect out of the NATO meeting?" he asked, as he took his first sip. Since they had been good friends for so many years, there was a clear understanding that even though Seth was a producer for a top cable news network, anything they discussed on civilian time would never appear in public. He raised his glass. "That's smooth."

"It should be. Even greater coordination. Particularly on what are called 'non-military' threats, like GPS spoofing, cyber-attacks, grid security. Unlike the previous go-it-alone Administration, he wants to build a coalition of consensus. That's what he'll focus on with the NATO leaders. And that's why he's taking the Speaker, to keep building bi-partisan support at home."

"*And* even though the Speaker's a crazy conservative, she was a kick-butt fighter pilot," Seth added.

"Yes, that, too. Now that his Progressive Agenda is taking hold, he wants to show her and the other conservatives that he's also concerned about defense. Some of the stuff I work on that needs to be strengthened." Tom threw a long ball to the back fence, and Beau took off.

"The Progressive Agenda may be taking hold, but not quickly enough. Not nearly enough. Rhodes doesn't really have the guts to push it through, and the country needs it. There are still too many people clinging to their Bibles and all that, years later."

Tom looked knowingly at his former apartment mate. "I know. But it's a start, and the elections should give another boost."

Seth nodded. "Yes, but the president should push harder. The nation needs strong leadership to push the God Squaders out once and for all. Their self-righteous moral crap drives me crazy, and some of them in the House are the worst. My turn." Seth picked up the ball and tossed it.

"I know. Rhodes is an old D.C. hand who tries to win people over with facts and arguments, like they used to do."

"That won't work with these people. My parents were never much on our Jewish roots, but I got tired of the God Squaders in high school telling me that I'm going to Hell. So I guess I also get tired of them trying to bring God into almost every subject and conversation, as if we still live in the Middle Ages."

Standing, Tom raised his glass. "Let's get a refill and check on Natalie. Like I said, we all agree on the policies, but Rhodes wants to try to get there with some bi-partisan support, which takes longer."

"Too slow. It's a recipe for disaster. We need to fix the country, not worry about conservatives' feelings."

Nodding, Tom started for the door. "OK. OK. After the midterms, there should be clear sailing."

"I hope so. Come on, Beau. Let's go see what Natalie's made for us."

Callie Sawyer and her daughter, Grace, had walked to a park that afternoon to meet several of Grace's friends. An hour later they were almost home to their ground-floor apartment when their landlord, Kristen Holloway, came down the steps from the row house above their apartment and started toward them.

Kristen had been Callie's older friend and mentor since before Grace was born. They had met, and Kristen had impacted Callie's life while working for Callie's father, David Sawyer. She had moved to Washington six years ago to pursue her commercial real estate career, buying the

row house in a downturn. When Callie landed her job as a writer for
*Genetic Policy* two years earlier, she asked Kristen about rental units in
the District, and within a month she and her daughter had moved in
below her friend.

When Grace saw Kristen on the sidewalk she ran and hugged her.

"How's my Goddaughter this afternoon?"

"Fine. We've been to the park!"

"It's a great day for it. Hi, Callie."

"Hey. You look great. Where are you off to?" At fifty, Kristen—tall,
auburn/gray hair, freckles and a disarming smile—was a striking figure.

"Our Singles Group at church is going to dinner and the symphony.
Should be fun."

Callie knew that Kristen, unmarried herself, had taken a volunteer
leadership role with a small group of the younger single women at
Church of the Good Shepherd. On a regular basis their church
sponsored events and mixers for all its singles as an alternative to the bar
scene.

"Have a great time. The sitter's staying late with Grace, and I'm
headed to a birthday party with a bunch of people I hardly know. Emily
Schofield invited me, from Senator Bradshaw's office. And you won't
believe this, but she wants to introduce me to Tom Sullivan. Isn't that
Richard Sullivan's son?"

"Really? When you first moved here I sent an email to Richard to tell
Tom about you."

Callie smiled. "I remember. Well, we never connected. Maybe he
heard I have a daughter, and that slowed him down. Anyway, I hope to
meet him tonight."

"Given the circumstance of how I first knew Richard—what, twenty
years ago?—I was never close with either Tom or his older sister. But I
hear he's pretty smart."

"Do you ever see Richard?"

"No. The occasional email. He and Janet have a very good life
together, and, even though she forgave us years ago—there's just no
reason for me to be in their lives."

Grace pulled her mother's hand. "I'm hungry."

"Just a second, dear. Yes, I understand. You and I have both learned a lot about forgiveness, which we don't need to revisit. Anyway, I guess a lot of Congressional staff people will be there tonight. I'm looking forward to it. It's been a while."

"Enjoy yourself. And if you want to stay out past the sitter's time, just text me and I'll come down and watch Grace."

"Thanks. You never know. Tell the others hello for me. Get some culture at the symphony. And we need to talk this weekend. Grace told me her teacher had each student stand up today and tell the others what sex they think they are, and why."

"In the third grade?"

"Yes. I need help with what to say to the teacher."

"Truth, with love. But we'll talk."

"Have a great night."


The gathering at Seth Cohen's was well underway, with young professionals in the row house and the backyard, talking, or focused on their screens; the sun was just setting behind the tall trees on the next block, and Beau moved from person to person, offering the ball for a throw.

Washington attracted people right out of school who wanted to *do* something. Not just make money, study a subject, or raise a family. These bright men and women, the youngest just out of college, the oldest pushing thirty-five, all wanted to do something that would make a difference to the nation, and perhaps the world. The entry points were as a Congressional office staffer, or as an analyst at a department like Treasury or State, or at an agency like the EPA or DEA. Or at a think tank, lobbyist firm, news network, regulator, law firm, journal, contractor, state agency, or interest group. Positions were often transitory, and people moved from job to job as they learned what really interested them and networked with others who shared their interests.

In just a few years an entry-level job could lead to a more senior position creating policy papers or writing draft legislation. With a little more experience and subject matter focus, one could ascend to a Congressional Committee staff position, which tended to be more stable as the politicians came and went. Or to a subject matter expert at a think tank, a chief lobbyist, or a Congressperson's chief of staff. And everyone tended to know everyone, or someone who did.

Because of the emphasis on the government *doing* something, most of the young people tended to be liberal and progressive—believing that some new program could cure almost any problem. Critical theory, embedded in the nation's educational programs for decades, had convinced many of them that the nation consisted of oppressors and victims. They, the majority, were in D.C. to ensure that more equity flowed to every victim identity group.

But given the recent years of a more conservative Executive Branch and House leadership, it was becoming possible to find a libertarian or even a conservative in the mix, though they were still definitely in the minority.

These were the friends of the original apartment mates—Tom, Seth, Emily and Clayton—who eight years later were gathered to celebrate Seth's thirty-fourth birthday. Adding in their spouses, significant others and friends, any such gathering virtually ensured that every branch, department, agency and interest was well represented. And that many overlapped in their responsibilities and perspectives. And for those unattached, there was always the opportunity for a weekend liaison, or more.

And of course members of Proklor's army were also in attendance, listening, lying and learning useful information for future action. Balzor, Nepravel, Obman, and several others all had charges and responsibilities that intersected at a gathering like this. With the non-believers—the great majority this night—their emphasis was always on keeping each person's focus on himself or herself: how is this conversation or connection going to help me?

With the few believers in attendance, if a demon could stand the pain of getting near the internal spiritual light and heat, he sowed voices of *Unworthiness, Doubt and Conformity*.

And with every human they looked for opportunities to encourage jealousy, hook-ups, infidelity—anything they could use later to create distrust or to gain leverage. So they were always busy, and many had other similar gatherings to monitor—including Senator Bradshaw's dinner party—that Saturday evening.

After studying at Oxford, Tom Sullivan had begun his career with a large international bank, which meant a job in New York. But because his interest was in cybersecurity, and because he wanted to be at the center of things, after six months in Manhattan the bank transferred him to Washington to interface with the experts at the National Security Agency. That's when he answered an ad and moved into a huge flat in a renovated older apartment building on Columbia Road with Emily and Seth, who had also answered Clayton Hunt's ad.

After several years in the bank's employ he was well placed, along with his mother being a former Congresswoman, to take an entry position on the newly formed White House Cybersecurity Team, and now he was the second person in the group, behind Olivia Haas, a brilliant former consultant whom President Rhodes brought in when he was elected.

At thirty-four, Tom was on the slightly older side of those celebrating that evening. He refilled his drink at the bar on the patio and was about to walk over to one of the attractive Florida media producers talking with Seth when Clayton Hunt, no longer in uniform, and his wife Andrea, came in. Tom pecked Andrea on the cheek and noted her girth with a smile and a nod. She shrugged her shoulders. They chatted at the bar while Clayton poured a glass of bourbon and a diet cola.

When Andrea turned to a friend, Tom said to Clayton, "I suspect you may be working on the same thing I am for a trip to Camp David."

"You would be right. Not easy, especially to prioritize. Which is worse, beheading or poison?"

"Exactly. But he's right that we've got to think out of the box. We're due for something."

Clayton nodded. "You know, I really hate to sound like an old man, but look how many are on their phones in the middle of Seth's party. What's so important on a Saturday night?"

Tom smiled. "You do sound old! But I guess we are. These folks have never known a time when they're not, like, sending or receiving. Is it any wonder that no one can keep a secret in this town?"

"Well, most of what we're working on better stay out of texts, or we'll really be in trouble."

"At least you're at the Pentagon." He took a sip and saw Emily. "Most of these guys think a security clearance just means they have juicier stuff to share with their friends."

"Not good. Well, I need to say hi to Seth and Natalie. Let's talk later."


As Air Force One sped east over the North Atlantic, it was joined in the early morning darkness by two F-35's from Lakenheath in the UK, replacing the Iceland-based escorts which had accompanied the flight during its middle leg. It was considered prudent to have two U. S. Air Force fighters tucked in close behind the president's plane.

"Delta One on station," reported Major John Grantham to the crew in Air Force One.

"Good morning," came the reply. Grantham's wingman, Captain Adam Hassan, clicked his mic button twice to acknowledge.

Onboard Air Force One were President Alexander Rhodes and Representative Rebecca Gordon, the Speaker of the House. It was unusual for them to travel together, but it was an unusual summit in the Czech Republic to which they were headed, along with their senior staffs and press representatives. Each had tried to sleep, but now they were sitting in the president's office, sipping coffee and talking with Peter Sloane, the National Security Advisor, about the upcoming three days in Prague.

The Western Allies plus Russia and Turkey were coming together, with representatives from their executive and legislative branches. Their goal was to try to craft a common response to the crisis created by the interconnected issues of Iran's just announced, previously secret nuclear weapons capability, the increasing attacks on Israel by her neighbors, and the calls from the newly empowered Islamic blocks in several Western parliaments for European governments to disavow any support for the Jewish state.

Speaker Gordon had attended graduate school in Germany and spoke the language fluently. She was considered an expert on Europe, even though it had changed dramatically in the twenty-five years since she was a student. Given unprecedented pressure from many of the indigenous parliaments, and several Muslim members of his own party who hated Israel, President Rhodes had asked the Speaker to join him and to help push a strong, united policy.

"The Sunnis in the Middle East may be nervous about Iran's new weapons, but *every* Muslim leader in Europe, Sunni and Shi'ite, appears to be emboldened by the power that Iran now possesses," said the president, slowly rotating a mug of hot coffee in his hands.

"Yes, Mr. President, and it will only get more difficult. What were steady streams of refugees from Syria and North Africa have now become near-majorities in many cities and regional governments."

There was a knock on the door and an Aide entered. "Madame Speaker, there's a call for you from Congressman Mentz. He says it's about the Budget, and he needs to talk with you, if you're available."

The president smiled. "Go deal with the Budget, Becky. We need it. Come back when you can, and we'll continue our conversation."

"And I'll go check on those position papers," said Sloane. "We should review the final drafts before we land."


As Clayton and his wife Andrea moved to the backyard, Tom walked over to Emily Schofield and her husband, Logan, who was originally from Nicosia, Cyprus. The couple had met when Emily was on a study abroad program in London. A few years later, when Logan landed in D.C. on a six-month secondment from the Bank of England with the U.S. Federal Reserve, they'd renewed the relationship. Married three years ago, Logan had moved from regulator to lobbyist, a role at which he appeared to excel. He had recently been hired away to become the lead internal lobbyist coordinator for Juggle, the California search engine whose budget in this area exceeded $50 million.

They shook hands, and Tom pecked Emily on the cheek. "What's up?"

"We're good," Emily replied. "Have you recovered from this morning's run? Logan's been complaining."

Her husband smiled but touched his knee. "A full minute faster than last week. Were you trying to kill us?"

"No, no. Just fighting the aging thing. I feel good. How's your search engine?"

"I guess it's OK. But the rumors about more restrictions on our data use is worrisome."

"*Our* data?"

Logan smiled. "Well, the data we collect."

"On your customers."

"Well, yes. But it's the key to our business."

"You've been saying that ever since you got there."

"And it's been true for at least that long. Emily, what would you like?"

Tom walked with them to the bar on the patio; Seth turned around and Emily gave him a birthday hug.

While they caught up, Tom noticed a tall young woman with dark hair making her way onto the patio.

"Callie!" Emily called out and gave her a quick wave. Callie smiled, and soon Emily had introduced her to all the friends in reach.

Tom watched her during the introductions and was the last to shake her hand. "Glad you could join us. What would you like?"

She smiled. "Some white wine would be great, thank you."

A few minutes later they were standing together next to an outdoor table, sipping their drinks. Callie was wearing a dark blue knit shift dress and gold jewelry.

"So, Emily said you're a journalist."

"Well, sort of. I edit a journal on genetic research."

"I know enough to know that I don't know. A big field."

"Yes, and new, really interesting subjects every month. Many with both moral and policy implications."

"Which means regulation and funding issues. Which is why you're based in D.C."

Her smile broadened. "Emily said you're really smart."

He took a sip. "She did? Maybe I used to be, but now I work for the government."

Beau came up and presented a tennis ball. Tom took it and held it up. Beau sat, locked on.

"Is he yours?"

"Yes. He likes to visit Seth and Natalie."

"Isn't your father Richard Sullivan?"

Tom, who was about to toss the ball, stopped and looked quizzically at Callie.

"Yes. How did you know?"

"I think my friend Kristen Holloway told him that you and I should get together when I first moved here."

His eyes widened. "That's you?"

"I guess so."

"I should listen more closely to my father."

She smiled. "And you're in cyber security, at the White House. Sounds pretty interesting."

"It can be, at least on some days."

Tom threw the ball into the yard. Beau spun around to chase it, and in his excitement bumped into the table, spilling a drink onto Callie's dress and shoes.

"Oh, no. I'm sorry," Tom exclaimed. "I'll get a towel."

"It's OK. No big deal. I've got some napkins." She crouched and began wiping the tops of her shoes.

"Here are some more...You seem pretty unflappable."

"That's one of the benefits of having an eight-year-old daughter."

"You have a daughter?"

Callie stood. "Yes, she's a mess, but she's the love of my life."

"I'm impressed."

"Just another big mistake that God turned into something wonderful."

"Hmm."

Nepravel noted that Balzor, who had left to check on Senator Bradshaw, had been right. The spiritual light inside Callie was bright and painful. He couldn't stay with them, but instead had to dart in and out of their conversation. And he didn't like what he heard.

Across the city in the large auditorium at Capitol University, Vice President Evan Carpenter and his wife were seated at the head table enjoying dinner with the leaders of the "My Body-My Choice Forum." He was there to give the Keynote Speech for the group's annual Fundraiser, which in turn gave liberally to Progressive candidates around the nation. Even in the noisy hall they could hear the shouts and the clangs from the Pro-Life protesters just outside the venue. The student newspaper had encouraged the university's activists to help protect free speech by engaging the "Right Wing-Fascist Hate Mongers" whom they expected to show up to protest the event. Extra police were brought in to protect the auditorium and to separate the two groups outside. Because so few people were praying for the event, the invisible demonic force on hand was large. And ready.

An hour later Tom and Callie had dined around with most of the guests, enjoying Seth's incredible brisket and ribs. Now they were walking together in the backyard, while one or the other tossed a tennis ball Beau's way.

Nepravel hung back by the bar, unwilling to follow them into the yard. The spiritual light in Callie was radiant—it hurt him to look her way. And several prayer vectors of light had actually landed near her. He suspected that the Holloway woman and her friends were praying for her!

"So what exactly does one do all day at the White House when focusing on cybersecurity?" Callie asked.

He thought for a moment. "Surround yourself with smart people, work hard, and hope that you stay at least a half step ahead of the bad guys."

"And what are they trying to do?"

"*That* is the great question. Of course we know they want information on our people, and that China and Russia are behind a lot of it, so they also want defense secrets, industrial secrets, and access to everyone's emails. Most of our work is focused on blocking those two from stealing us blind."

"My Dad actually did a lot of real estate work in Russia years ago—back when my friend Kristen worked with him. It was different then, I think. I've read that much of their technology is based on ours—stolen from us."

He nodded. "But what if they can go further now and get inside processes and manipulate them, from factory production lines to air traffic control to voting rights to stored 'facts' to, say, genetic test results—and we don't know it. Then what? What if they can hack and use A.I. to make what's true and what's false suddenly unverifiable? What would that do for business or government?"

"Not to mention our personal lives."

He stopped. "Exactly. What we think to be true could then actually be a lie—but we wouldn't know." He smiled. "So, to answer your question, we start with the basics of protecting the information in the Executive Branch as best we can, mostly with strong rules and procedures. I'm a big fan of rules and procedures as the foundation for protection. And then we try to imagine the bigger picture of what might be coming at us. Sometimes our team has to make recommendations that can affect a lot of people, and I'm OK with doing whatever we have to do to protect ourselves."

"Sounds like a lot."

"We're never bored."

At that hour another gathering was in full swing at the row house of Senator Henry Bradshaw, the President Pro Tem of the Senate. He and his wife, Margaret, were hosting his party's Minority Leader in the House, Nancy Cantrell, her husband, and the Chief Whips and their spouses, as coffee and dessert were served in their classically decorated dining room.

When Balzor arrived from Seth Cohen's, he was surprised to find General Bespor and Zloy mingling with the group and interjecting voices whenever they could. There was no concern about any spiritual light at this D.C. address. Balzor and the others moved from person to person, reminding them of their *Intelligence, Superiority,* and *Rational Thought.*

Henry Bradshaw looked down the table to his right. "Nancy, do you think it's wise for the president to be seen so closely with the Speaker in Prague, trying to tamp down Muslim demands in the Mideast? She's one of the wackiest."

The Minority Leader shrugged a bit. "We've spent two years focusing on our domestic agenda, which has gone well enough for first steps. Obviously we need to do more. But to get the majority we need some independents, and the Speaker appeals to a number of them, particularly on foreign policy. So I think the president's OK to have her with him. And this weekend *is* the anniversary of 9/11."

"But she never quits. Faith, faith, faith. You would think she and her caucus sit around examining their Bibles for answers to every question."

Cantrell smiled as others nodded. "Exactly. But they're holdovers from the past, and thankfully voters are getting tired of it. As we push our better agenda, giving benefits to every American family, people will certainly see the real differences between us."

"And hopefully vote for reason over blind faith."

Cantrell raised her wine glass to Bradshaw. "Well said. Yes. Here's to rational thought over blind faith. I like that."

When Tom Sullivan went for refills for Callie and himself, he found Emily Schofield at the bar. She raised her eyebrow inquisitively.

"Yes, you're right, she's very interesting. And she reminded me that my dad told me to look her up a couple of years ago. I should have. She has a lot going on. We've talked about almost everything imaginable. A smart lady."

Emily smiled. "Good. So maybe you'll ask her out?"

Taking the drinks, he shrugged and returned her smile. "You never know. Maybe I'll ask her over to my place."

He walked to where Callie was talking with Seth and handed her a fresh glass.

"Seth says The Network may be interested in a piece about human gene research."

"Yeah, you know, the pros and cons. Which side would you rather be on, Callie?" Seth asked.

"It depends on the specific topic. That's what's so fascinating. Some good, some bad."

"OK. I'll contact you this week. Now, please excuse me, I gotta see Natalie about the cake."

Tom said, "I've enjoyed our discussion. By the way, where do you live?"

She told him.

"That's not far. And my house is only about a block out of the way."

"A beautiful area."

"Yes. In fact, why don't we walk over there for a nightcap after the cake?"

"Just the two of us?"

"Yes. Well, Beau will join us."

"Mmm. Maybe not such a great idea."

He smiled. "Why not?"

Just then her phone vibrated, and she read a text. "Speaking of cake, my sitter and Grace baked brownies tonight, and now we're out of milk. She thinks I should stop and get some for breakfast."

"Simpsons is on the corner on the way. They're open late. I'll walk with you and we'll get some."

"Oh, no, I couldn't ask you to do that."

He smiled. "Of course. It's almost on my way, and you can't walk by yourself."

"Well, I could, but thank you. Yes, that would be nice."

"Good, then let's go help Seth and Natalie get his cake out."

It was still an hour before dawn as the president, the Speaker and the National Security Advisor resumed their conversation on Air Force One. "Becky," said President Rhodes, "most of the European leaders with whom we're about to meet don't have a clue about how to turn the immigration wave around. You can hardly recognize the assimilation tin can which they've kicked down the road all these years, it has so many dents."

Nodding her head as she returned her mug to its holder, Speaker Gordon agreed. "Only the Russians and the Turks have had long experience dealing with the Islamic radicals, and their historically violent solutions would of course not be accepted today. And in the past the radicals didn't have a nation-state with nuclear weapons threatening to annihilate anyone who disagrees with their view of Allah's world. Has there been any reaction to your proposal?"

Sloane responded. "Some, mostly positive, but that's what we hope to work out in Prague."

"It's a lot of money, but if we and Western Europe tie the payments to the voluntary, permanent return of immigrants to rebuild their homelands, there is some chance we can both defuse Europe while seeding the Middle East with people who naturally belong and have a personal stake in its future."

The president sighed and nodded his head. "The alternative appears to be more large-scale riots and even worse in Europe, as well as more destruction in the Middle East. We've got to find a solution that encourages everyone to embrace peaceful answers."

"A stronger, rebuilt military would help move them in that direction, Mr. President. I just hope we're not put to the test until we rebuild. Our military is a little ragged in many areas. Can we use this meeting in Prague to add to the Budget with a bi-partisan fix for Defense when we return?"

The Commander-in-Chief smiled. "That's another reason I like you, Becky: You're always dealing. We'll see. We'll discuss it on the way home. And I'm glad you're with me, Rebecca. As a former A-10 pilot you've got the gravitas we need to convince the Russians, Turks and others that we mean business. Hopefully that alone will buy their agreement."

Now she smiled. "I doubt a one-woman former combat pilot can pull that off, Mr. President, but I'll give it my best." She picked up her coffee and looked out the window.

As the three planes sped to the east high above Belgium's coast, Captain Hassan notched back his speed ever so slightly and moved his F-35 from its normal wingman position to directly behind his friend and mentor, John Grantham. Flipping two switches, he armed his Vulcan cannon.

Major Grantham keyed his mic and turned his head just in time to see the explosive rounds exit Hassan's cannon at point blank range. His last living sensations were of the shock wave and heat as his fighter exploded.

Everyone on Air Force One felt the bump and saw the flash from the fireball; the plane started to shake from the damage to its horizontal stabilizer. In the cockpit the captain yelled, "Break right! Release flares and chaff." But it was too late. The missile from Captain Hassan's F-35 detonated inside the port inboard engine. The wing disintegrated and broke off, sending the plane and its occupants into a six-mile death spiral to the dark earth below.

Captain Hassan keyed his mic on the Center Frequency. "Allah Akbar!" he shouted joyfully, then switched off the transponder and turned south.

At the same time Vice-President Carpenter was concluding his after-dinner speech at Capitol University. In the balcony, which had previously been empty and locked off, twenty protesters wearing black suddenly unrolled banners and began denouncing the gathering with cries of "Baby Killers!" and "White Privilege Kills Black Babies!"

As security personnel rushed to the stairs in the back of the hall, two men dressed as waiters emerged from the kitchen door on the side of the room and began screaming profanities up at the protesters. Secret Service agents ran to cut them off, but one of them pulled a handgun from a hidden holster at his back and fired at those in the balcony.

Before the Secret Service could react, there was a fusillade of rifle fire from above, taking out the waiters and spraying the dais. Two agents tried to protect the Vice President; others drew their weapons and fired toward the rifle shots. In the ensuing chaos, twelve were wounded and seven were killed. Vice President Carpenter died almost instantly with a hollow point bullet to the head, his wife with one to her heart.

Tom and Callie were standing at the kitchen island finishing their cake with Seth, Natalie and the other two original apartment mates.

"Wonderful brisket, Seth," Clayton offered. "As good as we had at home."

Seth smiled. "Now that's a..."

It was hard to tell which phone vibrated first, because almost instantly they all were. Tom glanced at Callie, then took out his phone and read the text. He frowned. "They want me at the office. Actually, at the White House."

Seth read his text. "The Network says there've been shots fired at the vice president's speech, and they want me in."

"Oh, no," Callie said, putting down her plate.

"Code Red Foxtrot," Clayton read. "Damn. I gotta go. Honey, can you get a ride home?"

"Sure," Andrea nodded. "Go."

"Clayton, can you drop me near the White House on your way? Natalie, can Beau spend the night?" Turning to Callie, Tom said, "Sorry I won't be able to help with the milk."

"Another time'll be great. I hope everything's OK."

He grabbed a paper napkin and wrote. "Here's my number. Text me, and I'll let you know."

Putting on her coat, Natalie said to Andrea and Callie, "Stay as long as you want. Last one out just pull the door closed with Beau inside."

"We'll take care of it."

Outside they could hear more than the usual number of sirens, seemingly from every direction.

Clayton gave Andrea a long look while squeezing her hand, then turned to Tom as the others said their abrupt goodbyes.

Across town the same vibrating began as Henry Bradshaw's dinner party was winding down. He had barely glanced at his phone when one of the two D.C. police officers assigned to him that night burst through the front door.

"Everyone move to the central hall, away from the windows," she ordered.

"What is it, officer?" Bradshaw asked.

"Not sure. The Secret Service radioed to take defensive positions. They're on the way. Please, move to the hall."

"The Secret Service?" Bradshaw repeated, turning to Margaret as they walked from the dining room.

"The vice president's been shot!" Nancy Cantrell read on her phone.

"Has the president landed in Prague?"

"It doesn't say."


"What does that Foxtrot code mean?" Tom asked from the passenger seat as Clayton sped along Pennsylvania Avenue.

"It could mean several things—none good."

Tom's phone buzzed. He saw it was Seth and answered on the speaker.

"I'm still in a car headed to the studio, but they called me. No one's heard from the reporters traveling with the president for half an hour, and there're reports from northern Belgium of a huge fireball falling from the sky and destroying an entire village."

"Damn!" Clayton said under his breath, shaking his head.

"I know neither of you can comment officially," Seth continued, "but have you heard anything?"

"No," Tom said. "But I should be at The White House in a few minutes. If something has happened to Air Force One, I suspect I won't be able to talk for several days. They made me the White House's interim Continuity of Government Officer 'til they could find a permanent replacement."

"What does that mean?'

"I'm supposed to keep us up and running in an emergency."

"OK. But I may come across some information that could help."

"Then call me."

"And me," Clayton added.

"OK. Stay in touch."

In Senator Henry Bradshaw's hallway it sounded to the guests like every siren in the district was headed their way. Then blue and red flashing lights reflected from the walls.

The front door opened and a muscular man in a suit, wearing an earpiece, entered and looked around. Two men and a woman came in behind him and fanned out inside. He took out his badge and ID.

"Officer Mills, I'm Senior Agent Clark Talbot. Thank you for your quick action securing the home. You can join your team outside now." The police officer nodded and departed.

"Senator Bradshaw, I'm to take you and your wife to a temporary command post. Please come with me."

"Command Post? What's happening? Is the vice president OK?"

Glancing at the other guests for a moment, Agent Talbot replied, "We'll give you a briefing on the way. For now, it's imperative that we leave. Please follow me." He turned and walked to the door, checked with the agent there, who nodded.

Bradshaw turned to Nancy Cantrell. "I'll call you as soon as I can."

Outside, they put the Bradshaws in a black SUV with Talbot in the passenger seat. A moment later the six-car convoy departed, lights flashing.

General Bespor sent Balzor and Zloy with them, while he left to report to Prince Proklor that the events they had planned for so long were beginning to happen.


Emily, her husband Logan, Callie Sawyer and Andrea Hunt were alone with Beau in Seth's row house.

Emily shrugged. "I just got a text from Rob, our Chief of Staff. He says to stay put—he's trying to contact the Senator now."

"You don't have a set plan for emergencies?" Callie asked.

"We practiced once. But we were all together in the office when we started."

Andrea surveyed the home. "Well, whatever's going on, this place is a mess."

Callie nodded. "I'll help, then I better get home. Here, Beau, a small bite for you."

Logan looked up from his phone. "My parents just texted from Cyprus that the Russian News Service is reporting both the president and vice president are dead or missing."

"Impossible. Fake news. They aren't together," Emily replied. "We'll give you both a ride. Logan, these plates go in the sink."


A block from the Bradshaws' row house the convoy detoured briefly through an empty, unlit parking lot. While there, the two middle SUVs extinguished their lights and peeled to the right, while two identical SUVs, lights flashing, took their place. The convoy then continued out the other side.

In the silence of the parking lot, Agent Talbot and the driver waited and watched, then the two SUVs turned on their normal headlights and departed in another direction.

Turning to the passengers, Talbot said, "Information is still coming in, but we believe Air Force One was shot down over Belgium, perhaps by one of our own. Everyone on board is lost, including the president, the First Lady, the Speaker, and all their staff going to the NATO conference. Separately, the vice president was killed in a shoot-out between protesters inside the university where he was speaking." He paused as that information registered on the passengers. "We're not certain of the actual threat, so we're improvising."

"You mean you're here because I'm the acting president?" Senator Bradshaw half-asked, half-stated.

"Yes, sir. You are now our first priority, along with the Secretary of State, who was already in Prague. In the last thirty minutes we've shifted more assets to him and will look for a way to get him home."

"What do you mean?"

"If Air Force One was taken out by one of our own, then we don't know who to trust, or what the level of threat really is. So air travel becomes a problem. And that's why we're using the dummy convoy."

"Where are we headed?" Margaret asked.

"A military base is the safest place to go while we try to figure this out. So the convoy is on the way to Joint Base Andrews, a logical choice. But we're on the way to Fort George Meade in Maryland, which has the advantage of direct connections with the NSA and Cyber Command. We need to swear you in, sir, and then you need to communicate to the nation what has happened."

Clayton pulled to the curb on 17$^{th}$ Street. Their cell phones buzzed. Tom read the headline from Seth's News Network: "Air Force One Shot Down Over Belgium. All Onboard Believed Dead."

They stared at the news for a long moment, then looked at each other.

"The president, Speaker, their staffs. Anything more on the vice president?" Clayton asked.

Tom opened the car door. "Not here. My boss was on Air Force One. The president invited me to join them for the trip."

Clayton met his eyes. "It's gonna be tough. They need you."

"Should we even be here? It's an obvious target. 9/11." He got out.

"Same for the Pentagon. We'll see. I'll be praying. Check in when you can."

"Will do." He closed the door and Clayton took off.

As Tom walked to the Employee Gate, Nepravel caught up with him. The police, backed by Marines with M-16s, were double checking the ID's of the staff members in a short queue. When he made it inside the West Wing he saw that not many had come in yet. Or maybe they hadn't been told to report. He headed toward Olivia's office but ran into Allen Linder, one of the four Deputy Chiefs of Staff.

"Thank God you're here, Tom. You're the COG Officer. We need you in the Situation Room."

They started towards the stairs. "Who's there?"

"Besides the duty watch team, Diane, Garrett and I are it for now. President Rhodes had his senior team with him, including his Chief of Staff."

"What about the vice president?"

"You haven't heard? He was killed in a shootout with protesters. And his wife. His Chief has gone to tell their kids."

"What?"

"Something terrible's going on. We're trying to conference in Senator Bradshaw, who's now president. The Secret Service has him safe and on the move."

They descended beneath the West Wing and entered the Situation Room, a state-of-the-art communications center with three conference rooms, manned 24/7 by personnel from Intelligence, Homeland Security, and the military. Diane Marsh and Garrett Crose, two of the other Deputy Chiefs, were sitting across from each other at one end of the large conference table. The president's chair next to them at the end was empty. The screens in the room all had live feeds from secure government sources and the news networks. Crose motioned for the two men to take the next seats, just as a handheld video of Senator Bradshaw, riding in a vehicle, came up on the center screen, and he began to speak.

"Mr. President, this is Garrett Crose in the Situation Room at the White House. Most of President Rhodes' senior staff were with him on Air Force One. Diane Marsh and Allen Linder, the other two Deputy Chiefs, Tom Sullivan, the Continuity of Government Officer, and I are here. More mid-level staff are on the way in."

"This is unbelievable," Bradshaw said in a low voice, his head moving slightly side to side.

"Yes, sir, it is. I understand you should be at Fort Meade in forty minutes."

Bradshaw looked up at Agent Talbot, behind the camera, and nodded. "Have there been any more attacks?"

"None on government officials or buildings, but there are reports of what could be terrorist attacks on others. We're checking."

Bradshaw nodded again and looked to his wife, then back to the camera. "What should we do?"

"As soon as you get to Meade, you'll be sworn in. But before that, as acting president, we need you to officially raise the COGCON Level from Four to One. The Pentagon and Homeland Security Advisor have already raised the DEFCON and Security Alert systems to their highest levels, so the military and security services are ramping up their readiness, but only the president can raise the COGCON level."

"What's that?"

Diane Marsh looked at Tom, who responded. "Mr. President, it's the highest of the Continuity of Government Conditions and authorizes the Emergency Relocation Groups in every Executive Branch agency to move to their alternate locations, to be ready to run the government from outside the immediate Capital Area."

"Oh, yes. I remember. Of course, go ahead."

Tom took a pad from the center of the table and began writing a brief Executive Order.

Allen Linder spoke. "Mr. President, we need to communicate something to the nation. No one from the White House Press Secretary's staff is here yet, if any of them is even alive or available. When you get to Fort Meade, we recommend a short video message, including your swearing in."

"What should I say?"

"That's up to you, sir. But we can draft some points and send them to you."

"Emily Schofield is my Press Secretary. I'll try to find her and loop her in with you."

Tom looked up. "I know where she is, sir. I'll call her, give her a head's up, and get her input."

"Yes, thank you. Can she and the rest of my staff join us at Fort Meade?

As Tom rose to deliver the COGCON order to the Communications Watch Officer and to call Emily, the others at the table looked at each other and nodded their agreement.

"Good. I'll feel better with them."

Crose paused, then said, "That's of course fine, Mr. President, but none of them has experience here at the White House, or in the Executive Branch."

"I know, Mr, ah, Crose, but they're good people, and I think we'll all have plenty to do. We'll have to work together."

"Yes, sir. By the time you get to the base, we'll have an Action List ready for you."

"Good. Thank you. Let's hope there are no more attacks."


Clayton ran into Ahmad Rashid in the hallway just outside their work space at the Pentagon. Rashid was in his uniform, but Hunt was still dressed for the party.

"What the hell?" Rashid asked, touching his ID badge to the reader on the wall. Hunt followed.

Inside, about half their team was in place and online, checking their assigned areas for issues or threats. As Hunt booted up, Megan Buckley, one of the Air Force officers assigned to their Threat Group, said, "We've only got intermittent returns, but it looks like the F-35 that shot down

Air Force One is heading across the Med for Algeria or Libya. Control heard 'Allah Akbar!' just as Air Force One disappeared."

Ahmad asked, "Clayton, is there a carrier in the Med that can intercept him?"

"We haven't had enough carriers to have one in the Med for six months."

"Then can we have Tomahawks ready to go when we know where he lands?"

"That we can arrange, if we have a president to authorize launching them."

Buckley turned to Rashid and added, speaking slowly, "The pilot is Captain Adam Hassan. Took out his wingman before the president. Bastard."

The room was silent. The phone next to Clayton rang. He listened, then stood up. "We've just moved to COGCON ONE. We're going to Site R at Raven Rock immediately. A van will be at Door WE-2 in fifteen minutes. They'll bring the others tomorrow. No phone calls or texts. Let's move."


Fred Palmer was one of a handful of doctors left performing abortions in St. Louis. But he refused to live there, to protect his family from a long string of death threats. He drove in on every other Thursday and stayed at different motels near the Women's Clinic until departing on Sunday afternoon, since most of his clients wanted the procedure on a weekend. Fred loved the comfort food at Ray's Diner and usually availed himself on Saturday evenings.

As he walked to his car after dinner that night, the side door of a van parked next to the sidewalk opened and Dr. Palmer was hit in the chest with two shotgun blasts. The shooter threw a dozen "Jesus Loves Children" flyers around his writhing body and closed the door; his partner drove them out of the lot.

The two demons who had been working on the shooters for weeks smiled and rode off with them. They needed to be there to ramp up the appropriate voices if either of the men started to have any feelings of remorse.


Emily and Logan Schofield, Callie Sawyer and Andrea Hunt were just drying the last plates from the party when Emily's phone rang.

"It's Tom. I'll put him on speaker. Hey. Logan, Andrea and Callie are here. What's happening?"

"Uh, OK, but none of this gets repeated, to anyone. Emily, Senator Bradshaw is now the president, and he needs your help drafting a video message to go out tonight. He's on the way to a safe destination. He'd like you and his staff to join him. I'll text you separately where he is. You and Logan should pack a bag, and he can drive you out. When you're in the car, call me back, and I'll give you more details. Tell Logan to bring his passport—I'll do my best to get him on the access list."

"Bradshaw is president? What about...?"

"No time. Call me when you're on the way. The text is coming. Callie and Andrea, if you have friends outside D.C., you may want to head there. I suspect Clayton will soon be at a remote location as well."

Andrea said in a low voice. "It's that bad?"

"No one knows. I gotta go. My main duty now is to assist the new president, so, Emily, I'll be joining you. Oh, can I impose on one of you to take Beau? He's well behaved."

Callie said, "I'll take him. No problem."

As the Schofields put on their coats at the front door, Logan said, "We offered you both a ride home."

"That's OK. You need to go. Andrea and I will be fine. And we've got Beau."

As they closed the door on the Schofields, Callie turned to Andrea. "I need to get home to my daughter and think about where we might go. Would you like to spend the night with us?"

"Uh, actually, yes. If you have room and don't mind."

"Between our apartment and my landlord, who's a great friend, we have plenty. Let's walk."

"Yes. And I picked up on something you said. You're a believer."

Callie nodded.

"Then let's stop a minute and pray."

Callie held out her hand. "Thank you. It's so important."

The two women bowed their heads and prayed for the nation, the new president, their families, and their friends.


Seth Cohen flashed his security badge at the armed security guards standing by the dedicated elevator in the lobby of The News Network's D.C. Studio, but one of them stopped him.

"I'm in a hurry," Seth snapped.

"Yes, sir, everyone is. Give me your badge, please. It should just be a minute."

He took the badge from around his neck and handed it to the guard, who put it under a scanning box, then, satisfied, carefully compared the photo to the man.

"Thank you, sir. Go ahead."

When the doors opened upstairs on the massive two-story Studio and News Bureau, there was another security checkpoint, behind which Seth heard raised voices and saw an intern running with papers. He strode down the hallway separated by a soundproof glass wall from one of their two brightly lit studios, where he could see the senior on-air personality with a map of the Capitol Area behind him, and a map of Belgium to his right.

To his left, off camera at the moment, a panel of four experts were sitting down and adjusting their mics. They were all in casual clothes. Behind them were Obman and the three other fallen angels assigned to The Network. With no prayer cover and few believers on the staff, they had complete freedom to move inside the building, and Obman sent regular reports to General Legat about what they saw and heard. So far they were very pleased.

Seth walked quickly past his own office to the Senior Producer, Rachel Shaw, who was holding court around her desk with six others, all standing.

"Who's coordinating video with Europe?...Who's at the White House and where is Senator Bradshaw?...Any more on how it happened?...Is someone digging into the groups at Capitol University?...A medical briefing at the hospital?...Hannah, we need experts in the next thirty minutes on Presidential Succession, the F-35, local hate groups, Muslims in the Air Force, and Senator Bradshaw."

"I was with him yesterday," Seth said, "and with his Head of Communications tonight."

Rachel and the others turned. "Then he's yours. Find him and dig in. Whatever you need."

Seth nodded, left for his office, and pulled out his cell phone. Obman saw him and told Pitow to follow Seth wherever he went.

Harry Calloway had been depressed for several weeks, and that night as he sipped a beer in the tiny apartment he could no longer afford, Zoldar made sure that Harry's depression was made even darker with voices of *Despair* and *Trouble*.

He had graduated from college two years after the financial crisis had cost his parents their home in suburban St. Louis, leaving him with a huge amount of student debt and no job prospects equal to his expensive education in computer apps. His parents downsized and did their best to care for the special needs of his younger sister, but the drugs needed for her care became more and more expensive. Harry moved to New York, determined to make the American dream work and to save his family.

After several years of laboring at low-level jobs in coding, he and a friend had borrowed $30,000 from the bank to pursue the development and marketing of an app which they were sure would change the restaurant industry. But some immigrant woman with better connections had apparently beaten them to that space, their loan was in default and would destroy Harry's precarious credit rating, his friend had disappeared, the bank wanted his car, and his parents could no longer afford the drugs that his sister needed.

Zoldar revved up the thoughts that already pummeled him.

*I'm a failure. The banks, the system, and those with privilege have pulled me down for their own advantage.*

He'd heard as much for months, not only from Zoldar, but from politicians and talking heads on television. Harry was just a regular white guy, and the experts all said that the American Dream should be rigged against him to give others a better shot. How was that fair? He was a victim. Zoldar reinforced his growing despair. The experts were wrong, and Harry would do something to fight back against those destroying him and his family. He ran his hand along the barrel of the AR-15 he'd bought a week ago when the idea of how to retaliate first occurred to him.

Callie unlatched her ground floor door and found Kristen Holloway on the couch, watching the news. She stood. "Grace is sound asleep, despite all the sirens."

Callie unbuttoned her coat. "Thanks. Meet Andrea Hunt, a new friend. She helps good people fly more easily at Homeland Security, and her husband works at the Pentagon. And this is Beau. They're spending the night with us."

Kristen shook her hand. "Glad to have you. When are you due?"

"Six weeks."

Kristen bent down and patted the Lab. "Glad to meet you, too."

Callie continued, "Beau is Tom Sullivan's, who told us we ought to move out of the D.C. area tonight, if we have a place to go, before he and almost everyone else left for their offices."

"Really? I have good friends in Annapolis. I can call them."

Callie glanced toward Grace's room. "I...I'm not sure. I don't want to put any of us in danger, but right now I feel like maybe we're supposed to stay here and pray."

Just then Kristen's phone beeped with a text. "There's a prayer vigil starting at church—through the night."

Callie silently nodded.

"How far is it?" Andrea asked.

"Three blocks. Two can go, and one can stay with Grace and get some sleep."

Andrea patted her front. "Show me where the essentials are, and then you two go. I'll hold the fort here, also praying."

That night in the Oval Office Prince Proklor limited the attendance to his inner circle of senior generals—he wanted the others out—watching, influencing, and reporting back as the mayhem around the nation ramped up. The mood was guarded but upbeat.

"No divorces today, of course," Temno began as they settled into their usual places around The Resolute Desk, "but over 3,000 abortions. A good Saturday."

"A great Saturday!" Proklor said, looking around. "Well done. Getting both that Muslim pilot and the abortion extremists to act within an hour of each other was brilliant. Pass down my personal congratulations to those who planted and coordinated those voices so perfectly. They will be elevated. Again, well done."

Bespor bowed slightly. "We will. And all our sector leaders are watching for any new ways to sow hate and confusion as the anarchy begins."

"Good, good. It's starting, finally. The days ahead should be full of great things for us, after so much work." He smiled. "As someone said, 'the fields are ripe for the harvest.'"

# 3

*Democracy will soon degenerate into an anarchy, such an anarchy that
every man will do what is right in his own eyes and no man's life or
property or reputation or liberty will be secure, and every one of these will
soon mould itself into a system of subordination...to the wanton pleasures,
the capricious will, and the execrable cruelty of one or a very few.*

John Adams[1]

Sunday, September 13

It was 12:30 on Sunday morning when Tom Sullivan arrived at Fort
Meade in a van with Diane Marsh, Allen Linder and three members
of the Situation Room watch staff. Garrett Crose stayed at The White
House to coordinate.

The three Deputy Chiefs of Staff were in their early 40s, veterans
of D.C. who had worked up through Congressional staffs, think tanks
and law firms, creating resumes of action, organization, and results. And,
given their key positions with President Rhodes, each had a Moderate to
Progressive worldview.

From the Security Gate their van was led to a conference center
which had been cordoned off with vehicles and soldiers. In the lobby
they deposited their cell phones in the usual lockers provided for that
purpose, then entered a high-tech conference room with several screens,
a central table for twenty, and empty chairs along each wall. , Tom found
President Bradshaw with Rob Thompson, his Senate Chief of Staff,
Emily Schofield, and four others from the Senator's former staff, plus
several senior military officers. Allen Linder walked over to the
president, shook his hand and introduced the others from The White
House. Behind the president, Garrett Crose was on a screen.

"Thank you for the list, Allen," President Bradshaw said, as he sat
again in a chair at the center of the table and ran his hand through his
ample gray mane. "We've been working through it. Threats, issues and
people. There's a lot."

---

1. http://libertytree.ca/quotes_by/john+adams

Other screens on the wall had network reports from Belgium, Capitol University, St. Louis, and even Boufarik, where a telephoto shot showed an F-35 parked in the distance on the tarmac at the Algerian Air Force Base in the early morning light.

Bradshaw continued, "They've already broadcast a video of that son of a bitch Muslim pilot, telling how he has always loved Allah more than America, where he was born, by the way. He's about to hold a press conference, two days after 9/11, after killing the president and many, many key leaders. And how the hell is he connected with a group protesting the vice president's forum being shot up by a BLM anti-abortion splinter group at a university in D.C.? And these other attack we're hearing about? Who or what is next?"

The room was silent. Balzor, Nepravel and several other demons invisibly circled within the group, undeterred by the thin prayer cover at this location or for these individuals. They sowed strong voices of *Confusion, Hate and Doubt* among the participants.

Garrett Crose spoke on the screen. "The Navy is ready with a submarine launched Tomahawk to hit the F-35. We just need your authorization."

"So our first retaliation against this attack is to destroy a $100 million piece of our own equipment? Is that the best our military can do? Brilliant." Brashaw paused and looked around the room. Finally he said, "Yes, go ahead, if that's all we can do."

Emily broke the ensuing silence. "Senator...uh, Mr. President, we've almost finished your address. The networks are standing by for a feed at 1:30."

He thought for a moment. "Will they know where we are?"

"We don't mention your location."

Bradshaw frowned. "But will everyone working with the networks know where the feed is coming from?"

Emily stopped and looked at The White House team. "I'm not sure."

Tom replied, "We can bounce an encrypted feed through a couple of other locations to The Situation Room, then release it from there. To the world it will look like it's coming from The White House."

Bradshaw turned. "Good idea. And who are you, again?"

"Tom Sullivan. Continuity of Government, and Deputy Cybersecurity at The White House. My boss, Olivia Haas, was on Air Force One."

"I've known Tom a long time," Emily said. "He's good."

"All the better. You're now the Head of Cybersecurity." He looked around. "And we should *all* be thinking about secrecy and deception. Someone is obviously out to get us, and they mean it. We need to be *very* careful."


At 2 am, the networks broadcast a recorded video which they had received moments before, written in part by Emily and Tom. Henry Bradshaw addressed the nation from what appeared to be the small conference table in the White House Situation Room.

As the camera slowly moved closer, a voice said, "The President of the United States, former Senator Henry Bradshaw."

"My fellow Americans, over the past few hours we have sustained terrible attacks on our nation. Terrorists downed Air Force One over Europe, killing President Rhodes, the First Lady, Speaker of the House Rebecca Gordon, and their senior staffs; they were on their way to a NATO Summit. At almost the same time, terrorists killed Vice President Carpenter and his wife at a speech he was giving at a local university. And there have been several strikes against groups and institutions which may or may not be related to the first two acts of cowardice, perpetrated by our enemies.

"With their tragic deaths our Constitution provides that the new head of the Executive Branch, the president, shall be the President Pro Tempore of the Senate. Until several hours ago that was my role in our government, as the senior most Senator from the majority party in the Senate. For those of you who don't know me, I have served our citizens for over forty years, as a municipal executive in my home state of California, and then in the Congress, and finally in the Senate.

"Although I took the oath of office as president tonight,"—a picture of him, Margaret and a military judge standing in front of a flag with his hand on a Bible appeared briefly on the screen—"so that our government will continue to operate as our Founders intended, this moment in our history is not at all about me. It is about the men and women in uniform and in government facilities all across our nation who are at this moment both defending us and beginning the process of bringing these terrorists to justice.

"We have raised the Defense and Homeland Security Departments' alert levels to the highest possible all across the globe, and through a well-rehearsed process implemented after 9/11, key federal decision makers and their staffs have begun dispersing to remote sites to ensure the operational continuity of our government, no matter what may occur.

"At this early hour all of these—and many other—processes are in their first phases, so there are bound to be some disruptions and missteps. But I want to assure you that my new Administration will quickly ramp up to full effectiveness, and our first priority will be to keep America safe.

"I've issued Executive Orders to close our national air space, as we did at 9/11, and to seal our borders. These moves will inconvenience many of you, but they are necessary this morning. Hopefully they will be temporary. I have also sent orders to all fifty governors federalizing the National Guard, so that troops will be ready, if needed, in any capacity in the coming days. I have tasked each governor to immediately implement local plans for Guardsmen to protect key infrastructure points such as water resources, dams, bridges and airports.

"Tonight I ask every American to keep the families of our fallen leaders and loved ones in your thoughts and prayers, along with those who must now take on new responsibilities. We have many tremendous tasks ahead of us in the coming days, most of them unpleasant, and all of them unexpected. As we address what must be done in the next hours, days, and weeks, I ask each of you to assist us with your own skills and talents. Much will be asked of all of us, but that is how it has always been. Working together, we will get through even this darkest hour, to what we must believe, as impossible as it now seems, will be an even better nation.

"That is our clear hope for the future. But for now we are focused on safety and security. Please stay close to both local and national news sources and alerts. If you see something suspicious or out of place, let the authorities know immediately. It is much easier to contain a possible threat than to deal with its aftermath.

"Working together as individuals and banded together as local, state and federal governments, we will effectively protect our nation and defeat our enemies. We will do our part here in Washington, and I ask that each of you do yours. We plan to give updates no less than once a day until it is clear that the threat has been completely eliminated. While our first responders, military, and government experts ramp up their efforts in the coming hours, please give your children an extra hug and tell them that your government will protect you.

"Good night, and may God bless America."

The working group at Fort Meade watched the address on a monitor.

"You said what had to be said, and you set the right tone," Emily told the president. "It's very clear that America is still in business."

"I hope you're right," Bradshaw responded, slightly shaking his head and taking Margaret's arm. "The base has provided rooms for all of us next door. Unless there's more to do, I suggest we get a few hours' sleep, and we'll reconvene at seven."

Allen Linder said, "I'll take the first watch here. Diane, can you relieve me in two hours?" She nodded.

After retrieving their cell phones, the Schofields and Tom Sullivan walked down the hall to the lodging side of the conference center. Emily's phone buzzed.

"It's Seth." The three of them formed a huddle, and Emily answered on speaker. "Hey."

"That was a good talk. You put it together well."

"A terrible mess. Any news on your side?"

"We haven't heard from any groups yet, claiming responsibility. We have people on the way to every location to follow up. And that Air Force pilot's video, full of calm, rational hate for Christians, Jews and America, has gone viral on the Internet, particularly in the Middle East. He's being hailed in several capitals as a conquering hero, and there have already been early morning riots in Stockholm and Munich as his supporters demonstrate and clash with far-right thugs."

"What's next? We've got to find these people." Tom said almost to himself.

"Emily, The Network has designated me as point person with the new president and his staff, given our relationship and history. Is there any way I can get an early interview?"

She glanced at Tom, then said, "Not now. We're really trying to dig out of a hole, and we don't know how deep it is."

"I know you're at Fort Meade, so I could run up to do an interview after your morning briefing. And we can compare notes on any other news."

She shook her head. "Seth, no. Not right now. We'll think about it. I promise you'll get the earliest shot possible."

Tom frowned. "How do you know where we may be?"

"We installed those Friend Following apps on our phones two years ago when we were traveling overseas. I can see you're both in the Conference Center at Fort Meade."

Tom paused. "Seth, thanks. But that's classified information now, so don't share it with anyone.'

"It may be classified, Tom, but it's right here on my friggin' phone."

"I understand. Emily, I gotta talk with Allen." He turned and walked quickly back to the conference room.

Balzor and Nepravel, who had been hovering nearby and listening to their conversation, looked at each other as the spiritual light in the conference center started to brighten and turn much warmer. Apparently people had seen the new president's talk, had started praying, and now He was answering them. "Damn Him," Nepravel muttered, as he followed Tom but wondered how much longer they would be able to stand the light and the heat from the incoming answered prayers.

Early that Sunday morning Neal Jamison and Sam Stewart, young African American engineers at a bustling aerospace plant outside Savannah, Georgia, drove north on a dark two lane road in rural South Carolina. Originally from New York, the two friends had moved South to pursue their careers after excelling in robotics research as undergrads in Boston.

Both men traced their family roots to the rural South, and over the years they'd heard many stories about life in Georgia before the Great Migration North during World War II. Neither man had experienced much overt racism on the job—in fact they were already on leadership paths within their expanding company. But as they attended Critical Race Theory classes and talked with their friends, they realized that they were in fact victims of Systemic Racism. They hated being surrounded by the monuments and totems which proclaimed White Supremacy from the lawns of many county seats and college campuses within a hundredmiles, which still survived even after the protests several years earlier. The blatant racism was incredibly infuriating, and since it was seemingly unnoticed by their white colleagues, except in the required CRT classes, it made them even angrier.

So Jamison and Stewart decided to push back, and while they couldn't topple a statue on their own, they knew they could master a good spray painting. Late that night, after a couple of beers, they had headed to Hampton Pierce College and a particularly obnoxious statue of a Confederate Cavalryman guarding the campus entrance at its intersection with the small college town. Razum and two other demons had been working on their feelings of victimhood for months, and they rode along, revving up the voices.

*The rednecks at the plant are never going to accept us. Look at all the history, man. They're just using us. White Privilege. They never change.*

As they expected, they found the main street near the statue dark and empty of people—just a few parked cars. The Bible Belt still had some clout here, even if only with closing hours.

They parked and quietly unloaded their spray cans of black paint and step stools. Seeing no one, they quickly walked over to the statue and began spraying the base. Neal had written, "Black Li..." when he heard a shout behind him, followed by a car door closing. Razum smiled because his companions had roused the white boys across the square.

"What are you doing?" came the first shout as a shotgun round was chambered. Car lights came on.

They looked at each other, then leapt to the ground. They saw men's silhouettes running their way.

Dropping their paint cans, they took off running in the opposite direction. By sticking together they made it possible for the first blast to take them both down, and for the second to kill them. As Jamison gasped for air and felt blood pooling around him, the last sounds he heard were whoops of laughter.

Hovering over their bodies, ready to harvest their souls, Razum thought how easy this was becoming again—like before all that Civil Rights crap years ago—because the schools and their own companies were teaching everyone to be tribal. And it was actually better than before—no longer just in the South; the whole nation was splitting into racial camps, led from the top. "Thank you," Razum said, as Jamison's soul recoiled from its first look at eternity.


As Tom neared the door to their meeting room, two women and a man arrived and went inside. Tom followed them.

They found President Bradshaw still in conversation with Allen Linder and Diane Marsh at the conference table. Linder looked up and motioned for them to come over.

"Mr. President, this is Special Agent Tanya Prescott of the FBI. James Toomey, the Director of the FBI, has designated her to be the Senior Agent in Charge. As you know, on any domestic operation the FBI is the lead and the coordinator."

Prescott, of medium height, mid-40's, with high cheekbones and intense blue eyes, stepped forward and shook the president's hand. "We're the first of what should be about ten in another hour, connected of course back to all the resources at FBI headquarters. We should be fully operational in about thirty minutes. Director Toomey is in the air from Phoenix and will join us in two hours."

The president gave a small smile. "Thank you for coming. We need you."

"It's what we do. We'll begin working very closely with the other agencies, from the Secret Service where you're concerned to the NSA for foreign intelligence. At every relevant agency there'll shortly be an FBI team focused only on this. My team and I will handle the overall coordination."

"Have you ever done this before?" he asked.

Prescott paused, then said, "Not exactly this. No one has. But I *have* been on some pretty tight assignments—before transferring to the FBI I was the lead agent in charge for President Harper's trip to Moscow, and all that followed."

"Hmm. I know that was a tough one. Too bad the Kremlin has changed so much since then—maybe they could help us now."

"Unlikely with the current people there. But, excuse me, sir, we need to get set up."

Tom, who had been standing at the table and listening, spoke up.

"Sir, and Agent Prescott, if you want our location to be secret, we're going to have to take some steps."

The president said, "Agent Prescott, this is Tom Sullivan, Cyber Security at The White House."

They shook hands. Tom noted the strength of her grip. "Our group works on cybersecurity, which is usually about protecting key data and physical targets, like the power grid, from attack—and also about using cyber weapons against others."

"Yes, I know," Prescott smiled.

"So this is not my precise area of expertise, but I was just speaking with a friend and realized that right now we have a much more mundane but potentially dangerous threat—our cell phones."

Bradshaw's eyes narrowed and Linder shifted in his chair. "What about them?" the president asked.

"Just having them. Using them. Most of us have two phones—one official and one personal. We put them in the lockers to come in here, but then we pick them up again in the lobby. On either or both of these phones we may have installed apps that transmit our location, for all sorts of good reasons. You and your wife may have them on your phones. And some phones automatically send your location, unless you turn that feature off. Plus our watches and exercise monitors. In short, given so many of us here, hundreds of people may already know exactly where you are, to within a few feet."

The president reached in his pocket and handed Tom his personal phone. "I guess I just walked past the lockers and didn't think about it."

Tom quickly scrolled to Settings. "Yes, sir. Your Location Services is on, and your location is being broadcast to anyone with whom you text message. The signal probably won't connect from this secure room, but as soon as you go out into the lobby, you'll be transmitting."

"How do you turn it off, and why didn't anyone think of this sooner?"

Tom glanced at Prescott. "I'm turning it off now, sir, or at least it appears to be. Actually, hard to know for sure. And I guess no one foresaw the need to make your location secure as a Senator."

"What about my wife and all these other people? My staff members? Who knows what their phones are transmitting? And you think the watches are doing the same?"

"We'll get some help from Cyber Command. General Price will be here soon. We'll have to be sure our phones, watches and pads and laptops aren't transmitting location information, or any other information."

"What a mess."

"Yes. We could power them off, but I don't think we want to do that, given the critical need to communicate right now. And of course every government official and military member who's been deployed to a remote site has the same issue."

"How did no one ever think of this before?" Diane Marsh asked.

Agent Prescott spoke. "We have, as Tom said, for secure headquarters with plenty of landlines to use. Not for this situation."

Tom added, "I guess Continuity of Government policy never imagined hiding individuals' locations. But we can direct the MPs at every remote site to perform an audit on every device, official and personal, to reduce the risk."

"Thank you, Tom. I like the way you think. Keep it up. Now, unless any of you has more, I'm going to try to get a couple of hours' sleep, even if my bed is in someone's crosshairs."

As they broke up, Agent Prescott turned to Tom. "Good call. Let me get set up, and we'll compare notes in the morning."

The lights were burning all across the White House at four that morning, but in the seemingly empty Oval Office the spiritual darkness was palpable. Proklor was smiling in front of the Resolute Desk, listening to reports from his key lieutenants, assembled all around him.

"Most of you were with us for the Reichstag Fire in early '33. Only a month later our boy was ruling by decree alone, and did so for twelve incredible years—all done "legally". Doesn't this seem even better?"

There were nods and smiles. "Yes, Prince Proklor," Temno replied for all to hear. "With your planning, the targets were easily identified."

He nodded. "More to come. And you have our forces in Russia, China and elsewhere on strict orders not to encourage any military aggression?"

"Yes. As you commanded. Only cyberattacks and hacking. Nothing physical."

"The Americans must be allowed to come undone by themselves. We'll link with the other Princes once this last light is extinguished and there is only darkness."

He smiled. Just then Balzor and Nepravel materialized at the back of the meeting. Proklor waved them forward.

"Come. With these events you are now on the front lines—the most important decision makers are under your direction. Please, report."

The ranks parted and Balzor moved forward, followed by Nepravel, until they were standing in front of the prince, with Temno just to one side. They bowed. Balzor began, "It all went according to your plan—utter confusion—but we barely got out of Fort Meade. Once the new president spoke, the prayers began, and of course He knows where the president is, even if others don't, and so His answers to their prayers came down right on us. The heat and light were blinding. We stayed as long as we could, but the prayers kept increasing. They were all going to sleep, so we came to report."

"I see. And until the prayers overcame you?"

Balzor paused and glanced at Nepravel, who spoke. "It was exactly according to your plan, my liege. Complete chaos. We had room to maneuver, spinning up voices of *Fear* and *Revenge*. The new president is very fearful about more attacks, and about his own safety. And he only really trusts his own inner circle. When the answered prayers at Fort Meade die down, and sooner at other places, we'll watch carefully and ramp up more voices of *Hate* and *Distrust*."

"Good. Very good. Yes, it feels like Berlin, or Saint Petersburg two decades earlier. We had no idea those situations would advance so quickly—but they did, thanks of course to our earlier work." Proklor looked at Legat. "We need teams stationed all around Fort Meade, just like we normally have at the White House, so whenever there's a let up in the prayers, they can move quickly and find out what's going on, before the light gets too bright again."

"Yes, Prince Proklor."

He looked at the group. "And the rest of you—keep the strikes coming, in waves, with a few quiet days in between. The pressure and distrust will push them back into their tribes and they will descend into anarchy, where no one trusts anyone. That was the problem with those Muslim idiots on the first 9/11—they didn't listen to us. Four attacks at the same time on the same morning. When they were over, that was it. The believers regrouped and pulled together. Not this time."

Tom and Emily were pouring coffee in the lobby of the conference center.

"Did you get any sleep?' he asked, filling his cup.

"Not really. I kept adding to my lists. Logan, poor thing, helped me. You?" She reached for the cream and sugar.

"I met with Agent Prescott and General Price at Cyber Command two hours ago. They're working on our communication and location problems. And I texted Callie. She and Andrea decided to stay in the city."

"That was nice of you."

He shrugged. "She seems like a nice person. Thanks for inviting her. She said they've been up all night praying for us."

Emily raised an eyebrow. "Nice." Then she turned to head for the makeshift Operations Center in the large conference room. "Last night seems like a week ago, doesn't it?"

He nodded and opened the door for her. It was where they had started at midnight. At one end of the conference table were President Bradshaw, Rob Thompson, Diane Marsh and Allen Linder, who waved them over. The monitors had the Situation Room and The News Network streaming live. Tom and Emily took seats. Diane was finishing.

"And so the FBI, Pentagon and NSA briefers will be here at 7:30 with domestic and foreign updates. I suggest we all attend, if that's all right with you, sir."

President Bradshaw, his eyes red, looked up from his mug and nodded. "Yes, until we have some idea of what's really going on, we need as many trusted people as possible in the decision making."

She continued. "Most departments have deployed their advance COG teams to their remote locations, with more personnel following this morning. With National Guard troops deployed to most airports, our air space should reopen at noon for a limited number of flights. The borders later today." She looked at the president.

He paused before he spoke, looking from face to face. "I'm obviously new at this. Diane, thank you for the update. But we have a lot of important *specific* issues. The downing of Air Force One—identifying the remains and bringing all those bodies home for a lot of funerals—including a presidential funeral. The vice president, his wife, and others murdered. Funerals. The Air Force pilot and the F-35 in Boufarik—I assume the Russians, Iranians and Chinese are on the way with cash, though hopefully we'll destroy it. Appointments to replace all the people we lost on Air Force One. Protecting our military bases, water sources, power grid, internet access, and transportation arteries. Is it safe for anyone to fly? Should the government in Washington even open for business tomorrow? When will it be safe to return to the White House, and where should we work until then? Deciding on a new vice president. How are foreign governments reacting? Are our enemies probing for weaknesses? *All* those issues and many more are on our plate without any new attacks, which could happen this morning. And, of course, how are all these acts linked, and to whom? So don't we have a lot of specific problems to solve, and how do you propose to tackle them all?"

Garrett Crose, on the feed from the White House Situation Room, spoke. "Mr. President, for better or worse the federal government is huge, and there are teams already working on almost every situation you just mentioned. They will be reporting up through their chains of command starting this morning. All National Security Council members will be here in person or by link at noon. On the big picture issues like whether to open tomorrow, and protecting our resources, we'll start those discussions shortly, to make recommendations to you and to the NSC. We've already looked at every position believed to have been lost on Air Force One and have a specific recommendation for the acting replacement—basically moving the next best person up."

Diane Marsh added, "As terrible as this is for leadership, the rest of government is intact: except for your governor appointing an interim Senator to replace you, and electing a new Speaker of the House and President Pro Tem, the Legislative Branch is in place. And the Judicial Branch. Almost all Cabinet members. All of our Defense and Policing capabilities—the SecDef and Chairman of the Joint Chiefs were already in Prague with the Secretary of State. And all state and local governments, plus local law enforcement."

"So we have an incredible amount to do, both in trying to figure out what happened and who did it, and in moving forward," Allen Linder said, "but we have resources working on most of it now."

The president nodded. "But given the attacks on Air Force One and the others, we don't know whom to trust, what they may now be planning, or how they're connected."

Linder continued. "We'll begin there in a few minutes with your first agency briefings. For now, by the way, if you concur, we thought it best to have two Co-Chiefs of Staff—Rob with you, and Garrett at the White House. They'll be in regular contact and coordinate your schedule and briefings."

"Fine. Fine."

Tom spoke up. "On communication, we've got to take some quick actions."

"Go on."

"As we realized last night, we're all silently giving out important information which could be used by an enemy, even before we start moving around again and talking to each other, which is a second problem. All the phones and devices in the Legislative and Executive Branches, except those used specifically for classified information and police work, are completely open. Even the 'official' ones. Like yours, Mr. President, when you arrived here. We've got to rein them in. We've got to think much more about security and control, starting with the basics."

The others waited.

"General Price of the National Security Agency and I met with the FBI Director when he arrived. The general will be one of the briefers at the National Security Council meeting. But he and the FBI team immediately agreed that active monitoring is a real-time threat. We're going to start with a Core Group—right now the NSA team is configuring twenty specially developed smartphones for this group's exclusive use, with a unique 25 digit authentication key and a daily change algorithm that will make hacking into the Core Group network impossible. Only General Price and I will have copies of the 25 digit authentication key and algorithm, in our personal safes.

"Once these twenty are baselined—we should have fifty by tomorrow—they'll be limited to encrypted text and voice on our own special military-grade Trusted Network when talking to another phone in the network. They'll be numbered and we'll keep a record of who gets each one, starting with us and expanding to those who are critical to security.

"They won't ping normal towers but will instead use a tight, guarded government frequency range available on our secure towers in major cities and near military bases. They'll have a crossover interface so we can talk unencrypted with phones outside the special Trusted Network, but those other phones will have no access inside. It will take phone-level authentication to join the special network, and a second authentication for one phone to communicate with another inside the encrypted group. These phones are very, very secure.

"That solves our second problem. The first is all our existing cell phones, pads and computers. They either are now, or can with a click or two, be disclosing our locations. And if they've already been compromised, their microphones and cameras may be turned on when we don't know it. And then even our conversations could be compromised. My recommendation is that everyone in the Core Group who'll get a new phone should turn in our cell phones now. Tag yours, and a special team will go through them and delete any function that includes location, behavior, etc. They will become the dumbest of dumb phones, but you can still talk and text on them—with no security."

He pulled out some adhesive labels.

"And we've got to require an audit by a cyber digital forensics team of every other device you have, besides your phone, to delete any location information, and to check for indicators of compromise. So tape your name and device password to any iPad or laptop you need to use. Outside of our Core Group, the FBI and I recommend that everyone in government submit to an audit of their phones and devices for these same reasons. We'll give those devices an internal certificate for use, once they pass the inspection and then we can configure them to report back if anyone tries to hack into them."

There was silence as the implications sank in. Then the president looked around the room. "When we leave, everyone get your phones and give them to Tom."

Rob Thompson asked, "How long will it take to inspect and certify every device of every government employee?"

"Not sure, but we'll start at the top of each department, staff and agency with actual physical inspections. At lower levels, we believe the audits can be done remotely while VPN'd into our network. General Price has a group working on it now."

More silence. Finally the president said, "Good work, Tom. You may have saved many lives. Thank you for taking the initiative this morning."

"I'm sure there'll be more, and that all of us will have similar areas to cover. For now, turn off your laptops and tablets, and we'll try to roll out the Core Group phones and the first inspections before lunch."

Clayton Hunt, Ahmad Rashid and the other members of the Threat Identification Group had evacuated to Site R at Raven Rock, just across the Pennsylvania line, north of D.C. They had practiced a COG evacuation twice before, but this was the real thing. Assembled in a windowless room they checked the threat networks displayed on their screens with a sense of serious urgency, and occasionally they followed feeds from other Department of Defense sources, along with the major cable networks, as shown on wall monitors.

To this point it was like any other Sunday morning. There had been no noticeable change in the activities which each of their groups monitored. Then Clayton received a message in his earpiece and clicked a few buttons on his console.

Simultaneously on two of the large screens in front of them there appeared a News Network broadcast from Boufarik Air Base, showing Captain Adam Hassan at a podium with his F-35 visible behind him on the field, guarded by two half-tracks. On a second screen was an overhead satellite image of the airport on the Algerian coast and the surrounding fifty miles. A white dot, superimposed on the aerial, was inbound from the Mediterranean.

Hassan was speaking to what appeared to be a large group, with a bank of microphones in front of him. "American Crusader ideals and laws are opposed to every teaching of the Prophet. Allah's decrees and his Sharia Law describe the true and proper world, submitted to his will. Living under the Crusaders' Constitution while studying his laws made me realize how holy and true are his ways. The two are incompatible. I am glad to have struck a blow this morning for real truth. I renounce my service in the Crusader force and swear my allegiance to Allah."

As cheers erupted on the Network screen, those watching at the TIG could see the white dot cross the coastline.

Suddenly there was a huge explosion on the field, and Hassan was thrown from the podium. The entire area behind him was engulfed in flames and thick smoke.

Megan Buckley offered, just loud enough for everyone to hear, "Not enough collateral damage. Muslim pricks."

Clayton turned to Ahmad, who was staring at the screens. Finally the Marine said, "What a terrible day. So many lives lost."

"Yes," Ahmad answered. "A terrible day for our country."


Later that Sunday morning Callie, Kristen and Andrea entered the sanctuary at Church of the Good Shepherd. Built as a simple brick structure over a hundred years before, the church had been added to and enlarged, with classrooms in a day basement, where Grace was now in Sunday School. The sanctuary was filled beyond capacity with members, neighbors and passers-by. The senior pastor, Robert Ludwig, had dispensed with the scheduled service and his planned sermon on "Marriage: One Man and One Woman." Instead the congregation knelt together and offered prayers of confession and supplication for the nation and for the new government. Andrea prayed especially for Clayton and his team. Callie asked for wisdom for Tom, Emily and the new president. And every ten minutes or so they sang hymns.

No demon could come near, but several were encouraging a group which was gathering two blocks away.


"Damn it, Seth, where are you?" Rachel Shaw demanded through Seth's cell phone.

"Turning off the Parkway now. We'll be up in ten minutes."

"The BBC, our main competitors, and half the world are already broadcasting from outside Fort Meade, and you're not even there yet?"

"We will be."

"I thought you had an 'in', Seth. How did the rest of them know where the president is, and you didn't?"

"It won't happen again."

"You're right. Not if you want to keep it." She hung up.


Late that morning Tom stepped out of the Core Group discussion—there had been no new developments other than the Boufarik raid—and met General Nathan Price and two officers carrying faraday bags outside the conference room. The National Security Council was scheduled to begin in thirty minutes in the larger Secure Operations Room at NSA Headquarters itself, a short drive from the Fort Meade Conference Center.

General Price was powerfully compact, his uniform chest covered with medals, his hair short.

"Thank you for the fast work, general," Tom said, as they shook hands. "Come in."

The president and the others looked up from the table, covered with coffee cups. On the screen, Garrett Crose raised his hand in recognition from the White House.

Tom began, "I think you all know General Price, the Head of the NSA, whose facilities are not far away on the base at Fort Meade."

"The base commander and I are glad to be of service, but sorry for the circumstance."

President Bradshaw nodded. "Please thank your team. They've been most gracious."

"I will. Now, here are the Core Group phones. They're as secure as any phones on Earth. They will only connect via secure government cell towers. You can talk and text, but no email. They're numbered and logged. Once we've distributed similar phones to the NSC members, Mr. Sullivan will have the log and some additional phones which he can distribute to those who need them, under his control. And we expect to have your other devices back to you this afternoon, checked and secure. But for now, only use these."

"Thank you very much, general," the president said, as he accepted a phone from one of the officers and signed the log. "I know you'll be part of the NSC briefing this morning, but give us a quick summary. Did the NSA have any warning or indication about these attacks?"

The general shook his head. "No sir, we did not. Nothing. As you know, we're focused on every type of communication offshore, as well as protecting our domestic systems, and we have seen nothing in the last days or weeks to indicate what just happened."

The room was silent.

"Thank you, General Price. Hopefully your domestic counterparts will have some actionable information at our briefing."

"Yes, sir. And if they do, we'll of course help in any way we can."

Thirty minutes later the Core Group was walking toward the exit doors to several waiting SUVs. President Bradshaw and Rob Thompson were in the lead.

Behind them, Emily quietly asked Tom, "Did you see Seth's report from outside the gate?"

"Yeah. Every other network is out there, too."

When they were outside, the president turned to them. "Emily, if you agree, you'll be the new White House Director of Communications." She nodded. "Tom, I need someone with your experience whom I can absolutely trust on the security side of all this. Emily knows you and tells me you're the best. While Rob and Allen work on filling in the positions we lost on Air Force One, would you accept becoming the acting Deputy National Security Advisor so that you can really help us through this mess?"

Tom paused. "I'm certainly no Peter Sloane. But, yes, of course. I'll do my best."

"Good. Good. Then maybe you ought to ride over with Tanya Prescott and General Price, and the three of you can begin comparing notes on what we should do to find who's behind this."

Emily and Rob joined the president in his SUV. As the Secret Service driver pulled away, Balzor materialized with them, sliding through a lapse in the prayers for the office, meaning almost no spiritual heat or light bothered him. He immediately began ramping up the voices inside the riders.

Bradshaw turned to his two long-time confidants. "Thank you, both. This isn't easy, and I really need your input. While it's just the three of us together, let me say what I suspect you're already thinking: Everyone else here—from the Deputy Chiefs of Staff to the entire National Security Council—were appointed by President Rhodes.

"You know I had the greatest respect for him—he was certainly one of us and a whole lot better than that Bible-thumping idiot before him. I'm no spring chicken, but I'm afraid Rhodes was starting to lose his edge. I think conservatives like the Speaker were starting to get him to think about compromising our programs, when we're right on the verge of having full control. As terrible as this is, it could be a real game changer.

"I'm sure his team are all great people and doing their best at this difficult time. But at the end of the day, I suspect the three of us have a more active approach to winning and to governing than they do. Not to mention the vision for the equity and social justice we want for oppressed Americans. Assuming we survive the next few days, I think friction is going to be inevitable."

Rob nodded. "Yes. We need to work together now, obviously. But every president has the right to appoint his own team and to pursue his own programs."

"So, of course we'll focus on the crisis. But Rob, put a couple of our former Senate staff to work quietly figuring out whom we should designate and appoint to key positions, now that our team has the Executive Branch, as well as control of the Senate. And let's get Drew Boswell and his Tech friends involved—quietly—to give us some suggestions on good people who can really help us in decision-making roles.

"I assume Jacob Welch, the House Majority Leader, will be elected Speaker. A conservative Uncle Tom from South Carolina, so we'll have to tread lightly—can't attack him head on, at least not soon. Our candidate to be the new vice president will be critical. Someone who shares our vision for America and can be approved by both houses of Congress."

"Yes, sir. I'll be on it this afternoon."

"And, Emily, given the reporters outside the gate, it looks like Tom was right about too much information getting out. Please think about how we can put out the information we need to, while limiting what others know, until we understand what's really going on."

"Yes, sir."

"I hope President Rhodes' remaining senior team has some idea about who killed him on Air Force One, and almost simultaneously killed the vice president while he was surrounded by Secret Service agents, for God's sake. And why. I assume we're next on someone's list. Security has to guide us on all our decisions."


Alexei Nobikov landed in Larnaca, Cyprus, on the late afternoon flight from Moscow. He'd spent four days in the Russian capital, the first two with his group's senior staff, reporting on his team's activity. Then he helped his elderly parents get their dacha ready for winter. After attending Orthodox Church that morning, he'd been driven to Moscow's Sheremetyevo Airport, and now another driver in a new BMW was taking him to his home in Limassol on Cyprus' south coast, where many Russians had lived and worked for several decades.

He and his wife, Anna, enjoyed their relaxed life on Cyprus. Childless, their home had five bedrooms—they usually had a steady stream of visitors from their homelands. They'd met when they were students at Moscow University. She was from Uman, in Ukraine, and they'd always had many family members and friends in both countries, as was the norm for those who grew up in the Soviet Union.

A cyber expert who had trained in computer technology and then as one of the first exchange students at Boston University during the more hopeful early days of detente in the late 90s, Nobikov headed a disinformation team that was known to only a few outside the top echelon of the Kremlin.

What had begun a decade earlier as a passive window on the West to gather information had become, with the change to more aggressive policies from the Russian leadership in recent years, an agent for dissemination and internet intrusion.

Nobikov, who had set up the original fact-finding operation and now also published a travel blog for cover as a journalist, had been forced to expand his focus, as his superiors directed. His only alternative had been to resign, which would not have been good for him or his family. And the leadership's increasing demands kept him focused on the very latest technologies, which always interested him.

But then his country invaded Ukraine, after blaming the West. Alexei, like most Russians with international experience, was torn between his natural patriotism and his understanding of truth vs. lies, so he suffered from an ever-increasing tension which remained unresolved.

While Western intelligence focused on threats coming from Russia, Alexei Nobikov appeared to be a freelance journalist and the owner of one of the legitimate internet service providers, InternetOne, on Cyprus, inside the European Union. Through this window his team had almost unrestricted access to every aspect of worldwide social media outside of China, which blocked even Russian experts, as well as daily opportunities to create and to plant false information in and about Western companies, governments and institutions. And they had dark cash available to help fund competing activists.

Alexei's ten-person team of young specialists were as highly trained as any cyber experts anywhere in the world, but he was careful to ensure that they were not hackers—they didn't break into networks or steal information—that was the job of others. Alexei's team was kept busy simply gathering, assessing, and trying to covertly influence everything on the internet for his government's advantage. And all the while the turmoil within him intensified, with no easy resolution in sight.

Riding with Nobikov was his Number 2, Svetlana Pankratova—highly unusual for a Sunday evening, but then a lot had happened in the last twenty-four hours. Two years earlier Sveta had been assigned to his Cyprus internet company from Moscow to help their operations become more aggressive, and Nobikov assumed that she had a direct personal link to his bosses. So, while he'd privately shared his growing concerns with a few members of his team—the ones he'd recruited at the beginning—he maintained the proper public face of total loyalty to the state. He and Sveta had never discussed their country's most recent aggressive actions, other than the usual quick comments about the latest news reports. Unspoken, the issue hung between them, as with many Russians.

Sveta handed Alexei a two-page report. "All morning their social media has been going crazy. Besides the usual calls for patriotism and coming together at such a time, almost every imaginable interest group has been blaming and threatening others. Greens. The Gun Lobby. Muslims. Skinheads. Black Lives Matter. Jews. Russia haters. White Nationalists. China haters. Conservatives. Liberals. Antifa. All of them. There appears to be real fear, and real hatred. Everyone is pulling back into their Identity Tribes and looking for enemies."

"Good. Have we been exploiting it?"

"Of course. I called everyone in. We've been piling on wherever we can. Dmitri is working on some new websites to put up tomorrow. I've instructed our donor fronts to increase their giving over the next three days—to all these groups. And we may try to spoof The Network."

"Excellent. America has taken a big hit. As usual, we'll do our best to confuse them, and to make it harder for them to recover."


Since it was past time for Grace's lunch, Callie and Andrea walked with her down the front steps of The Church of the Good Shepherd. Kristen remained behind with others to pray for the nation.

On the sidewalk fifty feet past the church's steps in both directions, behind short temporary barriers, stood groups of protesters with signs reading "Love Is For Everyone" and "God Loves Gay Marriage." Behind them, a block away from the spiritual heat, hovered their invisible encouragers.

Turning toward home and holding Grace's hand tightly, Callie began to walk, followed by Andrea.

There were shouts. "You're all bigots!"

"We love each other, but Christians hate us!"

They were almost past the protesters when Andrea turned to a young woman holding a sign reading "Gay Love is The Law" and said, "No one preached anything today about this. We've all just been praying for our country. Don't you know what's happened?"

"Yes, of course. And good riddance to three of the worst hate mongers."

"What?"

"The three of them. They hated us and opposed our right to marry."

"What? The president *pushed* your agenda. Now you've won. It's the law. Marry whomever you want."

"They opposed us for years, and only switched because they knew we'd win. Hypocrites. People like you bigots who oppose us even now want to turn back the clock. Well, see what happened to them! I hope the same thing happens to you."

Callie had stopped and was listening.

Andrea, her pregnancy as well as her disbelief obvious, inched a bit closer to the woman. "My husband is serving our country right now. I've spent the last two hours praying for all of us, not thinking about who should marry whom. You should be ashamed, talking about murder that way."

The woman advanced a step and three men joined her. "Ashamed? Me? No way. You rich, white, homophobic bitches pray for the nation one minute, and against oppressed people like us the next. I know. I've heard you."

"What?"

"You heard me. And if you have to add another white-privileged baby like yourself to this overpopulated world, I hope they are gay, or transgender. Then you'll see what oppression feels like."

Holding even tighter to Grace, Callie moved to face Andrea. "Come on. This is no place for us, or for an eight-year-old."

"But how...?"

"Come on."


Tom sat next to Emily in the first row of chairs behind the main players around the conference table at the NSA Headquarters, located inside Fort Meade, for the new president's first National Security Council meeting that Sunday afternoon. An NSC meeting was usually chaired by the National Security Advisor, but Peter Sloane and his senior staff had all been onboard Air Force One. President Bradshaw, flanked at the center of the table by Rob Thompson and Allen Linder, ran the meeting himself.

In attendance, either in person or by remote video connection, were James Toomey of the FBI, the Chairman of the Joint Chiefs, the Director of National Intelligence, plus the Secretaries of State, Defense, Treasury, Homeland Security and Energy. And the Attorney General, the other White House Deputy Chiefs of Staff and the White House Counsel. In addition, many key members from their teams, like Tom, Agent Prescott of the FBI and General Price, the Head of the NSA, surrounded them in the room. The meeting lasted two hours, and when it concluded, Tom heard the president's frustration.

"You mean the most talented people with the best systems on the planet don't have a clue who's behind these attacks?" Bradshaw fumed.

After the silence, the Secretary of Defense spoke on one of the screens from an executive jet returning from Prague. "As you've heard, sir, we have leads and suspicions, but nothing definite yet."

His hands on the table's edge, Bradshaw looked from the screen to the others in the room. "Well, until we have more than that, we'll keep the government in dispersed mode. What do you call it, Tom?"

Tom responded to the sudden glance from the president. "Continuity of Government, sir."

"Yes. Continuity of Government. By the way, meet Tom Sullivan, the first member of my new National Security Advisor team. Please stay focused, and we'll meet here again tomorrow, unless something comes up sooner. Emily, please prepare a report I can give to the nation this afternoon. Thank you."

Logan Schofield waited in a chair by the coffee bar in the lobby of the convention center for Emily and Tom to be dropped off after the NSC meeting. He had spent the day watching the news and reading. When he looked up, his wife and their friend came in the front door.

He hugged Emily. "A tough day, I bet."

She ran her fingers through her hair. "Yes. Too long. I need a nap and a change of clothes."

"I'm ready," Logan replied with a grim smile.

"Here's the list, dear. I hope you can find it all."

"I'll do my best. And thank you, Tom, for arranging the pass with General Price. I doubt I could get back on the base today just by saying I'm married to the brightest woman in the Executive Branch."

Tom smiled. "Of course. But it comes with a price. I'm as tired of my clothes as Emily is of hers. Here's my list and my key. Can you help me out, too?"

Logan paused. "We all have our roles to play in the crisis."

"Good man. And if you can't find something or figure out what I wrote, just grab what you think works. You're a sophisticated European—I'm sure your choices will be fine."

"I'll be back as soon as I can." Turning serious, he said to Emily, "And, really, get some rest. You'll feel better and make better decisions. I'm proud of you."

She pecked him on the cheek. "Thanks. But I have to review the notes for the president's report to the nation tonight."

"Try." Logan nodded to Tom and left for his car.

As the door closed behind Logan, Tom turned to Emily. "Can we talk about a couple of things before trying to get some rest?"

"Sure. But let's walk. My brain is clogged."

They went out the side door and began walking around the parking lot. It was warm, and the late afternoon sun felt good on Tom's face. He noticed a mobile surface-to-air missile launcher in the adjoining lot, and another on the opposite corner.

"Who would've imagined eight years ago when we answered Clayton's apartment ad that we'd be advising the president in the middle of this?"

She shook her head. "Yes, it's crazy. Do you feel the responsibility like I do?"

"Yes. To get it right. Everything. Not to miss anything, or to screw up. I really hate the uncertainty. The not knowing—waiting for the next attack."

As they walked in silence, Armored Personnel Carriers arrived with additional soldiers to seal off the area. Finally Tom said, "After realizing what a threat just our own phones are, and listening to the NSC briefers today, I'm struck by how the people attacking us have access to everything, but we know nothing about them. It seems impossible, but it's true. We're so open with everything. The haters can find out anything they want, and coordinate in secret. But we know nothing about them, and can't find them."

"What's the answer?"

"Maybe until this ends we need to tighten down on information. And if we temporarily impose some stronger rules and procedures for communications, then it'll be much easier to see who's trying to get around them. We can focus on those people and hopefully figure out what they're planning, and stop them."

"How do we 'tighten down on information'? And figure out who the bad ones are, much less stop them?"

"I have some ideas. We can build on the restrictions used during Covid—people generally accepted them. But we need even more. I want to talk to Agent Prescott and General Price before proposing anything. You know me—I want the details to be right."

"OK. I've been thinking about communications. We've got to project resolve and control. But like you're saying, maybe we should also plant some deceptions."

"That's probably an excellent idea, especially right now." He stopped and smiled. "I'm going to find Tanya. Good luck on a nap, and on the report. Let's compare notes again later."

President Bradshaw nodded to the Secret Service team standing outside the door of the best suite at the conference center that the Base Commander could organize for him and Margaret. "Thank you," he said, as he opened the door and went inside. Margaret was watching the news but turned it off, walked over, and hugged him.

"What a mess," he said, as he leaned back a bit and loosened his tie. "I need a drink."

"We both do." She smiled. "I had them bring some of your favorite."

Five minutes later, drinks in hand and seated by the window with a panoramic view of the parking lot, Margaret waited for him to speak.

"No one can figure anything out. Whoever is planning these attacks is doing so completely off the normal grid. Underground. It's really scary that all these generals and advisors have so few answers. See that young man walking in the lot with Emily? That's Tom Sullivan, a cyber guy at the White House. Emily's known him a long time. He's had the only good advice so far—and it's to turn off our cell phones!" He shook his head. "Did you give everyone's addresses to the Secret Service?"

"Yes, and I called the kids. There are agents at all three houses, and once the schools reopen, teams will accompany the grandchildren."

He was silent. "I can't let on, but I'm really, really concerned. Our country has grown so big and so complicated—it's hard to control. Apparently bad people can hide right under our noses. Remember when we were surrounded in our car by those neo-Nazis after my speech at Berkeley ten years ago, and they broke the window?"

"I still have nightmares."

"Well, this is much, much worse. And I feel about as helpless now as we did then. I hate being out of control, being unable to help. I bet those same right-wing lunatics—'Christian' White Supremacists—are behind this, somehow teamed up with Muslim fanatics. They all hate the better nation that America can become—is becoming—with diversity, equality, social justice, and progressive leadership."

"They've always hated people like us, Henry."

"I think a strong central government with progressive policies is the only way to prevent chaos and to hold the country together."

"Like Franklin Roosevelt during the war."

"Yes, this is war. And a few of Rhodes' White House people are actually praying about it! I saw three of them huddled in the conference room and praying after the NSC meeting."

She smiled. "It's normal at a time like this, dear. Remember after the first 9/11. They're not doing any harm."

He raised his hand. "OK. But I don't like having advisors who are dropping to their knees every few minutes to pray to a mythical being. We all need to be on the same page, with faith in ourselves, not in some Biblical Santa Claus who's going to save us. It's hard enough as it is, without two different teams." He turned towards her. "But we're starting to work on that, too. And we've got to find whoever's behind this quickly. The nation expects it."

After a long night and morning of monitoring no unusual financial activity at the DEA headquarters in Arlington, Natalie Ellis had finally been given a couple of hours off. She drove home through mostly empty streets and was impressed by how their friends had left the row house. She took a few ibuprofens for her headache and lay down on the couch. She switched on the TV and turned to The News Network.

By chance, Seth was on with a live update from outside Fort Meade, standing in a grassy area with the front gate in the background.

"...and so we're waiting on today's update, which we expect shortly from the new president. There's hope that..."

There was an interruption on the screen and Seth was replaced by a sign which read, "No Fake News! Tell the truth or worse things will happen."

Natalie sat up and read the message again. Then the screen went blank. A few seconds later the Network anchor in D.C. came on. She started to speak, but the screen again went blank. Natalie reached for her phone. Ten seconds later, another studio interior came up, and a person was just sitting down at a desk when that screen went blank. Natalie dialed Seth. Voicemail. She left a terse message and a third studio came up, this time with "Los Angeles" visible behind the chairs. Someone, seemingly a technician, not a newsman, said, "We've just experienced an interruption in Washington and New York. Regular programming should resume shortly."

Natalie dialed Seth again.


Kristen Holloway had driven Andrea to the Hunts' suburban home that afternoon. They and Callie had agreed that if Clayton did not return in a day or two, Andrea could rejoin Callie at her apartment. Now Callie and Kristen were attending a candlelight prayer vigil in their church's sanctuary, which was again nearly full. Callie had volunteered for an hour downstairs in the Nursery, and her daughter Grace was helping her with the younger children. They were coloring Bible story books around low tables with five others. Three infants were in cribs in a room next door with another volunteer.

Nepravel was two blocks away. The spiritual light from the believers and their prayers hurt his eyes, and he dared not venture closer, in case an angel happened to show up, drawn by the same light. But Nepravel felt great—all afternoon he'd been stirring up the voices in four of the earlier protesters at the church, encouraging them to return with a serious purpose. Now he could see them coming up the sidewalk.

Callie was sitting next to Grace in the Nursery, with the younger children around them. She could hear the congregation above them beginning the second chorus of "O God Our Help in Ages Past" when the window near them was smashed by a large rock and then a Molotov cocktail glanced off the curtains, shattered on the floor, and splattered burning gasoline across the room in a fireball, hitting the curtains, Grace, and the little boy next to her. The backs of their clothes caught on fire. All the children started screaming.

Grace lunged for her mother, and Callie grabbed the burning boy as he raced for the door with the others. She pulled them to the floor, rolled them over, and lay on top of them, smothering the flames with their bodies and hers. But now the curtains were blazing, as was the carpet next to them. She heard pandemonium outside the room, as screaming children tried to run upstairs and adults rushed down.

The fire alarm went off. Holding the two children tightly, she began to crawl toward the door, the pain searing her palms. She saw adult shoes in the doorway, and then the sprinklers kicked in, showering the room with water. Above the shoes came a fire extinguisher, deployed on the worst flames. Someone took the little boy from her grasp, and she collapsed on the floor with Grace, who held her mother like a vice, too scared to cry.

An hour later Nepravel departed to report at Sunday night's session with Prince Proklor at the White House. He hated that the church was still standing, but he'd heard many people, even members, saying "This has gone too far," and "When is someone going to teach them a lesson?" Which, after all, if you couldn't stop believers from praying, was the next best thing. He'd been watching humans for several millennia, and he knew that hatred mixed with fear was powerful enough to overcome almost anything, even faith—and he knew that Proklor would be pleased. It had been a good twenty-four hours.

# 4

*Religion in America...must nevertheless be regarded as the foremost of the political institutions of that country.... I do not know whether all the Americans have a sincere faith in their religion; for who can search the human heart? But I am certain that they hold it to be indispensable to the maintenance of republican institutions. This opinion is not peculiar to a class of citizens or to a party, but it belongs to the whole nation, and to every rank of society.... Christianity, therefore, reigns without any obstacle, by universal consent.*

Alexis de Tocqueville

Monday, September 14

Most of the demons who focused their lies on the humans working in the upper levels of government passed their nights meeting in a well-known local university's faculty lounge, or in an abortion clinic a mile northeast of the Capitol. Balzor and Obman, senior sector leaders, were in charge of the abortion clinic as a key stronghold. Given their large numbers and the daytime purpose of the modern two-story building, they were never concerned about an angel showing up. And the occasional incoming light and noise of an answered prayer was swallowed by their overwhelming darkness.

They returned to the clinic each night as their charges finally went to sleep—something spiritual beings did not require. If human eyes could see them, they would look like men from all walks of life, but with scars remaining from their original defeat, like a platoon regrouping after being routed. They were permanently angry. Edgy. Hateful. Committed to fighting back against the power which had defeated them, or at least to taking as many humans as possible with them to their fate. Always just below the surface was the shared anger and disbelief of two millennia: *He made us first, but He made them in His image. They had nothing to do with that. So why does He offer them a way out, and not us? Damn them. Damn Him.*

Killing humans was always enjoyable, but since everyone would eventually die anyway, their main focus was on deceiving as many as possible, keeping them from hearing the truth—ensuring their eternity without God. In the abortion clinic's several large meeting rooms as well as in smaller offices, their forces usually met in the early hours of the day and talked, comparing notes and contriving strategies for the people they confused and misled.

Each demon was totally out for himself—there was constant tension and one-upmanship to gain notice and rewards, which occasionally boiled over into jealous fights. But they'd also learned across the ages that they succeeded best when they worked together. So they shared new tactics, technologies and lies which appeared to work well. They were early adapters of the newest trends and technologies, pushing their constant agenda of self-centeredness, pleasure, self-promotion, and tribal identity.

Early this Monday morning there was a sudden surge of accomplishment, a realization that beyond deceiving their personal charges, their years of work to undermine America and her institutions were now finally coming to fruition. Nepravel, returning from the White House, recounted to all who would listen, with no lack of self-importance, how pleased Prince Proklor had been with his report on the Church of the Good Shepherd fire, and how the coming nationwide anarchy and destruction were now inevitable.

Obman and Balzor did their best to channel their subordinates' enthusiasm into a renewed focus on spinning up constant lies and on looking for new opportunities for hate and despair in the quickly changing D.C. landscape.

Tom could hardly move from the chair at his desk when his alarm went off that Monday morning at 5am. He and the others on the Core Team, along with most of the National Security Council, were still at Fort Meade. They had decided Sunday afternoon not to open key government offices in Washington until there was a clearer picture of what was going on. Sunday's NSC meeting had produced nothing new, and the president's televised update eighteen hours after the attacks was simply a general encouragement, with nothing specific about the perpetrators, their demands, or their goals.

Earlier on Sunday Tom had been in the make-shift Situation Room at the conference center, talking with Tanya Prescott and General Price, when the take down of The News Network occurred on the large monitor behind them. Within a few minutes Seth called him—Tom answered, and they learned that somehow the network's signal had been hacked, and power had been cut to their studios on the East Coast, an extraordinary feat of cyberattack and coordination. Seth was clearly angry and incredulous. Neither Tanya nor General Price had a ready explanation for how it was done, and when they walked over to another console, Seth again asked Tom to interview the president. Tom put him off, but promised to tell Emily.

After the president's update to the nation, Tom, Emily and Logan had donned clean clothes and grabbed a quick Sunday night dinner together at the conference center's restaurant. Their conversation was muted—the pressure to push back against the attacks, to do something, was palpable, and the tension grew by the hour as the nation's military and law enforcement agencies were unable to connect any dots between, or explain, what was going on.

They had just poured coffee after dinner when Emily received the first email from Kristen, forwarded through Andrea, about the firebomb attack on Church of the Good Shepherd. Callie, Grace, and others were in ambulances on the way to several hospitals. It appeared that the structure had received some damage, but would survive.

"What the hell is going on?" Tom said aloud to his friends.

He texted Callie, wishing a speedy recovery to everyone, and saying that he hoped to see her again soon. Any thought of resting on Sunday night had evaporated with those attacks. He stayed up doing more research, making calls, and writing detailed recommendations. Whoever was behind this was very clever and very skillful—in Tom's own experience, starting at the bank and continuing through with the government, that usually pointed to the Russians or the Chinese. He would have to focus everyone more closely on how anyone could be directing and coordinating these attacks without being detected by the best of U.S. countermeasures.

He didn't remember putting his head down in the middle of writing his email to the president, and it occurred to him this morning that his fatigue might influence his decisions.

But this had to stop. The president had made him responsible for finding solutions—as the Acting National Security Advisor, a huge responsibility—and he thought he now had the best plan for moving forward. After throwing water on his face, he returned to his laptop and pressed Send on the email.

Clayton Hunt and Ahmad Rashid had bunked together at the Pentagon Raven Rock COG site in southern Pennsylvania. A few minutes after they awoke that Monday morning to begin their next shift, there was a knock at the door and an MP returned their cell phones. Overnight they'd been checked for malware, and all data sharing apps had been removed. When powered on, the screen displayed a new Department of Defense Certificate for several seconds, including a serial number and an inspection date.

Clayton was shaving in the bathroom when Ahmad, half dressed, turned his phone on; there was an urgent text to call his wife, Mariam.

She was breathing hard and obviously upset. "Where have you been?"

"I told you last night, we had to turn our phones in to be checked."

"In the middle of the night someone threw a rock through our living room window. I turned on the light and it was there on the floor, glass all around it."

"Are you and the boys OK?"

Clayton stopped shaving and listened.

"There was a note attached to the rock. It said, 'Go home, Muslim scum. We know where you live.'"

"Damn."

"What should we do?"

Clayton motioned. Ahmad told him what had happened.

"Tell her to call Andrea and move everyone over to our house this morning. Andrea's group is working from home today, and we can help."

"I assumed you were up since I got your email. Thanks for coming by." President Bradshaw handed Tom a cup of coffee in his suite's small kitchen. Both men were wearing dark pants and white shirts, but no ties. The door to the bedroom was closed. "Here, have a seat at the breakfast table." The older man took out his tablet and re-read Tom's email. "I can see you're as frustrated as I am. You think these measures will work?"

"I can't be sure. We've never tried them. I just know that these people must be communicating in some way to do their planning, which we've got to intercept, no matter the collateral damage. And they're using hate-speech and rhetoric to stir up others, which we've got to stop before more law-abiding citizens decide to defend themselves any way they can."

"Your ideas look promising to me, but will we be able to do what you're proposing?"

"The technology is in place. Legally, these measures are not in the Constitution—in fact, they contradict some of the Bill of Rights, but there've been many instances of localized martial law in our history. It was only implemented across the entire nation one time—by President Lincoln during the Civil War. Through my Mom I got in touch with Chief Justice Warner last night. She said, off the record of course, that whatever she thought personally about it, hearings could take weeks. Hopefully that's all the time we'll need to get a handle on this."

"So if we have to, we ask for grace, not permission, as President Rhodes might have said?"

"Yes. I don't see any other way. It's really just a step up from the mandates during the Covid pandemic, which gives us a great precedent for action. And of course we won't call it martial law. I thought we'd say that for thirty days we're going to implement a list of Temporary Emergency Action Measures, or TEAM, for everyone's protection."

"I like that, and I'm sure Emily will, too. Are you prepared to sell these to our Core Group, and then to the NSC? Today?"

Tom paused. "It won't be pretty, but, yes, because we've got to stop these people. And, sir, there is one more important issue. If your Core Group concurs, I recommend that you go ahead now and issue a confidential Executive Order to the FBI authorizing them to start adding these new functions expeditiously. With Director Toomey's contacts and weight behind them, Tanya's team will have to work covertly with some key outside vendors, like the major internet service providers and search engines, and it may take them a couple of days to get the protocols back in place from our earlier PRISM work. Some of them may agree to do so only with the authority of your executive order. This way we can shed some light on domestic internet traffic *before* the other side gets notice of what we're doing, which could be really important."

"OK. And I may be able to help us there. I'll make a couple of calls, and then I may have some key friends in the Tech industry for you to talk with."

Tom nodded. "Great. That would be very helpful."

The president stood. "All right. Let's do it. I like your approach. Straightforward. Our people need help, and we can give it. So let's do it. By the way, Tom, if you don't mind me asking, do you pray about this sort of stuff?

"Uh, no. I used to pray some, when I was younger. But not now. Not for years. Maybe I should. Why?"

Bradshaw smiled. "Just curious, since you've been at the White House a while. I tend to believe more in people and rational ideas than in a magical God and prayer. From Climate Change to this mess, we've got to come up with answers based on the actual truth as we know it—ourselves. I'm glad you feel the same. And, by the way, I know our party is much more on the side of rational truth and social justice. Faith is not rational, so how can it tell us what to do? Crazy. Guns, Gas and the Gospel just *add* to our problems." He paused. "Please brief Rob and Emily on your ideas, and then we'll start with the Core Group."

"Yes, sir. See you at eight."

Harry Calloway awoke that morning in his downtown New York apartment and smiled. He had been watching the news all weekend and was impressed with how others seemed to be setting the stage for the nation to focus on the revenge which he had been planning. Zoldar convinced him Sunday night that now was the perfect time to make his statement. He had written a two-page letter to the Network, explaining his just and valid complaints.

When he left the apartment with his large rucksack for the long walk uptown, he didn't bother to lock it. And once he dropped his letter in the mailbox at the corner, he knew there was no turning back.

"So everything you've just proposed, Tom, is technically possible?" Allen Linder asked from his end of the conference table. The Core

Group had been expanded slightly to combine the key surviving members of President Rhodes' personal advisors and President Bradshaw's staff from the Senate. Everyone was in attendance that Monday morning, and Tom was seated in the middle of the long table, next to the president.

"Yes. I've run all of these measures by Tanya Prescott and General Price, and a few others, and the 'wiring,' if you will, can be put in place within two days after the president authorizes it."

"What about Congressional approval, or oversight?" Linder pressed.

Rob Thompson answered. "As Tom suggests, we'll declare a State of Emergency for thirty days and govern by Executive Order. It makes sense to inform the Congressional leadership of our key steps, but not to seek legislative approval. There's too much at stake, and there's no time."

"And, frankly, a lot of what we plan to do must remain secret to be effective," Tom added.

"So we're going to scrap the Constitution and its protections?" Diane Marsh asked. "How are we to do that?"

"I'd rather say that we're going to suspend some provisions for thirty days," Tom answered. "At the discretion of the NSC."

"Unless, of course, at today's NSC meeting there is more clarity about who is attacking us and why," the president added. "I don't like these measures any more than you do, but we have to do something to counter these attacks, and there are numerous examples in our history of steps like this when widespread violence or revolt was threatened."

From the screen Garrett Crose said, "But they were to counter localized problems, like in Hawaii after Pearl Harbor."

The president clenched his fists on the table. "Aren't we beyond local, Mr. Crose? We're trying to separate charred pieces of the President from the Speaker in Belgium, the vice president was murdered and a church was attacked here, a doctor was killed in St. Louis, and two black men were gunned down in South Carolina. How local does that sound to you?"

Crose raised his hands in surrender. No one else spoke.

"All right," the president said. "We'll wait to hear the full briefing at this morning's NSC meeting. If there's no progress, then Tom, assisted by Agent Prescott and General Price, will lay out our plan of action. And I'll sign an executive order this morning authorizing the FBI, NSA and other agencies to begin putting covert measures in place, to be ready if the full State of Emergency is declared.

"Let me emphasize two very important points. First, as Tom indicated, some of these steps, like the one I just mentioned, must remain top secret in order to be effective. So no one here, nor at the NSC, says anything to anyone. Under the State of Emergency, leaking will immediately become subject to imprisonment.

"Second, if you don't agree with this approach, then get off the team now. So long as you remain quiet, no questions will be asked. Just let Rob know you're departing. But if you stay, I expect 100% buy-in and loyalty. The nation needs action, and I need everyone on my team to be of one mind on this, and on any other actions we take. Speak your piece on any subject, but once we decide, I expect us to work as one. Does everyone understand?"

As Jennifer Stanton rode the subway to work that Monday morning in Manhattan, she paid closer attention than usual to everyone around her—a leftover from her training at The Naval Academy, her alma mater. She had almost slipped her Glock 19 into her purse, but without a New York carry permit, and given the probable increased security because of the attacks, she didn't want to be arrested. So she'd left the gun in the drawer by her bed.

The Credit Bank of New York's leadership had made it clear in an email on Sunday that they expected to be up and running as usual, in defiance of whomever was trying to intimidate the country, and that was fine with her. She just wanted to be as safe as possible.

And she worried about Tom. Since their short call on Friday morning a lot had happened—too much—and she wanted to be sure he was alive and OK. She'd sent him two texts that weekend, with no response. He was either incredibly busy, or worse.

The tension after the first hour of the NSC meeting was palpable. It had begun well enough with detailed updates on the most pressing matters, like identifying and returning the bodies from Belgium, holding one or a series of state funerals, filling the many key vacancies expeditiously, and restarting commercial aviation. Teams continued to work on these and many other issues. They decided to fully reopen the nation's air space because there were no identifiable threats. And that discussion led to the admission that none of the agencies charged with protecting the country could offer any new information on any unusual current threats, domestic or foreign; nor were they prepared to speculate on who was behind the attacks, how they were coordinated, or what the goal of the perpetrators might be. All of which drew the president's withering rebuke.

For this meeting Tom was seated on the other side of Rob Thompson from the president, and as he looked around the long table he could sense a variety of reactions, from remorse to anger, as the president's words sank in.

"So, given that our ordinary methods of intelligence gathering and evaluation are not working, and the threat to our nation continues at the highest possible level, we're going to try something extraordinary. I've asked Tom Sullivan, the acting Deputy National Security Advisor, and FBI Director James Toomey to brief us today and to ask for your input. And let me emphasize that while everything said in this meeting is confidential, from this point on there is to be complete secrecy, for reasons that will soon be clear to everyone. Tom."

"Thank you, Mr. President. Unless there is substantial improvement in what we know about these attacks by noon tomorrow, then at that time the president will sign an executive order creating a nationwide State of Emergency, intended to last thirty days. The goals of this declaration are twofold. First, to intercept, identify and destroy whoever is behind these attacks, by whatever means are at our disposal. Some of these means will be open and obvious, but others will be clandestine, secret and protected—and not all the details will be communicated at first. The second goal is to shut down the hate speech and other un-American activities that are inciting violence among our citizens. We will not tolerate those who threaten their fellow citizens with words or actions. There will be no repeat of January 6th!

"During this time, the nation will be governed by Executive Order—basically organized around this Committee—with regular briefings for senior Congressional leaders and the Chief Justice of the Supreme Court. The FBI"—Tom nodded to the Director and to Agent Prescott—"will be in overall operational control, as directed by this body, the NSC. Each of you and your departments will have increased responsibilities and exceptional powers to accomplish those responsibilities. To assist you, the National Guard will be federalized and all civilian law enforcement will be placed under federal control. Regular military units will be authorized to operate domestically to maintain order and to keep our citizens safe. *Habeas Corpus* will be suspended, and most individual rights, as we know them today, will be modified to take account of the current situation.

"Once the two goals are accomplished, meaning that the attacks have been stopped, the State of Emergency will be lifted and individual rights will be restored. FBI Director Toomey will now give us a brief overview of how his organization will lead the technical side of this action, while bringing in other agencies as well."

There was some shuffling of papers and a few coughs, as the FBI Director looked around the table and began.

"The simplest way to understand what will happen is that all the tools and policies that the NSA now deploys overseas on foreign nationals and organizations will be focused for these thirty days domestically as well, by the FBI, the NSA, and our military assets, all working together. We expect that within 48 hours of declaring the State of Emergency, after conferring with the largest service providers, we'll have access to all emails, texts, and phone calls originating in or passing through the United States, along with scans of social media. Encryption will be illegal. Anyone found encrypting information will be arrested, and encryption software providers will be required to give us the keys for decryption, or face immediate shutdown.

"In addition, when applicable, we'll use security cameras, license plate readers, facial recognition, and drones to track the physical movement of anyone suspected of being involved with these attacks, or anyone suspected of inciting hate speech or violence of any kind. There will be many more details announced as these protections for our citizens roll out, but our government has strong capabilities, and we'll use all of them until these attacks are stopped.

"Special Agent Tanya Prescott, whom most of you have met, will, with her great experience, be the FBI's senior person on this team, coordinating the implementation with Tom Sullivan, General Price, and the other key agencies."

"Thank you, Director Toomey," Tom said. "So each of your departments' assignments now are twofold: from your operational perspective, what specific policies and procedures do you recommend to accomplish these goals? And what specific information that can be learned from the new, unrestricted intelligence gathering power of the nation's agencies will be helpful to you in fulfilling your part of this mission? The president would like that input from you no later than eight in the morning. Again, this information and our intentions are not to be shared outside this room. Are there any questions?"

Jenny Stanton walked across the plaza in front of the Manhattan skyscraper which housed The Credit Bank of New York, returning after an early sandwich and latte. As she entered the right side of the large lobby through one of the many glass doors and was about to descend three steps into the slightly sunken chrome and glass public area, Harry Calloway, dressed in jeans with a black jacket, entered through a center door to her left, took the AR-15 out of his backpack, and began shooting people in the lobby, starting with the security guards at the reception desk.

There were screams as the shots echoed like cannon explosions in the enclosed space, and bodies fell.

"The banks took all our money!" he yelled, then reloaded a clip and began shooting again. One of the elevators opened directly across the lobby from the shooter, who concentrated his shots and hit everyone standing inside in a matter of seconds.

Jenny was twenty feet to the shooter's right, obscured by a large chrome column. The outside door was right behind her. She could have run out and down the street.

*Son of a bitch!*

To Calloway's left, an older man in a business suit picked up a vase, and a younger man in a delivery uniform grabbed a chair. They ran towards him, weaving and yelling to get his attention. As the shooter turned towards them, Jenny rushed out from behind the column, swinging her purse. She was almost on him when he turned and fired point blank at her chest, ripping two huge holes in her back as the tumbling bullets exited.

Her final leap carried her forward and she fell on him, knocking him down, grabbing his face and scratching his eyes, as life drained out of her.

Following Tom's question at the NSC meeting, there was silence around the table. Tom noted that a few of President Rhodes' cabinet members looked at each other. Finally Thomas McCord, the Secretary of State, focused on Tom and said, "As you know, I've just returned from Prague. Are you saying that, after being in office less than forty-eight hours, your new team is going to declare a State of Emergency and basically impose martial law on the nation, with rules stricter than anything during the Covid pandemic?"

Tom swallowed but held the older man's gaze. "Yes, we are. But having been awake and working most of that period with good people like you who've been advising presidents for a long time, and who so far have little concrete information to share, I hope you'll look at this declaration as a way to better protect our citizens and to give that 'team,' almost none of whom President Bradshaw appointed, more ammunition to find out what is actually going on. And unlike during Covid, most ordinary life will go on unaffected. Just don't attack the nation or speak hatefully about your fellow citizens."

As McCord sat back in his chair, frowning, an aide entered and walked to the FBI Director.

The president said, "Thank you, Tom. And Director Toomey. Now..."

James Toomey interrupted. "There's something going on in New York that we should see." One of the wall screens switched to The News Network, where a young male reporter on the street in a canyon of tall buildings was trying to move against a wave of people running toward the camera, pushed on by police.

"...I was doing a story on food trucks when I heard people screaming and saw them running from the Credit Bank of New York building over there. We understand there's an active shooter and multiple injuries. Many people are said to be down."

From behind Tom's chair, Emily said, "Wasn't that your bank?"

Watching the screen, he nodded. "Yes. I have several friends there."

Jenny Stanton lay for a moment on top of Harry Calloway, her hands on his face. He pushed her off and wiped his eyes just as several men grabbed his arms and legs and two others sat on him. While another man picked up the rifle and opened the breech, two people rolled Jenny over and applied pressure to her wounds, trying to stop the bleeding.

There was a lot of shouting as the first police officers arrived. Others tried to help the large number of people who had been shot near the elevators.

Jenny vaguely heard the noise and dimly saw the man and woman kneeling over her, their arms soaked in her blood. The sights and sounds diminished further as she tried to cough, but could not. For a moment she experienced total darkness and silence.

Then, even though her eyes were closed, she suddenly began to see again, and to hear. As if her head were raised, she could see her battered body, and she saw and heard the shooter grappling with the people next to her.

A moment later her perspective rose still higher above the crowd, and she looked down on her full body, the pool of blood surrounding it, and the chaos in the foyer. She looked up for the first time with spiritual vision, able to take in the world's full reality, just as spiritual beings did. The bank lobby appeared to be crowded with dark forms—floating in the air over the bedlam below. Incredible. Some of the people seemed to have a light inside them, but most did not. Then she noticed souls arcing up out of the lifeless bodies of others who had been in the lobby at the wrong moment.

Finally it hit her that *she* was one of those souls, as she continued to rise, leaving her body, the one she had lived in for nearly thirty years, behind on the floor.

The night before Zoldar had alerted the sector leader in Midtown to be ready for a harvest that morning, and the area was swarming with demons ready to begin the ancient ritual of leading souls to the Judgment Seat.

Jenny continued to rise—she went right through the glass roof of the bank lobby and out into the air. She heard sirens and screaming. What an experience, floating above the world she had walked in only moments before.

But then she felt a chill and looked up to see four men—men?—dressed in contemporary clothing, moving—floating?—towards her and then surrounding her. They said nothing, but Jenny felt a terrible sense of dread—their lifeless eyes belied the smiles on their faces.

Without wishing to, Jenny found herself being transported in the middle of this circle, up and up. She couldn't stop, couldn't escape. There was no one to help her. On they went.

Eventually she discerned a light in the distance which seemed to be coming closer; they traveled toward it. Brighter and brighter it shown. But as it came closer, Jenny began to smell something sick and putrid. When the light was just in front of them, she looked over to the man on her left, and he had been transformed into a dark and terrifying form of pure evil and hate. She screamed. He smiled, but kept one eye warily on the figure before them.

They paused in front of the light for a moment, and when it turned to lead them, Jenny could see that it was actually another male form, tall and powerful. Somehow she knew that this was an angel, and that she was surrounded by fallen angels. Where were they going? How could this be? Angels and demons?

They traveled for how long Jenny did not know but eventually approached an area giving off an even greater light, if that were possible. The creatures next to her became more agitated, though to this point they had said nothing.

As they came into what was an infinitely huge and brilliantly lit throne room, the four demons stopped, but the angel led her on. There were more angels like the one leading her, but also magnificent, winged creatures with two heads and four wings, flying with one set of wings while covering their faces and feet with the other set and shouting, "Holy, Holy, Holy is the Lord God of Hosts." And voices from all sides were lifting a steady harmony of praise and worship, proclaiming His glory and His righteousness.

Jenny realized that she had arrived at the Throne of God.

The Light appeared as a large human form, seated on a huge throne. Next to Him, at His right hand, was a Lamb, alive, but with his throat cut, as if the Lamb had been sacrificed. Jenny could barely stand the brilliance. She could not understand how this could be happening. A God, just like in the Bible. How could it be? Why had no one ever told her it would be like this?

In the next moment Jenny began reliving her entire life on Earth, from childhood through school, the military, grad school, and her jobs. Her clear achievements. The parents she mostly ignored. The brother who never measured up. The lies she had told to get ahead, and the successes that had followed. The men she had slept with. The gospel story of salvation she had rejected several times as a myth. The talents she had been given, but which she never used to help others, focused on herself. The anger she had harbored against rivals. Her bravery that day in the bank lobby.

She was alone with her Creator, who was judging her, just as He had always promised He would.

When her life review was completed, the Light spoke. "She has sinned and cannot partake of Heaven, where there is no sin." Then the Light addressed the Lamb, and asked, "Is her name written in the Book of Life?"

The Lamb, also surrounded by brilliant Light, replied, "No, Father. She did not believe."

"Then she is to be cast into Darkness," were the last words Jenny's soul ever heard God speak, for all of eternity.

She cried out. "This can't be! I'm a good person. I've done many good things. I saved those people today!" She started moving away from the throne, but not by her will. "Please. No one told me it would be like this. Please give me another chance. If I had known it would be like this,

I would have listened. What do you want me to do? I'll do it. Anything! Please..."

As she left the throne room, she realized that the four demons were waiting for her. Seeing them, she screamed in terror, but the closest one to her laughed. Now that she belonged to them, he could speak. "Oh, but someone did tell you about all of this. Many times. But you chose not to hear. We helped with that, but you clearly didn't want to believe. And now you are ours. Forever. This is what we live for!"

Jenny's soul was led away to an eternity without God.

At the NSC meeting they watched the mayhem in New York for five minutes, as The News Network tried to get better camera angles and more information. Finally the president said, "Secretary McCord, and everyone else, this looks bad. I hope it isn't. But there could be no better reason in front of us for the action we've been discussing. Please get to work in tight, trusted groups and feed your department's recommendations as soon as possible to Rob, Tom, Agent Prescott and General Price. Thank you."

He stood, and everyone else did as well. Tom pulled out his phone and scrolled to one of the texts from Jenny. He pushed Call Back, but after several rings her recorded voice asked him to leave a message.

As the president left the meeting he walked with Rob Thompson and spoke softly. "I think you better speed up the process to nominate a new vice president. If anything happens to me, Secretary McCord would have a claim to be president, and he probably knows it. We haven't gotten along since he was just a Congressman from North Carolina a decade ago."

Rob nodded as Tom caught up to them at the exit.

"Well done, Tom," the president said. "It was your idea, and you explained it perfectly. I helped get Director Toomey confirmed two years ago—he shares our ideas on the role of government and is big on tech—I think you'll work well together."

"Thank you, sir. General Price and Special Agent Prescott are no slouches. But there's still a lot to do."

"Yes, but we've lobbed most of the balls into their courts for the afternoon, so why don't you stand down for a few hours? Get some rest, or at least think about something else, if you can."

"Uh...OK. Maybe I'll figure out how to get my car and a few more clothes from home. And check on a few friends at Credit Bank."

"Good idea. Let us know when you're back, and we'll text you if anything comes up on New York or anything else."

"Thanks for giving me a ride," Tom said to Logan Schofield from the passenger seat as they entered downtown D.C. from the Baltimore-Washington Parkway. Nepravel had joined them in the car outside the gate. So far he had learned little that would be useful for future actions, but he intended to trail Tom while he was away from the overwhelming prayer cover at Fort Meade.

"Driving appears to be my main contribution to national security at this point. And Emily gave me another list. Besides, there's not much traffic for a Monday. Wasn't Credit Bank of New York where you worked?"

"Yeah. I'm waiting to hear from a friend. I just hope she calls when I'm in range of one of our special towers."

After a moment of silence, Logan said, "My parents on Cyprus say the European and international news organizations are blaming the attacks on right wing thugs and fundamentalist Christians."

"Neither of those sound like something Air Force Captain Hassan would have joined."

Logan paused. "You're right. Good point. I don't know."

They drove by Callie's church, still surrounded by yellow tape. Logan dropped him outside his row house. Tom opened the door with his key, looked around, walked over to his working table and sat down. Nepravel, who had from experience quickly checked the area for other spiritual beings, came in through the back wall. Tom's phone vibrated, and the display read "CreditBankNY." He smiled.

"Hello!"

After a moment of silence, an unfamiliar female voice said, "Tom?"

"Yes."

"Tom, this is Melanie Tate. I work with Jenny Stanton at Credit Bank. I got your number from a pad on her desk."

"Yes, I remember she talked about you."

"Well, I have some terrible news. You're with the government, so I assume you've seen about the attack on our building."

"Yes."

"I'm afraid Jenny was in the lobby when the shooting started. They haven't released all the names yet, but they've confirmed to us that Jenny didn't make it. She apparently attacked the guy just as he shot her, and she knocked him down."

"She's dead?"

"Yes. I'm very sorry."

He was silent for several moments. "How many others?"

"We're not sure. At least twelve dead and ten wounded."

He paused. "Terrible. And Jenny knocked him down?"

"Apparently. Then two guys grabbed him on the ground and the police arrived a minute later. She probably saved several people."

"Thank you. Please call or text me when you know more. I'll try to come to her funeral. And talk to her parents."

"OK. I think we're going to have a lot of funerals to attend."

"Yes. Very sorry. Thank you again. I hope the wounded recover quickly." He hung up. He thought of Jenny's smile. The yellow pad on his desk was open to the list of hypothetical threats he had started for his boss, Olivia Haas, who was now dead, to give to a president who was now dead, after chatting with a great young woman who was now dead, just before meeting another great young woman who was now injured.

*I need to see Callie. And was I really making this list just two days ago?*

He looked at it and realized that none of the seventeen threats he had listed had occurred.

*Do they have a list like this?*

Nepravel quickly read the list and committed it to memory. He smiled, imagining how he could use it with General Bespor. Then he moved next to Tom and reminded him that his job was critical to the future of the nation, and that he had no time for anything or for anyone else.

Tom couldn't think. He knew he had to rest. He went upstairs to his bedroom, kicked off his shoes, and lay down.

Nepravel decided that instead of watching Tom sleep, he would take a swing through the White House in case any of his other charges were working, looking for more examples of what they might be planning. He would circle back to Tom in the evening.

Tom had just put his head on the pillow when his secure phone rang. "Hello."

"Tom, it's President Bradshaw. Is now a good time? Are you alone?"

"Yes, sir."

"Good. I've got Andrew Boswell, who heads Juggle, on the line with us. He thinks he can help us."

"Hello, Tom. A pleasure to meet you."

Tom sat up and turned on the bed. "Hello, Mr. Boswell. Yes, the same."

"The president described to me your plan for what needs to be done over the next thirty days to catch the pricks who've attacked our nation, and I told him I think I can get the key players who used to be in PRISM—and a few more—to join us, without any dissenters."

"That would be a great help, sir."

"And if I understand correctly, you'll not just be gathering information, but also regulating what people say about each other in speeches and on social media."

"Yes. We've got to stop the hate speech and the lies."

"I think my friends who head Facegraph and Sifter can be a big help. They already have monitoring algorithms that will just have to be tweaked to help ensure that people see only the truth, and positive opinions about the new measures."

"That would be great."

"I'm prepared to start making calls this afternoon."

The president spoke. "Tom, Drew is an old friend. He and his peers can really help you and the team collect data on all the calls and searches across almost every phone and computer in our nation. Plus in most other countries, through their contacts and networks, some formal, some informal. Would that be helpful?"

"Yes, of course."

"Good. He suggested, and I agreed, subject to your OK, that to get everyone onboard without dissent, for this extraordinary month while they're helping to gather this information, we'd reciprocate by relaxing the government's privacy restrictions, allowing them to keep and to use the data they gather in any legal way. Do you see anything wrong with that?"

"Uh, you mean without any notifications?"

"Yes," the president responded. "As part of our State of Emergency we're going to need all the data we can get to analyze and to search through. Everyone will know we're doing it. Drew and the other Tech firms will be helping us gather every bit of personal information, without regard to anyone's privacy considerations, which we'll need if we want to find the bastards, and we'll just let them use what they find to help build their businesses. Only during this extraordinary time. It seems like a reasonable trade to me. And they have direct contacts with similar service providers overseas."

A picture of Jenny Stanton flashed in Tom's mind. "Well, it does sound reasonable. Let me run it past Agent Prescott."

"Her boss, James Toomey, and I have worked together before," Boswell said. "A good man—I'll bring him in on the plan. I'm sure there'll be no problem."

"Tom," the president added, "please do tell Agent Prescott, General Price and the others that Drew and his friends are prepared to jump in with both feet, but there's no need for them to know about the companies retaining what they find. It won't impact what the NSA will be doing—except to ensure they have even more data. Let's keep this understanding between us, though we'll issue a confidential Executive Order to that effect. But only we need to know until this is over. OK? I think you'll find that Drew and the others will be very helpful, and there won't be any surprises implementing what we need to do on any of their platforms. Right, Drew?"

"Yes, Mr. President. I can assure you that you'll have 100% compliance, and then some."

"So, Tom, unless you object, let's proceed in this way. The government and free enterprise will be working together at a very difficult time."

"OK. Yes, it will be great to have your help, with no dissension. We look forward to working with you, Mr. Boswell."

"Please, call me Drew. And I think you know Emily Schofield's husband, Logan, who works with us."

"Yes, I do. Very well. Another good person."

"Good people have to stick together in tough times," the president added. "Tom, thank you. Oh, please issue one of our Core Group phones to Drew, so he can stay in the loop without any issues. Drew, get your guys ready to give us everything you've got, so we can find these killers."

They said goodbye. Tom turned off his phone and lay down again. He was too tired to think. In a few seconds he was asleep.

The Hunts lived in suburban Virginia in a two-story redbrick home on a large lot that Clayton and Andrea hoped to keep, even when he or they were transferred to new assignments in the coming years. It had four bedrooms and a level, fenced backyard. Over the past two months they had turned the smallest bedroom into the nursery for the boy they were expecting.

Mariam Rashid had arrived late that morning, and after lunch her two sons were having quiet time in the guest room while the wives talked, seated with coffees at the island in the large, open kitchen. Andrea and Mariam had known each other for a few years, as their husbands' careers had occasionally intersected, but they were not close friends. After chatting about children and the vagaries of military family life, their conversation turned to the attacks.

Andrea said, "I couldn't believe the level of hate from those LGBT people at the church yesterday. They were actually glad the president and the others were killed. And then the fire, and the brick thrown through your window last night."

Mariam shook her head. "Welcome to our world. Ahmad and I were both born here to parents who fled the radicals in Pakistan. Our parents were welcomed here, have done well, and taught us that we owe everything to this country. But we are Muslims, and so there is always that issue, that question."

Andrea studied Mariam for a moment. "And the Muslim Air Force pilot shooting down Air Force One didn't help."

"Exactly. We get it. It's terrible. We know our history. We know Muslims didn't found America. Mostly Christians did. Ahmad and I believe in individual freedom and the Constitution. But we're also Muslims. We believe that Mohammad has revealed Allah's one true path to eternal salvation, and we try to live it. So we will always be suspect. What are we to do?"

Andrea smiled and stood to get the coffee pot as the boys stirred and came down the hall. "For now, stay safe here with us. Hopefully this will be over soon, and our husbands will be home. And we'll keep talking. Hey, guys, how about some cookies?"

Tom awoke after two hours with the beep from his alarm. Thirty minutes and a shower later, his body was recovering, but his mind was still spinning. He called his parents to check in and tell them he was OK—without any details—and asked them to call his sister. They said they would pray for him and the president.

"Good. Thanks," he nodded as they said goodbye. "I'll try to call again in a day or two. It's pretty crazy right now, and I'm working on some new stuff."

After sending a text he gathered some clothes and other items to be as self-sufficient as possible. In a final walk around the row house he picked up his paper L-Pad, locked the door, and drove off in his hybrid crossover.

After a quick stop on the way, he found a parking spot in the same block as Kristen Holloway's row house, got out, and rang the bell for the lower level apartment. After a moment, Kristen opened the door. "Yes?"

"Hi. I'm Tom Sullivan. I hope I have the right address for Callie Sawyer. Is she here?"

Beau barked and then whimpered from behind the door. Kristen smiled. "Yes, Tom. I'm Kristen Holloway. We met many years ago at your parents' home. I was a real estate agent. I came to your home a couple of times. Callie got your text. Come in."

Tom started to reply, but Beau immediately jumped up to greet him, tail wagging. Tom patted him.

Callie was lying on the couch in jeans and a light sweater. There were bandages on parts of her hands. She had apparently been reading to Grace, who was lying next to her, and who now eyed the stranger warily.

"Oh, hi!" Callie exclaimed, smiling. "Thank you for checking on me—on us. Grace, this is Tom. Beau is his dog."

"How are you?" he asked, continuing to pat Beau.

She sat up and looked at her hands, then at Grace. "Remarkably well, considering what could have happened."

"Would you like some coffee, or tea?" Kristen asked.

"Uh, yes, that would be nice. Maybe some hot tea? I've been drinking a lot of coffee. Thank you. And I brought some milk." He held up a small bottle.

Callie smiled. Kristen held out her hand to Grace. "Can you help me upstairs? I've got some special teas that we'll bring down."

When Tom and Callie were alone, he sat in a chair opposite the sofa.

"I can't stay long. But I just wanted to check on you, to be sure you're all right."

"I enjoyed Saturday night—until it all happened."

He paused. "Me, too."

"Is it as crazy as it seems? Are we in trouble?"

"I, I think we may be. The biggest problem now is getting a handle on who's behind it. We're still trying to figure out how to figure that out."

Callie thought for a moment. "That's not good."

"No, so we've got to try some new things...But, look, can we just take a few minutes and talk about other things?"

She shifted. "Sure. About what?"

"Well, about how I should have called you a long time ago when my Dad gave me your number."

She smiled again. "I suspect you've met a lot of women in D.C. without needing your Dad's help. Particularly one with a daughter."

He was serious. "I guess. But I really enjoyed talking with you. And...and I've lost quite a few people I was close to in the last forty-eight hours. I'm just glad..." His voice trailed off and he studied her face in the silence.

She finally spoke, nodding slightly. "Yes, when I think what might have happened to Grace and the other children at our church, it gives me chills."

"Speaking of your daughter, is her father in the picture?"

Callie paused. "No. Not really. It's his decision, not mine. Someday when you're bored, we'll take a walk and I'll tell you the whole story. For now, suffice it to say that either Kristen or I could be the woman with the jar of perfume anointing Jesus' feet, and weeping. But, just like with that woman and with Kristen, He changed everything for me. And the unexpected joy is my daughter, Grace. She's a miracle."

Tom thought for a moment. "Did you ever consider just having an abortion?"

"For about a minute. I was new in my walk with the Savior who gave me new life and who creates every life, including Grace's. It wasn't convenient, and it's actually hard a lot of the time, but how could I kill a child He created in His image?"

He held her gaze during a long silence. "I don't think I'll be bored for a while, but I want to hear the story."

"Then come back when this calms down, and we'll take that walk."

Grace and Kristen returned downstairs carrying a tray with their teas. Callie sat up and carefully took the mug with her bandaged hands. Tom had Beau lie down.

"We can have a tea party," Grace said, smiling, and offering Tom a shortbread from the colorful box she was holding.

"Thank you." He took a cookie as Kristen joined them in another chair. "I understand you're in the third grade."

"Yes," Grace replied. "It's hard."

"I bet it is. Tell me about it."

She did, and they chatted together until Tom looked at his watch and realized it was getting late.

"I gotta go. Lots on my plate. Not sure when I'll be back. Can Beau stay a little longer?"

Grace looked at her mother. "Please."

Callie smiled. "Of course. He's already almost part of the family."

Tom stood. "Thank you. Thanks to all three of you."

Nepravel had returned from the Executive Office Building to find Tom gone from his home, and he only just caught up with him as he left Callie's apartment. He was distressed that Tom had spent time with two strong believers, and on the ride back to Fort Meade Nepravel turned up the voices of *Pride, Unworthy, Priorities* and *Lust.* Tom had fought actively for so long against the quiet voice of the Holy Spirit inside him that in many ways he was more immune to God's truths than someone who had never heard, and Nepravel wanted to be sure that he stayed that way.

Nepravel had promised Balzor and the generals that Tom would remain ineffective and would never be a problem for them, like his father was after Nepravel had lost him years before. After all they had invested in Tom's hostility to the truth, Nepravel was not about to lose him just because the latest target in a long line of his female conquests happened to be a follower of the cursed Son, and he was glad when the voices he amplified took immediate hold and kept repeating their lies. It was very personal for Nepravel.

Emily Schofield was at the desk in her room sifting through her notes to prepare a draft for the president's Monday evening report to the nation. She was considering possible deceptions to propose to the Core Group to try to slow down whoever was behind the attacks. So far police could find no connection between the gunman at New York Credit Bank and the other atrocities—he was described as another "lone wolf," which Emily thought was impossible. She knew the president was going to be frustrated, and they couldn't mention anything about their plans for a possible State of Emergency—half-baked speculation would only fuel the uncertainty.

A text came from Seth: *We REALLY need to talk. Call me. You'll want to hear this.*

She dialed his number. "I'm sorry, Seth. I haven't left this place, and the issues keep piling up. I promise I'll get back to you for an interview."

"OK, but this won't wait," he said, an edge to his voice. "A very reliable personal source inside the gate with you called to tell me that

President Bradshaw is about to declare martial law, probably tomorrow. Is that true?"

She paused. "Be at the Main Gate in ten minutes. I'll send someone to get you."

She hung up and walked over to their large conference room, where she told Al Linder about Seth's call, and what she proposed to do. He concurred.

Seth was escorted by an MP when Emily met him outside. They smiled and hugged. She thanked the MP and led Seth inside to two chairs at the far end of the room. They could see Linder and others in the Core Group talking and taking notes, but they couldn't hear what was being said. Seth looked around at the people, the laptops, and the trash.

"So this is where you've been since Saturday night?"

"Yes. Since your party. Seems like a month ago. We go over to a larger conference room full of screens in the NSA for the NSC meetings."

"Where's the president?"

"He and the First Lady are here. Probably resting. Look, for now, no pictures and no descriptions." He started to protest. She held up a hand. "That could change. It's fluid. We're here to talk. You're the only reporter inside. OK?"

He relented. "OK. But I need you to confirm or quash the martial law report. It's huge, and I need to know, quickly."

"Who called you?"

He smiled. "You know I can't tell you. But it's someone I've known, and who's reliable. And he or she is inside here with you."

Emily maintained a blank expression. "You can't use it. You can't publish it."

He frowned. "Is it true? An Administration only two days old is going to impose martial law on the nation?"

"You can't use it. In fact, we'd like your help to question the credibility of anyone who might try to bring it up."

"My help? I'm a journalist."

She smiled. "Yes, of course. But on Friday you met with us and we talked about helping each other. It's the same principle."

Seth frowned. "But I've been catching it from my boss since she sent me here. The government has done precious little, and now I've learned about a potential game changer, and you want me to sit on it?"

"A leak, Seth. Completely unauthorized, illegal and potentially very damaging to the nation—and to the agenda we share."

"Is it true?"

"If it were, planning for it would need to be mentioned after the fact, not before. Those who want to harm us might take steps if they knew a State of Emergency were coming, making it harder to counter them, or to stop them."

He glanced over at the others at work. "Emily, we're great friends. I've done what you've asked. But this is huge. Why would I agree to cut short my career, when someone else is likely to break the story anyway?"

"Our intent is to enhance your career—a lot, if you just help us a little. Unless and until an actual declaration occurs—and it might not—don't run the story yourself or speculate about it. If others publish it, use whatever means you can to question the veracity—you can talk about unnamed sources in the White House denying it. In fact, we'd like you to run a story tonight in which you cite credible sources that the president is at a secret location in West Virginia, closely following several leads at each site where an attack has occurred. And, for helping at this crucial time, you'll be given the first one-on-one, exclusive, on the record and on video interview with the new president."

He paused. "You're talking about in a few days, max?"

Emily nodded.

"OK."

Alexei Nobikov was in his fourth-floor office near the waterfront in Limassol, Cyprus late that evening, looking between the written report on his desk and the live posts on his computer screen, when Sveta Pankratova knocked at his open door.

"This is excellent stuff," he said to her. "Tell Dima I'm pleased by how he so quickly mined The Credit Bank's public reports and local newspapers to come up with these articles and online posts. Higher rates of loan denials to African Americans, at least in one state. The glass ceiling for qualified women managers. Portfolios heavy in carbon fuels. Sounds to me like they're bad people who deserved it!" He smiled.

She put several more samples on his desk. "Yes. And these new ones. Incredible childcare. Flexible work schedules for new mothers and fathers. Special loans for green energy start-ups. Sustainable offices. Sounds like they're good people who didn't deserve it."

He nodded. "Of course. Are the chat rooms still active?"

"Yes. They haven't let up. Everyone's angry."

"Great work. The takedown of The Network was brilliant, and Moscow sent a note to congratulate the team. Go home to your family. With the social media fuel we've added, this pot will boil nicely for many hours. And the funding should keep it simmering for weeks. Maybe I should take a trip over there—it's been a while. There's a cybersecurity conference I can cover, and I can check in with my old university and tech friends, see what they're thinking. We don't want to miss anything."

After Sveta left his office, Alexei swiveled his chair and looked out at the dark sea beyond the lights beneath his window. Then he did something that had been his habit several times a day since becoming a believer in America all those years ago—he silently prayed for wisdom, grace and guidance to help him and the others protect their country, Russia, but also improve it, from the inside. And soon.

Tom Sullivan drove back to Fort Meade, hoping to meet Emily and Logan Schofield for an early dinner, and parked near the conference center restaurant. Nepravel had to exit the car outside the gate due to the spiritual light and heat from the incoming prayers. He would have to monitor other humans outside the fort to keep up with their plans.

Tom was surprised to find Seth Cohen waiting along with the Schofields in the lobby. They shook hands. Tom looked at Emily, who smiled.

"We decided to bring Seth at least partly into the tent, so he can have a background understanding of what we're dealing with. He won't be attending official meetings, and he can't publish anything without my review. But he'll eventually have the first sit down interview with President Bradshaw, and we all think it's a good idea for him to share some time with us this evening in the trenches."

"Great," Tom responded somewhat flatly. "Always glad to have you, Seth. Just, please, abide by Emily's rules, for real."

Tom's seriousness was deep, and the others felt it.

"Are you OK?" Emily asked.

"A brave woman I've known for several years was killed at Credit Bank this morning. I understand she was a hero. And I visited Callie Sawyer this afternoon, recovering from the fire at her church." He paused and looked at Emily. "She said to tell you all hello, and thanks for inviting her." Emily nodded as they turned to walk to the restaurant. "But I know I'm no different than most people in the nation today, mourning our losses and wishing I could do something to help stop these attacks. So I'll get past it. Seriously, Seth, glad to have you."

"You *are* doing something, Tom," Emily said, as she took Logan's hand and they turned toward the restaurant. "We all are."

"I know. But is it enough?"

Jerry Kimble had been angry about the fracking in his part of Pennsylvania for years, since the first reports of possible groundwater contamination and increased seismic activity had surfaced. He'd attended public meetings, which is where Razdor, a local sector leader, had singled him out six months earlier because of his special skills. Razdor had ramped up several internal voices to add to Jerry's natural thoughts about the effects of fracking on their three children, and late that night Razdor was riding in Jerry's pickup truck through the dark backcountry about fifty miles west of Jerry's home.

Jerry knew the route well, even in the dark, because he had been scouting the area for several days, mapping large concentrations of natural gas condensate tanks, the by-products of a successful fracking well. The tanks held the heavier, "wetter" gas, like propane, after the "drier" methane was pumped away. Two days ago he'd found exactly what he was looking for: several large tanks mounted on a concrete foundation next to some storage buildings, surrounded by a security fence several hundred yards to the side of a paved road. On the other side of the road a rising terrain with stands of trees separated by fields.

After driving a little further he turned left on an even smaller road and began a gentle climb. Twenty minutes later he had parked his pickup and hiked the last bit through trees and underbrush to the edge of a clearing, using the skills he'd learned a decade earlier as an Army Special Ops sniper. And all the while he was being encouraged by a voice which sounded like his own, but was really Razdor's.

He lowered his backpack to the ground and put on his night vision goggles. Immediately he had a clear view down the hill and across the road to the natural gas condensate tanks. Five minutes later he was in a comfortable prone position, his sniper rifle loaded with a special incendiary round.

Jerry's intent was to discourage more fracking, and he knew three other tank locations which would lend themselves to a similar attack if the oil companies didn't heed the warning he was about to send them.

His finger tightened on the trigger, and Razdor's soothing voice was full of rationalizations about how corporations never listened until they were forced to do so. Jerry knew that tonight's message would be hard to ignore.

His training proved effective. The round he squeezed off produced a huge explosion and fireball that temporarily blinded him. But he could take apart and store his rifle by touch alone, and a minute later he was headed towards his truck, the path now illuminated by the raging fire in the valley behind him.

Unknown to Jerry, but reported to Razdor earlier that evening by other demons, when Razdor encouraged Jerry that this should be the night, three vans of migrant working families, including teenagers and children, had parked on the other side of the tanks behind the storage buildings, just outside the fence, where a spigot provided fresh water.

The conflagration consumed them all.

After dinner, Tom spent most of the evening with Tanya Prescott and her FBI team, working with General Price at the NSA, going over the requests for information and assistance which were coming in from the other NSC departments in anticipation of a State of Emergency.

Tom told them part of the story about Andrew Boswell's offer to bring the other high-tech companies onboard, which they welcomed. And he helped prioritize the requests with the team drafting the details of the Executive Order. Tanya reported that all the major telecom company CEOs had responded positively that afternoon to the secret visits from members of her senior staff, armed with the President's Executive Order—and probably helped by Boswell's behind the scenes calls—reinstating all the data mining and surveillance protocols which had previously gone under the loose name of PRISM.

The general told Tom that the back doors to every email, text, search and post initiated in or passing through the United States should be open and operational by midnight. Collection and review for keywords and known bad actors would begin as the data streams became available—there would be so many that, even though aided by Artificial Intelligence, both the NSA and the Pentagon would be helping the FBI with the review process.

As Tom entered the lobby of the conference center to head to his room, he noticed Emily coming through a side door.

"I just gave Seth to an MP for an escort to the gate. He had a full night and watched the president's report to the nation from inside the studio."

"Anything new? Or from the NSC?"

She shook her head. "Not really. Looks like the State of Emergency is on."

"General Price is optimistic that his team will be starting on the cyber side within a few hours. I just hope the telecom employees at the connection sites are as agreeable as their CEO's. Someone may try to sabotage what we're doing."

"Speaking of which, that was the trigger that got Seth inside tonight, which I couldn't tell you earlier. Someone called him to leak the State of Emergency announcement, and the only way to slow him down was to offer the stick of probable national damage plus the carrot of the first interview with the president."

"Someone from our team told Seth about our plans?"

"Apparently. He won't divulge his source, but he says it's someone with us, here."

"Does the president know?"

"Yes. He's livid. We're planning his announcement for 1 p.m. tomorrow. We don't think we can wait."

"Agreed. The NSC teams will be up all night, drafting. Then we can pull it together at our eight o'clock meeting. Full implementation will take several days, but we need it to clamp down on this information free-for-all before there are more attacks. And I can't believe that someone on the inside wanted to blow it."

She nodded. "Pretty discouraging."

"Maybe if we send one or two to jail, it'll make others think twice."

As soon as Seth was outside the gate, walking to his car to head for his hotel, he dialed Rachel Shaw at the Network. One of Obman's lieutenants joined him for the drive and listened in.

"I've been inside Fort Meade with the president's team for the past three hours."

"What? Do you have video?"

"Not yet. That was part of the deal to get inside. But they've promised us the first on camera sit-down interview with the president."

"Awesome. When?"

"Not sure. But soon."

"Listen, we've heard a rumor that they're going to declare martial law. Is that true? Can they?"

Seth paused. "I, uh, suppose they could, but they didn't say anything about it, and I've been with his senior advisors all evening."

"OK. So what *can* you say from your visit?"

"On camera, nothing. To you, they're scrambling, working hard, trying to figure out who's behind the attacks and what to do."

"Doesn't sound encouraging, if *they* don't know."

"Glass half empty? Maybe it's half full. I don't know. They're trying hard. Anyway, tomorrow I'll push again to get the interview set up."

"Fine. Good work. When you do, let's coordinate your questions. Stay with'em."

# 5

*We have no Government armed with Power capable of contending with human Passions unbridled by morality and Religion... Our Constitution was made only for a moral and religious People. It is wholly inadequate to the government of any other.*

John Adams

Tuesday, September 15

At ten that Tuesday morning Tom, Emily and the Core Group, expanded by the FBI and NSA senior team members, met with President Bradshaw in the Conference Room to finish the details of the Executive Order.

On the screen behind them, almost muted, The News Network cycled through three major stories: the horrendous, deadly blast at a Pennsylvania oil well, which had temporarily stopped all fracking operations in the U.S.; the increased security measures at all banks and financial service firms across the nation, following the previous morning's New York shootings; and speculation about the president's upcoming address early that afternoon.

Thirty minutes later President Bradshaw spoke. "I think you've got it. The measures are strong, but balanced. Hopefully they'll be enough to let us find and stop whoever is behind all of this. Thank you. Starting at noon I've got calls with key Congressional leaders and the Chief Justice to bring them up to speed. General Price, if all goes well, in a few days we'll be out of your hair and back at the White House."


Ironically the White House was where Prince Proklor had chosen to watch the president's address, along with his most trusted generals. The security and maintenance staff kept the president's house open even though no officials were there, and a television in a break room down the hall from the Oval Office suited Proklor perfectly.

The rest of his demonic army was spread out across the nation in offices, schools, restaurants, some churches—anywhere people gathered without prayer cover. Since they were creatures, not creators, the fallen angels were not omniscient, nor did they know the future. They had to act and react to events and opportunities, just like humans. So they watched and leveraged every new event and technology to increase the impact of their fixed number on an ever-increasing population.

From information gathered from outside Fort Meade, Proklor anticipated that the president was about to give them new tools to work with, but he could not be sure until he heard the speech. He was sure, however, that each of his skilled messengers, having observed what motivates people in general, and Americans in particular, for decades, would be able to undermine the president's words with voices to make most people at every gathering increasingly scared, angry or discouraged.

Of course denying personal salvation was always their first priority with every human, but discord was next in line. At tonight's meeting they would assess what new opportunities may have been given to them to sow hate and to drive people deeper into their tribal Identity Groups.

What great names this new generation of humans had coined! Identity Groups. Systemic Racists. Oppressors. Tribes. Identity Politics. Victims. No more "One nation under God," but groups of constantly warring factions. Sometimes Proklor smiled at how easy it was to make Americans distrust each other.

"My fellow Americans, this is the fourth time I've spoken to you since the terrible events of Saturday evening."

President Bradshaw was seated at a large desk inside an NSA Conference Center meeting room, converted to a studio, but the background was electronically altered to look like the Oval Office. The Core Team had debated the best setting for the president's address, and, led by Emily Schofield, they had settled for a look of continuity. Bradshaw wore a blue suit, white shirt, and red tie. He looked rested and focused. The Core Group watched from behind the single camera.

"During that time additional attacks on our nation have continued, even increasing in intensity. No one has claimed responsibility. Our exceptional law enforcement and counterintelligence experts, despite having the best people and systems in the world, have been unable to determine who is behind this murderous offensive, making it almost impossible to stop. Their inability to do so is caused largely by artificial constraints placed on them by recent laws and judicial interpretations.

"Obviously in normal times we hold our Constitutional rights to be the foundation of our nation as Americans, but 250 years ago how could the Founders have imagined the implications of their ideas in a world of instant international connectivity, in which a single person can do so much harm to so many?

"Hopefully one day we'll again have the luxury to debate these questions academically. For now, in order to preserve and protect our historic union, we need action, not debate. And quickly.

"Our Founders understood that exceptional times call for exceptional measures. Today I am announcing steps which follow their lead.

"Under the authority entrusted to me as President of the United States to defend and protect our Constitution, and as provided for in the National Emergencies Act of 1976, last night I signed an Executive Order declaring a State of National Emergency across our land. This action is taken with reluctance, but also with the input and assistance of experienced counselors who served under President Rhodes, as well as those on my staff, and in the armed forces.

"Under it, for a period of thirty days, our usual rights and processes will be suspended, and the nation will be governed by Executive Orders from the Executive Branch, as advised by the National Security Council, or NSC.

"The twin goals of this thirty-day State of Emergency are to identify and stop those coordinating these attacks, and to eliminate all forms of hate speech, thereby defusing the possible divisions among us. Our overall effort will be called Temporary Emergency Action Measures, or TEAM, and I urge everyone to give those working for our defense your strongest personal support.

"A series of Executive Orders will flow from the experts at the NSC. I will personally review and approve each of them. Some of these will impact all of us. Some will impact only a few. All of them are designed to accomplish quickly and effectively the twin goals stated above. If that happens in less than thirty days, we will rescind the State of Emergency.

"As will be more clearly spelled out in the orders themselves, we will need absolute transparency and openness in all our normal dealings, like our emails, phone calls and travel, so that those who are trying to do us harm will more easily stand out. We'll need to monitor news and public gatherings for possible divisive statements that will cause one group of Americans to feel less valuable than another group. We are all valuable, and all equal!

"We are particularly sensitive to the fact that our national midterm elections are scheduled for only eight weeks from today. Objective policy debate must be protected, while hate speech and divisiveness must be prohibited. We ask everyone involved in the election process to follow guidelines of common sense and goodwill when proposing policies or debating issues. Specifically, political ads must be positive in nature, supporting a candidate or a policy, not attacking or demonizing an opponent. Hopefully we will strike the proper balance, but make no mistake—these are not normal times, and violations will be punished in order to preserve our liberties.

"To implement these orders I have federalized the National Guard and authorized our military branches to operate within our borders when specifically tasked by an order from the Executive Branch. We will all be better protected under limited martial law—your local officials and our national civilian agencies like the FBI will remain responsible for handling most enforcement issues, but the armed services will be empowered to arrest and detain those suspected of violating any law or Executive Order.

"There will undoubtedly be some rough edges as we implement this strategy to safeguard our nation. If you hear grumbling, please remind those doing so that this is a limited action designed to protect and to shield our citizens at what is clearly an unprecedented and dangerous time for our country. We are asking that all of us give up a few of our rights for a limited time so that our nation will have the power to overcome those who wish us to do so much harm.

"Within the hour the first operational orders will be released to the press and posted on a new Homeland Security website, USTEAM. Please watch that site closely in the coming hours and days for new orders and procedures. This is a serious time, and violators of laws or orders will be treated with severity. We cannot afford to be asleep or forgiving when the very future of our nation is at stake.

"I ask that we pull together and fight back as one nation, not allowing terrorists, whether a misguided group or a rogue nation, to divert us from our place as the greatest and freest nation on earth. May God bless you and your family. And may God bless America."

The extra video lights went out. The president lingered in his chair. Those behind the camera moved towards him, not speaking. He stood. "I've just done what no other president has ever done. And I hope never has to again. Now we really better find these bastards, and make our nation safer and better. Tom, are the orders going out?"

"Yes, Mr. President. And General Price's team, along with the FBI and the military, are already reviewing the data streams and making recommendations to the new NSC Command Center here at Fort Meade, connected to law enforcement."

"I know it's a huge undertaking to coordinate all of this. Thanks to all of you. Now, Al, Diane, Rob and Emily, do you have more normal governing issues not related to the attacks that we need to be working on?"

Rob Thompson nodded, holding up a sheaf of papers. "Yes, sir, we do."

"Then let's get to it. Oh, first, let's send Secretary of State McCord on a two-week trip explaining the State of Emergency to our allies and others. He'll like the interaction, and he won't be here. Now, Tom, keep us informed as the emergency measures take hold. Let's hope for quick results."

# Declaration of a National State of Emergency With Respect to Attacks on the United States of America and its Individual Citizens

# A Proclamation by

# The President of the United States of America

By the authority vested in me as President by the Constitution and the laws of the United States of America, including sections 201 and 301 of the National Emergencies Act (50 U.S.C. 1601 et seq.), and in order to protect and defend the nation at a time of great peril, it is hereby ordered as follows:

Section 1. *Establishment*. From today for the next four weeks through October 12$^{th}$ a State of Emergency exists across the nation and territories of the United States of America. This State of Emergency may be rescinded, modified or extended by future executive order.

Sec. 2. *Responsible Free Speech*. During this State of Emergency all forms of speech, communication, and assembly shall include no hate speech, derision or exclusivity attributed to the race, religion, national origin, gender, sexual orientation or political views of any other person, except in ways which uplift or correct previous wrongs. All citizens and residents shall be treated equally.

Sec. 3. *Communications*. All forms of communication, including speaking, writing, video presentation, publishing, broadcasting, advertising, and all forms of electronic and internet communication, shall be subject to unrestricted governmental review to ensure that there is no violation of the provisions of Section 2 above, and also no conspiring, planning, inciting, colluding, or encouraging of any acts of violence, sedition or treason in violation of any law or executive order.

Sec. 4. *Encryption.* Encryption of all communications in Section 3 is henceforth unlawful and punishable by fine or imprisonment, as adjudged by an appropriate court or tribunal.

Sec. 5. *Assembly.* It shall be unlawful for more than fifty persons to gather, physically or electronically, for any purpose whatsoever without securing a permit to do so from the appropriate authority. Exempt from this provision are sporting events, houses of worship, and entertainment venues whose meetings were already scheduled as of this date.

Sec. 6. *Enforcement.* All branches of the U.S. military are hereby authorized to operate within the country to assist all domestic law enforcement agencies—local, state and national—with the discovery, investigation and prosecution of any violation of a law or executive order.

Sec. 7. *Detention.* Anyone suspected on reasonable grounds of violating any law or executive order may be detained by legal or military authorities for up to the duration of this Executive Order.

Sec. 8. *Implementation.* The National Security Council, through its Cabinet level members and agencies, shall be responsible for creating, administering and enforcing every executive order resulting from this Proclamation. To be lawful, every such executive order must be signed by the president, and will then take effect immediately.

Clayton Hunt, Ahmad Rashid, Megan Buckley and the rest of the Joint Forces Threat Identification Group had watched the president's speech an hour earlier at their individual consoles inside their COG site in southern Pennsylvania. They were emotionally at a low ebb after the high anticipation of their first two days at Raven Rock, when they had expected to identify one or more foreign aggressors. Instead, the normalcy of the intercepts and intelligence leads coming to them was now almost numbing, and they had run out of small talk. There was mostly silence.

The door opened and the Air Force colonel in charge of Raven Rock came in. Everyone stood as she went to the front of the room.

"At ease. Please, take your seats. I hope you saw the president's announcement. I've just received orders for our command to begin filtering and assessing domestic input along with our offshore intercepts. Apparently the volume of information is now so great that the NSA is going to divide the intake and use all available resources—civilian and DOD—to review it. In the next few minutes, from our usual FBI, DEA, and law enforcement channels, we'll begin receiving first and second level inputs which are purely domestic, for our evaluation and action recommendations. Our actions will be monitored at a new NSC Command Center at Fort Meade. Please treat these as you would our foreign evaluations. Any questions?"

After a moment of silence, Buckley asked, "Should we now use two-person review, given the potentially sensitive and personal nature of the domestic intercepts?"

"What do you mean?" the colonel asked.

"Well, suppose there was an intercept that seemed to implicate an African American group. Or a White Supremacist group. As we learned in our DEI training on CRT, since some people are racists but don't even know it, are we sure that all threats will be treated equally by a random individual assignment within our group?'

"Or a Muslim related intercept?" Ahmad injected, looking at his teammate.

"Oh. OK," replied the colonel. "We're a team, and unless and until I think any member is not carrying out our assigned duties to the best of her or his ability, without any personal preference, we'll continue using our normal procedures: one person to review and two people for action. Got it?"

Buckley nodded. "Yes. But you've taught us that we're all racists, so I hope it works."

That afternoon in the Conference Center the president joined a meeting in progress with his Core Team of Rob Thompson, Allen Linder, Diane Marsh, Garrett Crose and Emily Schofield. They brought him up to date on the long list of issues and actions that needed immediate attention. State Funerals were being planned for President Rhodes, Vice President Carpenter, and Speaker Gordon. Contingencies were being considered for moving some operations back to The White House, with stepped up military defenses and a larger perimeter. Phone calls of varying lengths were scheduled with the heads of state of thirty countries over the next two days, to introduce the president and to review the day's extraordinary steps.

While the others continued to go through their lists, President Bradshaw read through eight proposed new executive orders from the NSC agencies. Each was accompanied by a one-page explanation of why the order was necessary and how it would be implemented, and signed by the Secretary of the relevant Cabinet level office, or his or her first deputy, along with the initials of at least one of Bradshaw's Core Team. He signed all of them and gave them to Linder.

"I want to thank you, Allen, Diane and Garrett, for your great help these past three days. We've effectively pulled our two teams together and done what's best for the country. Thank you. Since we don't have a televised update tonight, I hope you'll stand down and call, or go see, your families. Let's regroup early in the morning."

"Thank you, Mr. President," Garrett replied. "Diane and I will let Allen file the executive orders, and we'll definitely take a break with our families. See you here, first thing, for our regular briefing."

The three former deputies to President Rhodes pushed back their chairs, packed their briefcases, and departed.

"Let's adjourn to my suite," Bradshaw said to Rob and Emily. As they passed the MP officer at the door he said, "When Mr. Sullivan comes back, ask him to join us in my room."

Peyton Tidwell was studying alone in his dorm room at Hampton Pierce College. Late the previous Saturday night he'd been sitting in the back seat of his older brother's car, drinking beer with him and their two cousins, who worked nights at his uncle's restaurant. They talked about girls, football and the sorry state of good jobs for white people. Unseen by them, their conversation was being amped up by Revno, reminding them that they were victims of the tide of illegal immigrants and uneducated blacks.

They had parked at the town's deserted main square. Alerted by Razum's fellow demons, Revno prodded the men to look up. They caught a glimpse of two black men heading toward their most historic Confederate statue.

"What are those boys up to?" Revno planted in their minds.

The three older men got out. Peyton's brother retrieved his shotgun from the trunk. Peyton joined them on the sidewalk.

"Those boys are up to no good," his cousin whispered.

"Take a look, but don't take the gun," Peyton offered.

"What if they're armed?" his brother asked.

"Come on," the second of the cousins said.

"Stay with the car," his brother commanded, and threw him the keys.

The three set off with Revno next to them, whispering ever lounder in their ears. Peyton stayed by the car, but when he heard his brother yell, he jumped into the driver's seat, closed the door and turned on the headlights, illuminating the campus green.

After two blasts and more yells, the older boys ran back to the car. As they jumped in, Peyton exclaimed, "What the hell?" He doused the lights and drove off. The other three alternated between shaking and laughing. Peyton watched in the mirror, but no one followed them.

Ten minutes later, parked in the cousins' neighborhood, they could hear the sirens downtown. They swore to each other not to say a word to anyone about what happened. If anyone asked, they'd been parked here, not in town, when the shooting occurred.

By Monday Peyton decided that he needed to provide a little extra cover, in case anyone recalled some of his cousins' coarser remarks over the years. He called his brother, who agreed that it would be a good idea.

So from his dorm room he joined several social media threads decrying the senseless murders of the rising engineers, and condemning anyone who would resort to such violence.

Unfortunately for Peyton, the keyword scanners used by the FBI and the Artificial Intelligence algorithms employed by the NSA linked these remarks to his earlier statements on what Peyton had thought were secure White Supremacist sites on the Dark Web, along with his location at Hampton Pierce College and a transcript of the phone call with his brother. The social media content anomaly and the phone call, along with their location, caused the scanner at the NSA to issue a Further Action ticket to Clayton Hunt's Team at Raven Rock. He and Megan Buckley, after reviewing the data, issued an Action Directive.

The result was that two unmarked cars pulled up to the dorm late that Tuesday afternoon, and Peyton was about to be visited by four well-armed FBI agents.

When the Secret Service Agent opened the door to the president's suite, Rob and Emily found the new First Lady on a sofa in conversation with the House Minority Leader, Nancy Cantrell, each holding a glass of white wine. Everyone greeted.

Bradshaw beckoned to his younger subordinates, "Please, have a glass of wine and join us."

"Thank you," Emily said, taking a glass from the First Lady and sitting on one of the two sofas which joined three chairs around the coffee table.

When they were all comfortably seated, the president began.

"I asked Nancy to drive up and join us this afternoon because the five of us worked closely for several years on our party's key progressive policies and strategies when we were all in the Legislative Branch. Now that we also have the Executive, I think it's crucial that we coordinate and strategize how to use this remarkable circumstance to advance our full Progressive Agenda, just as soon as this immediate crisis is behind us—assuming that happens, of course. I want us ready to move quickly with the upcoming elections, and we should be taking preliminary steps while everyone else is focused elsewhere. It's the perfect time to put in place an unbeatable Progressive majority."

He looked around. The others nodded. "In the House, Nancy, I'll call on the other side to elect someone as the new Speaker who's more 'in the middle,' in the spirit of national unity, but in an election year I doubt they'll do it. I assume Jacob Welch, the Majority Leader, will get it."

"I can work with him," Cantrell said. "He doesn't like being called an Uncle Tom by other African American members, so we have some leverage to get things done."

"We can appear to do the same in the Senate with the new President Pro Tem. The Governor in California is coordinating with us whom to appoint as my replacement in the Senate. Rob already has some staff people working on whom we should nominate as vice president. And then there are the elections. It's too early in this emergency to decide how to position ourselves for keeping the Senate and flipping the House, but I want a team working on different approaches, to be ready to go when this all plays out.

"Nancy, I'd like you to take this whole effort quietly under your wing, so that it's off the Executive plate for the time being. We've got a lot right now dealing with this mess, but hopefully we'll find the perpetrators and end the emergency in a week or two. I want our strategies in place long before that. What do you think?"

Nancy Cantrell leaned forward, looking at Bradshaw. "This is an historic moment. Through this awful tragedy we Progressives have been given an incredible opportunity. We can't waste it. Generations will look back on these weeks and months as a key turning point in American history—when our nation moved from the ashes of despair to a more just, diverse and equal place for all of us. Our educational institutions, most corporations, and the military leadership are ready. We just have to move. So, yes, we'll quietly create a team off the grid and begin working on every aspect of our agenda immediately, from new people to strong programs, and the election. Maybe we should call it Project Phoenix."

"Good. Good." Bradshaw nodded.

They raised their glasses in a toast. "To a better, more progressive future," Rob said.

As they sipped, there was a knock, and Tom Sullivan came in. "You wanted to see me, sir?"

The president waved him over. "Yes, Tom. Here, have a seat and a glass of wine. You remember Minority Leader Cantrell."

Tom nodded. "Yes, we met several times in the White House." Cantrell smiled and handed Tom a glass as he joined them around the coffee table.

"How's it going?" Bradshaw asked.

He took a sip. "It's of course very early, but the interfaces with the internet and social media providers appear to be working well, with no glitches or sabotage, and, as you've seen, the detailed recommendations for additional executive orders from the departments are coming in. I think you should have thirty more to review this evening."

Bradshaw nodded. "Good, Tom. It looks like you've come up with a good set of action steps that should find and defeat these people."

"Thank you, sir. I hope so."

Emily Schofield leaned forward. "Tom, are *all* phone conversations, texts and emails now open to our intercept and review?"

"Yes. Except for some highly classified DOD and law enforcement phones, which will remain encrypted."

"Even ours?"

He paused and put his glass on the table. "Well, no. Our new phones cannot be monitored, unless, I guess, the president authorized it. As you know they're on a special, concealed and encrypted network that requires two stage authentication, and we issue the individual passwords. Every system requires a key to get inside in case of an emergency, but the one for this network is heavily encrypted and not saved electronically—only General Price and I have a hard copy. Our Core Group and anyone on this network can talk with each other without worrying about being hacked or monitored by anyone, even a government agency."

Emily sat back. "Good." She glanced at the president. "We just wanted to be sure. Obviously our group needs to be able to communicate at the highest level without worrying about a possible intercept or leak."

"Yes, of course."

Rob said, "And only the most trusted officials, those actually involved in this emergency, should have access to these special phones."

Tom nodded and reached for his bag. "I'm controlling them myself, and I've got the list here. Would you like to go over it?"

"That's a good idea," Bradshaw said. "And then you and Emily should review together the placement of any new phones."


Mason Neal and Joshua Weber had grown up on adjacent farms in northern Kentucky, where they still worked their families' land. Now in their late 40s, they'd played high school football together and shared closely in all aspects of starting and raising families. They also shared a tragedy: both of their youngest children had died of opioid overdoses. Mason's son recovered from a college baseball injury only to be hooked on the painkillers which the doctors prescribed. Three months later, Joshua's daughter slid into drugs at school after her mother, the love of Josh's life, died of breast cancer.

The two young people died within a month of each other, and the two fathers never recovered from their grief, which over time turned to anger. As more and more details emerged about the roles of doctors, salespeople, and Big Pharma in creating the tsunami of addictive drugs, Josh and Mason looked for someone to blame. One night six months earlier, over beers on Josh's porch, where he now lived alone, they watched a Network expose´ and realized that it was not supposed to be this way, and that the Drug Enforcement Agency, while dutifully charting the explosive rise of opioid use in the nation, had done absolutely nothing to question or to stop it. And Vonyat, their local demon, whispered in Mason's head that their children were dead because of inept, corrupt, fat bureaucrats with big paychecks. Someone had to pay.

At Vonyat's suggestion that night they'd searched online under Timothy McVeigh, and found detailed instructions on exactly how to build a bomb like the one he used in Oklahoma City. Over the next several weeks the outline of a plan emerged, constantly encouraged by the demon, and they began acquiring the ingredients and materials that they would need. Given their farming operations, they had a legitimate reason to acquire the large amount of ammonium nitrate required, and for years they had mixed explosives to remove stumps from cleared land. Finally, they had built large, two-axle heavy equipment trailers since they were teenagers. By the late summer they had everything they needed to teach those responsible a lesson, and began assembling the bomb in a large shed behind Josh's barn.

That night as they unlocked the shed and surveyed their nearly completed work with a flashlight, Mason said, "If they're really going to bring on this State of Emergency, we probably ought to get a move on before they make it more difficult, 'cause unlike McVeigh, I don't intend to get caught."

Josh nodded. "I think we can be ready for the trip to D.C. in a week."


Tom started on his sandwich at a working dinner while sitting with Tanya Prescott and General Nathan Price at one end of a huge U-shaped table. They were monitoring the information ramping up at the NSC Command Center, hastily created at Fort Meade inside the NSA compound. To be manned 24/7 until the crisis passed, and coordinated by the senior FBI team, there was a seat for each of the key Cabinet offices, as well as for the CIA, DOD, NSA, and other agencies tasked with gathering information or enforcing laws and executive orders. A member of President Bradshaw's Core Group—from either the White House or his earlier Senate Team—presided on a rotating basis. There were a few large screens on the walls that could display situations around the globe, but the main purpose for the Command Center was to share high level information, make decisions, and send enforcement directives to the relevant agencies. With the new information expected from the measures in the State of Emergency, all the participants expected to be very busy.

Despite his weariness, Tom found the people and the activity exhilarating. Most of these functions had individually existed three days ago, but he, Agent Prescott, General Price, and a few others had actually been responsible for pulling them together, issuing the necessary commands, expanding their reach, and causing the process to function—all relatively smoothly, so far. He looked around at the thirty or so busy people, listened to the constant buzz of information, and for the first time since the original attack felt that they should now be able to identify and stop the perpetrators. He realized he was nodding to himself as he read through intercept reports and noted the recommended actions to be taken. Voices of *Well Done, Pride* and *Success* played in his head, amplified by the demons who braved the spiritual light and heat.

*The Constitution is important, but finding and stopping whoever's behind this has to take priority.*

Tom was quietly guessing that either Artificial Intelligence or an intercept would provide the key lead they needed back to the Russian, Iranian, North Korean or Chinese military—everything Tom knew about cybersecurity and communication, the scope of the attacks and the coordination required, not to mention the deception involved, meant that the attacks were probably coming from offshore. And when they had the proof, the U.S. would have to retaliate.

An hour later he said goodnight and took the base shuttle over to his room in the conference center. On the way he called and checked in with his parents. Like most Americans, they were mourning the nation's losses and worried about the future—but proud that Tom was in the thick of it. While he had to be vague about everything around him, he told them that he was hopefully optimistic. His words encouraged them, and they reiterated that their church was continuing a 24-hour prayer vigil, with Tom specifically on the list. He thanked them and said he would check in again soon.

Reaching his room, he questioned whether to call Callie. Not only because it was late, but also because he had only met her three nights before, and he didn't want her to think him pushy. But he found that he enjoyed talking with her. She had a kind of uplifting peace about her, and a lot of common sense. And she was beautiful. He decided he would give it three rings.

"Hello?"

"Callie, it's Tom."

"Oh, hi." Her voice brightened. "I didn't recognize the number. It looked crazy."

"I've got a new phone."

"How are you?"

"I'm fine. More importantly, how are you?"

"My hands are much better. I think I'll go into the office tomorrow."

They exchanged small talk for several minutes. Callie confirmed that daughter Grace, friend Kristen, and Beau were all well.

"When I come to town again, can I see you?"

"Yes, of course. Please come by—either the apartment or my office."

"How's the church building?"

"When I went in to pray this afternoon, I heard they plan to start repairs next week."

"Good. Are you all still praying there, even with the damage?"

"Yes, around the clock. I added your name—and I called Andrea Hunt to get your friends' names—to the list. It's so important."

"Hmm. Thank you."

"Tom, when I walk outside and head to the church, I just feel this weight. It's, like, oppressive. Like evil. All around me. I've never felt it so heavily before. I'm almost running by the time I get to the front steps."

He paused. "Really? That's kind of weird."

"I know. It's probably just a reaction to all this. But when it's happening, it feels so real, so dark. Like I'm surrounded. I just want to get away. But when I pray they go away."

"They?"

"Yeah. I know it's strange. But I feel like there are spiritual beings talking to us. So I pray. For all of us."

He smiled. "Well, you keep working on the spiritual ones, and I'll keep working on the real ones. Hopefully I can see you soon, and we'll compare notes."

"OK. I will. So we have even more on our list to discuss."

He almost laughed. "I generally like people who keep lists. I'll call you as soon as I can."

"I hope so. Good night."


At midnight in the Oval Office only Prince Proklor's inner circle met with him. Given their need to better understand what the president's speech and the increasing number of Executive Orders might mean for their strategies, Proklor had ordered all the others to attend every meeting and to listen in at every Cabinet level office which was not subject to prayer cover. Even that was becoming more difficult as churches and individuals increased their prayers and made them more specific. Lesser demons at the sector and street levels were ordered to report back on how the new, additional Executive Orders were being received in homes, offices and meeting places.

As was their custom, Temno began with the two daily numbers they watched most closely. "2,598 divorces and 2,712 abortions."

Proklor nodded. "We can count on them to split up their families and to kill their children no matter what else is going on. They really are predictable." He looked at Legat, who spoke.

"The new president thinks he can stop the mayhem with his new emergency measures, but they have no chance. Our forces are too entrenched. The splinters are too great."

Temno nodded. "We'll keep dividing them until each group feels it must attack others in order to defend itself."

Proklor smiled. "For now, wait several days to give them some hope, then ratchet up the attacks at all levels again. Keep everyone alert and reporting back if they encounter anything unexpected. This is new ground for them and for us—the Land of the Free under martial law. We must stay close and analyze every opportunity to divide them further."

# 6

*It is the duty of nations as well as men to own their dependence upon the overruling power of God, to confess their sins and transgressions in humble sorrow yet with assured hope that genuine repentance will lead to mercy and pardon, and to recognize the sublime truth, announced in the Holy Scriptures and proven by all history: that those nations only are blessed whose God is the Lord.*

Abraham Lincoln

Wednesday, September 16

At Wednesday morning's NSC Command Center briefing, attended by the president and his Core Group, each Cabinet office and agency reported on the first hours of implementing the State of Emergency. With only a few outbursts by libertarian pundits and a couple of cases of apparent sabotage by those tasked with routing internet traffic from private service providers to the NSA and the DOD, the first day appeared to be a success. And there had been no identifiable attacks.

Thirty minutes into the meeting the Secretary of Homeland Security recommended that over the next few days they begin moving Executive Branch functions back to the White House and adjoining buildings, and that Congress and the Supreme Court reopen as well, with one major caveat: a large section of the most popular parts of the capital would be temporarily sealed off to the general public. From the White House to the Supreme Court, including much of the Mall, all traffic, both vehicular and pedestrian, would be restricted to those on official business. In addition, this area would be cordoned off by the military, and portable anti-aircraft batteries would be stationed around the perimeter.

"I know people want to see their government back in action, and inside that island we could presumably get a lot done without a lot of distractions," President Bradshaw said from his seat. "But there is obviously the issue of safety."

After a five-minute discussion Bradshaw told the HS Secretary to draft an Executive Order to implement the recommendation.

As the meeting broke up an hour later, Tom and Emily walked to the exit together.

"I'm looking forward to getting back to the White House," Tom said. "The FBI was asking last night for volunteers to be in the first group, and I gladly raised my hand."

Emily smiled. "Well, you're young, single and, I guess, expendable."

"Thanks a lot."

"Actually, I volunteered, too. But the president wants me with him until he moves, probably on Friday. Will you help me find my way around?"

"Sure. It'll be good to have us all together. And I think the other COG remote sites will be shifting people back to their offices by the end of the week. With the strict measures in the State of Emergency, I think we'll be OK."


Following the arrests the previous afternoon of Peyton Tidwell, his brother and cousins on murder, domestic terrorism and hate crimes charges, NSA and FBI resources were focused on the hate groups associated with these four individuals, plus the next three circles of their acquaintances, and on the websites which they had visited on the internet, including the Dark Web. As a result, twenty-three teams were en route that morning across the nation to confront and question those suspected of participating in or planning similar hate crimes.

Tom and the agency deputies on duty monitored their progress, along with a steady flow of other enforcement actions, from the new NSC Command Center. Tom noted each arrest or detainment with great pleasure—finally they were pushing back for real and getting somewhere. It felt good. Now they just needed to connect the dots and find out who was actually behind all these attacks.


The president, Rob Thompson and Emily Schofield were having salads at the table in the president's suite, with Nancy Cantrell on the speaker phone. The House Minority Leader began, "Mr. President, I think with your staff's help we've settled on a compelling vice presidential candidate. We want to run her by you before we take any more steps."

Bradshaw put down his fork and picked up his iced tea. "Great. Go ahead."

"It's Congresswoman Patricia Reynolds." Emily and Rob looked at each other and silently nodded.

Cantrell continued. "She's from the just-murdered Speaker's state. You may recall that she was a conservative in their state legislature, but she changed to our side before running for Congress ten years ago. She's now a strong Progressive who fights for social justice, but I believe we can sell her as a uniter, as someone who understands both sides of most issues, in this difficult time when we all need to pull together—and it's a great story for our media friends."

"And where does she stand on Reproductive and Transgender Rights?" Bradshaw asked.

"She's solid."

"You're sure?"

Emily interrupted. "Yes, I can confirm that. In fact, as a pro-life feminist she became a pro-choice feminist because the conservative party leaders in her state started talking about imprisoning women who have late-term abortions, and that was too much for her."

"And she's a great speaker," Rob added. "Very polished, but down-to-earth and inclusive. I think she'll be well received. And remember, she doesn't have to win a popular election—just a majority in the House and Senate. If we move quickly and set her up right, it'll be tough for conservatives to vote against her, even if they have issues, given what's happened."

"OK," the president said. "Start the vetting and let me know when I should call her."

"And, just to reiterate," Rob added, "the policy team from our former Senate staff is working with the Leader's staff to refine a new, powerful Progressive Agenda that will advance real social justice."

The president thought for a moment. "And how about people? We need to get committed people in a lot of key positions, probably right after the midterm elections in November. We may have a once-in-a-generation chance to put together the people and the policies America needs to bring about real and lasting progressive improvements for all our people."

Rob nodded. "Drew Boswell and his Tech Roundtable have given our team a list of names and positions which will ensure that the government and the best companies are always working together. And, by the way, what do you think of Drew Boswell as Secretary of State, given all his international experience and connections?"

The president smiled. "He'd be awesome, and I'm sure Secretary McCord will soon realize he's finished with our party unless he fully embraces the power of our Progressive policies. We can nudge him in that direction.

President Bradshaw sat back. "You know, we've been so close before. It's our time. People are counting on us. Our friends in Big Tech and the media control what the nation sees and hears. Maybe the stars have finally aligned, after this terrible mess. But with the midterm elections coming, let's get our new V.P. through Congress before we announce our agenda."

After lunch Tom found Tanya Prescott sitting at the main console in the NSC Command Center, focused on a screen and communicating through a headset. Tom waited until there was a break, then touched her shoulder.

She removed the headset and swiveled her chair. "The intercepts and connections are ramping up. We're seeing a great increase in the number of Action Items from law enforcement on their own, plus from our special assets, both civilian and military. The tech firms have really helped us open the floodgates."

Tom nodded. "That's really good, Agent Prescott."

"Please, Tanya. Later today we'll start to focus our Artificial Intelligence resources on all this information. That should make even more of a difference, and hopefully lead us to the instigators."

"AI should connect a lot of dots. Do you think it's coming from Russia, or maybe China? Iran or North Korea?"

She paused, then spoke. "Could be. Others know more about China than me. Before transferring to the FBI to try to spend more time with my teenagers, I was on advance teams with the State Department. And since I'm half-Russian, and speak the language, that's where a lot of my career focus has been." He nodded. "As I think you heard, I was there for the attacks on both countries' presidents ten years ago and was at the point of the spear when we stopped it. Pretty intense. I was so proud of so many professionals in both countries. But then, as you know, the leadership in Russia turned dark, paranoid and corrupt two years later, then attacked Ukraine, and here we are."

"So it *could* be from there."

"It could, of course. But I will also tell you that there are a lot of great Russians who hate how their government has turned out and wish they could change it. But when the bad guys have all the guns and all the power, it's hard for good people to act, wherever they are."

"Hmm." There was silence for several moments as the FBI agent studied him.

"And not to get too philosophical, because there are good and bad people everywhere, but the huge difference between Russia and China is that Russia is fundamentally a European, Christian nation which gave the world Tolstoy, Dostoyevsky, Pushkin, Tchaikovsky—you can actually discuss with anyone in Russia Good vs. Evil, Right vs. Wrong, God and Satan, Salvation and Damnation. You may not think exactly the same way on these subjects, but he or she certainly understands the concepts. In fact, the average Russian is much more 'spiritual' than the average American. What they're sadly missing now are true facts, which distort the Good vs. Evil conclusions of many Russians. I don't find that to be true with most Chinese, at least in public, for whom the good of the collective State is the only consideration in anything and everything."

Tom smiled. "Wow. That's some pretty deep thought."

She returned his smile. "I told you—I'm half-Russian."

She stood. "Let's get some coffee. Are you going back to the White House?"

"Tomorrow. I'll stay here tonight, watching the process. And I've got to follow up with each of the internet providers, to thank them. Whenever you and I need to talk, we've got our phones."

"How many are on the Trusted Core Group circuit now?"

"We're up to sixty-two. All the NSC Cabinet level members and key staff."

"Good. Director Toomey wants me to give him updates, day or night, when anything breaks."

"What kind of a guy is he?"

She paused. "We're a bit different."

"How so?"

"Well, we both very much want to stop the bad actors. But that's really my only focus—I'm pretty simple. Get the truth and get the bad guys." She smiled.

"And Toomey?"

"He wants the same. But he's also got one eye on how any particular investigation could impact him—his career. He's the perfect blend of brilliant lawman and politician. I guess that's why he's the Director. And I've heard that along the way he hasn't shied away from bending a rule or two to be sure justice was served, so to speak."

"Sounds like he may be the right man for right now."

She was silent again for several beats, holding her eyes on Tom. "Maybe. I hope so. And the Hate Speech Review notices will start going out this afternoon."

"We'll probably get push back from some quarters on those, but they're certainly necessary. Everyone can just chill for a month," Tom replied.

"Agreed. After we get our coffee, join me and we'll monitor what's happening together. It should start to get interesting."

# 7

George Washington

Friday, September 18

Friday morning Teri Grantham was walking back to her parents' home from an adjoining field in rural Maryland. At thirty-four and five years out of the Army, Teri ran a one-woman drone video business which was hugely successful, from high end real estate sales presentations to fence and pipeline monitoring for the farms beyond her own ex-urban home northwest of Baltimore. She was one of the best drone operators in the area and actually taught classes on drone applications.

She'd left her parents' home an hour before, telling the assembled family members she needed to walk. But the truth was that she'd had it with mourning the savage murder of her older brother, John, in his F-35 at the hands of that Muslim A-hole—her brother's friggin' friend and wingman! The family had come together early last Sunday, and they still didn't know when, if ever, they'd have John's remains to bury. Growing up, Teri had been a tomboy and had idolized John—it's why she went into the military herself. Now this Muslim low life—whom they'd had in their home as a guest—had killed him, not to mention the president, the Speaker, and several hundred dedicated Americans. Enough with mourning; it was time for action.

As she neared the house again she was glad to see her younger brother, Brad, coming out of the lower level to meet her. Brad had been in the Supply Corps in the Navy. Out of the service with a promising AI logistics job and a girlfriend, he'd never given up his passion for hunting and firearms, and he was beginning to build a small rifle collection.

Brad shook his head as she came closer. "Hey, I'm about done with this. I can't watch Mom cry anymore."

As she hugged him, Ranit, a demon who prided himself on exploring the newest technologies, was standing next to them and whispered to her for the fourth time that morning. "Show him. He'll love it."

After a pause, Teri said, "I'm with you. It's time to teach these people a lesson." She took her phone out of her pocket. "Let me show you a video I think you'll like."

Tom walked out of the National Security Advisor's office in the White House—he still couldn't call it his own—on his way to the Situation Room when he ran into Emily, carrying a box of personal items.

"I think my office is over there." She smiled.

"Welcome to the Mad House." He took the box and walked a short distance down the busy hall with her. "In here."

He put the box on her clean desk. "Tanya Prescott and I have a daily virtual check-in at eleven. Come down and join us if you want. I think we're close to ID'ing the scumbags who torched Callie's church."

"No hate speech, please," she quipped, then looked around her new space. "Thanks for the invite. Maybe later. Right now I want to get moved in before the president arrives. He's on the way. Seth's interview is this afternoon. I've got to review the questions he's submitted."

"I doubt he'll try any curve balls."

She nodded. "But I gotta check anyway. The president wants to be totally prepared."

"I never disagree with that approach. See you later."

Richard and Janet Sullivan, Tom's parents, had moved to Atlanta four years earlier for several reasons. His law firm needed a steady senior hand in the real estate area of its Atlanta office after the untimely death of one partner and the departure of another. Janet's board work in international healthcare benefited from proximity to the headquarters of the CDC and CARE. And Susan, their oldest child and the mother of their granddaughters, was married to a man she met in college who continued his career with a high-tech company in the growing cluster around the Georgia Tech campus in Midtown.

After a brief search they'd joined a vibrant church—one of many in the city—and began putting down roots with their neighbors and church members. Richard now served on the Board of Elders. Since the terrible events of the previous Saturday night, the church's 24/7 Prayer Team had expanded to pray for specific people and groups in the government and military, and Tom's name had been on their list since Sunday's service.

Richard was about to leave his Buckhead high rise office for a lunch meeting when his cell phone buzzed: Stan Conway, their pastor.

"Stan, hey. How are you?"

"Better than I deserve, as always. You?"

"Except for regularly worrying about Tom and our nation, we're good."

"Well, that's sort of why I'm calling. Since you're an attorney with some gray hair, and Janet served a couple of terms in Congress, I need some advice."

"What's up?"

"Late yesterday afternoon I got an email—I think a similar one was sent to every church on every list, everywhere—notifying me that until further notice we have to submit our sermons to the Atlanta Regional Homeland Security Office for review at least forty-eight hours prior to the service, or they cannot be delivered."

Richard frowned. "Why?"

"Checking for hate speech, trigger words, or divisive un-American statements, according to the email. Which are all banned under the State of Emergency."

Richard sat in his chair and swiveled to look at the view. "The way the president explained it the other night it sounded reasonable, but I never imagined what you're now describing. It sounds exactly like the new rules at a 'woke' Christian school we're suing on behalf of a group of parents—the Board has made Freedom of Speech into a set of rules open to regulation and abuse."

"I hadn't thought of that connection, but, yes, that's my point. So we're coming up on forty-eight hours before our main Sunday service, and I'm looking for advice. From your experience and perspective, should we send it in? Or ignore it?"

"Nothing in my experience—or Janet's—equates to this new world. I'm sure those in charge are trying to do the right thing, and I think our son may be in the middle of it, though they've maybe gone a bit overboard. Can you—we—comply this week, and then see what happens after things shake out a bit?"

"That's about what two others have suggested as well, so, after praying about it, I guess we'll send it in. And keep praying."

"Let us know, and I'll tell Janet. See you on Sunday."

Although all three branches of government were reopening in Washington, the situation was far from normal. Barricades stretched from 18th Street west of the Capitol to 4th Street on the east, and from H Street to below the Mall. All of the museums and open spaces within that area were closed to the public, and there was a large and obvious military presence, including Armored Personnel Carriers and mobile surface-to-air missile batteries.

At 2 pm Seth Cohen approached a newly erected checkpoint on the north side of Lafayette Square with his press credentials and passport. After a ten minute wait and a phone call, he was escorted across the square by an MP, who then handed him off to a White House Security person. They waited just inside the portico at the entrance to the West Wing.

Emily Schofield walked out to the lobby and gave him a hug. "We're so glad you could come."

"Me, too. Thanks. What about my camera team?"

"Give us a few minutes to talk first. Come to The Roosevelt Room."

He followed Emily down the hall. She smiled. "I'm still learning my way around. Tom is around the corner as the Acting National Security Advisor."

They entered The Roosevelt Room. "We thought this would be the best place for the interview. What do you think?"

Seth realized that he was across from the Oval Office and a few hundred feet from the Press Briefing Room, where he normally hung out with the other White House reporters. Today there were no other reporters; he was the only member of the press in the building. Rachel Shaw at The Network wouldn't believe it.

"Would you like some coffee?" Emily said, smiling and indicating a chair at the end of the table. He shook his head. She closed the door. "Can you believe it was exactly one week ago we met in the senator's office to talk about your series on the Silent Progressive Majority?"

"What a week. Who saw it coming?"

"No one. And a lot has changed. In fact, almost everything. The president wants me to share with you that there are difficult times immediately in front of us, but in the bigger picture, the Progressive Majority may soon not be so silent."

"What do you mean?"

"Seth, based on our relationship, last Friday's meeting, and your help with the Executive Order, the president has asked me to take you into our confidence. But first I need your iron-clad commitment that what we talk about here always stays between us."

He nodded. "Of course. But maybe some coffee would actually be good."

She smiled and walked over to the sideboard, speaking while she fixed two cups. "Despite the current difficult trials—or really because of them—the better world we've all hoped for may actually be attainable, and not just as a campaign slogan, but in fact."

Emily handed him a cup, but remained standing next to him. "We now have both the White House and the Senate, plus many conservative members of the House already calling for ways to minimize the impact of the attacks on the average family. With the right nominations, policies and regulations, we think the Guaranteed Income Act and other progressive initiatives will pass almost immediately on an emergency basis—and then of course once people start receiving the funds, they'll become permanent. Worst case, we'll be really well positioned for the elections, when we could win big. We may be on the cusp of creating a much better and more just America than you or I imagined only a week ago."

As she sat next to him, he said, "I've been so focused on the attacks and the responses that I hadn't thought about that."

"Yes. Isn't it amazing? While we of course have all the right people working on defending us right now, another small group is quietly planning for the future."

"What an opportunity."

"Yes. But we can't talk about it. We want you to be in on the big picture so you can help keep the focus on the attacks and on our defenses. That's why we need reasonable questions with strong answers. And good coverage. OK?"

Seth paused. "And with that approach we continue our special relationship?"

She took a long sip and then nodded. "Exactly."

He smiled. "OK. I'm in."

"Great. The president will be very pleased." She set down her cup and turned over her pad. "Now, we need to know who leaked the story about the Executive Order."

After several moments' silence while Seth stared at her, he said, "Whoa. I guess I'm an idiot. I didn't see that coming."

Emily didn't smile. "As we've just agreed, there's much more at stake here than one person or action. We can't do what we've just laid out if there's someone calling the press after every decision we make."

There was silence for a long moment while Seth considered his options. "Diane Marsh."

"Really? How? Why?"

"We go way back. Same hometown. She's a little older. When I first arrived in D.C. she introduced me to several good contacts. Helped me get the job at The Network. Of course we're both Liberals, but I'm much more Progressive than she is: ten years ago that didn't matter so much. She was just being nice."

"And why?"

"She's hated your boss for a long time. You'd have no way to know, but she was Haley Fitzgerald's roommate when Senator Bradshaw was caught with her in that hotel room. I think it's always stuck in Diane's craw how Bradshaw's people—before your time—tried to blame Haley. Drove her out of town and into drugs. Terrible. A different day then, but Diane's never forgotten. And I think the idea of him declaring martial law just pushed her over the edge. So she called me."

It was Emily's turn to think. "The Senator—the President—has history with a lot of us."

Seth cocked his head.

"Nothing. And whatever happened all those years ago can't jeopardize how we deal with an enemy who's trying to kill us today. Or our Progressive future. I get it, but I'm very disappointed."

"What will you do?"

"It's not up to me. The president, and I guess Tom, the Security Advisor, will decide."

"Mmm. I hope they're not too hard on her."

"Seth, she can't be trusted. She sits with and advises the president. This isn't a video game. It's real life and death. What would you do?"

"OK. I get it. Agreed. Is there anything else before we talk about the interview and I get my crew inside?"


At that hour in Limassol, Alexei Nobikov and his wife, Anna, were sipping wine on their apartment's balcony. All afternoon he had huddled with Sveta and his team to craft ways around the new requirements against hate speech and political attack ads. The U.S. government was starting to block or delete some of their more strident social media postings and websites. But his group was creative, and they were re-designing their ads, messages and sites to appear to be more positive, with the divisive messaging buried in the content—not as potent as headlines, but they would increase the frequency to compensate.

After arriving home he had finished packing for his week-long trip to the U.S., and they were chatting about the friends he would see and the news Anna wanted him to gather about their families. He tried to visit the U.S. and take the nation's pulse every quarter, and this certainly seemed like a good time. In the morning he would fly to Boston via London to spend a few days with old friends from his graduate school days and attend a Cyber security conference—it always amazed him how Americans so freely shared the latest issues and technology with anyone who attended a conference, but he couldn't complain. Then on to D.C.

Besides calling on legitimate contacts in the internet industry, he also looked forward to spending time with his niece Katherine—his sister's oldest—who was in graduate school at American University. Childless, Alexei and his wife doted on their six nieces and nephews, the four oldest of whom were in school or working in the U.S. or Europe. Given the uncertainty and corruption now rampant in his country, sensible people, even the most secular, who wanted the best for their children steered them toward a future in the West, or at least to experiencing life there for a few years.

And he also appreciated that their perspectives gave him a window into what young people were saying and doing. Ironically, that helped with his real line of work as the head of an important Russian disinformation team outside the motherland, targeting the U.S. with half-truths and lies. He wished they were still mostly just information gatherers, which is how they started, but the new leadership was adamant that they actively intervene. So Alexei followed their orders. The alternative did not seem attractive. But then there were all the lies those same leaders made to his own people. What to do?

Given the move-ins and Seth's team setting up in the Roosevelt Room, President Bradshaw asked to hold a truncated meeting of his Core Group and key NSC staff in the Situation Room. It was also a test of their new set-up.

With the president and his Core Group's physical dispersal from Fort Meade, given the need for quick decisions during the State of Emergency, they had agreed to keep a virtual connection open 24/7 between the White House Situation Room and the other key departments in the NSC charged with those responsibilities. One member of the president's Core Group would always be in the Situation Room, and able to reach the Commander-in-Chief immediately. This structure quickly came to be known as The Emergency Council.

While the newly applied electronic countermeasures were still searching through all available data looking for a common thread of culpability, security cameras, facial recognition, and the NSA's supercomputers were allowing them to pick some low hanging fruit.

From his seat next to the president, Tom looked up from his notes. "Adding the NSA's capabilities to those of the D.C. police and the FBI, we've been able to positively identify the three fire bombers at Church of the Good Shepherd last Sunday." He nodded at a screen on the far wall, where a picture taken at a Rainbow Rally showed more than ten people with banners, but circles were drawn around two men and a woman. "They're currently under surveillance in hopes of discovering a broader connection, but we expect them to be taken into custody by Monday at the latest."

"Members of the LGBQT local leadership?" Diane Marsh asked.

"Yes. They picketed the church that morning," Tom replied.

"Why?" the president asked.

"The pastor had planned a sermon opposing Gay Marriage, but the events of Saturday night changed that."

The president nodded. "That's why I'm so glad our State of Emergency bans hate speech along with actions. We've got to turn down the rhetoric. Maybe there would have been no firebombs if the pastor had not been so homophobic. Thank you, Tom, for including both hateful words as well as actions in our State of Emergency. It's fair and balanced."

Tom looked at his notes and disliked what he had to say next. "Thank you, sir. Unfortunately, that's the most concrete new result we have this afternoon. All the rest remains in process."

"All right. Thanks, Now, I have my first network interview in about an hour. Each of you please give us an unclassified update on major projects that I can use in the interview—the clean-up in Belgium, the scaled-back state funeral schedule, fully restoring our government, early results from the State of Emergency. All that. Garrett, please start."


As Mason Neal and Josh Weber worked behind the closed doors of Josh's shed on his Kentucky farm that afternoon, Umer watched as they measured and installed several lengths of hose. Through the sector leader in his chain of command, Vonyat had asked for help, and once the leadership understood the potential, they'd sent Umer from his regular assignment in Afghanistan, where he encouraged young people to blow themselves in half, then harvested many startled souls for the Abyss. Umer had witnessed several key breakthroughs in the development of the V-1 flying bomb's warhead in 1944, and he'd been present while McVeigh and Nichols assembled their bomb in Oklahoma over fifty years later. He'd arrived at Weber's farm an hour earlier and, with Vonyat, had examined the men's work while they connected the oxidizer and the fuel.

"They have it right," he finally said. "It should work. A huge blast. Almost as big as Tim's. It should kill a lot of people."

Vonyat smiled. "Good. Report your findings, as will I. Now we just want to be sure they don't get caught, so we can use them again."


The technicians in the Roosevelt Room were breaking down the cameras and equipment following the presidential interview, and Seth, after thanking President Bradshaw, was on the phone with Rachel Shaw to be sure the key moments would be the lead on The Network News, with the full interview on as a special later that evening.

Emily Schofield and Tom Sullivan had been in the room the whole time, and she was very pleased with the result. Their preparation had paid off. Not only were Seth's questions reasonable, mirroring what most Americans wanted to know, but his follow-ups were not too pointed, allowing the president to respond in ways that were positive and helpful. In addition, Emily was able to plant, through the president, several untruths that Tom and Tanya Prescott had suggested they include in the conversation: problems with facial recognition software and license plate readers, imperfect ability to see all activity on the dark web, and difficulties monitoring cell phone calls—all untrue but designed to encourage bad actors to increase their activity, hopefully leading to an intercept.

Tom and the president were in conversation at the door. Seth clicked off his call and walked over to Emily, who was reviewing her notes. He smiled. "I hope that went well for you."

"Yes. And for you?"

"Great. Thank you. Rachel sounded very pleased."

"Good. If things stay calm we'll have to widen the press circle on Monday, though still with reduced numbers. Anyway, glad old friends could help each other."

"Are you busy this weekend? Would you, Logan and Tom like to come over for a drink, to pick up from last Saturday?"

"I'm sure Logan would love to. And me. But I just don't know. This is all still new. Can we call you tomorrow afternoon?"

"Sure. Natalie and I expect to be home."

"OK. We'll talk. Now let me find the right person to escort you back outside."

Tom had asked their original Core Group to meet in the Situation Room at five that Friday afternoon. When he and Emily walked in, Allen Linder, Diane Marsh, Garrett Crose and Rob Thompson were seated at the central table, talking about the day's events. He took the seat at the end, Emily next to him, with Nepravel between them. He knew he had to stay focused on Tom to ensure the right outcome here.

Tom continued. "I've asked you here to talk about something serious. Hopefully we'll get to the truth."

There was silence as everyone looked at him and waited. In the silence Nepravel spun up two of the most powerful voices in his arsenal for leading humans astray: *Anger* and *Pride*.

"Diane, we've been told by someone you contacted that it was you who tried to leak the news about the potential State of Emergency while it was still in the planning stage, when that information could have significantly hurt our chances to actually implement the Executive Order. Is that true?" *And are you trying to destroy all that we've done to protect this nation?*

The others turned to her. She never stopped looking at Tom, but was silent.

*Anger* increased. "I repeat: is it true? Did you directly disobey orders from the president and from me not to disclose this possibility outside our Core Group?"

She sat more upright. "Only because the order was unlawful, coming from inexperienced people who were clearly exceeding their authority."

Allen Linder grimaced. After a pause, Tom continued, "You're wrong. Everything we planned and then executed is covered by emergency powers which Congress gave the president, and which we cited. And who were you to make that decision? The president gave everyone the opportunity to step aside if you didn't agree."

Her own anger was rising. "But only if you were quiet. And I could never be quiet about that man trampling on our most basic rights in the Constitution. He's a bad guy. Once he has power, he'll never let go."

"You have no idea about that. Whether you like him or not, he's the president—as specified in that same Constitution. And our nation was and is being attacked. We're in the midst of a war, and you tried to sabotage us."

"No. I stood up, as provided for in our whistleblower laws, to leak information to the press when there is a clear abuse of power underway."

Tom sat back in his chair. Emily glanced at him. "Those laws don't matter now," he said.

"We'll let the courts decide that. I claim my free speech rights as a citizen and as a whistleblower trying to prevent a crime." She looked at the others. "I did the right thing."

Tom leaned forward again. "No, you didn't. Had you been successful, you could have torpedoed much of what we needed to do these first days, and endangered others. I have friends who are dead and injured by these attacks. We must find out who's doing it. You're neither a whistleblower nor a hero." Nepravel smiled at the put-down.

He stood and walked to the door. When he opened it, two Secret Service agents entered. "And now you're under arrest."

"What? You can't arrest me."

"Yes, we can. And we are. Or call it detention, if you want, as provided for in the State of Emergency. Whatever you call it, you'll be taken into custody and will be charged."

"But I have two small children. I have to get home tonight."

"You'll have to make other plans for them. Right now you'll be transported to the stockade in Maryland and held until further notice. We can't allow anyone to sabotage what we have to do to protect the country."

The two agents went to her chair and asked her to stand, which she did, glaring at Tom and Emily. One took her encrypted phone and gave it to Tom, while the other put handcuffs on her. They walked her to the door, where she made them pause. "He's a bad man, and the country will suffer because of what you're doing."

"But hopefully we'll still have a country," Tom replied. The agents led her out.

After a long silence, Garrett Crose said, "I had no idea. Where did that come from?"

Allen Linder nodded. "And in case there's any question, Garret and I may be from President Rhodes' team, but we're one hundred percent onboard with what we have to do to protect our nation. You don't have to worry about us. We're with the president."

Rob Thompson said, "Thank you, Allen. There's an awful lot left to do, and we don't need any bad actors. And thank you, Tom and Emily, for dealing with this. A mess. Will there be any public notice?"

Tom replied, "Yes. We have to set the public example that those of us in leadership have to abide by the same rules as everyone else. Announcing her arrest should show the nation that we truly mean business."

"The president agrees," Emily added. "I'm preparing a statement now." The others nodded.

Tom stood. "It's been a very long week. But we're back in the White House and hopefully our efforts will turn up whoever is behind all this. I know we'll probably be here much of the weekend working with the NSC briefers, but everyone try to get some rest."

Nepravel finally relaxed and left to report the good news to Balzor that a potential problem had been silenced.


Early that evening Callie Sawyer left her daughter Grace with Kristen, planning to spend an hour praying with others at Church of the Good Shepherd, which had been open 24/7, except for one day after the firebomb attack. As she entered the church, through another door came Natalie Ellis, Seth's girlfriend. Callie waved.

"Hey. Good to see you. What a week."

Natalie carefully shook the hand she extended. "Yes. Are you OK?"

"Pretty much. Certainly OK enough to pray. Do you come here often?"

"Off and on. Several times this week. My father is Jewish and my mother is Catholic, so I grew up in both faiths. I sometimes come to services here. From what I can tell, the people and the teaching seem to be God-centered."

"Yes. I've been a member since we moved here. Thank you again for having me to Seth's party."

"Of course. But it was a long time ago. Have you heard from Tom?"

"He came by to check on us once, and he says he hopes to come over this weekend."

"I think he's a great guy. I know Seth likes him."

"Yes. We'll see. Now, shall we go in and pray for them, and for so many others?"

"Lead the way."


At midnight Prince Proklor's inner circle met with him in another well-furnished Georgetown row house, this one owned by

Congresswoman Patricia Reynolds. They'd actually been there all evening, watching and listening as she, her husband, and her senior advisors met with Minority Leader Nancy Cantrell and her state's senior senator. The politicians had been discussing all aspects of nominating Reynolds as the new vice president, and Proklor wanted to learn firsthand about their strategies and goals before believers started praying for her and it became impossible to get so close.

The last guest had left thirty minutes ago, after securing Reynolds' promise to give them her answer by Monday, and the ground floor was now dark, at least to human eyes. The generals surrounded their leader. As always, Temno began with "2,789 divorces and 2,912 abortions. Both slightly up."

Then each of the generals reported either by department or geographic area the key results learned from their army in the field. The news was generally very good. People appeared to be fearful and on edge, not sure whom to trust or what might happen next. A few groups had protested the State of Emergency, but local police had dispersed them, and street leaders reported from across the country that there was almost unanimous support for the extra measures initiated by the government. People wanted to be safe.

As the last report finished, Proklor looked around at their faces. He'd known them for millennia. This closely knit group of haters had not only misled tens of thousands of people to keep God's Truth from saving them, but they had also ensured that millions of humans never had the chance to steal their rightful places in heaven, and they'd been responsible for the early deaths of more people than they could ever count. The first moves in the final stages of their plans for America appeared to be working well. "Let them feel better—safer—for a few days, and then we'll hit them again. Their despair will be palpable. They'll turn against each other even more. Anarchy will undo them. Everyone will be a victim of someone else's group. They'll pull back even more into their Identity Groups. America will break apart."

# 8

*The moral principles and precepts contained in the Scriptures ought to form the basis of all our civil constitutions and laws.... All the miseries and evils which men suffer from vice, crime, ambition, injustice, oppression, slavery, and war, proceed from their despising or neglecting the precepts contained in the Bible.*

Noah Webster

Saturday, September 19

Seth Cohen slept a little later that Saturday morning. He and Natalie had watched The Network's broadcast of his interview with the president, and he had to admit that it went pretty well. He suddenly might be a rising star in the political news universe, and Rachel Shaw had called to congratulate him.

The bedroom door pushed open and Natalie in her nightgown came in carrying two cups of coffee and the newspaper under her arm. "Here you are, Superstar. Looks like parts of your interview are on the front page."

He took the coffee, and she returned to bed. She unfolded the paper and was about to pass the front section to him when her eye caught a headline at the bottom of the page. She read for a moment.

"Don't you know Diane Marsh, the Deputy COS to the president?"

"Yes. Why?"

"There's an article here. Says she was arrested late yesterday for leaking classified information and possible treason. Wow. She's in jail."

"Let me see." He tried to take the paper from her, but she pulled it away and moved it to her other hand.

"Just a minute. It quotes Tom as saying that she called a network news reporter to leak secret plans to defend the nation. Why would she do that? So you and Tom are both on the front page this morning." She was smiling as she turned to him, but his expression did not match hers.

"She called me."

"What? Then how did they find out? You wouldn't give up your source. Particularly a friend. She must have also called someone else as well."

"I...I'm not sure. Maybe all that new technical gear they've got can listen to everything."

She thought for a moment. "It must be really powerful."

Natalie passed him the paper and he read both articles, sipped some coffee, and picked up his laptop from beside the bed. He logged in and opened his email. The top message was highlighted in red and was from the FBI. The subject line read "Notice of Criminal Violation". The text was short: "The recipient of this Notice is either using encryption or a VPN (Virtual Private Network). Both practices are illegal under the current State of Emergency. If the recipient does not cease these practices within the next 24 hours, she or he will be subject to a fine, immediate imprisonment, or both."

Brad Grantham drove out to his sister Teri's home in Maryland that morning. They'd spent much of Friday online, looking at designs and applications, and now he wanted to see the real thing.

After greeting him at the front door with a hug and a mug of coffee, she led him around to the windowless workshop she'd added to the back of her house two years earlier, when she needed a secure place to perform maintenance and to store her growing inventory of both large and small drones. She unlocked the steel door, flipped the light switch, and led Brad into the space. There was a large metal worktable in the middle of the room. Shelves on two walls held smaller drones and bins with sorted parts. Another wall was clearly for communication gear. A desk, computer and large screen took up the fourth.

On the worktable was her largest drone, fitted with long legs so that the video camera beneath the body had plenty of room to swivel like the ball turret on an old bomber. It had four rotors and looked like it could carry a large load.

Just then Ranit came through one of the walls. Overnight he'd met with a group in the Middle East—demons he'd known from the bloodiest battles of the Crusades, when they'd worked together to create atrocity after atrocity, and who now specialized in evaluating the best advances in drone technology among modern warring armies—and Ranit had some refinements he wanted to be sure the two humans considered.

Brad walked around the drone and touched it a couple of times. "Yeah, I see what you mean. If it can keep that video camera perfectly steady, and you can control if from two miles away, with what we saw yesterday we should easily be able to retrofit it with an assault rifle."

"It can use GPS coordinates, and both low light and infrared sensors for flying and targeting." She nodded toward the desk. "I can show you some videos I've taken."

"Sounds like it should be good for day or night ops. Let me take a closer look at the mount, and we'll see what we need to order or modify."

Ranit was pleased. It appeared that his charges were already well advanced in their understanding of the technologies required to create a stable and nearly undetectable aerial gunship. Americans continued to amaze him.

Tom Sullivan woke up in his own bed after his first full night's sleep in a week. He'd picked Beau up on the way home the night before, and he got up to let him out.

Ten minutes later, after he fed Beau and stirred cream into his coffee, he realized that at this same hour last Saturday Emily had been driving Logan and him to a parkrun—in a completely different world. He thought how good it would be to run, but all the sleep actually left him a little tired and fuzzy. So he took his coffee to the table by the front window and unfolded the newspaper he'd picked up just outside his door.

Like Natalie, he was drawn to the two articles about yesterday's events at the White House, and after reading them he was quite pleased.

Hopefully anyone else in government who was thinking about sabotaging their plans would understand that the president's team—with him as the Security leader—was playing for keeps. Yes, he was pleased. He wondered if the two government reviewers they'd installed at the paper had required any changes in the article before publication, or if this was purely the reporters' work. He'd have to ask.

After finishing the front section he glanced at the time. He needed to shower and walk over to their neighborhood coffee shop. When he'd seen Callie briefly to pick up Beau, he'd asked about getting together, and she'd suggested coffee that morning.

When he left his row house he had an invisible accomplice for his walk. Nepravel had assigned Zloy to check on Tom, not knowing that he was planning to meet Callie. Nepravel worried about the ramp up in prayers for Tom and the other presidential advisors, and he wanted Zloy to experience what that might mean for a demon near one of them.

Ten minutes later, as Tom approached the coffeehouse, he saw Callie coming from the opposite direction, wearing jeans and a light sweater over her blouse. On seeing her he broke into a smile. She waved, and he held the door for her.

"Good morning, I hope you and Grace slept well."

Pausing before going inside, she said, "We did, thank you, though we missed Beau. And now Grace is having cereal with Kristen."

The rustic interior was packed, but a couple was just rising from a table in the far corner. "Perfect. There's a table. What would you like?"

"Cappuccino would be nice. And some kind of terrible sweet roll—maybe we can split it."

"Or maybe not."

Zloy glanced quickly around. Besides Callie's obvious internal bright spiritual light, there were a few other believers in the shop, but not enough to deter him if he stayed focused on Tom. As usual, there were also other demons looking after their assignments, but no one that he knew well. None of them was pleased to have Callie and her spiritual light added to the increasing brightness inside the shop, and one of them looked at Zloy like it was his fault. Zloy ignored him and concentrated on protecting Tom.

A few minutes later Tom and Callie were seated with warm mugs and two plates between them.

"Do I understand that you and Emily have moved back to the White House?"

"Yes. We're up and running, though with all the new people it's a little rough. Next week should be better."

"How's your work?"

He leaned back. Zloy fed in the voice of *Pride*. "Crazy. But with the Executive Order and the new regulations, I think we're on a path to find whoever's doing this. And, at least for the last few days, there haven't been any new attacks. Maybe something we're doing is working."

She nodded. "I hope so. What you're doing must be very difficult. We've been praying around the clock at the church."

*Pride* again. "Good. And on the church, I can't really say anything, but we may be close to nailing the people who bombed you."

"Really?" She looked down and rubbed her hands. "Sometimes I think how close that was to a real disaster. Those children." There was silence between them for a few beats. Looking up, she continued. "As I've told you, many of us feel a terrible sense of dread, of evil, in the neighborhood. In the city. Only when we get inside the church and join in prayer does the darkness lift and turn to hope. Natalie was there last night; she joined us. She even said she sensed the difference, the divide."

"Natalie? Really? Is she still going to the DEA every day?"

"I think so. You should join us at the church, too. And our pastor, Robert Ludwig, has an amazing new book on grace."

Zloy was annoyed that the number of incoming prayers seemed to be increasing, but he held on and ramped up *Busy*. "Yes, maybe, but not this week. From noon today I'll be back at the White House. I'm the Acting National Security Advisor, for goodness sake. At thirty-four! Three doors from the president. Me. The job has always been a combination of experienced, gray-haired intelligence input plus coordination of more input from key intelligence agencies. For me, it's certainly mostly coordination, because I have little else to offer."

"I'm sure you're exactly what President Bradshaw needs right now. God has put you there for a purpose."

*Pride* and *False Humility*. He took a sip from his mug and again was quiet. Finally he nodded. "I don't know. I just feel very inadequate at a time of huge peril to our country. So I'll be at my desk most of the weekend setting up a weekly briefing schedule for others' input that I hope will keep us out of trouble...But, look, I'm tired of talking about these issues. How are you, and what are you up to?"

She smiled. "We're fine. Routines, like work and Grace's school, are good. Research and ethical questions on genes haven't slowed down, so there's always something new to ask or to write about. And I enjoy teaching a class at AU every Thursday."

"I didn't know. What on?"

"Advanced business writing. It's actually pretty popular, including a lot of foreign graduate students. I enjoy it. We assign different topics, and while I'm specifically focused on improving their English writing techniques, I actually learn a lot of interesting new stuff while I'm reading their work."

"Interesting."

"Yeah. So all that keeps me pretty busy. And my faith keeps me pretty happy."

*Skepticism*. "Is that what it is?"

She turned her head slightly. "What do you mean?"

"I...I don't know. I've just noticed a...a confidence, joy, something, about you that's different...I like it."

Zloy was baffled. Where did that come from? Were the prayers blunting the voices that quickly?

She looked down. "Not sure. But thank you. And I like being with you."

Again there was silence between them. Tom finally reached for his roll and took a bite. As he looked at Callie, Zloy turned up his trump card: *Lust*. After a moment, Tom asked, "Would you like to come over to my place for dinner one night this week, if we can find a day that works?"

She smiled. "I don't think that would be such a good idea. How about if I take us *out* to dinner, to thank you for all that you've done?"

"Uh. Sure, if you want. I'll have to check the schedule."

"That'll be nice. Just call or text when you know—I'll be here."

Tom smiled. "Great. Probably Friday."

When they broke up thirty minutes later, Zloy was glad to escape the increasing spiritual heat and knew he had to find Nepravel. These two could not keep meeting together.

Razdor had been working to contain a problem since early Tuesday, when Jerry Kimble learned that his single incendiary round into the fracking tanks in western Pennsylvania had killed three families, including seven young children.

Jerry had been an Army sniper in Afghanistan and understood that occasional collateral damage occurred with any attack. But since returning from the war he'd begun attending church with his wife and kids, and while his faith was certainly not uppermost in his life, he understood that killing so many innocents was a terrible sin. And he had done it.

He'd stayed home from his equipment sales job for two days, complaining to his wife and boss about a flare-up of his chronic back pain. But for most of both days he just sat in his chair in the den and thought—and even tried to pray.

That's where Razdor had found him on Wednesday, and he berated himself for not foreseeing what might happen with Jerry. He had to counter quickly the arguments which Jerry's conscience were playing in his mind. Razdor needed Jerry to attack again, and he certainly couldn't let him turn himself in. The authorities were looking for an international conspiracy, not a single misguided veteran.

So Razdor asked for and got help from demons who understood and motivated those who had been around death and destruction in war. Several of them had joined Razdor at Jerry's house and business since Thursday, telling him that he had only acted for the good of his family and others, and that it wasn't his fault that those immigrants—probably illegals—had decided to park there for the night.

As Jerry drove his twelve-year-old son and three friends to their Fall baseball practice that Saturday afternoon, he tuned out the youthful bantering in the backseats of their minivan. Instead, Razdor was right at his ear, whispering what Razdor wanted him to hear and believe.

*Yes, it was terrible. But it wasn't my fault. I didn't choose to hurt them—that would have been sin, but that's not what I did. I chose to defend my family against powerful interests who want to harm us and our land. Look at Jesus in the temple with the money changers. He was righteously angry, just like me! I bet at least a few of them got injured as he turned over their tables and scattered their animals. Some pain must have happened, even when the instigator was the Son of God. So how was I supposed to know about those people? I did the right thing.*

Not lost on Razdor, who was very smart, was the fact that he didn't have to make this up. He could describe the events in the temple from experience, because he'd been there. When he was together with the others at night, Razdor told them he never wanted to see Jesus like he did that day—angry and punishing those who maligned his Father. But they all silently knew that they *would* see Jesus again, just like that. And that realization motivated them even more to bring every one of these putrid human creatures with them.

On the news that night Jerry heard that the fracking companies, after taking several days off because of the explosion, would resume operations again on Monday. To Jerry that was unbelievable. Later, after everyone else was asleep and he was on his third beer in their den, Jerry opened his laptop and went to a website dedicated to saving the nation from the coming disasters which fracking would cause. Razdor was right behind him as he opened the site, which he did not realize was hosted on the server of a small internet provider on Cyprus. The first item in the newsfeed read, "The Lone Gunman of Western Pennsylvania." With carefully chosen words the article went on to praise the strong hero who had shown the world the dangers of fracking. And it imagined that there might be more pushback by patriotic citizens until the fracking stopped.

Razdor whispered to Jerry. "You're a brave man and a hero who needs to show the world your original intent—to harm the big corporations without hurting anyone. You can do it. You *should* do it. Who else is going to stop these greedy killers?"

A few minutes later Jerry was looking at the map he kept under a special password showing the other storage tank sites he had marked. *I'll need to visit them again to pick the ideal target. Or maybe more than one. The bastards.*

# 9

*I've lived, Sir, a long time, and the longer I live, the more convincing Proofs*
*I see of this Truth — That God governs in the Affairs of Men. And if a*
*sparrow cannot fall to the ground without his Notice, is it probable that an*
*Empire can rise without his Aid? We have been assured, Sir, in the Sacred*
*Writings, that except the Lord build the House they labor in vain who*
*build it. I firmly believe this, — and I also believe that without his*
*concurring Aid, we shall succeed in this political Building no better than*
*the Builders of Babel: We shall be divided by our little partial local*
*interests; our Projects will be confounded, and we ourselves shall become a*
*Reproach and Bye word down to future Ages.*

Benjamin Franklin

Sunday, September 20

After spirited hymns and two scripture readings, it was with a heavy
heart and mixed emotions that Pastor Robert Ludwig took the steps up
to the pulpit at Church of the Good Shepherd that Sunday morning. He
looked out on the congregation at their 11am service and glanced down
at the printed pages on the lectern in front of him. He was divided about
what to do. Finally, after a few increasingly awkward moments of silence,
he looked up and began.

"All of you know what a difficult time we find ourselves in. For us
it's both 'over there' and 'right here', since we were attacked last week.
Many of you have known me for the ten years I've been blessed to be your
pastor, and I hope you have a sense of my faith and my conscience.

"Whether you've been with us twenty years or twenty days, I want
you to know that I find myself in a difficult position this morning.
Under the Executive Order enacted by our government—a government
for which I appreciate many of you work in various capacities—we were
required to submit the full content of the sermon I had written to preach
this morning to a new government reviewer—a censor.

"After consulting on Friday with several senior elders and others, we
acquiesced to the requirement and sent in the draft of the sermon, which
touched on the attack, our response, and our future. I am unhappy to

report that the reviewer or reviewers did not like some of the text and the ideas, and they struck them out, forbidding me to speak those words under penalty of arrest and incarceration, because in their minds my words were exclusionary, verging on hate speech.

"The irony is that I'm not even allowed to tell you what those ideas and text were, because I would then apparently be violating the same order.

"As you can imagine, I don't agree with their conclusion, and so I have been in a quandary about what to do, as both a follower of Christ and an American. Last night I consulted again with the same wise advisors. And I spent most of the early morning in prayer, seeking His guidance.

"I have decided that for this week I will bow to the authorities whom God has placed over us in this time of national emergency. I will conform to their demands. Tomorrow our elders will meet and consider whether we should have a different response in the weeks ahead.

"For now, I will not give a censored, redacted version of what I had originally written because, frankly, without the words they've excluded, it no longer makes sense, particularly to us as believers.

"So, instead of a sermon this morning, we're going to have an extended time of scripture reading and congregational prayers, followed by hymns. Please begin by praying for the nation, for the decision makers in our government—by name if you know them—and for our church elders, that we will all be led to decisions which honor Him and uphold His truths in our country.

"Now, please join me in prayer."


Late that afternoon Mason Neal and Josh Weber pulled out of Josh's farm in Mason's heavy duty pickup truck, pulling a large twin-axle, enclosed trailer. They were headed to D.C. and a drive-in storage unit they had rented online using a fictitious name and paying with one of several prepaid gift cards Mason had purchased for cash when he visited his son at college in Texas.

They had decided to divide the bomb's ingredients into two parts and to make two trips. They had made up a story about a fictitious farm friend they were helping, to explain why they were transporting fertilizer—it wouldn't stand up to much scrutiny, but they didn't expect to be stopped. They intended to drive the speed limit and stay off the interstates. The trailer blocked any view of the pickup's rear license plate, and in Kentucky front license plates were not required.

# Wednesday, September 23

Three days later, on Wednesday morning, Tom was up early. It was still dark. Sitting with a cup of coffee he reviewed and edited his To Do List on his "L-Pad". He wasn't a total Neanderthal—he always transferred items from the pad to his electronic calendar. But he just liked the touch, feel and look of the yellow paper, as he wrote out new issues and connected dots.

Nepravel arrived from the Northeast Abortion Clinic, where his sector usually waited and trained while their humans slept, to read Tom's list for insights. And to keep the voices spinning in him which would inoculate him from God's truths, particularly given his inexplicable infatuation with Callie Sawyer. Nepravel was much happier with Tom's summer conquest, Erin MacNeil, who posed no spiritual threat.

Tom and his predecessor's staff had created a robust briefing schedule for the president at the White House; so far Tom had made every one of them. And he and Special Agent Prescott believed they had made great progress both in opening all civilian communications for review and in reducing the amount of divisive rhetoric. There were some early complaints in both areas, but the government's responses had been firm—a lesson learned from Covid: Allow no deviations, or there would be chaos. Tom knew they had to be firm to achieve the results they needed, and, happily, the FBI leadership under James Toomey felt the same.

And that was the frustration that hung over his every waking minute—so far they had been unable to connect any single perpetrator to any other. Not even the Air Force pilot who shot down President Rhodes; if he had accomplices or sympathizers, they had so far eluded the NSA's most powerful tools to uncover them. They had to keep digging and applying the pressure.

At that same hour in Atlanta, Richard Sullivan was awake and on his knees with his church's 24/7 prayer list, which included Tom, praying for his son and the many others tasked with the responsibility to defend the nation. Janet would take her hour's turn in twenty minutes.

And that's what so angered Nepravel as he tried to memorize Tom's To Do List. Before the attacks and all the believers' prayers that followed, he had enjoyed unhindered access to Tom and his other charges. Now Nepravel could only get a glimpse of Tom's intentions because the light, heat and voices—the damn believers' voices—in the incoming answered prayers were just too much. And he'd even narrowly avoided an angel on Tom's street on Monday, apparently drawn by light from the prayers. He thought he'd seen "Church?" on Tom's list, but he couldn't be sure, and now the intense heat was just too much to stay there.

He and the other street leaders with similar prayer challenges had to rely more and more on second-hand information. Nepravel had to invest valuable time in the non-believers who worked around Tom and whose lives were not covered in prayer, hoping to see or hear clues for inside information and intentions. Of course he and the other demons could readily track the presidential team's past actions. But what were they thinking and planning?

He'd talked with Zloy at the abortion clinic about which of Tom's colleagues would know the most, with the least prayer protection. Nepravel did his best to assemble valid information that he could pass to Balzor and above. But, unable to get close to Tom, he worried that he might miss something important, and he knew that Prince Proklor hated incompetent fallen angels almost as much as he hated humans.

Alexei Nobikov had been in Boston for three days, taking notes on the latest US initiatives for cybersecurity. Later that afternoon he would fly to D.C. to spend time with his niece and to take the pulse of the nation's capital. With his several American former engineering classmates who still lived in Boston and who were mostly in internet-related Tech start-ups, he shared the latest insights from Europe on the next big things and the most promising new technologies. They had been friends for many years, through different regimes and trials in the U.S., Russia and Europe, and they felt that their personal and professional relationships transcended those details. None of his friends dealt in any state secrets, so they talked and speculated freely on the future. But even their conversations helped shape how Alexei conducted his real business, and he always asked a lot of questions.

Alexei's relationship with America was complicated, made more so by recent events. He genuinely admired America and all the personal freedoms it offered each individual, particularly since he had lived in the country as a student and had experienced the final years of lies and repression under Soviet rule. One result of that American freedom had been a deepening of his own Christian faith from an aloof orthodox church attender like his parents to strong faith in a personal Savior, made possible by a student ministry in the U.S. which didn't exist in Russia. And by a mentor at the church he attended during his two years in Boston who took a profound interest in him as a rare graduate student from the crumbling Evil Empire.

But for the last decade his job had been to help advance his own country's interests at America's expense. His American friends had no idea that Alexei really visited regularly to gauge the mood of the country, the divisions, and effectiveness of their work to exploit those divisions. Now there were the recent attacks and the State of Emergency. He was looking for new themes and ideas that could potentially pit one group of Americans against another, using race, gender, political divisions, religion, income, anything where his team could first drive a wedge and then constantly widen the divide.

But the lies and repression of the failing Soviet state had returned to his homeland.

He was not pleased that his team was trying to help Russia rise by bringing America down. Particularly since his country was more and more adopting the Chinese Firewall approach to the internet, and to life itself, restricting access to more and more sources and choices.

Until recently he had rationalized his actions against the society he most admired by noting how strong and advanced America was, and therefore how much his own country needed help to catch up and to make headway on the world stage. When he had occasionally questioned his own actions, he figured that whatever he might do to pull down America would only be a small dent, whereas that seemingly small advantage could be huge for helping Russia. So he had worked hard over the years, immersed in both countries, turning the freedoms he personally admired in America into an opportunity for his government to exploit.

But what now? His country was clearly on the wrong path. The inner tumult continued. In his quiet times of prayer he asked to be successful enough to stay in his position, but not successful enough to really bring America down. In his quietest moments, he couldn't imagine what the world would be like without America.


President Bradshaw had continued his daily reports to the nation until moving into the White House. Emily then reduced that schedule to twice weekly, and she moved the location to the Press Room. Given the restrictions on movement inside the Exclusion Zone near the center of power, it was impossible to include the entire accredited press corps. Instead, Emily's team announced that they would pick twenty journalists to attend each briefing on a rotating basis. She also allowed a few questions, but in the name of national security, for the time being they had to be written and submitted in advance. For this first White House briefing, Seth had been selected to attend.

At 11am from a door to the left of the podium came a small group of men and women who took seats in the front row of chairs, and then the president entered from a set of double doors behind the podium. Taking out a few notes, he addressed the thirty or so people in the room, and the television cameras.

"Today marks the first full week since we inaugurated the State of Emergency, and I am pleased to report that there have been 3,496 arrests or detainments as a result of information developed through our enhanced law enforcement capabilities, many of which were for violations of our State of Emergency—encrypting messages or expressing hate speech, for example. But also included in that total are more traditional crimes that are more easily investigated using these capabilities, plus some who appeared to be planning future attacks, and, most importantly, those whom we believe instigated the firebombing of the church here in the nation's capital, as well as those who murdered the two African American engineers in South Carolina.

"The details on those arrested have been widely covered in the press. Our civilian and military professionals are constantly following up on new and credible leads, many provided by private citizens, and we expect to determine who has been behind these attacks in the very near future.

"As importantly, there have been no new major attacks since we implemented the State of Emergency. We believe that even in those cases where we have not yet found the perpetrators, our current readiness—enhanced by our ban on hate speech and the reduction of internal divisiveness—has at least deterred them from additional attacks. By maintaining the high alert status allowed by the State of Emergency, we plan to remain vigilant and to continue to make anyone think twice about any type of attack on the citizens of our great nation.

"After consulting with the Rhodes family and weighing the implications of all the options, we have determined to hold one Memorial Service for all of those who died ten days ago. It will be a week from today, at The National Cathedral here in Washington. We hope most of you will join with us via television in the celebration of so many incredible lives, so tragically cut short, but attendance at the service in these times will be by invitation only. We will be announcing information on the service in the next few days.

"While remembering the fallen and defeating those who are attacking us are our first priorities, it's also important that we move forward to a safe and better future. A first step will be to have a full federal government in place to serve the American people, and that means replacing the fallen vice president as quickly as possible. We are joined today by Congressman Jacob Welch, the newly elected Speaker of the House, and Congresswoman Nancy Cantrell, the Minority Leader, as well as the senior members of both parties in the Senate. We have all been meeting together this morning, and I am pleased to say that we agree that all leadership roles should be filled by exceptional people who will unite us, rather than divide us. I am pleased to announce in that spirit of bipartisan cooperation that the Executive Branch will today nominate Congresswoman Patricia Reynolds to become the next vice president of the United States."

The congresswoman rose from her seat and joined the president at the podium.

"Patricia Reynolds is the perfect person to assume this responsibility at this time, when we need to be united, and to work together. Over the years she has actually been a member of both parties and understands the governing principles which drive Americans of all political beliefs. During her five terms in the House, she has worked tirelessly across the aisle to move meaningful legislation which has benefited all of us. A gifted speaker with a keen intellect, and the mother of three teenagers, I am very pleased that Patricia has enthusiastically agreed to serve as the nation's vice president, as soon as she can be confirmed by both the House and the Senate. Based on this morning's discussions, and with the genuine spirit of unity here in Washington, I believe her confirmation can be accomplished by early next week. Patricia, please say a few words."

The congresswoman, almost as tall as the president, with brunette hair flecked with gray, wearing a conservative blue suit, stepped to the microphone.

"Thank you, President Bradshaw, for your faith in whatever gifts and abilities God has given me. I pledge to use them for the safety and betterment of all Americans." She nodded to those seated in the front row. "I look forward to the confirmation process in the Senate and House, where I have many friends in both parties. I hope we can then quickly move on together to defeat our enemies and to create an even better nation for all our citizens."

They shook hands, and she remained just behind him.

"We have several questions from the press who are with us today, and Emily Schofield will answer most of them. But one particularly intrigues me, asking whether we've seen any connections between those detained which will lead us to those ultimately responsible. Let me say that we have just made these arrests, and while, for example, one may not see a similarity between a militant Anti-Abortion group and a White Supremacist group, we are digging now to learn about any common mentors or infiltrators who could also be connected to those who killed the president and vice president. We don't have those connections yet, but we're confident that we'll find them. Now, if you will excuse us, Congresswoman Reynolds and I have a lot to cover this afternoon, as do those who will be confirming her, so Emily Schofield will take over the briefing."

The front row stood and exited with the president and vice president-nominee.

In the hallway behind the Press Room the leaders shook hands, and Bradshaw turned with Reynolds towards the Oval Office. "Perfect tone, Patricia. You couldn't have said it any better."

"Thank you, Mr. President. I have my eyes on the prize. Our staff will be setting up meetings with key Congressional leaders starting this afternoon."

Tom, sitting at his desk a few doors from the Oval Office, signed off from his daily video update with Agent Prescott. They shared their frustration at the lack of progress in connecting the attackers to a single enemy, and the Special Agent in Charge promised to revisit all possible leads with her senior FBI team that afternoon.

Before heading downstairs for a quick lunch with Emily to hear about the daily briefing, out of curiosity he logged on to his favorite bookseller to look at three books by Callie's pastor, Robert Ludwig, which she had recommended for this challenging time. But when he typed in Ludwig's name, the website responded with "Temporarily Not Available." Not just those three books, but everything he had ever authored.

He assumed that this block was because some of Ludwig's previous statements contradicted the terms of the State of Emergency on hate speech. He was impressed with the efficiency of the bookseller in conforming to the government's requirements, but he was still curious. Maybe Callie had copies she could lend him. He would ask her on their date.

Ahmad Rashid was standing in the Hunts' living room, his young boys wrapped around his legs, talking with Andrea. His wife Mariam was gathering their last items from the bedroom down the hall.

"Thank you again for letting Mariam and the boys stay with you," Ahmad said.

"We had a great time. I'm glad we had a chance to get to know each other better." Andrea patted her stomach. "And Mariam gave me some good advice."

He nodded. "When I go back tomorrow, Clayton should be able to come home for at least a day or two."

Mariam heard him as she rolled a small suitcase into the room. "Have you been busy?"

"Actually, we have. I obviously can't talk about it, but there's been a flood of input we've had to parse through. And many of the sources have been new for us—mostly domestic. It's taken some getting used to."

"Thank you, Andrea," Mariam said. "The boys' school opens again tomorrow, and things seem to have calmed down. And the fathers have volunteered to spend the night there on a rotating basis for extra security. We should be all right."

The women hugged. "I hope so. But if there's another problem, you're always welcome here. I'll be praying for you, and for the other kids at the school. What's the name of their school?"

"The Family and Friendship Mosque International School. Thank you. And we'll be praying for you. Tell Clayton hello and thanks."

Ahmad stood aside for Mariam, then held the boys' hands as they went through the front door. He smiled. "See you soon."


Stan Conway in Atlanta and Robert Ludwig in D.C. were part of a network of Bible-believing pastors who met monthly online and regularly prayed with and for each other and their churches. The two had also met several times over the years in person, and now they were on the phone together from their offices.

"How's your building?" Stan asked.

"The repairs should be finished this week. Thanks to God's protection or the ineptness of the perpetrators, or both, we had only minor personal injury, and the damage to the building was mostly cosmetic."

"That's great news."

"Yes. I wish I felt the same about this State of Emergency. We've been working through the psalms in our sermon series, and this Sunday I'm preaching on Psalm 139. I plan to reiterate God's teaching that the baby in the womb is just that, a baby. And so abortion is clearly murder, and detested by God. And of course David, the author, writes that he hates those who hate God. He must not have known about our speech requirements."

Stan smiled. "No, but God did." He was quiet for a moment. "And you think that will run afoul of the censors?"

"I hope not, but I'm afraid it may. Did you submit your sermon last week to the 'reviewing authority'?"

"We decided to do so last week, because it was new, and we want to live under authority. But we may have the same problem this week. In the message I remind the congregation that Jesus allowed himself to be worshiped, unlike any other major religion's founder, and he stated that he is *the* way to the Father, not *a* way. I suspect they'll want me to drop that reference to God's Truth."

"And will you?"

"The elders and I have a tentative meeting on Saturday morning, in case those are the instructions, so we can discuss what to do."

"Good. Please let me know. We've already had our meeting, and, after almost a week of prayer, we've decided not to allow God's Word to be censored. Even in a time of national emergency. The Truth is the Truth, whatever the circumstance."

"I admire you, Robert, and I'll let you know."

"Please don't admire me or our elders. It's about God's Truth and our Constitution. Pretty straight forward, really."

"You'd think so. But these are complicated times. I'll let you know. Thanks for calling."

Early that evening Mason Neal and Josh Weber were making good time on the interstate, returning home with an empty trailer after transferring its contents to a storage unit in suburban D.C. They exited and pulled into a large rest area with a truck stop and a couple of adjoining family restaurants. It was early evening and the parking lots were nearly full.

They hesitated near the back of the lot and watched a couple park and then leave their car to walk inside. After waiting another minute, and with no one in sight, Mason pulled their truck and trailer behind the car to block the view from the restaurant and the one security camera they could see on a light pole. Josh jumped out of the passenger seat and in less than a minute was back inside. He nodded and slid the Virginia license plate beside his seat. Mason pulled off, and they continued their trip home.

# Friday, September 25

The three Intelligence Briefers left the Oval Office in the White House early that Friday morning. Tom and the other members of the Core Team, with VP-designee Patricia Reynolds added, remained seated on the sofas in front of the president, who was at his desk. He stood and walked over to a chair in front of the fireplace.

"Tom, two weeks ago tomorrow night we were attacked, and we implemented the State of Emergency ten days ago. What have we got to show for it?"

The Acting National Security Advisor looked down at the notes in his lap. He knew this was coming and had prepared as best he could. "We're all frustrated by not finding the underlying perpetrators, but in every other way the State of Emergency has been very productive.

"Most importantly, there have been no new attacks. We've arrested or detained many individuals who either participated in the first wave or appear to have been planning new events. Plus we've arrested several thousand criminals who were not prepared for the extra power of the NSA and DOD to connect dots and to use Artificial Intelligence to predict behavior. As a result, crimes, and particularly violent crimes, are way down.

"Finally, though there's no precise way to measure it, anecdotally it appears to police chiefs and to pundits that our restrictions on hate speech have lowered the decibel level significantly across the nation. So, with the one very important exception, our strategy has been a success, and the nation is much better for it. There are even several pro-State of Emergency websites now, calling for more security measures."

President Bradshaw thought and nodded. "OK. Fair enough. Emily, let's use some of that in our next briefing. But, Tom, we've got to identify the people behind this."

"I know, sir. I know."

"Where is Diane Marsh?"

Allen Linder looked up. "She's been moved to Fort Leavenworth for the duration."

"I still don't understand that one." The president shook his head and exchanged a quick glance with Emily Schofield.

"Neither do I," Linder said.

Garrett Crose was next. "Changing subjects, the Memorial Service next Wednesday is well along in planning. It will begin at ten, with everyone seated—by invitation only—by nine thirty. We've put together a high-level team of military and civilian experts who've run previous presidential funerals and the last two Inauguration Days to coordinate with the National Cathedral, the choirs, and the Rhodes, Carpenter and Gordon families. We should have the full draft program for your review this afternoon, along with all the special security measures, which will be enormous, given who will be in attendance. An invitation list, including domestic leaders and foreign heads of state, is in the final review stage."

Emily added, "And your speech is well along. We should have good stories about each key person for you to share."

The president looked around at his team. "Good. Thanks. How, uh, 'religious' will it be?"

Linder looked to Crose, who spoke. "All three of them, and many of the others killed that day, were Christians. Their families have asked for scripture readings and prayers."

"Hmm. But citizens of other faiths, and of no faith, will be celebrating their lives and service to the nation as well. Is this a funeral service for them as individuals, or a remembrance of their dedication and service to the nation?"

Garrett did not hesitate. "I think it's both."

"Well, particularly with the restrictions during these thirty days, please emphasize more of the latter. It won't do for someone to say or pray on national television, with the entire government assembled, that, for example, Jesus is the only way to eternity. That's not the divisive message we want to send today.

"We've got to come together. Please be sure that there are also speaking parts for representatives of other faiths. They're equally American, and are equally touched by these events."

"Yes, sir."

"Thank you. It doesn't have to have Christian taglines to be a moving ceremony, celebrating so many good people." He paused for a moment. "What about your progress, Patricia?" he asked, showing a small smile.

The vice president-designee leaned forward. "The process is going well. We've already touched many of the necessary bases, with more meetings and interviews coming today. We're hoping, and discretely pushing, for votes in both chambers on Monday."

"Any problems?"

Rob Thompson spoke up. "None major. A few members from the other side have objected to issues on which Patricia spoke or acted years ago, even in her state legislature, but, with real bipartisan help"—he nodded to Allen and Garrett—"we think we've focused them back on her experience and personality, and calmed those waters. The new Speaker, Jacob Welch, has known Patricia for years, and he believes she'll easily win approval. We see no reason not to expect majorities in both chambers."

"Excellent. Excellent," the president repeated. "It's important to get you on board. We've got a lot of work to do."

Twenty minutes later, after discussing other upcoming legislative matters, the meeting broke up. Tom stood and, as the room emptied, walked out with Emily.

"How's Logan?"

"Fine. He's at an all-day online meeting with Drew Boswell about new opportunities for Juggle in the current environment."

"I suspect there are some... By the way, Callie and I are having dinner tonight."

Emily stopped in the hall outside the Cabinet Room and smiled. "Really? Your place, as usual?"

He shook his head. "No, we're actually going to a restaurant. And she even offered to buy."

"Amazing. That's great. I've got a good feeling about the two of you."

He shrugged as he turned toward his office and smiled. "We'll see."

Brad and Teri Grantham drove her enclosed transport truck out to visit their parents late that morning. After an hour of coffee and conversation, they then drove further back into the adjoining fields where they believed they could operate without being seen.

Thirty minutes later, after Brad walked a large pumpkin out into a grassy meadow and they made several final checks, Teri launched the modified photography drone, and Brad stood next to her with his own hand-held console.

She flew the drone up and off to their right until it was nearly impossible to see. First she took it on a broad visual sweep of the area to be sure they were alone, then expertly brought the drone down and toward the pumpkin. Like Teri, Brad could shift from wide angle to zoom on his console, and soon he was focused on the target.

"Weapons free, Bro," Teri whispered.

The morning silence was pierced by the crack of the AR-15 rifle high in the air, as a puff of dust flew up next to the pumpkin. There was another crack, and the pumpkin exploded.

She glanced over at him. "Good shooting!"

He nodded. "This is actually amazingly easy. Well done, Sis."

Twenty minutes later the drone and the controls were secured in the back of the truck. They climbed into the cab, and as she started the engine, Teri smiled over at Brad. "Now we just need to pick the right targets, and I've got some ideas."

Tom rang Callie's doorbell at seven that Friday evening, dressed in a blue blazer and khaki pants, with a subdued solid shirt and no tie. Callie and Grace answered together, Callie smiling, but Grace not so sure.

"Hi." Callie beamed. "We're so glad to see you. Aren't we Grace? And thank you for all the calls, checking on us."

Tom bent down a bit and extended his hand. "I'm so glad to see you're both well."

Grace tentatively took his hand after a little nudge from her mother. "What do you say?"

"Thank you." And finally a small smile. "Is Beau here?"

"Not this time. But he says hello, and he plans to come back." Tom focused again on Callie, wearing dark blue pants and a gray sweater. "You look great."

"Would you like to come in? My sitter is here to look after Grace."

"It's a beautiful night. Why don't we just walk over to Eighth Street. We have reservations at Carpathia at seven thirty."

"OK. Let me get my coat. Grace, please say good night, and I'll be right back."

As they walked on the tree-lined sidewalk in the Capitol Hill area, Callie brought Tom up to date on Grace, Kristen and the increased security measures she noticed everywhere she went.

He told her about security inside the Restricted Zone and about Emily's important role at the White House with the new Administration.

"Yes, I've seen her on TV. She's good with the reporters."

He then described what he knew about Seth, Natalie, Logan, Clayton, Andrea, and others whom she'd met at the birthday party two weeks ago. "And, listen, Seth texted me. He and Natalie want to have the original apartment mates—plus spouses, or you know—so eight of us—over tomorrow night. Just to chill and talk about all that's happened in the two weeks since we were there. Would you like to come?"

She looked at him for a moment. "Sure. I think I can ask Kristen to look after Grace. Thanks. By the way, I called Andrea, and she said they had a Muslim family staying with them. A friend of Clayton's?"

"An officer on his team. Muslim-Americans. They apparently had a threat on his wife and kids."

"Awful. I guess anyone can throw things," she said, recalling the fire bomb at the church.

"Yes, sadly. But we think we have the ones who attacked the church in custody."

"Such hate. The evil around us. By the way, Kristen and Andrea feel it, too."

"Do you feel it now?"

She looked at him as they walked, and she smiled. "Well, actually, no. Not right now. Not with you. But often."

From two blocks behind them Nepravel was cursing. He simply couldn't get any closer to the couple. Besides the light and heat from the incoming prayers for Tom, there was the strong spiritual light burning brightly in Callie. Hopefully the prayers would die down, and he could move in. Until then, how could he get close enough to hear what they were saying or to plant voices in Tom, to keep him headed where they needed him to go? What would Bespor and Balzor think, much less Prince Proklor? They had to find a way to separate these two, or there could be real trouble.

He was so focused on them that he almost missed the angel descending behind him. He finally noticed unusual spiritual light reflecting from the fronts of row houses on each side of the street and turned just in time to dart out of the way as the large, shining, male-like figure moved purposefully just over him and took up position a half-block ahead of the chatting humans.

Nepravel hadn't been this close to an angel for years, and he was shocked when he first looked up, before the brightness blinded him, to think that he once looked like this powerful creature.

"Damn. Damn!" he cursed, as he rubbed his eyes.

When he could see well enough to follow the spiritual lights in front of him, he started again, but he stayed well back.

Before the couple reached Eighth Street he could see that the angel had stopped and was standing in mid-air over the Restaurant Carpathia, ready to ward off any of their forces who tried to enter.

How would he know what these two would discuss? How could he leave Tom alone with a believer like Callie for the whole evening? He needed help. He and Zloy would have to watch them as they came out, then follow and monitor their conversations for the rest of the night, listening for clues and restarting the voices in Tom. He recalled that Zloy was attending a "Free the Washington Four" planning meeting for those accused of attacking Callie's church at the Out and About Bookstore not far away. As Tom and Callie entered the restaurant, he took off to find him.

Carpathia was one of Tom's favorite restaurants, with great Balkan dishes. The interior was fashioned from dark wood with rustic paintings of harvests and feasts; a long bar ran down the left wall. The place was already noisy, and every table looked taken. They stopped at the front stand, and Tom inquired about their reservation. The young lady apologized for the twenty-minute wait and suggested they get a drink at the bar.

Callie smiled and nodded, and they walked that way. There was one free barstool about halfway down the row. On the next stool a young woman was seated but turned away in a conversation with two men, one younger and one older, standing beside her. Tom motioned for Callie to take the free stool, which she did.

Recalling Seth's party, he asked, "Would you like an Old Fashioned?"

She nodded, and Tom leaned toward the bartender to order two.

"Ms. Sawyer?" the young woman, who had turned slightly, suddenly asked.

Callie shifted. "Yes. Oh, Katherine? Hi!" They shook hands. "Tom, this is Katherine Tikhonovsky, one of my Advanced Business Writing students. She's doing a graduate degree on Artificial Intelligence in Marketing."

As they shook hands, Callie said, "This is Tom Sullivan. He works in the White House."

"Nice to meet you. This is my Uncle Alexei. Alexei Nobikov. He's visiting from Cyprus. And this is my friend from school, Patrick Tomlinson."

The men shook hands. "A pleasure to meet you both," Alexei said. "And if you are helping Katherine, Ms. Sawyer, I can only say thank you, for her mother—my sister—and for me."

"Please, it's Callie. And it's my pleasure. She writes really interesting papers."

"And what do you do in the White House, Mr. Sullivan?"

"Tom. A little of this and that. Helping to get things rolling again."

"These are certainly challenging times for all of us, particularly here in D.C."

"I have a good friend, Logan Schofield, from Cyprus. His parents still live there."

"Have you ever been?"

"Unfortunately, no."

"A beautiful island with both sunny beaches and snow skiing! You should come. Both of you."

"Thank you. And what do you do?"

"I own a piece of an internet service provider on the island and manage the company. Along with a little freelance journalism. I thought I better come visit Katherine and see what's going on here, with all the challenges."

Tom nodded. "Yes, there've been quite a few lately."

Alexei smiled. "They were just telling me about a group of low-tech entrepreneurs at their school who've revised the old system of delivering personal, sealed notes around town, like before the telephone, to get around all the electronic collection going on. Isn't that interesting? They've apparently got hundreds of students with bikes, and all the delivery infrastructure left over from Covid, delivering personal letters instead of dinners. And people are paying. Only in America!"

"Hmm."

Alexei reached into his coat pocket. "If you'd ever like a European ground level take on what's happening on the internet, or anything to do with the security measures we're taking, or being forced to implement, please give me a call or send an email. I'll be glad to fill you in. Here's my business card."

Tom took it and, after a glance, put it in his pocket. "Thanks. You never know. Sorry I don't have a card, but hopefully one day life will be normal enough for me to order some. Patrick what are you studying?"

"American History and International Communications."

"Sounds like quite a combination. Where are you from?"

"Cincinnati. Katherine and I met this summer on a study abroad program in London."

"Glad you're here. Katherine, what are you working on?"

Their drinks arrived and they chatted for several more minutes. The hostess came over to tell Tom their table was ready.

"What about these folks?" Tom asked. "They were here before us."

The hostess started to respond, but Alexei said, "Oh no. Go ahead. We didn't have reservations. We were actually going somewhere else, but as we walked by, the menu looked interesting, so we came in. We're fine, catching up on family things."

"OK. Nice to meet you. Maybe we'll all vacation on Cyprus when this is over."

"Sounds perfect. Just let us know. We'll be glad to see you."

They all shook hands again, and Tom and Callie followed the hostess to their table.

When they were seated and their waters were poured, Tom unfolded his napkin and said, "I'm really glad we could get together. But, listen, while I'm thinking about it, it's probably not so good to introduce me as someone who 'works in the White House.'"

She looked flustered. "Oh, Tom, I'm sorry. I didn't think. It just came out."

He smiled and raised his hand. "I'm sure it's fine with them—you know her. But, in general, all of us would prefer to keep a low profile."

"Sure. From now on, you'll be 'my friend in the government.'"

"How about just 'friend'? Or even 'good friend'?"

She brightened. "Yes. Much better."

As they picked up their menus, he said, "You have a great smile. And you're always 'up.'" He paused. "You remind me a little of my friend Jenny, who was killed trying to stop that bank shooter in New York. I wanted to attend her funeral, but there was just no way, with all this going on."

Callie waited, then asked, "How long did you know her?"

He signaled to their waitress for two more drinks. "We were friends for a couple of years. I met her when I worked at the bank here, but she was always in New York. Like you, a smart woman and full of life."

"Were you friends, good friends, or really good friends?" she said, as the breadbasket arrived.

He looked away for a moment. "If you're asking whether we slept together, we did. I guess I'm not proud of it, but no one seems to worry about that anymore."

She smiled. "I think God does. A lot." She paused. "But you can't outdo me. I'm the unmarried one with the daughter. And if you check a little, you'll find videos online with me in them, from before Grace."

"You?"

She nodded. "Me. My boyfriend at the time made them. I was known as Samantha."

"That's crazy. And you talk about it?"

"Not with everyone I meet, but yes. With you. I'm not proud. But I think I told you when we met that what others meant for evil, God meant for good. First He used all that stuff to change me. Then Grace. And she's amazing."

"That's from the Bible."

Callie smiled. "Yes."

"I used to read it."

"You should try again."

"Maybe. But, listen, now that we've caught up on everyone we know, and we've even shared secrets about ourselves, tell me what you've been working on, so long as it's not related to terrorists or crimes."

The waitress arrived with their drinks, and they paused to order their dinners.

Callie sipped her Old Fashioned. "Well, I've been reading new reports on DNA codes—it's actually something that might interest you, as a cyber-crypto-codes-sort of guy."

"What do you mean?"

"The latest research in DNA replication shows not only how complicated and full of intelligent code DNA is, but how there are actually parity check codes, like I think you use for encryption, that must correctly match each time a new, daughter strand of DNA is created, signaling that the replication is correct, or else it's discarded."

"Really? And why does that pique your interest?"

"Because how could including a check code be the result of a random, chance process? Clearly it took some sort of designer to decide that one was needed. Just like with the codes you write. There's an intelligent design in the DNA code to replicate life, which is amazing itself, and then there's this check code, to be sure it's correct. Isn't that incredible?"

He took a sip and reached for a slice of bread. "Yes, I guess. But couldn't the check code be the result of a random evolutionary process?"

"Think about it. It's much deeper. It's just the opposite of a random process, which doesn't know right from wrong—only chance. But this check code means that someone or something outside of the process itself *knows* what's right, keeps it, and throws away what's wrong. That's exactly the opposite of evolution."

He laughed. "Maybe you're right, and I love your enthusiasm! OK. I'll look into it."

"Great. Be careful—you might find God again. I'll send you a couple of links to whet your DNA appetite."

"Thanks, and speaking of recommendations and links, I tried to order those books by your pastor—Robert Ludwig—but they weren't available. Do you have a copy I could borrow?"

She turned serious. "Not available, or blocked by the government?"

"Uh, I guess blocked, though I'm not sure why."

"Robert found out about it early this week, and he told the church at our Wednesday service."

"It may be the Artificial Intelligence algorithm being overly cautious, connecting previous writings and statements to possible future statements or actions."

"Which one? Statements, like discussions? Or actions, like firebombing? They're different."

From inside Tom came the planted voice of *Reason*. "Right now we have to be careful. They can be almost the same thing."

"What? Debate and violence are not the same things."

*Logic.* "They can be. The president even remarked that if your church hadn't scheduled a message opposed to Gay Marriage, it probably wouldn't have been attacked."

"Do you agree with that?"

"Not completely. But I understand the motivation, and that's why we've implemented these restrictions for another three weeks."

Callie leaned forward. "What if the censor tells Pastor Ludwig he has to delete parts of his Sunday sermon?"

*Pride.* "Then he should. For the sake of the nation. We're all in this together."

Her eyes narrowed. "All in what together? A nation where free speech and freedom of religion have always been strongly defended, even in the most difficult times?"

"Yes. And they're being defended now. We just need a cooling-off period so one group can't attack another."

"Attack one another or debate one another?"

"Again, right now, they're the same, and we need to control both."

"They're not the same and never have been. Where does it end? And when? And who decides?

"In three weeks. Back to normal."

"Don't be sure. And if Robert doesn't delete what the censor demands, should he be arrested?"

Tom paused. "That's what the Executive Order provides.

"So, yes? Arrest him?"

"Yes."

The server arrived with their meals. They each picked up a knife and fork, eating in silence.

Finally Callie said, "There's more to it, Tom. I know you're focused on protecting us, but in my experience, the old saying that power corrupts is always true. Once you give someone more power, it's hard to take it away."

He tried to smile. "We'll see. Give us a little more time to find out who's doing this, and then we'll get back to normal."

"Maybe. In the meantime, I expect to be visiting my pastor in jail."

"Actually, there's no visiting someone in detention. But let's hope it doesn't come to that."

She put down her fork, closed her eyes, and gently shook her head.

Prince Proklor and his key team met in the Oval Office at midnight. They again had every local fallen angel out in bars, restaurants, streets and homes—in D.C. and across the nation—looking and listening for openings they could leverage to divide people.

Temno opened. "Abortions are up, as usual, for this time of year, after the summer holidays. 3,216 yesterday. 2,849 divorces."

Proklor smiled. "Isn't it amazing, when you think about it? Remember how we used to have to tear the babies away from their screaming mothers for the Moloch sacrifices? Now they *volunteer,* and even pay to have them 'terminated'. What a great gift for everything else we're doing. All those mothers hounded by guilt, or needing constant justification. And, the great bonus is that no one defending abortion is likely to want to hear about Him on any other subject. Guilt with nowhere to go! Congratulate Voena again on what his team has accomplished."

"Yes, your liege."

"Now, back to the next few days. These should be critical. Reports?"

Temno began. "As you directed, we've given them a week of relative calm and allowed them to rebuild confidence in their defenses. While we can never be perfectly sure, it looks like the big events we've been encouraging our targets to undertake will happen on Monday or Tuesday. And, importantly, each of them should be repeatable—not just one-off events. Generals?"

The demonic leaders in charge of each targeted area reported to Prince Proklor in turn.

When the last one finished, Proklor nodded. "Good. Very good. This will be like nothing they've ever experienced. A second wave of destruction, with every group and tribe blaming every other. The Land of the Free will be the Land of Hate and Anarchy. Who knows where it will end? Great work. Proceed."

# 10

*The religion I have is to love and fear God, believe in Jesus Christ, do all the good to my neighbor, and myself that I can, do as little harm as I can help, and trust on God's mercy for the rest.*

Daniel Boone

Saturday, September 26

While it was still dark that Saturday morning at the Northeast Abortion Center, Balzor and Obman circled their forces together in the largest open space. They reiterated how important the next few days and weeks would be in the Prince's plan to create anarchy throughout the nation. Balzor reminded them to redouble their efforts to watch for and to pass up the chain of command anything they saw or heard that could be useful for creating even deeper division and distrust.

The forces in the stronghold responded enthusiastically to their leaders' encouragement. They were ready to get on with the final steps towards total anarchy in this wretched country.

As the meeting broke up, the two leaders were talking. "All those years molding Senator Bradshaw's beliefs turned out to be so important. It just shows we never know where our efforts will eventually pay off," Balzor said. "Now that he's surrounded by prayers day and night, I think the voices we planted and nurtured all those years, not to mention his own pride, will hold up until we can get close to him again."

Obman nodded his agreement. "And the people around him do almost as well as Nepravel and Zloy at repeating our lies, even when we're not there." The two street leaders approached the two sector leaders. "Something else?" Obman asked.

Always afraid to point out a problem, but fearful for his own future, Nepravel nodded.

"Tom Sullivan and Emily Schofield, two key advisors to the president, are spending a lot of time with believers. The light shining from within the believers plus the constant incoming prayers, particularly for Sullivan, make it impossible for us to stay near them. And just a few hours ago a pretty boy showed up and stood guard over a dinner meeting between Sullivan and Callie Sawyer! We have no idea who else they met, or what they said. We need help to stay close to them and to keep Sullivan doubting. Schofield doesn't seem to be a problem, but we don't like it."

Balzor asked, "Who's praying for them? His parents?"

Zloy answered with a slight bow. "Yes, and *her* parents. And both of their churches. And Robert Ludwig's church here. By name, and around the clock, with teams. That Kristen Holloway woman has started a national prayer newsletter from Ludwig's church that goes out to hundreds of churches every morning with names to pray for, and specific requests."

Obman and Balzor exchanged looks. "All right. We'll let Atlanta know, and hopefully they can cut down those prayers. We'll assign more forces to Schofield and those around the president, to ramp up the voices and to stir up hate when they're not with the believers, or protected by prayer. As you know, there are plans underway to eliminate Robert Ludwig—there are more ways than firebombs. Anything else?"

Nepravel nodded. "That should help. We can't let their infection spread any further."

Tom went into his White House office that Saturday morning in jeans—almost everyone on their team no longer distinguished weekends from other days. He felt badly about his argument with Callie at dinner, but he knew he was right. Nepravel, who was with him, fed in the voices of *Pride. Confidence. Control.* The government needed exceptional powers to stop this attack, and it wasn't asking too much for everyone, including pastors and newscasters, to go along with it for thirty days. Look how almost everyone had come together under Presidential leadership during the Coronavirus pandemic, for almost two years. Why not now for just thirty days?

As was required—and good practice—he entered Alexei Nobikov's data from the business card into the Foreign Contact list under his name. If there were any issues, he would get a reply notification.

He had just finished his daily video update with SAC Tanya Prescott—with nothing remarkable to report other than more arrests and detentions for 'normal' crimes—when Patricia Reynolds came to his door. She was not yet confirmed as Vice President, and so for optics sake she was not working in that office, but the president had installed her with a small, hand-picked staff on the second floor.

A tall woman in her early fifties with just the right amount of gray in her hair, she was wearing a tasteful business suit. She smiled. "May I come in?"

He stood and waved her in. "Of course. How is your Trusted Core phone working?"

She took one of the chairs in front of his desk. "Fine. Thank you for setting it up. It's nice to be able to communicate without worrying about being listened to. Maybe we should figure out how to get these safely to a larger group of good people." She paused. "Listen, I like to know the people I'm working with. The president speaks very highly of you and trusts you to be his advisor on National Security. So I thought I'd spend a few minutes on a Saturday to get to know you better."

"Thank you." *Pride. False Humility.* "But with so few real qualifications, I view my role more as National Security Coordinator, to bring in the experts who really know about these issues. And to help coordinate between the White House and the NSC as we push back against the terrorists. Eventually they'll hire an adult to replace me."

"Humility and reflection are qualities not always in abundance in this town. I appreciate your perspective. By the way, I briefly knew your mother when she was here in Congress—we met a couple of times when I was still in the state legislature—but I know that she accomplished a lot."

"Yes, I'm blessed with great parents."

"And she was—or is—a conservative Christian, as far as I know. So, how about you? How did you wind up advising a progressive President?"

He paused for a moment. "Well, actually, I'm pretty apolitical. I was a teenager when my parents became believers, and I 'accepted Christ' in high school. But then in college I woke up, if you will, to understand that there are many equally good faiths—and good people with no faith. So I haven't been too much into Christianity for quite a while—but my parents certainly are." He smiled. "They're probably praying for us right now. How about you? I understand you also changed."

She nodded and thought. "Yes. I don't advertise this, but since we're going to be working together, I had an abortion when I was in college. It was safe and legal. But I was overcome with grief and guilt. After a few months of depression, I found an outreach from some great people who happened to be believers, and they led me to repentance and forgiveness. It was wonderful. Years later after law school I ran for the legislature because I was angry about some education policies, and I won! Crazy. I was always pretty much middle-of-the-road on most fiscal and social issues, and of course Pro-Life.

"But then there was a push to not only stop abortions, but also to arrest and jail women who had an abortion. I couldn't go along with that. After months of arguing with my colleagues, I switched parties. I don't like abortion, but I don't want women arrested. And over the years I've come to see that much of the progressive program is helpful to people. However they got there, there are large groups who simply can't take care of themselves, and progressives make a good case that the government has to do it. So I support more of the big government program than my roots would suggest I might. I guess I'm a 70/30 progressive, if there is such a thing.

"The only problem I've had to deal with is that it's almost impossible to pick some Progressive issues to support and some not to. It seems that you're either into all of it, or others think you're not on the team at all. I've had to bite my tongue and cast a few worrisome votes to stay onboard with my colleagues, but it's what they expect."

"Like what?"

She paused. "Well, most recently this transgender thing with girls in sports. And locker rooms. I have two daughter-athletes, and it makes no sense to me. But I can't say anything, or they'll come after me. You learn quickly that there can be no breaks in the Progressive line. But that's just between us."

Tom nodded. "I understand. And your faith?"

She paused. "I guess it's still there, in moderation. My husband and I attend church when I'm home. But we're not crazy evangelicals. The church and the Bible have their place for teaching us, but so do reason, other faiths, and equal treatment laws. We try to balance."

"Sounds reasonable. Sounds like we've come to some similar conclusions."

She stood. "Well, thank you for your time. I have some final interviews this afternoon before the votes on Monday. If your mother ever comes to town, I'd love to see her again. She was and is a great role model."

"Sure. And I hope all goes well with the vote."

She turned to leave. Nepravel, who had listened to their conversation, was delighted that two former believers were so confidently dismissing real truth in the name of 'reason', and congratulating each other. He'd found over the last several hundred years that this approach almost always worked well.

Two neatly bearded men in jeans and work shirts, one in his early-thirties and one about ten years older, were having sandwiches on a bench at the edge of Anacostia Park on the south side of the river in D.C. For the past three months, Ablet Sabri and Kahar Bosakov had been doing odd jobs and generally lying low in the large Uyghur community in the capital.

Ablet, the elder, had been recruited three years earlier by radical Islamists in their hometown on the western side of China's Xinjiang Province, after most members of his family had disappeared into Chinese internment camps.

Singled out for his intelligence and zeal, Ablet was designated early on as a potential leader. Two months later he recruited his younger cousin, Kahar, into his cell, and the cousins spent a year training at a secret jihadist camp in the Afghan mountains. Their natural hatred for Han Chinese and the Chinese Communist Party was steadily fueled by terrifying reports from home and by their daily Islamic studies.

For the forces of darkness opposed to God's truth, a radical Islamist camp like the one Ablet and Kahar attended took far fewer resources than a similar operation in the West—Islam itself always leveraged the demons' usual lies through its teachings and practices. So there were only two demons required on site to make sure that the darkness was complete and all-encompassing for each participant.

After they completed their training, English language instruction, and Islamic indoctrination, Ablet spent two weeks on his own at another site for training to securely run a team, and then he and Kahar were sent on a circuitous route which included being smuggled as VIP's—with a hefty fee paid to a friendly drug cartel, and retribution promised in case of failure—across the porous southern border into the United States.

Met on the U.S. side by like-minded militants tasked each month with infiltrating more jihadists into the country, they were driven to D.C. and given fake I.D.'s which were good enough for securing low level employment and affordable housing.

For the next three months they settled into their new environment, rented an inexpensive apartment, and secured construction jobs. As the leader, Ablet awaited further instruction, expected to come via a letter or text with a previously agreed, coded message. His cell had pairs in five other U.S. cities; they would act in unison under his command. Only Ablet knew what was actually being planned—for security even his cousin Kahar was not privy to the specifics. But, given their training, Kahar expected their mission to be violent, and his final act on earth before attaining Paradise.

Ablet and Kahar typically attended the Family and Friendship Mosque, where they kept mostly to themselves and occasionally wondered if any of the other twenty or so young, single Uyghur men at the mosque were also secretly part of some other group.

The demons who monitored the mosque members were informed by their counterparts across the world about the mission, and they kept a close eye on the two cousins.

While they waited, Ablet enjoyed as many American pleasures and freedoms as his budget would allow. Kahar, more studious by nature, occasionally joined his cousin, but, like his father, who had disappeared into the Chinese camps, Kahar mostly enjoyed reading, especially history. And the nearby public library had an amazing collection.

"What shall it be tonight, cousin?" Ablet asked with a smile, folding up his sandwich wrapper. "The Kitty Klub, or more Kittyhawk?"

Kahar didn't really mind Ablet's needling. "How about a little of both? The story of the Wright brothers is almost impossible to imagine. Two regular guys who changed the world."

"Like us?"

"Perhaps. So first I'll read a bit. But then The Kitty Klub is also impossible to imagine."

Ablet's smile grew larger. "Good. Yes. There is hope for you yet."

That afternoon Mason Neal and Josh Weber put the finishing touches on their second delivery and closed and locked the shed. Vonyat and Umer had been close to them since they'd returned from their first trip, encouraging them at every step and drowning out any doubts that might crop up about moving forward. As the two men walked to the house to get lunch and their travel gear, Umer confirmed to Vonyat that all of their technical preparations appeared to be in order. And he promised to be in D.C. when they arrived.

An hour later the two men pulled away from the farm, towing the white trailer. Its Kentucky license plate was valid, and registered to Josh. The extra Virginia plate was in Josh's bag.

"Do you still want me to come with you?" Callie asked, when she opened her front door for Tom early that evening.

He smiled. "Of course. If we're really going to be friends, then we have to be able to talk honestly."

She nodded. "OK, then. Come in, and we'll say goodnight to Grace and Kristen."

Unseen by them the powerful angel from the previous night was standing in the street behind them, facing out. And when they started walking, he was there, too.

Twenty minutes later they joined the others at Seth's row house, placing a bottle of red wine on the kitchen counter as they said hello to Seth and Natalie, Emily and Logan, and Clayton and Andrea.

"I'm so glad you could come," Natalie said to Callie as she took her coat. "I told Seth I want to go to your church tomorrow. I really like the music, and the, I don't know, peace there."

"Great. Let's meet about 10:20 in the front hall, after I put Grace in Sunday School. Is Seth coming?"

"I doubt it. But we'll see."

"Maybe if he comes, I can get Tom to join us. Or vice versa. Like you said, we'll see."

"What are you talking about?" Tom asked, returning with two glasses.

"You and Seth coming to church tomorrow."

"Really? Me? We'll see." He walked with Clayton toward the kitchen.

Callie and Natalie shared a glance as Andrea walked over.

"Still no baby?" Natalie asked.

"No *visible* baby. But there's very definitely a baby," Andrea gave a pat to her abdomen as she replied and smiled.

After fifteen minutes of standing and chatting, the four couples took seats on the sofa and chairs around the large coffee table in Seth's living room.

"Two weeks ago tonight," Seth said, as they settled in. "Seems like another world."

As others nodded, Emily said, "It was."

"And I can't believe," Andrea added, "that the four of you who randomly roomed together ten years ago are now playing such important roles in all this. It's either crazy, or a God thing."

There were quiet nods.

"How's everyone holding up under the Emergency Actions?" Tom asked.

Clayton took a sip of his wine. "I can't talk about details of course, but, as you know, Tom, you've given us a lot more firepower to go after bad guys of all types, and it's working."

Natalie added, "As we follow money through the system, the ability to instantly access any and every bank account in the nation is awesome. I'll be over at DEA next week, and our instant window into the companies that the drug cartels set up with new accounts, close others, and transfer money is incredibly helpful. We're interdicting a lot more shipments and bringing many more prosecutions."

"But a bank lobbyist friend tells me that it drives the banks crazy," Logan pointed out. "They're losing legitimate customers who are looking for alternatives because they don't want the government looking at every check and deposit they write."

"If they're not doing anything wrong, why would they care?" Tom asked.

"Because they don't want the government knowing everything about them," Andrea said. "As someone who deals in the records of people's private lives every day, I can promise you that giving the government—or anyone—unchecked power is a recipe for disaster."

"But we have to stand up to them," Emily injected, looking across at Tom in support. "Find out who they are, and destroy them, before they destroy us."

After a moment of silence Seth said, "I get it. I'm all for what Tom and Emily are doing. We need to crush these people. Two weeks ago I imagined that the government might be able to read my emails and texts, and listen to my calls. Now I *know* they can, and are. For our good. But I will say that having a government censor actually sitting at a desk in our studios and checking the content of our stories and opinion pieces is a bit unnerving."

"I read somewhere that most news organizations learn after a few days what the guidelines are," Clayton said, "and self-regulate. The censor is only needed for close calls. Is that true?"

"Yes, I guess it is," Seth conceded. "We know pretty much what we can say, and what we can't."

"That doesn't concern you?" Logan asked.

"Well, yes, I guess so, if it kept on forever. But we can do it for thirty days." He glanced at Emily and Tom.

Callie, who had been silent, said, "What if your message can't wait thirty days? Or what if the censorship lasts longer? What right does the government have to tell us what we can say or not say for a single day, much less thirty?"

Emily smiled. "Wow. I'd say the government has the right—actually, the obligation—to protect us—and *all* of us, not just those with privilege."

"Is telling Seth's network what they can show and telling the pastor of our church what he can say from the pulpit tomorrow protecting us?"

"At this particular moment, under this threat, yes," Tom said.

"It's too high a price. Either we have our Constitutional rights all day, every day, or we don't. Where will it end?" Callie asked, slightly shaking her head. "Unintended consequences."

"Probably not well," Andrea added.

"You don't know that," Clayton countered.

"You're right, I don't. Hopefully we'll come out of all this and go back to being a free nation."

"We're free now," Tom injected, clearly annoyed. "Surely you know that. We're just defending our freedom."

Andrea pursed her lips and shrugged. "We'll see."

Callie turned slightly to face Tom. "Then come with us tomorrow to Church of the Good Shepherd. You can hear Robert Ludwig yourself. You, too, Seth."

With all eyes on him, Tom paused. Finally he looked at Callie. "OK. I will."

"And you, Seth?"

"I'm not a Christian. Why would I go?"

Natalie said, "Because I'm going."

He thought for a moment. "OK. If you and Tom go, I'll go."

Pastor Robert Ludwig usually didn't go out on Saturday evenings before preaching the next day, but his wife wasn't feeling well, and their thirteen-year-old son needed to be picked up after a friend's birthday event. Now the two of them were driving home east of the Capitol.

Proklor wanted Ludwig's voice silenced, one way or the other, along with those of about thirty other well-followed pastors, with the next round of their attacks expected soon. Balzor had placed Timor, one of his most senior street leaders, in charge of a plan to rid them of the pastor's constant proclamations from The Book, and his incessant prayers. Actions like the one planned for tonight were rare because of the timing involved, but to silence Robert Ludwig it would be well worth it.

Timor hovered over that part of D.C. while another demon followed as close to Ludwig's car as he could, given the bright spiritual light inside, and another sat next to a teenage boy driving another car to his friend's home for a party. The boy had downed quite a bit of bourbon before leaving his bedroom. He was on a fairly busy arterial street with only a few stop signs and ample streetlights. So the demon made sure he didn't notice that his headlights were off, and that he was driving with one hand while keeping an eye on his girlfriend's text thread.

From above them Timor coordinated the timing as Ludwig slowed down to stop at the four-way with the arterial street. He looked both ways and saw no cars either stopped or approaching.

"Go!" Timor instructed the demon with the teen driver, who silently encouraged the boy not to be late for the party.

Ludwig began to move into the intersection when suddenly to his right on the sidewalk a jogger in bright yellow running gear failed to heed the obvious danger and ran in front of his car. Ludwig slammed on the brakes to avoid the jogger, and just as he did a car with no lights barreled through the intersection from his left, without stopping. He and his son both yelled. Clearly they had just avoided a deadly collision by inches.

His hands gripping the wheel, Ludwig looked from the speeding dark car to his son, who was facing forward and shaking. Then to his left. The jogger was gone. There was no one at all on the well-lit sidewalk.

# 11

*May I always hear that you are following the guidance of that blessed Spirit that will lead you into all truth, leaning on that Almighty arm that has been extended to deliver you, trusting only in the only Savior, and going on in your way to Him rejoicing.*

Francis Scott Key

Sunday, September 27

The Church of the Good Shepherd was in walking distance of their row houses, so Tom went first to Callie's and then, together with Grace and Kristen, they, Natalie and Seth arrived in the entrance lobby of the historic structure only a few minutes apart. Nepravel, Zloy, Timor and the others had to stop following several blocks away. The spiritual heat and light emanating from the gathering felt to them like a raging fire, and no demon in his right mind would venture closer. Nepravel thought that he saw at least one angel in the midst of all that heat . *Damn!*

Callie greeted Natalie and Seth with a warm hug and introduced them to Kristen and several of her friends. They then made their way to one of the wooden pews in the center of the sanctuary.

Pastor Robert Ludwig and the morning's worship team were in a room behind the sanctuary praying for the upcoming service, that God would use it for His glory, and to reveal His truth. Each person knew that, after much discussion and prayer, the elders had unanimously voted not to accept the government censor's required changes to the morning's message, and Ludwig found himself a little nervous about their decision, but also very much at peace.

By 10:30 the building was filled to standing room only in the back, and just before the first hymn, he greeted everyone in the sanctuary and announced that there was overflow seating in the community room, with a video feed.

Led by a powerful organ which somehow seemed to unite everyone, they sang traditional hymns that even Seth found familiar. The prayers were moving, giving thanks for God's protection, and asking for His mercy, forgiveness, continuing protection and guidance in this difficult time. The Old Testament reading was Psalm 139, announced as the text for the upcoming sermon. The Epistle reading was 1 Corinthians 1, and the Gospel was John 3. After the offering came the sermon hymn, "A Mighty Fortress is Our God." Tom felt a chill and the hair on his arms stood on end as Martin Luther's lyrical attack against the forces of darkness ended with "...The body they may kill, God's Truth abideth still. His Kingdom is forever."

Pastor Ludwig walked to the pulpit and delivered a thirty-minute message on Psalm 139. The "song" had been written by King David in about 1050 BC when he was made King of Israel. Ludwig noted that David's psalm celebrates God's all-powerful omniscience and omnipresence as being a given—not something that needed to be debated or proven. Ludwig then concentrated on the fact that the all-powerful God who creates and holds every star and every molecule in the universe together, somehow actually focuses intently on each individual person, whom He has made in His own image, male and female.

Ludwig told the congregation that the first third of the psalm reiterates how God knows each of us as a single person, not as a group or tribe, including our thoughts and actions, even before we do. We cannot escape Him, for He made us, He knows us, and He is everywhere.

"If we try to hide from Him, David acknowledges that He always knows where we are, and that He will deal with us, even in the darkness that we think is hiding us."

Then the pastor went on to remind them that the middle verses of the psalm confirm that God is the Creator who individually "knit me together in my mother's womb. I praise you because I am fearfully and wonderfully made; your works are wonderful...all the days ordained for me were written in your book before one of them came to be."

Ludwig used these verses to remind the congregation that abortion must be the same as murder. "You and I are not the result of random events. God *creates* each one of us in His image and knits us together in our mother's womb. Whether we like it or not, we are His. And by the way, that's the truth behind Jefferson and the others writing in our Declaration of Independence that 'all men are created equal, that they are *endowed by their Creator* with certain unalienable Rights, that among these are Life, Liberty and the pursuit of Happiness.' This unalienable Right to Life is given to us by our Creator, not by any government, and not by random events, while we are being knit together by Him in the womb.

"Today we are rightly concerned about the terrible events that have caused so much death in our nation over the past two weeks. It is clearly wrong and the result of evil. And yet on average *every day* in our nation for the past forty years we have killed more babies—over 2,000 per day—than the total number who have died in all these attacks put together. Can we imagine that our Creator God has not noticed this government-sanctioned evil as well, and that He might have some consequences in mind?"

Ludwig paused and took a sip of water from a glass at the lectern.

"Getting back to the text, if roughly the first third of David's psalm is about God knowing us as individuals, and about how we can never escape from His grasp, and the middle third describes how He created each one of us and ordains every day of our lives, then the last third is David's plea for God to destroy his enemies, specifically those who hate God and are in rebellion against Him.

"This is a legitimate request from one born of the flesh. Revenge and 'getting even' are hard wired into us as human beings. They are 'knit' into us in the birth process. It is completely natural for David to hate those who hate God.

"And here we turn to the transforming power of the New Covenant. In the third chapter of John read for us this morning, Jesus tells Nicodemus, a learned intellectual, that having been born once in the flesh, he now must be 'born again' in the Spirit to enter the Kingdom of God. Nicodemus scoffs and asks how can one re-enter his mother's womb to be born again. Jesus makes it clear that he is talking about spiritual rebirth, specifically about believing in him as the Son of God, who willingly served as the passover lamb to bear the sins of the world so that we don't have to.

"And one result of that radical, revolutionary concept is Jesus' admonition in the Sermon on the Mount to love, not hate, our enemies.

David could never have arrived at that conclusion. Only through God's grace and our rebirth as His spiritual child through faith in His Son is it possible to love our enemies. To pray for them. To realize that their actions are the result of Satan's lies to them. It is Satan who is our real and only enemy, and we should pray that God will defeat and deflect his plans and strategies.

"I'm not advocating pacifism here in the light of obvious evil. The God-given obligation of government, in which so many of you serve, is to protect its citizens. But in doing so as the government I'm reminding us that individually we are called to love and to forgive our human 'enemies'—which is a radical idea and only possible with God's grace—focusing our spiritual firepower as believers on our one real enemy and his forces. Pray. Speak truth. Tell others about the God who transformed you and lives inside you. Live as an example of love, even in this difficult time.

"In summary, David's psalm reminds us that 1) God focuses first not on the group, but on the individual, whom He has made and whom we should protect and love from before birth to last breath, that 2) we as individuals can flee from Him, but He always knows where we are and will deal with us, and that 3) His offer of re-birth is utterly transformative, turning us from hateful revenge to genuine love and forgiveness.

"He is the all-powerful Creator Father, the Savior Son who willingly died for you when you hated Him, and the ever-working Spirit who can transform you, if you ask Him. Let's pray."

After a time of open prayers for the nation and its leaders, and a closing hymn, the service ended. The friends moved toward the lobby, chatting as they went.

Pastor Ludwig was shaking hands at the door. Callie stepped ahead and introduced Tom, who said, "Thank you. Your message sounded like what I used to hear growing up. No wishy-washy maybes. Very clear and understandable."

"Thank you," Ludwig responded, smiling. "That's how I think God communicates with us, when we let Him, and when other voices aren't drowning Him out."

Tom nodded and moved forward. Callie introduced Natalie and Seth.

"I need to think about what you said," Natalie offered. "I had never really thought about a fetus that way. Along with how we can run from God, but we really can't hide. He always knows where we are. Maybe that's me."

"Come back any time, and if you want to talk more, just shoot us a text or an email," Ludwig replied.

"Thanks, I might."

Seth shook his hand. "Just visiting. My first time. You're a good preacher."

"You're kind. Aren't you on TV?"

"Uh, yes. The Network. Seth Cohen."

"I thought I recognized you. You're also a good speaker. And keep digging for the truth. You never know where you might find it."

"I will. Thanks."

"And come back. We can compare notes on what you find."

"Maybe I will. Thanks again."

"Nice to meet all of you. See you tonight, Callie."

As Callie nodded, Kristen walked up with Grace, who, by pre-agreement, she had collected from Sunday School. They greeted her and shook her hand, then descended to the sidewalk.

"Well, what did you think?" Callie asked, looking at Tom. "Should Robert be arrested?"

Tom shrugged. "I don't know if he defied any specific reviewer's requirements, which would not be good. And he said that abortion is government-sanctioned evil. Also not good. But, actually, I was struck most by the first part of his message. I remember that God chose David to be King of Israel because he was 'a man after God's own heart,' or something like that. I guess that's what we would call a 'believer' today. So does this psalm mean that God will come after everyone if they try to hide from Him, or just believers?"

Callie thought for a moment. "Or maybe both. I know He came after me when I hated Him and wanted nothing to do with Him. He sent Kristen. That's when He changed me. Now, as a believer, I hear His voice nudging me when I try to rationalize something, or correcting me when I'm tempted to believe a convenient lie."

Natalie said, "That's interesting. So it can be both?"

Seth raised his hand. "Hey, this is getting really deep for this simple Jewish guy. How about lunch over at Hoagies?"

Callie smiled. "Yes. That's what David was. And Jesus. Simple Jewish guys. And, yes, lunch sounds great. Kristen, want to join us? By the way, thank you all for coming."

"It'll have to be quick. I'm due at the office this afternoon for an update," Tom said.

They nodded and started walking together to the delicatessen two blocks away. The angel hovered over them as they went.

While church was finishing President Bradshaw and the First Lady were hosting a working brunch at the White House in the West Sitting Hall and the adjoining Private Dining Room. Patricia Reynolds, Nancy Cantrell, Rob Thompson, Emily Schofield and four senior staff people on their party's Project Phoenix team had gathered at ten to go over their progress to date; papers were scattered in piles on the tables and the floor in the hall; now they were moving into the dining room.

"This is still taking a little getting used to," Margaret Bradshaw confided in Cantrell, as they took fresh coffee from the sideboard.

"I can imagine," the House Minority Leader replied, smiling. "But let's hope you're here for many years."

"And that you're Speaker for many years after these elections."

Once everyone had a pass at the offerings on the sideboard and were seated at the table, the president said to Rob and the team members, "You've done a remarkable job of summarizing and prioritizing our goals for the next months and the next years. Climate Change. Guaranteed Citizenship. Renewable Energy. Reducing World Tensions. Bank oversight. Guaranteed Incomes. Abortion Protection. Free Tuition. Expanding the Supreme Court. Debt forgiveness. Wealth redistribution. Slavery reparations. Corporate Liability. Gender Protection. It's all here. And the recommendations for replacing the Cabinet Members we inherited from President Rhodes. Thank you."

Rob Thompson said from the middle of the table, "And, as you requested, we've looked specifically at what we can propose on each subject for the upcoming midterm elections, depending on how things go in the next few weeks, and then beyond, assuming that we keep the Senate and also win the House."

"Yes, starting with Patricia's confirmation as vice president tomorrow."

"I think we're set there," Cantrell said. "We've been loving up on the other side over the last two weeks for 'bi-partisan unity,' and Patricia should actually sail through the House tomorrow. Obviously the Senate will be no problem." She nodded across the table at the nominee.

"OK, then," the president continued, "well done, and let's hope there are no more attacks so we can lift the State of Emergency a few weeks before the elections. That way the ads we're designing will be ready to roll with a message of unity, great accomplishment, and coming together."

Emily said, "Yes. And we're designing your Presidential Reports to the nation to include increasing references to the need for Progressive programs to be adopted as the answer to this crisis, and to make a better America, without being too obvious."

"Good. Good," the president said.

An hour later, after another review, the Phoenix Project staff departed, and the others adjourned to sofas and chairs in the Sitting Hall.

"I'd like to thank you again, Nancy and Rob, for this great work. Looks like we'll be ready to come out of the starting gates fast, no matter the situation. As you've heard, campaign funds are pouring in for our candidates and our PAC's, led by Juggle, your husband's firm, Emily. Let's hope it's peaceful, and back to normal. But I, uh, did want to ask this group a sensitive question. As we remake our inner circle and replace old-school people like Secretary McCord, I think we need someone with Tom Sullivan's expertise on this inner-inner team, and I'd like to invite him to join us, but I haven't known him that long. I know he's serious, but is he committed to a better, progressive America, and is he a loyal team player?"

Emily cradled her coffee cup. "I think I've known him the longest—ten years. We roomed, or apartmented, together when we first came to D.C. He comes from a conservative Christian background—you've all known or heard of his mother. But Tom has shaken that off and is, really, quite Progressive in his views. He's mostly focused only on the task in front of him, whatever it might be, and right now it's defeating the enemy. And on himself—one day pretty soon he'd like to be making a lot of money with a big bank or consulting firm. He probably sees success at both goals as being linked, so he'll be focused on success. He's a great, smart guy. Loyal to individuals. Again, he's focused on getting the job done."

"I actually spent some time with him yesterday morning," Patricia added, "and I'd say the same. Helpful. Wants to win. Not a crazy Christian. More a rational, former Christian, like I think I am. He seems OK to me."

Rob signaled his agreement. "He's done everything we've asked, and been ahead of most of the 'experts' on key issues. Remember, Tom came up with our two-track State of Emergency, when no one else had any idea what to do."

"I think he may have attended Church of the Good Shepherd this morning with my friend Callie. It just came up last night when we were together. I actually introduced them. He agreed to go on a kind of dare."

"OK, then. Emily, take a read on that, and then, unless you see a problem, we'll start including him in our planning sessions."

Emily nodded.

Tom walked Callie and Grace home from Hoagies after their lunch and more discussion of what they had heard that morning. Callie knew that he was in a hurry, but she asked him to step inside their apartment. Grace ran to her room.

"Here," she said in the entranceway, picking up two books and a DVD from the table by the door. "Since your all-knowing censor has blocked Pastor Ludwig's words on the internet, I thought I'd share them with you the old-fashioned way."

"They're only blocked temporarily."

"Whatever. Good. You can read these and be ready when the government will let you get more for yourself!" She smiled.

He looked at them. "What are they?"

"They're perfect for you. This is Robert's short book on *The Choice for Christ*. The title says it all. Then this is a great book by Gary Thornton, *The Foundations of America: A Study in Christian Faith*. And I know you'll enjoy these two DVDs, which are a weekend presentation the two of them did together at Church of the Good Shepherd a few years ago. The place was packed and I was mesmerized. All this stuff I didn't know about our history. Sitting where you're sitting, you should know it."

"Says you?"

She laughed. "Yes! Says me."

"OK, OK. I'll take a look. Thank you." He closed the short gap between them. "Let's get together this week."

"I'd like that. But first, your homework." She touched the items in his hand. "And don't let anyone see them. They might want to burn them."

Now he smiled. "OK. I'll guard them." He moved closer, leaned in, and kissed her on the lips. After a brief moment, she pressed back.

They pulled back and smiled. He turned to go, holding up his homework.

"Call me," she said, and closed the door behind him.

Teri Grantham and her brother Brad used the light Sunday afternoon traffic to drive into D.C. in Brad's car to scout the targets they had picked out on the internet. After two hours they settled on a secluded, tree lined parking lot behind a small warehouse on the north side of the downtown area.

From the map, confirmed by driving, this location was nearly equidistant between three mosques and Islamic Centers.

Sitting in the parking lot, Teri said, "This should do. No houses around. I only see one light pole, over by the building. If we park in that corner, we should be invisible."

Brad nodded. "This week?"

Ranit, seated between them, focused on Teri and ramped up visions in her of the mayhem they would cause.

"Yes, as soon as we have a clear night. We've waited long enough to send our message. Tomorrow or Tuesday. I'll rent a small van. My truck would be too obvious on security cameras."

Ranit smiled.

In the White House meeting at midnight there was growing anticipation for how the second wave of attacks would open the gates of anarchy and escalate identity politics into identity warfare. While motivating humans to action was always imprecise, it looked like several of their most promising targets were ready to carry out their plans. The seeds planted by individual thoughts had been watered and encouraged to grow by the demons' voices, and now it looked like the harvest was about to happen.

After so many positive reports it was therefore troubling to Prince Proklor when Bespor sounded a warning. "My liege, two of our best sector leaders tell us that along with the increased prayers there are now more angels appearing in their areas—more than they've seen since the week after the World Trade Tower attacks. The angels are making it harder for us to tell what their leaders might be planning, and now it appears an angel may even have taken human form to protect that Pastor Ludwig. We haven't seen an angel do that for years. And the result was that Ludwig preached a message against us with lots of government people in attendance. The appearance of angels is troubling."

Proklor was silent for several moments, realizing that the prayers, teachings and now actions of some scum-believers might derail what his forces had worked for decades to achieve. They could not let that happen.

"Well, then, we must move quickly. Instruct all your forces to ramp up their messaging. It's time for the harvest."

# Monday, September 28

Late that Monday morning Tom was in his office at the White House. He had just finished reading the report on Alexei Nobikov as a result of entering the Russian's name in the database. The summary gave a read-out on his history, including his earlier ties to American education and research, and his current position as CEO of a Cypriot internet service provider and occasional journalist. There was one yellow caution flag which caught Tom's attention: there was an unverified question whether Nobikov's company might be a front for Russian social media misinformation. And perhaps also black cash funding of causes in the U.S. To date there was no credible proof—just unverified speculation.

Tom thought for a moment, recalling how they had met in the restaurant, and the innocent connection between Callie and the man's niece. He put their meeting down as a coincidence, not a targeted encounter, but you never knew. And he clicked on the tab for notifications whenever Nobikov's name came across the system.

Emily knocked at his open door and took a step in. She was holding an iPad and smiling. "We have a new vice president. Patricia was just confirmed by Congress."

"Great news. One more step to normalcy."

"Yes. Very important. She's been sworn in already, but we'll have a ceremonial swearing in tomorrow morning in the Rose Garden. And thanks for your support at Seth's on Saturday night. I'm surprised some of our friends are so afraid to let the government protect us. Did you go to Callie's church yesterday?"

"We did. Seth, Natalie and me. Nice people. The service reminded me of ones we had at home when I was in high school."

"And the message? Was it a problem?

"Uh, it may have been. He came down pretty hard on abortion, the psalm talked about hating people who hate God, and he quoted the Gospel of John that having a relationship with Jesus is the only way to eternal life. Just like I used to hear. Seems like a pretty narrow view of God—one I certainly don't believe in."

"Hmm. Yes. If there is a God, why would He keep some people out of heaven? And abortion is so important to women." She walked over until she was in front of his desk. "Did I ever tell you that I had one when I was in college? I don't know where I would be today if I'd had a baby then."

Tom paused. "I don't think you did. That's tough. I may have been on the other side of one several years ago, too. Or at least a miscarriage. I was never told exactly, but I think so. But then there's Callie and Grace. I'm sure she—or they, someday—have a different opinion."

Emily nodded. They held each other's gaze for a moment. "Anything else about the service?"

"No, it was all a pretty straight forward born-again Christian service and message. He seems like a bright guy and a great preacher. I can see why Callie, as a believer, enjoys it."

"But not for you?"

He smiled and shook his head. "Not for me. I'm a logical thinker, not a blind believer. I guess I do believe in some higher power, but not in a God constrained by any man-made religion."

She turned. "OK. Good. I should get back to the final plans for the Memorial Service."

"And I've got to check in with Tanya. See ya."

Early that morning Mason Neal and Josh Weber had stashed their trailer in the self-storage unit in the D.C. suburbs and then driven further out to an inexpensive motel to wait. They wanted to minimize any chance that their truck or their faces would turn up on surveillance cameras in the D.C. area. Their plan was to leave the trailer early the next morning, camouflaged as a public works project, in a designated taxi stand on the street running down the side of the DEA Headquarters. The bomb's timer would be set to explode in mid-morning for maximum damage to the people inside.

They settled in to binge watch an episodic TV show about life under a fictional dictatorship in America, and to drink beer. Umer and Vonyat took turns as lookouts and as encouragers.

The four D.C. police officers who arrived at The Church of the Good Shepherd office just before noon were unaware that Pastor Ludwig usually took Mondays off. So by the time they had sorted that out with his assistant, checked with control, and driven several more blocks to the Ludwig home, the pastor, his wife, and two elders and their wives who lived nearby were praying in the Ludwig living room. A Network news van, which monitored the police frequencies, also rolled up. The reporter and cameraman had a clear view across the lawn in front of the Ludwigs' small but tasteful two-story brick home.

While one officer went around to the back, the others stationed themselves at the front door, and the lead officer rang the doorbell.

When Ludwig answered, the officer told him that he was under arrest for violating the directives of the National State of Emergency. He asked Ludwig to come outside and directed the others in the house to stay there, except for the pastor's wife.

Other church members, reacting to a text sent from the office, arrived by car and by foot. As Ludwig stood silently, his wife beside him, the lead officer read him his Miranda rights, and then one of the others cuffed his hands behind him.

"What are you doing?" someone yelled from the sidewalk.

"This is America, not China," another shouted.

The leader nodded to the officer returning from the back of the house; she went over to the sidewalk and ordered everyone to move away from the patrol cars.

Ludwig said to his wife, who appeared to be shell-shocked, "It'll be all right. Tell the boys I'll be back soon."

The officers with Ludwig turned toward the street. The leader said to the thirty or so people who had assembled, "Everyone stay back. This is a lawful action under the State of Emergency, and if anyone interferes, he or she will also be subject to arrest."

They walked Ludwig to the first car and put him in the back seat. The leader motioned for the crowd to give way, and they drove off.

Other elders had arrived during the process, and now they stood outside with Ludwig's wife and talked about what had happened. They agreed to meet at the church, hopefully with their attorney, at three that afternoon. And they agreed not to talk to the press until after their meeting.

The Network reporter tried to interview some of the men who seemed to be from the church, but when she was politely rebuffed, she focused on the neighbors for background information on the pastor and his family. Then she and the cameraman set out on the short drive to DCNet to file the story.

Clayton Hunt and Ahmad Rashid had duty that Monday at the Threat Identification Group in the Pentagon. At noon they took a break from reviewing email intercepts and had lunch together down the hall in one of the canteens. They put their trays down on a table by the window.

As they sat down, Ahmad said, "Thank you—and Andrea—again for your help with Mariam and the boys. Those were a scary few days."

"Of course. No problem. Hopefully with the State of Emergency those kinds of vigilantes won't resurface."

"I understand the reaction, in some ways, after a Muslim Air Force officer killed the president and so many others. Terrible. It makes everyone, even Mariam and me, question our faith. Or at least how some interpret it. Terrible. And it leaves a cloud over every Muslim, even those like us who love and appreciate our country."

Clayton nodded. "I got a text from Andrea just before we left for lunch that the government is apparently arresting preachers, rabbis and imams across the nation for violating the new No-Hate restrictions. So it's not just happening in the Muslim community. Apparently there's a lot of hate out there. Crazy."

"We can't all splinter into our own corners, our tribes. If we do, America will no longer be America. Look at China, where the central government is rounding up Uyghur Muslims by the tens of thousands and sending them to 're-education camps,' sterilizing the women, and using them all for forced labor in factories supplying clothing to U.S. manufacturers. It's terrible. We've got quite a group of Uyghurs here in D.C., and at our mosque. Mariam and I have been working with them; their stories of persecution are just terrible. We can't let America do like most other countries and divide up, persecuting the groups who are out of power. That's the opposite of 'Rule of Law.' It's 'Rule by Power.'"

"Agreed." Clayton said, shaking his head. "I didn't realize you were so involved with the Uyghurs here."

"Yes. They hate what's happening to their families, but most of them are afraid to say or to do anything, because the Chinese have spies and cameras everywhere, even here, and there's retribution at home if a son or daughter speaks out here."

"Can these U.S. manufacturers make a difference?"

"Are you kidding? They're even more afraid to raise a peep. The Chinese government will cut off their supplies and their access to the world's largest market."

"What's the answer?"

"We're thinking about that now. And I may need your help. We'll see."

"OK. Good. Just don't go off in a corner on your own." Clayton smiled, "How will I win you for Christ if you're off in your corner where I can't bug you?"

Ahmad laughed. "You're right. What would I do without your tracts and podcasts?"

"Yep. You know Andrea and I have been praying for you and Mariam for years, but we've ramped up since all this started. And, hey, I read the Koran, like you asked."

"You did."

"I couldn't make heads or tails out of much of it, as you know, but parts made sense."

More seriously, Ahmad said, "We're taught that 'making sense' is not the issue—it is the divine word of God, as given to his Prophet, whether we understand it or not."

"I know. And I get that, I guess. But you know how powerfully simple and understandable is the idea—built on the need for justice, as in the Koran—that by God's sacrifice of his Son for us, our debt has been paid for all time. No need for works or rituals. Done. We just have to repent and believe. Easily understandable, my friend. But so freeing, and so powerful."

Ahmad reached for his hamburger and smiled. "See, there you go again. The Son of God. We come to this same place every time we talk about it. I understand. But how can God have a son?"

Clayton smiled. "Because God has always been a triune entity, the first and most fundamental of all relationships. Three and yet one. Amazing."

"You're right, it would be boring if I were stuck in my own corner without you."

"That's the end of today's sermon. What are you guys doing this week?

"Actually, tonight and Thursday I've volunteered to be part of a rotating group of fathers and other men who stay at our sons' school, next to the Family and Friendship Mosque, in case anyone shows up wanting to spray paint, or worse. Since this all began we've been augmenting the security staff every night, just in case they need help."

"Will you be armed?"

"No. Just eyes, ears and persuasion in numbers, if needed. So far, there've been no incidents."

"I hope it stays that way. We don't need anything more to divide us."

As a routine part of his update with SAC Agent Prescott, and in preparation for that afternoon's NSC meeting, Tom received a list of the 36 men and women of faith who were being arrested that day for violating the Hate Speech directives. And he immediately noticed that Robert Ludwig was on the list.

When he returned to his office he picked up his cell phone, then put it down, thinking about the State of Emergency. He sat at his computer and wrote a short email to Callie: "Please don't call, text or write. I'll come by tonight."

Richard Sullivan, Tom's father, was in his Buckhead office that afternoon and finished reading a short email from Kristen Holloway. He called his pastor, Stan Conway.

"Richard, hey. I was about to call you. Is it about Robert Ludwig?"

"Yes. I just got an email from someone I know in D.C. who goes to Church of the Good Shepherd. The church elders are asking everyone to pray for their pastor—he's been arrested for violating the State of Emergency. Can you believe that?"

"I got a call from one of them after they had a meeting this afternoon. They've also been served with a notice from the police that for the duration of the emergency they can't talk about any details of the arrest, or specifically what 'hate speech' was involved, or give any type of interviews, because all those would be further opportunities to communicate or to condone the banned language. If any of the elders, or even other church members, violates the notice, then the elder board is also subject to being detained. And they had to take down the usual video archive of his message."

"Do you have any idea what he said?"

"His message was on Psalm 139. We actually spoke about it on Wednesday, and he sent me a copy of the draft. It's not hate speech."

"Incredible."

"And the worst thing is that I caved to the censor in my sermon yesterday and rewrote the parts she didn't like. But Robert didn't. I have to say that I'm embarrassed and ashamed."

"Because you're not in jail and still able to pastor our church?"

"I guess there are priorities to serving as pastor, and in this case I failed. Anyway, we're adding Good Shepherd's prayer request to our church's list, and sending it out to our larger network. We'll have our own elder board meeting this week to talk about next Sunday."

"OK. In the meantime, don't do anything rash. And if you send me Ludwig's sermon, I'll also take a look."

"Sorry I'm late," Seth said, as he closed their front door, put down his computer bag and gave Natalie a quick kiss in the kitchen. "A crazy day."

She looked up from the salad she was preparing on the counter. "I bet. I want to hear about it. Here's a glass of red. I'll join you on the patio."

A few minutes later as they settled into chairs with their wine, Natalie waited for him to speak. Unseen to them, Obman had followed Seth home from work; he also wanted to hear Seth's summary of the day.

Seth took a sip and then looked over at Natalie. "I am, to say the least, confused. As I texted you earlier, they arrested Callie's pastor for violating the Hate Speech directives at yesterday's service. I guess for talking about abortion and Jesus. I don't know."

"Can't you read the complaint?"

"It only states that Robert Ludwig failed to follow the government's restrictions on banned speech. No details. And, get this, we had a video crew which happened to be right there when they arrested him. The reporter put together a great package with footage of the arrest and interviews with the neighbors, but the government won't let us show any of it."

"Why?"

"They say it gives more credence to the hate speech to talk about it. Rachel is livid. The censors ordered her not to take any action."

"Can they do that?"

"No one knows. But no one wants to join Callie's pastor in jail to find out."

"That's terrible."

"Plus over thirty other priests and imams around the country. And even a rabbi! But other than saying just those facts, we can't report on any details."

"Were you offended by what he said yesterday?'

"Not really. But some could be, I guess. It sounded like he was condemning us to hell if we're not Christian believers."

"I think that's what Christians think Jesus said. And they've been believing it for two thousand years. Good news, I guess, for those who do believe."

"But hateful for those who don't...divisive."

She paused then said, "But I heard Ludwig say on a sermon I downloaded that the offer of salvation's *available* to everyone. Not dependent on race, country, income, education, social status, criminal record, anything. What could be more inclusive than that? It's a choice, not a designation based on our background, or a reward."

"I guess. It just sounds sometimes like they think they're better than the rest of us."

"Does Callie seem that way?"

"No, I guess not. Not Callie. Ludwig really didn't bother me, the way he put it. And those prayers. Where did those people learn to pray like that? They obviously believe that God listens and answers. Amazing. Anyway, all these government actions sounded so rational and reasonable when Emily and I talked about them ten days ago. And it's all for a good reason. But I just don't know...Anyway, how about you? How was your day?"

"Fine. Busy. It's my last week at the Drug Enforcement Agency before I rotate back to our offices. It's a little crazy. Even with the enhanced intercepts, we haven't found any connections between the attackers and the cartels, or their financial covers. Very frustrating."

Seth shook his head. "It makes no sense. *Someone* has to be responsible for these attacks. In the meantime, the government is writing the news."

Obman left to return to DCNet, convinced that they would have to work more on Natalie—she seemed to be hearing the truth from that damn church and, even worse, speaking it! But he also planned to report that Pastor Robert Ludwig appeared to be removed as a problem, at least for now. Was the American government about to start following most other nations in choking off God's truth? That would be incredible and could potentially change everything. Everywhere. Bespor and Prince Proklor needed to know.

Tom had not communicated with Callie since sending her the short email that morning. After leaving the White House he drove home, changed, and as the sun was setting put a leash on Beau and walked over to her row house. He found a handwritten note on her front door.

"Tom—we're at the church praying and talking. Come over and join us. Callie."

He looked at the note for a long while. One voice inside him—the tiny flicker of the Holy Spirit left from twenty years earlier when Tom made his confession of faith, but now nearly out—said to do just that, to turn all of this over to God. But the other, louder voices reminded him that this church was now flagged in their system, the pastor was in jail, they were having a meeting about it, and he'd been there yesterday—he couldn't afford to get any closer if he didn't want a lot of questions at work. As much as he liked Callie, he finally took the paper and wrote below her note, "I'll call you in the morning," and returned it to her door. Then he walked home with a detour by the park for some ball tosses.

Nepravel and the six other demons Nepravel brought with him to "flood the zone" around Tom that evening had been effective. Their combined voices had won out, and the angel stationed at the Church of the Good Shepherd to protect those praying never noticed Tom, several blocks away, in the spiritual darkness that surrounded him.

But when Tom got home he noticed Callie's stack from yesterday on the table in the front room. He picked them up and was about to put them down again when he wondered whether the second author, Gary Thornton, might also need to be reined in during the emergency. So he opened Thornton's book on the foundations of America, and began reading. The first chapter opened with a quote from George Washington's Inaugural Address in 1789:

*No people can be bound to acknowledge and adore the Invisible Hand which conducts the affairs of men more than those of the United States. Every step by which they have advanced to the character of an independent nation seems to have been distinguished by some token of providential agency...We ought to be no less persuaded that the propitious smiles of Heaven can never be expected on a nation that disregards the eternal rules of order and right which Heaven itself has ordained.*

Tom, who knew a lot about the history of the first president, both as a military leader and as a chief architect of the revolutionary American experiment, had never heard, or at least noticed, Washington's reference to Heaven's rules. He kept reading.

Jerry Kimble's wife thought he was getting a head start on a business trip when he left their home that evening, but in fact he—with Razdor next to him in the passenger seat—was headed out to fulfill his responsibility to stop the plague of fracking. The Lone Gunman of Western Pennsylvania planned to show his resolve again tonight.

In several other places across the country a few angry individuals or small groups who considered themselves to be victims of others' wrongs prepared to make amends with actions in the next day or two. Each was acting for specific, unconnected reasons to defend their group from others. But the timing was closely coordinated by the demonic army under Prince Proklor's control. Local strongholds had been working on their subjects for months, even years, ramping up their belief that whatever offense had first angered them now required action, fanned by Identity-enforcing docudramas and ever more divisive opinions on cable television and websites.

It included those abused by Catholic priests and Scout leaders in churches and schools. Neighbors enraged by the opening of a Muslim Student Center in their upscale community. Native Americans angry over 150 years of abuse and neglect. Groups fed up with abortion doctors killing children. Gays with multiple long-standing grievances. Transgender advocates tired of being oppressed by parents. Parents tired of seeing their daughters oppressed by transgender women. There were many reasons for Americans to be angry with each other and to want to get even. With demonic prodding, a few individuals concluded that action was not only right, but inevitable. And the time was now.

But the largest and potentially most deadly event was expected to occur in Washington the next morning.

# 12

*My only hope of salvation is in the infinite transcendent love of God manifested to the world by the death of his Son upon the Cross. Nothing but his blood will wash away my sins. I rely exclusively upon it. Come Lord Jesus! Come quickly!*

Benjamin Rush

Tuesday, September 29

At the White House meeting that midnight only Temno, Legat and Bespor met with Prince Proklor. All the other generals were in the field, encouraging their forces either to trigger a disaster or to sow seeds of hate, confusion and despair between warring groups as soon as an attack took place.

Although Bespor's report on the D.C. area focused on the upcoming events expected in the next hours, he mentioned Obman's observation that the new State of Emergency restrictions had effectively sidelined their Saturday night target, Pastor Ludwig, and also dampened the appetite of others, particularly more conservative news organizations, to push back against the government. These appeared to be two positive results from measures originally designed to defend against their attacks.

Prince Proklor listened to Bespor's report but then quickly agreed with his general's suggestion that they move to the area near the Family and Friendship Mosque, where they felt very much at home. As at most mosques, the spiritual darkness of Islam had been a great boon to the demons over many centuries.

As Satan's four most powerful leaders circled slowly around the mosque, Proklor observed, "Where would we be without the imams? Even the most peaceful ones make sure we send thousands of their people to the Abyss every day. Those people never have a chance, believing all the lies we told Muhammad all those years ago, and the imams keep teaching. What an investment that was!"

Temno nodded. "And the violent ones are the best. I laugh every time a suicide vest goes off! The look on their faces a few seconds after they pull the trigger and realize we're not virgins at an oasis—and see what they've actually done—it's just incredible."

The others smiled. "It never gets old," Bespor added.

It was a little after one in the morning when the Grantham siblings turned their rental van into the empty parking lot they had identified on Sunday afternoon. It was a crisp and clear night, with the first traces of cooler weather. A perfect night for flying a drone.

When they parked in the back corner of the lot, Ranit exited the van with them and surveyed the area. Spiritually, it appeared that the area was theirs.

They used the body of the van to block the view of their work from the street and from the warehouse with its single light pole, in case there was a camera. Within a few minutes the incredibly quiet drone and its AR-15 rifle were airborne, piloted by Teri. The controls were in a harness that she wore, while next to her Brad followed their route on a similar gunner's console.

The GPS coordinates for the Family and Friendship Mosque, which included a school, and the two other downtown Islamic centers, were pre-programmed into the flight plan. The drone rose to 400 feet and, without any lights, flew off almost invisibly to their first target.

The Granthams had agreed when they first decided on this course of action that even though a Muslim traitor had killed their brother and the president, their family were not killers. Their mission tonight was to send a message of warning to all Muslims who called themselves friendly to America, but who thereby provided a safe haven in which the radical killers could move and work. They would no longer be tolerated. They should leave and go back to whatever wadi they came from. And take their children, who would only make America worse.

Ahmad Rashid and three other men, one of whom was Kahar Bosakov, had volunteered to augment the security that night at the school adjoining the Family and Friendship Mosque, with which it shared a parking lot and a large, glassed-in entrance foyer. While two of the men slept on sofas in a nearby room, Ahmad and Kahar were sitting with the lone security guard in the foyer, reading and talking. Ahmad, who'd met Kahar earlier but had not spent much time with him, enjoyed, as always, telling a new arrival to America about how the country had transformed his family and given him opportunities which were unimaginable almost anywhere else. Kahar had not said much during the previous hour but had listened intently to the older Muslim's recounting of experiences which did seem to conform to his own observations of this place, so unlike his home.

"It's beautiful," Brad said to his sister, as she stabilized the drone's hover a hundred yards from the mosque's entrance, which shone like a bright light in the darkness. "Can we get closer?"

"Sure." Teri reduced altitude and moved in. They had studied all three targets extensively and knew that from the view on their screens the mosque itself was to the left, and the school to the right. The entrance was lit, but from their elevated angle they could not see anyone inside.

"Ready?" he asked.

"Weapon free," she responded.

From his tours in Afghanistan Ahmad knew the sound of incoming rounds. But for a moment he could not connect what he was hearing to where he was. Then there was breaking glass in the lobby and the security guard behind the desk next to them screamed, his leg a bloody mess.

"Get down," he yelled to Kahar. "Behind the desk." He was already loosening his belt to use as a tourniquet and moving toward the guard.

More rounds hit the floor and walls nearby, and then it was quiet, except for the guard's loud groans.

"I'll help," Kahar said, taking the belt and applying it to the guard's leg as he had been trained.

Ahmad pulled out his phone and dialed 911, telling. them to send an ambulance with the police. "Now!"

The Granthams flew their drone to its second target for the night. Proklor and his generals nodded to each other, then moved just across the bridge into Arlington, Virginia, to await what they expected would be the main event of the day.

Josh Weber and Mason Neal rose at five that morning and drove, accompanied by Umer and Vonyat, to their self-storage facility, which opened at six. Ten minutes later they drove off towing the plain white trailer with a Kentucky license plate. They headed away from D.C. on the interstate, then exited two miles later and reversed their course toward Arlington and the Pentagon City area next to Reagan National Airport.

Their preference would have been to place the trailer and its bomb under or almost touching the building, but the increased precautions of the last decade made that impossible. So they had settled on a four car taxi stand in the widened road outside the building. It was close enough so that the explosion plus the shrapnel would do a lot of damage to the same people who had done nothing to protect their children from early deaths.

As they drove they listened to the news, which was all about overnight attacks on two gas storage areas in Pennsylvania and on three mosques in the D.C. area. The latter was apparently from an airplane or drone. The details were sketchy, and officials were vague about any leads.

From the driver's seat Josh tipped his coffee cup to Mason. "That's pretty awesome." He smiled. "But just wait 'til the News at Noon!"

Mason laughed and touched his coffee to Josh's.

They arrived at the location about thirty minutes before sunrise. There were no taxis parked that morning, so they pulled into the designated area and got out wearing yellow, official looking vests and hard hats with medical masks covering their faces. Josh quickly unfolded a large orange Road Work sign on a tripod to block any view of the back of the trailer. They had practiced for a week, and in under two minutes they deployed eight orange cones around the trailer and affixed Arlington Department of Environmental Services signs to each side, complete with the logo and color scheme which they had copied from the internet.

When everything was set, and blocked by the Road Work sign, Mason unlocked the back door, reached inside, and activated the timer on the detonator. Then he closed and padlocked the door. Josh handed him the stolen license plate, which he exchanged for theirs. Taking their plate, they went to the front of the trailer and unhitched it from the truck. As a final precaution Josh took a bucket of mud from the back of the pickup and threw the contents on the truck's tailgate, bumper and license plate. From trial and error they knew that this preparation would obscure the plate for at least ten miles of driving.

They took one last look around. They saw what appeared to be an official Department of Environmental Services work trailer, pre-positioned for a project that morning. Satisfied, they returned to the cab and drove off, again heading east for several miles before reversing for home. Umer and Vonyat stayed with the trailer, waiting.

Tom's phone had buzzed at four, and he had been with Rob Thompson in the basement of the White House in the Situation Room since five that morning on a video connection to James Toomey and Tanya Prescott at FBI. There were also feeds from The NSA, The Network and from a local station in Pittsburgh. The regular duty officers were managing inputs from their adjoining stations outside the large conference room.

With the sun almost up, Director Toomey was describing the new damage in the areas around the two gas storage facilities using real-time satellite images when President Bradshaw joined them in jeans and a casual shirt. The two men stood, but Bradshaw signaled for them to sit, and for the briefing to continue.

"The only good news this morning is that in none of the five target areas do we have any reports of a fatality. A security guard at one of the mosques was badly wounded."

"And how does someone shoot up three mosques in ten minutes without a small army?" the president asked.

"Sir, probably with a drone. Maybe two. That's our working assumption."

"Where did it take off from, and land?"

"We don't know. Obviously it was dark. They're almost impossible to see or hear."

"You mean you can just fly a drone around a major city and shoot at anything you want, and no one can stop you?"

"With some warning there are potential countermeasures, but right now the defensive technology is limited to a pretty localized area that you're trying to protect, like the White House, or a stadium."

"Great. And what about the gas explosions? Drones as well?"

"We don't know. Perhaps. But it takes a large incendiary round to penetrate and ignite a tank, so it's more likely a sniper rifle."

Bradshaw paused and then looked at Tom and Rob. "Do we have any credible leads to who did the attacks?"

"No, not yet," Tom answered.

He looked up to Agent Prescott on the screen. "So we obviously don't have any connections between the two."

She shook her head. "No, sir."

"Great. Call me if anything changes. We've got the vice president's swearing in ceremony at nine. All the press will be here. Emily needs your input on what we can and should say by eight." He left the room.

Seth had also been awakened early and was already on the way to the White House briefing room. He'd tried to dress quietly, but Natalie got up to tell him goodbye. Now as she dressed and ate yogurt with berries she kept one eye on the news. It was not good. All the D.C. Metro area had been placed on the highest threat alert by the Regional Security Network. Not a good start to a Tuesday.

She decided to get a jump on the traffic, since she was up anyway, and headed off to work.

Forty minutes later, a little after eight-fifteen, she settled into the office she had used for almost a month on her rotation to DEA. The rightful occupant was on maternity leave, and from the tenth floor Natalie had a great view to the northeast of the Pentagon and the Washington Mall, in the distance to the left of the hotel across the street. She put her computer bag on the desk and looked out, holding a cup of coffee. The public works trailer parked below didn't register as she watched the traffic cross the bridges into the city.

Matt Davis and Sara Bryant had been partners on the Arlington County Police Department for almost a year. With the mosque shootings in D.C. only hours before, their captain had ordered all available units into the streets that morning and encouraged them to keep an eye on the sky in case the early assessment of a drone attack proved to be correct.

Matt, the more senior of the two and nearly six inches shorter in height, drove their cruiser as they patrolled their assigned beat around Pentagon City. "I've seen videos of rifles mounted on drones," Matt said, reaching for his coffee in the center console, "and I remember thinking that would be a hell of a weapon to go up against."

Sara nodded as they drove west on 12th Street to the intersection with South Fern Street. Matt was about to turn left, but Sara pointed right and said, "Let's go up Fern. Yeah. Now maybe we are. And at night. Wonderful."

It had just turned nine o'clock as they passed the DEA Headquarters on their left and the hotel on the right. When they stopped at the traffic light at Army Navy Drive, Sara was looking in her side mirror and said, "Hey, go around the block again."

"Why?"

"Something wasn't right about that DES trailer."

"Eyes like a hawk," he smiled. "But remember we're supposed to be watching the sky, not trailers."

"It'll just take a minute."

Ahmad Rashid spent several hours at the hospital answering questions with the police while their mosque's security guard was in the ICU. Unfortunately neither he nor Kahar had seen or heard anything except the incoming rounds, which was not helpful to the investigation.

Now he was driving, exhausted, back to the mosque, and talking to Clayton Hunt on his hands-free phone.

"I feel like I've got to go, Clayton. Mariam says there's a big meeting. People are angry. They want to fight back."

Clayton was walking to their command center in the Pentagon from the parking lot. "I understand. No one expects you here today after what happened. Will the guard be OK?"

"Not sure. The rounds just missed his bone."

"OK. You try to calm everyone down, and we'll try to find whoever did it. Check back this afternoon after you get some rest."

Matt pulled the cruiser up behind the DES trailer. "See," Sara said. "That's not a local government license plate, and it doesn't end in L."

"Wow. You do have good eyes."

"Run it, and I'll take a look." She got out and he, as was procedure, turned on the cruiser's blue flashing lights, which reflected off the windows of the hotel.

Natalie was working on a report at her desk but noticed the blue reflections and stood up to look down at the street. She saw the driver of the police cruiser get out and walk over to his taller female partner next to the DES trailer, holding an iPad.

She could not see Umer and Vonyat who had stayed behind to hover over the trailer and to report the upcoming results to their stronghold. They had been unhappy to see the police cruiser approach. And when Sara Bryant exited the car, they were angered to see the bright spiritual light shining in her. A believer, she would be difficult to influence with voices of *Uncertainty* and *Impatience*. Umer appealed to Bespor, hovering nearby with Prince Proklor, and within a minute the area was filled with demons whom the prince summoned from all over the city.

Matt looked up from his iPad. "Son of a gun. You were right. That plate was reported stolen last week."

"So what's it doing here, on a public works trailer?" She looked around and suddenly felt a terrible oppression and a deep chill. Her voice changed to a near-whisper. "Next to the DEA Headquarters and a tall hotel?"

"I'll see if Spike's available, and you check with DES," Matt said, as cars streamed steadily past them on the busy street.

Sara snapped a photo and sent it with a text to the dispatcher at Public Works. Unfortunately he was coordinating a water main break and didn't see it when it dropped into his In box.

"Spike can be here in less than ten. I told'em to come on." Matt looked at the two buildings and the traffic. "I don't much like this."

They walked around the trailer again and noticed that the DES signs looked less than professionally done. They returned to their cruiser, and Sara called DES on the county radio circuit. After two tries the dispatcher came on the line. She pointed him to her text and asked if they had a project scheduled on Fern Street. As Sara heard a police siren approaching he came back on the line thirty seconds later. "We don't have a project there, and we don't have any trailers like that."

The K-9 patrol cruiser pulled up behind them and the driver turned off the siren. He got out with Spike, a German Shepherd, one of ACPD's two bomb-sniffing dogs. As soon as they approached the trailer it didn't take an expert to tell that Spike definitely had a "hit." His handler nodded, and Matt immediately got on his radio.

Natalie had watched the commotion from her window, including how the officer with the radio kept looking up at her building and pointing. The handler put the dog in the cruiser and started running up the drive to the hotel, while the female officer dodged the traffic and crossed the street to her building. Natalie gasped as the officer leapt to the curb to keep from being hit by a car which accelerated directly toward her.

Natalie knew something was happening and unplugged her laptop, put it in her bag, and grabbed her coat. As she exited her office into the open area outside, others who had been looking out their windows either came to their doors, or were clearly on the way out.

A tsunami of demons flooded the building, their eyes wide with excitement at the prospect of what was to come. They screamed silently with the powerful voices of *Confusion, Don't Panic and There's Nothing to Worry About*. Nepravel, Balzor and Obman arrived from the Capitol area and joined the fight to keep everyone calm and at their desks for just a few more minutes. Obman immediately recognized Seth's girlfriend. He spoke to her.

"Wait a minute," she thought. "Most people aren't leaving. I shouldn't overreact. I'll never get this report done."

Natalie stopped walking and felt a little foolish. She turned to go back to take another look down from her office window when a middle-aged woman in accounting, Valerie, grabbed her arm and said, "Let's go." Valerie, who had been at the DEA for years and had two sons in high school, had acted as Natalie's liaison when she first arrived for her assignment.

With Obman still at Natalie's side, Valerie quickly led her to their floor's elevator lobby. They noticed others starting down the stairs in the central stairwell, and followed. As they rounded the turn to the eighth floor, the evacuation alarm went off with a piercing shriek.The emergency lights flashed. A voice came over the loudspeaker. "Evacuate the building using the stairwells. Evacuate the building using the stairwells. Walk west toward the Museum and away from Fern Street."

Almost immediately the stairwell was flooded with people and the descent became a slow crawl.

As the two officers returned to the trailer and more sirens converged on the area, Matt directed the K-9 cruiser to go south and block traffic heading north from 12th Street, while he and Sara pulled their cruiser into the intersection with Army Navy Drive and prevented any cars from driving south. Others would have to block Army Navy Drive east and west of the interchange.

As they directed traffic, they could see guests and staff from the hotel walking east, and workers from the DEA headquarters walking west. More cruisers took up positions to expand the perimeter, and a helicopter arrived overhead. The hotel soon appeared to be emptied, but people were still streaming down and out of the office building.

A minute later the ACPD SWAT Team Mobile Command Center pulled into the intersection, and Sara recognized members of the Bomb Squad getting out. Their captain jogged over. "Great job. Now pull over to Hayes Street. You're too close here."

Sara nodded and ran west on the sidewalk while Matt started the cruiser. She noticed that there was no traffic on I-385, a short distance to the north. She also saw that most people were exiting out of the northwest corner of the DEA building, on the side away from the trailer, into a courtyard with a similar building further to the west, the DEA Museum and Visitor Center. Sara jogged into the courtyard and over to the headquarters' main entrance doors. As she looked beyond the people streaming out, she could see others heading to the doors on the opposite corner, which would put them directly in front of the trailer on Fern Street.

When Natalie and Valerie reached the lobby, they moved west with the crowd towards the exit on the Museum side. Valerie, right behind Natalie, glanced to her left and saw quite a few people going to the less crowded exit on Fern Street.

"They're going the wrong way," she said, and left Natalie to warn them.

Sara radioed her intent to Matt and wedged her way through the tide coming out of the lobby. Natalie stepped back to let Sara slide past her inside, and just as she did the trailer exploded with a huge fireball and pressure wave, throwing nails and shrapnel in all directions. All the glass on the east side of the DEA building was shredded, and a portion of the building's facade nearest the explosion collapsed, as did the ceiling in the lobby.

Sara was hit by glass flying through the lobby and fell back on Natalie.

Those moving toward the southeast exit on Fern Street were hit by the full force of nails and glass, and were decimated.

The closest police officers and SWAT team Bomb Squad members were gravely wounded or killed, including the Captain. Only those working to get the tracked robot out of the back of their van were untouched.

Matt, whose cruiser had been protected by the building, got out and ran toward the main entrance doors, as people in the courtyard screamed, and the wounded crawled forward or lay still.

Proklor and his staff looked on and smiled. He was glad they had called in so many of their forces to confuse people to remain inside the building, or to go out the wrong exit. Now they would be helpful in rounding up the large number of souls suddenly freed from their bodies by the explosion and the carnage. All would be taken to the Judgment Seat. If several millennia of results were predictive, Proklor knew that this event would produce a great harvest. A good morning.

Clayton Hunt's Target Identification Group Command Center was on the outside ring of the Pentagon on the south side of the complex, and despite the thick walls, they felt the explosion from across I-385.

Megan Buckley looked at Clayton from her console. "What the hell was that?"

A minute later, as reports started to stream in, they knew that a third major attack had occurred that morning.

Valerie was halfway across the lobby, walking next to the windows, and had just raised her hand to yell for attention when the bomb exploded. She felt excruciating pain as the blast pressure ruptured her eardrums and collapsed her chest, just before the splintered glass and metal shards tore into her. As she hit the floor, everything went dark and silent.

But then her vision, hearing and sense of smell all returned, all at once, and in a riot. The combined effect was like snapping her out of a deep sleep, and she looked down at her mangled, bloody body. What was she seeing? How could anyone with exposed inner organs be alive? And then it occurred to her: her body was dead, but she was alive. How could that be?

She looked around at the chaos and heard the screams. She could taste metal and smelled burning flesh. But her vision was different from just the minute before. She saw some sort of dark creatures circling above, and recognizable spirits—souls?—rising from the bodies of those around her. She felt no pain, and was thankful, as she watched the badly wounded but still living victims writhing from their deep cuts and lacerations. And she saw blood splattered on all the columns, and on the ceiling.

As her perspective rose—not from her action—she could see that on the far side of the lobby there was also mayhem and people in great pain, but not the total destruction and death immediately around her.

As she continued to rise she somehow went through each of the upper floors and noticed that the effects of the blast continued on these floors as well, but there were only a few dead or wounded bodies.

She was trying to understand exactly how all this could be possible when she broke through the roof and could look down on the entire area, including the courtyard between their two buildings, the adjacent hotel, and the surrounding streets. There were people running everywhere, and the cacophony from approaching sirens grew louder and louder.

But arriving outside what struck her the most was the army of those same dark spiritual beings circling and then lining up in groups around the many souls—that's all she could imagine they were—rising with her from the devastation below. They were everywhere. And those that weren't circling the souls were watching from the perimeter, pointing and apparently talking to themselves.

Suddenly four of them approached her, and she could instantly feel their hate and disdain. But then they passed near her and went on to circle Roy Gardner from HR, whom Valerie saw several yards away. He was looking her way and suddenly seemed to be in utter terror as they drew close to him.

For a moment Valerie thought about her husband and her two sons. Where were they, and were they OK? Did they know what had happened? What *had* happened?

Then another four of the dark spirits came up to her from the opposite direction, but they, too, passed her by. She was looking around, seeing so many of her colleagues surrounded by these creatures, when she looked down and noticed that she appeared to be radiating an inner light. She looked up again and saw a few others with this same light in them, and none of them was surrounded by the dark figures as they rose. But everyone else was. What was going on?

Then several bright lights started to appear from much higher up and very far away, coming toward this awful scene. As the lights approached, they spread out, and suddenly Valerie was confronted by a large, intensely bright male-like figure only a few feet in front of her. She tried to turn, to escape, but she could not.

"Don't be afraid," he said in a calm voice that seemed out of place for the majesty he displayed. "I have been sent to help you."

She looked around at all the mayhem on the ground and the activity in the air and was ready to let someone help her. She relaxed just a little and decided to follow him, though she was aware that her wishes didn't matter. He moved up and away, and she simply followed.

Tom had returned upstairs to his office at eight-thirty after reviewing with Emily a draft statement of outrage and determination over the gas explosions and the mosque shootings for the president to open the morning's ceremony in the Rose Garden. While that event began, Tom caught up on the Pennsylvania explosions and noted that there was nothing new or actionable from either law enforcement or their covert intercepts.

He looked at his watch and took out his phone to call Callie when it and his laptop surged with alarms, and the Situation Room Duty Officer sent a high priority text asking him to return.

In the Rose Garden Patricia Reynolds had just been sworn in again by the Chief Justice and was beginning her remarks to the press at the podium, with President Bradshaw standing to the left behind her. Garrett Crose came to the president's side and spoke to him. There was a brief exchange, and then the president stepped forward, interrupting his new V.P.

"Patricia, forgive me," he said loud enough to be heard on the live news feed. He turned to the audience. "And all of you, as well. There has apparently been another attack at or near the Pentagon, which we have to deal with. The Secret Service asks that you all please move quickly to the Press Room, where you will shelter in place until we know more. Right now we're needed in the Situation Room. We'll give you a full report as soon as we can."

With that he, the new V.P., and the members of their immediate staffs walked quickly up the stairs behind the podium and into the White House.

Thirty minutes later, closeted in the Situation Room with his Core Group and linked to the FBI and the key Secretaries of State, Defense, and Homeland Security, it was clear to President Bradshaw that the nation was again—or still—under a deadly siege from an unknown aggressor.

The first reports and pictures from Arlington, just across the Potomac River from where they were sitting, were horrendous. There would be many deaths and terrible casualties. And it would have been much, much worse except for the brave actions of two front line police officers who noticed something out of place and acted.

"If two officers on the ground can get it right with nothing but their eyeballs and guts, why can't the most sophisticated intelligence network on Earth give us a single heads-up on what's about to happen, or a lead on who's behind three more attacks in less than twelve hours?" he fumed at Tom, James Toomey, Agent Prescott, General Price, and everyone else in the room and on video links.

There was a long silence. Finally Tom said, "We'll follow up on the new information and hopefully have good leads in twenty-four hours."

The president turned even darker red. "Tom, you, Agent Prescott, General Price, and all the others," he waved his hand, "have been saying that for over two weeks, and while you've done a great job of arresting bank robbers, drug pushers, and the lowest members of the terrorists' food chain, you have no idea who is actually leading and planning these attacks. That is totally unacceptable to the American people, and to me."

There was another long silence. A little calmer, the president said, "Rob, clearly we have to postpone tomorrow's Memorial Service. We can't assemble the whole government in one place to make an easy target for another bomb. And the measures in our State of Emergency are obviously not strong enough. We need to tighten down more, until we find and destroy this enemy. I want every member of the NSC to propose new steps in your areas that we should take under the State of Emergency to unmask these people. Give Tom Sullivan and Agent Prescott your recommendations this afternoon. We're not going to play around anymore. Those who promote hate among us will be removed from our midst. Those who attack us will be destroyed. We are a peace loving, free people, and we won't be bullied. Am I clear?"

He stood. "Good. Let's meet again at noon for a full update. Meanwhile, keep us posted on any leads." He turned and walked toward the door. "Emily and Rob, I'd like to see you in the Oval Office in an hour."

Emily, who had been sitting next to Tom at the conference table, leaned nearer and asked, "Isn't that where Natalie's been working?"

He grimaced. "I think you're right."

"I saw Seth in the Rose Garden. I'll tell him we'll try to let him know if we get any news on her."

He nodded, and she stood. "I hope you find these bastards."

Seth had joined the other reporters in the Press Room and was one of the first to learn that a bomb had been detonated outside the DEA in Arlington. He immediately called Natalie's number, but there was no answer. He called his office and told his boss, Rachel Shaw, that he was "trapped" at the White House and that Natalie had been at DEA. Rachel assured him they would do everything possible to find out about her as they reported on the attack, but that he was not the only one "trapped"—a directive had just been issued telling everyone in D.C. to stay in place until 2pm. Only emergency and essential vehicles would be allowed to move in the greater D.C. area until then.

When he hung up he heard more sirens and could see trucks arriving with troops. Shortly the White House was surrounded with armed defenders.

A staff person came out and promised a press briefing before noon. She saw Seth and gave him a note from Emily, saying they would let him know if they heard about Natalie.

He sat at the back of the room and every few minutes dialed Natalie's phone. And, he couldn't believe it, but he found himself praying for her.

Alexei Nobikov had returned to Cyprus on Sunday from his visit to Boston and Washington. On Tuesday afternoon he was at his desk as news reports were ramping up from the mosque attacks and then from the bombing in Arlington.

Sveta Pankratova came to the open door of his office. "I've called everyone in. We should have new postings on all the websites and chat rooms by the end of the day. Both haters and victims."

Nobikov nodded from his chair. "Thank you. And thank you for the report on Tom Sullivan. Cybersecurity and now National Security Advisor. Quite a rise for a young man. And his mother was a Congresswoman. He must be in the thick of the president's policy decisions as they deal with these attacks. We definitely need to keep our eye on him. My niece takes a class from a woman whom I guess he's seeing. I'd love to figure out a way to understand how he thinks."

She nodded, and when he said no more, she smiled and walked away. He turned in his chair and looked out at the Mediterranean Sea just beyond the beaches two blocks from his window. In the silence as he was thinking, suddenly he heard a quiet voice within speak words which startled him, telling him to pray. The voice wasn't audible, but almost. He looked back at the empty doorway, then turned again and bowed his head. He was startled because the voice said that he was to pray for America.

Officer Matt Davis had rushed to the main entrance of the DEA building, and just inside the tattered doors he found Sara Bryant alive but unconscious, badly cut from the face down by multiple wounds and bleeding profusely, lying on top of another woman's back. Many others, some terribly wounded, lay around them. A few were moaning. As he took off his shirt to press against Sara's worst wounds, the other woman stirred and tried to move. Matt lifted Sara a bit, and the other woman slid from under her and rose slowly to her knees.

"Are you OK?" he asked. All around them were groans, cries for help, and a few muffled screams.

"I—I don't know. I can hardly hear. I think so." Blood trickled down the back of her right arm from a surface laceration.

"This is my partner. Sara. We were clearing the building. Can you hold my shirt here while I try to get help?"

Natalie nodded, moving to a better position. "I think I saw you out the window. Yes. Go."

For twenty minutes Natalie knelt next to Sara in the chaos, keeping pressure on the wounds on her head and chest. Several times she looked for Valerie. Once she quickly pulled her phone out of her purse to call Seth, but there was no service. Her head was splitting, but as she looked around she knew that she had been very lucky. Sara had saved her life, both by emptying the building and by taking the brunt of the blast when it came. Tears formed in Natalie's eyes, and she bent down to whisper in Sara's ear. She unashamedly whispered strong, specific prayers for Sara, and for all those around her.

Natalie's prayer combined with others on site and many, many more incoming prayers from around the country and the world. In the midst of the devastation, the spiritual light started to brighten. Obman, who had been planting voices of *Despair, Defeat, Anger* and *Revenge* in the survivors noticed the change and looked up in time to see several angels arriving, sent by God, he imagined, and drawn by the spiritual lights in the believers who had died. They ordered the demons to leave. Obman hated them but had to obey—so he and the others pulled back.

Forty minutes after the blast, Natalie was riding in an ambulance next to Sara, who was still unconscious. Natalie's arm had a bandage, but the EMT focused on Sara. Matt had given Natalie a scrap of paper with his cell phone number. She put it in her purse and tried again to call Seth. This time the call went through and he answered.

"Natalie! Are you OK? Where are you?"

"Yes. I'm OK. I've got a lot to tell you."

Valerie could not be sure how far they travelled, or how long it took, but she and her guide were approaching a brilliantly bright, immense room. There were more angels like the one leading her, but also magnificent, winged creatures with two heads and four wings, flying with one set of wings while covering their faces and feet with the other set and shouting, "Holy, Holy, Holy is the Lord God of Hosts." And voices from all sides were lifting a steady harmony of praise and worship, proclaiming His glory and His righteousness.

Valerie realized that she had arrived at the Throne of God.

The Light appeared as a large human form, seated on a huge throne. Next to Him, at His right hand, was a white Lamb, alive, but with his throat cut, as if the Lamb had been sacrificed. Valerie realized that it was just like in the Book of Revelation, which their couples' small group had studied the previous year. Incredible!

In the next moment Valerie began reliving her entire life on earth, from childhood through school, her jobs, marriages, the years of raising their sons, her return to the DEA. Her clear achievements. Her friend Julie's insistence that she consider the truth of the Gospel. Her devastation, repentance and surrender to her Savior after the trials of her failed first marriage, her affair, divorce, and a guilt-filled abortion. The parents she increasingly cared for. The brother who never helped her, but to whom she had witnessed for years. The gifts she had been given, and which she used with her husband and their church to help others. Her bravery that day in trying to help others in danger.

She was alone with her Creator, who was judging her, just as He had always promised He would.

When her life review was completed, the Light spoke. "She has sinned and cannot partake of heaven, where there is no sin." Then the Light addressed the Lamb, and asked, "Is her name written in the Book of Life?"

The Lamb, also surrounded by brilliant Light, replied, "Yes, Father. Her sins are atoned for by the Blood of the Lamb. She believes. She is my adopted sister."

"Then welcome, my daughter, into the Wedding Feast of the Lamb," were the magnificent words Valerie's soul heard from God Almighty. "And now, meet your brother and Savior, and all your many brothers and sisters."

Valerie's soul leapt for joy. Slowly she moved beyond the throne room into a large, beautiful field with green grass and wildflowers, with a stream of crystal clear water running through it, and a brilliant sky above. There, waiting for her, was Jesus. He took her in his arms. She collapsed. He lifted her up.

"Here. You're home. Well done, good and faithful sister. You have all eternity ahead of you. There's so much to do, and so many to meet. Let's walk a bit and then sit. We have a lot to talk about."

Tom was again in his office. He had intended to find out what happened with Pastor Robert Ludwig that morning, until the attacks derailed him. Now he checked the morning report and read that Ludwig was being held at the Federal Detention Center in Maryland. He dialed Callie's number.

Immediately she asked, "Are you OK?"

"Yes. I'm fine."

"I've been so worried since I didn't hear from you."

He smiled. "I've been a little busy."

"I know. I'm sorry. But isn't that where Natalie's working?"

"I think so. We're checking."

She was silent for a moment. "And I think one of those mosques is where Andrea's Muslim friends go, and to the school."

"I didn't know. We're not aware of any injuries beyond the one security guard who's in bad shape."

"Did you hear about Pastor..."

"Yes. Listen, we're going a little crazy here. How about if you stay home tonight, and I'll come over as early as I can?"

"That would be good."

"In fact, you guys just stay home all day. I don't want anything to happen to you. We still have those stories to share."

After a pause for a smile, she said. "We will. Grace loves to bake. We'll have some cookies waiting."

"Great. See you then."

A few minutes later, Emily came to Tom's door. "Seth just called. Natalie's alive but on the way to the hospital. That's all I know. But the president would like you to join us."

"Uh, OK. Do you know which hospital she's in?" He closed his laptop and picked up a legal pad. They walked the short distance to the Oval Office, where the president motioned for them to take seats on the sofas. He joined them in a chair.

"Tom, we need to have a short conversation, moved up by these terrible attacks today. You know better than most that we call the group in the Situation Room our Core Group, and it is, for dealing with this mess and for implementing government policies. Sometimes, as you've seen, I have to get upset with them to keep them all focused.

"But we have another small team—the one that will design and enact the policies that the rest of the government will follow. Patricia Reynolds, Rob Thompson, Nancy Cantrell, Emily, plus the newly elected President Pro-Tem of the Senate, Gerry Veazy from Ohio, who also happens to be our Progressive Majority Leader, and four members from my former Senate staff are the leaders. Gerry and I have known each other for two decades. He's been a great booster for our causes in the Senate. Hopefully after the elections in six weeks Nancy will be the Speaker of the House. Then we'll control all three branches, and we can finally get things done.

"Tom, we need someone with your abilities and judgment on the security side. You may not be the oldest or most experienced in that area, but we've watched you through this and like the way you reach out and coordinate the best experts in the field. If you'd like to join this team, we'll drop 'Acting' from your title and stop looking for a replacement. But the choice is yours. Everyone on this team is committed to transforming America through a progressive program of diversity, social justice and true equity. If you'd like to be a part of that future, then we're inviting you to join us. If not, that's OK. Again, it's up to you."

Emily smiled at him from the opposite sofa. Tom was not prepared for this conversation. He had just been thinking about how he had failed and about new ways to spoof the unseen enemy into revealing more details. But the thought of being the actual National Security Advisor at this time of great threat, and the responsibilities that came with it, were potentially life changing. Despite not yet uncovering the attackers, the president apparently liked him and appreciated his work. Emily must have put in a good word. And what doors might this open in the future? How could he turn down the president of the United States asking for help at this difficult time?

Tom looked over at the president. "I'm in."

Bradshaw smiled. "Good. Good. We look forward to your input. Now, back to the situation. I believe these attacks today have changed everything—and God forbid there are more tomorrow. Anti-Muslim. Anti-business. Anti-law enforcement. And these will just stir up more hate and more counter attacks. We've got to stop them. We've got to clamp down more. I want our new V.P. to spearhead our National Unity Task Force to bring down this enemy. With your help, push the NSC, FBI and law enforcement to double down on our surveillance and interdiction until we find and destroy these people.

"We'll announce her new role as the Head of the Task Force at our noon meeting and then publicly this afternoon. Hopefully the American people will accept this as a positive step, even if we haven't found the bad actors. But we will. Please help Patricia get up to speed very quickly. Emily and our team have been working on probable members for the task force and an announcement. Today's attacks have moved that up, which is why we're meeting with you now.

"But another important thing we have to do, and the two goals work together—is to win the midterm elections in November, to give America a chance for a much better tomorrow when we finally do crush these terrorists.

"We expect the headline for our election campaign to be National Unity, but the subtext will always be our progressive agenda. How it's better for everyone to rise together, particularly after everyone has suffered together. Emily and her team will work that theme into the news on a daily basis. The Project Phoenix team—that's what we call this small group—will be recommending specific people as seconds to the Cabinet Secretaries we inherited from President Rhodes, to fill the important next-level positions in their areas.

"We can't change policies and dismiss the old Cabinet when we're also calling for National Unity in the elections, but we can do it right after the elections are over. And these six weeks will give our future Secretaries of State, Defense, etc., time to learn the ropes in their departments—and for you to introduce them to the realities of this new world we're in. So, for now, we'll continue on with who we have. But we wanted you to be aware of our greater goal for the nation so that you can do everything you can to help the new appointees, as well as be on the lookout for any possible sabotage of our plans, like Diane Marsh tried."

Tom took it all in and nodded.

"We're glad to have you on our other important team. When you hear about a strategy or a person or a program proposed, you'll know how it fits into the larger strategy we've undertaken. Any questions?"

"Not now. I'll do my best to help, with a first priority to stop the attackers." He looked at Emily, who was smiling.

"Good. A lot to do. Emily, it's probably not safe for us to visit the mosques today, but let's get their leaders on the phone, or invite them here. Tom, with all the cameras in D.C., there must be a lead on who parked that trailer by the DEA. We need answers. I'll be back in the Situation Room in a few minutes."

The president stood, and Tom left for his office.

When he walked into it a voice told him "This is now *my* office, not a seat I'm keeping warm for someone else." *Pride. Elite Accomplishment.* "The president has confidence in me, shared his vision for the nation with me, and asked me to join his inner circle." *Entitled.* "A great opportunity and a great responsibility."

He *had* to find the attackers. And very soon.

As he sat down his Trusted Core Group phone rang. Tanya Prescott. "We may have some good news."

The expanded Core Group and NSC heads met in the Situation Room in person and via video links at noon. The Secretary of Homeland Security and FBI Director Toomey gave them an overview of what was known so far about each of the three most recent attacks. While the first two were bad, the damage and the death toll from the DEA bombing held everyone's immediate focus.

As the update was concluding, Tom, sitting three chairs down from President Bradshaw, could sense his rising frustration. As the president was about to speak, Tom said, "Mr. President, turning from what has happened to who may have done it, the FBI has some new information."

All eyes turned to Agent Prescott on a video screen. "Yes. Here is a close up of the back of the trailer in a photo taken by one of the police officers who first thought something was not right. The license plate is, in fact, stolen, and not one used by Virginia governments. The trailer appears to be homemade—a very good job—so there will not likely be any identification numbers on any parts that may have survived the blast, as there were in Oklahoma City.

"But if you look closely you'll see three scratches on the right-hand door—perhaps made when it was opened up against a wall or a post with a nail. We don't know, and the scratches are not that pronounced, but they're visible."

"All morning we've been running the footage from surveillance cameras on the interstates and roads radiating out twenty miles from the DEA building, looking first for a trailer like this, and then for those scratches. The camera resolution and computer search capability required wouldn't have been possible a year ago, but now they are. I'm pleased to report that we have a positive match, and a valid license plate."

"Excellent, Agent Prescott," the president exclaimed. "And Director Toomey."

Toomey nodded. "Yes. But these developments must remain absolutely secure. We have a lot to do before we make a move."

Everyone nodded. Tom felt a glimmer of hope.

An hour after the travel ban was lifted Seth made it to Natalie's hospital bed. She was connected to an IV and a monitor and had several bandages, but she was sitting up, watching the news, and smiled when he came in. He immediately gave her a kiss.

"I'm so glad you're OK! When I didn't hear from you for an hour, it wasn't good."

She nodded. "It wasn't a good hour. I tried to call, but the service was out. And imagine how glad I am to see you!" They held hands. She clicked off the TV. "It looks as bad on TV as it did on the ground."

Seth just watched her. "Can you talk about it?"

She paused. "I would probably be dead except for a tall female police officer who apparently first spotted the bogus trailer and then happened to be standing right next to me when it detonated—she took the glass and shrapnel that would have hit me."

"Where is she?"

"Here somewhere. We came in the same ambulance, but she never woke up. An hour ago they said she was in surgery."

"What's her name?"

"Sara Bryant."

"I'll pray for her."

"You'll *pray* for her?"

He nodded. "Yes, after seeing how those people at Callie's church prayed on Sunday, when I didn't know what might have happened to you, I decided to pray just like they did. For you. Those people clearly believe God is real and answers prayers. Christians don't have a monopoly on prayer. Jews have prayed to the same God from the beginning. So I decided that if He actually could be real, I need to be praying, too. I prayed for you all morning."

Natalie waited to see if he was joking, but he wasn't. "Yes, I prayed for Sara in the ambulance. And for all the others."

"So let's pray now. For her, for them, for Tom and Emily and our nation."

He took her hand in his, and they bowed their heads.

Tom spent an hour that afternoon reviewing with Vice President Patricia Reynolds all facets of the requirements and restrictions in the current State of Emergency, and the logic for each one. He also went over a detailed Org Chart showing all the departments and agencies involved with implementing and enforcing the Executive Orders under the operational control of the FBI.

Then they had a lengthy video conference from the VP's office with General Price in which they discussed how to put more pressure on those advocating hate, and on those carrying it out. General Price believed they had every source open for intercepting messages or money movements that would indicate an organizer. And he promised the VP that his team would reevaluate what else could be done, including planting stories of deception in order to ferret out the perpetrators. And they discussed making better public examples of those who violated any of the prohibitions on hate speech.

Meanwhile the news continued to come across on all three attacks. Late in the day Tom watched a piece with Seth standing as close to the DEA HQ as the police would allow. A great part of one side of the building was missing. Tom imagined that Seth would now be even more motivated to help them find the attackers.

And they all expected to hear something any minute from the lead on the trailer which the FBI had opened up with its forensic video work. Tom worked late in his office, then said goodnight to those still there and headed to Callie's.

"Am I too late?" he asked when she opened the door to her apartment.

"Come in. Grace has been hoping to see you and to offer you her cookies."

Callie's daughter came into the living room in her pajamas, carrying a plate of cookies.

Tom said, "I'm so glad to see you. And thank you." He took a cookie and, after Grace gave the plate to her mother, he hugged her. She hugged back. They stood together and chatted for a few minutes about Grace's day, and then Callie said it was time for bed. Tom was left alone for five minutes while Grace brushed her teeth and said her prayers. Tom looked at the titles on Callie's several bookshelves.

"Now, what can I get you?" Callie asked, returning from the hallway. "A beer, or wine?"

"A beer would hit the spot. It's been a long day. Thank you."

She smiled and went to the kitchen. A few minutes later they were seated in comfortable chairs around her coffee table. She tipped her wine glass to him. "Thank you for working so hard to keep us safe."

"I'm afraid we didn't do a good job today. Too many dead at the DEA. And we were just lucky with the other two."

"I saw a text from Emily to a group about Natalie. Any further word?"

"Seth thinks she's going to be OK. I may not know the latest. We've been crazy. But I'll certainly let you know."

After that general catch-up, each took a sip and waited for the subject that hung in the air between them. Three blocks away, Nepravel, who had followed Tom from the White House and who was afraid to leave him alone with Callie on such an emotional day, crouched behind a parked truck, occasionally peering at the angel who had been next to Tom all day and now was standing by Callie's front door. The demon was about to give up and move on to Emily when he glanced back and noticed that the angel was gone. He waited, then crept forward. A minute later, not believing his good fortune, he went inside and settled next to Tom, despite the bright spiritual light inside Callie, ready to listen and to add to their conversation. But always with one eye out for the angel's possible return.

Callie asked, "Did you do your homework?"

Tom nodded. "Yes. Gary Thornton's book is fascinating. I read three chapters."

She smiled again. "You get an A. Please keep reading—and take those famous notes of yours. I want to see what you think is important."

"OK."

"I assume you know that Robert Ludwig was arrested yesterday. Do you know where he is and what he's been charged with?"

"Yes."

She waited, but he said no more. "Well, when can you get him out? He obviously didn't do anything wrong."

Tom pursed his lips. "Actually, he did."

"You were there. You heard him. What did he say that could lead anyone to arrest him?"

He paused. "During this special, short period, we're asking everyone, particularly those in the public light, to refrain from any kind of speech that could be considered divisive or hateful. We're trying to lower the rhetoric that can divide us and focus instead on the things that unite us. In his case, Robert Ludwig submitted his draft sermon for review but then blatantly disregarded the changes that the reviewer required. He violated the restrictions in the State of Emergency. So that's why he and about thirty others were detained yesterday."

"'Reviewer'? You mean censor? Since when does an American pastor, or any American, have to ask for permission to speak his or her opinion?"

"Since we enacted the temporary State of Emergency, like I just explained."

"Then what did he say that was so incendiary and divisive? You actually commended him on his talk when we left."

"I haven't seen the reviewer's mark-up and don't expect to. Presumably the church has it. From being there I imagine that his attack on abortion—which is legal in some form in almost every state—was considered too pointed against women. And repeating or implying that you have to believe that Jesus was the Son of God who died for your sins in order to avoid Hell is also a bit divisive, don't you think?"

"Is the Son of God."

"What?"

"*Is* the Son of God. Not *was*."

"Oh. OK. Is the Son of God."

"But that's not Robert Ludwig's idea. Or the Apostle John's. Or mine. Or any believer's. It's what *Jesus* said. And his offer is freely available to anyone and everyone. It's not divisive—it's inclusive!"

"But if you don't choose to believe that way, then you're excluded. And that's divisive."

"Wait. You just said it's a choice. As they say, choices have consequences. But to become a believer no one is holding a knife to your neck or requiring to know your parents' lineage, as with some religions. The choice is open to everyone, with no pressure other than your own conscience—and maybe God's leading."

"And the next thing you know, these people come out against a woman's right to protect her own body, and against gay people getting married. How divisive and hateful is that?"

"Is it divisive to tell a child not to put her hand on a hot stove?"

"What?"

Callie shook her head. "Never mind. Just trying to obey the One who made us—seems like He might know what's best for us."

"I think I've proven the point. Christians can be very divisive. Not always, and not all Christians. But some. Like the statements that Robert Ludwig made. And that's why he's detained. He violated the law. And blatantly, on purpose."

"But not the Constitution."

"We'll have that back in a few weeks. For now, the State of Emergency is the law." There was a long silence between them. "I'm sorry I can't help with him, but I can't. He chose to break the law and, as you just said, choices have consequences."

Callie didn't say anything. She just silently shook her head.

He stood. "Well, I guess I better be going. It's late and we all got up very early this morning."

She stood as well, but did not immediately look at him. Finally she turned and took the empty bottle from him. Almost in a whisper she said, "Keep doing your homework. I think it's really important." She moved to the door.

"I'll let you know when I hear more about Natalie," he said, picking up his computer bag.

"Thank you."

"I'll call you later this week."

She just nodded and opened the door. Tom and Nepravel left together into the night.

It was dark when Josh Weber and Mason Neal pulled their pickup into Josh's farm in Kentucky. They had taken several back roads since leaving D.C., and twice the news reports on their phones weren't good enough—they'd pulled off to watch the events on a big screen at a truck stop and a sports bar. They were very happy with the damage they'd done and were already planning a second target—the big pharmaceutical company that had pushed oxy on their children while racking up obscene profits and bonuses for their management.

Josh stopped the truck between the house and the shed where they'd made the bomb. He switched off the ignition and was turning to Mason when headlights pulled into the driveway behind them. Then other lights came on all over the property, several focused on their truck.

A voice came over a loudhailer. "This is the FBI. You are surrounded. Open the doors slowly and come out with your hands up."

There was a great sense of accomplishment at Prince Proklor's expanded White House meeting that midnight. The generals had invited the sector leaders and a few key street leaders, so the Oval Office was packed with dark, human-hating energy. Proklor nodded to Temno, who began.

"As you will hear, it's been a great day for destroying America. And even our base tracking numbers are up: 2,915 divorces and over 3,000 abortions—3,056 to be exact. Well done, everyone."

Proklor then hovered just over the Resolute Desk. "Yes, well done. This second wave of violence two weeks after the first caught them completely by surprise. And we should have more tomorrow. Generals, your reports please."

Twenty minutes later, after each of Proklor's direct reports had either detailed the mayhem of that day's assaults or predicted the carnage expected tomorrow, the prince summarized. "Here we see the beginning of the end. America used to be proud of the strength of its diversity. We know that was only possible because the majority shared the same faith in Him and His principles. After the fifty years we've spent destroying that faith, their diversity will now be their undoing. Tribe against tribe. Oppressor against Oppressed. Belief against belief. Color against color. Opinion against opinion. Now they will attack each other. America is coming undone. More people will die. We can only wonder: What will come next?

"Go back and encourage your troops to step up their lies for another great day of harvesting more of these putrid people tomorrow. Well done."

The Oval Office emptied, but Proklor asked Bespor and Temno to remain. When they were alone, Proklor said to Bespor, "Tell me more about what your sector and street leaders are seeing and hearing from the people around the new president."

# 13

*All the good from the Saviour of the world is communicated through this Book; but for the Book we could not know right from wrong. All the things desirable to man are contained in it.*

Abraham Lincoln

Wednesday, September 30

Tom had a fitful night with little sleep and finally got out of bed at five. Besides the terrible events of the previous day which needed his total attention, he replayed the conversation with Callie and wished it had gone better. *Logic.* How could he intervene for someone who so fundamentally defied the State of Emergency? *Pride.* He would have no credibility if he even brought it up. It would probably end his quickly improving career. Yet he had been at the church, and it didn't sound like hate speech to him. Just the opposite, really. *Justice.* But Robert Ludwig had made his choice and would have to live with it.

He was in the office by seven, in time to read a report that three older Catholic priests in Indianapolis had gone missing the night before. That in itself was strange, but all of them had been charged five years earlier with sexually assaulting teenage boys several decades ago. Nothing had ever been proven. Was this just a coincidence, or another example of the hate and violence which seemed to be engulfing the nation?

In his early morning video briefing with Special Agent Prescott he learned that interrogations of the two alleged DEA bombers had begun in earnest. And the NSA/FBI enhanced computers were cross checking every person within a hundred miles of the Pennsylvania explosions against military records for sniper or sharpshooter competence, and then using cell phone records and license plate readers to track their movements over the past two weeks. Hopefully there would be a breakthrough.

At a little after eight Kristen Holloway began an internet video meeting with Richard and Janet Sullivan in Atlanta, and David and Elizabeth Sawyer at their retirement home in Charleston. All five had cups of coffee around their three breakfast room tables.

"Thank you for joining me after all these awful events. I felt led by our mutual faith, which I trace back to Richard and Janet's first impacting me two decades ago, and then to my opportunity to touch the Sawyers' daughter, Callie, when she was at the bottom in her life nine years ago. So you've known about each other, but I'm not sure you've ever met. I wanted to get you together because Tom and Callie have now met and are getting to know each other at this difficult time. Tom has a big job at the White House for a relatively young man. Callie has a big faith. There may be difficult strains. There may be great opportunities. They're both great people, as are you, and I just want to be sure that you, as their parents, are praying for them both."

David Sawyer said, "Thank you, Kristen. And you certainly impacted us, too."

"Well, God has obviously impacted all of us."

Richard asked, "Is Tom aware of your pastor being arrested?"

"Yes. He was actually at the service with Callie, me and some other friends on Sunday."

"He was?" Janet said. "I don't think he's been to a church service in years. Callie must be something."

They all smiled.

Richard turned serious. "But I think it's going to get worse. Our pastor here in Atlanta knows your pastor, and this coming Sunday we may also refuse to adhere to whatever the government censor tells us. As may other churches around the country."

"What does Tom do in the White House?" Elizabeth Sawyer asked.

"He advises the president on issues like arresting pastors who refuse to comply with the State of Emergency," Janet said.

"Oh. Goodness."

"Yes," Kristen said. "So you can see why I hope you will redouble your prayers for these two, and for the many young people here in D.C. who are thrust into positions where extra wisdom and judgment are needed, but so many of them have no faith to guide them."

"Thank you, Kristen, for getting us together," David Sawyer said. "Yes, Elizabeth and I will pray, and we'll add Tom—and Callie—to our church prayer list."

"Let's start now," Richard said. "And then, ironically, I've got another call with our church elders in thirty minutes."

The five of them bowed their heads and prayed fervently for Tom, Callie, and everyone making decisions that would impact the nation—that God would be glorified in every action.

Seth was used to juggling a lot of balls at one time, but today was already crazy. After checking on Natalie at the hospital—she continued to improve—he went to the White House for an early briefing on the arrest in Kentucky of the suspected DEA bombers. There was as yet no news on their motives, nor any information on the other attacks, now including what appeared to be the late-night abduction of three priests.

After the public briefing he was called behind the scenes to an off-the-record strategy session with Emily and the new vice president, in her office, on how best to roll out and characterize the new National Unity Task Force. Emily and her assistant were suggesting some angles that The Network might pursue about Patricia's earlier work when word came that two Philadelphia policemen, their wives and small children had been found executed in their homes overnight, with gang markings all around. The officers had been spearheading a drive to rid a large section of the city of gang influence, and this was the first known case of retaliation against entire families. Some in the city were immediately equating it to the worst quarters of Latin America.

Emily stood and looked at Seth. "We gotta go. Let me quickly walk you back to the Press Room. I'll call you this afternoon."

As they walked, Seth said, "They almost killed Natalie, Emily. She was very, very lucky. When are you going to nail them?"

"We think we have those two, but not sure if there were others involved. Tom, the FBI and the military are really focused."

"What if she'd been killed?"

"I don't know, Seth. I don't know."

At The Network, Rachel had called a working lunch meeting to be sure they were covering all angles of the crisis, so Seth left for DCNet. Zloy, sent by Obman, started following him once he was clear of the prayer cover over the White House, always eager to participate and to learn.

To>Katherine

ANobikov: Are you OK after the attacks?

KatTikh: Yes. We're fine. But the attacks were terrible.

ANobikov: Please be careful.

KatTikh: I only go out with Patrick, and we stay away from crowds.

ANobikov: Good. I've been praying for you.

KatTikh: Thanks!

ANobikov: I liked your teacher and her friend, Tom. The next time I'm there, let's invite them to dinner.

KatTikh: OK. I think she's a believer. We may visit her church.

ANobikov: Wonderful.

Andrea opened the front door to their home and welcomed all four of the Rashids. Clayton, who had duty scheduled later that afternoon, joined them from the den and took a roller bag from Mariam. "Come in," the Hunts said together.

Ahmad followed Mariam and their two boys inside, pulling a large bag. "Thank you again." He closed the door.

"Follow me, boys," Andrea smiled. "You'll be in your same room. OK?"

They nodded hesitantly. Mariam took their hands, and they followed Andrea down the hall.

"I can't thank you enough, Clayton," Ahmad said.

"No problem. What happened?"

"After the attacks on our mosque and the others, there are those who want to seek some kind of revenge. A tiny group, but vocal. I've spoken out against them, telling everyone that we must not seek revenge. But this group thinks that Allah demands revenge, and therefore I and others like me are not true Muslims. So we've been threatened."

"I'm sorry. Does anyone know you'll be staying with us?"

"Only our parents. And they understand the situation."

"We're glad you're here." He smiled. "Put your bag down, and then maybe you and I should hit the grocery store before I have to go in."

During her lunch break Callie drove from her publisher over to the hospital in Arlington where Natalie was recuperating. When she found the room, Natalie was alone and sitting up, looked almost normal, and smiled.

"Hi. I'm so glad you came."

"Of course. And Grace picked out these flowers for you. How are you?"

"They're beautiful. I'm much better. The ringing has nearly stopped. I may go home later today or tomorrow."

"That's great." Callie put the flower vase on the table next to the window and sat in the chair next to Natalie's bed. "I guess it's been pretty awful."

"Yes. All those people killed or maimed. A woman I barely knew convinced me to leave with her, then she went to help others and was right next to the blast when it hit." Natalie choked. Callie waited. "While I held a shirt on an officer's wounds, I could hear people all around us crying and, I guess, dying."

Callie shook her head. "Terrible. I'm so sorry. Was that Sara?"

"You know Sara Bryant?"

Callie smiled. "Yes. Sara goes to our church."

"She does?"

"Yes. She was there Sunday. You might have seen her. Hard to miss."

"I guess, but it didn't register. She literally saved my life."

Callie looked down. "I checked on her before coming to see you. She's still in ICU, and the prognosis is not good. We're praying for her—and you."

"She might die?"

Callie nodded.

"And you know her?"

"Yes. For a couple of years. She's a great girl. A strong believer."

Natalie was silent for a moment and then said. "You said something right after church that really stuck with me. That God had been coming after you, even when you fought Him, and He sent Kristen. That's...that's how I feel right now. We live near your church and I went a couple of times and liked it. Then I met you and enjoyed our conversations. You're so...so calm in the midst of storms. And then going to church and hearing your pastor, and all the people praying. And the hymns. And then to find out that Sara is a believer who saved my life...goes to your church...and now she may be dying...Could God be coming after me? That emptiness I've felt for so long. I don't think you have it. Or Kristen. What is it you both *do* have?"

Callie smiled again. "I think it's God's peace. I had that same emptiness, but His peace replaced it. Whatever happens here and now, I know I'm really a citizen of Heaven who just happens to be spending some time—important time, but still temporary—here. Whether I die today or in sixty years, Heaven is where I'll be for eternity. With God and all the other believers. Imagine talking with my great-grandmother, not to mention the Apostle Paul!

"And I know what you mean about the emptiness. Believe me—for me it was an aching, gaping pit—and you're right, I don't have it anymore, because by His grace I confessed all that I had done, which was a lot, and surrendered my life to God's Son. The emptiness has all been replaced by His peace. He paid the price for my sins instead of me. It's incredible, really."

"If you knew what I've done...how could He forgive me?"

Callie shook her head. "It doesn't matter. That's between you and Him. He loves you and wants you to be His child."

"And you think that's what Sara believes?"

"I know she does. We've talked about it."

"How do I get what you and Sara have?"

"It's simple, but powerful. The Bible says that if you believe in your heart and confess with your mouth that Jesus is Lord of your life, you'll be what Robert Ludwig called born-again, as one of His children. His forever. Being born-again isn't a marketing catch phrase. It's a state of being. You're born again when you sincerely confess your past and surrender your future to Him. You become a new creation, adopted as His daughter, forever. He will never let you go."

"Can I do that now? With you? Will you help me?"

Callie smiled again. "Of course. It's the greatest privilege I can imagine. Here, hold my hand, and let's pray."

As the two women bowed their heads and Callie led Natalie in an ancient prayer, every demon in and near the hospital turned their eyes towards Heaven and cringed as the gathering roar of the Holy Spirit filled their ears. Then they had to look away, or hide, as the most radiant spiritual light in the universe descended and filled Natalie's hospital room with perfect brilliance, hesitated for a moment, and moved on, leaving behind in her a flame which would now burn eternally, plus a new powerful voice which would grow stronger and louder when properly fed and nurtured.

When she finished praying, Natalie opened her eyes and laughed. "I feel new. Now what?"

"Do you have a Bible at home?"

"I think so."

"Then read the Gospel of John when you get home, and I'll bring you some other good things for a new believer to read and consider. I think you'll enjoy them, and learn a lot. And Kristen leads a Sunday School class at church for new believers. She's very good. Lots of wisdom and insights. You should try it."

"And we should pray for Sara, and the others."

"Yes, let's do that now."

The NSC briefing via secure video link took place in the Situation Room for the president and White House staff late that afternoon. Tom had coordinated the agenda with the key reporting departments and called on each in turn. The Core Group and NSC members learned that:

There was overwhelming physical evidence at the farm in Kentucky to link the two suspects to the DEA bomb, from ingredients to their laptops. They were under interrogation, and deep traces were being done on all their prior communications to find links to the others with whom they were assumed to be working.

Just that afternoon the government's advanced techniques, including AI reviews of records, phone tracking, purchase tracking, and license plate readers had turned up a probable suspect in the fracking gas explosions, and officers were on the way to make an arrest. Already the suspect's communications and background were being combed for links to terrorist groups and foreign entities.

Focused media monitoring and instant taps had uncovered conversations which appeared to be promoting revenge attacks for both the mosque shootings and the police family murders. Several individuals in Philadelphia and D.C. had already been arrested, including two imams and four police officers.

SAC Tanya Prescott was finishing up from a video screen. "On the mosque attacks, drones at night are very difficult to guard against across a wide area. But we do have location-specific countermeasures that work reasonably well. While we already have some deployed in the capital, they were not focused on houses of worship as targets. We're bringing in additional assets from across the country today and will be beefing up anti-drone security at many potential targets over the next twenty-four hours."

"Thank you, Agent Prescott," Tom said. "Finally, we have detained almost two hundred demonstrators and thirty-five individuals—mostly clerics—for violating hate speech regulations, and we plan to be even more vigilant in this area. Under the leadership of the vice president's National Unity Task Force we're working on enhanced guidelines in new Executive Orders for all social media platforms for self-review, mandatory recording, and interdiction, coordinated with on-site government personnel. We will now require anyone speaking at a gathering of any type of more than twenty-five people to submit the proposed text for review at least seventy-two hours before it may be delivered. Anyone violating this order will be arrested and detained. We are determined to remove those who would divide us. At this time of major attacks, we need unity. Mr. President, that concludes the prepared briefing. We're of course glad to answer any questions."

Everyone looked to the end of the table. The president nodded. "Thank you, Tom. Thank you all. Finally, a generally positive report, despite this second wave of attacks. And one indicating that the extraordinary steps we took with the State of Emergency are actually effective and paying off. The arrests in the DEA and fracking attacks show the value of the powerful technology you've deployed, and the early arrests for revenge attacks in the other cases show the value of our heightened hate speech vigilance. Emily, please include those points in our next address to the nation."

He looked around the table. "Now just find out who's behind all of this. As soon as we think it's safe the vice president and I will be traveling to the sites and the people impacted, to show them even more that their government cares and is working for their protection. Our thanks to all of you. Please keep digging and watching." He rose and left the room. Everyone stood and then resumed their seats.

Tom spoke again. "We have your departmental recommendations on how to further enhance the safeguards in the State of Emergency. Together with the vice president," he nodded toward Patricia Reynolds sitting across from him, "and the members of her task force, we'll draft amendments to the Executive Orders over the next couple of days and send them around for your final review. Then the president will again address the nation. Thank you all for your fast work. It looks like our measures are starting to make a difference."

Jerry Kimble and his family were sitting down to dinner when they and their neighbors heard a loud voice exclaim through a megaphone in the driveway. "This is the police. Open the door and come out with your hands empty, and in the air."

Their forks stopped in midair, Jerry's wife and boys looked at him.

He frowned, then looked at each of them in turn. "Whatever happens, whatever you hear about me, remember that I did it all for you, and for our country."

He rose and walked to the front door.

When Tom returned home that evening he was tired and not very hungry. He almost called Callie, but decided to wait for the immediacy of her pastor's arrest to cool down. Instead, sitting on his bed, he checked in with his parents, who wanted to hear about what he was doing. He of course had to talk in generalities. They ended by saying that they loved him and were praying for him.

He saw Gary Thornton's book on his bedside table. He opened to where he had stopped, lay back on his bed, and began reading. The next chapter began with another quote, this one from Alexis De Tocqueville in *Democracy in America,* about the Frenchman's impressions while traveling in America almost two hundred years earlier.

*Religion in America . . . Must be regarded as the foremost of the political institutions for that country; for if it does not impart a taste for freedom, it facilitates the use of it . . . I do not know whether all Americans have a sincere faith in their religion - for who can search the human heart? - But I am certain that they hold it to be indispensable to the maintenance of republican institutions. This opinion is not peculiar to a class of citizens or a party, but it belongs to the whole nation and to every rank of society.*

Thornton then went on to describe how organized Religion relates to individual Faith like Democracy relates to personal Choice. Religion and Democracy are generally big, passive concepts. Faith and Choice require individual action. He argued that in America there is an inseparable connection between the individual's right to choose his faith, or not; and his right to vote for a candidate, or not. Europe in De Tocqueville's time was run by institutional Religion and Top-Down Government Rules, not by Bottom-Up individual Faith and Choice.

And that's what fascinated De Tocqueville about the new country. Everyone seemed to know, without being told, that in order to make good choices you needed knowledge, wisdom and virtue. And the latter two were best derived by having Faith. It was the shared general Christian faith, woven into every aspect of the society, that provided the common wisdom and virtue for the entire nation; and that simple fact was acknowledged by everyone at the time, whether a Christian or not.

These two interlinked concepts, empowering and even requiring the *individual* to make personal decisions of serious consequence, both secular and eternal, drove the American revolution and energized the new country, summarized in one word: Liberty.

Tom finished the chapter and put the book down. He realized he needed to think more about Thornton's words, but right now he was just too tired. Hopefully, tomorrow.

The joy of accomplishment at the Northeast Abortion Center that midnight was tempered by the anger over losing Natalie Ellis, given her proximity to so many other humans who were important to their success. Obman was livid, knowing that this news would not go well with General Bespor.

"How did Callie Sawyer get to her, and you weren't there?" he shouted at Zloy in one of the rooms adjoining the larger meeting area. Balzor and Nepravel were also there, watching.

Cowering a little but determined to hold his ground, Zloy replied, "Callie Sawyer's not my responsibility, and Natalie Ellis was stuck in a hospital bed. You told me to focus on Seth Cohen, which I did back at DCNet, and I gave you a full report. I can't be in two places at once."

Balzor tried to calm down his fellow sector leader. "We don't have enough forces to watch all of them, all the time. It happens. I'll go with you to tell Bespor. And we warned them just a few days ago about the prayers and the angels."

"All right," Obman sighed, slowly shaking his head and looking between Zloy and Nepravel. "You know what to do. She's lost to us, so make her completely ineffective at infecting others. Pile on the voices of *Guilt, Unworthy, Busy, Doubt, Rejection, Pain*. Natalie Ellis cannot become another Callie Sawyer! Or Kristen Holloway."

The two street leaders nodded. Nepravel added, "Actually, we've got to do more to quarantine Tom Sullivan from all of them. I discovered he's reading Thornton's books on faith in America. From Callie Sawyer. He needs more of our voices. We can't let the tiny voice still left inside him from twenty years ago get his attention."

Balzor added, "We just learned that Sara Bryant passed."

Obman raised his head. "Good riddance. She's obviously not ours to keep. But at least she's gone. What right does she have to be in Heaven with Him, where we belong?"

In the Oval Office that night there was the usual meeting of dark spiritual forces, but only attending were Proklor's six closest generals, who were already assembled in the iconic room when the prince appeared in their midst. He looked at them in turn, then said, "We've been a strong team over the millennia, and your advice has been excellent. Today is no exception. I have just been with our Master and the other world leaders."

The generals were surprised and showed it.

"No reason to be concerned," Prince Proklor assured them. "Just the opposite. Your observations have led me to recommend a change to our strategy, and I am pleased to tell you that Satan himself has approved it."

The generals were speechless. Finally Temno said, "What is it, my lord?"

Prince Proklor smiled. "We've been pushing and pushing for total anarchy. For their society to split apart in violence, revenge and retribution between tribes. But the constant feedback from your forces has disclosed an even better outcome: using their new technology to achieve total control of every word spoken and every action taken. Instead of anarchy, we will achieve the opposite—complete control."

The generals remained silent, waiting.

"Think about it. With divisions, splits and near-chaos, even though the believers would be isolated, they could still exist as one of the warring factions, and continue to talk about Him. But this new ability to watch everyone and to control every word means that believers can be completely silenced. Their meetings monitored. No outreach. No one talking about Him. No one at all. Not even an underground. After all, that's always been our goal in America: to stop people from telling others about Him. The church will die. No more believers.

"We've never really cared which party or group was in power. Yes, some are better for us than others. But the goal has always been to destroy the church. To silence it. No more salvation messages. No more testimonies. No one will learn about Him because *no one will tell them.* Total control is much better than anarchy. The threat of anarchy fuels it, but their new technology makes it possible. You helped me see it. So from now on we're going to continue to add the anarchy fuel, but the goal is to be sure that those who want control will always win, and then, through them, we will control everyone. Just like we did in Germany, and the old Soviet Union."

Temno said, "An even better outcome. Like how we control China, the Muslim world, and most of Russia."

Proklor smiled. "Exactly. But China, Russia and others have a different culture. Total control was easier there to implement. No one thought it could be done in America. Too individualistic. Too much emphasis on choice and freedom, buttressed by the choice and freedom in their underlying faith. So it wasn't possible until we spent the last fifty years destroying those foundations. Now that their faith is marginalized, the combination of fear and the new technology will allow us to crush it completely. No more faith. No more choices. No more individuals. Everyone in America will submit to their government's common control—just like in China. But only because of what we have done!"

"Brilliant," Bespor said.

"The Master wants us to work with our brothers in China and Russia to bring America together with them in one great worldwide Cloud of Darkness. No more light from America, or from anywhere. The world will be divided between these three powers, and we will rule each of them. It will be our time."

# Thursday, October 1st

When Natalie awoke that morning in the hospital, she pulled up the Gospel of John on her phone and continued where she had left off. Then she prayed.

Unknown to her, Callie, Kristen and others at the Church of the Good Shepherd were praying for her at that same hour.

And unknown to all of them, Natalie's prayer, like the prayers of all new believers, had a special direct line to the Throne of Grace, bringing great joy to the Listener.

President Bradshaw put his cup down on the coffee table in front of the sofas in the Oval Office. As the morning news started to arrive he'd asked the vice president, Rob, Emily and Tom to join him and the First Lady before going down to the Situation Room for their daily briefing.

"Yesterday we were supposed to hold a Memorial Service for President Rhodes and Vice President Carpenter at the National Cathedral," he said. "We couldn't do it out of fear for what might happen. Instead we're still dealing with their deaths plus the new death and destruction from Tuesday's attacks, and now missing priests, two police families killed *at home* by a gang, fires at two Women's Clinics last night and another unarmed black teenager killed by police while in custody. Does anyone get the feeling that our nation is coming apart?"

No one spoke.

"We talked optimistically the other day about the upcoming elections and getting back to normal, along with our progressive agenda. Given the last two days' events I'm not sure we'll get back to normal any time soon. Until we have something more concrete about who's doing this, and until these attacks stop, at the very least I think we have to prepare quietly to extend the State of Emergency for another two weeks, or a month. And that will put it very close to the November elections."

Patricia Reynolds nodded. "I agree. As you pointed out yesterday, the arrests we're making and the crimes we're preventing are a direct result of the teeth in the State of Emergency. Without it, we have no idea what might have happened. The American people will support that conclusion and the extension. Otherwise there might be total anarchy."

After taking a bite from a croissant on a plate in front of him, the president continued, "And the animosity in some of our critics' words. The hatred. Why is that? We just asked for a cooling off period. Some of these faith-based people are crazy, or provoke craziness in others. A church firebombed. Shootings at mosques. Muslims planning revenge. Hate speech about women's rights. Priests kidnapped." He glanced at Patricia and Tom. "You two used to be Christians. What is it about belief that drives some people to do crazy things?"

"I...I guess some of them think they hear from a higher power, so they don't have to live by the law of the land," Patricia responded. "I think we should reach out to the friendly major denominational leaders to comply with the State of Emergency for the sake of our long-term freedoms, and isolate the few who won't. I can start making calls today."

Tom nodded. "Good idea. And the drafts of this weekend's sermons are due in a couple of hours for review. We'll run them through our AI scanners and then focus on any outliers for follow-up questioning. We're already into that with several imams over their proposed calls for revenge at their Friday services."

Rob spoke. "Clearly they have to stop, or suffer the consequences. We can't have groups of people who think they're above the law just because they're clerics or pastors. Particularly ones with a microphone and a following. They only encourage more divisions and more hate."

Tom leaned forward. "We'll tighten the restrictions in the expanded orders, the draft of which you'll see by Monday, Mr. President, and we'll be sure the public is aware of what happens to them—the consequences for violating the rules."

Emily nodded. "Let me have the draft as soon as you can, and we'll start working on talking points for Patricia and her task force. And we'll see you Friday evening to go into more detail."

"All right," President Bradshaw said, standing. "Patricia, I think you and your team should coordinate with Tom, the FBI and NSA about extending the State of Emergency. Nothing public yet. But we can't relax our guard while we're under attack. Just get everything we'll need ready.

And on the election, we need to figure out—quietly, without involving any of the bureaucracy yet—how we would run it during the State of Emergency, then alert our key fundraisers, friends in High Tech, and ad people about what might be ahead. Now let's go down and see what the briefers have to tell us."

In suburban Maryland Brad Grantham tapped at his sister's front door that morning. She invited him in for coffee and breakfast. They had agreed not to discuss anything other than meeting together on their phones or by email, given what they read about heightened security. They would conduct their future business in person, and as an extra precaution, they switched off their cell phones and left them in the entrance hall, while Teri scrambled eggs and they talked in the kitchen.

Brad had brought the morning papers and spread them out on the kitchen table. "I'm miffed our message to the Arab a-holes got lost after those farmers blew up the DEA. What the hell were they thinking?"

Standing at the range, Teri said, "Well, whatever they thought, they got caught pretty quick. Not a good plan." She turned and smiled. "But we're still here and no one has a clue."

Brad nodded. "I like drones at night. You can't see'em and you can't hear'em. If we stay careful, we should be able to shoot up mosques for a long time—until they leave, or stop attending."

"Bastards."

"Where's next?"

She served him a plate. "John was Air Force, but Colorado Springs is a hike. How about Annapolis? I was looking online at a new mosque there, not far from the Naval Academy. Would that send a message?"

Stan Conway was on the phone with Richard Sullivan in his law office that morning. "I got a call from a pastor friend in Dallas who wants to put together a loose network of churches around the country. Like us, they want to do the right thing with the response to the government's orders. He wants to connect the lay leadership. Could you take that role for us, to listen and report on what they're thinking?"

"Sure. Who do I call?"

Beau was a black blur of wags as Seth opened the door to their row house and Natalie stepped inside. He pushed a ball against her leg, and she smiled as she tried to bend down, but Seth intervened.

"He's a surprise from Tom. He thought Beau would be good company while you recuperated." He looked down. "Give her a couple of days, Beau, and she'll be good as new." He then walked beside her to their bedroom, the Lab trailing expectantly.

Soon Natalie was in comfortable jeans and a light sweatshirt, propped on several pillows on their bed. Bandages on her right arm and the top of her head were the only physical reminders of the blast two mornings earlier.

Seth held up the bag of clothes she had worn to work that morning, retrieved from the hospital. "Should we just throw these away?"

"I'll have 'em cleaned and I'm keeping them."

He smiled. Beau circled and settled next to the bed. "OK. Would you like something to drink? Some lunch?"

Ten minutes later Seth was sitting next to the bed as they nibbled on turkey and cheese sandwiches and sipped hot tea.

"Thank you for getting me."

He smiled. "Of course. We're lucky that you had so little damage."

She started to smile but then turned serious. "How many people died? Eighty-two?"

"Eighty-nine, and some are still in ICU."

She shook her head. "And all those wounded. All those screams."

"I can't imagine."

"I think Sara Bryant's memorial service is next week at Callie's church. I have to go."

He nodded. "After what you told me, and the reports from our guys, she was the real hero."

"We're only here talking together because of her." They were silent for a moment. "And I want to go to their service on Sunday morning."

He took a bite of his sandwich and sipped some tea. "OK."

She put her sandwich on the plate and turned to him. "In fact, I need to tell you something. I feel like, like God's been chasing me for the last year. Getting my attention. Their church. Callie. The sermons. Now Sara.

On Tuesday He *really* got my attention. Callie came to see me yesterday. We talked. I asked her how to get the peace that she and the others have. She told me, and I gave my life to Christ."

Seth frowned. "You gave your life to Christ? How?"

"I prayed. I asked him to forgive me for all that I've done that's not right, and I asked him to take over my future, to make me the person he wants me to be. I feel so good. So right."

He looked at her. Finally he said, "What does that mean?"

"I'm not completely sure. But whatever it is, it's good. And it's real. I'm going to study with Callie's friend Kristen. I'm reading the Gospel of John. I'm praying. It's all new, so I don't know. But I'm glad that He's in charge now, and not me."

Seth thought some more. "What does that mean about us?"

She smiled. "I don't know. I love you. You're amazing. Somehow we'll figure it out. Or He will."

"Hmm. Well. A lot has changed in two days."

She nodded. "I'm alive. Sara and almost a hundred people who went to work that same morning, aren't. There has to be a reason why He saved me." She smiled. "I want to find out, and I'd love for you to help me."

"That's a lot to take in. Give me a couple of days to think about it."

"Of course. And keep praying, like you did on Tuesday."

"Uh, OK."

"Now, may I have some more tea?"

To>Callie

Tom: I think Natalie is home.

Callie: Great. I saw her yesterday. She looks good.

Tom: Want to help me host the group at my place this weekend? Maybe Saturday evening.

Callie: Sure.

Tom: I'll ask everyone. Stay tuned. Come an hour early, about six. Can't wait to see you.

Early that afternoon President Bradshaw and the First Lady visited a hospital with over twenty victims of the DEA terrorist bombing. They spoke with several people, many heavily bandaged, in their beds. Afterwards he gave some remarks, scripted by Emily, about how individual law enforcement actions and the State of Emergency had both prevented a greater tragedy and made swift arrests possible, ensuring the perpetrators could not strike again.

Later that day Vice President Reynolds and a group of Christian and Jewish leaders, along with several reporters, visited the Family and Friendship Mosque to meet with the leaders and to show their solidarity with those who were attacked early Tuesday morning. Among the large group from the mosque gathered in the meeting room were Ahmad Rashid, in his Army uniform, Kahar Bosakov, and, in the back, Kahar's older cousin, Ablet Sabri.

Ahmad described to the visitors and the mosque members what happened that night, and he urged everyone to let law enforcement and the military determine who was responsible. Kahar, who seemed nervous and out of place, nodded when Ahmad mentioned how he had applied the tourniquet to the guard's leg, but otherwise said nothing, staying close to the Army officer throughout the event.

The vice president gave a short but powerful talk echoing Ahmad's plea that no one try to take revenge into their own hands, but instead allow the government, with its new, enhanced, effective powers, to find and arrest the demented terrorists who would attack a house of worship.

Prayers were then offered by senior representatives of all three faiths.


To>Clayton and Andrea, Emily and Logan, Seth and Natalie, Callie

Tom: No one feels like a party, but would you like to come to my place on Saturday night? We can talk some more. Callie and I will make something. 7?

Clayton: May we bring a couple who are staying with us? He's Army. We work together at the Pentagon.

Tom: Yes, of course.

# 14

*The laws of nature and of nature's God...of course presupposes the existence of a God, the moral Ruler of the Universe, and a rule of right and wrong, of just and unjust, binding upon man, preceding all institutions of human society and of government.*

John Quincy Adams
Friday, October 2

At mid-morning the first of what would be several days of funerals and memorial services began all around Washington and across the nation for those slain in the DEA bombing.

The Department of Homeland Security had issued a carefully worded statement exempting funerals and memorial services from the requirement to submit public statements beforehand, while suggesting that speakers should focus on those being remembered, rather than on any nationally sensitive subjects.

The president directed the committees which had been working on the still un-celebrated Memorial Service for President Rhodes and Vice President Carpenter to expand their work to include one or more larger celebrations of service at all levels, to be held once the threat of attack was over.

Tom was at his White House desk on his daily video conference with Tanya Prescott at the FBI Command Center.

"We're in two massive data searches. The first is through everyone involved with the Child Molestation case against the church in Indianapolis. And then all the known gang members the police were targeting in Philadelphia. A few leads have popped up, and we're coordinating closely with the local police and the FBI in both cases."

"What about the attacks on Tuesday? Any connections?" Tom asked.

"It's maddening. We've put all three men—two in Kentucky and one in Pennsylvania—through the ringer, and we've checked and rechecked their backgrounds, emails, texts, phone calls, website visits...everything. The two farmers in Kentucky come across as misguided fathers looking to avenge their kids' deaths by opioids. Terrible. They meant to kill a lot of people. And the salesman in Pennsylvania appears to be a misguided nut worried that fracking will harm his family. But, just like with the first wave, we can't find any connection between them and the mosque shooting, or between them and anyone who acted three weeks ago. The attacks certainly look to be well thought out, coordinated, and timed. But we can't find any common thread or connection. Maddening."

Tom remembered his optimism and confidence right after the declaration of the State of Emergency and the ramp up of the NSC Command Center with all its power. He had been so sure that long before now they would have found the perpetrators and halted the attacks. But they hadn't. He was letting down the trust the president had placed in him.

He knew that Agent Prescott and her Director were just as frustrated and worried, and there was no point in pushing her, but he had to ask. "Are there any overseas connections at all? Even seemingly insignificant? Russia? China? Iran?"

"As you would imagine, we have telltale evidence of them all piling on to inflame the affected groups after the attacks, but we haven't been able to connect them with causing the attacks in the first place."

Tom shook his head. "I guess I would suggest we look deeper, if we can. There must be something. Are these Americans all just acting on their own, with no one controlling or teaching them? Seems impossible."

The SAC spoke up. "Three senior volunteers and I will stay here this weekend and go back through everything we've done every hour since we started. There must be some connection."

"Thank you, Tanya. If anyone can, I know your team will find it. In the meantime, we have your group's input to further enhance our intelligence capabilities, and we'll incorporate them into the next round of improvements."

That afternoon Stan Conway in Atlanta convened a virtual meeting of his church's Board of Elders online. There were twenty people on the screen, including several staff members.

After ten minutes of fervent prayer for guidance, Stan addressed the business at hand. "We heard back from the government censor two hours ago, and there are parts of Sunday's sermon they want to modify or delete."

"What are they?" one of the elders asked.

"Does it really matter?" another said. "Isn't it the principle?"

There was a momentary silence. "Yes, I think that's what we've got to decide. The principle," Conway answered. "Richard, what did you learn from your conversation?"

"I was on a call with about thirty men and women from churches around the country. Stan asked me to join in the call because he knows the pastor in Dallas who pulled the group together. Several of them reported that the vice president personally called the heads of their denominations, asking them to abide by the State of Emergency for the sake of defeating America's enemies, and for our long-term freedoms."

"Hogwash," someone volunteered. "They just want total control."

"That may be," Richard continued, "and several of those on the call said exactly the same. But then others pointed out that it's only for two more Sundays, and that we should be able to deal with it for that long."

There followed a thirty-minute discussion of their options, from going to jail to abiding by the orders.

Finally, sensing a consensus, Richard proposed, "I move that we issue a statement as our individual church, and in agreement with the others in this group, that we strongly oppose any government censorship of any free speech, particularly speech in pursuit of our Freedom of Religion, as guaranteed in the First Amendment to our nation's Constitution, but that in the spirit of temporarily assisting our duly elected government officials in defending us from our enemies, we will abide by the terms of the State of Emergency for two more weeks."

After more discussion, the Board of Elders adopted the resolution, but with three No votes. Pastor Conway said that he would read it at the beginning of Sunday's service and post it on their website. And that he would make the changes required by the censor.

Several members were still unhappy, but they agreed to support the majority. Richard said that he would share their resolution with the church network.

As Tom drove out to the vice president's Residence at the Naval Observatory off Massachusetts Avenue early that evening, Nepravel rode with him and reminded him how lucky he was to have been elevated at his age to be one of the new president's closest advisors. *Personal Accomplishment.* If there were a good ending to his current responsibilities, his future was almost unlimited in either public service or in the private sector. *Pride.* His personal future looked bright, but it would be much brighter when they caught or destroyed whoever was behind all this.

Patricia Reynolds had invited Tom, Emily, Rob, Nancy Cantrell, Gerry Veazy and eight members of the full time Project Phoenix team to drinks and a working dinner. Their goals were to design and sync the details of an expanded and lengthened State of Emergency with the midterm elections, and to devise strategies to maximize the results for their party's followers. The first goal was focused on the other official Executive Branch advisors, and to the nation. The second was just as important, but would be enacted within their own progressive ecosystem of officials, Tech financiers, and the friendly media. Thanks to their donors, particularly from Drew Boswell's efforts with his High-Tech firms' executives and investors, they were sitting on a pile of campaign cash that could be deployed quickly.

Tom, with Nepravel invisibly at his side, entered the cozy living room of the Queen Anne style home, and he was greeted by the VP and her husband, Mark. Most of the guests were already there, including Emily and Rob, who were talking with the new President Pro-Tem in the Senate, Gerald Veazy. They were also joined by three other demons whose charges were present. Nepravel nodded to the other fallen angels, expecting a productive evening of rich information, unhindered by prayer cover or believers' input.

Tom picked up a glass of wine and joined Emily's group for some small talk. Patricia Reynolds walked over.

"Tom, we're here to talk about big picture strategy tonight, but I have to ask a question." She held up her Trusted Core phone. "This is such a great help. Could we expand this idea from a Trusted Core to, say, a Trusted Citizen? Could we somehow tag people as trusted individuals so they could get more sensitive information, or could have access to a special, more secure network—similar to our phones—because of who they are and their support for our ideas? Like our Trusted Traveler program—you first earn it, and then you renew to maintain it?"

Emily said, "It would certainly make our lives easier, knowing who we can trust, based on their past actions. And wouldn't it then make it easier to focus on the bad guys?"

Tom nodded. "Could be helpful. I'll look into it."

"Thanks. It would be great to have it up and running soon, given the election." The vice president smiled and walked to another group.

When Nancy Cantrell arrived, Patricia Reynolds asked the staff to set up more chairs, and they got down to business. The junior member of the Project Phoenix team took notes as they started their discussion, which an hour later continued in the beautifully furnished dining room.

By the end of the evening they had settled on several action items and strategies, all of which would be expanded in meetings early in the week.

National Policy:

Because of the government's recent success in both stopping attacks and arresting many of those responsible, and because of the continued constant threat of new attacks, the State of Emergency will be extended by an additional four weeks until November 9$^{th}$.


1. Free elections are the bedrock of our nation. The midterm elections on November 3rd will proceed as planned, using both in-person and mail-in ballots, as determined by each state.

2. For those campaigning in person, on television, by social media, or in any form, free speech will be fully protected, but hate speech will not. Anyone using hate speech will be warned once, and then detained. The offending communication will be removed from public access.

3. Any microphone or camera connected to the internet will be subject to monitoring by law enforcement.

4. Rewards of up to $1 million will be offered for information leading to the arrest and conviction of anyone perpetrating an individual

hate crime, and of up to $5 million if the information leads to those behind the coordinated attacks.

5. The national Memorial Service for President Rhodes and the others killed in the attacks since then will be held as soon as it is feasible to do so.

Progressive Action Steps:

The election will be portrayed as a referendum on the successful measures taken to defend our citizens and our freedoms vs. the chaos and anarchy which would have resulted without strong leadership.

1. Campaign material, social media influencers, and media friends will equate our current shared suffering with the immediate need for national sacrifice, equity, and social justice in all our policies going forward. The unified message will be that only the Progressive Agenda of Diversity, Equity and Inclusion can deliver that shared justice.

2. Any calls for lifting the State of Emergency will be equated to promoting anarchy and will be questioned as probable foreign interference in our election process.

3. Electing Progressive candidates will be portrayed as the only way to ensure that core American values triumph over those who hate. Progressives are the true Patriots.

4. The national Memorial Service will be delayed until after the elections.

# Saturday, October 3

Since Tom had been out late, he struggled that Saturday morning to meet Seth at their neighborhood Sports Center for a round of racquetball, a personal competition they'd begun in college. Tom liked to break-up his parkrun schedule with an occasional match, and Seth had called Friday morning to set it up, adding that he'd like to talk with Tom over coffee afterwards.

Tom was a few minutes late arriving because of the National Security updates he had to check on his encrypted laptop and special phone. There were no major overnight developments, and it appeared that most houses of worship were complying with their censors' requirements this weekend. Even better, the number of requirements was way down—it appeared that self-censorship was starting to work.

It was not Tom's best racquetball performance; Seth won two out of three, with a six point rout in the last game. Now, forty-five minutes later, they were cleaned up and ordering coffee and bagels at the same shop where Tom and Callie had met two weeks earlier.

Nepravel had gone to Tom's home that morning to check on him after their productive evening with the vice president, but found him gone, and had only now caught up with him.

Tom had asked Seth about Natalie's condition when they'd first met at the courts. Seth's response had been positive. Tom expected them both to join their group at his place that evening.

As they sat down in chairs at a small table in the busy coffee shop, Tom asked, "Has Natalie talked at all about the explosion and what she went through?"

Seth nodded. "It must have been really terrible. Natalie wound up trying to stop the bleeding from the police officer who saved her life by shielding her."

"Is that Sara Bryant, who goes to Callie's church?"

"She went there. She died of her wounds."

"Sorry...I'd heard that. So many deaths."

Seth took a long sip and then put down his cup. "And that's kind of why I wanted to talk with you this morning. Sara. Callie. Natalie."

"What do you mean?"

"When I brought Natalie home on Thursday, she told me that when Callie came to see her in the hospital, she—Natalie—'accepted Christ as her Savior' after praying with Callie. She told me she felt God had been, like, chasing her for a year. With her near-death experience and Sara's sacrifice, He finally got her attention. So she gave up and surrendered her life to Him."

Tom had not expected any of this. "Hmm."

Seth continued, focusing intently on Tom. "So why I wanted to talk to you is to try to understand what all this means. You said you had some sort of conversion experience as a teenager. And you've been around these born again people for years—like your parents. I want to understand what this means, to 'accept Christ.' What has she done? Will she change? What happened?"

Tom looked down at his cup for a several moments, thinking. "Has she already changed at all?"

"Well, it's only been two days. But, actually, yes. She doesn't seem as anxious. She keeps saying she feels happy, at peace."

Tom slightly nodded. "Yeah. The same thing happened with my parents. And with others I've known. And, I guess, at least for a while, with me."

"What? What happened?"

Tom spoke slowly to his friend. "The textbook answer would be that if you believe there's a spiritual side to life and a personal, Creator God, and that there's more to reality than we can see and touch, then Natalie has asked God to forgive her for all of her sins, has committed to having a relationship with His Son Jesus as her Savior, and has been filled with God's Holy Spirit to guide and protect her for the rest of her life on earth, insuring her of spending eternity in Heaven."

Nepravel was aghast at Tom's perfect recall of the truth.

Seth raised his hands and shook his head. "That's all?" He seemed incredulous. "Is that your answer, too? Did that happen to you?"

Tom thought again. "I guess it did. But it was a long time and a lot of experiences ago."

"So is the Holy Spirit inside you, guiding you?"

Tom shrugged his shoulders. "Some would say so. But I don't think so. I moved on years ago and have never looked back. I doubt the Holy Spirit would have time for me now." He smiled. "I believe Christianity is just one of several Mesopotamian Myths—people seeking explanations in a world full of the inexplicable. We all need a savior, so we invented one—or several."

Nepravel, next to their table, nodded, though his spiritual eyes occasionally caught what appeared to be the small flicker of a spiritual ember in Tom. Nothing to worry about, though, so long as the voices in Tom, emphasizing pride and 'reason', kept suffocating it.

"OK. So is Natalie deluded? She certainly seems to believe something real has happened to her. And it's affected her."

"Well, people can be deluded, and think it's real. I guess if she believes she's been born again, it can't hurt you, can it?"

"Only if she starts looking to God to make decisions. And decides, say, to move out because we can't 'live in sin' without being married."

Tom nodded. "Yeah, I guess that would upset the apple cart. That would mean she's serious. But, look, over the years I've met lots of girls who say they're Christians, but we've still had a good time. Hopefully that's where Natalie'll wind up."

Seth paused. "I guess. I don't know what to hope for. I love her, so maybe I should hope that this is actually real for her, even if it breaks us up. Or maybe we *should* get married."

Tom's eyes widened. He raised his coffee cup. "Wow. That'd be a change. Maybe the Holy Spirit *is* real!"

Seth lowered his head and nodded, then looked up at Tom and took a sip. "I don't know, but Natalie's no dummy, and she thinks so."

Nepravel was not amused and noted that Natalie might already be a problem. He had seen this kind of transformation many times over the centuries. It always amazed him that there was apparently such power in confession, and it just redoubled his resolve to keep the false voices turned up high in all these young people, to prevent the truth from breaking through the dark noises they managed.

Gary Thornton, the older historian who had written the book Tom was reading, lived in Tom's neighborhood and held the door open to the coffee shop as Tom and Seth came out. The three men politely nodded. Thornton didn't recognize either of them, and he thought it strange that he felt a chill as they walked past.

Nepravel was following the younger men to the door but had to turn away and go out through the back wall because of the infuriating, intense spiritual light coming from whomever was holding the door.

Five minutes later Thornton was seated alone, as was his custom on many Saturday mornings, and began reading the newspaper with his coffee and croissant.

On the front page of the second section was an in-depth story about Sara Bryant and Matt Davis, their local upbringings and their backgrounds. The story mentioned that the Memorial Service for Police Officer Bryant would be on Tuesday morning at The Church of the Good Shepherd. Thornton had visited there several times and knew Robert Ludwig well from the weekend seminar they had done together. And he knew of Ludwig's detention. From somewhere Thornton heard the almost audible thought that he and his wife should attend the service.

To escape the national focus on their mosque, Ablet Sabri had instructed his cousin, Kahar Bosakov, that they should leave D.C. for a few days. Kahar had always wanted to see Gettysburg, and so they had driven to an inexpensive motel in southern Pennsylvania the night before. They were having lunch in the back corner of a fast-food restaurant between their visit to the museum and their self-guided driving tour of the battlefield itself.

Picking up his hamburger, Kahar said, "I hated all that attention, but what was I to do? I had volunteered to help with the security that night, and if I'd stayed away from that big meeting, that might have brought even more questions."

"Yes, yes," Ablet agreed, reaching for his drink. "You did OK. But we needed to leave. All those young men talking about revenge, and anger toward American Jews and Christians, even though they are our enemies, is something we don't want to get caught up in. We have our own mission to revenge real grievances for our family and our faith at the hands of the Chinese devils, and we can't be connected in any way to whatever is happening here."

They ate in silence for a few moments. Then Kahar said, "It's ironic, isn't it? The Chinese government is so powerful at home that we have to come here, to America, to find a way to attack them. Only the freedom everyone has here, like that Army officer, Ahmad, at the mosque keeps saying, allows us to plan such a thing. Freedom is the ocean in which all the fish can swim, and they either live in peace, or attack each other."

"Very philosophical, cousin. But surely you're not thinking that American Christians and Jews are our friends. Our faith teaches us they're conniving liars, not to be trusted."

Kahar put down the last of his hamburger and looked at his cousin. "Yes. But the American government has never attacked me or our friends or our family. The Chinese government, on the other hand, is trying to destroy all of us, and our faith. Other so-called Muslim governments are doing nothing. So we have to come here, to where there is freedom, to have any chance to fight back."

"What can I do to help?" Callie asked, as Tom opened his front door. "And I brought a bottle of Chardonnay to add to the mix."

He was once again stopped in his thoughts by how beautiful she looked in just jeans and a cream top, her dark blue eyes shining beneath her jet-black hair.

"Are you OK?" she smiled, holding out the bottle and leaning down to pat Beau.

"Uh, yeah. Sorry." He took it. "Thank you."

They walked into his row house's living room, which blended back through a large, fixed opening into the dining area. "What are we having? And, again, how can I help?" She took off her light coat, which he hung by the door.

"My nearly famous Greek chicken. Slow cooked for a couple of hours. I don't think I'm very Greek, but it's a great dish for ten. Easy. And a huge Greek salad. We can cut up the veggies in the kitchen."

"Yum. Ten?"

They walked through to the kitchen, which included Tom's breakfast nook and table, looking out over the backyard, where the chicken was grilling.

"Yes. Clayton and Andrea are bringing a couple who're staying with them. Would you like some wine?"

On the street outside, Nepravel, Zloy and two others arrived from the abortion clinic where, with Bespor and Balzor, they'd discussed how important it was to watch the group gathering that night and to derail any conversations which might lead to any more losses or embarrassment.

As a result, lesser demons had been sent to prepare the non-believers attending the dinner with potent lies and visuals, and to travel with them to Tom's home.

But from two blocks away Nepravel and Zloy were angered to see that same angel, shining with God's holy spiritual light, standing guard outside Tom's row house.

"What brought him?" Zloy cursed.

"Too many prayers," Nepravel answered. "The three of you taunt him from the street, and I'll try to get in the back. And maybe we can get some help to keep him distracted."

Ten minutes later Tom and Callie were standing at the kitchen island wearing aprons and cutting cucumbers, tomatoes, onions, and peppers.

"It's nice of you to have everyone over tonight."

He paused. "With so many people killed on Tuesday, I don't want to call it a celebration, but I do want to celebrate that Natalie is alive—that we're all still alive."

Callie nodded. "Yes. Are you coming to Sara Bryant's Memorial Service on Tuesday at the church?"

"I'm planning on it. At ten?"

"Yes. And can you come to church with us tomorrow morning? I think my Russian student and her boyfriend, whom you met at the restaurant, are going to come."

The combined spiritual light from the angel in front of the house and from inside Callie was intense and very uncomfortable for Nepravel, as he came in through the back wall. But he'd heard the question and wanted to influence the answer.

Tom stopped cutting a pepper and looked at Callie. "The Memorial Service I want to do, and I'm sure it will be crowded with lots of good people. But your regular Sunday church service is a different situation. Your pastor refuses to abide by the State of Emergency. He's been detained. It's in the news. The message your church sends in general is divisive to a lot of people, despite what you, and even I, might think in regular times."

As she started to speak, he held up his hand. "I know. Look, I'm the president's National Security Advisor. I'm not sure how or why, but I am. I can't possibly attend a service at your church until this is over. Your pastor is defying rules and regulations I helped write and which I believe are important for our safety. Besides the fact that I think he's wrong, showing up at Church of the Good Shepherd again would be severely career limiting for me, to say the least."

Nepravel, constantly turning to withstand the spiritual heat, smiled.

Callie, who stopped cutting as Tom spoke, frowned. "You needn't worry. The Elders decided that for these last two weeks of your State of Emergency, we won't have a message. We're simply going to sing, read scripture, and pray. No sermon. So your career should survive, whether you attend or not."

He moved closer to her. "Callie, I know where Pastor Ludwig is. I check on his status and his well being every day. It may not be the Ritz where he's staying, but he should be fine. I'll make sure he's OK. I like you a lot and I don't want this to come between us. I wish I could wave a wand and make it all go away, but I have the responsibility to deal with it for the safety of the nation, and I think we're doing the right things. Can we please call a truce on this one subject and just agree that we disagree? I'd much rather kiss you than argue with you."

She listened and thought for a moment. Finally she shrugged her shoulders and smiled. "OK. But this is the only pass I'm giving you."

"Agreed. Now, watch that knife in your hand." He reached for her and they kissed. She put the knife down and let him pull her close as they kissed a second time.

Tom was in the backyard at the grill when the doorbell rang; Callie greeted Emily and Logan. As they were coming inside, Seth and Natalie also walked up the three steps to the landing. Natalie still had a bandage on her head. She and Callie hugged, while Seth watched. They all went inside, where Tom greeted them wearing his apron.

Natalie admitted to still being a little weak and took a large chair next to the coffee table in the living area. The men went to fix drinks.

A few minutes later Clayton and Andrea arrived. Behind them came Ahmad and Mariam Rashid. She was wearing a headscarf.

From near the front door, Clayton said, "Please meet our friends, Ahmad and Mariam. Ahmad and I go way back—all the way to Afghanistan, where we served together. Now we work together at the Threat Identification Group in the Pentagon. They and their two boys are staying with us for a bit."

Tom walked over and shook their hands. "Welcome. Three of us go back about a decade with Clayton, too. We're glad you're here. Please come meet everyone. Dinner should be ready in about thirty minutes."

The couples mixed and chatted while Tom kept an eye on the chicken and answered Callie's questions about where to find things. As was usual at D.C. gatherings, each couple—each individual, really—had an interesting story of current responsibilities and previous assignments, not to mention the terrible recent events, so the conversations were animated by many questions and answers.

Ten minutes in, Emily intercepted Seth on the way to the bar. "That piece you were working on right before all this started, 'The Progressive Silent Majority.' How far along is it?"

"I think we got it about seventy percent done. Why?"

"We'd like to talk about rolling it out soon, probably with some additions from the last month."

"Sure. We can do that. Talk Monday?"

"Yes. But I think you know what we need. Let's just compare subjects we want to be sure you cover so it's a thorough documentary."

He smiled and nodded. "We'll be on it."

A little later Tom announced from the kitchen that dinner was served and invited everyone to get a plate. On the back table by the window were a large platter of grilled chicken, salad, roast potatoes, and fresh bread.

They were standing by the island and were about to begin serving themselves when Callie interrupted.

"Would anyone mind if I said a blessing?"

They all looked around, and Tom smiled. "Of course, please." She bowed her head and the others followed.

"Father, thank you for your many blessings, and for our time together this evening. We especially thank you for protecting Natalie at this difficult time, and we pray for the families of all those killed or injured this week, to somehow give them Your Peace in the midst of their grief and pain. Please give our president and all who govern us Your wisdom and guidance to protect our nation. Be with us tonight in our conversations. And please bless this food and the hands that prepared it, that it will nourish us to serve You better. In Your name we pray. Amen."

Nepravel had had enough. The heat from the four believers was intense, but as the spiritual light and believers' individual voices from the answered prayer began to fill the space, he couldn't take the pain any longer. He quickly left through the back wall, hoping to avoid the pretty boy in front. He and his fellow demons would have to work after the dinner to spin voices in the non-believers and to find out what had happened. And he hoped their recent voice plants in the non-believers would help energize the discord they wanted among these people.

Everyone at the kitchen island smiled. Natalie said, "Thank you."

Tom handed her a plate. "Dig in."

When they were seated with full plates around the dining table, with Tom and Callie in the end chairs, Tom thanked everyone for coming and proposed a toast to Natalie. They clinked their glasses.

After several bites of the delicious food and a long sip of her wine, Emily said, "You realize it was three weeks ago right now that we met at Seth's for his birthday party? And then the world changed."

Everyone fell silent. Tom had a flashback to the previous White House, President Rhodes, Olivia Haas, all those killed on Air Force One, Jenny Stanton, and this week's DEA attack. And so many others.

Seth finally almost whispered. "Yes, it was a different world. Three weeks."

Logan said, "And so many of you around this table are on the front line of trying to stop it. It's remarkable. My wife never stops working."

"Nor my husband," Andrea added.

"We've won some battles, but we don't even know what war we're in, or who's behind it," Tom sighed, picking up a piece of bread. "We've got to do better."

"Forgive me," Ahmad said. "Mariam and I are your guests, and you don't really know us, other than Clayton and Andrea. But what if there is no single group behind it? What if different individuals and groups are just seeking revenge for past wrongs, real or imagined?"

Logan said, "And what if Islamic Jihadists are actually behind it all, and that's just a great smokescreen?"

Emily put her hand on his. "Logan, you have no idea. Why would you say that?"

"Ahmad was in their mosque when it was shot up—he was almost hit," Clayton said, frowning at Logan, who looked at Ahmad across the table.

Logan continued, feeding off voices planted in him over many years. "I grew up on Cyprus. My uncle and his wife were murdered by Muslims during the 1974 invasion by Turkey, and the rest of our family were uprooted and moved to the Greek southern side after the civil war divided the island. I know what happens when radical Muslims decide to attack."

Tom was surprised by Logan's sudden tough edge.

Ahmad smiled. "You know more than me, but my reading is that the war was started by the Greek junta in Athens, as a diversion from their failures, and trying to add Cyprus to Greece. Turkey, which at the time was only nominally Muslim, simply reacted."

"Not true. And the Turkish side is still a backwater. What good has ever come from a Muslim country? The religion keeps everyone down, straight-jacketed, starting with women." He nodded toward Mariam. "Surely—I assume you're Americans—you both see that."

Again there was silence.

Tom was about to speak a calming word when Ahmad said, "Yes, we were both born here. To Pakistani parents fleeing hatred and revenge. Our extended family loves this country and all that it stands for. And we've studied history."

Seth asked, "Actually I've always wanted to ask this question. I know Muslims are supposed to live their daily lives totally by Sharia Law, which speaks to almost every action and relationship. But when Sharia Law and our Constitution or our laws are at odds on any subject, which takes precedence?"

"Obviously, the Constitution," Mariam quickly replied.

Logan jumped in. "Then how can you be a good Muslim, and how does anyone else know whether what you just said is actually true? I'm sure the bastard who shot down Air Force One would have said the same thing if anyone had asked him before he climbed into his plane."

Ahmad nodded. "On the first question, how can a Christian who believes that marriage is a God-ordained permanent union between one man and one woman be both a Christian and an American, given the new laws on same-sex marriage? You just do it. As do we.

"On the second, no one ever knows what's in someone else's heart. In the 50s Senator McCarthy asked the same loyalty question of 'normal' looking white Americans who might have been communists. Maybe a few were. Most were not, or at least not violent in any way. It's the chance we have to take with each other to protect our liberties.

"And, trust me, we feel it all the time. We're staying with Andrea and Clayton because I pushed back against several men in our mosque who want to take revenge for the drone shootings, which I opposed, and they threatened us. So we wind up asking this same question about other American Muslims. It's both complicated and simple. Only Allah knows the heart, but as Americans we have to trust each other."

Logan shook his head. "It's not that simple when people are out to kill you."

"Actually, I think it is. It's just not easy. Look at the Uyghurs in China. They're being persecuted, even killed, not so much because they're Muslim, but because they profess *some* power higher than the Chinese government, which that government can't allow. The government has gone group by group for decades, systematically eliminating every ethnic, political, cultural and religious group which in any way challenges their absolute authority."

There was a pause while everyone took a sip. "And God can and does change hearts," Clayton offered. "He certainly changed mine, and it would be easy to pigeon-hole me as a white Southern officer in the military."

Emily nodded. "Yes. I've known you for ten years, Clayton, even lived in the same apartment with you, Seth and Tom. You do have a heart of gold. Here you've taken in our new friends to help protect them. But as an African American interested in social justice whose ancestors were brought here as slaves, I challenge us to go beyond just getting the heart right.

"Your ancestors, Clayton, probably enslaved mine. Or similar people. Your ancestors got wealth from slavery which has been passed down to you. Mine did not. And my grandparents couldn't buy houses where yours could, by federal regulation. In every other instance in America when the government takes something from someone, that same Constitution says that there must be just compensation. Don't you think that white people, or the federal government, owes quite a bit to me and my people?"

Natalie broke the ensuing silence. "Wow. How would you organize that? Who would pay?"

Emily looked at her and Seth. "I don't know, but after World War II Jews in Israel got reparation payments from Germany. Someone figured it out. Trust me, if there were a will, we'd figure out how to do it." She looked around at the table. "And I personally hope we get there soon—it's way past time for my people to get what they deserve."

"You're serious?" Andrea asked.

"Very much. It's in the Fifth Amendment—the Bill of Rights. With the proper Congress elected, I believe we'll get it done."

Another long silence while most of them cut their chicken or loaded their forks. Finally Clayton said, "Natalie, it's a miracle you survived. We felt the explosion through the walls of the Pentagon across the interstate."

She looked up at him. "Yes. I feel the same. A miracle. And, Ahmad, I understand the bullets from the drone just missed you. How does that feel?"

"Clayton and I were just missed by a lot of bullets when we were on patrol." He smiled. "I believe that Allah—God—is in charge of all such things. He orders our days."

"Yes, I guess I do, too. But in my case I know I'm only alive today because of the sacrifice of two women who warned me, tried to protect me, and ultimately gave their lives so that I lived. They're no longer here, but I am. I'm left asking *Why?* I think God must have a purpose in this—a purpose for me. I really want to understand it. Tom, what do you think?"

"I, uh. I'm not sure," Tom replied. "I'm *very* glad you're here. I just don't know what, if anything, is actually controlled by God, and what just happens."

"Then what's the purpose for living, if all of this is just random?" Callie asked from the other end of the table.

"To do the best we can for the most people," Emily offered. Logan nodded.

"But who defines that?" Callie asked. "If there's no God to set the rules, who knows what's 'best'? It can change from moment to moment and from person to person."

"Or from God to Allah," Logan noted, looking between Callie and Ahmad.

Silence again. Finally Tom said, "Look, we're here to celebrate Natalie. Some of us believe in God, some don't. That's OK. Natalie's apparently been touched by it all, which is understandable. Besides being happy for Natalie and Seth, we *can* agree, I think, that it's up to us to find whoever's doing this—whether it's a small group masterminding it like I believe, or some crazy random revenge all happening at once, like Ahmad suggested. Either way, we've got to stop it, and it's up to us."

Natalie looked up. "You may be right. But maybe, like with me, it's up to God."

"Or," Callie said, "maybe both."

Ninety minutes later Tom and Callie were alone in the kitchen, drying the last serving pieces.

"That got pretty intense," Tom said, lifting the salad bowl to its shelf. "I don't think in all our years together we've ever had a conversation quite like we did tonight."

"Yes. Personal. Divisive. Glad we settled back between the usual D.C. guardrails for the last hour."

He turned to her. "That about does it. Thank you for the help—all night. You were great. I hope you enjoyed it. Here, give me the towel, and let's have a night-cap in the living room."

When she offered the towel, he took her hand and, after checking her eyes, pulled her close again, and they kissed with an urgent intensity.

She finally pulled back and smiled. "OK, but I can't stay long. It's getting late."

He held on. "I don't guess there's much chance of a spend the night party."

She removed his hands but kept smiling. "No. I don't think so. For several good reasons. But let's have the nightcap, and then I can call a car, or we can walk. I've had a great time. Your friends are really interesting."

"We'll walk. And you've apparently had quite an impact on at least one—Natalie."

They started toward the front of the row house. "I was in the right place at the right time for God to use me."

"Apparently. Do you do that often?"

She shrugged.

"I'll put the nightcaps in cups, and we can walk and talk."

"Perfect."

When they arrived at Callie's apartment's door, he hugged her and they kissed again. Then she let herself in, and Tom turned to walk home.

Kristen was on the sofa in Callie's living room, dressed in jeans and a pullover, reading a book. "Hi. Grace is fine. How was your evening?"

Callie hung her wrap, smiled, and shook her head. "Fine. Crazy."

Kristen put down her book. "Would you like some herbal tea and a chat?"

"That sounds like a great idea. I'll check on Grace and change."

A few minutes later Kristen was back on the sofa, and Callie was in a large chair across the coffee table from her in her pajamas. Each was balancing a cup of tea.

"So tell me about your dinner," Kristen said, testing the tea's temperature.

"Tom is an amazing guy with amazing friends," she answered, pulling her knees up into the chair. "Four of them have known each other really well for ten years. They're very open and comfortable with each other, which is great, but they also don't mince any words." Callie went on to describe the guests and the issues addressed at the dinner. Kristen winced at some of her descriptions.

"And of course Seth's girlfriend, Natalie, suffered in the explosion and gave herself to Christ this week. She's amazing, and she wants more information about your Beginnings Class tomorrow at church. But then Emily, who actually introduced us, seems to think that faith is crazy, for losers. So it was all pretty interesting."

"And how about you and Tom?"

Callie looked into her teacup for a moment, then back at Kristen.

"I wish it would work. He's intelligent, charming, caring. And appears to have a great future. But he isn't a believer. At least not that I can tell."

Kristen nodded and took a sip. Callie continued. "When we talk about anything spiritual, he obviously talks the talk. He knows what faith is. He just refuses to have anything to do with it. Like he's moved on, knows more, is smarter, and anyone who believes is sort of deranged. And of course I can't imagine a long term relationship with any man who hasn't submitted his life to the Lord." She paused. "It's actually kind of sad. One day soon I'll have to spare us both a lot of wasted time and break it off."

She looked up at her friend, clearly distressed.

Kristen said, "We've both known people like that. 'Inoculated' I heard one pastor say. They think they know just enough about our faith to keep from getting the rest of it." She paused and sighed. "I met Tom when he was fourteen. You know the story of how his parents and I went through a tumultuous year of pain, but eventually we all found God's grace, forgiveness, and peace, thanks mainly to Tom's father, Richard. And I thought that a year or two later Tom became a believer. But I could be wrong. I can ask them."

Callie shrugged. "Whatever happened then, I can assure you that he thinks he's moved on, and, like I said, it's sad. He's a good, typical, secular man, but he will always be less than the man I could give myself to because he thinks he's in charge, that it's all about him and his abilities. How could I marry someone—if that ever came up—who doesn't believe that God *has* to be the third person in the marriage if it's ever going to work?"

Kristen turned on her side and smiled. "I know. I know. Look at me. Where are the Godly men?" A silence ensued. "Let's pray for Tom, and you, and Natalie and all the people who were there tonight, that God will show each of them His Truth, and move each of them closer to Him."

Callie nodded. "Yes. Please, lead us." They bowed their heads, and Kristen prayed.

Overnight at the abortion clinic Nepravel reported that he had followed them to Callie's apartment but could not learn much about what had happened—he had to stay back because of the angel hovering about them.

Others, however, had more positive reports. Emily and Logan Schofield, according to Zloy, were incensed by some of the insensitive and stupid things the Hunts and their Muslim friends had said. And apparently Natalie couldn't express her new faith well enough to interest anyone—the Schofields felt embarrassed for her. And Seth was questioning their future together.

So while no disaster seemed to have occurred from the dinner, it was clear that they had to break up Tom's relationship with Callie and cement him as a permanent skeptic before she could have any more impact on him. Tom was gaining too much power in the White House for them to let his permanent lack of faith remain even the slightest question. Nepravel, having spent a busy summer with Tom, said to Zloy, "I think the answer is on the way."

A little later, as they assembled for the larger meeting in the main space at the clinic, a new arrival materialized, still appearing to be in the rugged, dusty wardrobe of his last assignment at a training camp in Afghanistan.

He looked around. "I'm Mavlan. Is Balzor here? I'm supposed to report."

Zloy nodded. "Hey, Mavlan. It's Zloy. We were together in Cambodia all through Pol Pot's Killing Fields. Balzor's over there."

"Those were good times. Looking forward to the same here." He moved over to Balzor. "I worked with the Uyghurs at the camps in Afghanistan, and the leader wants me here to help keep them on track for the finale next month."

Balzor smiled. "Glad to have you. The prayers are getting to be ridiculously frequent, and aimed right at us. With the Uyghurs you may be able to work without all that."

"I hope so. They're so full of hate that it shouldn't be difficult to keep them focused. I know Zloy over there from before. Can he show me around in the morning?"

"Yeah, sure. And as soon as you check their voices and motivations, let us know if you need anything. They're probably enjoying America."

"One more month. Then they're ours forever."

Balzor nodded and turned to the others to start their nightly meeting. He introduced Mavlan and then reported that on Friday he was able to spend most of the day in the White House, along with several other senior sector leaders. Apparently believers were praying less for this progressive president, or they'd simply lost interest. Whatever the cause, the prayer light and heat was reducing daily, and Balzor believed their forces would have a free run of the Oval Office and of all the president's meetings with his staff within a week. And the vice president. This would give them both more intelligence and more opportunities to make Americans suffer.

# 15

*If in the opinion of the People, the distribution or modification of the Constitutional powers be in any particular wrong, let it be corrected by an amendment in the way which the Constitution designates. But let there be no change by usurpation; for though this, in one instance, may be the instrument of good, it is the customary weapon by which free governments are destroyed.*

George Washington
Tuesday, October 6

Tom was in the office, as was his habit, early that Tuesday morning to check on developments with Tanya Prescott and General Price, and then to attend the daily Intelligence Briefing with the president, held that morning in the Oval Office.

The SAC's focused work that weekend had produced several possible connecting leads—it was inevitable that people out to commit violent acts would visit some of the same websites and experts. And so the FBI with the NSA and local law enforcement were following up on every possible connection. And that was the main message of the briefing—follow-up on all the previous attacks and arrests. Thankfully, there had been no new attacks.

As the others left the Oval Office, Tom lingered by the Resolute Desk, where President Bradshaw was sitting. Unseen by them were Balzor, Nepravel and two other sector leaders.

"I'm going to attend the Memorial Service for the policewoman who was the hero in the DEA bombing last week."

"It's at that pastor's church, isn't it?"

"Yes. Robert Ludwig. Church of the Good Shepherd. Ironically, that's where she attended."

"It'll be good to see a member of our Cabinet there—shows we're concerned about all our people, particularly first responders, even as we have to enforce strict rules on whoever violates them. Good balance. And that reminds me—Patricia told me about asking you to look into the possibility of creating something like the Trusted Traveler program we've had for years, only broader. A voluntary program to identify and reward people with no history or inclination to violence, treason or terrorism, so that we can better focus on the bad actors."

"Yes. I have a meeting this afternoon with an assistant secretary at Homeland Security who helped set up the traveler program. If we do it, I think we should house it at DHS, but of course it will focus on much more than travel."

"Of course. And, listen, Drew Boswell should be able to help us there, too. Juggle has a lot of experience gathering information on people and summarizing their behavior."

"We'll see. Sure."

"Let us know if you learn anything at the Memorial Service."

"I will. And you'll have the detailed draft for the extended State of Emergency this afternoon."

Tom took the Restricted Zone East-West shuttle van over to the zone's eastern boundary next to the Supreme Court. As he rode, he thought how nice it was to be able to move around this large area without all the pedestrian and vehicular traffic that used to clog the area before the attacks. Getting out, he sidestepped a small group holding placards by the checkpoint calling for an end to the State of Emergency. They were watched over by a contingent of police, who were also taking their pictures, and there was no media coverage. From the checkpoint it was a ten minute walk to The Church of the Good Shepherd.

He and Callie had agreed to meet outside; by 9:30 there was already a crush of people. She waved from the steps, and he followed her inside to a pew near the front where Kristen was holding seats for them. Natalie and Seth were there, and as Tom moved to sit between the two younger women, he saw Clayton, Andrea, Ahmad and Mariam four rows back. The men were in uniform. They exchanged greetings.

Nepravel, Zloy and a host of others assigned to the humans in attendance could not go anywhere near the church. The spiritual light and heat from all the believers was as intense as Nepravel had ever experienced. Bolts of incoming prayers were landing all around, and three brilliant angels covered the building with their protection. It was no place for a demon.

Tom had seen photos of Sara and her family on easels in the narthex. Now he read a short history of this remarkable woman in the Order of Service. The oldest of four children, Sara had apparently focused her life on service, first in the Army, and then both on and off-duty in her police work, and in several of the church's outreach ministries.

A little after ten an honor guard of Arlington County police officers in dress uniforms silently preceded Sara Bryant's casket, draped in an American flag, down the central aisle, her family following immediately behind. The casket stopped in front of the raised platform, and her family filled the first three rows of pews.

The assistant pastor greeted everyone and said that Sara had chosen the hymns they would sing and the scripture they would read as an exercise during a Women's Retreat in which each attendee was asked to imagine how she wanted her life to be remembered and celebrated.

There was then a moment of silent prayer, after which the organ announced the powerful opening to John Newton's "Amazing Grace."

As he stood to sing, Tom felt chills run down his arms. The choir and the congregation filled the church with triumphant praise.

After two prayers the pastor announced that Sara wanted to be remembered by how God had used her imperfect talents to touch the lives of others. Four women in succession gave testimonies about how, when in high school, college, the Army and the police force, Sara had changed the course of their lives for the better, pointing each one to the peace and joy of a relationship with their Savior.

As the last one finished, she said, "Sara touched a lot of people. As the next hymn begins, I'd like to ask those of you who know that Sara impacted your life in a personal way to stand in her honor."

Natalie immediately stood, as did Callie, and many others. A moment later, Seth stood as well.

Everyone then stood and sang "How Deep The Father's Love For Us." As the powerful song came to its final verse, Tom heard several audible sobs in the sanctuary.

The final speaker was a young man about Tom's age named Ryan Hopkins. As he started to speak, Callie reached for Tom's hand.

Ryan told the congregation that, as many of them knew, he and Sara had been engaged to be married in November. He recounted a brief testimony of his early life without faith, including several relationships over the years, some drug use, and a dark future. He had been led by an old high school friend to surrender his life to Jesus Christ five years earlier, at home in Seattle, and then a year ago he had moved to D.C. to start a new job. Another friend had recommended the Church of the Good Shepherd, where he found a real home. And then he met Sara.

The smile that broke out on Ryan's face startled Tom. His whole countenance changed at the mention of her name. He described how they had come to know each other in an outreach ministry, and in the church's high school ministry. Their friendship had grown into something more. Ryan couldn't explain it—it was like nothing he had ever experienced with a woman before. She was so good, so intelligent, so exciting to be around. He loved just talking with her, going places, serving together. They had just booked their honeymoon and were deep into wedding plans.

She was to be his radiant bride, pure on their wedding day, because both of them had been bought at a great price, and they were committed to honoring God in every aspect of their relationship. And Ryan hoped to love her sacrificially, as Christ loves the church.

When Callie dabbed her eye with her other hand, Tom was struck by how similar the two young women appeared to be.

"And now she's gone," Ryan said. There was a moment of silence. "We will not be married." He wiped his eyes. "But I have a year's worth of incredible memories—she changed me with her love and her example of faith in action. And though her body lies here in front of me, she is not really here. She is alive. She's in heaven, loving and being loved, and helping others, just like she did here." He smiled through his tears. "And I know that I'll see her again. Isn't that incredible? I'll be with Sara and all the other believers, forever." Another pause.

"This is in one way a terrible, terrible day. But ours is an amazing eternity. Meeting my savior and meeting Sara are the two greatest things that have ever happened to me. And whatever happens in the future, I will meet them both again, and I know that God is in charge. If you've found a soulmate, hold her or him close. Speak your love. And if you haven't yet found Christ as your savior, ask Him into your life today. It's the most important thing you will ever do.

"Sara, I love you. You've been His for years, and now you're with Him. I cannot be sad." Again he smiled. "I rejoice, because Sara lives."

Ryan finished and rejoined the family. The assistant pastor led the church in final prayers, and they sang "It Is Well With My Soul." Tom felt chills. And he noticed that tears were streaming down the cheeks of both Natalie and Callie.

After the casket, the honor guard, and the family departed, the guests began to file out. As Tom turned to his friends, he felt both drained and energized. Natalie was still teary, but smiling.

Seth turned to him, mildly shaking his head. "That was incredible. I've never been to anything like that."

Callie whispered, "They were so in love. She knew he was the right one—she talked about him a lot. Imagine having anyone love you that much."

The two other couples joined them, and the women hugged.

"A truly remarkable person who touched so many people in such a short life," Ahmad said to the three men, who all nodded.

"On earth," Clayton added. "As Ryan said, she's not here, but she's well, and with her Savior forever."

They began to walk out, and when they were near the back of the church, Kristen, who was leading the way, suddenly stopped. "Gary, I'm so glad you're here." She shook hands with an older man and his wife, then turned. "Everyone please meet Gary Thornton. He's been on several panels here, and our women's group had dinner with him. Thank you for coming."

He nodded. "I remember Sara was at our dinner. She asked great questions."

They all shook hands. As Tom reached forward, he glanced at Callie. "Actually, I'm about halfway through *The Foundations of Faith in America*. How did you find time to do all that research and correlation?"

Thornton smiled. "I'm old. I've had lots of time. And I have great assistants. What do you think of it?"

"It's certainly different from most of what I was taught in school."

Thornton nodded. "Yes. I hear that a lot. How long can our nation last without knowing our real history?"

Callie said, "Tom does a little work at The White House."

Tom smiled. "And Callie gave me your book."

"Then why don't the three of us have lunch one day soon? We can talk about all that history, and you can ask me whatever you want."

Tom looked at Callie, who was beaming. "Uh, OK. Yes, that would be interesting. Thank you. How will we set it up?"

A few minutes later Tom said goodbye to Callie and the others on the sidewalk. He wanted to take Callie to lunch, but he had to finish the new Executive Orders.

"Thank you," he said to Callie. "I'll text you this afternoon. What a coincidence to meet Gary Thornton."

She smiled. "Yes. What a coincidence. Let's have dinner again soon."

He nodded and walked west. From somewhere he heard a faint voice. *What just happened? Are those people real? All that joy in the midst of their terrible loss. How could anyone be like that?*

When he reached the Restricted Zone checkpoint and showed his badge, Nepravel was finally able to rejoin him. He was appalled to find that all the voices he had planted over the past weeks were gone. Silenced. Tom was in great danger. *He* was in great danger. As Tom settled into a seat on the shuttle, Nepravel went to work, ramping up *Doubt, Unworthy, Unproven, Impossible, Too Busy, Too Important,* and *Pride.* He had a suspicion that the last three might prove to be very important before the day was over.

As Seth and Natalie walked back to their apartment, she quietly said, "Did you see that?"

"What?"

"All those people. All that joy. All that love."

"Yes. I told Tom it was crazy."

"But it was *real.* That's what God has been chasing me for. What Callie helped me pray for. *That's* the life I want. I'm still not sure exactly what to do to get there, but I know those people have what I want. I'm going to talk with Callie and Kristen about how to learn more."

They walked on in silence. "You really have changed."

She thought for a moment. "Yes. I'm free. But I'm His. Does that make sense?"

He looked at her and smiled. "I guess. Well, actually, I'm not sure. But I'm trying."

She took his hand. "Thank you. I love you."

Tom spent the afternoon reading through what he hoped was the final draft of the expanded and extended State of Emergency.

Under his personal hands-on coordination, but with the new VP's Task Force as the publicly visible lead, the Core Group had pulled together input from all the NSC stakeholders, including the FBI, Military Intelligence, the NSA, CIA and others on how to improve the effectiveness of their search for the perpetrators, as well as on how to better control hate speech with an election season in full swing.

Unknown to Tom and the others in the Core Group, except for Emily Schofield, the proposed State of Emergency enhancements had been reviewed and tweaked by members of the Phoenix Project to ensure that the wording in the government's official actions also encouraged a Progressive victory in November. And Drew Boswell's friends at the largest social media platforms adjusted their algorithms to make it almost impossible to find anything negative online about the extension.

Tom finished reading the final product and was pleased. These new steps would better protect the nation, end hate speech for the duration, and coincidentally further enhance his rising star status with the president and the party's leadership. It felt good.

He had just returned to his desk from delivering the draft to the president's secretary when his phone vibrated. He immediately thought of Callie, but when he looked at the readout, it was a different woman's name.

"Erin? Hey, how are you?"

"I'm fine. Busy. How 'bout you? I haven't heard from you in a while."

"I...yes, as you can imagine right now, after the attacks."

"You couldn't even call once?"

Tom and Erin MacNeil had met at a seminar sponsored by the Information Initiative, the institute where Erin worked, in early August. Erin, like Tom, was interested in cyber security, and their initial conversation had expanded into dinner that same night and a taxi back to his row house. Then they'd spent a weekend together at the beach.

He paused. "You're right. I'm sorry. I should have. The weekend you had to go to L.A. for your job is when the first attacks happened, and I've been covered up every minute since. But I should have called."

"Our beach weekend seems like a long time ago, doesn't it? A great time."

"Yeah. A great time." He smiled.

"It was. But the result is I'm pregnant."

Tom said nothing.

"And, yes, if you're wondering, I know only you could be the father."

"I, uh...Oh."

Erin paused. "That's how I feel, too. But, listen, I'm not calling to harass you. I know we haven't seen each other since then, and that's OK. I'm a big girl. I'm about ninety percent certain I'm going to have an abortion, but I thought I'd call and check to see if you have any strong feelings one way or the other. This is also your potential son or daughter we're discussing, as well as mine."

"I think it's totally your choice."

"Yes, ultimately. But I wanted to find out if you have any interest in helping to raise a child now. I don't mean to get married. You're a great guy, but we hardly know each other. I mean, just, if you've always wanted a child, or you think it's important, I'm doing my best to seek your input."

"I, uh...thank you. No. I don't have any strong feelings to want a child right now. I obviously haven't thought about it, but like you, I'm really busy."

"Yes, I get it. I have to decide pretty soon. Right now, abortion seems like the best answer. But I'll let you know."

"Yes. And, uh, I'll be glad to pay for it. Or share. Or...I'm not sure what one does in this situation."

"Me neither. My first time. But I'll let you know. OK?"

"Yeah, sure. Just let me know what you decide."

"OK, I will. Be safe. Bye."

"Thanks. You, too. Goodbye."

He put the phone down. Erin. Beautiful. Sandy red hair. Smart. Younger, maybe twenty-six. From Texas, he recalled. A cyber security expert with a great laugh. She'd come on like gangbusters, and he, of course, had been happy to go along. As he had with so many others over the years.

Pregnant? Seemed impossible. Didn't she say she took the pill? He actually couldn't remember. Their weekend rental on the Eastern Shore. Pregnant? A baby? A voice told him it was almost quaint that she'd called him to get his input. Why did she even ask? *Self-importance. Busy.* He had too many big responsibilities—all critical to the nation—to imagine taking on even shared responsibility for a child. And she had a career as well. Crazy.

*Just have the abortion.*

Late that afternoon President Bradshaw finished reading the updated draft Executive Order that Tom had delivered, then headed up to the residence for a simple dinner with Margaret. Balzor was at his side. The voices inside the president were reliable and strong, so Balzor liked to work on his imagination, feeding him ideas.

"You look tired. Bad day?" she asked, as he loosened his tie in the bedroom.

He smiled. "Not so bad. I guess I'm getting used to mayhem and constant sparring. Budgets. Briefings. People. Rob, Emily, Patricia and I are still having to work through the people whom Rhodes installed. Beyond dealing with the current attacks, our ideas on a faster pace to a better future don't generally match theirs, to say the least. How was the new Food Bank opening?"

They walked to the bar in the West Sitting Hall. "Well organized with a lot of people. The press were all over it."

"Good, good. Thank you. They should serve a lot more people with the increased warehouse space."

He fixed their drinks and they sat together in comfortable chairs by the window.

"What's the answer to the Rhodes people vs. our Progressive policies?"

He took a sip and sighed. "There's so much up in the air now. The attacks. The State of Emergency. The elections. It's difficult to change teams at a time like this, but we're going to have to. The election is key to the nation's future. Rhodes' people all talk a good, classic, liberal line, but they're too passive, too open to compromise with conservative whack-ohs. Our own team wants *real* change. Over the years we've been close to having a working, filibuster-proof Progressive majority in both houses, but we've never quite made it. Now we're almost there. Think of all the Progressive policies and social justice reforms we can finally implement, and once and for all transform the nation, if we can just win a few more seats next month."

She nodded. "It's been your dream for a long time."

He thought for a minute, looking out the window. "We simply must win. The nation needs our solutions. Maybe the State of Emergency—and the changes we're about to make—will give us some additional opportunities."

"What do you mean?"

"I'm not completely sure. But I'm going to talk with Drew—then with James Toomey, and with Tom."

# Thursday, October 8

Before she had washed the sleep from her eyes that morning, Teri Grantham received a text from her brother: *Turn on the News. Lunch at your place?*

Teri clicked on her TV as she poured coffee in the kitchen. On every network the only story was about a savage attack on both the Muslim and Jewish Student Centers at Duke University the night before. It had apparently been conducted by an armed drone, like their mosque attack. In Durham, despite the late hour, there had been students inside each building, ironically located only a block apart. Six were killed and several were wounded by the high-powered rounds fired as the drone apparently hovered just outside the well-lit windows.

Although no one had claimed responsibility for the attacks, because it was in the South and both Jewish and Muslim students were targeted, the pundits on the networks all speculated that it was probably an Alt-Right White supremacist group, perhaps even fringe-Christian radicals.

After watching for ten minutes, Teri put down her coffee and confirmed meeting with Brad for lunch.

"Today of all days," President Bradshaw fumed from his seat at the end of the table in the Situation Room, surrounded by Patricia Reynolds, Tom, Emily, his Core Group and the key NSC departments responsible for battling whoever continued to attack the nation so viciously. "I think we still have to go ahead with the address to the nation tomorrow." He was referring to the upcoming announcement about the State of Emergency which Emily had booked with the networks for eleven on Friday morning. "Tom, what do we know?"

"Unfortunately, not much yet, sir, beyond the casualties and damage." He nodded to Agent Prescott on one of the large monitors on the wall.

The SAC said, "Since the two buildings are so close together, the drone—or drones—could have been launched from anywhere on that side of Durham, blasted both properties with multiple rounds, and been

314

gone, all in a matter of a few minutes. As you know, locating a drone at night over a large urban area is almost impossible. And even if you detect it and it's identified as a threat, there's no readily available countermeasure. In this case, a few people reported the noise and saw some muzzle flashes, but that's it."

"So what's the answer?" the president asked the table.

"We talked before you got here, sir," Tom answered, "and we think it's to focus on the people. Track back using records of purchases, user courses, known users, and associations to find everyone with access to a large drone that could be modified to support a rifle."

"Can we add an Executive Order requiring drone registration?"

After glancing around the table, Tom answered, "Yes, of course. Give us a day."

"Patricia, can you cancel whatever you were doing today and fly down to Durham this morning to visit the hospitals and meet with the leaders? And Tom, why don't you go with her? It'll be good for you, and you'll be back this afternoon."

Their cell phones turned off and left in the entrance hall, Teri and Brad Grantham sat down to lunch in her kitchen. He'd stopped by their favorite Bar-B-Q place on the way out, and she put the plates on the table as he deposited three morning newspapers on the island.

"Who the hell did that?" he fumed. "Friggin copycats."

"Only worse. They killed people. And attacked Jews as well. Terrible."

He reached for the ribs. "I guess it was inevitable that someone would copy us. But in only ten days? How many drone and rifle combinations can there be, ready to go?"

"I've been thinking about that all morning. I know some people in the drone business in North Carolina. Like me, here. We sometimes talk and share tips. Look, is your rifle registered anywhere?"

"No."

"But other people have seen you with it?"

"Yeah, of course."

"So could you quietly get another one just like it, and 'lose' that one for a while? Maybe bury it?"

"Why?"

"In case anyone starts connecting the drone and rifle dots, and finds us, I'd like your rifle's bore not to match whatever slugs they pulled out of that mosque. I'll bury the special sling we made. And let's talk about where we were that night."

"Yeah, I can do that, today."

"And then we'll lay low for a while. I actually hope they catch whoever killed those students. That was never our idea."

Ranit, who had been invisibly listening to their conversation, was again struck with the incredible human capacity for self-delusion, even without any assistance.

Tom had texted Callie from Air Force Two, suggesting that they walk over to Eighth Street for dinner that night, since the weather was so nice. She agreed and they decided to return to the Balkan restaurant they'd enjoyed before.

Tom said hello to Grace and "Aunt Kristen" while Callie finished getting ready.

"Wanna help with our puzzle?" Grace asked, pointing to the jigsaw pieces and the almost finished border on the coffee table.

"Sure." He joined her on the sofa by the table and almost immediately found a missing piece, which he handed to her to insert.

"Good job," Kristen said from the chair. "We've been looking for that one."

"Yes. Good job."

Five minutes later they told Grace and Kristen good night and left them bent over the puzzle. As they walked, Tom started to tell Callie about his brief but poignant trip with the vice president to Durham, beginning with visits to seven students in two hospitals.

They wound up waiting at seats in the bar again, and Callie nodded when he suggested Old Fashions.

"Being here again reminds me of my student Katherine and her friend Patrick Tomlinson. Did I tell you they came to our church on Sunday?

"You said they might."

"Well, for yet another reason, you should've been there." She smiled and pointed her finger at him. "Turns out the younger people are both believers—and she mentioned her uncle on Cyprus is as well. They may come back this week."

"Good. Alexander Nobikov."

"You remember his name?"

"He gave me his card, and I ran it through our system. Seems to be a legitimate internet service provider and journalist. Maybe other stuff, too. You never know with internet people."

She smiled. "Like you? And—you won't believe this—Patrick is interning with Gary Thornton and writes synopses of new books and articles on American History for him. How's that for a coincidence? So maybe all of us will get together."

"Great. Let me know. But, look, here's your drink, and let me tell you about today."

She settled back, took a sip and nodded. "Sure."

"The VP was of course the lead. I just went along, asked some questions, and took notes. It was terrible. Last night, with the lights on and with big windows in each building, the drone apparently just hovered outside in the dark and opened fire on rooms full of people. In both buildings there were still blood stains everywhere. Awful.

"Patricia met with some of the parents at the hospital. And with two couples who lost their children. I don't know how she does it. I could barely speak." He shook his head.

"Is there any idea who did it?"

"Ironically, the killings have brought the two communities closer together. They apparently for years have had joint projects and make a real point of getting to know each other. But, sadly, there are also apparently calls to find out who did it, and to take revenge."

"Ugh."

"Yes. Our federal team is helping the Durham police comb through any connections between White Nationalists or Alt-Right Christian extremists, and drone operators in the area."

"Christian Extremists?"

"Yes."

PARKER HUDSON

"Hmm."

The hostess arrived to take them to their table. Callie insisted that this round was on her, and paid the tab.

Nepravel had ridden on Air Force Two and joined the VP's group for the interviews and discussions. On the return flight, focusing on his main responsibility, Nepravel had used Tom's immediate, strong emotional response to what he saw and heard in Durham to ramp up voices that reinforced the need to clamp down hard on all those who sowed division and hate, no matter what the short-term costs might be. Tom heard his own voice say that he owed it to the nation and to the president to stop this dissension.

But now Nepravel was once again outside on the sidewalk, a block away from the restaurant. That same angel was standing watch over Tom and Callie. Nepravel vowed to find out who was doing all the praying for them, and, as best he could, to stop them.

They almost knew the menu by heart so they were ready to order when the waiter brought their second round of drinks, and the restaurant's signature bread basket.

"Mmm," Callie said, slowly enjoying her first taste of the baker's finest.

"Too bad we have to order anything else, but I think they'd notice."

She nodded, smiled, and took another bite. "Grace loves to bake. Wouldn't it be great if they had classes here?"

"It was fun doing the puzzle with her. She and Kristen are great pals."

"They're inseparable. Did I mention how blessed I am to have both of them?"

He turned more serious and took a sip.

"So, when you found out you were pregnant nine years ago, did you ever think about having an abortion? You were pretty young."

She looked down, then at him. "That was the least of it. As I told you, I'd been making movies with my boyfriend. Kristen had befriended me, 'cause she was a believer and knew my Dad at work. My best friend in the movie business died from a drug overdose. Kristen was amazing. She flew out to California to be with me. Crazy. God was clearly chasing me, using her. In that same week I found out I was pregnant and, with Kristen's help, surrendered my awful life to the only one who could save me. He washed it all away. It's gone. My terrible story is now embedded in His great story. I'm a completely new person." She smiled. Almost laughed. "Isn't God incredible?"

He just looked at her. She continued.

"So, since becoming pregnant was all part of His plan for me, how could I abort that child? Grace saved me—both His grace *and* the child. And now you know her. Can you imagine killing her?"

"Hmm. Well, you wouldn't have killed the Grace we know. She was just a tiny fetus."

"Who else was that fetus than the Grace we know? They're the same. I would have killed Grace."

He took a long sip. "OK. So, in your case the pregnancy was part of a larger plan for you to be saved. How about for the more 'plain vanilla' case where a girl just finds herself pregnant?"

"God has a plan for everyone, Tom. Mine may have been more intense at that moment. But every baby is precious in God's eyes. Each one is made in His image. How can anyone kill a baby?" Callie paused. "Tom, why are you asking? Is something going on?"

He looked down to put butter on another piece of bread. "Well, uh, a girl I know is unexpectedly pregnant, and she...asked my advice on what to do."

Callie leaned forward. "Are you the father?"

"She says I am."

"Are you?"

"I, uh, guess so."

Callie slumped back. The waiter arrived with their salads. After he left, she asked, "What advice did you give her?"

"I haven't seen her since—since August. She had ninety percent decided to have an abortion when she called, but she wanted to hear from me. She has a great position at the Information Initiative. I told her to go ahead." Callie was silent, looking at Tom. "I'm not ready to be a father. You know what I have on my plate for responsibilities."

She spoke softly. "I wasn't 'ready,' either, to be a mother. Who is? So your convenience is more important than a baby's life?"

"That's not fair. I'm working to save lots of lives!"

"Not that one. And he or she is pretty defenseless."

"Look, it's not a baby. It's a fetus."

She shook her head. "It's a baby. I'll send you a link to pictures that show the results of abortions at different stages."

"I doubt I'll watch it."

"How about adoption?"

"And put her through childbirth?"

"Yes. Her career will hardly take a bump. Or yours, for that matter."

"Well...that seems more like only her decision. When I was about fourteen the girl next door to us got pregnant, and she had her baby. My sister Susan's best friend, Amy. She had a boy. He almost died on the way to the hospital. My Dad was in the ambulance and prayed all the way there. I guess that all turned out OK."

Callie nodded. "Yes. You should tell her. Soon."

"It's asking a lot of her."

"Give me her phone number. I'll tell her."

"No. No. I'll do it. But abortion just seems so much easier."

"Not for the baby."

"You have strong opinions."

"Tom, I really don't. I just know that there is right and wrong, in God's eyes. He made us. His truths. He hates murdering babies. And He hated much of what I was doing. He saved me from that. So I can help save babies. It's not my opinion. It's His truth. Do you realize that since 1973 on average we've killed one baby every thirty seconds, 24/7/ 365? Two babies a minute! For decades. If you're looking for a reason why God may be allowing attacks on our nation, you might start there. Hopefully with the Supreme Court ruling it will slow down a bit. But it's still the individual's decision. We have to choose sometimes, right or wrong. Good or evil. Tom, I'm asking you to choose."

He paused as the waiter delivered their main courses and refilled their waters. "OK. OK. I'll call her and tell her."

"Good. Let me know. I'll be praying for her—and you. Do you mind telling me her name?"

"Uh, I guess not. Erin. Again, I haven't seen her for quite a while."

"I understand. I'm the last one to throw a rock."

Tom's phone vibrated. He read the message.

"The president wants me to have breakfast with him in the morning."

Callie nodded and took a bite of her lamb. "We roll out the update to the State of Emergency at eleven. He probably wants to talk about it. I expect Emily'll be there, too."

"Mmm. I'm just glad it's almost over. We need our pastor back."

Tom didn't say anything as he typed his acceptance for the morning.

# Friday, October 9

After walking Callie home and thinking more about Erin, Tom slept for six hours and was in his office at the White House at seven, reviewing the overnight information. At seven thirty he walked to the entrance to the Residence, and a few minutes later he was seated across from President Bradshaw at a small table in the private kitchen. A buffet was provided, and Tom had chosen scrambled eggs and bacon.

Balzor and Nepravel joined them to listen in and to add their influence. The flurry of prayers following the original attacks had made it difficult to get this close, but the reduced number of occasional incoming prayers for the president in recent weeks posed no problem for the demons and would attract no angels. Unless God Himself sent one of His messengers on a mission, they were safe to sow their voices and their lies with impunity.

As the two men ate and sipped their coffee, Tom briefed the president on his trip to Durham, and on the massive resources being devoted to connecting the dots between drone operators and possible terrorist organizations. The president nodded and agreed how tough it must be for the parents and friends of the students who were attacked.

When Tom finished, he asked, "Are Emily and Rob going to join us?"

"We'll see them a little later for the Executive Order update. For now I want to talk just with you."

The younger man was surprised. He picked up his coffee mug and sat back. He of course could not see Balzor move closer to the president, whom the demon had been speaking to daily for many years, while Nepravel moved next to his own chair.

"I hope you agree, Tom, that the upcoming election is critical to the future of our nation—maybe our very existence. And with the State of Emergency still in place, I imagine there may be a lot of angst and a lot of drama as the election approaches. Do you agree?"

"Yes sir, I do."

"And unless we can govern effectively through the crisis, the attacks may increase again, and the chaos may get worse."

Tom nodded.

"So we've got to not only win, but we've got to control both the House and the Senate with majorities that can actually pass legislation. No more gridlock. Agreed? Well, it turns out that given past voting patterns, achieving that control this year means winning in twenty key Congressional Districts and seven Senate races that are now very close. Can you imagine? So much potential change in the hands of so few voters."

Tom nodded again.

"Given the physical attacks we've seen this month, don't you think we're in for cyber attacks—your specialty—and don't you think those specific races would be particularly attractive to a dedicated group, or a country, to cause us real harm?"

Tom leaned forward. "We've always thought our election process was a key target, which is why Congress passed the Federal Election Protection and Integrity law a few years ago, but I hadn't really focused on how few altered votes it might take to make a really big difference."

"Exactly."

"What are you thinking?"

"I think we have to build a fortress around those particular races. Here's a list of them." The president took a handwritten note from the table next to him and handed it to Tom. "And we have to start by understanding whether someone could hack inside each of them and change the results, even with the new, federally mandated processes and systems."

"It could happen, but it's pretty unlikely, given how different and diverse the polling places are, using different systems and machines. And it's now illegal under the new Federal Election Law to connect any voting machine to the internet—the results have to be delivered by hand from each precinct to the county or state Election Management System on a secure flash drive or memory disk, with two-person control.

"And under the new law the FEIC is now the single central collection point for the results from each state's EMS. The communication and tabulation software they use was developed with Juggle's help, and it's very secure and accurate. And they run tests with every state's EMS several times right before the election, to check for integrity."

"OK. But is there a way that you, the National Security Advisor, could really make sure, for us? Sort of test the testing process?"

Tom thought for a moment. "I think so. I could get the connection keys for these races from the FEIC team and have some white-hat hacker friends I know try to get inside each race, to see if they can. And then we could ask the FBI or NSA to check the integrity of the FEIC's electronic reporting connection to each one."

"That sounds like a good plan, Tom. I want us to be sure that no one hacks any election results, and particularly in these key races. But this has to be done totally off the grid. We don't want to be accused of interfering with the process, or of embarrassing any Secretary of State or Election Commissioner. That's why I wanted to speak privately with you. We want to test each race for security without anyone knowing about it. So that, if we find any vulnerabilities, we can then mount a real defense, not tipping off any election officials beforehand, and actually catch those who might do the attacks on election night. Sort of like an ambush, I guess."

Tom looked at the list and thought for a moment. "Well, if there are twenty-seven or so key races, I could farm out twenty-seven different assignments across a wide group of experienced cyber experts, some friends and reformed hackers, implying that each one is the only test case we're focused on. And I could then compile the results to be ready to make any defensive assignments to, say, Tanya Prescott's team, right before the elections. And I'll ask her to check the communication integrity between each reporting station and the FEIC. I'll just need to get the various communication algorithms and codes from the FEIC."

President Bradshaw smiled. "That's what I hoped might be possible. Something you and I can work on together, look at the results, and make a decision on whether an attack might really work, then catch those as they try to do it. And if we do, I think it may tell us who's been behind all the attacks."

Tom nodded. "I think I can get the ball rolling. I'll have to be careful to spread the messaging out, and to approach it as a favor, rather than an official request, except for the test of the FEIC."

"Exactly. Yes. Please proceed. And, again, no one needs to know for now except us. We'll bring others in if it looks like there could be a real threat to the nation."

As Tom stood to return to his office, Balzor and Nepravel nodded to each other. Another new avenue for adding dissension seemed to be opening.

Ninety minutes later Jacob Welch, the nation's first African American Speaker of the House, and his party's Minority Leader in the Senate, Caleb Powell, left the White House together for the short drive back to the Capitol. They had just attended a briefing in the Oval Office with the president, vice president, and their two counterparts from the president's party in the House and Senate. The invitations had come by phone the previous evening. The subject was a surprise to them both.

Sitting behind the driver, Welch turned to the Senator from Indiana. "I can't believe they're going to extend the State of Emergency for another thirty days, including the election."

"I think we both expressed how disappointed we are. Basic rights being trampled."

"Even if he's right with his facts and figures on the results so far, the Constitution doesn't say that we have these rights except in certain situations. They're supposed to be sacrosanct."

"But he's right that previous Congresses have passed legislation that gives the president the right to declare a State of Emergency and to rule by dictate."

"I don't think the Founders imagined anything like this—only a limited action in time and place. Not the whole nation in total lockdown for two months. And during an election. All the 'temporary' restrictions we made during Covid are now coming back to haunt us—as 'precedents.'"

Senator Powell looked out his side window and shook his head. "Do you think he's played us, with all his talk of unity and pulling together in this time of attack?"

"There's a very good chance. And we've grown complacent. Until a month ago we expected to pick up seats in a conservative nation governed by a liberal President and Senate. Maybe even flip the Senate. We weren't prepared for the change at the top, and his unity talk may have lulled everyone to sleep for too long."

"While rolling out a buffet of 'free' gifts and entitlements to whet enough swing voters' appetites for more and more government."

"Don't you think people can see that?"

"I'm not sure. We've got to refocus all our efforts on the election."

"Yes, Jacob. But the State of Emergency doesn't help. And I suspect if we try to push against it, they'll do their best to label us as unpatriotic, dangerous, and divisive. Maybe even arrest us."

"We've got to try. Imagine our nation governed totally by secular progressives. The Founders clearly knew that our rights are 'inalienable', given by God, not man. Once you give up that truth and consign them to any group of people, no matter how well intentioned, then they will always be subject to some group's interpretation or manipulation."

"I think that's where we are, Jacob. It's incredible. We'll soon be prisoners in our own land, unless we speak and behave a certain way that meets their approval."

"We may already be."

Prince Proklor had decided to watch the president's address on the State of Emergency from the headquarters of The Network. He and his key generals had arrived a few minutes earlier, and as they moved invisibly through the area, they were impressed with the high level of activity in the producers' offices, the newsrooms, and the well-lit studios. He had wondered whether their targeted attack in Durham would have its intended effect, and he was pleased to see that Obman was there with the reporters and panelists, already whispering "truths" into their ears.

He knew Seth Cohen from previous reports and noticed him on a monitor from the White House lawn being fitted for a mic.

Tom, Emily and the Core Group were just behind the cameras in the Oval Office as the president began his address.

"My fellow Americans, the American Revolution lasted eight years and upended every citizen's life. No one was the same afterwards. More recently, our grandparents' generation united and fought to save the world from the tyranny of fascist forces in World War II for over three and a half years of bloody conflict.

"I mention those two heroic conflicts in which the American people triumphed as a way to put our current struggle into context. We have now been under attack from unspecified forces for a month. Though I know it seems like much longer, it has only been four weeks. And I believe the end is almost here, if we persevere and don't give up now that victory is in sight.

"When we originally scheduled this update we expected to talk about many days without any attacks, due in large part to the successful measures in the original State of Emergency. But, tragically, there was the hate-filled gunning down of innocent Jewish and Muslim students late Wednesday night in Durham. Yesterday, Vice President Reynolds visited the injured and the families of those killed and assured them that all Americans are standing with them.

"As terrible as that attack was, it serves as the perfect backdrop for where we are, and why we are taking extra measures today.

"The fact is that because of our emergency measures, attacks have been thwarted and perpetrators have been arrested, both after and before they act. And yet some people still hate and want to harm others for nothing more than their religious faith. Sadly, in this particular case, they were successful.

"So the last forty-eight hours tell us two things: First, our emergency measures are very successful, and, second, we must stay vigilant and combat hate of every type.

"Added to this difficult situation are our midterm elections in less than a month. These elections are sacred and most go ahead, as America has always done, even in our darkest moments. I am pledging to everyone that we will ensure free and fair elections, while also deterring attacks and eliminating hateful thoughts, words and actions.

"There is a lot to do, but with your help we can accomplish all these goals together.

"For the sake of our nation's continued safety I am announcing this morning an extension of the original State of Emergency for an additional four weeks, through November 9$^{th}$.

"The midterm elections on November 3rd will proceed as planned with balloting as determined by each state. For those campaigning, free speech will be protected, but hate speech will not. After one warning, any person or group which violates this requirement will be detained. And, to more quickly react to such cases, we're deputizing our most reliable technology partners to allow them to enforce these regulations through their social platforms.

"And we are implementing rewards of $1 million and more to encourage anyone who has information on violent attackers to come forward to help the nation.

"There are other specific details and enhancements that will be in a series of updates later today. Please visit our USTEAM website to see them so that you and your organizations may fully comply.

"Finally, in the spirit of the upcoming elections, although we are extending the prohibition on hate speech for thirty days, we are going to release immediately anyone who was detained under this provision in the original State of Emergency. Everyone deserves a second chance, and we hope that with this release we can create a foundation of mutual trust and agreement on the principles that we Americans hold so dear.

"Again, these are difficult times. But it will only be for one more month. We can win over the forces of darkness and hate, together. We are very close. We must defeat this enemy. As our great Declaration of Independence states, we are all created equal, and we must treat each other with mutual love and respect. We must win these battles, and we will. May God bless America."

The demonic spirits filling the Network's D.C. headquarters were delighted with the next thirty minutes of reporting and analysis. Seth added a few details which Emily had given him, like the need to monitor all microphones connected to the internet—now deemed a public connection—to ferret out possible violent acts or motives. He and the panelists back in the studio uniformly praised the president's team for their difficult and heroic action to save the nation from chaos during the all-important elections.

And at the end of this special coverage there was a trailer for the upcoming Network documentary, "The Progressive Silent Majority."

Alexei Nobikov and his team of nine on Cyprus also watched the president's address in their conference room. As Bradshaw finished, Alexei felt even more conflicted. The U.S. president was doubling down on more restrictions on freedoms, and more central control, not only of actions, but also of ideas. *Is he going to create another Russia, or even China?* was his immediate thought.

Alexei's team focused on planting false news, creating fake websites, and generally adding fuel to the warring sides in every divisive argument in the U.S., while always appearing to be homegrown. The group's technical skills were equal to anyone's, and they shared Alexei's fascination for using the internet and social media to influence people's actions and opinions. *Maybe by sowing dissenting voices to the president's latest move, we can for once actually help America.*

But then his Number Two, Svetlana, sitting next to him, said "He's going all-in. Think for a minute. We of course usually add dissension and arguments whenever we can. But is this case different? Don't we want the president to succeed in this clampdown? Doesn't that concentration of control at the center make it easier for us in the future, if he can pull it off?"

The others around the table were silent. Alexei knew that at least five of them probably agreed with him that the world would be worse if America gave up her freedoms, but it would be dangerous to openly say so. Instead, Alexei said, "I think you're right, Sveta. Less freedoms and more central control over everyday life can only be good for our purposes."

"Then I propose that we focus on ways to support him. Testimonials. Editorials. Patriotic reminders to do one's duty. And of course lots of funding."

"Yes. Good idea. Let's create some drafts this evening, and we'll ramp up the support even more starting tomorrow."

He looked around and then pulled his notes together. "Thank you all."

As the meeting broke up, Alexei rose and walked into his office, where he sat at his desk and looked out at the early evening sky over the blue Mediterranean. On one level he couldn't argue with Sveta's approaches—it was what he was tasked to do by the leaders in the Kremlin.

But another voice also spoke to him, the one from the spiritual light inside him, the one that had kept him in turmoil since his country invaded Ukraine. He said a prayer for guidance. He thought about his student days in America, and about his niece's experiences at university in D.C. The voice spoke to him more clearly, and he realized that their work was no longer just trying to bring America down a notch or two—they were actually trying to make America more like Russia, or even worse, China, with more central controls and less freedoms. Was it possible that America would become another Russia? Or even a China? Is that what he wanted?

The news spread quickly through the Church of the Good Shepherd's email chain. At seven that evening the church was packed—including Callie, Kristen and Natalie—to welcome their pastor, Robert Ludwig. A police car had returned him to his home an hour earlier.

The tenor of the gathering was one of thanksgiving and praise. They sang several hymns and offered up heartfelt prayers.

Then Ludwig addressed them from the pulpit. "I'm so glad to be home with my family and back with all of you."

A loud "Amen" was called out from the back of the congregation, and several people clapped. Ludwig smiled and nodded.

"Yes. Amen. Thank you, Lord, for your kindness, mercy and faithfulness. Besides my family, you all know that you are my greatest joy and my greatest responsibility. While I was away I spent hours praying for each of you, by name. And I know you were praying for me. Thank you. Again, thank God."

He paused for a moment. "You should also know that as a condition for my release today, I agreed with the government's demand that I not speak about the events that led to my incarceration, nor about the detention itself, during the State of Emergency. Thinking that would be for only a few more days, I agreed and gave my word. Only on the way home did I learn that the State of Emergency has been extended for another month, until after the elections. I'm prayerfully considering the ramifications of what I just told you, and our possible options."

He smiled. "And for that, I need your help. This is a time of confusion, violence, and discord. What we so need are God's truth, clarity and guidance. As I prayed for us in confinement it became clear that our next steps, whatever they are, must be united. By ourselves we are powerless. But united and acting in His will, no force on earth can stand against us. So I'm asking everyone in the congregation—and believers beyond our church whom you invite to join us—to pray specifically for His guidance, for a word from Him about our next steps. Please, in the coming hours and days, pray, fast if you can, and listen. Seek His wisdom. And if you feel so led, share His leading with me or with one of our Elders. Whatever we do or say, we want it to be with His power, not our own." He paused. "For now, let's continue to thank God and ask Him to bless and defend this nation."

The congregation prayed for another thirty minutes and then closed with a hymn, "Be Thou My Vision."

As the church service ended Tom was at home finishing several hours of work at the table in his kitchen, looking out on his yard as the sun dipped below the horizon. He had decided he could not work on the president's special request on the election that morning from his office in the White House. There were too many people coming and going, and too many official records. So after lunch he had moved home, made a list on his L-Pad, and spent the afternoon calling and texting friends and contacts in the area of cyber security.

He already had twenty individual experts who had agreed to look quietly into the voting system for a specific race that November, and Tom was sure he'd nail down the others he needed later that night or over the weekend.

His doorbell rang. He was not expecting anyone, but he walked to the front of his home and opened the door.

"Callie! I... Great... Did you call? Come in."

She walked past him without smiling and stopped in the foyer as he closed the door and turned to her.

"Can I take your coat?"

"I won't be that long." He could see that she was not happy. "At dinner last night you must have known that the president was going to extend this stupid State of Emergency for another month."

"It's not stupid. But I knew. And I agree with the need to do so."

"So when I said stuff like, 'It's only for a few more days,' you knew that wasn't really the case, but you said nothing."

"How could I? It's policy I can't talk about."

That seemed to make her even angrier. "And Pastor Ludwig is back, but they tricked him into agreeing not to talk about anything until after the State of Emergency, but didn't tell him about the extension."

"Callie, *I'm* the one who pushed to get them released today. That was my idea, and the others accepted it. I think Emily actually came up with that condition, but it makes sense."

"Sure. Tricking someone makes great sense."

"Come sit down."

"No. Don't you see what a mess you're making of our country? You...how are you going to run elections if people can't speak freely?"

"They can speak freely. Just no divisive hate speech."

She folded her arms. "And who decides that? An election *is* a division. A choice. By design. And you, Tom, have to choose. Are you going to keep helping them shut down our freedoms?"

"I'm helping to protect the country."

She twisted her upper body a bit. "Did you call Erin about the abortion?"

"Not today. I had a special assignment from the president that I had to work on."

"So maybe she killed your child while you were on special assignment? Great."

"I...I'll call her."

"Friday is the biggest day for abortions."

"OK. I'll call her."

Callie was quiet for a moment, looking at him. "Tom, I keep saying you have to choose, but really you already have." She shook her head. "There's no point in continuing to see each other. A waste of your time and mine. Even if on one level I enjoy being with you and like you, on the most important level I could never really be with you. You don't get it. There's right and wrong. Life or abortion. Freedom or repression. Light or dark. Absolutes that you can't parse into shades of gray.

"From where I sit, you've chosen the dark. It's too bad, for many reasons." She moved past him to the door. "There's no point calling me anymore, unless it's to tell me about your child. Go on about your important business." She opened the door and looked back at him. "I hope you're a great success." She walked out, closing the door behind her.

He stared at the door. *What the hell? Chosen the dark? Are you kidding me? I'm defending the damn country! It's easy to get on a high horse when what you say doesn't matter. But the president and the country are actually depending on me. So, yes, I'm here, working tonight. And I haven't called Erin about that fetus. But I am trying to stop the damn bastards who want to kill us all. That's what I'm doing!*

Zloy, who had followed Callie when she didn't head home after the church service, was delighted, both by their argument and by the voices that Tom pulled up from their earlier plants. He couldn't wait to report these developments.

# 16

*For avoiding the extremes of despotism or anarchy . . . the only ground of
hope must be on the morals of the people. I believe that religion is the only
solid base of morals and that morals are the only possible support of free
governments. Therefore education should teach the precepts of religion and
the duties of man towards God.*

Gouvernor Morris

Saturday, October 10

Tom had so much on his mind and his plate that he contemplated
texting the Schofields to beg off their parkrun that Saturday, but he woke
up early after a fitful night and was able to review his Security updates
and still be ready when the couple arrived to pick him up. And he knew
from past experience that the run would help clear some of the fog in his
brain, at least for a few hours.

He climbed into the back seat as Logan drove off.

Emily turned from the front passenger side and smiled. "Good
morning. How are you?"

"I guess I've been better. I think Callie dumped me last night."

"What? Where did you go?"

"Nowhere. She made a point to come over just to tell me. She was
pretty angry."

"It's none of our business, but if you want to talk, I did introduce
you."

He nodded. "I know. I know. I actually really like her. But she's
very, very mad about everything to do with the State of Emergency, and
particularly the extension."

"Why?"

"Well, we locked up her pastor because he wouldn't follow the rules
against hate speech. Letting him go yesterday somehow made it worse
in her mind because of the extension. And she thinks we're ending free
speech, which we're obviously not."

They rode in silence for a few moments. Then Emily said, "There's
something about some Christians. Especially the 'evangelicals.' They

think they know everything and won't bend on anything. 'God's rules' and 'God's laws.' Give me a break. I didn't know she was like that when I invited her to Seth's party. I'm sorry. And now she's apparently somehow filled Natalie with that same stuff. Crazy."

He raised his hand. "No. It's fine. She's actually good and fun to be with. She certainly let's you know where she stands. But despite what she thinks, I have to focus on what I know is right, to help protect the country."

"Exactly. And thank goodness not all Christians are like her. I think Patricia has pulled together a large group of denominational leaders—and others, like rabbis and imams—who are endorsing what the president has decided we have to do to be able to hold fair elections while we're under attack."

Logan added, "That's good for the elections, but watch those imams and mullahs. I couldn't believe that Muslim friend of Clayton's. He comes on like some Pakistani Patrick Henry, but I think the Muslims are putting up a smokescreen to divert us from who's really attacking us. It has to be them. They hate us—they hate everyone who isn't a Muslim."

Tom tapped Logan on the shoulder. "That may be a bit over the top. We have no indication of that."

"See, the smokescreen's working!"

Emily shook her head. "Getting back to Callie, it's tough. But there really is a divide between Christians like her and the rest of us rational human beings."

"Yes," Tom said, "you're right. A divide."


After the run, some tosses with Beau, a shower and some breakfast, Tom settled in at the kitchen table to make his last calls on the special project for the president in the all-important battleground races.

Nepravel, delighted by Zloy's report the previous night on Tom's break-up with Callie, was making his usual Saturday swing through Tom's home to be sure the voices of deception were up and running. They appeared to be reminding Tom of his own importance to the nation, and of how illogical were most Christians.

Satisfied, Nepravel was about to move on when Tom's phone vibrated. It was a video call.

"Hi, Dad. What's up?"

"It's actually both of us. How are you?" Richard Sullivan replied.

"Fine. I'm fine. Hi, Mom. Very busy, as usual."

"Even on Saturday morning?"

"Yes. I did the parkrun, and now I'm working on a special assignment for the president in the midst of all this other stuff."

His mother, Janet, said, "That sounds important."

"Well, I guess it is, a bit. And time-constrained."

"But how are *you*?" she asked.

"Uh, I'm fine. Trying with everything we have to find the people doing all this."

"Hmm. Yes. I can't imagine how you do it. With all that, do you have any other life? Are you seeing anyone?"

Tom had to smile. "Well, Mom, I was. A little. Until last night. She doesn't like the State of Emergency, so she decided to break it off."

"Is that Callie Sawyer?"

"Yes. The girl Dad suggested I look up a couple of years ago. I guess I should have."

Richard said, "Kristen Holloway, whom we know, apparently had a big impact on her."

"Yes, that's what she says. And I guess I met Kristen Holloway when I was in high school. Am I right that she came to the house once or twice, and wasn't she there that night Amy went to the hospital in the ambulance and had her baby? And you were all on Mom's reality TV show?"

"Yes," he said. "You have a good memory."

"Not really. I only recently thought of it and wanted to check with you. It was quite a night."

"So you and Callie broke up?" Janet asked.

Tom paused. "Well, I'm not sure we were ever really together, but I do like her, and I think we're at least in a long recess. She's not crazy about what we're doing to protect the nation, so I doubt I'll see her until this all settles down, if ever."

Richard said, "That's another reason why we called. I have a virtual meeting with people from about thirty churches around the country who are ready to tell the government censors good-bye. Do you have any input or insights for me on that?"

Tom frowned. "Dad, you know I can't talk about that. Just, please, follow the law. And the regulations in the State of Emergency. Do you expect more than twenty people? Did you register with the Government Online Portal so the meeting can be monitored? Just bend, if you have to, for another month, and we'll get through this."

"But the government has taken away our rights. And I didn't set up the meeting, so I don't know about all that ridiculous registration stuff."

"Actually, the government is protecting our rights from those who want to destroy us."

"Our lives and property, maybe. But not our rights. We basically have none. The government listens to everything and censors everyone."

"Dad, maybe, from your perspective, but ultimately to protect those rights for the long term. It's only for another thirty days."

"That's what they said thirty days ago."

There was a silence as the two men looked at each other.

Janet said, "OK. It's a tough time. But like with Covid, I'm sure we'll get through it. And I have to admit I've enjoyed the more positive ads this political season. Much less tearing others down. They're being forced to talk about what they will do, not what their opponent has done. It's actually refreshing."

Tom nodded. "It is, and we *will* get through this. Hey, Mom, back on our neighbor, Amy, for a minute. I don't remember: did she ever consider an abortion?"

"Yes. In fact the school set it up and she and your sister actually went to the abortion clinic. Our church and others prayed for days. It was Susan, sitting in the waiting room, who suddenly felt the urge to talk Amy into canceling the abortion and having the baby. It was incredible. Now he's in school somewhere, twenty years later. Why?"

"Just wondering. I never knew those details."

"Well, you were fourteen and had some issues of your own."

"Yes, I remember."

Richard smiled. "Look, whatever happens with all this, you know we're incredibly pleased and proud of what you're doing. It's amazing. And we're praying for you."

"Yes, I know."

"OK, we'll let you get back to your special project. Have a great weekend."

"Thanks. You, too. Bye."

Tom looked back at his project call list and thought that maybe he should call Erin that afternoon.

Nepravel hated the sight of the older Sullivans, and the father's voice was particularly grating. Prayer! But he felt Tom held his own without too much damage, so he left him to his phone calls and moved on to his other White House charges.


Ten days after the attack on their mosque and the vice president's visit, the calls for and against revenge had died down, and the Rashids had moved home again. Now Ahmad was ascending the steps of a neighborhood library next to a commercial area on the south side of D.C., responding to a call from Kahar Bosakov. He found him standing in the small foyer, three books under his arm. He smiled when he saw Ahmad.

"Thank you so much for coming," the younger man said, reaching out his hand.

"Of course. I'm glad to see you."

Kahar looked around for a moment. "I really want to talk with you, but I don't want my cousin to know. I come to this library on Saturdays—I'm reading lots of history. Anyway, he thinks I'll be here most of the afternoon.

"I noticed a coffee shop up the street. Would you like to go there?"

"Yes. That would be great."

Ten minutes later they were seated at a table with coffees on the far side of the half-empty café. After answering Kahar's inquiry about his family and commenting in general on recent events, Ahmad asked, "Tell me more about you and your cousin. Ablet, yes?"

Kahar leaned forward. "Yes. We're obviously Uyghurs. We were lucky and escaped from Xinjiang Province with just the shirts on our backs a year ago. A refugee organization in Afghanistan helped us get here, and we're trying to make money. The mosque and the other Uyghurs have been very helpful. America is an amazing place."

Kahar paused to sip his coffee, and Ahmad nodded. "Yes, it is."

Mavlan had been checking on his other Uyghur charges and had looked in a couple of places for Kahar. He arrived and took position between the two Muslims.

"That's the thing—why I wanted to talk with you. You're a Muslim, like us. I am so filled with hate for the Chinese who have killed or imprisoned almost our entire family, and many of my friends. I want—and I think the Prophet teaches—that we must kill the Oppressor. Take revenge for all that they have done to us. They are Godless oppressors. Worse even than the People of the Book who don't revere Allah and his Prophet."

Ahmad nodded. "In my job I read reports about what's going on in Xinjiang, and it is truly terrible. Forced labor. Sterilization. Re-education. Genocide. All done, controlled, and covered up by the Chinese government."

"Yes! And no one cares. Some governments talk. But no one does anything. Not even Muslim countries! The Chinese have the rest of the world in their pockets. Everyone is afraid of them. Meanwhile, our people are 're-educated', tortured and killed. This is what makes revenge so important."

Ahmad did not respond, but held Kahar's gaze, noting the anger in his eyes. Mavlan was pleased with his words.

Kahar continued. "But since we were together that night in the mosque, I've watched you. You seem to oppose revenge. You've argued to let the infidel police—or military—take care of finding who did the shooting, and arresting them. Several of the men have spoken out against you, yet you don't change. I wanted to talk to you to find out how you live your faith and yet don't feel that we must fight back."

Ahmad reflected for several moments, sipping his coffee. "That's an excellent question, Kahar, worthy of a lengthy discussion, which I'm glad to have with you. Let me just say that I've studied the Koran extensively, and I believe that Allah is all supreme. But there are passages which seem to contradict each other, particularly as it relates to violence, revenge, and jihad. I believe one can make the case for peaceful conversion of non-believers, and allowing Allah to take revenge, as much as one can make the case for the opposite. Particularly as an American who also believes in individual freedom and respect for law, I choose to live by the more non-violent passages, as it relates to my personal response."

Mavlan was repulsed. He'd never heard a Muslim speak like this in Afghanistan. At least not the ones he'd help train.

"I understand that there are some who do not agree, but I think they should then not live here, where Rule of Law, not rule by any group, religion or tribe, is the key to how it all works. Almost uniquely in all the world. There are radical Muslim groups in Europe that frankly scare me, just like there are radical groups here who wrap themselves in Christian trappings but genuinely scare my Christian friends. And as an officer in the Army who has actually killed people, I also acknowledge and support the government's role to defend us, including from violent Muslims. Remember, Christian Americans defended their nation against Christian Germans in World War II. If people are attacking America, which I'm sworn to defend, then, even if they call themselves Muslims, I will do my best to defeat them."

Kahar listened intently. "Rule of Law. I read that a lot. Is that like Sharia Law?"

"Sort of. Except Sharia Law sets many rules for exactly how we're supposed to live, almost hour by hour and relationship to relationship. Rule of Law, as it's used here, means setting the framework for people to then be able to choose how they live and what they do, so long as they don't harm others. American law, on purpose, leaves a lot of room for individual choices—for good or for ill—but the point for now is that the Rule of Law here is supposed to apply equally to everyone, not just to some, and not just because one group is in or out of power. Our Muslim faith is protected in this country, founded by Christians, because the laws apply equally and to everyone."

"That's not what the Chinese do."

"Exactly. Their idea is total control of every decision, action and relationship, to bend it to the 'good of the state'. And so there is no place for any faith that believes in a power higher than the state. It must be crushed, along with everyone who believes, or in any way defies what the state dictates."

Mavlan spoke into Kahar, who thought for a moment. "So if there is no Rule of Law protection in China, are we justified in taking revenge on the Chinese, on those who oppress us?"

Ahmad paused. "Another very good question. What is our personal responsibility when a government demonstrates repeated evil acts, like genocide? What should—could—good Germans have done to prevent the killing of so many Jews and others in the all-powerful Nazi state? That seems like a question which must be answered by each individual, given where he or she is, and what opportunities he has."

"Well, I'm here, and there may be opportunities to take revenge on Chinese here."

Ahmad thought for a long moment. "Yes, I guess you could. But it might have the opposite effect of reinforcing the Chinese story that Uyghurs are terrorists, and may also impact Americans in a way that will not help your cause here."

Kahar frowned. "Then what may I do to help my family and my people? The Chinese are everywhere and see everything. If I or any Uyghur does anything, even here, they will know and will punish our families even more."

Ahmad paused again. "You have excellent questions. Let me think. Perhaps some of us here can help you and this cause. Let's keep talking. You've met Mariam, my wife, at the mosque. If we can get a few friends to join us next Saturday, will you tell them what's happening?"

Kahar thought for a moment, and then nodded.

Mavlan was surprised by this conversation and decided to ask others for help.

That afternoon from his den Richard Sullivan logged into a virtual meeting. He expected to see the same thirty people whom he had interacted with ten days earlier, so he was surprised to see over a hundred men and women from all across the nation.

The pastor from Dallas who had sent the invitation greeted everyone before leading them in a short prayer.

"Thank you for joining with other brothers and sisters who are concerned about our nation. We're happy to have with us Pastor Robert Ludwig from The Church of the Good Shepherd in Washington, who was released from prison yesterday. Robert has asked to say a few words to us."

"Thank you all for joining in today. I gave my word as a condition for my release that I wouldn't talk about the events that led up to my confinement, nor about the confinement itself, other than to say that I was not physically mistreated in any way—other than being locked up for speaking."

He went on to share with this group the same message he'd given his congregation the day before: he asked them to join their churches together to fast and to pray for guidance from the Lord before they adopted or rejected any course of action.

"Our nation is clearly at a crossroads, a time for decisions, perhaps for action, certainly an election. My hope is that we will hear from Him and know that whatever we decide to say and to do is only from Him. If you agree with this approach, then please ask your pastors, elders and members to pray and to listen. Then let's convene this group at the end of the week to see if we have a consensus for a path forward."

Ludwig's proposal seemed reasonable to Richard, and apparently to many others. Within five minutes it was adopted, and Richard called Stan Conway, his pastor, to report.


Erin MacNeil was on an extended walk/jog that Saturday afternoon through downtown D.C., enjoying the combination of urban storefronts and vistas on the Mall that were so unlike the small town in Texas where she grew up. As she listened on earphones to a podcast about Zero Day Attacks and Ransomware, she hugged the western perimeter just outside the Restricted Zone and headed north—it was still a couple of miles to her favorite bookstore-café where she loved to browse the rows of obscure and interesting titles.

Her phone vibrated, so she pushed the Accept button.

"Erin?"

"Yes. Hi, Tom. I'm walking. How are you?"

"Fine. I grabbed a few miles this morning at the parkrun."

"Good. I love walking in the afternoons in the fall here."

"Yes. It's a beautiful day."

She slowed her pace a bit. "What's up?"

"Well, two things, really. The first has to do with our concern with a particular Congressional race in this year's election, that it might be an easy target for a cyber attack. I was wondering if you might use your previous, less-discussed cyber skills to check it out and let me know if you agree. Could it be compromised? All off the grid, of course."

"Uh, yeah, sure. You want me to try to hack into the voting process to see if I might be able to manipulate it?"

"Yes, exactly. Don't do anything, of course. Just let me know what you learn."

"OK. Where is it?"

He told her, then added, "Thank you. I'll send you some links. That will really help us. And then I was also just calling to find out whether you'd made a decision about the, uh, abortion or not."

"Not completely. But it seems like the right thing. I've gone to the Northeast Women's Clinic for a consultation. They were really nice."

"OK, good. Listen, I, uh, know this sounds crazy, but I know a person who feels really strongly about abortion—that it's killing a baby. I told her a week ago that I knew someone considering one. Anyway, after talking with her, I promised that I'd call you and at least raise the point."

Erin paused at the crosswalk for a busy street as cars moved past. "So does she want to have the baby for me? I've heard all that. All my life. If I told my parents about this, that's all I'd hear. To me, it's just a growth.

Something I can deal with. I'm twenty-six and just got a great promotion at the institute. I don't need a holy roller preaching to me about a fetus."

"No, no, she's not like that. She got pregnant nine years ago and had the baby. A single mom. Seems to be really happy."

The light turned and Erin started walking again. "I bet. That's what I need! A child, so I, too, can be a single mom. Sounds great."

"Adoption?"

"You want to have this baby? From all I've heard, it's not much fun."

"OK, OK. I get it. Actually, I agree. I just thought I'd play devil's advocate."

"What do *you* think?"

"As I said, I think it's your choice, and at this point it's just a fetus. So, yes, go ahead."

"I expect I will. One Thursday or Friday soon, so I can recuperate over the weekend."

"Good. Let me know. And, hey, would you like to have dinner at my place tonight?"

She laughed. "I really would like to see you, but since I haven't heard from you for more than a month, I'm actually going out with someone else. Do you always call girls you've impregnated on three hours' notice for dinner?"

She picked up her pace on the sidewalk as she waited for him to reply.

"I, uh...Sorry, you're right. Not good. I'm just very busy, and the time gets away. How about another night, this week or next?"

"Sure. Tell you what: I'll make an appointment at the clinic and then we can get together."

"OK. Let me know. And I'll send you the info on that race."

"I will. Bye."

Erin started to switch back to the podcast, but then decided just to walk and think. *We had such a great weekend. Tom's an amazing guy—now he's the National Security Advisor to the president. Crazy. I know he's been busy, but why didn't he call me even once? I'd love to see him again.*

While working in his basement office, Richard Sullivan received an official email early that evening notifying him that he had participated in an online meeting of more than twenty people which had not been properly registered, though it was still recorded by the government. The email stated that this was a warning; if he participated again during the State of Emergency, he would be subject to possible penalties. In the meantime, the content of the meeting was being reviewed for any other violations, in order to keep America safe.

He walked upstairs and showed the email to Janet, who was putting dinner on the table.

She read it and handed the copy back to her husband. "That's crazy. Do you think Tom knows anything about this?"

Tom was actually relieved to have a Saturday night to himself. And he was pleased that he'd found IT friends or acquaintances to quietly tackle each of the important election sites which most needed protection from hacking. They should be reporting back to him within a week.

In the living room he watched the last half of a college football game, with one eye on his cell phone, as always. He heated up some leftovers for dinner. At his work table by the back window he switched on his secure laptop and scrolled through and answered the constant flow of issues and questions that always pursued him as National Security Advisor—those related to the recent attacks, as well as to the more usual, longstanding challenges for the nation.

A little after nine he closed the laptop and was headed for the stairs when by his TV he saw the two DVD's Callie had given him with Robert Ludwig and Gary Thornton talking about The Foundations of America. Since he'd met both men he decided that he'd have a quick look at the first one.

Ninety minutes later he finally went upstairs. Callie had been right. Tom already respected Thornton's research from reading the book, which he was half way through, but the two men played off of each other very well as they drove home with example after example how the Founders had relied on Christian principles to create the nation's unique government structure, and assumed—even warned—that a requirement for the republic's survival was that this faith remained woven into the tapestry of everyday life—Virtue, Freedom, and Faith all supporting each other.[1] If one is removed, the structure will collapse.

After changing and getting in bed, he opened Thornton's book to the next chapter. He was struck by the quote at its beginning:

"They who can give up essential liberty to obtain a little temporary safety deserve neither liberty nor safety." —Benjamin Franklin

As he started reading, he thought, *Franklin must have lived in a much simpler world.*

Kristen Holloway had been at church the previous night and heard Robert Ludwig's admonition that they all fast and pray about what their next steps should be. She passed on this request to the large nationwide prayer chain which she and others had connected over the years, and she was pleased to receive a similar request from the separate group with which Richard Sullivan had met that afternoon.

One of her favorite Christian writers had prepared a book which compiled Bible verses by topics, so the reader could use them to pray scripture back to God. In the quiet of her bedroom that night she began reading and praying from her comfortable chair, then slipped to her knees and continued, using verses about Government, the Church, God's wisdom, Evangelism, and several others.

She put the book on her bed, changed into her nightgown, slipped into bed, and picked it up again. When she did, it opened to the section on Spiritual Warfare, and the first verse listed was Ephesians 6:12:

"For our struggle is not against flesh and blood, but against the rulers, against the authorities, against the powers of this dark world and against the spiritual forces of evil in the heavenly realms."

She felt a chill and read the verse again. *Is this what God wants us to pray about?*

# Wednesday, October 14

Just before noon Richard and Janet Sullivan slid into a booth across from Stan and Becky Conway at a local Atlanta barbeque restaurant. After catching up on each family's latest doings and ordering their lunches, they focused on the purpose of their meeting.

Each was a member of a different Biblically based group. The men were engaged with others in organized ministry, Stan as a pastor and Richard as a lay leader. Janet retained membership in a loose group of current and former Christian Members of Congress. Becky Conway had served for years as a leader in the Pro-Life movement. Each national group had recently adopted the old-fashioned phone-tree approach for communicating, to keep the number on any one call at ten or less, thereby conforming to the State of Emergency's requirements. It was cumbersome, but they were getting used to it. And each of them had to report to their group later that afternoon or the next morning, after four days of prayer and seeking God's guidance; hence the reason for their lunch together.

Janet Sullivan stirred sweetener into her iced tea and said, "I guess I've had twenty conversations with former congresspeople, and of course a few of them hated the original State of Emergency and now want to fight the president's extension tooth and nail."

The Conways nodded. "Same with our group," Becky said.

Janet continued. "But the interesting thing I heard from most of them was that this is now something beyond our usual political and policy differences, particularly with the violence, the absence of anyone claiming responsibility, and the lockdown on speech. Several told me that as they prayed, they sensed this is more like a concentrated push, a broad-based spiritual war, than an attack by any single group."

The waitress arrived with their sandwiches and sides. Stan blessed their lunch and asked for wisdom. There was a moment of silence as they began to enjoy the food.

Stan began again. "Yes. I've gotten calls and texts from members who've fasted and prayed, and they believe that rather than pushing back directly against the government's specific dictates, our responsibility as the Church is to push back against the one who's behind *every* effort to subvert or to destroy God's truth."

Richard looked up from his sandwich. "That just gave me goosebumps. Last night I got a text from one of our high school students who'd been praying as you asked us to do on Sunday, and he wanted me to look at two verses I'd never really noticed before."

He pulled out his phone and typed in the search engine. "Here. Ephesians 3:10-11. 'His intent was that now, through the church, the manifold wisdom of God should be made known to the rulers and authorities in the heavenly realms, according to his eternal purpose that he accomplished in Christ Jesus our Lord.'"

They all sat silently for several beats. Janet said, "So...the *church—us—*is to make God's purpose known to the dark spiritual powers?"

"Not God Himself, or the angels, telling them, but us?" Becky added. "*We're* supposed to show the demons what God's manifold wisdom is?"

"That's what Paul writes," Stan said. "And you're right, I haven't exactly focused on those verses. Like with evangelizing our friends and families, where He says that the rocks could shout His truths, but instead He wants us to do it."

Richard spoke. "I guess it means that the good angels could lecture the demons on God's purposes, but His strength is more fully revealed if we, who are weak, teach them."

"Wow." Janet looked at each of them. "How do we do that?"

As Wilson Smith drove his Ace Delivery van from Carrboro into Chapel Hill that afternoon, he couldn't believe his good luck. Nor did he notice as Zaraz, his personal demon, arrived and moved inside him.

Wilson, aged forty, had grown up in Carrboro, next to the North Carolina university town. After his father abandoned the family when he was four, and his mother died when he was six, he'd bounced from foster home to distant relative until, after several run-ins with the juvenile authorities, he'd attained his eighteenth birthday, but without a high school diploma.

Carrboro used to be a sleepy suburb of Chapel Hill, but in Wilson's lifetime it had become an even more progressive city than its progressive neighbor, with lots of immigrants and "others." As a young man Wilson had watched them get the jobs that he should have had, building businesses and wealth by stealing it from people like him, who he believed were the true Americans. Their brazen success in his country made him angry, and he had drifted further and further into websites and organizations which spoke up for people like him.

Zaraz liked to hang out with men who frequented these sites—he'd taken immediate notice of Wilson and had turned up the volume on the voices feeding him lies and hate. The world, the flesh and the devil reinforced each other in Wilson's mind, and three years ago his hate had become so intense that Zaraz was able to move beyond planting voices and instead actually possessed Wilson for the first time. Now he did so whenever he wanted. Demons like Zaraz were only able to accomplish this feat in a small number of people, but the results were always powerful: Zaraz and Wilson were one.

When drones first entered the general market Wilson had been attracted to them because they allowed him to see over fences and behind woodlands to spy on what less-desirable people were up to, without being detected. In a "coincidence" arranged by Zaraz, Wilson had a wild fling one weekend with a young woman in a local real estate office who the next Monday was asked by their top broker if she knew anyone with one of the new drones. Wilson had quietly been doing all that firm's aerial photography ever since, along with other jobs by word of mouth. He preferred cash payments for his work, and his drone business remained well below the radar.

To level out his income when the weather or the market made drone photography less productive, Wilson drove a local delivery van. It wasn't the best job in the world, but it wasn't bad, provided benefits, and Wilson met a lot of people. Two years ago he'd delivered a package that was identical to one he'd ordered for himself from a very patriotic group.

So he'd circled back to that house at the end of his route and left a note in the mailbox.

Now he and Trey Dunham were best friends, sharing their anger and looking for a way to push back against the tide of foreigners, Muslims, Blacks, and Jews who were obviously destroying America. Trey had escaped an abusive relationship with a foster parent to spend two tours overseas in the Army. He was very good with all types of weapons.

Wilson had introduced Trey to a group who called themselves The WhiteStorm. Their leader owned a farm twenty miles north of the Research Triangle, and in an isolated barn behind a hill on his farm the group of about twenty men and several wives/girlfriends stashed weapons, met several times a month to hear talks and to watch videos, and took target practice. Trey and his skills fit in perfectly.

The two men had been sharing beers at their favorite honky-tonk in town when the first bulletins about the drone attack on the D.C. mosques hit the screens above the bar. One reporter speculated that the shots appeared to have come from a drone hovering near the buildings.

Zaraz/Wilson took a long pull, put down the bottle, and turned to his friend. "Damn, Trey, we could do that."

And they had, at the Muslim and Jewish Student Centers at Duke, the week before. It had been glorious—much better than they could have imagined. Hopefully the bastards would get the message that even in liberal North Carolina, they were not welcome. And no one had any idea who had done it. Wilson and Trey wanted to tell their friends at WhiteStorm at their next Saturday night meeting, but there was always concern about informers, so they kept quiet.

Now he had just heard on the radio that there would be a large gathering in ten days on Saturday evening at a UNC auditorium to discuss proposals for "Mideast Reconciliation" between Jews, Christians and Muslims. There would be hundreds of people there listening to the six speakers—and Wilson was sure they would all be people with whom he would disagree, to say the least.

*What a great opportunity.*

Tom was in his office that afternoon coordinating with his three senior assistants the briefings coming up for the president on issues that had little to do with the attacks or the State of Emergency—the "normal" business of the National Security Advisor: the implications of changing governments and their policies overseas, foreign military movements, key intelligence intercepts collected on the leaders of friendly and unfriendly countries and their opposition parties, strategic international businesses, and terrorist organizations.

As their meeting ended and his staff filed out the door, Tom's Core Group phone vibrated. He checked the caller, stood and answered it while he closed his door.

"Hello, Mr. Boswell."

"Drew, please."

"Yes. Hello."

"I'm checking to find out if our High-Tech group, and especially my team at Juggle, is giving you everything you need. Any issues with the enhanced data you're receiving?"

Tom sat again behind his desk. "No. It's great. They've been incredibly helpful. I doubt we're missing any data. We just need to connect the dots to find out who's behind all this."

"I'm sure you will. I've worked closely with James Toomey at the FBI from when he was a field agent. A good man. I was one of his key supporters for the Director position. Before Congress interfered a decade ago, we used to share information all the time, kind of like we're doing again now. He understands what has to be done to defeat the bad guys."

"Yes. I work daily with Special Agent Prescott, but Director Toomey is always involved as well. We're applying the most powerful tools we have."

"Good. And listen, if you ever need back-channel connections to your counterparts in other countries, I've been at this a long time and know almost everyone. We have operations all over the world, even in China and Russia—and through those we also know a lot of other important people. How they control things in those countries isn't pretty, but it works for them."

"Uh, OK. Thanks. Who knows where this might all lead?"

"All right. Just checking in. If you need me, call. Anything. OK?"

"Yes, thank you."

Tom hung up and looked out the window. There was a tap on his door.

"Come in."

"Something important?" Emily asked as she cracked the door and looked in.

Tom smiled. "Just a call I needed to take. Come in."

She stopped halfway to his desk and smiled. "Seth's documentary, 'The Silent Progressive Majority' is airing next week on The Network, and he wants us to see a preview. Logan and I would like you—and a date—to come over Saturday night to watch it with us. And Logan is going all out on some serious food and drink because apparently Juggle's revenues have been through the roof the last two weeks."

Tom nodded. "Great. I'd love to, but Erin MacNeil is coming over for dinner."

"The girl from Texas you met at a seminar?"

Tom nodded.

"You do move fast. Perfect. Bring her."

He looked at his desk for a moment. "Actually, we have a little history, and I told her we'd have a quiet dinner. I really can't change that."

Emily turned. "Well, OK. We'll miss you. But I understand how a 'quiet dinner' at your place might turn out." She inclined her head. "If you change your mind, come on."

He smiled. "Thanks. I will."

# Friday, October 16

Tom's first meeting that Friday morning was with Andrea Hunt and three members of her team, plus two from his, around the conference table in his office at the White House. Emily Schofield and her assistant also joined them. When Andrea came in they shook hands and Tom gave her a peck on the cheek.

Andrea looked down at her enlarged front. "Ten days."

"How do you feel?"

"Actually, wonderful. Clayton says I've been nesting like crazy, but everything seems to be ready at home, the office is running well, and now I just want to be sure these guys are in sync with you before I bail out to maternity leave."

"Great. Everyone, please have a seat."

After a few minutes of introductions and general discussion, Andrea led off. "We understand your goal is to devise a voluntary system that Americans can join, like our Trusted Traveler program, to, in essence, establish their identity, credibility, and lack of being any kind of threat to the nation. For lack of a better term, we've been calling it 'Trusted Citizen.' Is that right?"

Tom nodded. "Yes. The immediate goal is to eliminate as many people as possible from our big data searches, so that we can more quickly focus on possible bad actors. But the program could eventually also include positive rewards."

"Like what?"

Emily said, "We're not sure. We hope that's what our combined teams might brainstorm. Basically things like easier access to college admission, perhaps a separate security line at public events with your Trusted Citizen—I like that name—ID card, even a boost on your credit rating. So far we've imagined the program would be ongoing, and that, like with a credit score, one would earn points for continued excellent behavior over the months."

Andrea said, "Excellent behavior. What do you envision there? In our traveler program, we look through public records for things like arrests, convictions, lawsuits. What are you thinking we'll be scoring for Trusted Citizen?"

Tom and Emily looked at each other, and she indicated that he should answer. His assistant passed him a piece of paper and he glanced at it.

"Since we're trying to eliminate searches of bad behavior which could lead to violence, that kind of behavior would lower one's score, and vice-versa. So we imagine that things like hate speech, racism, or job discrimination would clearly work against you. Volunteering to work at a homeless shelter and giving extra amounts to approved charities would raise your score. All with the goal of rewarding good citizenship and discouraging bad actions."

"I see," Andrea said. "That's far beyond what we're doing now, of course, but I guess the concept and the analytical structure are the same."

Emily spoke. "We realize it will take time to come up with the categories to grade and the parameters for doing so, but we also think it's very important, so we should start the process. Obviously this will not even be proposed to Congress until after the elections."

"And this program will be voluntary?"

"Of course," Emily said. "But we hope people will want to join it."

"It'll give the government a lot of power over people's lives—who wins and who loses."

"Hardly more than is already there. We'll just organize it better and make it work positively for those who want to participate. We think most people will want to join in, and then we can look hard at those who don't."

Andrea was silent for a moment. She looked at her team. "Do you have enough to continue what we've already started?" They nodded. "All right, then, we'll get to work on the details over at DHS and get back to you with questions and, eventually, a first draft. And hopefully I'll go have a baby."

They all stood to leave. At the door, Andrea, Emily and Tom were together. Andrea said to Tom, "Have you heard about the initiative we hope to pull together to highlight the persecution of the Uyghurs?"

"Yes, Emily mentioned it to me when we got coffee this morning. It sounds really good."

"Logan is actually excited about helping," Emily said. "Wouldn't that be a great result after our get together at your place?"

"Yes. Yes, it would. Let me know how I can help."


It felt odd to Richard Sullivan to be without his cell phone as he walked, dressed in jogging clothes, with Janet and the Conways, from the parking area at the Atlanta City Golf Course over to a secluded area of picnic tables at the adjoining Tennis Center. They were carrying several boxes of sandwiches and chips. But at least his phone was in the same city. The other twenty men and six women attending their outdoor gathering had flown or driven in that morning, and they'd agreed to leave their cell phones at home.

By a little after noon the other "joggers" were there, including Robert Ludwig from D.C., their de facto leader, along with pastors and church elders from around the country.

For the first thirty minutes they ate lunch, introduced themselves, and compared notes on how current events had impacted them. Then Ludwig asked them to be seated as best they could at the tables. He stood where everyone could hear him, and Richard took notes on a legal pad.

"Thank you for coming on short notice and with some unusual stipulations," he began. "We wish we could have invited more, but you understand. We have a phone tree in place with over three hundred participants, so whatever we decide today will be disseminated to everyone by this afternoon. Our first order of business is to pray."

The group spent ten minutes lifting up prayers for guidance and protection. The resulting spiritual light and heat were too much for the three demons responsible for this area, and they had to back off, though their leader said he would mention this unusual activity to their sector leader.

Ludwig continued. "We're here to make recommendations back to our home churches about how to respond to the extension of the State of

Emergency. We don't need to spend much time on its deficiencies. Let's focus on what we should do."

There followed almost an hour's discussion. At one point a police drone flew overhead and circled back to take a closer look, but Richard felt secure with their jogging clothes and paper plates.

One of the first pastors to raise his hand was an African American from Midland, Texas. He reported that as his congregation fasted and prayed, several courses of action became apparent, but the one most repeated was that they should put on the Whole Armor of God and pray and act against the forces who were ultimately behind all the hate and violence, no matter the immediate details: Satan and his demons.

A Women's Ministry leader from Colorado Springs, invited by Kristen Holloway, rose and agreed with the pastor from Midland. Her group, and those with whom they were connected, had reported the same message. She took out a pocket Bible and read from Ephesians 6:

"Finally, be strong in the Lord and in his mighty power. Put on the full armor of God, so that you can take your stand against the devil's schemes. For our struggle is not against flesh and blood, but against the rulers, against the authorities, against the powers of this dark world and against the spiritual forces of evil in the heavenly realms. Therefore put on the full armor of God, so that when the day of evil comes, you may be able to stand your ground, and after you have done everything, to stand. Stand firm then, with the belt of truth buckled around your waist, with the breastplate of righteousness in place, and with your feet fitted with the readiness that comes from the gospel of peace. In addition to all this, take up the shield of faith, with which you can extinguish all the flaming arrows of the evil one. Take the helmet of salvation and the sword of the Spirit, which is the word of God. And pray in the Spirit on all occasions with all kinds of prayers and requests. With this in mind, be alert and always keep on praying for all the Lord's people."[2]

When she finished, there was a general nodding of heads and several comments of "That's what we heard, too."

Ludwig spoke. "So prayer, and relying on truth, righteousness, peace, faith, salvation, speaking the word, and more prayer. All directed at the

Prince of Lies and at the lies of his minions. Spiritual Warfare, with us as the combatants, rather than legal or physical confrontation with the authorities, which we'll trust God to do. Is that what you've heard and believe we should do?"

Heads nodded and several people said, "Yes."

"Then what if we encourage pastors all over the country to preach for the next month on Ephesians 6? And I'd like us to create lists of actions and examples in each of Paul's Full Armor categories that we can share with others. Let's divide into working groups and write down some ideas. Becky, will you coordinate on Faith as a shield? Stan, on Truth as the connecting belt? Others? Richard, do you have some extra paper?

"Just before we start, let me take a minute to mention something that has come to us about uniting people of faith in America to stand up for all human rights. We need to shine the light of truth on the terrible plight of the Uyghurs in China. Stan and his church here in Atlanta are interested, and beyond how we might help them, the symbolism with what is happening here could be powerful. I have fact sheets here for you. Let us know if you're interested.

"Now, back to standing firm against the real enemy in all this evil."


Tom Sullivan was alone in his office that afternoon, finishing up a video conference with Tanya Prescott.

"Now that we have access to all the 'On mics' in the country, the flow of information is really enormous," she summarized. "Thank goodness we have AI to sort through it all to find the bits that we need to know."

Prescott was referring to one of the provisions in the extended State of Emergency, which allowed them access—through the various service providers and search engines like Juggle—to listen in and to mine information from all of the microphones that were turned on 24/7 in every smart device, intelligent speaker, automobile hands free mic—virtually every home and car in the country that was connected to the internet and not intentionally turned off.

It was amazing what people would say when they forgot that just because they couldn't see another person present did not mean they were alone. Almost 300 million adults and teenagers had a lot of daily conversations, and even with the combined processing power of the tech giants plus the NSA, there was still typically a lag of a couple of hours for a potentially actionable conversation to be reported. But the results had been dramatic.

"As you know, Tom, arrests are up and crime is down in every category and in almost every jurisdiction, thanks to these powerful tools. Do you think people are noticing?"

"I hope so, Tanya."

"But of course it makes it doubly frustrating that with all this power and all these leads, we still haven't connected back to find the attackers."

Tom nodded. "I know. It seems inconceivable that they're smart enough to avoid and evade what must be the most powerful dragnet ever deployed. No private group has that expertise and technical power. It must be a nation-state. Have you looked again at Russia, China and Iran? North Korea?"

"Many times. Daily. Each has tried to add to the dissension here, but we can't connect them to the actors themselves. Let me ask you a question that's been bugging me—Is it possible that there is no connection? That all of this has just randomly happened as a result of all the divisive rhetoric we've heard for so long, separating us?"

Tom paused, then shook his head. "There's too much all going on at once. There must be a connection, a purpose. Could there even be a rogue group, using some government's resources? This may sound crazy, but what if we asked the Russian and Chinese governments to help us find whoever is doing this? Include a carrot and a stick for helping us?"

"That would be very unusual. Maybe crazy. But I'll think about it. Maybe our break will come today. We'll stay on it, Tom. Have a good weekend."

"Listen, before you go, I have a new subject for you. The president is understandably really concerned about election security this time around, particularly with about thirty key races. We'd like your team to monitor and test the communications links between the new Federal

Election Integrity Commission's tabulators and each state or county's Election Management System during the week before the election, as an added safeguard."

"Sure. I think we have a team already on that, but glad to help and report to you. Just get me the codes for the links between the EMS in each state and the FEIC, and we'll set it up."

"OK. Thanks. Have a great weekend."

"You, too."

He closed his secure laptop and was about to go in search of a coffee when his Core Group phone vibrated. He didn't recognize the number.

"Hello."

"Mr. Sawyer, hi, this is Patrick Tomlinson. We met at Carpathia Restaurant with Kate Tikhonovsky and her uncle a few weeks ago, when you were with Ms. Sawyer."

"Yes, Patrick. How are you?"

"I'm fine. I hope you are. As you may have heard from Ms. Sawyer, I actually intern with Professor Thornton, and he met you at a Memorial Service and talked about having lunch."

"Yes, I remember."

"Well, he's traveling a lot but asked me to set up a lunch with you and Ms. Sawyer. I called her, but she said I should just call and set it up directly with you, and she gave me this number. Is that OK?"

Tom had a moment of sudden sadness as Callie's face flashed briefly into his mind. "Uh, yes, sure. When would you like to get together?"


When Tom arrived home that evening he was delighted to find that the mail had brought the first twelve envelopes from the people to whom he'd assigned the task of checking on potential attacks for hacking the upcoming election. He'd instructed each of them to use his home address and to report by snail mail—for the moment he believed the written word was still the most secure, and he didn't want any connection between this assignment and the White House.

He let Beau out the back, changed clothes, went back for a few ball tosses, opened a beer, and sat in his recliner. Thirty minutes later he was actually impressed. At least in these first cases, his hackers had found no way to change the data from off-site in any of the local voting machines or county tabulators.

He would share the good news with the president on Monday.

# 17

*God who gave us life gave us liberty. Can the liberties of a nation be secure when we have removed a conviction that these liberties are the gift of God? Indeed I tremble for my country when I reflect that God is just, that His justice cannot sleep forever.*

Thomas Jefferson

Saturday, October 17

Just before 3 am Natalie silenced the alarm on her phone as quickly as she could. Next to her in bed, Seth moaned and said, "You're really serious, at this hour?"

She swung her feet to the floor.

"I figure I can sleep later, but I have lots of years of not praying for anyone to catch up on."

He rolled over. "Whatever. I think you're crazy."

She nodded as she headed for the bathroom. "Yep. I know. I'll be back in a little while." *I would have said the same thing a year ago. Now it seems like the most important thing I do.*

A few minutes later she knelt in their living room, using their coffee table as a lectern. She spread out the three pages that Kristen had emailed her, and she opened her Bible.

Taking over from Callie a few blocks away, it was Natalie's hour on the front line, joining other believers across the country who had volunteered to weave their voices together every hour of the day and night, to ask God for His forgiveness, guidance, wisdom and intervention, and to pray against Satan and his forces. And she added a prayer for a meeting she was to attend that afternoon with Callie and Andrea.

Balzor, Nepravel and Zloy were sitting together in one of the conference rooms at the Northeast Women's Clinic where they typically passed the night. A fallen angel from Silicon Valley had just finished briefing their

362

group on a new virtual reality sexual experience which he claimed was more addictive than a narcotic for some men.

Balzor looked at the other two. "Sex must really be something. I can't imagine. Whatever it is, we've used it forever to lead men, and some women, wherever we want them to go. Why would He put such a powerful force inside these darlings of His?"

Nepravel shook his head. "Not sure. I thought that was where we were headed with Tom Sullivan and that Sawyer woman, to finish them off, but their break-up last week is just as good."

"And he's still got that issue to deal with," Zloy added. "That other woman is pregnant and set to come here for her abortion. They're meeting tonight to talk about it."

"I plan to be there," Nepravel said. "And..." He noticed the corner of the ceiling, where a warm spiritual light started to glow. It began as a small dot, but then grew, and as it did so, it made the three demons uncomfortably warm, and partially blinded them.

"Damn," Balzor cursed, shielding his eyes. "What's that?"

"Prayers! Here?" Zloy exclaimed.

They moved out into the larger common area, where others were similarly retreating from the periphery rooms and shielding their eyes. As they massed together the darkness of their combined force absorbed the spiritual light from the answered prayers, giving them relief.

Nepravel hissed to Balzor, right next to him, "It's one thing for those people to pray for each other, but these prayers must have been targeted at *us*. Who told them to do that?"

"I don't know, but it's got to stop. I'll speak to Bespor."

"We've got too much to do to be worrying about incoming prayers."

As Teri Grantham worked at her computer to format a photo shoot she had completed that morning for a nearby farm, she did not see Ranit circle in and perch next to her.

He had come with instructions he had never received before—they were going to encourage Teri to give up the White Supremacist shooters in Durham—men it had taken them five years to motivate to the violent action at the Jewish and Muslim student centers. His sector leader had explained that there was a larger plan to make the new government restrictions appear to be working well—arresting this group would be a key factor. And, anyway, they would still have Teri and her brother.

As she worked on sequencing the aerial photos, Teri remembered having drinks at a trade show six months earlier with two drone guys from Chapel Hill who, on their third round, espoused some racist views about minorities of all kinds. They had actually offended her at the time, but she'd shrugged it off because they were also pretty funny and had some good ideas on how to expand the business. She now recalled one of them wondering whether you could put a rifle on a drone.

She heard her own voice speaking to her. *Maybe they pulled off the Durham attack on Wednesday. And maybe if the Feds focus on them, they'll focus less on everyone else. North Carolina isn't that far from D.C., and the Feds might think they did both. I wonder if that Anonymous Tip Line is really anonymous. Probably not. So maybe just a typed note mailed to the FBI with no return address. And have Brad drive it a few states away to mail it.*

After his usual parkrun that Saturday morning with Logan, Tom had spent a couple of hours cleaning up his row house in anticipation of Erin joining him for dinner. It had been a while, so he gave Beau a bath with the hose in back. Near the end of his chores he took some time with his bedroom, and even the bathroom.

Nepravel was right there, determined to help Tom navigate the evening, starting from early in the day. He knew that one of the best ways to ensure the outcome he wanted was, as with almost any man, to get early visuals into Tom's mind.

*You never know, and it's been a while,* Tom thought to himself, remembering his enjoyable encounters with Erin. *Callie would never come here on her own, but Erin is a different story. Can't hurt to have everything in good shape, just in case.*

At a small meeting room in the library which Kahar visited most Saturdays, he was seated with the Rashids, who had invited two other couples from their mosque, plus the Hunts; and Andrea had asked Callie and Natalie to join them.

After Ahmad introduced him, Kahar described again, with growing passion, the terrible practices which the Chinese Communist Party were using to wipe out the Uyghurs, their culture, and their faith in Allah.

When he finished, the group asked questions and talked for over an hour about what they could do to bring attention to the Uygurs' plight. They agreed to meet again soon.

As Erin MacNeil relaxed in her bath that afternoon, Voena was nearby and making sure that her mind focused on the evening with Tom Sullivan.

*Tom's a great guy. Really fun. And we have a lot to talk about. I'm glad he asked me to help with that voting thing. Maybe he and I do have a future. Not the baby—and not marriage, not now. I guess if I were older—not ready for that. Career. Could he love me one day? For now I'd just be happy to be his girlfriend. Spend time together. There are certainly worse men to hang out with!*

Tom spent a couple of hours that afternoon in his White House office clearing up loose ends from the week. On the way home he bought some flowers for the dinner table. He took the steaks out of the fridge and opened a bottle of red—he assumed Erin was not laying off alcohol—and fixed himself a whisky and water. He looked around the place and decided that it looked pretty good. And Nepravel, who had just returned from planting voices in his other charges, amped up the visuals again.

His front door buzzer rang just after six, and he opened the door. Erin smiled—she was as beautiful as he remembered. "Come in. I'm glad you could come."

He helped her out of her coat and she turned around. She was wearing jeans and a low-cut green sweater. Unseen to them Voena also came in, and nodded to Nepravel.

"Don't know what you might have planned for dessert, but I brought some awesome eclairs from a shop near my apartment. Amazing." She handed him a white box.

"They'll be perfect. Do you remember Beau? We're having steak, salad and baked potato. OK? Can I get you a drink? Wine? Whisky?"

"Hi, Beau. Sure. How about some red wine?"

"Over here."

"And here's my report on that Senate race." She handed him an envelope. "As you asked, after trying for a couple of days, I think it would be really difficult to mess with the votes unless you had physical access to all the voting machines in the district. So possible, but not probable. I just wish they also had paper back-up."

Tom took the envelope and put it on the sideboard in the dining area he used for his bar. "Thank you. Yes, with the new federal law and strict standards, counties can save money by doing away with paper ballots, which I'm not sure was a good idea. But I'll focus on it tomorrow." He smiled, poured a glass for her, and refilled his whisky. They touched glasses.

She smiled again. "Thanks for having me."

"Let's sit down and catch up." He motioned to the sofa and chairs. "But first I'll bring out the chips and salsa."

A few minutes later she was seated on one end of the sofa, he on the chair next to it, with their drinks and chips on the coffee table. Nepravel and Voena were perched next to them, ready to add their voices.

She caught him up on her work on cybersecurity at the Information Initiative, focusing on how to protect against hacking of manufacturing systems. And of course keeping a company's entire supply chain safe from bad actors and cyber attacks.

"It's incredible how easy it would be to mess with most companies' orders and processes. They usually have some protection, but not enough."

She leaned forward for some chips and smiled. *Lust.* He looked and smiled back. "But then you know all that—you're the National Security Advisor to the president, for goodness' sake."

*Pride.* He shook his head. "You'd be surprised. Just summaries. There's so much, and more every day with the data mining we're doing."

"I can't imagine. What a responsibility you have."

"Hmm." He took a long sip of his whisky. "So, tell me about your plans."

"With the abortion?"

He nodded.

She sat back. "I made an appointment at the Northeast Women's Clinic for Thursday afternoon in ten days—on the 29$^{th}$. I have a friend at work—she had one a year ago—who'll go with me. I'll take Friday off. Should be OK." She looked at him.

He paused. *Relief.* "Yes. It should be. I'm sorry you have to go through this."

She shrugged. "It comes with the territory. I'm not ready to be a mother or to pause my career, so it happens. I know women my sister's age, in their thirties, who would have it, married or not. But not me. I have too much living to do." She smiled and handed him her empty wine glass. "I assume you're the same. Just don't tell my sister, or my parents."

He took the glass, raised it to her, and walked to the bar.

"Yes, I agree. Too much living to do."

As Tom refilled her glass, Nepravel turned to Voena. "It's going well."

Voena started to speak, but suddenly felt uncomfortably warm and noticed a shaft of light arcing down and starting to glow on Nepravel's chest. He quickly got up.

"Someone's praying!"

Nepravel also moved away. "Damn."

The light touched the two humans as well. The demons could see the tiny spiritual light inside Tom flicker once, but very weakly. Erin was unaffected.

"I don't like this," Voena spat as they backed away from where the light from the answered prayer had landed.

Nepravel, away from the light, said, "I think we're OK. They both seem to have the same idea for how the evening should end."

"Yes." Just then another arc of spiritual light illuminated the living room, and the two demons moved outside. "This has to stop. I'll check back in a couple of hours and report."

Nepravel agreed. They left Tom and Erin listening to their own pre-programmed internal voices, which by now were well in sync.

Even though the bombing was still fresh in her memory, Natalie was glad that eight of Seth's friends from The Network, including Rachel Shaw and her wife, Sally, along with Emily and Logan, could join them for a screening of Seth's "The Silent Progressive Majority" at their row house. Seth had worked deep into many early mornings to edit the original work to account for the new reality of the State of Emergency, along with the midterm elections. He seemed to be very pleased with the final product, and Natalie looked forward to finally seeing it.

She was sorry Tom and Callie had broken up, and that Tom could not join them.

As she greeted their guests, Natalie knew that the others gathering in her home still considered her to be a bit of a celebrity, having survived the DEA bombing, but she couldn't stand that thought. She knew she was saved physically and then spiritually by others' sacrifices, and by God's grace, and she made sure that anyone who asked her knew those truths. But generally she never mentioned it, or her new faith, except to Seth and her growing number of friends at The Church of the Good Shepherd. She felt she still had so much to learn about the new life she'd been given as a gift.

After getting Emily a glass of wine, Logan went in search of hors d'oeuvres, and Natalie turned to Emily.

"Have you talked with Tom about Callie?" she asked.

"He's not saying much. I think she broke up with him, but I'm not sure why. Tonight he's having dinner with Erin MacNeil. You may remember him mentioning her this summer. Not much mourning for the Callie relationship."

Natalie shook her head. "I guess not. I saw Callie today, and she isn't saying much, either."

Emily changed the subject. "Seth has been great to work with, on this and other projects. Really the whole Network team. Great insights."

"Seth enjoys working with you in the White House, though he says it's a bit crazy."

"Until we get our own team in place, I suspect it will stay a bit crazy. We're working on it. Let me go say hello to Rachel and Sally."

Natalie nodded and turned toward the backyard, where she saw Logan and Seth in conversation.

Thirty minutes later they gathered in the living room around Seth's large screen, pulling chairs from the dining area and also sitting on the floor.

Rachel Shaw stood. "I'm glad we could get together with Seth and Natalie to get a first look at this documentary, on which so many on our team have worked so hard, under Seth's steady direction." Several raised their glasses. "And of course I also want to recognize Emily Schofield from the president's team, who shares with Seth the title of co-inspirer. And Logan, her husband, who works for Juggle, our key sponsor. Seth, any words of wisdom?"

"Hopefully, you're about to see them."

The hard-hitting documentary focused on, one by one, seven American identity groups to show how they were victims of white, male oppression—African Americans, women, Native Americans, LGBTQ, Muslims, the under-educated, and undocumented immigrants. The general narration was done by a senior African American anchor at The Network whose voice was known to carry both wisdom and wit. There were plenty of facts about the uneven distribution of income, health and wealth. And other articulate, passionate speakers, including President Bradshaw when he was much younger, all clearly stated why each group had so many reasons to back Progressive programs to improve their health and to redistribute the nation's wealth.

By adding together all of the Americans in these separate groups, the result was "The Silent Progressive Majority"—those who wanted their grievances redressed, and the oppression against them to stop.

But it was clear in the script that they also wanted to be kept safe from attack—Seth, through the narrator, was careful to point out that their communities were the least able to rebound from physical harm or from hate speech.

The best solution for all these issues, strongly advanced in the documentary, was an expanded Progressive federal government with the strength to protect *all* its citizens from every attack, foreign and domestic, physical and verbal.

As the credits rolled there was applause from everyone. From his seat next to Natalie on the sofa, Seth raised his hand and nodded his head in acknowledgement. "Almost everyone in this room participated in making the final product a success, including Emily and Logan Schofield, and of course Natalie, who I thank God is here with us, and only because the government protected her when it most counted."

There was more applause.

Natalie, looking down at the glass in her hands, said just above a whisper, "Actually, it was not the government, but two heroic women who, I believe, had some sort of divine leading to save so many of us."

Rachel heard most of what Natalie said and quickly stood up. "Well, we've been almost an hour without refills, so please take care of whatever you need, and I'm sure Seth will be glad to answer any questions you have, one-on-one."

# Sunday, October 18

Light was just beginning to filter through the curtains when Tom awoke in his bed that Sunday morning. He was lying on his side and was delighted to find the still-sleeping form of Erin MacNeil right next to him.

*What a great night.*

As he quietly went downstairs for two cups of coffee, it occurred to him that some time spent with Erin might be quite pleasant.

*Why not? "Too much living to do" she had said. Should be a good time, without the intensity and—what?—'morality' of Callie. Definitely should be fun.*

A little later Callie and Kristen were sitting and having coffee in Callie's kitchen before walking to church. Grace played a video game in the living room—one of the perks Callie allowed on the weekend. Callie told Kristen about their meeting with Kahar and the others, along with some ideas for how to bring more attention to the Uyghurs' plight.

"Sounds terrible. Let me know how I can help," Kristen said. Then, putting her mug on the table, she added, "So, a week without Tom."

Callie looked at her own mug and nodded. "Yes. I have to say that in a maddening way I miss him. How can such a seemingly good, intelligent man be so blind, so clueless? Can't he see what he's doing is so wrong, on so many levels?"

Kristen smiled. "I suspect because he thinks he's doing the right things. That's the usual lie people listen to."

"Yes, he does. It's so bad."

"As we've been reminded so often this week, 'the Devil is a liar, and the father of liars.' He's the real enemy, and he's a great liar. He figures out—maybe through trial and error—exactly how to lie to each of us individually so we'll believe his lies instead of the truth. That's what Tom's up against. Plus he's smart, attractive and an overachiever—all good traits unless you also start to believe your own press releases."

It was Callie's turn to smile and nod. "Yes, that's him."

"So, if you and I are any examples, God sometimes has to go to great lengths to get our attention before we'll listen to Him. What's going on in Tom's life that God could use to get his attention?"

"A lot, I suppose. Seems like everything he's doing at work is a potential disaster—for somebody. And I told you about the possible abortion. Did I mention that Gary Thornton's assistant called to set up the luncheon we talked about at Sara's Memorial Service?"

"No. Are you going?"

"Not now. But I told the assistant to go ahead and set it up without me."

Kristen thought for a minute. "Pastor Ludwig has asked us to pray directly against Satan and his forces—that their plans for us will be destroyed. So let's do that, but specifically let's pray against the plans they have for Tom, and that Tom will be open to hearing God's truth instead."

"Yes. And will you share that prayer with the others on your prayer chain?"

"Of course, starting with Tom's parents."


At that same hour President Bradshaw welcomed his long-time friend, campaign contributor, and Juggle CEO Andrew Boswell to the Residence in the White House.

The two men, dressed in slacks and casual shirts, shook hands as the escort turned to leave. "Drew, thank you for coming on a Sunday morning, when things are a little more informal and not quite so open to notice."

Boswell smiled. "My pleasure, Mr. President. Whenever you need me."

"Let's go into the private kitchen and have some breakfast."

A few minutes later the two men were seated at the same comfortable table where the president and Tom had talked a week before, with coffee and plates of eggs, bacon and toast before them. They chatted for a few minutes about their families and Juggle's business.

"I notice your sales and stock price have been on a tear of late, Drew," Bradshaw said.

"Yes, they have." His friend smiled. "Seems like we've found new ways to connect buyers with exactly what they want. Thank you for the help."

"Good. Good. And thank you for all your help, including with High Tech's contributions to the upcoming elections, both financial and, shall we say, with friendly algorithms."

Boswell nodded, and they each took a bite of their breakfast and a sip of coffee.

"Drew, I asked you here this morning because I want these elections to really mean something, to set a new Progressive course for our nation. And not just for two or four years."

"You know we're on the same page there, Mr. President. We've been so close to achieving that before. The country needs it."

"Exactly. We can't fail this time. We can't. It's too important. Listen, I understand from Tom Sullivan that Juggle helped create the tabulation and reporting software for the Federal Election Protection Commission."

"Yes, under the new law centralizing all election results with the federal government, which Congress passed a few years ago. I'm glad to say that it works well."

"Even with all the different machines and procedures out there?"

Boswell laughed. "Yes, the law gives the states two more years to come into the single Federal standard compliance for the voting machines themselves. Until then we interact with the various Election Management Systems that combine the local machines' results, and so we issue system security updates to the software right up to the election itself."

"I see. Interesting. Let's come back to that. On a related subject, have you ever thought about how much we could accomplish for our people if a huge part of each year's budget didn't have to go to the military, to the Defense Establishment?"

"It's enormous. About half of all discretionary spending."

"Exactly. What if we could take both China and Russia off the table as possible enemies, or even as perpetual competitors?"

"It would free up incredible resources to push progressive programs and to pay down our debt. Everyone should find something to like, even conservatives. But how would that be possible?"

"Drew, this is just between us, and I'm just asking for your opinion. As I understand it—please correct me—both of our main competitors—China and Russia—have created their own internal realities for their people. In each country the government controls the internet, the media, and entertainment. And the government tailors what people can see and hear. People in China and Russia are basically told what to believe about almost everything—and most conform. Is that right?"

"Yes. The new generation in China really doesn't know anything else other than what they're told. Russians still have access to a few mostly U.S.-based alternatives to their State's information monopoly, but they're closing down access to those, too."

"Well." Bradshaw leaned forward and lowered his voice a bit. "What if we did the same thing here? Not quite as openly, but just as well. For our own protection. And, with the government's help of course, you guys in the Tech world could quietly run the implementation and the monitoring? Like we did before with Trailblazer, PRISM, and the other partnerships, only this time you block or remove untrue and unhelpful information. I mean, we wouldn't block an entire site, like they do in China, but instead we use Artificial Intelligence, or whatever, to just remove the harmful ideas and content on every site that could mislead people who don't know the truth.

"Between the earlier Covid lockdowns and our State of Emergency, I think in many ways we're almost there. Tom and DHS are working on a system to reward good citizens' behavior, and they may need your help there after the elections. Between Progressive corporations, universities, high schools and the media, our message already dominates almost every corner of the public square, every day. If we can just silence a few more voices, our Progressive truth will be the only truth anyone ever hears, or believes, or even knows about, which should give us a free path to govern for decades for the good of everyone. What do you think?"

Drew poured coffee in both of their mugs from the silver pot on the table. "I agree that virtually all the pieces are already in place, and they're working well. Most people wouldn't notice any change, and half the country would applaud us anyway."

The president tapped the tabletop with his index finger. "Exactly. And Drew, here's the final piece that no one could pull off before without our current technology. What if we had an understanding with Russia and China that the three of us could create and control whatever reality we wanted in our own countries, and that the other two wouldn't interfere or compete?"

Boswell sat back and thought for a moment. "You mean, sort of divide the world into thirds, and give each of us the uncontested right to control what happens, and what people think, in our third?"

Bradshaw nodded. "Yes. Asia to the Chinese. The countries of the old Soviet Union and their near neighbors to the Russians. And the Americas to us. We'd all agree to dial-down our military spending, to stop trying to one-up each other. Leave each other—each region—alone. And use those savings to help our people."

Boswell considered the president's idea.

Bradshaw continued. "Once we set it up and get comfortable with each other, think of all we can achieve. No more hacking each other and trying to steal secrets and information. We can share—government to government and company to company—our best practices and innovations, because we won't have to compete. We'll help each other. Imagine having the huge Chinese economy on our side as a partner, not a competitor."

"What about Australia, Japan, Korea and Taiwan? And Ukraine? Even Europe."

"They'll have to deal with a new reality, to finally figure out how to work with their larger neighbors without us sticking our nose in to help them. Europe can putter along as one large, pleasant museum for the rest of us to visit. On our side, we'll be able to handle Cuba and Venezuela without interference. It may take a year or two for the world to adjust, but think how much more peaceful that world will be. And together we three leading nations will come down hard on the Muslims and the Israelis. We should be able to dictate what peace between them will look like, and then enforce it. What do you think?"

"You're right, everyone would be better off. And, again, the pieces are there. But it would mean walking away from several major treaties and alliances with our allies."

"Breaking a few alliances to achieve world peace, and to save hundreds of billions of dollars a year, will be worth it. Once we've done it, everyone will agree. Which is where these elections and you come in. We've got to win, and with a bullet-proof, super- majority in the House, and a filibuster-proof Senate, to pass whatever agreements and treaties might be necessary in the first 100 days."

"Yes. And me?"

"I need a back-channel person I can totally trust to secretly propose this vision to the presidents of China and Russia, to find out if they're agreeable. From everything you've told me, you know the most capable 'Drew Boswells' of those two countries—men you can meet with one-on-one and then trust to convey this plan to their political leaders without risk of disclosure until after the election, when we can roll right from the State of Emergency into this new world order, though we'll take our time to set the stage and do it carefully. I just want to be sure that both China and Russia are onboard."

Drew nodded. "Yes, I know just who to talk to. When would you like me to start?"

"Can you do this in person, preferably without translators?"

"Yes, both of these men have degrees from U.S. universities. And I can fly out quietly tomorrow or Tuesday, as soon as I can set up the meetings."

"Drew, you'll be doing the world a great service if you can help with this huge step to permanent peace and understanding."

"It's your vision, Mr. President. I'll just be the messenger. But I'll try to get it right."

"Good. Now let's circle back to our first subject and talk again about how to win this election, maybe with a little extra help from your team."

That Sunday in hundreds of churches all across the country there were announcements that starting immediately and continuing for the next month the sermons, Sunday School teachings, small group discussions, and mid-week prayer services would focus on the believer's role in Spiritual Warfare, with the relevant Biblical texts listed in each church's bulletin and on its website.

That evening in their home office Clayton and Andrea Hunt logged into an online meeting they had set up with Seth, Natalie, Emily, Logan, Callie, Ahmad and Mariam.

After general greetings, Clayton led off. "Thank you for joining us. Andrea and I want to plant some seeds and continue a conversation we had at Tom's dinner, but with what we hope might be a very positive outcome for many people."

Andrea continued, "We've gotten to know Ahmad and Mariam really well over the last month. They've stayed with us twice to hide from people who've threatened their family—both radical "super-patriots" and radical members of their own mosque. And we've listened to them recount the much more terrible plight of the Uyghurs, one of whom we met with yesterday."

Clayton said, "From those discussions, and after prayer, we've come up with an idea that we hope might both help the Uyghurs and also help heal some of our own differences, which we want to run by you for your input, and possible help. If you think it makes sense, we can also talk to Tom."

"Please go ahead," Callie said from her living room.

"In an uncanny way," Clayton began, "it seems to us that the Uyghurs today are in almost the exact same situation in China as the Jews were in Germany in the late 1930s and 40s. Each group was and is being persecuted and exterminated by their own government simply because of their race and their faith, but it's all done behind the tightest secrecy that technology will permit, and with enough doubts and denials offered by officials to deflect any real inquiry."

"And, just like then," Andrea said, "if any family member who has escaped the tyranny speaks out or calls attention to the truth, then his or her family back home suffers even more, so it's almost impossible to hear first-hand witnesses."

"Also like then, America remains on the sidelines, generally aware that something bad is happening, but unwilling to force an investigation in the full light of day, or to bring other pressure, because a lot of business relationships are involved," Clayton said. "So the evil continues and people suffer.

"Our idea is to unite Christian, Jewish, Muslim and secular Americans to publicly denounce this genocide, and to call for an immediate international investigation, along with strict sanctions on the Chinese government if no investigation is forthcoming. It's a way for all Americans of faith—and of no faith—to show in a concrete way that, despite, or because of, the current attacks, and our other differences, we are united in this country on the foundational principles of personal freedom and human rights.

"Seth, starting with you, given your Jewish background and media savvy, what do you think?"

"I, uh, think it sounds like a good idea."

"Logan, I know you have some strong thoughts about Muslims," Clayton said. "What do you think?"

Logan glanced at Emily. "On the face of it, it sounds good. I know I came on a little too strong when we had dinner—Emily has mentioned it several times, and I'm sorry. Certainly not all Muslims. And I don't want anyone to suffer, particularly for no reason. I'm glad to hear more."

"Me, too," said Emily. "Given my position, I may not be able to demonstrate, but I can help behind the scenes with the D.C. government, at least."

Natalie asked, "What do you plan to do, and when?"

"On the what, we'd like to hope we can interest the leaders of all faiths, and actually become a national movement to hold the Chinese government accountable. A large demonstration, with diverse speakers, probably here in D.C. and simultaneously in the other five cities where the Chinese have consulates, would show that Americans care about *all* human rights, not just for those in our own 'group'. It could be really powerful, and even healing.

"On the when, it turns out that the Nazis concocted Kristallnacht, which began the open persecution of Jews, on November 9$^{th}$ and 10$^{th}$, 1938. And, coincidentally, November 12$^{th}$ is the anniversary of the Uyghurs' 1931 revolt against China and the formation of the first East Turkestan Republic. So, to connect the two government sponsored genocides, we thought an event on the 12$^{th}$, which this year is a Thursday, would help connect those dots and shine extra light on the Chinese darkness."

Andrea added, "The elections will be over and even the extended State of Emergency should be ended. Not that a demonstration of human rights should raise any issues, but those restrictions should be behind us, and hopefully we can focus on healing ourselves around an unselfish cause to help others."

"Sounds really good to me," Natalie said. "Callie, do you think Church of the Good Shepherd and others will get behind it?"

"I'll talk to our leadership about it. Maybe we could help sponsor an event here."

Ahmad added, "And the same with our mosque, and many American Muslims. Who knows, Callie, maybe our mosque and your church can work together."

"That would be impressive," Seth said. "I'll check at The Network, but I can't imagine why we wouldn't support it. And I have several friends in the Jewish community here, and back home. I'll make some calls."

Clayton smiled. "Thanks, everyone. Ahmad and I will be glad to meet with any pastors, imams or rabbis to share the vision with them, in person or online. We only have a month, but let's see how far we can get."

Ahmad and Mariam Rashid logged off the video call in their den. Ahmad stood. "I'll put the boys to bed."

Mariam looked up at him from her chair. "This could be incredible, for many reasons. I'm all in. But there's something about Kahar that still doesn't sit right with me."

"What?"

"I'm not sure. Like he's leaving out something. Did you ever get the details on his family, or how he and his cousin got here?"

"No. He changes the subject. Maybe he's embarrassed."

Mariam paused. "Maybe. Or maybe he just doesn't want us to know."

Ahmad shrugged. "I'll ask again. And maybe I'll dig a bit into how Uyghurs in general are able to escape all that mess and come to the U.S."

She stood and smiled. "Yes, I think that's a good idea. It's so terrible for them. I'd like to know myself."

# Saturday, October 24

Tom was up early the next Saturday morning, sitting in an undershirt and shorts at his work table, sipping coffee, and scrolling through the messages and notices on his Core Group special phone. He occasionally bent down and scratched Beau's head. He imagined the dog was unhappy about being ousted from his spot in the bedroom on several recent nights, and Tom tried to make it up with pats and treats.

It had been another packed week for him and the nation, as the midterm campaigns swung into full but slightly abbreviated action, and Tom's team continued to do its best to coordinate briefings for the president on all the National Security issues confronting the country.

On Wednesday Tom had quietly shared with the president the first reports on potential election tampering issues. The Chief Executive appeared to be pleased with his progress, and was relieved that hacking on a scale large enough to change outcomes seemed almost impossible at the level of county voting and reporting. Tom expected to hear from the last of his contacts within a few days, and the results were certainly promising if you thought that election integrity was one of the foundations of the nation.

With Gary Thornton's assistant they'd set lunch for that coming Wednesday. Tom had never heard of the "Meat and Three" restaurant where they would be meeting, but Patrick Tomlinson, the young assistant, assured him that the food was great and the booths large. Patrick also hoped to join them.

So Tom had finished Thornton's book two days ago, and he'd then spent thirty minutes checking some of the Founders' quotes which Thornton referenced—he found himself wondering how these pillars of rational enlightened reason could also possibly live by such deep faith in the supernatural, personal God portrayed in the Bible. Were their declarations really what they believed, or just a show for the voting populace? He wanted to have some examples ready to discuss at their lunch.

When he finished going through his current messages, he refilled his mug and poured a second one, then walked upstairs.

"Hey, sleepyhead," he announced to Erin, who was just waking up in his bed, "Logan and Emily'll be here in forty minutes. We've got a 5K to do."

Erin slowly propped up on one elbow, took the mug from him, and smiled. "I'm not sure I have any energy left after last night...and I can't imagine how you could."

"Come on. I'm not *that* old. In fact, there may be some more gas in the tank now," he grinned as he put down his mug and pulled back the covers.

"No way."

Nepravel, who had joined them on his usual morning rounds, was quite pleased that Tom seemed to have traded Callie's truth challenges for Erin's challenges of a different type. But he didn't like the spiritual temperature in the room, and several incoming answered prayers touched Tom while Nepravel watched. Happily Tom was almost impervious, particularly at this moment, and Nepravel left to check on the other souls to whom he was assigned.


President Bradshaw and Margaret were enjoying a quiet breakfast together in the private kitchen and watching a replay of "The Silent Progressive Majority." They had been busy on Wednesday night when the documentary originally aired on The Network, and they were enjoying it now.

"That's so true," Margaret said, after the narrator commented on the need to spend more for better public schools in low-income neighborhoods.

The president's Core Group phone vibrated, and he looked at the Caller ID. He used the remote to pause the TV and answered. "Drew, how are you?"

"I'm fine, Mr. President. And you?"

"Margaret and I are fine. Having breakfast together."

"Good, then I won't keep you. Say, are you certain these phones are secure?"

"Yes. Both Tom and General Price vouch for their complete security against hacking or interception."

"OK. Well, I have good news. Both the presidents of Russia and China have received your message, and have responded."

"Go on."

"The Chinese are in complete agreement with your proposal, and the Russians are strongly considering it. Each thanks you for it. The Chinese will await our lead on implementation, but they look forward to working with us."

"Excellent, Drew, excellent. Well done. I think we should go ahead, don't you?"

"Yes, Mr. President. We will. And the other help we discussed with the elections is on track as well—almost done. I remain at your disposal to assist, as does the entire Juggle team, and the other key tech players."

"Then, please, draw up a draft plan for how we can phase in the final internet controls here after November 3rd, and you and I can strategize together on who to bring in on the plan, and when. Just the two of us for now."

"Sounds good, Mr. President. I'll do it, and by myself."

"Excellent. I think we're in great shape now to win the election, and then to change the world for the better—in many great ways."


Two and a half hours later the Schofields' Subaru pulled up for the second time in front of Tom's row house. They had made a slight detour on the way back from their parkrun to let Erin off at her apartment, but she and Tom agreed that she would come over later with a bag packed for a few days, and to help him cook dinner for their guests.

"Thanks, as always, for driving," Tom said to his friends as he opened the back door. "Nice pace today, Logan. You pushed me."

"She's cute," Emily said, as he got out.

"Yes, she is. She definitely is," he said with a smile, as he closed the door.

"And maybe not as much baggage as Callie," Emily offered through her open window.

"Well, some, but different, for sure. A nice person."

"And cute."

"And cute," he replied, backing toward his front door, and waving. "Thanks again."

Tom went inside and had just downed a power drink when his phone vibrated.

"Hi, Mom," he said to the small screen.

"And Dad," his father added, coming into view. "How are you?"

"Fine. Literally just got back from our parkrun. I'm letting Beau out now."

"How was it?"

"Pretty quick this time. I feel it."

"Getting old?" Janet asked.

"No," Tom said, smiling and thinking back to the first reference to his age that morning.

"Well, we look forward to seeing you on Tuesday for dinner," she said.

"And you're representing your church?"

"Yes," Janet said. "I knew Patricia a little bit when I was in Congress, and I think her invitation went out to about a thousand churches, synagogues and mosques around the country to come together and talk about how to reduce hate speech, and to bring unity. Our church asked us to go, so we are."

"Good. Yes, dinner will be great. And, by coincidence, I'm having lunch the next day with Gary Thornton, the author."

"I've read his books," Janet said. "That should be interesting. Please tell him hello for me. We met once a long time ago."

"I will. But right now I gotta go—a ton of stuff to get through."

"OK. We'll see you Tuesday. We love you."

"Love you, too."

He hung up, took out another power drink, and went upstairs for his shower.

A little later he was seated at his table downstairs, alternating between his To Do List for the week and his grocery list for his shopping date with Erin once she arrived. His Core Group phone buzzed again.

"Tanya. Happy Saturday."

"Same to you. Sorry to bother you, but I thought you'd be interested. While our high-tech wizardry has been at work this week, an unmarked envelope arrived at FBI Headquarters and went unopened for a couple of days. Late yesterday someone finally noticed it, and it's an anonymous tip about two guys in the Chapel Hill area who have a drone and a high level of skill with rifles."

"Really?"

"Yes. A joint team is gathering in Durham now to pay them a visit this afternoon. And there's a conference tonight in Chapel Hill on Mideast Reconciliation, so a lot of potential targets for whoever attacked the student unions will be in that area."

"I hope they're the ones, and you get them."

"I'll let you know. And one more thing. You know we review all draft sermons, and all public addresses, before they can be given, looking for hate speech."

"Yes, of course."

"Well, as the AI algorithms went through the thousands of drafts submitted on Thursday checking for hate speech, it took a supervisor to review the individual outputs and to realize that almost a thousand of them are about the same subject—spiritual warfare. We've never seen that before, and it just seems impossible that it's a coincidence."

"Like someone is coordinating them?"

"Yes. Few if any of the sermons themselves had any noticeable hate speech, so they're OK. But we were wondering. So we went back and pulled up the recorded phone calls and emails from the leaders at several of the larger churches where we've had issues in the past, and with the help of our voice recognition software, we found that, as we thought, over the last week almost all of them have been encouraging each other to give a message on that topic."

PARKER HUDSON

"Spiritual warfare? Like, demons and angels?"

"I guess."

"Seems odd."

"Well, pastor Robert Ludwig here in D.C. is one of them. And, actually, we heard your father talking about the same thing with his pastor on the phone."

Tom paused and said, "We really can listen to almost everyone, can't we? Well, let's keep an eye on it and see if there's anything harmful going on. If there is, we'll have to be all over it."

"Yes. In the meantime, we're focused on North Carolina."

"Good luck."


Callie had walked Grace to a friend's house for a birthday party, and now she and Natalie were about to enjoy sandwiches in the late October sun at a table in a small park nearby.

"Thanks for getting lunch," Callie said, unwrapping her corned beef special. "These are the best—and half will keep for supper."

"My favorite deli. And thanks for meeting. I feel like I need to talk with you. But first, speaking of supper, Seth and I are going to Tom's tonight. He felt badly about missing the documentary preview and wants to have us over, and introduce us to someone."

Callie pursed her lips. "Good for him. Probably Erin, whom he dated a couple of times before we met at your place the night of the attacks. They may be perfect for each other. But let's talk about you. I hope I can help." And she took a healthy bite.

Natalie opened her bag of chips and took one. "OK. Kristen's class for new believers has been wonderful—she's so clear and patient with every subject. Thank you, again, for recommending her. And I've gotten to know some of the other women in the class. Some pretty tough stories, but amazing as well."

"God transformed me completely, and that was no small task."

Natalie smiled. "Yes. That's what I think He's doing. After spending a year getting my attention, now that I'm His, He's working on me, changing me. Or trying to."

Callie nodded and took a sip of her drink.

"As you can imagine, living with Seth is at the top of the list. I love him, it's convenient, and I think he loves me. But God's word, as Kristen—and Pastor Ludwig—have shown me, calls for us to make a commitment, and to be married. And I've heard others say that unless God is the third person in the marriage, it will never work. So I just don't know what to do. Should I break up with Seth? Demand that he marry me?"

Callie swallowed and thought for a moment. Just then both of their phones vibrated and they saw a message forwarded by Kristen to their church's prayer team from Janet Sullivan. Each took a minute to read it.

Our son Tom is having lunch with Gary Thornton on Wednesday in D.C. Please pray for their protection from evil forces, for clarity, and for God's truth to be manifest. And please pray the same for the Vice President's conference on national unity that afternoon. There is spiritual war raging in our nation's capital, and we must engage with the enemy on our knees and with our voices.

Callie looked up at her friend. "I just got goose bumps. That lunch idea began at the Memorial Service for Sara. Remember when we met Gary Thornton at the back of the church?"

Natalie nodded. "I wish you were going."

Callie shrugged. "Maybe it's better for their meeting that we've split up. Anyway, we'll pray about it before we leave, but back to you and Seth. I'm no expert on marriage, but you certainly don't want to demand that he marry you. And if he does ask you, you'd have to decide if you want to spend the rest of your life with someone who may never join you in your faith. The Bible warns against that—it's called being 'unequally yoked.'

Knowing others in that situation, I suspect it's tough. Hard for God to be in a marriage if one of you doesn't believe He exists."

"Hmm. I can see that. Years of friction, or just a dull truce."

"I think so. So what you have, as in other situations, is God's Word telling us to behave in one way, for our own best outcome—not because He's a prude—and the world, the flesh and the devil telling us to behave exactly the opposite. And, as believers, we have to decide. Are we to trust God's commands and abide in His Son's love, or to be molded by those other forces and renounce His will for us? When I start there, I find that most tough decisions actually become pretty clear."

Natalie thought for a few moments while looking at Callie. She smiled and nodded. "Yes, when you put it like that, it does seem pretty simple. Not easy, but simple."

"Straight forward. Do you trust the One who made you and only wants the best for you, or do you trust those who either don't care about you at all, or want to destroy you?"

"Pretty simple." Natalie reached out and covered Callie's hand. "Thank you."

"It's not me. It's Him. Now let's pray against the spiritual forces trying to mislead you and Seth, and then for Tom—and even Erin—and all that's happening tonight and next week."


Wilson Smith and Trey Dunham had driven in Wilson's pickup truck far out into the country, to a field in the middle of a forest that Wilson had first spotted while surveying a nearby farm with his drone. Zaraz and Ranit joined them, and Zaraz enjoyed showing Ranit how he could almost completely control Wilson's thoughts and actions. Ranit, whose most recent possession had been an ISIS bomb manufacturer in Syria a few years before, was jealous of Zaraz's power over the human. But they also both knew that these men's time on earth might be short, given the plan that was now playing out.

Wilson/Zaraz and Trey spent the afternoon shooting aerial target practice and downing a few beers, so neither was home when federal agents and local police came calling at the houses they rented. After only ten minutes inside Wilson's house, the agent in charge was sure that they needed to find him, and quickly.

As dusk set in, the two lashed down the drone in the back of the truck and covered it with a tarp. Then they set out, using back roads, for a light industrial area on the north side of Chapel Hill—Wilson's delivery job had given him ample opportunities to assess the best places from which to launch his drone with the least chance of being seen.

They parked behind a vacant warehouse building on the edge of a treeless construction site that was advertised as the coming second phase of the development. A dumpster and the nearby buildings fronting other streets but adjoining the same pad meant that their corner of the lot was not visible from any street or window, and there was no security lighting facing their way.

"Nice," Trey nodded, as Wilson stopped and killed the engine.

"It's supposed to start at seven. Let's be in the air by 6:30 and hit a group of them walking up outside the front doors."

"Sounds like a plan," Trey said as he opened the door.

"Teach the bastards a lesson to leave us alone."


"Tell me about Seth and Natalie," Erin said, as she and Tom set his table for four, and Beau walked around them with a tennis ball in his mouth and one eye on the back door.

Tom put down the plates. "Well, Seth and I roomed—or apartmented—together almost ten years ago, and we'd known each other as undergrads. So we go way back. Two others from that same apartment you'll meet, I'm sure, soon. Seth's an on-air guy at The Network, well plugged in with the new Administration, mainly through Emily Schofield, the president's Communications Chief, one of our other apartment-mates."

She looked quizzical, and he held up both hands. "I know, sort of amazing how we started. The documentary was his idea, and he wrote most of it, but Emily had input. Anyway, Seth and I share stuff, but he knows he can't mention it unless I OK it.

"He and Natalie have lived together about six months, in a row house not far from here. They love Beau. She tracks the bad guys' money, and I was at their place the night of the first attacks. She was working at the DEA the morning of the bombing. She was almost killed, and many around her were. I think it really changed her. She suddenly has a strong faith, and is going to The Church of the Good Shepherd, where Pastor Ludwig is the preacher—we had to detain him for hate speech."

Erin smiled as she added the wine glasses. "Wow. Sounds like a TV drama."

Tom thought for a moment. "Yes, it is sort of crazy that our lives are so intertwined. They should be here soon—I'll get the salmon ready."


Wilson had entered the GPS coordinates for the historic meeting hall at the center of the UNC campus into the drone's onboard computer. As soon as he powered up and released it, the drone climbed almost silently to 200 feet and then headed south towards the target, the rifle slung underneath in its special harness. The sun was just setting, and they could toggle between normal and infrared views on their individual monitors.

The twilight and the streetlights gave a perfect picture as the drone began its descent over Franklin Street and headed for their target on Cameron Avenue. Trey, from his gunner's monitor, could see what looked like hundreds of people converging from every direction on the well-lit square at the front of the auditorium.

"Look at all of 'em," he said quietly to Wilson. "This'll be like shooting fish in a barrel."

"I'll bring the bird to a hover, and then it'll be weapons free," Wilson responded.

The drone stopped its descent and started to hover just above Cameron Avenue. Trey's finger tightened on the trigger as he picked out his first target—a man wearing a yarmulke—when the drone suddenly jerked up and climbed at a fast rate back to 200 feet.

"What the...?" Wilson exclaimed. As he and Trey watched, the drone pivoted and headed north, seeming to retrace its flight path. Nothing Wilson did with his controls could stop it.

"Damn. Must be some kind of countermeasure. Damn! It may be headed back here. Let's go."

They threw their controllers in the back of the pickup and took off. Wilson used no headlights until they were out of the industrial park. "See if anyone's following us," he told Trey, who turned to watch behind them.

"Where we goin'?" Trey asked, his voice almost cracking.

"The Barn. There's a meetin' tonight. We'll pick up some guns and supplies, borrow some money, and head west. My cousin lives on a huge farm in Mississippi. He's got some outbuildings we can hole up in."

"Do you think they ID'd us?"

"Not yet, I don't think. But if they get the drone, they'll sure as hell be able to trace it to me."

"Damn."

As they drove further north, two government drones were already following them in the dark sky.

Nepravel was livid. It was already too spiritually light, warm and full of believers' praying voices in Tom's home, with all the incoming answered prayers finding Tom—and even some touching Erin—but then Natalie showed up with Seth, and the brilliance of her new believer's faith nearly blinded him. He hoped Tom, Erin and Seth would be safe from any truth Natalie might speak, but he couldn't stay there to oversee their voices. As he departed through the side wall, an angel appeared and demanded that he leave and not return. An angel! He had to report to Balzor and the others—this could not go on.

The two couples spent time chatting and connecting in Tom's living room. Soon Tom put their salmon-on-a-plank on the grill, and refreshed everyone's drinks. There was a lot of praise from the hosts for Seth's documentary; he went through some of the more difficult issues they'd overcome to match the right speaker and visuals with each of the key identity groups who had been marginalized by past or present government policies.

Sitting beside Seth on the sofa, after taking a sip of her new drink, Natalie looked at each of them in turn and said, "What about Christians? I haven't been one for long, but I feel the discomfort and displeasure, the marginalization, and the government is definitely discriminating against us now."

The other three were silent in the awkward moment. Finally Tom said, "Isn't that a bit of an exaggeration?"

"Ask our pastor, who just got out of jail and has to submit his sermons to a government censor."

"That's not just Christians," Tom reminded her. "That's any and all of us during the State of Emergency."

"OK. That makes it much better and understandable."

There was another silence. Trying to break the tension, Erin smiled. "When did you become a Christian?"

"I doubt you really want to hear."

"Actually, I do. Tom said you were almost killed in the DEA bombing."

Natalie looked at Seth and took another sip. "Yes, but God started getting my attention for about a year before that. I've talked to others recently who also speak about God 'chasing' them, bringing other people into their path, or pricking their conscience about things for quite a while."

"Like what?"

"Well, on the one hand, I enjoyed science in school and would always pick up articles on new discoveries about the universe, or even about microbiology. For the last year or so everything I've read has pointed me to the fact that there must be a Creator. Have you ever studied the cell? It's incredible.

"Life is completely impossible as a random chain of events. The most 'advanced' science cannot account for it. Knowing what I now know, for example, I don't see how anyone could ever have an abortion, since God knits each one of us together individually in His image. Each one of us is unique, and a miracle. His miracle."

Erin frowned slightly and took a sip of her drink.

"So if He creates each of us, then maybe He has plans for us and standards of behavior He wants us to follow—for our own good. Those are the kinds of thoughts I started having. Driven by science, of all things. Very general, and yet focused on Him."

"I see."

"Yes. So at times I would think about what plans He might have for me—my purpose. And how I had not behaved as He would probably want. And then people started coming into my life who seemed to be different, and if I dug a little, it turned out that they were believers, followers of Jesus. Not many. And not religious, particularly. But each one was in a relationship with their Savior, the one who they believed had forgiven their sins and would be with them for eternity. They had a quiet joy. It was crazy, but these people got my attention." She smiled.

Erin turned to Seth. "Was this happening to you, too?"

Seth glanced at Natalie. "No. Not really. Every once in a while Natalie would mention something, but I didn't feel 'chased'. Unless that's what's happening now." He smiled at her. "We've been together most of this year, and she's really changed in the last month. Since the bombing. I have to say she really is much more at peace. Happy. I'm trying to understand."

Tom said, "That must be tough for both of you."

Seth and Natalie looked at each other for a moment. Then she turned back to their hosts. "I love Seth and we have a great, comfortable life together. Yes, maybe it's been tough these last few weeks, but mostly for Seth. He has a new person living with him, and she's got to figure out what her life is going to be like before he can figure out whether he wants to be part of it." She looked at Seth again. "Tough."

Erin asked, "And then the bomb exploded near you?"

"Yes. Very near. And it would have killed me but for two women who saved me. Both of them died saving me, and others. Both believers. One I held all the way to the hospital in the ambulance. How's that for getting my attention?"

Erin just looked at her.

"I didn't need to be asked, or prodded, again. I knew He wanted me. And when this other great woman, Callie Sawyer—she glanced at Tom—showed me the next day how to give up and to ask for His forgiveness and His help, I ran to Him. I didn't walk. I ran. And now I'm in His arms."

After a long silence, Erin exhaled. "Wow. This is pretty serious for our first time together. I just got chills."

Tom smiled. "Yes. Here, give me your drink, and I'll go check on the fish."

Wilson and Trey drove north in the dark. Twice they doubled back on the two- lane roads to make sure no one was following them. Convinced they were safe, they turned into the unmarked dirt road for the farm, entered the security code at the gate, and drove over the small hill and through the woods towards the barn where the WhiteStorm gathered.

There were cars, trucks and motorcycles parked in the gravel lot outside the barn, and when they went inside they found the group of about thirty people sitting on folding chairs in the near-dark and watching an underground video documentary on a large screen praising Planned Parenthood and the abortion industry for greatly reducing the number of African-Americans in the country.

Wilson shook hands with the large man standing by the door. "Is Blane up front?" he asked.

The other man pointed toward the back wall to their right. "He's over there."

"Thanks." Wilson and Trey walked over to Blane, who was standing with two others and watching the documentary.

"Hey," Wilson said in a low voice. "Can I talk with you for a minute?"

Blane nodded and moved to stand next to the two new arrivals. Wilson started to explain their situation and to ask for money and guns so that they could get on the road out of the state.

After less than a minute, Blane erupted. "You did what? And you came here? Are you crazy?"

"We weren't followed. We checked. Help us, and we're out of here."

Just then the man by the door yelled to Blane, "Someone just crashed through the gate. Lights coming this way!"

"Son of a...You idiots!" Blane exclaimed. "How many?"

"At least four cars on the surveillance. No, more. At least six."

Most of those in the barn heard this exchange. The video stopped and someone turned on the lights. They could hear a helicopter in the distance.

"NO!" Blane yelled. "Kill the lights! Wilson and Trey've brought the Feds down on us."

"Damn!" several yelled. "Do we fight?" A man ran towards their weapons vault.

"Yes," Wilson said to Blane. "There must be more of us than them. We can fan out and surround them in the dark while they focus on the barn. We'll hit 'em from behind. Let's go!"

As Wilson started to move towards the weapons locker, Blane grabbed his arm. "No! They'll have night vision, automatic weapons, drones and a helicopter. They'll chew us up. And then more will come."

"Are you afraid, great leader?" Wilson/Zaraz snarled.

"We aren't taking on a federal task force. Not tonight."

"You wimp...Then Trey and I will. And anyone who wants to join us."

The headlights from the incoming vehicles began to play off the walls and then suddenly went dark, and the helicopter was much closer.

Wilson looked around at his comrades. No one moved. He motioned to Trey. "Come on." They raced to the locker, took out a couple of rifles, hand guns and ammo, and then ran out the side door.

There was a moment of silence in the barn. They could hear the vehicles pulling up. "Turn on the lights," Blane said. "Anyone with a gun, put it on the floor. Have a seat like we're having a meeting. Get ready to tell these people the truth about why white people are better. Stay calm. I'll go out and meet 'em."

A moment later a bullhorn announced that law enforcement had arrived in force, that the barn was surrounded, and that everyone should come out with no weapons and with hands up.

Blane opened the front door wide, took a towel from the drink table, waved it in the opening, and slowly walked outside, his hands up.

After ten paces he was told to drop to the ground, and four officers approached and handcuffed him. They stood him up, and an agent who appeared to be in charge walked over with two others. Blane was surrounded by seven agents, with the helicopter making a racket just to the west. Blane started to tell them about the thirty peaceful people inside having a meeting when the first bullets found their targets. The agent in charge, two others, and Blane were hit and mortally wounded by high powered rounds from the edge of the clearing. In the immediate chaos, several agents from behind their vehicles fired on the barn, instantly killing four people in chairs, including two women. Faced with this slaughter, most of the men inside retrieved their guns and returned fire through the windows and the door.

After hundreds of rounds were exchanged, including a firing pass from the helicopter, twenty-six inside the barn were either dead or severely wounded. The second agent in command finally realized that her boss had been taken out and called a halt. As the law enforcement team cautiously moved forward to try to figure out what had just happened, Wilson/Zaraz and Trey crawled away, undetected by anyone, into the woods. Zaraz was ecstatic.

The rest of the dinner party at Tom Sullivan's had been less intense than the discussion about Natalie finding her new faith, and she and Erin had established that they had several mutual acquaintances across the city. As would be expected, much of the conversation was about the elections, Seth's documentary, and the State of Emergency.

Now Seth and Natalie were walking home on the sidewalk, holding hands. After traversing a block in silence, Seth said, "You talk about your faith better each time you do it, and it's obvious that it's deeply moved you."

"Yes, I guess it has. And I keep discovering new insights as I read God's Word and study with Kristen and the others at the church."

"In a way I'm jealous, and I'm trying to understand, but I guess God hasn't been chasing me, like He did you."

She smiled and looked at him. "I know. But maybe He is now, and you just need to listen more. And I know you didn't sign up for this when we decided to move in together."

"Hmm. I was wondering when that might come up."

They crossed a quiet street in silence. Finally Natalie sighed. "Yes. I love you but I just don't feel right about living together. Like it's not how God wants us to behave. Commitment. Husband and wife. I know that wasn't us before, and I know it's not you now. But it's more and more me. Callie told me that Christ gave the ultimate sacrifice to pay for my sins. I've been bought for a high price. Shouldn't I live like I recognize my worth to Him? I want to be in a right relationship with Him as the foundation for all my other relationships, which I also want to build. Would ours last if I moved to my own apartment and we stopped having sex? I hope so. Do you think it would?"

"I honestly don't know. Seems like a step backwards to me."

"Funny. It seems like a step forward to me."

They walked another block in silence. "Is that where we're heading?" he asked.

"I'm not sure. It's certainly not about you. You're a wonderful man, and I love you. But I'm trying to match my life to my faith, not because I have to, but because I want to."

"It'll be tough."

"Yes, it probably will. Be patient with me. And come to church with me in the morning, to hear more about the other guy who loves me."

"What?"

"Jesus."

"Oh...We'll see."

Wilson and Trey had crawled away in the underbrush from the gunfight at the barn, then, in the dark of the woods, they had run, clutching a rifle each, and little else.

Ten minutes later they stopped to catch their breath.

"What do we do now?" Trey asked Wilson.

"Go north—I think it's that way—to hit the road, then find a house we can break into. A car. Money. Drive fifty miles. Steal another one. Keep going to Mississippi."

"If they have the drone they'll know exactly who we are. And it's cold out here."

"Yep. You got a better idea?"

High overhead a government drone with an infrared camera tracked them.


Tom and Erin were in the kitchen straightening up the last few items from the dinner. Erin handed Tom the just-dried salad bowl to put away.

"Have you ever heard a story like Natalie's before?" she asked.

Tom walked around to the shelf behind the island. "Actually, I have. I guess several."

"Really?"

"Yes, when I was a teenager, my family went through a tough time. All of us in different ways. I guess it might have blown us apart. But Dad, and then the rest of us, found the kind of faith that Natalie described, and that faith, or He, saved us."

"Us?"

Tom was silent, then nodded. "Back then I was a believer, much like Natalie."

"What happened?"

"I...I guess I came to realize that Christianity is just another of the many faith myths that play to our natural need for something bigger, to sustain us. But that doesn't make it real, or necessary to be happy."

Erin turned to him. "Whatever happened to Natalie seems pretty real to me. It's changing her in big ways."

"Yes. Faith can do that."

"My parents are like that now. Only after I went off to school. They seem like different people."

"I thought they might be, from what you said."

She started drying a wine glass. "Mmm. Me having an abortion would not sit well with them. Their grandchild, they would say. Boy, Natalie doesn't like abortions, either, does she? And she arrived there from studying science. That's a new twist." She handed him the glass. "Hey, do you know that woman she mentioned? Was it Callie something?"

Tom took the glass and placed it in the cabinet above the plates and cups.

"Uh, yes. She's actually the one who asked me to try to talk you out of the abortion."

"Really? How do you know her?"

"I, uh, met her that weekend when you were away, when the first attacks happened. At Seth's birthday cook-out."

"So is she why I didn't hear from you for a month?"

He looked down, then back at her. "I guess she had something to do with it. But it was mainly how crazy everything got after President Rhodes was killed."

Erin put down the dish towel and looked at him for a few moments. "Did you sleep with her?"

"No."

"Did you try?"

He smiled. "I, uh, guess so. What's the big deal?"

"She wouldn't let you."

Tom just looked at her.

Erin raised her voice. "So you met this incredible woman of faith who changed Natalie, and probably others, who refused to go to bed with you, and told you to talk me out of an abortion—how did she even know about it?!?—and then...I bet she dumped you, didn't she, and that's when you finally called me."

"I, uh...there was so much work."

"Bull. Don't tell me you stayed at your desk for a month."

"I didn't say that."

In a more normal tone Erin said, "She must be pretty strong. Stronger than me. I'd like to meet her, since she knows all my secrets."

"What?"

Erin picked up her phone.

"What are you doing?"

"Calling a driver to go home."

"What? You brought your bag."

"I know. Imagine carrying your baby for a few more days and thinking that one day you might love me."

"What?"

"You say that a lot. I'm going home. Maybe we'll talk again. Maybe not. I've got to think about all this. Have a great weekend."

She left the kitchen and Tom heard her going up the stairs. His phone vibrated.

"Hello, Tanya."

"Tom, I hate to bother you on Saturday night, but I have some news I think you'll want to hear, and maybe pass to the president. That lead I told you about turned out to be right on, and we stopped a drone attack on the Mideast Reconciliation Conference in Chapel Hill. We captured the drone and the rifle, and we killed or captured over twenty of the perpetrators at their base—the details are still coming in—but we think these must be the same people behind the attacks on the student centers in Durham."

"Great news. How did we stop a drone?"

"When you're defending a specific target, like a stadium or an auditorium, it's not that hard. We have mobile units with pinpoint radar and RF interceptors on the frequencies the drones use. With that lead, we deployed units from Durham over to Chapel Hill in time to catch the drone before it attacked. We recorded its flight path and used our own drones to follow its track back to the launch point, then to trail the guys who launched it."

Tom heard Erin coming down the stairs with her bag, and he moved from the kitchen to the living room while still talking to Tanya.

"That's really great news. Congratulations." He held up his hand for Erin to stop, but she shook her head, gave him a curt wave, and walked out the front door, closing it behind her.

"Our team tracked them to a barn they apparently use for their meetings. When we tried to arrest them, someone fired, and there was a shootout with an unfortunate loss of life, including our lead agent and two other agents."

"I'm sorry."

"Yes. Bastards. Maybe this will finally lead us to the people who are behind it all."

"I hope so, and I'm sure the president will be pleased. Call or text again when you know more."

"I will."

As Tom hung up, he heard the car drive off.

# 18

*It is in the man of piety and inward principle, that we may expect to find the uncorrupted patriot, the useful citizen, and the invincible soldier. God grant that in America true religion and civil liberty may be inseparable and that the unjust attempts to destroy the one, may in the issue tend to the support and establishment of both.*

John Witherspoon

Sunday, October 25

Tom's alarm went off at seven. He'd been up for an hour during the night, reading the first reports on the Chapel Hill intervention and writing a cover text for the president.

Now he lay alone in his bed with Beau on the floor and the thought occurred to him that this had not been what he had pictured when Erin had arrived with her bag in the afternoon. Not at all.

He had his home, and his thoughts, to himself.

Nepravel was across the street, unable to manage the voices inside Tom. The incoming answered prayers were too many, and the spiritual light in Tom's bedroom was too hot and bright. Worse, as he watched, a brilliant angel descended and stood in front of Tom's row house. Nepravel cursed but could do nothing about it, at least for the moment. He went looking for Erin.

Through the bedroom's curtains Tom could see the sky turning gray. He smelled the coffee downstairs but decided to remain where he was for a few minutes.

He rolled over and bunched his pillow. *Callie seems to have an impact on my life whether she's here or not. She's gone. But now Erin's gone, too, thanks to Callie. And then Natalie and Seth—he'll be on his own soon, I bet, thanks to Callie. What is it about her?*

Tom almost jumped when he heard a voice inside say, "The truth."

He shook his head.

*No way. She doesn't have the "truth"—it depends on the person and the situation. She just has lots of strong opinions.*

"But God has the truth and she speaks it," he heard. "Maybe they both left because of how you treated them."

*No way. We're all adults. It's a new world. Women like having a good time as much as men. Callie certainly used to—I saw one of those videos. Holy cow. And what does she know about national security, to complain about what we have to do? Are we supposed to stand by and do nothing while our nation is destroyed? Give me a break."*

"It's all about you."

*What?*

"Your pleasure. Your success. Your rules. You. Not truth. I created you. You're headed for disaster."

*What?*

He threw the covers off. "Damn," he said out loud.

He went downstairs for his coffee, and to check his messages.


The law enforcement team at the barn had worked through the night caring for the wounded, interviewing the survivors, and gathering evidence. The acting FBI agent-in-charge made sure that a drone was always on station to watch the two figures in the woods, but their team, headed by Director Toomey himself in D.C., decided to wait until first light to make any overt move, unless the two men approached a house or a road.


Alexei Nobikov and his wife had attended church that morning in Limassol and had just finished lunch at their favorite seafood restaurant on the waterfront when a text message unexpectedly summoned him to the office, only a few blocks away.

There was always a team on duty, so he said hello, then went into his office and put on the headset for their most secure communications system and called his supervisor in Moscow, as directed.

An hour later he was home and standing by their bed, packing for a late afternoon flight to Zurich. Anna came in carrying two cups of tea. "What's going on?"

He took one and shook his head. "Thanks. I'm not sure, but I'm not happy—A possible initiative from the U.S.—and Grigory wants me to go to D.C., to check sources, and to be there in case an off the grid in-person meeting is required."

She stood in the bedroom doorway. "That's pretty unusual. How long?"

"He doesn't know. Their elections are in a couple of weeks. What he heard sounds far-fetched, which is why he wants someone there who can check without raising any suspicions."

"What is it?"

"What I know now is sketchy, but, if true, it would be a game changer."

"More power to those in charge?"

He nodded. "Of course. That's how they all think."

She shook her head. "Terrible. I'll miss you. I hope you get to see Kate."

He smiled. "Me, too."


Wilson and Trey had trudged generally north all night. They wanted to hit the east-west road which intersected the road to the barn several miles away, hoping to elude what they assumed would be a great number of emergency vehicles.

They were tired, cold and scratched from head to foot by their journey. From the edge of the woods where they stood, they saw a recently harvested field, on the other side of which was the road, and, thankfully, a home with at least two cars parked next to it.

Not wanting to be seen from the house crossing the entire field, they skirted around the edge of the field in the woods, planning a short walk along the road to the house. They hoped, with their rifles, to look like hunters out for an early shoot.

When they were about halfway along the road between the woods and the house, they heard several vehicles approaching from both directions. Then, unbelievably, a drone descended from nowhere and started circling around them.

"Damn!" Wilson/Zaraz yelled and started running back towards the woods. Trey followed. When he saw that the SUVs would cut them off before reaching the woods again, Wilson turned and started running diagonally across the end of the field.

The four SUVs stopped on the road and agents got out. One had a megaphone. "Police. Stop. Drop your weapons and put your hands up!"

The drone dropped to twenty feet and circled around them.

Zaraz gave Wilson the words. "You sons of bitches! We're the real Americans!" He raised his rifle and fired toward the agents.

Trey's "No!" was lost in the fusillade that followed. Both men went down.

A few moments later Wilson was standing again and looking at the agents on the road. He tried to raise his rifle, but it wasn't there. He looked down for it and saw it on the ground, in his hands! His whole body was on the ground. *What the hell?* Trey, too, was on the ground, but he was writhing in pain.

Some of the agents moved towards them and Wilson had a good view because he started rising. *What's going on?*

Now he could see the entire field, the road, and his body, with blood all around it. One of the agents was cautiously advancing towards Trey.

"Well done."

Wilson turned around to see the most horrific face imaginable on a grotesque, suflurous body, surrounded with stench, and rising with him. It was Zaraz. He cringed and tried to pull back, but couldn't. From a few inches away the face spoke. "You're ours. Forever. This is as good as it gets."

The realization of what had happened and what was about to happen suddenly flooded in, and Wilson screamed.

Since Tom unexpectedly had Sunday morning to himself, he decided to finish his summary of the election security reports to give to the president—the last two had arrived on Friday. Then to prepare for Wednesday's lunch he intended to watch the last thirty minutes of the DVD with Gary Thornton and Robert Ludwig. That reminded him of what Tanya Prescott had said about the sermons being coordinated across the nation that Sunday. So Tom noted that the service from The Church of the Good Shepherd would be streamed live at 10:30, starting in ten minutes, and decided to watch it online.

He brewed a fresh pot of coffee and settled into his most comfortable chair with his laptop. When the live stream began an assistant pastor gave the week's announcements, and the camera panned around the congregation. Tom saw Callie, Kristen, Natalie and Seth sitting together in the third row of the center section. And in the row behind them were Kate Tikhonovsky and Patrick Tomlinson.

Following several well-known hymns a lady walked to the lectern and gave the scripture reading. As soon as she announced the reference in Ephesians, Tom knew it was about Spiritual Warfare and Paul's admonition that believers put on the full armor of God to combat the lies of the devil. Tanya was right.

After another hymn and the offering, Robert Ludwig began his message by noting that for the next several weeks his sermons would focus on this text in Ephesians 6 because despite what anyone might feel from watching the news and focusing on immediate national issues, the most important struggle is always between Satan and believers over the souls of every unsaved person on earth—family, friends and colleagues. God's free gift of salvation is offered and received one person at a time, he said. Groups and institutions—like the family and churches—and even nations, can be critical in making God's gift known to the greatest number of people, but in the end its acceptance always comes down to an individual decision.

Ludwig continued that Satan works his lies to thwart every step of the process, to confuse and demoralize everyone from hearing about or accepting God's free gift. He does this by lying.

Which is why the first piece of armor Paul tells believers to take up is the Belt of Truth. Jesus told Pilate in John 18:

*"...The reason I was born and came into the world is to testify to the truth. Everyone on the side of truth listens to me."*

Ludwig went on to describe the two greatest lies that everyone struggles with: autonomy and self-sufficiency. They both stem from refusing to acknowledge that we are made by our Creator, which is why Satan's insistence that we are all just the result of random events with no purpose whatsoever may be his most powerful weapon in perfecting his lies.

He explained that autonomy is believing the lie that your life belongs only to you, that you can live however you please. When we make something—a work of art, a business report—we own it, because we created it. God is the same. He made us—even the most agnostic person must quietly recognize the impossible fine tuning required of the entire universe and of each tiny cell—He made us and so we belong to Him and are not autonomous. We are His and will eventually seek out His truths unless Satan can get us to believe that we have no Creator and therefore can behave however we want.

And Ludwig noted that self-sufficiency is believing that we have everything we need within ourselves, to be and to do whatever we want. But we were created to be dependent, first on our Creator, and then on others, in relationships.[3]

Tom was astonished to realize that Ludwig was using much better words to say what he had heard when he first awoke a few hours earlier, about himself.

"And the one word that sums up these lies is 'pride'—the belief that we are our own god. That was Satan's sin, and it's ours. Until we realize, make a choice, and confess our need to be saved from pride and from our other sins—our need for the one perfect Savior from our one Creator—we will continue to put ourselves first, to go astray, and to destroy. When we turn back to Him, ask for forgiveness and accept His gift and His rule over our lives, we'll be in relationship with our Creator, the healing process will begin, and eventually His truth and virtues will rule in our lives.

"And that Godly virtue, built one changed person at a time, is, when it informs the majority of our nation's people, the very foundation for our country. Without that Godly virtue, our Founders warned again and again, we won't survive as individuals, and we won't survive as a nation. That individual/national virtue is the critical juncture where the Christian gospel and our Founders' Constitution intersected 250 years ago, and continues to do so today. And that's why Satan attacks both so fervently with his lies."

Ludwig paused. "That's the end of the message this week, except for one important footnote, and it involves all of you.

"Under the State of Emergency neither pastors nor lay leaders can talk to a congregation or group about the unique claims of Jesus because some of those claims are thought by some in government to be divisive and hateful, and therefore banned.

"Without arguing the absurdity of that view, there is not yet any directive against any believer talking about Jesus' claims with another individual, one-on-one.

"My hope is that by silencing 'leaders,' the government has empowered each of you, faithful believers, to have this discussion with your family members, friends, colleagues and acquaintances. Talk with them. Start with your own testimony, the truth of which no one can refute. Pray with them and for them. When you dam a stream the water has to go somewhere, and I hope that from inside each of you a spring of living water will flow out, nourish the land, and begin true revival."

He smiled. "You can tell them that you know the secret that the government doesn't want them to hear! Find someone today and try it. You will be blessed, as will they."

After the sermon there were two closing hymns and the service ended, but not before Tom again saw Callie and the others starting to talk with those around them.

For a moment he wished he were there, then thought that Callie would probably be angry with him. Or, more accurately he realized, disappointed.

In the quiet of his chair he thought about Jenny, Callie, Erin and several other women previously in his life, and also about Natalie and her transformation. Was Robert Ludwig right that he, Tom, viewed these women from purely his own selfish perspective—for some fun, and for their affirmation of his self-proclaimed exceptional accomplishments? Was he that callous? Maybe.

And there was Seth with Natalie at church. That must be tough for Seth.

He tried to shift his mind to the To Do List he needed to make on his L-Pad for the next week, but he noticed the remote for the DVD, picked it up, and started to play the last half of the interview between Thornton and Ludwig.

From outside on the sidewalk the angel could see the continuing stream of incoming prayers for Tom, and he noticed that in response the small spiritual flame inside Tom started to flicker just a little more brightly.


Clayton Hunt was finishing up his eight hours on duty at the Threat Identification Group late that afternoon in the Pentagon. The day before they had been assigned by Homeland Security to the high-level coordination role for the Chapel Hill incident, and as the various teams in law enforcement investigated the actions and researched the people involved, Clayton's group was tasked with looking for threads and connections to other bad actors. Clayton was at his console, connected by headset to two others in their TIG space as well as to a diverse group pulled together from across the country with skills for this particular assignment.

The secure door to their space buzzed open. Ahmad Rashid came in and put his bag by his console next to his friend, who indicated that he was finishing up an online discussion.

A moment later Clayton swung the mic on his headset up and turned to Ahmad. "This is a live one."

"Good. About time."

"Yes. WhiteStorm they call themselves. Nice people. Twelve died and the same number were wounded in a shootout at their base camp, including three of ours. So this is murder, terrorism, and almost anything else you want to add. Ten of them were captured and are being interrogated. Two of them—we think the ones with the drone—got away; but we tracked them and moved in early this morning. They opened fire. One died on the scene and the other is in the ICU at the UNC Med Center after two surgeries."

"Any leads?" Ahmad asked as he logged into his console.

"Yes, lots. The one in ICU served in the same unit with Jerry Kimble, the shooter at the fracking tanks in Pennsylvania, only six months later. We're looking through all those records again, tracing every member for a year before and after.

"One of the women who was killed was the cousin of the Tidwell brothers, in South Carolina. And the apparent leader, a guy named Blane King, also dead, made a lot of trips to Europe, Turkey and the Middle East two years ago. Not sure why. We're tracking that down, and about ten other pretty interesting connections. They're all in the summary."

"OK. Thanks. Sounds like we may finally be near the mother lode. Now go home. Isn't Andrea due?"

"Yesterday."

Ahmad smiled. "Boy, your life is about to change. And thanks again for all your work on the Uyghur human rights demonstration. It seems to be coming together."

"Yes, I meant to tell you. We got our official permit from the D.C. police for Thursday afternoon, the 12th, after the State of Emergency ends earlier that week, at the Chinese Embassy. Logan actually helped us get it, and The Church of the Good Shepherd has been planting a lot of seeds, both with other churches and through social media to a much larger audience. With the permit, we'll really start advertising the issue and the demonstration. And we expect to get permits in the five cities where they have consulates—we've contacted friends in New York, Chicago. Houston, San Francisco and Los Angeles."

"Thanks. It will really mean a lot to the Uyghurs at our mosque—they've never seen a peaceful demonstration go well. Not to mention involving other American Muslims—as well as Christians and Jews, of course."

Clayton logged off and picked up his computer bag. "Sounds good. Text me if anything big happens here, and I'll do the same from home. Tell Mariam and the boys hello for us."


Tom divided his time that afternoon between his weekly To Do List on his L-Pad and Juggling queries about the beliefs of the Founding Fathers, to see if other opinions matched those of Gary Thornton. After he made the first query on his laptop he suddenly thought about possible surveillance from an overzealous AI algorithm wondering about his activity. He had to admit it was an unpleasant feeling, imagining that the government—at his own direction—was monitoring everyone's online searches. He did the rest of his queries using his Core Group special phone. For the most part, Thornton appeared to be accurate.

Tired of writing, Tom took Beau for an hour's jog/walk in the neighborhood. They passed Callie's row house and he almost stopped, but kept going. The same at The Church of the Good Shepherd, where a "24/7 Prayer Vigil for the Nation" was underway, according to the posted public notices.

Whether Tom was inside his home or walking, the angel sent by God and drawn close by the many believers' prayers attended him and protected him from any demon's influence or voices. As Tom walked he thought about all that he'd recently heard, and without the quenching action of the demons' voices, the small spiritual light inside him shone a bit brighter.

After returning with Beau, Tom had leftovers for dinner while watching The Network's Weekend Summary, which not-so-subtly reminded viewers about how the president's programs should be able to shift into high gear after the upcoming elections. And a piece about how the black ancestors of the conservative Speaker of the House, an African American, may have owned slaves on a Caribbean plantation two hundred years ago.

When the dinner dishes were put away, Tom sat again in his armchair and just thought. He noted how both restless and exhausted he was, like after a day of final exams. His thoughts caromed off each other, from Callie to those killed in recent attacks to Erin to the State of Emergency to abortion to Robert Ludwig to spiritual warfare to Seth and Natalie to the Founders to his own pride to all the other women to all his accomplishments to his failure in finding the attackers.

With most other people being fervently prayed for, the angel would have planted voices of truth—like he had done with Natalie several months earlier—but in Tom's case the Holy Spirit already lived inside him from two decades ago, and He was more powerful than any internal voice when He was not being quenched by willful unbelief. Given a small opening, He began to do His work.

Finally, about nine, Tom picked up his phone and started to call Callie, then stopped. What would he tell her? *That I just want to see you and talk. That the abortion is still on. That I treat women like transactions.*

He put the phone down.

# Monday, October 26

Early that Monday morning Tom joined the president and vice president in the Oval Office for the Presidential Daily Briefing. Given the violent events of the weekend, both James Toomey and Tanya Prescott from the FBI, and General Price from the NSA, joined the rotating daily briefer from the CIA, and as the six of them sat around the coffee table the Director referred them to the top secret information in their briefing books. He led them through the events as they had transpired on Saturday evening and Sunday morning in North Carolina, then shifted to the combined agencies' best assessment at this still-early stage of the investigation.

"With this group's leader and the drone operator dead, it's hard to nail down all the details, but even a cursory look at the people in the WhiteStorm—dead, in hospital, or in custody—suggests great potential resources and access across the nation and also in Europe. A couple of them are university lecturers, and one is a professor. They've studied and traveled overseas, including Germany, Austria, China, Hungary and Russia. We're tracking down all those connections."

President Bradshaw, turning the pages in the briefing book, nodded to his V.P.

The Director continued. "From license plate readers and cell phone records we've determined that several of them were in the D.C. area at the time of the drone attacks on the mosques, though we haven't yet placed the drone owner there—we assume that we will. Or maybe they have access to a second drone. We'll dig until we find it.

"Between the dark web and the seemingly legitimate university connections, we've already traced several of the members, unfortunately all dead now, to similar organizations in other key cities where attacks have taken place, and to a resource site on bomb manufacturing that we know the DEA bombers often visited. So there is much more to do, but it looks like this group may be directly linked to the other attacks. We may finally be on the verge of identifying the group behind all of this."

Bradshaw leaned forward. "Excellent, Jim, excellent. I always suspected that a White Supremacist Group with ties to some whackos in Europe were the ones. They have the history, the resources, and the network."

"When will you have enough evidence to move against their network?" Patricia asked.

"At least a couple of days. With such a large group we have a lot of leads to follow, and we want to be thorough and not spook anyone."

The president asked, "So we can say publicly that these particular actors appear to be a White Supremacist Group, but indicate, maybe, that we don't have many other leads?"

"Yes, that sounds OK."

"Tom, can you brief Emily after we finish?"

"Sure. Director Toomey, two questions," Tom asked. "After being so successful, why wouldn't they do a better job of concealing what they're doing, instead of holding a large meeting? And what connection would Adam Hassan, the F-35 fighter pilot who shot down Air Force One, have to this group?"

The Director shook his head. "Not sure on the first one. We're digging. Maybe some miscommunication. On the second, also not sure, but maybe it's 'The enemy of my enemy is a friend' sort of thing. More to follow."

"Understood."

The daily briefer continued through the book for another fifteen minutes. As they stood to leave, the president admonished everyone to keep him informed of any important developments. Tom asked to see him privately, but then said to the VP as she picked up her notes, "My mother and father are looking forward to your conference tomorrow. She remembers you from her days in Congress."

"Good. It'll be great to have them here, and I look forward to seeing her again. We hope to arrive at a consensus of believers from all the key faiths to support the ban on divisive talk and hate speech, at least through the elections and the State of Emergency."

"I know they'll try to help."

As the others moved toward the door, President Bradshaw walked behind his desk. When the door closed, Tom took an envelope from his computer bag.

"Here are the reports and the summary you requested, Mr. President. Happily, it looks like in all the 27 races you identified—and by inference across the country—my white-hat hacker contacts couldn't find a way to manipulate the votes as they are recorded, or in the tabulation process. Since the voting machines are never connected to the internet, and the new federal reporting channels are encrypted, it looks like this and future elections should be bulletproof."

The president took the envelope. "That's great, Tom. Thank you. I'll review the report and get back to you, but it sounds like there'll be no grounds for the crazies to allege vote fraud, as they've done in the past. That should make every American happy. Does anyone else know these results?"

"Only the individual hackers, and each one thinks his or her case is a one-off."

"Good. Good. I'll get back to you. Just between us for now. Please brief Emily on the WhiteStorm group, and let's give her lots of ammunition about them for her press meeting this afternoon."

"Yes, sir."


Tom stopped at Emily's office on the way to his own. She was at her desk, poring over several reports. When he knocked on the doorpost, she looked up and smiled.

"Hey. How are you? Worn out from your weekend?"

"Not exactly. Well, not as I had expected. I think Erin dumped me."

"Good grief, you do run through your women." Tom looked upset. She retreated a step. "What happened?"

"You're probably right, and it's worth a longer conversation. But not right now. I need to brief you on what may be a game changer."

"Sure. Come in. I was just looking at the flash results from our weekend polling."

He closed the door and sat down across from her. "And?"

"It's a mixed bag. We're getting high marks for protecting the nation, but people appear to be sick of the restrictions in the State of Emergency. Looks like the election may be close, despite all we're doing."

"Well, then here's some news from the attacks this weekend you can use—carefully for now—to show why those restrictions are important and effective."


"Drew, are you here in D.C.?" the president asked on his Trusted Core phone from behind his desk.

"I'm actually in Austin right now, sir, but about to take off and head your way."

"Can you swing by for a drink late this afternoon? I've got that list we discussed."

"Of course. About six?"

"Yes, perfect. See you then."


To>KatTikh

ANobikov: I just arrived for an unexpected visit. Are you free tomorrow night for dinner?

KatTikh: Yes, but Patrick and I were going out.

ANobikov: Please bring him. About seven?

KatTikh: Yes. Thank you!

ANobikov: I'll make reservations and text you.

KatTikh: Great.

ANobikov: See you then.


When Tom arrived home he found beneath his front door mail slot, along with the usual bills and notices, a personal letter with the Hunts' return address. After putting down his computer bag, dealing with Beau, and opening a beer, he sat in his lounge chair to read it.

Dear Tom,

With all the monitoring the government is doing now, I decided the best way to communicate privately with you is in an old-fashioned letter.

Any day now, God willing, our baby will arrive and I'll be on maternity leave. So I'll be off my several projects, including yours.

I'm sure our team will do a good job for you and the president. Maybe too good.

Having known you all these years, I want you to know that the Trusted Citizen project scares me. No matter what safeguards you think you will have in place, once a system with this much power is there, it will be too easy to override or ignore the safeguards.

I can imagine Americans becoming like the Chinese we read about today, where what you wrote in high school or what you say today can keep your child from getting into college, or prevent you from getting a good job.

I was a History major, and I know too many examples of Lord Acton's "Power corrupts, and absolute power corrupts absolutely."

As a Christian believer, I also know that our Founders, unlike the European intellectuals of their day, knew from their faith that mankind would never be perfected. Instead, they set up a system of checks and balances so that progress required consensus between imperfect actors willing to compromise for the common good,and could not be dictated by a supposed elitist group using raw power.

I know you know that. But I worry that you're helping create an all-powerful system from which we can never turn back.

Please think and pray about this. I've shared a bit of this with Clayton, and even though he's focused on using these new tools to catch the bad actors, he's also concerned. If you ever want to talk about it, I or we will be glad to listen.

God has put you in a very important place. Please, as you listen to others, also listen to Him.

I hope to see you soon with our son in my arms.

Love,

Andrea

He put the letter down and thought: *Does everyone have advice for me?*

At Prince Proklor's meeting that midnight in the Oval Office there was a rising tension. It combined anticipation that events which they had planned for so long were finally coming to a head, along with increasing anger over the unceasing prayer intervention by so many believers around the nation, and actually from around the world.

Rather than his forces deployed and doing their important work around the capital, the increase in prayers meant that large numbers of lesser demons had to surround the West Wing and the Oval Office. Only by massing together to create one huge dark, evil force could they bend and deflect the incoming answered prayers, taking hits on lesser demons on the perimeter, but protecting the leaders. Yet they all still caught pieces of the believers' voices, praying not only for particular people, but specifically *against them.*

In the relative calm at the center of this spiritual fortress, the Prince himself, along with Temno, Bespor, Legat and the other generals met and planned what they believed were the final moves to bring America in line with the rest of the ever-darkening world.

As they circled closer and tighter to the Resolute Desk, the Prince hovered just above them, and Temno began, "Both abortions and divorces are holding above 3,000 a day, as they have for the last month."

"Excellent," Proklor responded. "Hopefully they will continue to increase. Bespor?"

"As we expected, this president is now fully committed to 'his' idea of dividing the world three ways and controlling what Americans should think, just as the others do. He has no idea what the Chinese have planned for Taiwan next year, and this will only help them carry it off.

But for now our focus is on being sure the Progressives win the elections. Then everything will fall into place. The Chinese are ready to help with that, and probably the Russians as well." He turned to Legat.

"The president's side should win, given the advantages of the Emergency Orders and the successes we've helped create with the lockdown."

Proklor interrupted. "Good. Our forces are almost in total control. But I want him to be looking beyond this one election. We need to remain in control through measures like these forever. Start planting those seeds in him and his team.

"And I'm glad the Chinese are ready. I don't trust the Russians as much. Most there continue to push faith in the accursed Son—even their government does it! Our forces there are not as strong as they should be, and we have to fix that as soon as America goes dark. Two very different places."

"Yes. Tomorrow's conference is a big event for us, to show how the 'best people of faith' support the president. We hope to target several believers who've bothered us for years. Richard Sullivan will be there."

"Can we destroy him and his wife once and for all?" Proklor asked.

"We have put together a plan for them tomorrow, my liege," Bespor said. "They should no longer be a problem. And their son, Tom, in the White House, is firmly with us, just to add to their pain. There are many specific prayers directed at him; he's even had an angel over him once or twice. But Balzor, Nepravel and the others assure us that after years of work, our lies are holding in him. And in a few days he will have helped to kill his unborn child. After that, like most such parents, he'll become a committed defender of the president's entire Progressive agenda."

Proklor paused. "It is amazing how our lies all work together, isn't it? Believe one, believe them all. They're such simpletons. But we're only a week away. There are millions of souls in the balance. This is what we came here for. We can have no slip-ups."

Bespor and the others bowed.

# 19

*The Christian religion is the most important and one of the first things in which all children, under a free government, ought to be instructed.... No truth is more evident...than that the Christian religion must be the basis of any government intended to secure the rights and privileges of a free people.*

Noah Webster

Tuesday, October 27

The Sullivans' flight arrived in Washington on time that morning, and they took a taxi to the large hotel where they were staying for the vice president's "Faith and Unity Conference," scheduled to begin at noon. After they checked in, Janet lay down for an hour. Richard went downstairs to get their conference material, and he texted Tom and asked him to make reservations for dinner that night. After registering for the conference and glancing in at the huge ballroom set up with hundreds of round tables, plus a raised speaker's dais, he returned to their room and worked quietly on his laptop.

Unseen by Richard while he registered, the ballroom was filled with an ever-increasing host of demons, some from the Washington area, and some assigned to the participants arriving from all over the country. A few incoming prayers momentarily slipped through the oppressive spiritual darkness in the room, but there simply were not enough prayers to impact the concentration of hate and evil. And God apparently elected not to send an angel to expel them. So the demons held clear claim to the Faith and Unity Conference as their own.

"The coffee you ordered," Tom said, as he came through Emily's office door holding two mugs. She was sitting at her desk; he handed her one. She smiled and motioned for him to sit in one of the chairs. Then she took a sip.

"Just like I like it."

"I *have* been making coffee for you for almost a decade, you know."

She nodded. "Yes, we go back a long way. It's been good."

"Yes, it has. You're a great friend."

"And you. Sorry I said what I did about the women in your life."

He looked down at the mug. "Actually, you're right. And you've certainly tried to inject some good ones. Do you have a minute?"

She lowered the mug and looked at him.

"Like I said, the story with Erin is a little more complicated. She's planning to have an abortion day after tomorrow."

Emily paused. "I see, and you're the..."

Tom nodded.

"Hmm." She leaned back in her chair. "That's tough. I get it."

There was silence for several moments as they both sipped their coffees.

"I had an abortion when I was young. In college. After a summer as an intern, helping progressive candidates. Besides the almost-father, only Logan knows. It was crazy. It's partly why I'm here."

She took out a legal pad, wrote on it "President Bradshaw," and handed it to Tom.

"What?!?"

She quickly raised a finger to her lips for silence and motioned around the room with her other hand, while shaking her head.

"It was a different time. No blame either way. Consenting adults. Believe me, abortion was the *only* answer for that one. But even now I do sometimes wonder what that child would be like. A young teenager. Can you imagine that, given all that has happened and where we are now?" She smiled.

He stared at the legal pad. "Knowing you—and him—the child would have been incredible."

She sighed. "We'll never know. As the pro-life people say, I killed our baby. Sometimes I think that way, but most of the time I think of it as removing a growth. It's complicated. I understand what Erin—and you—are going through."

"I think it's totally up to her."

"Yes, but she's asked you, hasn't she?"

He paused. "Yes. That's why we missed going to Seth's. We had to talk about it."

"I see, and I'm certainly pro-abortion, pro-choice. But I also have to admit that there are those moments." Silence again. "Obviously this is all just between us," she said.

"Obviously. Thank you. It means a lot."

He finished his coffee and smiled. "Well, I better get back to work protecting the nation."

"And I'll do the same by helping to ensure the right team is elected. I'll be thinking about you and Erin. Aren't your parents in town to attend the vice president's conference on Faith and Unity?"

He rose. "Yes. I'm having dinner with them tonight."

"Great. I'll be going over to the hotel with Patricia. Her conference should put a final seal of approval from the *real* leaders in the religious world—the ones most people listen to—on all the good things we're doing."

"I hope it goes well. You've met my parents before—say hello if you get a chance. I'm sure I'll hear about it at dinner."


A little before noon Richard and Janet joined the group mingling and chatting outside the ballroom. Looking at nametags they found a few kindred spirits from other churches which were part of the prayer chain focusing on spiritual warfare. But there were not many, and they knew that The Church of the Good Shepherd had decided not to attend, given the earlier detention of Robert Ludwig.

Once inside they noticed several television cameras set up for The Network. They found their assigned table toward the right front of the ballroom and introduced themselves to the other six at their table as they arrived: a rabbi from St. Louis, a Muslim youth leader from Detroit, a pastor and his wife from a mainline church in San Diego, and a married gay couple from a Christian conference center in Minnesota.

At the same time ten dignitaries mounted the steps on the side of the dais and took their seats. As those in the room chatted, vice president Patricia Reynolds came in the back door and worked toward the front, greeting the participants and shaking hands. When she came to the

Sullivans' table she recognized Janet, who stood with Richard, and the two women shook hands and smiled. The V.P. thanked them for coming, nodded to Richard and the others, and moved forward.

A few minutes later, after greeting those on the dais, she stood at the podium and welcomed everyone officially.

"President Bradshaw and I want to welcome you here today from all over the country to discuss, and hopefully to reaffirm, as people of faith, our commitment to the American ideals of Freedom of Worship and Freedom of Speech. And to add another ideal: Freedom from Hate. We have some wonderful, knowledgeable experts with us to lead our break-out sessions after lunch, and our Keynote Speaker, Bishop Adrienne Davis, is a personal friend and an advocate for all that we're about. So, please, enjoy your lunch and your table conversations, and let me say a blessing." She bowed her head.

"In the eternal names of the God of Abraham, of the Universal Cosmic Spirit, and of the Spirits of Nature and our beloved departed Ancestors, we ask your blessing of Wisdom on our gathering today, that She will prevail in all our deliberations. And we give thanks for the food we are about to receive. Amen."

The side doors opened and servers entered with plates for all in attendance. Richard and Janet shared a look, then chatted with those sitting next to them, smiling as they ate.

After twenty minutes the vice president rose again and introduced the dignitaries on the dais, who were leaders in all the major faith traditions in the nation. She said that following the keynote address and a Q&A session, the conferees would break into smaller groups to discuss specific topics and to make recommendations on how to preserve freedom and also reduce hate during the State of Emergency and after it.

She then introduced Bishop Adrienne Davis, the African American Presiding Bishop in a major mainline denomination. Bishop Davis had impressive educational credentials and had devoted herself for twenty years to serving the Church, after ten earlier years in marketing and attending seminary. Most importantly, according to Patricia Reynolds, the bishop was a loving, married lesbian with a daughter and two grandsons.

After the applause Bishop Davis rose and gave a powerful talk on the need for love and tolerance in all things, especially in relationships and in speech. She gave several examples of how she had been hurt on many occasions in her earlier life because she was considered to be "different," and what a difference it had made when loving people began to tolerate and then to embrace her perfectly natural lifestyle. She had then been able to minister to others, with the result that the number of gay members of her church had grown exponentially.

"And that growth, that winning people from darkness and despair to Love, is because everyone in our church body is tolerant. We know that there is no exclusive franchise on truth—that truth is different for each of us—and so by actively expressing tolerance for different truth traditions we also make room for others to accept us, and thereby greatly reduce hate.

"For that reason I hope all of us will today confirm our support for the president and vice president in their quest to both protect us and to make us more tolerant."

There was loud applause, and many people stood to clap. Janet and Richard looked at each other, and Richard gave an almost imperceptible shake to his head.

As the applause subsided, Bishop Davis said, "Thank you very much. If there are any questions or short comments, we have time for a few before we break to our small groups. I understand there are microphones placed in the middle of the room and on the sides if anyone cares to join the dialogue."

Richard stood. Janet grasped his hand and shook her head. He smiled and whispered to her, "Truth is important—it's the first piece of God's armor that holds up all the rest. I'll be nice," and walked over to the central mic.

The young lady in front of him asked a question about dealing with bigots, and the bishop replied that one had to forcefully speak truth from her own experience and never be afraid.

Richard stepped to the mic. "Bishop Davis, thank you. Richard Sullivan. I'm interested in truth and tolerance. I always learned that truth is truth—fixed—and that tolerance means, particularly as Americans, that we freely allow others to express their opinions. But that doesn't necessarily make their opinions true. So my question is, do you believe, as a Bishop in the Church, that there are any absolute truths? Are there truths—whether from God or elsewhere—that are always true, no matter what we may think about them at any given time?"

Bishop Davis frowned. "Are you saying that it's wrong that I love another woman?"

A few people sat up in their chairs.

"No. I was just asking whether there are any truths, like perhaps those in the Bible, that are not open to personal interpretation. Or can each of us believe whatever we want to be true, with no consequences?"

"Before I answer that, I want to know whether you think love between two women—or two men—is wrong."

Janet squirmed in her seat and felt the looks of the gay men from Minnesota.

Richard paused for a moment. Then he spoke in a calm and measured voice. "I believe God's truth that any intimate relationship—if that's what you're asking—between two people outside of marriage between one man and one woman is wrong, whether it's having an affair, pre-marital sex, or gay sex."

"So you think it's wrong that I'm a lesbian?"

"What I think really doesn't matter. Because you asked, I told you what I believe God's truth to be, that it's wrong."

"Mr. Sullivan—that's your name, I think—you obviously don't like people like me, who don't happen to conform to your personal idea of white, male privileged truth, and so you think less of us."

"I never said anything about you. I simply said that sex outside marriage violates God's truth and His clearly expressed will for us."

"Well, that's who I AM. That's how God made *me*. Who are you to tell me what is true? You're a prime example of the hate that we don't need any more of in this country, dividing us instead of uniting us." She smiled. "Do you think I'll make it to heaven as a lesbian?" Then she looked back at the vice president.

More stirring in the chairs. The vice president started to rise, then sat down again.

Richard said, "I have no idea. It's certainly not up to me. I think we're saved only by faith in Jesus Christ and his shed blood, which atones for our sins. I assume you believe the same."

Her voice rose. "Mr. Sullivan, now you've offended every Jew, Muslim and Universalist here today with your hateful remarks. I know I'm going to heaven because God made me like I am, and He—or She—loves me. And all of us. That's why they sent Jesus—and Mohammad, Buddha, and the others—to show us how to live lives of love. That's all that matters: living for love. Not hate, like you espouse. What are you doing here?"

The vice president rose and stood next to Bishop Davis at the podium. She smiled and pulled the microphone her way. "Thank you, Bishop, and Mr. Sullivan, for that interesting interaction. There's no place for hate in America today, and the president and I are committed to wiping it out. Now it's time for our break. Our group sessions will begin in thirty minutes. You should have room assignments on your nametags. Please get some coffee outside in the foyer, and let's have a productive afternoon."

Janet stood, nodded to the others at the table, and walked toward Richard, who was himself walking toward the podium. She took the diagonal and met him in front of the dais.

"Richard, let's go. She won't listen to you," she said in a low voice.

"But she asked me questions and then twisted every answer I gave."

"It doesn't matter, dear. It's done. Let's just go before something else happens."

Bishop Davis had her back to the room, talking to the vice president, who looked down and saw the Sullivans. Her eyes opened a bit wider and she shook her head in a sign of disbelief.

Two reporters came up and started to ask Richard questions.

"Come on," Janet said, and she almost dragged her husband toward the back exit.

As the ballroom emptied, the hundreds of demons present were joyous. Particularly Balzor and Nepravel, whose run-in with Richard Sullivan twenty years earlier had severely damaged their standing.

They followed closely behind the Sullivans as they tried to walk and speak with friends, while dodging reporters and several people who were clearly hostile.

"Don't try to mess with us, Richard," Balzor said near the attorney's right ear. "You're in over your head. This is our territory."

"Someday you'll hear about the granddaughter you never had, aborted the same week you were in D.C. for a conference," Nepravel added.

As they reached the lobby outside the ballroom, what Richard and Janet did hear audibly was a large man, one of the conference organizers, asking Richard not to return for the breakout sessions, and taking his credentials badge.

"And we'll be turning over the tape of your remarks to the authorities," he added, then walked away.


Tom was finishing a late sandwich at his desk when his Trusted Core phone vibrated.

"Emily, how's the conference?"

"Uh, it's well attended, but I'm afraid your father has been asked to leave."

"What?"

"After the keynote address by Bishop Adrienne Davis, which was superb, your father basically accosted her for being a lesbian, citing 'God's truth' against gay love. It was terrible."

"I can't believe it."

"Patricia was embarrassed for the bishop, and the organizers asked your parents to leave. So I never got a chance to speak to them, though I wouldn't have gone near them with all the cameras around."

"OK, thanks for the heads up. Tell Patricia I'm sorry."

"I will. The next sessions are starting—Gotta go."

"See you tomorrow."

He almost called his father but instead put the phone down and stared at the bookcase on the opposite wall. Then he got up, closed the door and sat at his desk again, ignoring the report he was supposed to finish.

*Just what I need—a crazy, born-again father arguing in public to add to my plate. What was Dad thinking? I warned him. Where was Mom? Why would they jeopardize my position? What will the president and vice president think of them and of me?*

*Besides being responsible for stopping the attacks on our nation and finding the attackers, now I've also got to deal with Dad, Callie and Erin. And the abortion—that's my child.*

*What?*

*Emily still thinks about her abortion. With Bradshaw? Crazy.*

A new thought stopped him short. *Is God trying to get my attention with all this stuff? Chasing me, like Natalie says?*

*No way. I'm beyond that. But I am pretty focused on me.*

*Where did that come from? Isn't everyone? That's normal. This is crazy.*


Alexei Nobikov had awakened early in his hotel room due to jet lag and had worked for several hours on his laptop, while surfing the cable networks for the latest news and commentary, comparing the usual sources to try to triangulate the American mood.

When he went down to the lobby restaurant for breakfast, he noticed preparations underway for a large conference that afternoon on "Faith and Unity."

Thinking the agenda might give him some insights, after breakfast he donned a set of media credentials that he kept with him while traveling and investigated further. The result was that he was sitting at the press table in the back of the ballroom during the keynote speech as well as the escalating exchange between a participant and the main speaker.

As a mature believer in God's Word, Alexei thought the gentleman's question was reasonable, and he was surprised by the vitriol of the female bishop's response. It occurred to him that the lines of social conflict were definitely hardening in the nation once known as the champion of free speech and genuine tolerance.

When he walked out into the lobby he was almost next to the exchange between the same gentleman and the organizer, who took his credentials. As well as those of his wife.

As the Sullivans turned toward the elevator bank and Janet started to speak, they almost ran into Nobikov.

"Excuse me," he said. "My name is Alexei Nobikov, and I write articles on America for a journal in Europe. I watched your exchange with the bishop. As a fellow believer I found her response to you rather troubling. Do you have a few minutes to talk about it?"

Richard looked briefly at Janet and said, "Thank you. But I seem to have already said enough in public for one day. Though," and he looked again at his wife, "I was just trying to get to the truth."

Janet smiled. "Thank you, Mr., uh, Nobikov. Your support is refreshing, particularly from Europe. Where, may I ask?"

"My wife and I live on Cyprus, but we travel all over."

"Well, thank you again, but I think my husband and I need to take a little break."

"Of course. Here's my card, if I might ever have the pleasure of catching up with you and hearing your story."

Janet took the card and slipped it into her purse. "Thank you. We will. Enjoy your stay."


That afternoon Callie Sawyer was at her desk at *Genetic News* when she received an internal meeting request from the publisher's HR Chief, for 3pm.

When she came to his corner office on the third floor of the building from which ten separate scientific journals were published, he ushered her in, smiled, and offered her a seat at the small conference table on one side of the room. He sat across from her and placed a file on the table.

"Thank you, Callie, for coming on short notice."

"No problem. What's up?"

He opened the file, took out three printed pages, and handed them to her. "Did you write this?"

She looked down at a review she had written the previous week for her adult Sunday School class on "Creation, Intelligent Design and Evolution."

"Yes. For my Sunday School class."

"OK. Well, under your name at the end it lists your job title as an editor at our publication, *Genetic News*."

"I think that's standard practice at our church."

"Well, the problem is that it associates us with totally unscientific, absurd fantasies about how the universe was created, how life began, and how we came to be as humans—as all living things."

"But if you..."

He raised his hand. "Callie, this is serious. Two different employees found this paper online at your church's website, and complained about it. Your paper may have been seen by who knows how many people. And your pastor was one of the ones detained for Hate Speech, wasn't he?"

"Yes, which was ridiculous. And I didn't realize it would be posted online."

"Well it is. And those here who've read it don't think it's ridiculous. It's online right now, fueling myths and ignorance, not science and truth."

Callie was silent.

He continued. "Beyond that lapse in judgment, management cannot understand how an intelligent person such as yourself could believe this stuff. A Creator? 'Intelligent Design is shown in the outermost reaches of the universe and in the innermost workings of the cell.' Do you really believe that?"

"Yes. It seems obvious to me. Have you ever thought about..."

He again raised his hand, then took back the article and looked at it. "We hired you for your writing and organizational skills, Callie, which are many. But now we question whether someone with such extreme beliefs, counter to the scientific method we promote, and from a church where Hate Speech is practiced, should have editorial input into our articles, many of which are on the cutting edge of genetic research."

"I believe someday in the future we'll discover that what you call 'science' today and what I call 'intelligent design' are both somehow simultaneously true—we just don't understand how yet. And I've never changed anything about the scientific discoveries or conclusions reported by our contributors, and I never would."

He was silent for a moment. "You say that, but then, look at your beliefs. Who really knows what you might do? At a minimum, consider this an official warning of unacceptable performance, and have this paper taken down from your church's website. That's it for now, but management is considering other actions, if we deem them to be necessary after further review this afternoon. You should take the rest of the day off, and I'll let you know."

After making some calls to their pastor and others in Atlanta, Richard and Janet accepted Robert Ludwig's invitation for coffee in his office at The Church of the Good Shepherd.

An hour later he welcomed them into his book-lined study. His assistant took their coffee/tea orders and the Sullivans sat on a comfortable sofa while the pastor settled into a large, padded chair across the coffee table from them.

"Well, that didn't go how we planned," Richard began. "I'm sorry."

Ludwig smiled. "I watched her speech and your exchange on The Network. You seemed perfectly reasonable to me. She attacked you. But, as we've all been reading and praying about, we know who really attacked you."

Janet nodded. "I thought having some previous credibility with the vice president might make some difference, which is why I wanted to attend, despite the probable agenda. So I was clearly wrong, too."

Their mugs arrived and Ludwig thanked his assistant, who said to him, "Callie Sawyer called and wonders if she can see you this afternoon."

Ludwig was about to speak when Janet asked, "Is that the young woman who's a friend of Kristen Holloway?"

"Yes."

"We've heard about her from our son, Tom. If it works for you, we'd love to meet her."

Ludwig nodded to his assistant. "Tell Callie she can come any time—and there are some people here who'd like to meet her."

The assistant left, and they each took a sip. There followed a thirty-minute, wide-ranging discussion of the day's events, the government's takeover in the State of Emergency, their continued focus on prayer, and the need to encourage believers to vote against the president's Progressive Agenda in the upcoming elections, now only two weeks away.

As they rose to get refills, Ludwig said, "You know your son is right in the middle of all this, don't you? How did that happen?"

Richard stood aside for Janet to exit the study. "Tom's been a high achiever ever since high school. Goals. To Do Lists..."

"Takes after his father," Janet interrupted with a smile.

"And his mother. Most things he's touched have gone well, which we know is not always a recipe for wisdom or humility, particularly in young males. He became interested in computer science early on, won a big scholarship, and did well at The Credit Bank of New York. President Rhodes accepted a suggestion in a note from Janet, whom he knew in Congress, to bring Tom in at a starting level in the White House. He's still there."

Ludwig nodded.

Richard added with a shake of his head, "Oh, and I'm afraid he's never met an attractive young woman with whom he just wanted to be friends."

Ludwig nodded again as they poured coffee in the break room. "That sadly seems to be the way these days. But two things I don't understand—with you as his parents, where is his faith? And why is he a holdover with President Bradshaw?"

As they walked back to the study, Janet said, "On his faith, I think we failed. After Richard and I gave our lives to Jesus, when Tom was fourteen, he was really touched by the events of the night when our next-door neighbor's daughter—in high school with our daughter—had a baby that almost died in the ambulance going to the hospital. It's a long story, but Tom clearly was touched by what he saw as God's hand in everything that happened." They took their seats again. "He went regularly to a great student ministry at our church and accepted Jesus six months later. He was in Bible studies. But then he went to university, and the combination of peer pressure, temptations, and reading books which 'proved' that the Bible was just one among several such stories, simply turned him off. He thinks our faith is all a myth that has no impact or power in real life. We pray for him every day."

"And he's been on our prayer list for a month now," Ludwig said.

"As for President Bradshaw," Richard said, "we imagine that Tom's just really good at what he does and wants to get ahead by doing well, so the new president has kept him. Tom's known Emily Schofield, the president's Communications person, since he came to D.C."

"They're quite a team. Where do you think this will end?"

Janet shook her head. "Given the last six weeks, if the Progressives win this election, I worry they'll never give up control. They'll use 'we're being attacked' until all our liberties are gone."

"And the Gospel cannot be preached," Ludwig said.

"And the Gospel cannot be preached," Richard repeated.

"When you step back and look, it's really clear who's behind all this," Janet said.

The intercom buzzed. "Callie Sawyer's here."

Ludwig looked up. "Great. Please send her back."

"We can't stay long—we're having dinner with Tom tonight," Richard said.


Callie had driven to the church from her office. She thanked Pastor Ludwig's assistant and walked down the hall to his study; the door opened and he greeted her.

"Come in, Callie. And please meet Tom Sullivan's parents, Richard and Janet."

"Wow." She smiled and shook hands.

Janet said, "Sorry to surprise you, but we were in town for the vice president's conference, and we've heard so much about you from Kristen, and from Tom, that we stayed with Robert a few extra minutes to meet you."

"Here, everyone have a seat," Ludwig said.

"OK. But we're meeting Tom in a little while," Richard added.

Callie had two subjects to discuss with her pastor, but she shifted gears to engage with the Sullivans. "So you knew Kristen, who's my landlord, back when she became a believer. Yes?"

Janet smiled. "It's very public knowledge that she and Richard—a different Richard and a different Kristen, really—had an affair. God used that incredible mess to first change Richard, then me, and then Kristen. None of us is the same person."

Callie nodded. "And, as you may know, it was Kristen who first told me about the God who loves me and the Savior who died to clean up the utter mess that was my life. And I can tell you that at our church Kristen has powerfully impacted hundreds of women—and men—for the Lord."

Ludwig laughed. "Isn't He incredible? All that Satan intended to ruin you, Kristen, Richard and Janet, God turned around to bring people to His side."

Richard said, "To think that all the pain I caused Janet and my family planted seeds for your salvation, Callie, gives me chills."

"Yes, me, too."

"We understand you and Tom are not seeing each other anymore, but tell us more about you," Janet said.

They talked for fifteen minutes about Callie's job, current events, the Church of the Good Shepherd, and the Sullivans' experience at the conference. Richard looked at his watch. "This is wonderful, but we've really got to go, and Callie came to see Robert, not us."

Everyone stood and shook hands. Janet said, "We try never to get involved in Tom's relationships, but I have to say that I wish you two were still seeing each other."

Callie nodded. "Yes. He's a great guy. But I'm afraid we just wouldn't work, for some pretty fundamental reasons."

"I understand. Thank you for letting us stay. And thank you, Robert, for seeing us. We're heading back to Atlanta tomorrow afternoon."

The Sullivans left and Pastor Ludwig motioned for Callie to have a seat on the couch across from him, while he made sure the study door was wide open, giving his assistant a clear view inside, though she could not hear what was being said.

"That was a surprise," Callie said. "And it underscores the second thing I want to talk with you about. But first, let me tell you about what happened at work this afternoon, and ask for your help, and for prayer."

Ten minutes later Ludwig had encouraged Callie that he knew two well-funded journals/blogs, one on Intelligent Design and one on below-the-radar investigative journalism, called the Truth Action Forum, that would probably like to have her expertise, if her current employer let her go, and he committed to making the introductions.

"What's the second thing on your mind?" he asked.

"Actually, it's much more important. The Sullivans don't know it, but they have a grandchild who is about to be aborted. Day after tomorrow."

Ludwig frowned. "What?"

Callie explained all that she knew about Erin, Tom and the abortion decision.

"That's terrible, Callie. Day after tomorrow. We should pray."

"Yes, of course. But in this case, knowing Tom and now his parents, I want to do more. Or at least exhaust every possibility. I found Erin's phone number at her institute. You and I know several families who are desperate to adopt a baby. And you can add me to the list. I'd like you to call her and tell her that a church member you know would like to adopt her child, and that the church will pay all the expenses for the delivery. If necessary I'll do both, with help from Kristen and others, but there are many potential families here, and I think it's important for the church to act as the initial contact, to protect everyone's privacy."

He thought for a few moments. "Callie, that's quite a commitment."

"Not really. If no one else stepped up, Grace needs a sibling, and at the rate I'm going, that won't happen any time soon. I may be a single

Mom, but at least I know how to do it, and I'm blessed with an incredible support group at our church. For days I've been thinking, 'If not me, then who; and if not now, then when?' But I'm sure there are several better qualified families than me. Neither Erin nor Tom ever needs to know who started the process. But first things first. If you'll call her tomorrow, we'll really need a night of prayer to open her heart to what she'll hear."

"Yes, of course I'll call her. And, yes, we need to bathe Erin in prayer. Without divulging any names, we'll have the request out to our prayer chain in thirty minutes."

"Thank you, Pastor."

"No, no. Thank you, Callie. Let's pray now."

It was a short walk just past Lafayette Square to the restaurant where Tom had made reservations for their dinner, and so he left his office a little after six. As he headed across the square, he tried to calm his thoughts about what his parents had done to complicate his life in their short visit to the capital.

*All Dad had to do was just do nothing. How hard is that? But he had to speak up for 'the truth.' Always, 'God's truth'—at least as he sees it. Thank you very much.*

The truth is important. Maybe he encouraged others to speak up this afternoon.

*What?*

Watch the tape, listen to their exchange yourself, and see what you think. Be fair to your father. He only wants the best for you.

*Come on. He's a smart attorney. How could he let it happen?*

As he joined the sidewalk and neared the restaurant, a man in a blue suit who had been standing at the front door stepped in front of him.

"Mr. Sullivan?"

"Yes."

He opened his left hand to show a badge. "I'm Officer Pete Higgins with DC Metro, and we'd like you to remain outside for a few minutes, please."

"What? Why?"

"A small team is inside. They should be out soon. The lead officer gave me your photo and asked me to be on the lookout. Could we step down the block?" The officer took Tom's elbow, turned him around, and started walking down the sidewalk.

"What's this about?"

Just then he heard a commotion behind them at the door. From half a block away, he turned around and saw two plainclothes officers leading his father, handcuffed, out of the front door and toward one of two patrol cars which Tom had not noticed in the street. He started to move forward, but Officer Higgins held on to him.

"Our orders are to keep you away from them." Just then his mother emerged next to another officer, and several men nearby started taking pictures with their smartphones.

In a few seconds the first car departed with Tom's father in the backseat, and his mother got into the second one. As she did so, she looked up, and Tom was sure that she saw him. There was clearly shock on her face.

"Where are they taking them? And why?"

"Your father's being detained for violating the State of Emergency on Hate Speech, and we're taking your mother back to her hotel. We strongly suggest, and this comes from the top, that you not be seen with her any time soon. That's why we stopped you from going inside. Call her if you want, but it would not be good for you to meet her where you might be seen."

The second car drove off, and Officer Higgins released Tom's arm. "Do you need a lift?"

Tom stared at him blankly, then spoke. "I, uh, think I'll walk."

It was just over a mile to Tom's row house east of the Capitol; he found himself headed in that direction. It was a mild evening, and he'd made no plans for after seeing his parents. He knew he had to call his mother, but first he needed to find out what the hell was going on.

As he walked on the sidewalk he took out his Trusted Core phone and dialed Emily, who answered immediately. "Emily, you won't believe what just happened. I..."

"I know," she interrupted. "I was with Patricia when she and the president talked about it late this afternoon during a break at the conference."

"What? *They're* involved?"

"Think about it. Your Dad bombed the most visible event of the day, on live television, embarrassing the Administration. Then, DC security cameras showed them going to Callie's church to meet with that pastor who had to be detained under your orders. Who knows what they're plotting?

"By the way, we didn't initiate anything—the regular authorities did so after reviewing the tape—but when they contacted the White House because of you, we had to get involved. And we told them to go ahead and detain your father because he and that pastor might be cooking up something really crazy."

"I was in my office. Why didn't you contact me?"

"Think about it. For about a thousand reasons that would be the very worst thing we could have done. We had to let the system work without interference."

He walked several paces in silence. "So what now?"

"I imagine your father, like the pastor before, will be detained until the end of the State of Emergency—that's pretty standard now. And they'll ask him about his meeting at the church, and any others he's had. And the president wants to see you first thing. Oh, and please, don't say anything or do anything that could make this worse. We actually got several strong, public, ecumenical resolutions of support for our—your—approach to defending the country at the conference today, and we don't want any distractions to derail them."

He walked five more paces in silence. "OK. I gotta call Mom. I think she saw me outside the restaurant when Dad was arrested. I imagine the president is not happy."

"I guess not. Hey, Tom, you didn't say or do anything wrong. They did. We'll get through this, like we have everything else. You just need to put some distance between you and them. And now we have the leaders of the real faith community clearly behind us."

"Yeah. Great. Thanks. I'll see you in the morning."

He put the phone in his pocket and stopped at a red light, almost to Constitution Avenue. He looked around in the twilight.

*This place is beautiful. I love it. But it may all be over for me, after today.*

He walked east for fifteen minutes, then dialed his mother.

"Mom, it's Tom."

"Oh, thank goodness. Are you all right? Was that you outside the restaurant?"

"Yes, I..."

"Are you OK?"

"Yes, I'm walking home. Where are you?"

"At the hotel. We were so worried you'd come in and get caught up in the insanity. They arrested your father for 'hate speech'! They handcuffed him in the restaurant. In front of hundreds of people. In America."

"I just found out from Emily. What did he say at the conference?"

"What does that matter? In America you don't get arrested for speaking."

Tom was silent.

After a moment she continued. "Can you come to the hotel? I'm going to cancel our tickets home. I can't leave with Dad in jail."

"After they question him tonight or tomorrow, he probably won't be in jail—more likely at a camp in Maryland or Virginia. And most likely you won't be able to see him. They may question you, too. He should get out at the end of the State of Emergency."

"Question him? And me?" Her voice rose. "About what?"

"Where did you go this afternoon?"

"To the Church of the Good Shepherd. Pastor Ludwig. We'd met him earlier. And we also met..."

"Who?"

"Nothing. What's going on?"

"A national emergency, Mom. Attacks. You know that. And you know I'm in the middle of it. Yet Dad had to lecture a bishop on national television about 'God's truth'? This may be the end of my job."

Janet was silent. "If that happens, it'll make a terrible mistake even worse. Richard did not lecture the bishop. She asked loaded questions."

"Which he answered."

"Which he answered with the truth."

He walked several more paces in silence. "I can't come to the hotel. Someone might see me and take a picture. Not good for the National Security Advisor to be seen with people being arrested for hate speech."

"OK. I get it. Yes, you should protect your job. I'll call others to help us, and to pray. And, who knows, God probably has you there for a reason, so don't blow it."

"What?"

"I don't know. But think about all that had to happen for you to be where you are, right now, with all this craziness happening."

"Mom, most of what you call 'craziness' I designed."

"Yes. That's exactly my point. Keep at it. We'll be OK. We love you."

"I love you, too."

They hung up. Tom kept walking. With the sun down, it started to get chilly.

*What did she mean by that?* He almost laughed. *If there is a God and He has me here for a reason, He'd better move fast, 'cause I may not be here much longer.*

What Tom could not tell in the chill was the slightly increased spiritual warmth from the tiny flame inside him. The angel hovering over Tom, attracted by the many answered prayers arriving constantly from all those praying for him, protected him from the demons' voices of deceit. And because those voices were dimmed, the small flame was being fed by the truth spoken by believers like his mother.

As he walked he added his father's arrest and his mother's distress to the issues overflowing his plate. *Emily's right—I need to stay out of it, if I even still have a job.*

But they're my parents, and they've stuck up for me many, many times.

He hoped the WhiteStorm connections to European racist groups turned up some threads they could follow to finally link all these bad actors together—it was becoming an embarrassment, and he hoped the small but increasing calls in the press for a change of direction wouldn't upset the president's hopes for the elections.

*Erin's abortion is scheduled for Thursday morning. Maybe she and I can get back together when that's behind us.*

But what about the baby?

As he turned off the main avenue his phone vibrated with a text from the president, asking him to an early breakfast. He punched "Accept" and returned the phone to his pocket.

His route took him within two blocks of Callie's home. He thought of her, Grace and Kristen as he came to the cross street. He touched his phone with his fingers. *I'd really like to talk with her. She...*

He looked down the street, thought for a moment, then released the phone and headed for his own home.

# 20

*Upon my arrival in the United States the religious aspect of the country was the first thing that struck my attention; and the longer I stayed there, the more I perceived the great political consequences resulting from this new state of things. In France, I had almost always seen the spirit of religion and the spirit of freedom marching in opposite directions. But in America I found they were intimately united and that they reigned in common over the same country.*

Alexis de Tocqueville[1]
Wednesday, October 28

Alexei Nobikov was up early that Wednesday morning and from his hotel room talked to his wife Anna on Cyprus with his laptop's video chat.

"Yesterday was a little unusual. I attended a conference—with all that they're doing here now I don't want to mention any specific names or places—and saw a first-hand example of what seems to be coming. It was like a newsreel from the first days of the Bolsheviks. In America.

"But I met the couple involved, and then when I had dinner with our niece and her boyfriend, it turns out that I actually met the son of that same couple on my last trip here. Can you believe that? And Katherine's boyfriend, Patrick, who interns for an historian, is having lunch with him today...I know. I'm going to try to stay connected, in case these people have some insights that can help us. There's a small pool of press passes each day for foreign journalists at the White House—I applied for one online, and if I get it, I'll try to attend the briefing."

At that same early hour Tom was escorted to the West Sitting Room in the White House, where he sat in an upholstered chair while a server put eggs, bacon and other deep dishes on the buffet table in the small Dining Room. Nepravel came in through the closed western window and nodded to Balzor, who indicated that all was well, so Nepravel

---

1. https://www.azquotes.com/author/14691-Alexis_de_Tocqueville

moved on to his other charges, most of whom would soon be arriving in their offices in the West Wing.

Tom could make out the voices of the president and his wife in their bedroom, then the president answered a call. After about ten minutes the president opened the door and came out, dressed in gray suit pants and a white shirt, with a blue tie. He smiled and extended his hand. "Tom, good morning. Thanks for coming. How are you?"

"I'm fine, sir. But I've also been better."

President Bradshaw nodded and motioned towards the buffet. "Yes, I can imagine. A tough day—undermined in what you're trying to do for the nation by your own parents."

"And still no breakthroughs with the WhiteStorm attack, though the FBI thinks they may be close to linking them to at least some of the earlier ones."

"I think we're close, too, Tom. But your father. Has he always been full of such antipathy for those with whom he doesn't agree?"

"No. I watched the tape of the interchange last night when I got home, and he did simply answer the bishop's questions."

The president picked up a plate but paused at the first serving pan. "With hate speech and malice, Tom, towards another American. And one who even shares his faith. Are you defending him?"

"No. No, of course not. You're right. It was absolutely wrong. He should have just said nothing."

"Or, better yet, helped us defend our short-term measures in this extraordinary time, as all the other delegates did in their final resolution."

"Yes." Tom placed some scrambled eggs on his plate. "That would have been much better."

"Well, I hope you understand we had to deal with it—it was too visible. And we didn't want you to have to get involved in the arrest, which is why we had the officer head you off."

They walked over and sat at the small table. "Yes, I understand. Emily and I talked."

"Good. Good. Dig in. Listen, there's just one thing I need you to do." He paused for a moment. "It's important that there's no confusion out there, particularly with the election next week. The country needs to hear a clear message from the National Security Advisor that no one, not even his father, is above the law."

Tom picked up his orange juice and took a sip. "OK."

"So, here. I asked Emily to write a statement about the incident that we'd like you to read and sign, so we can get it out to the press today, to put this matter to rest." The president picked up a manilla folder that had been next to his seat and handed it to Tom.

Inside was a one page, typed statement on Tom's office letterhead. He began to read it and realized that it was a denunciation of his father as a white privileged religious bigot who had in the past allowed his faith to lead him into hostile statements about those who were not, like him, "saved by faith in Jesus Christ alone."

Tom had not finished reading when the president said, "You can finish it later, and of course let Emily know if she needs to tweak anything. But I think it's accurate, and it's vitally important, Tom, especially now, that we're all one team. Do you agree?"

Tom put down the folder. "Yes, sir. I do. Of course I agree."

"And Emily may decide it'll be a good thing for you to do a short video. Or maybe answer some questions from the press. She'll let you know."

Tom nodded. He felt light-headed. He picked up his fork, but wasn't interested. They talked for several minutes about the various investigations and initiatives that were underway.

"Eat up, Tom. This is the best breakfast in town."

Balzor smiled and nodded, even though he had never tasted food.


Thirty minutes later Tom sat at his desk in the White House, opened the manilla folder the president had given him, and read.


Contact Information: Emily Schofield, White House Communications

For Immediate Release
  The Office of the National Security Advisor
  The White House
  October 28$^{th}$

## National Security Advisor Condemns Hate Speech

For over a year I have been an advisor on National Security in the White House under both Presidents Rhodes and Bradshaw. Following the attacks on our nation which started almost two months ago with the assassination of President Rhodes and hundreds of others, I have assisted President Bradshaw as his National Security Advisor in countering those who would destroy our country, either with violent actions or with violent words.

Under the President's guidance I helped draft the provisions of the original State of Emergency's temporary regulations, and the subsequent amendments. I am, therefore, fully in agreement with all the steps our government agencies and law enforcement personnel have taken, and continue to take on a daily basis, to protect our nation.

These temporary restrictions on our normal liberties exist to ensure that we have those liberties for the long-term, and they must apply equally and to all of us.

I was therefore unhappy to learn that yesterday a member of my own family, my father, violated one of the key foundations of our approach to national safety—he engaged in hate speech. And he did so by condemning a woman of color and of the greatest faith in a national public forum designed to encourage unity and understanding.

While I of course love my father, and my entire family, I also love our nation, and I condemn the words he used to imply that another American is not worthy of God's acceptance because of how God made her. No rational thinking person could agree with that statement, and it grieves me that my father attacked her with such malice.

I stand firmly with President Bradshaw and with every action of this Administration to rid us of violence, and to silence those who sow the seeds of hate that lead to violence.

------

Thomas Sullivan
National Security Advisor

### 

Tom put the paper down and had an immediate image of his parents in their kitchen when he was younger.

*How did it get to this? Which parental lesson is this: Actions have Consequences, or Always extend Grace?*

Then he imagined his father being booked, fingerprinted, and put in a jail cell. And his mother on the phone with people all through the night. And many of those people knew him from childhood.

Emily knocked at his open door and came in. "Tough night, huh?"

"Yes, to say the least."

"Did you talk to your mother?"

"Yes. She understood about not getting together. And then the president and I had breakfast, and he gave me this statement that he said you wrote."

She nodded. "Is it OK?" He looked at her but said nothing. She continued. "Let me know if you think anything needs changing. He asked me to let him know when you sign it."

"My father just can't be quiet about his faith. I've told him for years to let up. He just won't listen."

He looked down at the page again, then picked up his pen, signed it, and held it out to her.

Emily took it. "Thanks. I'll get you a copy. Why do you think that is?"

Tom paused. "He thinks he's a sinner who hurt others and was headed to Hell until God stepped in. He'll tell you that when he 'surrendered' to Christ and was saved, God transformed him. So he wants that for everyone. And he won't be quiet, even when I ask him to."

"And even when it hurts others."

Tom nodded. "Yes. Even then. I love him, but I'm tired of it. He always just thinks about himself."

She started to leave. "If the press wants to talk more about it, I'll get with Seth and figure out how to do it as low key as possible."

"Thanks. Sadly, his faith makes him irrational. I'll just have to deal with it. Our team is protecting and making our nation better, even if he doesn't understand that—or won't. Maybe some time to be by himself and to think will help him."

As she turned, she said, "I understand. As I mentioned to you yesterday about how I wound up here, sometimes what seems bad turns out to be for a good reason."

He nodded. "Yes. Thanks." He smiled. "I've heard that before—most recently from my parents."


As usual Tom had several more meetings that morning, but he found it hard to concentrate.

So he left a few minutes early to take the Restricted Zone shuttle over to its southeastern corner, from where he walked four blocks to a restaurant in a row of shops on a side street. It was not fancy, with unpolished wooden floors and cream colored walls. But on opening the door he knew it was a good choice from the smells filling the air and the large portions on the plates at the front tables.

Nepravel caught up with Tom just as he opened the door, concerned about with whom he was meeting. The demon was about to go inside when from a booth in the left rear Tom saw Patrick Tomlinson's raised hand, and Nepravel saw the bright spiritual light spreading out from that area. He turned away as the humans greeted each other and Patrick moved over next to Gary Thornton, so Tom had one side to himself.

"Never been here before," Tom said to the historian, who smiled.

"One of my favorites. The collard greens and fried okra are to die for. I'm glad you could make it, with all that's going on."

"You mean my father."

"Yes. I saw it on the news this morning. Well, they didn't show what he said, just him being arrested. And they mentioned a connection to the Church of the Good Shepherd."

"All of which is true."

"And what do you do at the White House?"

Tom understood it to be an honest question, so he tempered his response. "Security. But, look, that's what I deal with all day, and I've been looking forward to grilling you at this lunch ever since Kristen and Callie introduced us, so is it OK if we set my father's problem aside for a few moments?"

Thornton smiled as a waitress approached them with menus. "Yes, of course. A good idea. Iced tea?"

They chatted for a few minutes about the state of Thornton's current research, with help from Patrick and another intern, and ordered their lunches.

As the waitress left, Tom said, "I finished your book and watched the seminar you did with Robert Ludwig. There's a lot I could ask you about. I have to admit that the evidence you present is pretty strong that the Founders of this nation did so on Christian principles, which we're not taught in school. Even the men who were not what I guess we would call 'born again believers' supported the Christian faith. They thought it was foundational to the virtue they believed we need to guide individual freedom and individual choices."

Both men across from him nodded, and Thornton said, "I think you've done your homework."

"That's what Callie said. But, look, that was back two hundred and fifty years ago. I'm a rational person. I guess I may have had 'faith' in high school, but it seems pretty irrelevant to me today. I try to live now based on rational thought, not irrational faith. What I want to know is how did the greatest thinkers, activists and leaders on opposite sides of the ocean take such different paths at almost the same time? The French and American Revolutions were started by smart men with great vision—why didn't the American Revolutionaries think like their French counterparts, sharing the same reliance on Reason? But instead, they focused on 'Faith'?"

Thornton sat back in the booth. "Tom, that's quite a question. Good for you. Patrick, do you have any ideas?"

The college student thought for a moment, then leaned forward a bit. "The Americans certainly used Reason to argue against Britain's control of their lives, but their reasoning was built on a foundation of faith—their belief that people and their rights are God-created and God-given. And because of the Great Awakening, led by George Whitefield, Jonathan Edwards and the other evangelists in the preceding decades, their faith was personal and individual. In fact, they were very aware that many of the colonies had different ways of officially expressing their Christian faith—denominations—which led them to focus not on any single church organization, but on the underlying faith itself."

Thornton nodded as he put sweetener in his tea. "Go on."

Patrick did likewise, then continued. "In France there was the monarchy and the Catholic Church, which supported each other. Both were huge top-down institutions requiring allegiance and strict conformity, not based on personal choice or individual freedom. So the only counter-weight was secular 'Reason', arguing that individual 'freedom'—Liberty, they called it—was needed to break away from these oppressive institutions, but a freedom not founded on any underlying principles other than 'equality' and 'democracy.' If anything, the French Revolution was anti-faith, anti-religion, and all in the name of secular 'Reason.'

"But without a Christian foundation of principles, one man's democratic majority became another man's oppressive nightmare, power corrupted them all, as it always does with us fallen humans, and their nation descended into the murderous Reign of Terror and anarchy. And that same path, with a few different details, was later followed in Russia, Germany, and China. So I think that 'reason' is a great *tool*—given by God, by the way, since we're created in His image—but not a good foundation for structuring a society."

"Wow," Thornton exclaimed with a smile. "You've been listening!"

Patrick sat back and shrugged. "I guess so. You're always making me read and think."

Tom sat silently, then said, "Yes. Wow."

Thornton looked at their guest. "And, getting back to you, Tom, for a moment, you're wrong to juxtapose faith and reason. *Everyone* believes in something, whether they'll admit it or not. And 'reason' is not a sufficient foundation for structuring a life, either. It's a tool. A foundation has to have principles. It has to answer the Big Questions: Who am I? Where did I come from? What is my purpose? What's after this life?

"The best foundation for an entire society, built on many individual but shared foundations, answers those questions. Marx tried and failed. Hitler. Mao. Darwin. 'Science'. 'Reason'. Take your pick. But the Founders of this nation believed in the personal God of the Bible, and in their own salvation through His grace alone, and structured our institutions to account for our fallen nature, so that no one group or faction could gain total control, as has always happened elsewhere. And they guaranteed that this foundation of personal faith—not a religious institution—would be constantly renewed in future generations by safeguarding the freedom of personal choices."

Tom looked at both men for several beats. "Can I say 'Wow' again? And our lunches haven't even arrived yet."

They laughed. "Yes, pretty heavy," Thornton admitted. "But you asked."

"I did," Tom said, as the waitress arrived with their plates. "And doesn't this look good?"

They took a break from the discussion to weigh into their food. Tom had ordered ribs with collards and squash casserole. He was immediately pleased with his choices.

They veered off to reflect for a few minutes on more current events, and Tom used that discussion to circle back to the question that fueled his curiosity. "So, given that the Founders' era was much simpler and slower moving, what do you think they would say about our current challenges?"

"I've actually thought quite a bit about that," Thornton said, "and I think I have an answer. Yes, events and information in those days were in fact 'slower', but that didn't make them easier to deal with. It may have actually been more difficult than today. There was at least as much fog and confusion, probably more. Communication was slow and imperfect. In a battle, until someone attacked, you had little idea where your enemy was, or what he was planning. You couldn't even see over a hill. Think about our Civil War, with families split, brothers fighting brothers, and everyone's neighbor a potential spy. What was that like compared to what you're dealing with today?"

"I guess it was pretty tough. Not knowing much. Like today. "

"Yes. So you stuck to principles—for governing, communicating, fighting—and trusted that those principles would get you through the fog of uncertainty. With, of course, most of the Founders would add, God's help."

"I see," Tom said, holding Thornton's gaze. "So you think they wouldn't be happy about our State of Emergency provisions?"

Thornton nodded. "Because those provisions take away our basic freedoms, put way too much power in the hands of a small group—something all the Founders feared—and will probably have many bad unintended consequences. That's usually what happens when you ditch your foundational principles."

Tom sat back. "I see. Uh, let's come back to that, but, Patrick, that was quite a summary you gave on the two revolutions—rooted in faith. Where did you learn all that? First, though, how's your friend? Is it Katherine? The one who takes the writing class with Callie."

Patrick smiled. "Oh, she's fine. We're good."

Thornton also smiled. "Beautiful and smart. Quite a combination. And a believer, too."

"I knew about the first two, at least. I met her."

"Just last night we had dinner with her uncle—Alexei Nobikov, who you met at that restaurant. He's back in D.C. this week. I told him about our lunch today, and he asked me to tell you hello."

"Thank you. He sure made Cyprus sound inviting."

"And he's a believer, too, which you might not expect. He learned about the Lord when he was here in graduate school."

"That is unusual. But, now, tell me how you learned all that history."

"Most of the details I learned from Professor Thornton while I've been interning with him for the past two years, but I grew up in Cincinnati, and my mother home-schooled us through eighth grade, so I also learned a lot about history then."

"Your family were believers?"

"Yes, still are. And I've always felt a special connection because I was supposed to be aborted, but God rescued me, and my parents adopted me."

Tom looked more intently at the younger man. After a pause, he spoke, "Tomlinson. Cincinnati. Do you know any of those details?"

"My parents arranged for me to meet my birth mother once, about five years ago, when she was in town. She was very nice, and explained that she'd been in high school, and that through a miracle she'd canceled the abortion at the last minute, and had me instead. Through an attorney the Tomlinsons agreed to adopt me. And I apparently almost died while she was giving birth. But I made it. And that's why I have such a strong faith in God and His purpose for me."

Tom stared at Patrick for a long while. Finally he said, "Is your birth mother's name Amy?"

Patrick looked shocked. "Yes. How do you know?"

Tom looked back and forth between the two men. "This is impossible. Amy was our next-door neighbor. My sister Susan convinced her not to have the abortion—in the waiting room at the clinic. My father, the one arrested yesterday, set up your adoption and rode with Amy to the hospital, praying for her, and for you."

None of them spoke. Tom invisibly shook. He repeated, "This is impossible. I was there that night—I think I was fourteen. You immediately went off with your new family, and I lost track of what happened to you. But now, here you are, twenty years later, sitting across from me at lunch, telling me about our nation's history, because of my sister and my father. This is impossible. Crazy."

Thornton and Tomlinson were also incredulous.

"You were there?" Patrick repeated. "The night I was born?"

Tom nodded. "Yes. And the night at dinner when my sister Susan told us what happened at the abortion clinic, when she and Amy hurried out, the nurse literally chasing them to come back." The three men were silent again. "My parents won't believe this. Or my sister."

"Or mine."

"I gotta think about this." There was another silence. Tom stirred his meal with his fork, then picked up the remaining rib. "Professor, if you don't mind. let's talk some more about the principles that the Founders thought were most important."

Given their responsibilities, Balzor and Nepravel both attended the lunch meeting in Patricia Reynolds' office with Emily, Rob and the Phoenix Team on maximizing the Progressive message in the final run-up to the midterms, including the best ways to leverage the reports of strong support from the religious leaders' Faith and Unity conference the day before. As the meeting broke up, the two demons met just overhead.

Balzor nodded. "It's going well. Reminds me of Berlin in 1933—at the tipping point. Remember, it took only a month from the elections to Adolf ruling by decree for twelve years. These people are almost in complete control, which means we'll be—again. Only this time, here, in America. Incredible. And, best of all for you and me, they've got Richard Sullivan in jail."

Nepravel was silent. Balzor looked at him, and he spoke. "Yes, yes. But I don't like all the prayers—for so many of these people, and against us. And angels! Sometimes I can't get near Tom Sullivan, and prayers are hitting almost everyone he knows. I can't always maintain his voices, and I have no idea what those two believers are telling him right now. It's got to stop, or there may be surprises, which our Prince doesn't like. We've got to stop these people from praying."

Balzor thought. "I'll talk to Bespor about attacking and discouraging the people who're doing the prayers, not just the ones they're praying for. I agree—they've got to stop."

"Yes. Our brothers in 'flyover country', as they call it here, can do something to help us. We can't let these people in D.C. hear other voices. We're too close. "


When Erin MacNeil returned to her desk from lunch there was a voicemail on her office phone to call someone she didn't recognize: Robert Ludwig. He said he would like to talk with her briefly.

He sounded sincere, not like a scammer, so Erin decided to return the call on her cell phone.

"This is Robert Ludwig."

"Mr. Ludwig, this is Erin MacNeil. You called me earlier today."

"Yes. Hello, Erin. Thanks for returning my call. I'm actually a pastor—at The Church of the Good Shepherd." Erin frowned, but didn't hang up. "I've actually never made a call like this before, so please forgive me if I search for the right words...One of our members asked me to call you because of a, uh, medical procedure that you may be having soon, and this member wants you to know that if you will instead go through with the pregnancy, all your costs will be paid, and the baby will be immediately adopted into a good family here in D.C."

Erin stood and closed the door to her office. "What? You know my private business and you're calling to get me to stop? Who told you about it?"

Ludwig paused. "That's why I'm calling, and not the member. I'm acting as a confidential buffer. If you'll consider the offer, we'll expand the circle by a couple of people. If not, no one will ever know."

Erin thought for a moment, her anger rising. "Except you and how many other people at your church?—my private business. I think I know who told you, and this is *way* out of line."

"Please don't jump to conclusions. That's why I'm the one on the phone."

"Well, we'll free up time for you to go save some souls this afternoon. I'm not interested. And I may call an attorney. Have a nice day."

She hung up. But just as she did so, the voices fueling her anger wound down and stopped; the incoming prayers from so many groups across the country finally had their impact.

As she put her phone on the desk, she thought, *Why are these people so focused on one stupid fetus? Just leave me alone.*

Because she's My daughter, created in My image, and I have a wonderful plan for her life that you cannot even imagine.

Erin's head snapped up, as if she'd heard an audible voice next to her. *Where did that come from?*

Alexei Nobikov had just finished lunch with an old friend from his graduate school days at a restaurant near the White House, hoping to gain some insights on the president's intentions, when he received an innocent looking text message about a missing book at the train station near Track 2. He had to read it twice, then said goodbye to his friend a little more hurriedly than he would have liked, looked at his watch, and caught a taxi to Union Station.

In his twenty years of service he'd never actually received a message like this—only in training. His credentials for the White House press conference would be ready for pickup at 3pm, but first he had to be just outside Union Station at 2.

Tom was walking in deep thought after his lunch meeting.

*What if Susan and Dad hadn't intervened twenty years ago? Amy would have had the abortion, and Patrick wouldn't be here.*

Erin is pregnant with your child. Your responsibility.

*Come on! It's her choice. Her body. And the Law. No way.*

He was almost to the gate at the edge of the Restricted Zone when his phone vibrated. He stopped.

"Hi, Mom. How are you?"

"Can we talk?"

He turned to retrace his steps for a block. "Yes, but always assume that someone is listening. How are you?"

"Oh. Uh, I'm OK. But I haven't been able to find out anything about your father."

"You probably won't. That's by design, I'm afraid. But I can check to make sure he's OK. I'm sure he is. The intent is to pull people out of circulation, not to hurt them."

Janet Sullivan was silent for a moment. "You may have accomplished that, but I suspect that after seeing what happened to us yesterday, there are thousands more people who are upset and praying for God's intervention."

Tom started to smile, but stopped. "I think the president would say that they can pray all they want—just don't say or do anything, at least not for the next two weeks."

"And I guess he doesn't understand that praying *is* saying and doing something."

Tom started walking toward the gate again. "Hmm. OK, fair enough. I think you're right about that for him. But, listen, you won't believe who I had lunch with today."

"Who?"

"Patrick Tomlinson."

"Really? He's here?"

"Yes. It's a long story—he's a friend of a friend, but he's Gary Thornton's intern. He set up the lunch and came with him."

"What did you say?"

"I told him how I was there the night he was born. And that Susan is the reason he's with us."

Janet was silent for several moments. "That's amazing."

"Yes. I'll tell you more, and I hope to see him again. But now I gotta go. When I find out something about Dad I'll call you."

"Thank you. And be careful."

"I will." He hung up, but looked curiously at the phone before returning it to his pocket.

Nepravel caught up with Tom at that moment. He was relieved to see no angel and only a few incoming prayers that he could deal with, but was appalled to see a tiny but steady spiritual light inside him. He moved next to Tom as he boarded the shuttle and spent the trip restarting the voices of *Pride, Reason, Impossible, Angry, Myth, and Too Intelligent*. By the time they reached the White House, Nepravel was satisfied that Tom was thinking correctly and was safe again, at least for the afternoon.

The simple text message had sent Alexei to the main entrance at Union Station at 2 pm, where, when he shook hands with a man in a Boston Red Sox sweatshirt, he received the key to a locker in the station. Inside the locker he found a plain envelope addressed to him, and he was now seated alone in the station's large Waiting Room, reading the letter written in Russian on simple white stationery.

Alexei,

Given the extraordinary measures now being employed where you are, I thought it best to use this antiquated but secure method of communicating with you.

Our government has been approached at the highest level by an unorthodox but credible envoy claiming to be from the president, offering a major détente in our relationship after the upcoming elections, and also asking us for some specific, covert help.

If the offer is real, the result could be very beneficial to us. But we fear that it may be a trap, to get us to act so that we may then be "caught" in a very public way and blamed for any and all issues, as has happened before.

We are considering the request and, if we go ahead, we expect to employ your team in much of it, to give us deniability as well.

But our leadership wants to know whether the offer and request are real, or a trap. If it is real, it would signal a new and much more equal and beneficial world order. If it is a trap, we want to avoid it.

We are therefore focusing all of our human and electronic resources, including your team, to find evidence about the true intent of the offer.

You have reported contacts with one or more high level individuals who should know the true nature of this offer. You are authorized to use whatever means necessary to discern the true intent, and to report as quickly as possible.

We await your input. After reading this note, destroy it.

There was no typed name at the bottom of the paper—only a signature. But Alexei knew it well. He frowned, folded the paper, and put it in his coat pocket. He then stood and rubbed the right side of his face, signaling to those watching him in person or on camera that he had received and understood the message. Then he left for a taxi to the White House.

Richard Sullivan, his wrists handcuffed together in front of him, sat alone in the third row of seats on the prison bus as it prepared to leave D.C. proper and head into the Maryland countryside. A large envelope with the record of his violations accompanied him on the seat. The federal officer in charge announced to the fifteen male prisoners being transported that they would be going to a former military base which was now a detention center.

From the front of the bus he added, "Given the nature of the charges against you, you can expect to be there for at least the duration of the State of Emergency. I strongly recommend that you not make any trouble while you're with us. We have other, less pleasant facilities, and additional charges will carry much longer terms. There is no talking while in transit." He smiled and stepped down to the curb.

As the bus pulled out, Richard turned to look at his traveling companions. There was nothing particularly noteworthy about any of them. One middle-aged man three rows back with graying brown hair, held Richard's gaze and slowly shook his head.

Seated at his desk Tom was on the phone with Agent Prescott, who said, "We're capturing conversations in cars through those GoStar microphones everyone has—people never think about them—and we picked up a conversation between the wife of one of the WhiteStorm members and her brother, who's visiting from Germany. We've connected him to a Neo-Nazi group in Munich. Turns out most of the former Army-types we've run into through this were at one time stationed around Munich, so we're doubling down with our counterparts there, looking for the connection."

"Good work. And you've reminded me to keep my thoughts to myself while I'm driving."

"Yes, always a good idea. I'll call you when we have more."

As he put down the phone, Emily came to his door. "Are you ready?"

"Not really, but I know we have to do it." He pushed back and stood up.

"The news cycle's quick. If nothing else stirs it, your father will be old news by tomorrow."

"I hope so."

They walked over to the briefing room, where on most afternoons Emily answered questions from the press, and entered through a door behind and to the side of the podium. Tom took a seat in the aisle near the door, while Emily climbed two stairs to the small stage around the podium and began the briefing with a summary of the day's news from the White House's perspective. Tom looked out at the reporters in the chairs and saw Seth in the fourth row.

After about ten minutes and some general questions, Emily said, "We have with us this afternoon Tom Sullivan, the National Security Advisor, who issued a statement this morning about his father's remarks and detention for Hate Speech. He wants to further clarify and give you the opportunity to ask questions. Tom."

A moment later he was at the podium. "Thank you, Emily, for allowing me a few minutes to talk about this issue." He turned to the reporters. "As you can imagine, this has not been an easy twenty-four hours for our family. I love my father very much. It's largely because of him, and my incredible mother, the former Congresswoman, that I have the opportunity to serve our nation and our president today. But as much as I love my father, I also love our country, and right now she is under attack, and extraordinary measures are needed in her defense.

"As Americans, we abhor divisiveness and hate speech, and I regret that my father's better judgment, usually so good, did not guide him yesterday in his remarks to the bishop. I think he may be under stress from his work, or has allowed others to influence his abundant common sense.

"But as he and Mom taught me years ago, we make choices, and there are consequences." Tom smiled just a bit, then turned serious again. "Well, this is one of them.

"I'm sorry he violated the requirements in the Executive Orders which I helped write and which I help this great team implement every day. When someone violates those lawful orders, there are consequences. He is no exception. I hope he accepts the consequences and actually learns from them, because we all want only what is best for our nation. Now, if there are any questions, I'll be glad to answer them."

Several hands went up. He nodded to Seth, who said, "Seth Cohen, The Network. Do you know where your father is now?"

Tom nodded. "I do. But, again, he is being treated exactly like anyone else in his situation would be treated, so I cannot reveal that. Nor will he have any outside interaction until the end of the State of Emergency."

He called on a female member of the press in the front row. "Peg O'Callaghan, *New Day*. In the last thirty minutes your mother, the former Congresswoman, has released this picture of herself smiling with then-Congresswoman Patricia Reynolds several years ago, along with a statement calling on the vice president to immediately release her husband and what she calls 'all other prisoners of conscience'. Do you have a reaction to her statement?"

Tom was not prepared for her question and paused for a moment. *What is she doing?* He regrouped. "I had not seen that, nor have I talked to her about it."

The reporter handed it up to him, and he took it. The two women in the photo looked quite happy together.

"I, uh, feel the same way about her actions. We must pull together and make some small sacrifices today to defeat this enemy, so that in the long run we will remain the great country that we are. Unity right now is the key. I regret that she has issued this. The vice president, like everyone in this Administration, will follow the rules as we have implemented them. It's that simple and that important."

She pressed. "Will your mother be arrested, too?"

Tom shrugged. "As I said, I don't know the details yet. Hopefully she won't break any laws."

Hands went up again, and Tom had a vague sense that he recognized a man in the middle of the group, so nodded to him.

"Alexei Nobikov, *Cypriot Life*. If your mother and father were here now, what would you say to them?"

Tom nodded again in recognition. "I would say to bend a bit along with everyone else so that none of us breaks."

"And if I might," Alexei quickly added, "What do you think they would say to you?"

*Truths don't bend. They're truths.*

Tom stared at him for a moment as those words went through his head. "I, uh, wouldn't want to speculate on that. As I said, I don't think my father is himself right now, so I really don't know what he might say. I look forward to getting him back soon with his mind and emotions functioning well again."

Emily stepped up on the podium, smiling. "Thank you, Tom, for sharing your insights with us on your father's problems. We'd better let you get back to defending us, and we thank you for all that you and your team are doing."

Tom moved to the side. "Thank you, all. By unifying and working together, we'll defeat this enemy. Have a great day." He stepped down and left through the same door. Emily restarted the press conference.

Walking back to his office, Tom found it hard to concentrate on finishing his last tasks that afternoon. *I think I just sold out my parents, like I've read about children doing in Germany and the Soviet Union. But I'm not a child.*

As he passed the president's secretary, she said, "Oh, Tom, he asked you to stick your head in the door."

He did. "Mr. President?"

The Commander-in-Chief looked up from reading a paper at his desk. "Well done, Tom. I watched. You did a great job. Your father—and your mother—are now isolated oddities. You're a natural with the right words to defend our cause. Thank you."

"Thank you, sir. We have to win this. And we will." The president nodded, and Tom turned and walked the short distance to his office.

His assistant handed him a file of papers to review, but as he sat at his desk, he received a text.

ErinM: Did you have Robert Ludwig call me?

*What the hell is this?*

TomS: No. About what?

ErinM: Guess

TomS: We should talk.

ErinM: Maybe next year. My business is MY business.

He held his phone, thinking about what to write next, when his assistant came in and picked up the remote to the monitor that was always on The Network, but muted, in the bookcase between his office windows. "I think you'll want to see this."

On the sidewalk outside a federal court house in D.C., Janet Sullivan was being interviewed by an older male reporter.

"...way beyond anything to do with protecting us and are now arresting innocent people for simply answering questions in a civil way, terming it 'hate speech', whatever that is."

"Have you spoken with your son, Tom Sullivan, the National Security Advisor, and one of the architects of the Administration's State of Emergency, about your husband's arrest? He gave a press conference a little while ago in which he said that your husband has been under a lot of stress, and is maybe unduly influenced by others."

"No, we haven't really spoken. He's a grown man, and I could say the same things about him. Hopefully the family side of this will heal, but I do agree with him on one thing—this issue is bigger than any one family. That's why I'm speaking out today. This Administration has gone way too far. Our rights and protections are all being stripped away in the name of this emergency. Soon we'll be just like China, with the government in charge of our lives, and no turning back. This is no longer America, except in one major way—the ballot box. I urge every American who cares about our future to defeat every liberal progressive candidate in the upcoming midterm elections, before it's too late."

"Thank you, former Congresswoman Janet Sullivan." The reporter turned to face the camera. "And there you have the statement by the wife and mother of two men embroiled in a battle over protection vs. individual rights. We'll have..."

Tom took the remote. "Thank you." He turned it off. "I've got to get some work done. But let me know if there's anything new."

As she left, Tom looked at the blank screen.

*Our family, fighting on national television over words.*

Over Truth.

*Come on. Who knows what truth is? Just bend for a while. It's no big deal.*


"She got really angry," Robert Ludwig said from his office on the cell phone to Callie, who was walking to the park with Grace that afternoon. "I guess I blew it. I'm sorry."

"Maybe it's my fault for even bringing it up."

"No, no. We have to try to save every baby we can. You did the right thing."

"Well, I think then we should redouble our prayers against the forces that want to kill her baby, and for Erin, Tom and his parents. You never know how He is working."

"I agree. I'll put out the word."

Callie laughed. "And not today, but eventually you can add me to the prayer list. My journal let me go this afternoon for my 'anti-scientific bias' and my 'anti-LGBTQ bigotry.'"

"What?"

"Yes. Apparently it got out in the office that they were checking on me, and someone went to HR and told them I'm a member of a church that openly practices anti-gay bigotry."

"Callie, that's crazy. I'm so sorry."

"I guess it doesn't really matter for how many reasons you get fired. And in both cases I know I'm not guilty—I'm just sticking to God's truth."

"You're a strong woman and a great role model for others."

"And an unemployed single mother."

"We'll work on that next. Let me get our phone tree going on Tom's child, and then I'll call my contact at Truth Action Forum. They should grab you."

"Thank you."

Late that afternoon Tom was back at his desk after a departmental budget meeting. His assistant let him know that the vice president had returned to her office. He walked around and found her in the hall, leaving for another meeting with two assistants.

"Hi, Tom," Patricia Reynolds smiled. The two invisible demons walking with her group were angered to see streams of spiritual light from answered prayers touching Tom almost continuously—and the terrible noise from the believers' voices. The intensity caused them to turn away while the humans talked.

"Hi. Listen, I see you're headed out. I just wanted to let you know how sorry I am about these last two days with my parents."

She shook her head. "I was embarrassed for the bishop, but I think we're OK. I hear you did well at the press conference, and your mother will never change. And it *is* a free country." She smiled again. "So, thank you. We just have to redouble our work to shut down all types of violence and hate speech."

"Yes. We are. General Price has some leads in Europe, and I'll be catching up with him next."

"Good. We're all counting on you. Now, I have to chair a meeting."

As she and her team walked away, Tom turned toward his office; his cell phone vibrated.

He answered. "Mom, I thought we agreed not to talk. Especially after..."

She interrupted. "This is not about opinions. I just want you to know that the same police officer who arrested your father called, and they're coming to pick me up for questioning now."

"Why?"

"Shouldn't that be *my* question?"

He paused. "OK. When you finish, let me know."

"Or maybe you can find me on one of your reports in the morning."

"Mom, I..."

"They're here. I gotta go. I love you." The call ended.

As he walked past his assistant he asked her to hold his calls and closed the door to the office. Sitting again at his desk, he thought about what he should say to Erin.

*Did Callie tell Robert Ludwig about Erin? Were they harassing her? Is Erin upset?*

What about your baby? Your child will be killed in the morning. Are you upset?

*Damn! Stop!*

Then his mind circled back to his parents.

*Why won't they just leave it alone? Maybe even publicly back off? It's just for a while. That would be such a positive thing for real Christians to do—to show the world their tolerance and love.*

His phone vibrated again.

He picked it up. "Patrick, hello. Thank you again. Lunch was about the best thing that's happened all day."

"Oh, you're welcome. I know Professor Thornton really enjoyed talking with you. And the story of how your sister and father saved my life two times—before I was even born—is just incredible. Without them, I wouldn't be talking to you."

Chills ran down Tom's body. "I, uh, yes....I already told my mother about it."

"Great. I'd love to meet your parents. But, listen, the reason I'm calling is because Katherine's uncle called me a while ago and wanted your phone number, to talk with you, he said, about some issue with your parents. He said you'd understand. Does that make sense?"

"I guess so."

"Well, I wouldn't give him your number, so he suggested I call and give you his. If you'd like to talk, he hopes you'll call him. We're having dinner with him again tonight."

"Uh, OK. Thanks. Please give it to me." He picked up his pen and wrote it down.

"He sounded like he really hopes you'll call him. And will you see Ms. Sawyer again soon?"

"I, uh, I'm not sure. Maybe."

"When you do, please tell her how much Katherine appreciated her help with the report last week."

"Yeah, sure. I will. And thank you for handling Mr. Nobikov the way you did. I'll see about calling him."

"Sure. Thanks. Have a great day."

*Oh, I am.*

He hung up the call and sat alone in his office, with thoughts and feelings ricocheting through his mind. Out of habit he took out his L-Pad to try to think about organizing the next day, but was frustrated.

*What should I start with? "Abort my child, who might grow up to be like Patrick"? Or "Check whether my mother has also been arrested"? Or "Return to Foundational Principles to protect our nation"? I seem to be doing a great job with all of those.*

He put the L-Pad on his desk and looked out the window, unable to focus. A few minutes later he reached for his In Box to see what papers he could just read and route.

Early that evening, Nenav, one of the three human-haters assigned to the Northeast Women's Clinic, headed out on his usual rounds to check on the women who had abortions scheduled for the next morning, to ensure there were no issues which might interfere with their Thursday morning quota of killing at least twenty babies.

He checked in successfully with the first five mothers on the list and was approaching Erin MacNeil's apartment when from several blocks away he noticed an unusual spiritual light radiating from her fourth-floor apartment, along with almost continuous incoming answered prayers. The heat and intensity kept him outside, and as he watched, an angel showed up!

Nenav was repulsed; he moved back several blocks. The prayers continued to arrive, the spiritual voices of the believers almost deafening, and he finally decided to move on to the others on the list. But Balzor would hear about this.



An hour later, as the sun began to set, Tom made a last check with Tanya Prescott about developments with the WhiteStorm connection in Munich—there was nothing new—and packed up to head home. It was a nice evening, so he decided to walk, hoping it would help clear his head. He started east through the Restricted Zone, thinking about the nearly impossible coincidences of the last few days.

*And should I call Alexei Novikov? At least he asked reasonable questions.*

Nepravel arrived on the sidewalk behind Tom after ramping up voices in other White House staffers and, like the other demons, was appalled to see the light from so many prayers touching Tom and diminishing the voices he'd set only a few hours before. And as if the bright light and the voices from the believers praying for Tom were not bad enough, he turned around just in time to duck as two angels arrived to escort Tom.

*What the hell? This has got to stop. I need help.* And he left to find Balzor.

Tom, oblivious to the spiritual battle taking place around him, walked on and eventually left the Restricted Zone for the residential area where, several blocks further south and east, he lived. He thought of

Beau—he should pick up some dog food at Simpson's store. As he came out with a small bag, he looked down the street to where Callie lived, and, without really thinking about it, started walking in her direction.

In a couple of minutes he was standing outside the door to her ground floor apartment. He could see lights on behind the curtains, as well as upstairs at Kristen's. From somewhere a feeling of calm descended on him. He took out his phone and called her.

She answered. "Hello...Is this Tom?"

He smiled when he heard her voice. "Yes. How are you?"

"I, uh, I'm fine. We're fine. You?"

"I'm OK. But I've been better. Are you busy?"

"Grace just had her bath and is in her jammies for bed."

"May I see her and tell her goodnight?"

"What?"

"I'm outside your door, if you're decent."

A pause. "Oh, goodness. Uh, yes. Give me a minute."

They hung up. Tom started to check his email, then decided not to. He thought about Callie, Erin, Jenny, and the other women he'd known since coming to D.C. It suddenly seemed like a lot. A few minutes later the door opened. Callie was in gray slacks and a long sleeve, cream top. She smiled.

"Hi. Come in. What brings you to this part of the neighborhood?"

Grace came around the corner from the hall; he set down the bag and gave her a hug.

"Is that for me?" she asked, looking up at him.

He smiled. "No, not this time. Sorry. I, uh, needed some dog food for Beau, so walking home I stopped at Simpson's, and here I am. I think you've grown."

"She has. At her check-up last week the doctor said she's in the top 10% for height."

"Very good. Well, you come by it naturally."

"What?"

"Oh, that's just a saying. You take after your beautiful mother."

"Oh." Grace looked at Callie and smiled.

He knelt down and showed Grace his phone. "And look, here's Beau in the kitchen. I've got a camera there so I can watch him when I'm gone."

"He's not doing anything. Just lying there."

"He's resting to throw the ball with me when I get home."

Callie looked at the phone with Grace and then said, "OK, it's past your bedtime. Let's go say your prayers, and then I'm going to have a chat with Tom."

"Goodnight, Grace," Tom said, as they left. He looked around the living area, remembering his several previous times there, and wished that he'd thought to bring some wine.

He was still standing when Callie returned.

"Would you like a glass of wine, or a beer?"

"Whichever is easiest. I don't think I've ever arrived with dog food at a woman's home before."

"Certainly is different," she smiled. "I have some red open."

"That'd be great. Thanks."

"Sit down. I'll be right back."

A minute later she was on the sofa and he was sitting in the adjoining chair. "Cheers. Thank you again," he said.

"I'm glad to see you. It's been, what, three weeks since we last saw each other?"

"Since you left. Yes. But I did see you on your church's streaming service on Sunday. And I met today with Gary Thornton and Patrick Tomlinson, which you helped set up."

"How was that? And I understand your father was arrested for hate speech yesterday. Is that right?"

Tom looked down at his glass. After a moment he said, "Yes. My mother was taken in for questioning today, and I haven't heard from her. I feel terrible for both of them. But sometimes Dad just won't back down."

They looked at each other for several beats. Finally Callie said, "Like someone else comes by traits naturally? I hope your thought-police let them go. My latest news is that I was fired from my job at the journal today because I'm opposed to science, and because I'm a bigot—the church."

Another pause. He shook his head. "Sorry. Not good. Maybe things are getting a little extreme with all this."

"Unintended consequences?" She paused. "I wanted to ask you: I was praying last night, and it occurred to me. What if all these attacks are not actually orchestrated by a single group or nation? What if they're just the result of Evil working through a lot of angry, misguided people?"

He shook his head. "It just seems too coordinated. We're going to keep looking. But you asked about lunch. It was really good. Thornton is amazing. I can't refute his research. But you won't believe how I know your student's friend, Patrick."

Tom told Callie about the improbable coincidences of his sister Susan and Patrick's mother, the hospital ride to save Patrick in his mother's womb, Patrick's impassioned defense of Christian faith as the foundation for America, and Alexei Nobikov turning up at the press conference.

When he finished, he looked at her. "I mean, like, how can that all be?"

Callie took a sip and nodded slightly. She was quiet for a long moment. Finally, she spoke slowly. "Do you remember Natalie—and me—talking about how God spent a year getting our attention before we each finally heard Him?"

Tom nodded.

"And how He sent people to do that in our lives? Someone said our faith is not a religion, but a romance. That God tries to woo us to Him, like a suitor. Not to accept doctrines, but to have a relationship with His Son. That's why the symbol of marriage is so important in our faith. We are all to be the bride of Christ. He will love us eternally, *if* we accept Him. I think He's been setting you up for a long time—including Emily introducing us—but has only turned up the heat in these last few weeks and days."

"Turned up the heat?"

"Yes. Forcing you to make a decision."

"A decision? About what?"

"Showing you exactly what life is like without Him—by you rejecting His plans for you. Then asking you how that life's working out?"

Tom looked again at his glass. "If there really is a God, and that's what this is, then not so well, in some ways, I guess."

Callie leaned toward him. "That *is* what this is about. And you don't have to guess. It's clear and it's terrible, for all the reasons you mentioned, starting with the death of your child tomorrow morning and including all the people you've locked up for speaking the truth, which includes at least one of your own parents. What more do you need to see?"

He paused again, thinking. "I guess it's pretty bad."

"And, by the way," Callie continued, "before you get out your L-Pad and start making lists to fix things, with God added as an extra resource to do so, this isn't about doing things. It's personal, about you. God wants *you*. That's always the point with any of us. He wants you to give up, to ask for His forgiveness, accept His free gift of grace for eternity, and begin a relationship with his Son, as the much wiser older brother you never had. He wants *you,* not your To Do List. Once you're His, you may wind up doing some great things. But maybe not. That's up to Him. The first choice is up to you."

Tom continued to look at her. "Up to me?"

"Yes. You just recounted a list of 'coincidences' that some would call a miracle—He can do that when He's after you. But He can't decide. Only you can."

"Believe that God is real?"

"Yes, but much more. Look at what the Creator of everything and everyone has done and said through history. How He's radically transformed people you know, starting with your parents and me. How He's miraculously organized over several years all these people and events in your life. And then don't just believe, but give Him your whole life—even the L-Pad—and trust Him, talk with Him, listen to Him, love Him, as He loves you."

"That's a lot."

"In some ways. But in some ways it's very easy."

"And you think that's why all this has happened."

"Yes."

"And I don't like you just because you're smart, talented and beautiful?"

She smiled. "Don't change the subject."

"I didn't. But, OK, did you tell Robert Ludwig about Erin, and ask him to call her? Or did he do it on his own?"

Now she paused, took a sip, and responded. "I told him, and I asked him to call her. As a buffer, a go-between. There're several couples at the church who'd fight over the chance to adopt your child. I wanted her to know."

"But how does that make me look to her? She knows I had to tell you—or someone."

"I guess I'm sorry, but not really. Where a defenseless baby's life is about to be ended, does it matter too much about how people feel? What did you say happened between your sister and Patrick's mother at the clinic when she was about to abort him?"

He told her.

"So if your sister—Susan—hadn't acted, as well as your parents, Patrick would never have been born. What a loss to the world that would have been. And now your own child is about to be killed. We'll never know him or her. How does that make you feel?"

He stared at his glass for a long moment, then spoke. "I...actually, after meeting Patrick, it makes me feel really bad. And sad...but it's her choice."

"That's a lie. She asked you. And it's only a choice under the laws of some states. What do you think God's law says about killing an unborn child?"

"So we're back to God?"

"We usually—no, we always—are."

"Hmm. OK. What about us?"

She frowned. "Us?"

"Yes, can we get back together?"

She put her hand out as if holding something. "Tom, I'm part of the mess you've made of your life—and of many others' lives. I told you I don't want to be part of that. God is waiting for your answer to His obvious offer to you. You know it. That's first. Answer Him, and then I'll be glad to talk.

"And, listen. One last thing. This isn't some intellectual exercise to be considered again next year, like switching management consultants. He is the *Creator of the Universe*. He made us, and everything in the universe, and holds it all together at His pleasure. This is about your eternal future. The Creator Himself is obviously trying to get your attention *now*. But He may give up and move on. Will you seek God, or reject Him? There's no middle ground. It's one of those choices we talk about, but it's real, it's the most important one, and it's you. Forever. And then maybe impacting Erin, your baby, even the nation. Only God knows. But it starts with you."

They sat again in silence. He drained his glass. "OK. Understood...Thank you. I've got a lot to think about. It's been quite a day." He started to get up.

"Yes. Me, too. Gotta find a new job." She stood. "If Grace didn't have to go to school, I could sleep in. I'll be up at one, praying for Erin and your baby."

"What?"

"Yes, at our church, and in many other churches. For Erin, you, your baby, all this national mess—the attacks, the victims, the answers—believers all over the world, actually, are praying around the clock for you, and against the forces of evil."

Tom walked silently to the door and picked up the grocery bag for Beau. He opened the door and turned. "Thank you."

She walked over to him. "It's what God told us to do. Now, make your decision. Continue on your own, or give it all to Him. He may be done with trying to get your attention. If he abandons you, it'll be terrible. It's time for you to decide."

"I'll try." He smiled, turned and left.

"Thanks for keeping me company a second night," Alexei said, as he stood and welcomed Katherine and Patrick to the bar at Carpathia. He hugged his niece and shook Patrick's hand.

"We'll be glad to carry this burden every night with you at our favorite restaurant," Katherine said with a laugh, sitting down on one of the two open barstools.

"Yes, thank you. 'Poor college students dine regularly with a rich foreign news correspondent' is a great story, at least for us," Patrick added, motioning for the older man to take the other seat.

Alexei smiled. "I wouldn't say rich, but I can spring for dinner again. Your usuals?"

A few minutes later they had their drinks and had discussed the difference between the weather in D.C. and Cyprus that day.

Katherine asked, "How did the press conference go?"

Alexei described the process of entering the White House Press Room to them, and the conference, including his questions to Tom Sullivan, whom he'd first met at this bar, and whose parents he'd met the day before.

"That's amazing," she said.

"I got in touch with him this afternoon and gave him your number," Patrick added, "and he said he'd look into it. So I hope he calls you. And if you think that's wild, let me tell you what I learned at lunch today about Mr. Sullivan and my birth mother."

When Patrick finished, both Alexei and Katherine were silent.

Alexei shook his head. "The three of us know how God works, and that is clearly a God story."

The two young people nodded. "I wonder if Ms. Sawyer knows about this," Katherine mused. "Actually, she asked me to join a prayer group she's in, and we pray about a lot of people and issues. My regular time is for fifteen minutes, at midnight. I'll get an email of prayer requests just before I start."

"Prayer can change everything," Alexei said.

As the hostess walked up to show them to their table, Patrick just nodded.

As Tom walked home from Callie's, voices swirled within him—not those planted by the demons, which had been almost totally silenced by prayer and Callie's witness—but the words spoken to him by his mother, Patrick, Erin, the president, Gary Thornton, the vice president, and, finally, Callie. What a day.

He let himself in, walked Beau in the back, fed him, and then poured a glass of red wine and sat down at his table and took out his L-Pad and a pen.

He tried to ignore the voices and was about to start making his usual To Do List for the next day when he twice heard Callie's pointed question: "How's that working out for you?"

*OK. I'll make a list of what we've accomplished.* He started to write, and had four items on the Pad when he heard, No, "How's your life working out for you without God?" is what she asked.

He stopped. The voice had been almost audible. He actually looked around, then patted Beau at his feet. He slowly folded the page over, tore off another, and looked at the two new, blank pages. He labeled them "With God" and "No God".

For the next hour he thought about the two headings, and about all that he had heard or seen, including in his past, and filled in the two pages, crossing back and forth between them.

Under "With God" he wrote:

He made me and everything.

Holds the universe together with his rules. Has rules for behavior.

Wants the best for me.

Purpose to the universe and to life.

Physical laws and limits.

Not happy with me. I've hurt people.

Women. Selfish. The baby? Not what he says.

Wants to communicate with us—Bible, complexity of life, stars, cells. Prayer?

Communicates through others? Dad. Mom. Callie? Patrick? Ludwig. Thornton.

Seems to transform people. Parents. Natalie. Callie.

Purpose for me. What is it? How would I know?

Amy, Susan, Patrick, Thornton, Kristen, Callie. Did he organize all that?

Miracles might happen.

There could be Good and Evil. Angels and Demons. Satan.

If he made us, there must be Heaven. Spend eternity there?

If I reject him, will he let me in? Why?

How will I get to Heaven?

Jesus? Is the Bible real? Salvation a gift. Grace.

Is there Hell? He says so.

He judges. He loves.


Under "No God" he wrote:

I am random molecules and events. But molecules from where?

No purpose to life or for me.

No right or wrong. No Good or Evil. Does that seem correct?

No rules. Anything is OK.

My rules.

Life is all chance.

No logic, reason or truth.

Go for it. Relax. Have fun, then die.

No Heaven or Hell.

But what if God is real, and actually who He says He is, and I reject Him?


He looked back and forth between the two lists. An hour earlier he was still comfortable—as he had been for fifteen years—that God was only a myth, but as he looked at these two lists, he realized that the first seemed much more like the world he had experienced all his life. The second seemed unpleasant, unreal, and almost bizarre. Not the world he knew.

And he realized that without thinking he'd added editorials to what was supposed to be the second list of facts.

The second one triggered a memory, maybe from high school. Maybe from C.S. Lewis:

"Christianity, if false, is of no importance, and if true, of infinite importance. The only thing it cannot be is moderately important."

*If there's no God, then this all makes no difference anyway. But if there is God, and I ignore him, what will happen to me? To those around me?*

Then one of the few remaining voices Nepravel had planted made it through to his mind.

*But right now, does this matter? Don't I need to focus on protecting our nation? My responsibilities? People's lives are at risk. I agree with Callie that God questions are important, but I can think about all that later.*

He put down his pen and pushed back from the table. It was getting late. He and Emily had a meeting with Andrea's team early tomorrow to talk about the Trusted Citizen program.

He put on Beau's leash and took him for a short walk around the block, then cleaned up, locked up, and took a shower. As was his habit, he checked messages on his special Core Group phone, answered a few, and put it down on his bedside table. Ten minutes later he tried to start a new novel which Emily had recommended about life in the South under Jim Crow, but the thoughts from earlier kept popping up, particularly on Erin, and he couldn't really focus. He wasn't very tired, but he put the book down and turned out the light.

The two angels were still stationed outside his home, and the number of prayers intensified as midnight approached.


Prince Proklor and his senior leaders met in the relative calm of the Oval Office with, once again, an even larger force of regular demons surrounding the White House grounds, their sheer weight bending the lights, heat and sounds coming in from the ever-increasing prayers.

Together they were reviewing the timing for the attack right after the elections that would give the government its rationale to rule by decree for the foreseeable future.

# 21

*Of all the dispositions and habits which lead to political prosperity, religion
and morality are indispensable supports. In vain would that man claim
tribute to patriotism who should labor to subvert these great pillars of
human happiness - these firmest props of the duties of men and citizens. . . .
reason and experience both forbid us to expect that national morality can
prevail in exclusion of religious principles.*

George Washington

Thursday, October 29

Tom rolled over again and looked at the clock—1:20. He had not slept.
At 12:30 he'd switched on the light and written down some reminders,
including to call Alexei Nobikov. He found that writing notes usually
helped clear his mind, but not tonight. He was about to turn on the light
again and try to read, when he thought of Callie.

*She must be praying right now for Erin, the baby and me. The baby.*

He remembered the link Callie had sent him with pictures of
aborted fetuses, which he'd never pulled up. Reluctantly, and maybe
because of the hour and his inner turmoil, he found the text and clicked
on the link.

Thirty seconds later he closed the phone, shaking his head. *My son or
daughter. Our son or daughter. Terrible. Or like Patrick. What were Amy
and Susan doing twenty years ago, the night before he was to be aborted?*

She is your daughter. Made in God's image. She will touch many
hearts, as Patrick has, if she lives.

*Damn!* He rolled over. But the thoughts wouldn't stop. *What is this?*

For the first time in fifteen years the other voices inside Tom were
completely silenced by the prayers and the witness of believers, and Tom
was able to hear the Holy Spirit clearly.

Callie asked: How is your life working out, without God?

He reached for the light but stopped and propped on his elbows. *I'm
successful, and we've saved many lives with my ideas and my actions...So
I'm good...But many people I've been close to are dead, in jail, or will have
nothing to do with me. So that's also how my life's worked out. I guess I've*

479

*used some good people. Particularly some good women. And they question whether I have principles. Now this baby.*

He rolled to sit on the edge of the bed, still in the dark. *I really don't want to think about all that right now. I have an important job to do.*

*But what if I did my work with God's help?*

Make your decision.

*I've made a baby who is about to be killed. I've made laws to lock up people for their beliefs, including my father, whom I've disowned. I've treated people like stepping stones to success or to pleasure, not with respect and love.*

*What if I listened to Him? What if I let Him be in control, like Callie, Natalie, my parents, and so many others who seem to have something I don't?*

Will you save your daughter's life?

He pictured Grace, a beautiful little girl with a great Mom, and Patrick, a bright and dedicated researcher—both were about to be aborted until someone stepped in.

He pictured the nation in turmoil and recalled all the Founders' warnings to keep God's truth as the foundation for every law and action.

God's truth. God's guidance. God's help.

A chill. He lowered his head. Another chill. He sank to his knees.

*I hear you. I've messed up. The truth is that I've sinned against You. It's been all about me...Forgive me, and forgive me for running away. Forgive me for thinking only about me. The nation's in a mess, and I've caused some of it. Help me to listen to You. Strengthen my faith that You'll guide me and that You want only the best for me. I surrender.*

*Callie's right—don't let me see You as just some extra new resource. Please take over completely. Let me live again a new life because Jesus took all my sins, freeing me. Forgive me. Guide me. I give it all to You. I give it all to You.*

He stopped. There was silence. But he knew that something had happened.

You are my beloved son. You strayed, but no more. Welcome home. Abide in my grace. Rely on my strength. You are home again.

More silence, his head still bowed. But he felt a peace.

Several more moments of silence, sensing the closeness of his Maker. Unlike anything he'd felt in a long time. Peace.

*I can deal with all the other stuff later, but right now I have to try to save this baby. Our daughter. Is that what You want me to do?*

Yes.

*I don't want her to be killed...What should I do?*

On her knees in her living room, Callie finished her appointed hour of prayer at 2am and went to check on Grace, who was sleeping soundly, her bear snuggled in one arm.

Callie was exhausted and concerned about all the issues on their Prayer List, as well as the personal ones she'd added. She'd never engaged in physical combat, but she felt drained by the force of the words she'd used in this spiritual combat to push back against the forces of darkness and to ask for God's intervention in the nation. And in the life of one small baby only a few blocks away.

The demons in the Northeast Women's Health Clinic once again had to huddle in the main meeting area, and even then bolts of spiritual light, energy and sound were not always deflected, striking demons on the outer fringe. As a result there was a lot of pushing and arguing, and none of their usual business—comparing tactics or fine tuning their personal strategies—could be done. No one could remember for the last fifty years an onslaught of unrelenting prayer like they were now experiencing.

And in the middle of all that, Nenav, Nepravel and others complained bitterly to Balzor that it was like this during the whole day around many of their charges, preventing them from keeping the voices ramped up.

An hour later, still in his bed, Tom's mind was racing. *I think Erin said she'd be early at the Northeast Women's Clinic. But what time? When do they open?* He checked online. *Seven. Ugh. I guess they want the women in before there's too much traffic or notice, and it's still dark. I'll set my alarm for six and call her. I'll offer to pay for everything if she'll just agree to let our child live.*

Nenav went to check that Erin was up at 5:30, but he couldn't get within a block of her apartment due to the light and heat from all the incoming prayers. Frustrated and angry, there was nothing he could do, so he left for the next mother on his list.

Erin had to fast that morning, so she was sipping water while putting on her make-up when the phone buzzed next to her bed. Her friend Tracy was to pick her up in forty-five minutes, so she hoped there was no issue. She walked over, picked up the phone, and saw it was Tom. She declined the call and returned to her make-up table.

Standing by his worktable in jeans, his well-chosen words of logical reasoning ready to go, he watched as his call to Erin went to her voicemail. He refilled his coffee mug, hoping to clear his head from lack of sleep, and dialed her again. The same result.

Concerned, he sat down at the table and scratched Beau's head with his free hand. *If I go to her apartment I might miss her. I guess I'll have to go to the clinic. But I'm sure they have lots of security people and cameras. Not good. I can't afford to be seen—or arrested!*

He was about to jump up when a new thought came to him. *God, I'm going to try giving things to you. Please show me what to do, because I have no idea what to do. But I'll try to go where you lead.*

The Northeast Women's Health Center was located in a commercial area in a two-story, free-standing brick building, surrounded by an eight-foot wrought-iron fence, with a gate to the parking area in front.

Tom parked two blocks away a little before seven. The sun would not be up for forty minutes. He walked toward the clinic on the sidewalk wearing jeans and a gray hoodie, with dark glasses as his final measure to try to avoid detection.

He wasn't sure what to expect, but from a block away he could see people with placards on the sidewalk on both sides of the street. Those next to the fence were kept twenty feet from the gated entrance by sawhorses, with a police officer at each one. Across the street, a larger group was lined up, single file, facing the clinic, with police officers stationed every thirty feet. It looked to Tom like it was all well-organized.

At that moment Nenav invisibly came up the middle of the street, noting the usual line-up of abortion supporters on the near side of the street, and protestors, most radiating bright spiritual light, on the other side. He looked away from their light. Happily, between their own legion still in the clinic from passing the night, and the supporters, the depth of the spiritual darkness was too great for many of the incoming prayers to get through, but Nenav noticed their intensity increasing as seven o'clock approached.

Tom, hands in his hoodie pockets, walked up to a young African American man on the edge of the group across the street, their pro-life sentiments clearly shown by the placards that several carried, and nodded to him.

He nodded back. "Almost seven. The first mothers will be here soon."

Tom stood next to him, eyeing the scene, and wondering what he could do.

He didn't have to wait long. A car pulled up to the closed gate, and a policeman asked the driver to roll down her window. As they conversed, people on Tom's side started to yell "Don't kill your baby!" and "God loves you and your child!"

Those on the other side, next to the fence, began clapping and yelling words of encouragement.

The gate opened and the car drove in. A pair of women came out of the clinic in blue medical uniforms, each carrying a blanket. It was hard for Tom to see exactly, but he believed the driver, a woman, and another woman passenger exited the car. The staff placed the blankets over them, obscuring their identities even more, as two more cars came to the gate, and the crowds yelled louder.

*Is that Erin? How will I ever know? This is impossible.*

Meanwhile, in all his years at this position, Nenav had never seen so many incoming prayers. The light and the voices from the believers were hitting all around him, and on their human supporters, several of whom took a break from yelling and clapping.

Tom was distraught. He was right there, but how could he reach Erin? In desperation, he cupped his hands and yelled across the street, trying to save their baby, "Erin, it's Tom. Don't do this! Let's talk!"

The first pair and their staff escorts entered the clinic, and the two other cars were inside the parking area with their doors opening and staff members approaching. Tom yelled again.


Erin and Tracy got out of the second car. As soon as Erin stood, a middle-aged nurse greeted her with a smile, asked her name, and draped a light blanket over her. The clinic had sent Erin a link to videos of what the protests and counter-protests looked and sounded like, to prepare her, but in the near-darkness of the morning the loud din was almost surreal. She had to speak loudly to give the nurse her name.

They turned to walk to the front door. Halfway there, as Erin focused on the asphalt, there was suddenly a decrease in the intensity of the noise from both sides, and Erin unmistakably heard a single familiar voice. "Erin, it's Tom. Don't do this! Let's talk!"

She tried to stop and turn her head, but the nurse, with her hand on her elbow, and with encouragement from Nenav at her side, propelled Erin forward and into the building.

Once the first arrivals and their escorts were inside, Tom hung his head and felt like a total failure—an emotion he was not used to.

"Here come the last two for this hour," the young man said, as two more cars pulled up to the gate. "It's usually five about every two hours."

The earlier scene was repeated for these arrivals, and Tom again yelled Erin's name.

When they were inside, the young man said, "I gotta go to work. All we can do now is pray."

Tom nodded and moved aside as the young man departed down the sidewalk. He looked at his watch. 7:15. He would already be late for their meeting in the White House, and the sun was fast approaching, meaning that it would be much easier to identify everyone in these crowds. He couldn't miss the meeting, and he couldn't be identified here.

He turned away and followed the young man, feeling terrible. As he walked, he thumbed a text to Erin.

ErinM: If you get this, I was outside the clinic. Please don't have the abortion. Life is too important. Let's talk.

The nurse took Erin and Tracy to a consultation room furnished with comfortable chairs and colorful artwork.

She smiled. "Please, take a seat. Erin, here's a clipboard all filled in. Please check that the information is accurate, update anything that needs to be, and sign it. The doctor will be in to see you in a few minutes."

When she left and they had taken adjoining chairs, Erin looked at the clipboard but then said to Tracy, "I could have sworn I heard Tom yelling from that crowd as we came in."

"Like, the father?"

"Yes." She was silent as she tried to focus on the form. "He would never do something like that. But I thought I heard him call my name."

"There was a lot of noise. Must have been someone else."

"You're probably right."

Dexter Jenkins was filling in that morning for another WasteNot driver who was sick with the flu. The big green truck with arms in front for lifting and dumping large trash containers was difficult to maneuver in tight spaces, so he tried to finish his route in central D.C. as early as possible. But Dexter, unfamiliar with the route, was behind schedule, and he arrived at the kitchen equipment company's dumpster, two buildings down from the clinic, almost an hour late.

He had only handled this property once before. He knew it to be tight, but he also knew he had to make up time. So he maneuvered in to pick up the dumpster and then backed up and turned a little too quickly. As he did, an unexpected bright light obscured his side mirror, but he proceeded anyway.

As a result, the right rear corner of his truck backed into the ground level electric transformer next to the adjoining building, causing a loud mini-explosion and a huge display of sparks.


Erin completed the form and pulled out her phone. She couldn't believe the text from Tom. She turned to Tracy and was about to speak when there was a loud bang, and the lights went out.


Tom navigated the short drive home carefully. He had not slept at all and had a terrible headache. And he was livid that he was powerless to stop the killing of his daughter—he realized it was irrational, but somehow he knew the baby had been a girl. He pictured Grace. And now she was dead. *Where was God? Were those just warm and fuzzy wishful thoughts he'd had at 2am, or was that really God? How could God let this happen?*

As he mulled that over, the thought occurred to him that he was playing with fire to keep jumping into bed with young women at every occasion, even if they seemed to be willing. Another child, and maybe another abortion, would easily be the result. And even without a child, it was like starting a relationship with a tsunami instead of a gentle shower.

*Not a good morning,* he thought, as he unlocked his door and hurried upstairs to change.

Ten minutes later, as he came down to let Beau out in the backyard, his phone vibrated. Clayton.

"Hey," Tom said as he walked quickly to the kitchen.

"Andrea had our son at five this morning! Isn't that great?"

Tom stopped at the island and smiled. "Yes! Wonderful. How are they?"

"Great. They're both great. Here, I'll send you a photo of Clayton, Junior, and Mom."

Tom let Beau out and looked at the picture of a tired but smiling Andrea with their pink new baby in a swaddling blanket. "Congratulations, Dad."

As he looked at the picture and spoke those words, they were unexpectedly like a knife to his heart. *Damn. What have I done?*

"They should go home late today or tomorrow, and we hope you can come over this weekend to meet him."

"I, uh, yeah—sounds great."

"Good. I gotta go. Already a lot of parent stuff to do, and he just got here!"

"Sure. Tell Andrea hello and congratulations. I'm meeting with her team in a little while."

"OK. Have a great day."

Before leaving he went upstairs again to his medicine cabinet and took three aspirin. On the way out he paused by the whisky at the bar, but decided against it.


"They're waiting in the conference room," his assistant said, meeting him in the hall in the West Wing.

"OK, thanks. Sorry I'm late. Crazy morning. A coffee, please." He turned into his office. "I'll get my file." He put his computer bag by his desk, picked up a paper note and wrote, "Erin, Dad, Mom, Alexei," then grabbed the Trusted Citizen file.

As Tom stepped out into the hall again, Nepravel came around a corner, whispering his lies into the head of a new, young staffer on the VP's team. He was suddenly aware of spiritual heat near him, and he was appalled to see the Holy Spirit burning brightly inside Tom. The light bothered him and the heat was intense. Not as bright as that Sawyer woman, but a real flame.

"Damn!" He retreated to the other side of the White House. He had to think. "When did that happen? I warned them! Tom Sullivan," he spat. "Has he stopped quenching the Spirit? Damn. What now?"

In the conference room, Emily, seated at the head of the table, and two members of her team were engaged with the three members from Andrea's group at Homeland Security whom they'd met earlier. Tom took a seat at the other end where there was an unopened folder and apologized for his tardiness by saying, "Did you hear that Andrea had their little boy this morning? She and the baby are fine."

Everyone brightened. "That's great news," Emily said, looking at him a second time, a brief note of worry on her face. "The, uh, DHS Team has made a lot of progress. In the folder are the parameters they're suggesting for achieving three ascending levels in the program, and the benefits at each level. Of course, the whole thing is voluntary, and no one has to do it, but it should really help you, Tom, on the security side to focus in on the bad actors."

"Hmm," Tom said, opening the folder. There were three pages labeled Silver, Gold and Platinum. On each one were the requirements to attain those Trusted Citizen levels, and the benefits that would then be enjoyed by a citizen attaining that level.

As Emily continued to describe the program, he glanced at the ascending requirements. Criminal record check. Social media check. Military service check. Public service check. Employer HR check. Email review. Check family members. Check others in social network. Number of years in the program.

"So what do you think, Tom?" he heard Emily say a little loudly, and realized that he hadn't been listening.

'I, hmm, think the requirements look very comprehensive. Can you give a quick summary on the potential benefits while I take a look?"

The most senior looking person on the DHS Team, a woman, said, "Yes, as you advance in levels you'll pick up things like automatically being added to the Trusted Traveler Program, extra points on your Credit Score, a discount on Medicare Supplemental insurance, and a bonus supplement on Social Security."

"So there will be a real incentive to participate."

"Yes," she said.

"And what will happen if you don't?"

"Nothing. It's completely voluntary."

"I see."

Emily said, "And this looks so good, we were talking before you came in about adding a Trusted Immigrant Program for those in the country on the path to citizenship."

"Legal immigrants?"

Emily frowned. "It won't matter. We don't want to discriminate, and for your purposes, I assume you'll want to know all you can about everyone here, legal or not."

"Well, yes, that's true."

They talked about the details for another twenty minutes, and then Emily concluded with, "So, thank you DHS team for this great first draft. We'll circulate it in a very tight, confidential circle and get back to you with any tweaks. Our goal, as you know, is to roll it out right after the elections."

When the meeting adjourned, Tom motioned to Emily to hang back.

When they were alone, before he could speak, she asked, "Are you OK? You look awful."

"Rough night. Erin had the abortion this morning."

"Oh. That can be tough."

He just nodded.

"Listen," Emily continued. "If she needs to talk with someone, I know some counselors who are really good in that situation. One I used myself is still a friend."

"Counselors? Why would you need a counselor if abortion is no big deal?"

"Well, it affects different women differently."

"And men?"

"I guess. I hadn't thought about it. Anyway, if she—or you—needs to talk with someone, I'll help."

Tom rose up on his toes, then settled back, and exhaled. "OK. Sure. Thank you."

His father had been processed into the Federal Detention Center—a repurposed former Army base surrounded by a double fence, topped with razor wire—and had spent the night in an open floor plan barracks with twenty-three other men, accommodated on twelve double-bunks, with the facilities at one end.

ᛏ They were awakened at seven and had walked as a group past several similar barracks to the Mess Hall, where they were eating breakfast at long, two-sided tables. They wore orange jumpsuits, and unarmed guards circulated among them.

From conversations in the twelve hours since arriving, it was clear to Richard that all of these men were being held for some violation of the State of Emergency, and mostly for Hate Speech. In his own barracks there appeared to be at least two imams, a rabbi, perhaps a Nation of Islam minister and—who knew?—maybe some White Supremacists. It occurred to Richard that this might be a volatile mix, and he hoped to discover some fellow "hateful" followers of Christ, such as himself.

The Daily Schedule posted on the bulletin board in the Mess Hall indicated that they had mandatory morning classes on Critical Race Theory and Controlling White Male Privileged Aggression.

Ninety minutes later Tom was at his desk, trying to review his notes for a follow-up briefing on the current broad range of threats from Iran and Korea, but he found it difficult to concentrate.

*What will I say to Callie about the baby? That I was there, but had to leave for a meeting? Will I ever tell my parents? And should I risk calling Alexei, given the other issues that might involve me?*

Another novel thought occurred to him. *I should pray about all of this.* He quietly did so, sitting at his desk. *Father, if You're there and You're real, please help me. I'm beyond being able to cope with all this. Please.*

Then he called Patrick Tomlinson and left a voicemail. "Hey, the overseas gentleman we've been talking about—can you arrange a repeat of our first dinner meeting together for Saturday night? I'll try to see if Callie can join us. Say, 7:30. Let me know. Thanks."

*OK. Now this.*

CallieS: Hope to have dinner with Patrick, Katherine and her uncle Saturday night, where we all met before. Can you join us? I'll come by at 7 and we can walk if it's nice. Let me know.

Late that morning Seth arrived at The Network and began putting the finishing touches on a story about the need to solve the Temporary Worker Program—encouraging the ideas of the Progressive Congress Members who were leading the initiative.

He had walked to work to give himself time to think about Natalie. She was clearly different now, and slipping away. He wasn't angry—she seemed very happy. And she tried to include him in her new life as a believer, but so far it was beyond him. They'd had no sex for quite a while, even though she remained loving. But he knew this could not continue, and he decided to try praying while he walked, as strange as that was to him, because Natalie said she did. He wondered whether God actually listened.

Now he was composing on his laptop with one eye on Rachel Shaw's office. When she arrived, he waited a few minutes, then went to her door.

"Hey. I'd like to run something by you."

She sat behind her desk and smiled. "Sure, come in."

While he spoke, he pulled out his phone. "As you know, Emily, Tom, another guy and I shared an apartment when we first came to D.C. But I've actually known Tom from our college days. So I've met his family several times. From those days his Mom has my phone number, and this morning she left me this message."

"Janet Sullivan, the Christian former Congresswoman?"

"Yes, and before that, a television producer. Here it is."

"Hi, Seth, it's Janet Sullivan. Hope you're well. I'm sure you know what's happened to my husband, so I've stayed in D.C. and plan to do as many in-depth interviews as I can about the absurdity of arresting Americans for what this government thinks is Hate Speech, maybe teaming with Gary Thornton. I thought I'd call you first—you can do the first interview, if you'd like. Just call me back and let me know. Hopefully we'll make some news."

Rachel was quiet for a moment, taking it in, while looking at Seth. "We can't do that. They'll rip the Administration and the people we're trying to get re-elected. No way."

Seth nodded. "I thought you'd say that, and I agree. I just wanted to check. She'll make news, I'm sure."

"But not our news."

He turned and left, putting the phone in his pocket. He felt a small touch of regret, but shook it off. *Gotta stay focused on the goal, which is not necessarily to report all the news.*

Tom got up from his desk to head for lunch downstairs when his phone vibrated. He looked, stopped, and closed his door.

"Erin. How are you?"

"I'm fine," she said, sounding matter-of-fact. "But the morning didn't go as planned. I didn't have the abortion."

"You didn't?"

"No, and not because I heard you or got your text, which I have to say was unexpected. There was some sort of accident and power failure at the clinic. After we sat with emergency lights and flashlights for an hour, they sent us home. I've rescheduled for Friday, the first slot they had after I get back from my Dallas trip."

"So you're still carrying the baby?"

"That would be the normal result of not having an abortion."

"Uh, sorry. I've been so worried about the baby, and, of course, you."

"Yeah. I heard you yell and couldn't believe it. Then your text. It's so unlike you. But this *is* my decision, and I'm going ahead. I don't want to have a baby."

"OK, OK. But can we talk?"

"Maybe some time. Not sure why we would. And right now I'm exhausted."

"Fine. Look, I'm really glad you're OK. I'll call you in a day or two."

"OK. You came to the clinic. I'll at least listen for a little while."

"Thank you."

She hung up, but Tom just stood there in the office, listening again in his mind to her message. *Our baby is still alive! I can't believe it...Oh, thank you, God.*

Later that afternoon Callie was sitting at her kitchen table, updating her resume on her laptop. The morning had been terrible—Erin's abortion weighed heavily on her. *What more could I have done?* she repeatedly asked herself, and the lack of sleep didn't help.

Finding herself at home on a weekday—the journal had given her an hour to clear out her personal belongings—and with Grace in school, she'd actually taken a nap.

She'd replied affirmatively to Tom's text about dinner—she thought the discussion would be interesting, and she wanted to support Katherine and Patrick.

*But what about Tom? Would he ever understand that there is only one truth, not many? Would he ever become a man who found his strength in God, rather than himself?*

Her phone vibrated.

"Tom? Are you still at work?"

"Headed home. Never slept last night. But I have great news. Erin didn't have the abortion."

"What?"

"I was there, on the sidewalk, but I failed. She called later—there was some kind of power outage. They couldn't do it."

Callie almost shouted. "Tom, that's great!" She stood up, smiling, the phone to her ear.

"Yes. But she's still going to have it. She's traveling next week on business, so she rescheduled for Friday."

"OK. A week to work and to pray."

"I told you—I failed. She heard me but went inside anyway."

"My grace is sufficient for you, for my power is made perfect in weakness."

"What?"

"It's what Paul wrote about when we finally come to the end of our own strength and abilities that we find out how much more He can do through us when we ask Him and let Him. We've got nine more days. Or, He does."

"And, listen. I made my choice at 2am this morning."

"Really?"

"Yes. You've been right. I chose God."

"You did?" The excitement was clear in her voice.

"Yes. I can't do all this on my own. And I've been a huge jerk for a long time. I prayed a lot. Then I was mad at God because I thought Erin had the abortion. God has a lot to teach me."

"Yes. All of us! Tom, that's two great bits of news at once. What else?"

He smiled. "Right now I'm too tired to think, but we obviously need to talk, and we can pick up again on Saturday night."

"Yes. I was tired, too. But now I'm fired up. I've got some people to call, give them the news, and get them back on their knees. Thank you!"

"Sure. See you."


At midnight in the Oval Office Prince Proklor was livid. General Bespor had just reported on how the expected abortion of the Sullivans' granddaughter had been thwarted—delayed—and Proklor was not pleased. The general did not report on the change in the baby's father, Tom, because Balzor, hearing the news from Nepravel, had decided not to report it yet. He wanted to see for himself, and to try to counter what had happened. Losing Tom at this critical moment would, he knew, be unacceptable to his superiors, and he didn't want to face them without a plan.

"You mean at our own safe house—the abortion mill where Balzor and the others spend the night—some angel was able to confuse a truck driver into shutting the place down? So Tom Sullivan is still potentially a father, not a killer?"

"They *will* kill the child, Prince Proklor. It is only a delay," Bespor said, cringing beneath the powerful prince's anger, his peers all gathered several steps behind him.

"The Sullivans and their friends have been thorns for twenty years. They must be silenced."

"Yes," Temno finally spoke up. "They will be. But the prayers have been terrible. More than we've seen since the first years we came here. Many who've been silent seem to be praying again, and they're aimed directly at us, on behalf of these people. Our street leaders can't get near their charges to maintain the voices. So some people are slipping away, hearing the truth again. And angels are showing up, like this morning."

Proklor was silent, contemplating. "Temno, Legat, take fifty of our best and fan out across the nation. Instruct our forces in every location to focus on stopping their people from praying. Whatever it takes, from *Busyness* to *Boredom* to *Irrelevancy*, our forces must silence these prayers for the next week. We have everything invested in the divided world that Bradshaw will deliver—meaning no more truth taught anywhere. He must win. *We* must win. Now, go, instruct our forces. It is to be their only focus. No more prayers from these people!"

# Friday, October 30

Exhausted by Thursday's events, Tom had gone to bed early and awoke at 5:30 without the alarm clock. Before he even rolled over, his mind shifted to his parents, then to Erin, Callie, the baby, the elections, WhiteStorm, the State of Emergency, Nobikov, Patrick, Thornton, Bradshaw, Emily—he was instantly engaged and almost overwhelmed. *Where to start?*

For the first morning in years, he thought: *With prayer. If Callie's right about strength and weakness, maybe I should try prayer. I haven't been feeling very strong.*

He slipped out of bed and knelt down, but he felt awkward. It had been a long time, and he'd said a lot of things about God and faith that made the sight of his hands folded in front of him hard to accept. But there they were, and again there were no voices to capture and amplify a rebuttal. It felt right. And as he began to pray, the growing spiritual flame inside him flickered even more strongly. His first prayer was for Erin and their baby. Then for his father.

Callie, too, was praying at that moment in her living room. Once she took Grace to school, she had no specific plans for the day. But, as she prayed, she realized what she had to do.

A little later that morning Callie dressed professionally in a classic blue suit and, using her journalist's bag to transport her laptop and several books, took a taxi to The Information Initiative on Massachusetts Avenue. There she found a comfortable chair inside the glass and chrome atrium from which she could see everyone coming and going through the institute's front entrance. As she glanced again at the picture of Erin MacNeil she'd printed from the institute's website, she prayed that Erin would be at work that day.

General Nathan Price was alone in his office at Fort Meade, about to head to a meeting with his senior team, when his Core Group phone vibrated.

"Hello Drew, how are you?"

"Fine, Nathan. How's the family?"

After a few moments of catching up, Drew Boswell said, "I thought I'd let you know that the guys over at CyTech mentioned to me they're looking forward to having you join the team when you retire next year. You'll bring a lot to help them, and they're excited."

Price smiled. "Thank you, Drew. I just want to finish here on an up note and help stop whoever's behind all these attacks."

"Yes. Anything new?'

"Not really. Your team's input has been crucial to allowing us to see all that we can, and to clamp down quickly, but still no real connections."

"OK. Listen, the president asked me to mention to you and to Jim at the FBI that with the election around the corner, he hopes you'll be careful not to accuse any foreign state of any shenanigans, unless you really have the goods. He wants these elections not only to be without incident, but to be seen by the American people to be without incident, as a real step forward."

"We agree, and we're on it. Jim and I coordinate all the time, and so far the preparation looks to be right by the book and clean as a whistle."

"Thanks, Nathan, have a great weekend."


Other than a single quick dash to the lobby restroom that morning, Callie had remained at her post. She was about to open one of the snacks she'd brought when she saw Erin come in the revolving door, her ID badge around her neck. As Erin started toward the front desk security check, Callie stood up, said another silent prayer, and walked towards her.

"Erin?" She smiled and moved closer.

Erin stopped. "Yes?"

"I know this seems a little bit crazy, but I'm Callie Sawyer, Tom's friend." She extended her hand.

Erin frowned and declined the handshake. "Good grief." She looked around. "How many of you are here, and what do you want?"

Callie dropped her hand. "Just me. No one knows I'm here. After what you went through yesterday, I just want to talk with you for twenty minutes, max. There's a coffee shop around the corner, as you certainly know, and I'd like to buy you a cup and tell you why you're so important to me." She prayed silently again.

Erin paused, looking at the slightly older, attractive woman. She *had* been through a lot, and Tom *had* come to the clinic at the crack of dawn.

Finally she said, "OK. Twenty minutes. But I've got a ton to do. I'm traveling early next week."

"Thank you," Callie smiled. "I promise I won't bore you."


Jacob Welch, the Speaker of the House, came out of his inner office and smiled at Janet Sullivan. "It's so great to see you." They embraced, and then he motioned her inside.

"Thank you for letting me come by," Janet said, as she walked into his office, followed by the Speaker and his female assistant, who closed the door behind them. "After all, I am the wife of a Hate Crime Detainee."

"Please, have a seat at our table by the window. This is Sandy, who's been with us for years. Yes. Terrible. I saw the replay. Any of us could have said the same."

They sat down.

"Richard and I want to extend our personal congratulations to you, the second African American Speaker—a man blessed with rare gifts of intelligence and leadership."

"You're very kind, Janet. I wish it had been under different circumstances—losing Becky like that was just terrible. And the way things look now, I may be the last conservative Speaker of any skin color for a long, long time."

"It seems impossible, Jacob. What's going on with the country?" Janet asked.

Welch was silent, looking out the window. "A lot. I'm worried."

"Will the election change anything?"

"We hope so, but we can't get our message out. We're slowed or stifled at every turn, either by the government censors, or by their Big Tech enforcers who we think dampen or cancel anything that starts to get traction, all in the name of 'National Security.'"

Janet shook her head. "Jacob, who would have believed this when we served together?"

"Or even just a few years ago? It's all happened so fast. I think the Covid lockdowns made the idea of restrictions on our freedoms seem normal, and now President Bradshaw has made them even feel preferable to some people—for protection. He obviously couldn't have planned the attack on Air Force One, but now, by constantly playing the National Security card or the White Supremacy card or the "I Am A Victim" card, his Progressives may win a majority in both chambers, even though our polls show most Americans also detest the loss of our freedoms. Though it's hard to tell which they think is worse. Bradshaw may capitalize on their fear. We may be only four days away from our government having, once and for all, *all* the power—and for a long time."

Janet paused. "Did you know our son, Tom, is in the thick of this? He's the acting, or maybe permanent, National Security Advisor."

"He's your son? I hadn't connected those dots."

"Yes. Do you think you could talk to him? He's a good person, and long ago he was a believer. But now he's all caught up in the drive to find the attackers. And he's apparently orchestrated a lot of it."

"I'd be glad to talk with him. But he may not want to be seen with me. Bradshaw's group is pretty tight, and I doubt I'm on their Most Welcome List."

"But you're the Speaker of the House."

"Exactly."

Callie and Erin took seats with their coffees at a table in the pre-lunch, nearly empty café around the corner from Erin's office.

Callie smiled. "I get it that this couldn't be more awkward for several reasons and on several levels, but I decided to put my own nervousness aside, after hearing what Tom did, to try to meet you."

Erin nodded and took a sip. "OK."

"As I've been sitting in your lobby this morning, praying and thinking about what to say to you, and not meaning in any way to offend or upset you, I've finally come to this. There are two people I want you to meet. Right now I only have their pictures." She opened her bag. "This is my daughter, Grace. And this is Patrick Tomlinson, a friend whom Tom actually knows. Both of them should have been aborted. Patrick's mother, like you, was actually in the abortion clinic. They're both remarkable people. Nothing else I could say could be as important as meeting them and seeing what they add to the world."


Nepravel was making his usual rounds at the White House that morning and trying to figure out where Tom Sullivan stood from listening to others, when he received an alert from another demon on Massachusetts Avenue. He couldn't believe what he heard, and hurried there. He arrived just in time to see Erin MacNeil, surrounded by bright, answered prayers, and Callie Sawyer, radiating God's Spirit from inside, enter the café together. The heat and the light were too much for him.

"Damn," he cursed, moving across the street, where he could not hear what was said. "How did that happen?"


Tom joined the President's Core Team along with the Phoenix Project leaders, spread out on sofas and chairs in the Oval Office to review the schedule of speaking events, media interviews and messaging that needed to be emphasized for the final run-up to the crucial midterm elections in four days.

Emily Schofield, in a chair next to the President and vice president, led off the discussion. "A lot always happens in the last few days before an election, and right now our polling shows a very undecided electorate. This stays in the room: Discounting both bases, swing voters in the middle don't like the attacks, but they also don't like the State of Emergency. Many are very keen to get the entitlements we're proposing. How that will all play out in these last ninety-six hours in about thirty races will decide our nation's agenda going forward. Right now, between us, it's a toss-up. We may even be behind a bit. But a lot can happen in four days.

"As we've discussed, the key emphasis in everything from here on is that our party represents the new world of Protection, Progress and Patriotism, whereas the other side wants the dangers of the old world filled with uncertainty, racism, hate speech, privilege and anarchy, which can no longer be tolerated. For the sake of our nation's future, we must win. So we've got to paint them as they really are—haters, bigots and racists on the wrong side of history and on the wrong side of tomorrow."

There were nods all around. "Exactly, Emily," the president added. "Well said."

"And let's hope there are no more attacks," the vice president said, glancing at Tom.

He had just been asking himself with a voice he hadn't heard for a long time if Emily's description was what his parents and other conservatives stood for, when he realized that the others were looking at him.

He shifted toward the V.P. "Yes. We have no indications of activity, like we did before WhiteStorm."

There was a moment of silence. "Tom, I've been thinking," the president said. "Who knows where we'd be today if it weren't for the State of Emergency which you originally suggested and have so well-orchestrated? Some on the other side are undermining our effectiveness by calling your ideas 'fascist' and 'un-American', and even encouraging our citizens not to abide by our lawful orders. The results could be disastrous for the nation. Can we issue an Executive Order today making it illegal to attack the State of Emergency, when it's so crucial to our protection?"

Tom paused. "Well, there is an election, and some people do think it's extreme."

"They can think all they want," the vice president inserted. "Just don't incite others to undermine its safeguards, which is a threat to the nation right now."

"Exactly," said President Bradshaw. "We didn't pick this timing. We're just trying to protect the nation. People—candidates—can focus on what they're *for*, but not try to undermine our defenses by attacking the government that's working so hard to defend them. That just makes no sense, and will only aid our enemies."

"OK," Tom said. "I'll ask my team to work on some wording."

Erin had not expected Callie's opening offer to meet her daughter and another young man, so the words she'd prepared as they walked to the café about her rights vs. a tiny fetus would have to wait. Instead, hoping to change the focus, she asked Callie about how she came to D.C., and where she worked.

The result was a natural opening for Callie to share her personal testimony with Erin, from her experiences making porn films, to Kristen's intervention, to God transforming her life, to Grace's birth, to moving to D.C., to losing her job the day before.

When Callie mentioned God, the voices planted inside Erin reacted with *Another Whacko,* and *Mistrust.* But she said, "You've had an interesting life, to say the least."

Callie smiled. "I guess so. All I know is, He's in charge, I'm not, and I'm His, so I look forward to every day."

"Hmm." Erin put down her cup and crossed her arms in her lap.

"And I want you to know, Erin, I'm ready to adopt your child as my own, to raise him or her as Grace's sibling. I'm also ready to be your Birth Coach, to get you through this in great shape. Yes, parts are painful. But most is wonderful. And there are also other couples at our church who will gladly adopt your child and pay for everything, if a currently single and unemployed Mom doesn't seem right to you. Or if you want to keep the child and experience the crazy ups and downs of motherhood, I'll introduce you to support groups that will help you with every step."

Erin paused, turned away for a moment, then looked again at Callie. "Thank you. But I'm not ready for any of that. I'm glad you've 'found Christ', like my parents, but that's not me. I don't want to go through all that for a fetus that I can just as easily get rid of." She stood.

"But it's..."

"No. Stop. It's not. I don't want to hear any more. I've got work to do. Thank you, but no. Please just leave me alone." She turned and left.


Late that morning Tanya Prescott knocked on Tom's open door. "You wanted to see me?"

Tom stood and smiled. "Yes. Thank you for coming. Please, have a seat." He joined her at the conference table, a file in his hand.

They talked about their mutual frustrations with the ongoing investigations, and then Tom pulled a paper from his file.

"Special Agent," he began.

She frowned.

"All right, Tanya. For a few days we've got to shift our focus. The president wants to be sure the election on Tuesday is completely without any question of credibility. He wants to be able to cite your agency's checks when it comes to the new Federal Election Integrity Commission reporting out the voting results from each state's or each county's Election Management System.

"So, I'm personally asking you to watch over the FBI's monitoring of all the communications back and forth between each EMS reporting site and the FEIC, starting from this weekend right through the final results. We know the bureau's assigned team will monitor any updates to the process before Tuesday, and then watch the reporting process carefully on Tuesday night until we're done, to ensure that everything is on the up and up. But I'll feel better about it if your team—the one that works closely with us—is also watching from the inside."

"I got it. I'm sure the assigned team will do a great job, but I'll also ride herd on it. If I or we see any irregularities, we'll report them. But let's hope not."

"Thank you, Tanya."


Richard Sullivan took his lunch tray and noticed a table for eight with one seat empty. He'd been praying for an opportunity since arriving at the Detention Center, and he decided that now was as good a time as any. None of the other seven men at the table looked like him. He walked over and asked if it was OK to join them. A large black man, picking up his fork said, "Sure, why not?"

So Richard sat down.

He introduced himself and began eating his lunch. A couple of men evidently knew each other and continued their subdued conversation. The others ate in silence, or commented on the food, or their plight.

After a couple of minutes, and after saying a silent prayer, Richard said, "They tell me I've been detained because I said there's a God who created us, and that you only get to Heaven by faith in His Son. That apparently makes others feel badly, like I hate them. I think just the opposite, but I'm wondering what you guys think, and why you're here?"


It was considered bad form in the White House to communicate using one of the rapidly expanding personal delivery services in D.C.—it was thought to undermine the transparency now expected under the State of Emergency for communication, even though the Core Group used their own special phone system to ensure privacy with each other—so Tom was surprised when, eating a sandwich at his desk, his assistant brought him a high-quality parchment envelope, sealed, with only his name and "The White House" written on the outside, and no return address. Tom thanked him and waited for him to leave, then opened it. It was from the Speaker of the House, inviting him to meet.


Alexei Nobikov called his wife Anna on Cyprus that afternoon and first told her about the extraordinary connection between Kate's boyfriend and "someone I met here in D.C." Like him, Anna was also amazed, and she reminded him that Kate's mother, his sister, had strongly considered an abortion as well—the sort of terrible 'birth control' left over from the common Soviet practice, but that he had talked to her and changed her mind. So both of these young people now dating each other were alive because someone spoke up.

Alexei thanked her for reminding him, then shared his general frustration with not being able to "find out what I need to know, and then, even if I'm successful, knowing what's best to do with that information," obliquely referencing the assignment from his real boss. "But I have another dinner tomorrow night where I hope to learn something, or at least open the right door."

She encouraged him to keep trying, and they finished, as they usually did, by praying together on the phone for guidance and protection.


Natalie had texted Seth that they should meet after work that Friday for a glass of wine and maybe dinner at an Italian restaurant they liked on Eighth Street, not far from Seth's row house. When she arrived, Seth was already sitting at a table outside, a gas-fired heater providing plenty of warmth against the late October chill. He stood up, smiled, gave her a kiss, and handed her a glass of Chianti.

"Thanks," she said, sitting down and putting her purse beside her.

"Long day?"

"Yes, but really interesting," she replied. "Callie, Kristen, two other women from Church of the Good Shepherd and I had lunch with Mariam and four Uyghur women from their mosque, in one of the

Muslim lady's homes. Tom's mother, Janet, was there, too. Kristen invited her. It was fascinating. And the food was delicious."

"I'll bet."

"Seth, we live in such a bubble. All these women have family members who've been killed, jailed, sterilized or just disappeared. By their own government." She shook her head and took a long sip of wine.

"Terrible."

"While we were there, I kept thinking what it might have been like to be in D.C. in 1940, sitting with Jewish women—our ancestors—in maybe even the same home, as they were telling Americans about what was happening in Europe. And no one listened or did anything."

"Yes. We need to do something. And we are. Rachel signed off today on doing a full coverage of the demonstration, and it should be one of the big issues we pivot to after the election. The Network is ready to go all in."

Natalie smiled. "Good. Really good. Thank you."

"I get it. I really get it. America for the most part at different times has failed both Blacks and Jews. Here's a chance for those of us alive today to make up in a small way for those terrible mistakes."

"Yes." She paused and took another sip. Then put down her glass. "And, look, why I really wanted to meet here today, I think you know. I'm a different person since the bombing. Not the woman who moved in with you. I love you very much. I want us to be together. But I was saved—physically and spiritually—for a price and for a purpose. And I can't ignore that. My Savior says He has forgiven and forgotten everything I did in the past, but now I'm responsible for the present, and living together outside marriage is not how we're supposed to be."

Seth nodded, but said nothing.

"So I have to move out. I've found a small furnished apartment not far from you, and I'll be moving there this weekend. I love you and want to keep 'dating'. I certainly don't want to hurt you. But we can't live together unless we're married. And I'm *not* putting pressure on you to marry me. I want to see what we're like together when the physical issue is off the table."

"I see."

"And, I'm sorry—one more thing." She smiled. "I want you to meet some of the guys our age at Church of the Good Shepherd. Callie has a couple in mind. And there's a retreat later in November for singles, with teaching. I *know* it's not your thing, but I really hope you'll consider it."

Seth looked away then returned her gaze. "You're right. It hasn't been my thing. But I've heard you talk about how God seemed to chase you for a year through different people, trying to get your attention. Maybe that's what's happening here, and I don't want to require a bomb blast to hear it." They both smiled. "So I'm not signing up for anything yet, but I'm willing to try it for a while, and we'll see where we wind up. I know I don't want to lose you."

She took his hand on the table. "Thank you. I couldn't ask for more."

When Tom arrived home after dark that evening he went through his usual routine, fed Beau, and, thirty minutes later, dressed in jeans and a jacket, headed out with Beau for a walk.

Unseen by Tom, Nepravel and Balzor arrived—the latter to see Tom's situation for himself. He was prepared to order Nepravel to suffer the pain of the heat and the light to restart the lying voices in the young man—voices hampered by all the recent prayers—including for the first time in years—Tom's own. But they were surprised to see, from two blocks away, the same cursed angel hovering behind Tom, protecting him from the work that had to be done. Balzor was livid and even more concerned for his own future if there were another Sullivan family disaster.

As Tom walked down the sidewalk he was joined by an older African American man who was similarly dressed.

Tom glanced his way but kept walking. "Mr. Speaker."

"Tom. Good to see you. Your mom says hello."

"Thanks. She and I are both glad this will soon be over."

"Will it? Listen, first. I have no phone or recorder with me. You?"

"The same. My phone's at home."

"Good. Then we can talk. And I meant what I said. You may think this is about to be over, but my older and more beaten-down bones tell me it's just beginning."

Tom paused for a moment for Beau to do his thing and looked at Speaker Welch. "Why would you say that? The election is Tuesday and the State of Emergency ends right after. Then we'll be back to normal, even though we're still looking for who's behind the attacks."

They started walking again and the Speaker said, "I know that must frustrate the hell out of you, and the whole team. I get it. Your mom mentioned how you feel responsible to bring the master-planners to justice. But what if there are no master-planners? At least no human ones? What if we're witnessing a whole lot of individual anger and hate, fanned for years by those who divide us into warring identity groups of supposed oppressors and the oppressed, and urged on by the media and those who gain power and money from exercising ever-more control over our lives? What if that's what's happening?"

Tom was silent.

Welch continued. "And now you've shredded the one protection we really have." Tom looked at him. "The Constitution. In the name of protection, you've destroyed the one, unique thing that actually *does* protect us."

"Mr. Speaker, with all due respect. We haven't destroyed the Constitution. We've only temporarily set aside parts of it for, as you say, our protection."

"Tom, there's no difference. You either abide by the Constitution, or you don't. Besides all the current injustices, like your father being in jail as we speak, what you've done, building on all the lockdowns during the Covid pandemic, will now make it easier for the next leader who needs to break the rules. And then the next. Pretty soon—maybe even next month—we'll start picking and choosing which parts of the Constitution are currently 'correct', and enforcing only those. It's coming."

They crossed a quiet street in silence. "Don't you think you're exaggerating?"

"Ask the generations of Black Americans before me, when the rights of the Constitution were selectively applied by a different but similarly determined group for their own gain, and Black people suffered. I'm only here today because of *equal* protection and *equal* enforcement—not equity protection! And the rights, given by God and protected by that Constitution, to Freedom of Speech, Assembly and Worship. You've messed with all of them."

"I..."

"The Founders had it right—since all people, even the best among us, will be corrupted by power, you can't give all the power to anyone, or to any group. They *will* be corrupted. They *will* abuse that power. As a believer who knows that we're all fallen, I know it simply has to be that way. It's inevitable. The Founders, mostly believers, knew it. That's why they set up checks and balances in a document that's hard to change. Radical action is supposed to only be possible with broad consensus, not an Executive Order. But you've just thrown it out. I shudder at what the consequences will be."

"So you think it's more important to protect the Constitution than to protect our people?"

The Speaker stopped in the middle of the block and looked at Tom. "Without the Constitution, you can't protect our people. One group at a time will become targets of those with power. Only enforcing the Constitution and its Rule of Law ultimately protects us all. Anything else is a quick passage to repression. You've gotten people used to the idea. It's coming."

Tom paused, not moving. "I guess I hadn't thought of it that way."

"I know. You're young. But God can give wisdom to anyone, of any age—and usually through other people. Listen to Him through the Founders, and through those who you love and trust. Listen carefully for His truth in what others are telling you. If you hear it, consider action. You have a huge responsibility."

"We have no idea what they talked about," Nepravel complained angrily to Balzor at the Abortion Clinic, as the latter prepared his report to Bespor. "Except it could not have been good for us. People are praying and talking to him, and that angel is here now several times a day. The truth may be starting to infect him! I won't be held responsible—I'm doing all I can. Can't our leaders stop all this praying?"

# 22

*When you become entitled to exercise the right of voting for public officers, let it be impressed on your mind that God commands you to choose for rulers, "just men who will rule in the fear of God." The preservation of [our] government depends on the faithful discharge of this Duty; if the citizens neglect their Duty and place unprincipled men in office, the government will soon be corrupted; laws will be made, not for the public good so much as for selfish or local purposes; corrupt or incompetent men will be appointed to execute the Laws; the public revenues will be squandered on unworthy men; and the rights of the citizen will be violated or disregarded. If [our] government fails to secure public prosperity and happiness, it must be because the citizens neglect the Divine Commands, and elect bad men to make and administer the Laws.*

Noah Webster

Saturday, October 31

After his walk with Speaker Welch, Tom had come home and looked again at the lists he'd made of his life with and without God. And then he took a big step and prayed that, as the Speaker said, he would hear and act only on God's truth.

He slept well for the first time in days and enjoyed the routine of going to the parkrun with the Schofields. Emily didn't run but helped at the finish line so she could spend most of the time on the phone dealing with election issues. She would be leaving that afternoon with the president on a barnstorming swing across the nation for Progressive candidates.

Tom almost beat his previous best time, and in the car he caught up with them about the plans for the demonstration supporting Uyghur Human Rights at the Chinese Embassy in two weeks. He was glad that Logan seemed to be genuinely interested, and he promised to be more involved if and when they nailed down any concrete leads from the WhiteStorm assault.

An hour later he drove out to the Hunts' home to meet Clayton, Jr. Tom couldn't believe that a living human being could be so tiny, alive, well and hungry. As Andrea cradled the baby in bed and Tom held the boy's small hand, he thought again about the probable fate of his own child.

"We've been thinking and praying," Clayton said, standing on the other side of the bed, "and we want to ask you if you'd be one of Clayton's godfathers. We've known you a long time, and we think you'll have a great influence on his life when he gets older and comes to know you. And if anything were to happen to us, we know you'd be sure to raise him in our faith. Whether you participate or not, we trust you with his upbringing."

Tom was taken aback. "Really? Me?"

Andrea smiled, "Yes, you. Actually, we think being a godfather might be good for both of you."

"Well, then, yes, of course. I'll be honored."

They chatted for another twenty minutes, then Clayton suggested that while Andrea fed their son, the two men could prepare some lunch in the kitchen from all the food that had materialized from their church members.

As they opened containers on the kitchen island, Clayton said, "You know this demonstration against the Chinese persecution of the Uyghurs has really gained momentum—in churches, mosques and synagogues. And in other cities. Ahmad thinks it could give new hope to the Uyghurs in their mosque. And did you know your mom has used some old ties to contact leaders at two mostly Chinese churches here? Wouldn't it be amazing if a large group of Chinese Americans join us? *That* should really speak to the Uyghurs and to other Muslim nations—and maybe even to the Chinese Communist Party."

"I had no idea about Mom, but it sounds like her. Just don't expect much coverage on the mainland."


Rachel Shaw had called Seth into The Network early that Saturday afternoon to help cover the upheaval caused in several places by the new Executive Order prohibiting direct criticism of the State of Emergency.

Seth stood with three others in her office. "We need to cover this big: Conservatives being openly unpatriotic and anti-American in their criticism of the clearly successful State of Emergency, which has protected us from much worse outcomes. Patriotic Americans should be supportive, not critical."

He started to say something about it being an election, but decided to remain silent.

That afternoon Tom was in jeans at his back kitchen table, with one eye on the arrests being made for violating the Emergency Order playing out on his TV. But his real focus was on the books by Gary Thornton, and on the notes he'd made earlier while watching the videos of the historian interacting with Robert Ludwig. He'd decided to go back through their material, trying to discern what he, Tom, considered might be God's truth as it related to all the issues they'd faced and decisions they'd made since the attacks began almost two months ago.

As he did so, the thought surfaced several times—*Is it really possible that there's no one group which has organized all this destruction and death? And if that could actually be true, what does it mean?*

Callie had related to Robert Ludwig and to Kristen how she had failed miserably in her meeting with Erin the day before, but knowing that she would see Tom that night, she waited to tell him in person.

When the doorbell rang she sent Grace to open the door. A few minutes later when she emerged from her bedroom, Tom and Grace were on the sofa, Grace still in her cat costume, reviewing the haul from her earlier Halloween walk-around. Tom looked up and smiled.

"Hi. You look great. And it looks like chocolate won't be an issue for a while."

"Thanks. We had a good time with a group of Grace's friends. The sitter's running late, but Kristen will be down in a minute, before she goes out, so we can go ahead."

"OK." Turning to Grace he said, "I met a new baby boy today—at the Hunts'—he was only about this big."

Grace looked surprised.

"Is everyone doing OK?" Callie asked.

"Yes. They seem very happy."

Ten minutes later they started out in light jackets for the Carpathia Restaurant on Eighth Street. It was a beautiful night, and the streets were full of parents and young Trick or Treaters.

Nepravel was again taking cover behind trees, trying to dodge the pain from the heat of the spiritual light radiating from the angel above Tom and Callie. He cursed. His only solace, as he remarked every Halloween, was that parents did such a great job of preparing their children to believe that the battle between Truth and Evil was just a game, a fairy-tale, with no reality. Who could do it better than parents, particularly believing ones, like even this damn Sawyer woman?

Tom said, "Thanks for coming. I know we're not 'together', but I thought it would be nice for Katherine and Patrick if you join us."

"Sure. I'm looking forward to seeing them again—and her uncle. Is your father still in jail?" Callie asked, as they headed down the sidewalk.

"Yes. Detention. I'm sure he's OK, but I'm staying out of it. We arrested a lot more people today for criticizing the State of Emergency. I didn't agree with that move, but four days before the election I decided to just let it go. Mom apparently called on Speaker Welch yesterday, and he and I spoke last night."

"Really? What about?"

"Protecting people by protecting the Constitution."

She smiled. "Sounds right to me...Listen, I want to hear more, but I need to let you know that I bombed out with Erin yesterday."

"You spoke with her?"

"Yes. I met her at her office. I offered to introduce her to Grace and to Patrick, for obvious reasons. And to adopt her child—your child. And to help her through her pregnancy. But she said she doesn't want to hear about it, and left."

"Wait. You offered to adopt our baby? So that child would be Grace's brother or sister?"

She looked over at him as they walked. "Yes. I should do it for any child, but particularly for one with such great biological parents. Don't you agree?"

He kept walking but said, "I gotta think about that. You would adopt my child. That would be something."

"And, trust me, there are many more qualified couples at our church who would jump at the chance. That's not an issue."

They continued, catching up on each other's news. "I think I had a good interview with the Truth Action Forum leaders that Pastor Ludwig put me in touch with. They're definitely not crazy-woke, like so many places now, and they're already interested in the Uyghur Rights demonstration we're planning, so maybe there's a job in my future."

"I heard details today from Emily, Logan and the Hunts. Sounds good. I know the Forum. I think they're good, but if you start working there, we'll have to have an understanding like I do with Seth on private vs public information. They like to dig. Anyway, I also made the two lists you mentioned when we talked last week."

They waited at a red light. "Really? What did they tell you?

"It seems hard to believe, but the world I actually see around me, and the one that makes the most sense to me, is the one with God."

She smiled and nodded.

He continued. "Those two lists, your story, and coming to the end of my own mixed ideas on all this mess—plus seeing my father and so many others arrested for just speaking—are what made me realize that, like you said, God has been trying to get my attention. Quite a few people have paid a high price for my stubbornness."

"When He finally got through to me years ago in California, I felt exactly the same."

They took several steps in silence.

"But now I don't know what to do—about Erin or the State of Emergency." Before she could speak, he added, "The Emergency should end in ten days. It should. But the Speaker's afraid we're just at the beginning." He shook his head. "I hope not. To think that I may have helped cause us to lose our freedoms. Surely the president will honor and abide by the Constitution. But then there's the baby. What's my responsibility in both these situations?"

As they neared the commercial district she said, "You're right. There's a lot. And you're right in the middle of it. But He must have put you here for a reason. And now, most importantly, instead of relying on yourself all the time, you can pray and listen for His voice of truth speaking through those whose wisdom you trust."

"It's such a mess, Callie. And most of it's my fault."

She took his hand and held it tightly. "But you're here for a reason. So listen."


Emily was sitting with the president and First Lady in his office in the single remaining aircraft fitted out to serve as Air Force One, as they made the short trip between two rallies in the Midwest early that evening.

He looked up from the binder in his lap. "This presentation is excellent, Emily. Some of your best work. It'll be great to roll out our own new senior team and our full Progressive program right after the election, knowing we'll be able to implement changes in January that our predecessors could only have dreamt about. Here, Margaret, take a look."

"Thank you. But our latest polls aren't encouraging. Some voters apparently think we're going too far, both with our programs and with the State of Emergency."

Bradshaw smiled. "Too far? Emily, we both know we haven't gone far enough. People need what we're bringing. And we're about to break through. It will be a great day for America." He paused and smiled. "I predict we're going to win a majority in the House and at least sixty seats in the Senate."

Emily shook her head. "That would be amazing. And great."

He nodded. "Yes. Trust me. We're going to do this, and then set America on a new path of peace and prosperity."

Tom and Callie arrived at the restaurant, and the angel took up station over the entrance. Alexei, Katherine and Patrick were already seated at the back of the dining room, with Alexei and his niece on a bench against the wall, and Patrick in a chair. There was an open bottle of wine on the table. Everyone smiled and greeted. Tom sat in a chair across from Alexei, and Callie took the empty bench seat next to Katherine, across from Patrick.

"I'm so glad you could join us," Alexei said, reaching to pour glasses of wine.

"Thank you for inviting us," Tom replied, nodding to Katherine as he spoke.

The bread arrived, and there followed a general catch-up on the two students' studies, Callie's unexpected job search, Alexei's travels and articles, and Tom's expanded focus on the integrity of the upcoming elections.

After the waitress took their orders and refreshed their wine glasses, Alexei put both hands on the table and said to Tom, "Again, thank you for coming, and for bringing Callie." He nodded to her. "She has so helped Katherine—our family will be forever grateful. And I understand that Kate is now praying with Callie, which is wonderful."

Tom looked at the two women and nodded. "I didn't know. Good."

"And I know you are very, very busy. But I wanted to have this dinner because I called my wife, Anna, and told her how extraordinary it is that we met here before, then I happened to attend the conference where your father had the issue with the bishop, and then I got a pass to ask you questions at your White House press conference.

"That same night I heard from Patrick how you actually knew his birth mother and were present at his birth. When I told Anna that Patrick was almost aborted, she reminded me that I had talked my sister out of aborting Katherine, and she said I must take you to dinner and celebrate how God has used and connected us."

Tom studied his glass for a moment. "It *is* extraordinary how this happened, particularly meeting Patrick again, and connecting with the two of you—and to an historian. Sort of crazy." Everyone was silent. "If you don't mind me asking, what did you say to your sister?"

Alexei sat back. "Well, when I returned to Moscow from studying computer science in the U.S. I was a new believer, but my younger sister wasn't. Twenty years ago in Russia housing was still tough, and she moved in with an older guy whom I didn't particularly like. They broke up, she moved back to my parents' apartment, and a month later she realized she was pregnant. The standard thing, left over from the Soviets, was to get an abortion. She mentioned it to me one day when I was over there. I hadn't been faced with this issue before, but I believed then and now that abortion is murder. So I argued with her for a couple of days."

"I never knew that, Uncle Alexei," Katherine said, next to him.

"There was never any reason. Two years later your mother became a believer and, as you know, married a wonderful man from your church who has been your very supportive father ever since. It's amazing how the Holy Spirit can speak so clearly to us when he lives in us, and other voices aren't drowning him out. But in those days my sister was very much a humanist. So I simply bombarded her with arguments about her own experiences as a human being, and did she want to deprive this new person of all those future experiences for just her own convenience? Looking back, I was terrible, but I think it really didn't matter what I said—like the parable of the woman badgering the judge for justice—it was my almost obnoxious perseverance—and God—that persuaded her to hold off the abortion. And a little while later she decided to have you." He smiled and raised his glass. "For which we're all very glad!"

"Or the five of us wouldn't be here tonight," Callie said, taking a sip.

"Thin threads," Patrick added. "That's what Professor Thornton calls them."

"Yes, thin threads," Tom said. After a pause, he asked, "When did you move to Cyprus?"

"Almost ten years ago. As you know, there has always been a strong connection between Russia and the Greek half of Cyprus because of our shared orthodox faith—and the climate is a bit nicer! When our economy opened up, I had a chance to interest some investors, and they agreed to fund our internet service provider start-up. We began in the Russian enclaves, but now we service the whole island. And, given the current situation, there are a lot of new Russian-speakers arriving every day."

"I bet you're a front for one of those Russian hacking operations we read about!" Patrick quipped.

Alexei smiled. "Not hardly. Not on Cyprus."

"Just kidding."

"I know."

Their meals arrived and while they ate, the conversation turned back to the three younger members of the party and their upcoming events.

As they were finishing, Alexei asked, "And what about the elections, Tom? I assume you're pulling for the president's party and agenda."

Tom waited a moment to answer. "Yes, I'm part of his team, and I agree with most of those ideas."

"But not all?"

"Not all. But right now I'm mostly focused on defending us against attacks and making sure the elections go without any issues. So I don't really think too much about the political agenda."

"I see. I must say, continuing the thread theme, that you've threaded the needle pretty well, trying to run an election in the midst of a State of Emergency."

Tom looked at Callie. "Thanks. Some would disagree with you. *I* might disagree with you. But we are where we are, and we're almost done." He could see Callie nodding, while focused on her glass.

They ordered two desserts with five forks.

"Excuse me for a minute," Tom said, rising.

"I think I'll join you," Alexei said, putting his napkin on the table.

The two men walked over to a hallway that led to the restrooms. Before getting to the door, Alexei said, "Can I have a quick word with you?"

Tom turned around. "Sure."

"I know this is awkward. You don't really know me, of course, and what I'm about to say is propelled as much by my faith as by my role, which you may or may not believe. I can only say about Patrick's comment, 'Out of the mouths of babes.' I do, in fact, work for the Russian government on occasion. I'm not a spy, trying to get secret information from you or anyone else here. Our team mostly watches and reports on what we see. And then we try to stir up different factions on social media. I'm not particularly proud of it, especially given our government's recent actions, but there it is. I'll quit as soon as I can find an alternative. I'm no enemy of America—in fact, just the opposite.

"But recently our government has been approached by a private individual purporting to be a messenger from your boss, offering what appears to be a new, more friendly approach to our relationship, and also to a large nation in Asia, after next week's election, that might move the world toward real peace. At least that's the theory—I personally am not sure I would agree.

"Anyway, I've been asked by our government to ask you to corroborate whether this individual and his proposal are legitimate, or just his own fanciful idea. And not a trap. A lot might change as a result of what he has proposed, and since our government has been blamed in the past for a long list of election ills, they want to be sure of its validity before moving ahead."

Tom's training kicked in. During his first years working at the White House he'd been approached by people at bars and parties, including several attractive women, who, he suspected, wanted either to compromise him or to learn classified information, and who made vague offers that money could be involved. He was instructed to let each conversation play out, without ending it, then report the details to the FBI, in case they could then use the opportunity to turn the contact to their advantage.

But this felt very different, assuming that what Alexei said was true, and a voice told him that he might trust him. But the rules were the rules, so he decided to thread the needle once again, particularly because one never knew when a conversation was being recorded. He quickly looked up for a security camera, but saw none.

"Alexei, I, uh, don't really work on foreign policy."

"In this case, with what has been proposed, I think you would definitely know about it."

A woman exited from the washroom and while she walked by, Tom took out the small L-pad he kept with him.

He wrote on the pad "Never heard of it." As he showed it to Alexei, Tom said, "Well, it's out of my area. Sorry."

Alexei looked at Tom and then at the pad, and nodded. They turned and continued their trip without speaking again.

Back at their table the dinner continued for another thirty minutes.

"When are you heading home?" Callie asked. "Hearing you talk, I really want to visit Cyprus."

Alexei smiled. "Of course. Come any time. And I suspect," glancing at Tom, "I'll be here for at least another week, looking for stories about the election."

It was a bit cooler as they walked back to Callie's, but the spiritual heat again kept Nepravel from getting close.

"Alexei seems like a nice guy," Callie volunteered, after they crossed into the residential area, "and I didn't expect him to be such a strong believer."

"I agree. But someone keeps telling me about the power of God to change people."

She smiled. "You're right. Good answer. Any ideas on how to persuade Erin, now that I pushed her away?"

"I thought what Alexei said, at least for his sister, was interesting—persistence."

"Yes, certainly in prayer, which our church and others are continuing."

"Hopefully that prayer will lead to some kind of action. Whenever I now think about the lives of Patrick, Grace, Katherine, and even Clayton, Jr., I don't want to lose this baby. He or she is too important." They walked in silence for half a block. "And I just want things back to normal. With the country, and, frankly, with us."

"What's normal with us? Or with you and Erin?"

He stopped and looked at her. "I guess I'm not sure. I really enjoy being with you and talking with you...But I've been thinking more about Erin and my responsibility for this baby."

"Hmm."

"I think the nation is almost there. The elections are on Tuesday and the State of Emergency ends a week later. Hopefully the new National Election Integrity Commission will ensure that the elections go off without a hitch. And I hope nothing triggers another extension of the Emergency, so we can release everyone and stop all these extra measures."

She quickly said, "*Nothing* should justify another extension—I hope you agree with that." He was silent. "And my Unintended Consequences Antennae predicts that whatever the next 'normal' is, it will be much more restrictive for all of us than 'normal' was in August. Look what Covid did in some states. Now you've given a new rationale for the federal government to restrict us even more, and all the time."

"That's sort of what Speaker Welch said."

They started walking again. "Did he also suggest that you listen when you hear the same thing from different believers you trust?"

"Yes." Another pause. "We'll see. Hopefully it will be the *old* normal. Whatever it is, we're almost done, and I'll be very glad."

They chatted more about Grace, Kristen, and Callie's upcoming job hunt. At her door, she said, "Would you like to come in?"

"Yes, of course. But it's been a long day. And I want to think—I'm going to try praying—more about Erin. Let's plan on something right after Tuesday's election. I think I'll be pretty busy 'til then. Or would that violate your 'not being together' rule?"

She thought for a moment and smiled. "I guess that would be OK. Yes. And, in fact, why don't you come to church with me in the morning?"

"Uh, hmm. Maybe I will. Save me a seat, and if I'm there, I'm there."

She nodded. "To hear God's truth it's best to go where God truth's spoken."

"Makes sense. Thanks for everything." He turned and walked toward his home.

Nepravel was enraged that the damn angel went with him.

From the phone in his hotel's Business Center, Alexei made a local call that he knew would automatically be re-routed overseas. There was a beep, and he said, "My friend knows nothing about your question, and he would. Be very cautious."

The president and First Lady were sitting in armchairs in his Air Force One office, drinks in hand, as the plane sped back to D.C. and the staff worked on final plans for the next two days.

"You were really good today, dear," Margaret said, "at all four of the events. Your dedication and passion for the underdog still come through after all these years."

He smiled and took a sip of bourbon. "Thanks. I'll get Emily to quote you on The Network."

"No, really. You're still the best."

"We're so close." His Core Group phone vibrated, and he answered. "Drew, where are you and how are you?"

"Leaving Singapore now so I can be home to vote. And I'm fine."

"Good. Good. We've had a good day. What's up?"

"I just confirmed again that our friends in China are ready to go on the post-election order. And on the extra help we discussed, the head of our Juggle coding team over there, someone I've known for years, farmed out the work to a couple of groups, so no one has the whole picture. He's run tests with the finished product, and we're all set. The updates will be sent to our U.S. team today to load on Monday."

"Excellent."

"I haven't heard from the Russians. They may be gun-shy after past elections."

"That's OK. We only need one, right? And we'll remember who helped when we divide up the geography to finally give us peace—they may wish they'd participated."

"Yes. But Beijing is concerned about something that's pretty important to them."

"What's that?"

"There's apparently a big anti-Chinese, high tech demonstration planned in D.C. and five other cities over the Uyghurs, the week after the election. Looks like there may be videos purporting to show human rights violations. The Chinese say the videos and the allegations are false, and that this will be a terrible way to launch our new relationship. They say if we can't control our side any better, why should they agree?"

"I haven't heard anything about this."

"You've been busy."

"Yes, but someone should have told me. Tell 'em that we're on it, and we'll take care of it. We can't have a bunch of Turkish Muslims in China, for goodness sake, screwing up all that we have planned for world peace once you're Secretary of State."

"Glad to hear it, sir. I'll let them know."

"Good. Travel safely, Drew, and we'll see you back in D.C."

"Same to you, Mr. President."


"Abortions and divorces are holding at a high rate, my liege," Temno reported to Prince Proklor at their midnight Oval Office briefing with the other generals, as the barrage of incoming prayers and voices were absorbed by lesser demons packed around the West Wing. "But the prayers and the witnessing continue at a pace we haven't seen in decades. It's terrible. Believers are speaking up about their faith to their friends and families, telling them to 'save the nation's foundations' by voting against President Bradshaw's Progressives in Tuesday's elections. Awful. And angels—they suddenly seem to be everywhere, damn them, attracted by the prayers."

Proklor hissed, "You were to instruct our forces to stop the prayers with distracting voices across the nation."

"Yes. Yes, they've tried. But people who have never prayed before have suddenly started—all because of the witnessing. The light and the heat here and in many of the key election cities are just too intense. Our sector leaders can't get close to their charges to plant voices or even to understand what they're saying and hearing. Even someone as important as Tom Sullivan—we haven't been able to get near him for days, and Balzor is worried he may be slipping back into his faith."

"No!"

Temno backed away a step and almost whispered. "He may already be lost. Balzor reports the Truth may once again be burning inside him."

"Damn!" He paused. "Do you have *any* good news?"

"Yes, great prince. Our voices *have* been effective in deterring the believers from praying for the president himself. Thankfully, they've given up on him. So we have complete access to him and his team—except that young Sullivan—and all our plans through him appear to be on track."

"Good. Surround and concentrate on him. Ramp up our voices in him and everyone around him. Guide them all you can. In fact, if Sullivan's a risk, use Bradshaw to get rid of him. No distractions. Focus."

# Sunday, November 1

Early Sunday morning Tom let Beau out and poured a first cup of coffee, then sat in jeans and a T-shirt at his table, starting through his usual routine of checking overnight developments on his secure phone and laptop. But it occurred to him that he should try a different routine. So he put down his devices, closed his eyes, and prayed—prayed for forgiveness, wisdom and guidance, and then for each of the many people and issues on his list.

When he finished he felt some relief—his first steps of reliance on God's leadership lifted the weight of his own heavy responsibility a bit, and the absence of any terrible overnight violent acts or intelligence intercepts meant that he could focus on what was already on his plate. *Which is a lot. But I guess not a lot for God.*

And one of those issues was Alexei Nobikov. What was his message about? From the Russian government? He would report the incident tomorrow, but it seemed genuine, not like some kind of a probe or a trap. And Alexei was strangely normal—even a believer.

As he ate some yogurt with blueberries, he was also torn about whether to go to The Church of the Good Shepherd that morning. *Wait a couple of weeks until after the election, the State of Emergency has been lifted, and my parents are out of the news. It won't look good for me to be there, and the president won't like it.*

But today another inner voice said *I'm not going to break any law, I want to worship the God who has done so much for me, and many friends will be there doing the same.*

In the end, he decided to go. *Compared to what others face, how brave do I have to be to attend church?*

Two hours later as he neared the church on the sidewalk, he saw Seth approaching from the opposite direction. He smiled, and as others entered the sanctuary, they shook hands.

"Hey. Where's Natalie?"

Seth shrugged. "She moved out yesterday. But not too far. I helped her. But we're OK."

"What?"

"Yeah. Not what I planned or wanted, but since she became a believer, she wants us to see what our relationship might be like if we're not living together. No sex. Just talk and doing stuff together." He laughed. "Who would have thought? But so far I'm actually enjoying it. She has a lot of great ideas. And here I am. Sunday morning at her church."

Tom looked at his old friend. "Wow. Callie and Natalie are something, aren't they?"

"Natalie would say it's God trying to get my attention—and I guess she learned that from Callie. So I guess He has."

Tom nodded. "Me, too—I'll tell you later. But, wait. Hold on a minute. I've been meaning to ask you all week—where are all the stories on The Network coming from about tying the WhiteStorm connections to the other attacks, like the DEA bombing? It's almost like your information is coming from the FBI, but the truth is, between us, there aren't any proven connections, and the lead agent I work with in the White House tells me her team isn't talking to anyone."

Seth shrugged. "You know, Rachel and others have their sources. I don't know—honestly. Maybe others at the Bureau—higher ups—are talking. But I know Rachel is focused on it. And, truth be told, on anything else that will put your boss in a good light before Tuesday."

"But it's just not true."

"A minor point with some of us." They went inside and found Calllie, Natalie, Kristen, Patrick, Katherine, Alexei and Gary Thornton standing and talking together in the aisle around the first few rows at the front of the church. Everyone shook hands and greeted each other.

"You came!" Callie said, kissing him quickly on the cheek.

"The decision would have been a lot easier if I'd known a kiss was included."

She moved close and said in a low voice, "Your mom is sitting near the back with the Speaker and his wife." She nodded her head to the right. "They came early, after taping a Sunday Talk Show interview.

When I told her you might come, she moved the three of them away, so as not to embarrass you or create a photo op."

He glanced up and saw them. "Really?" His mother slightly nodded to him.

Just then the organ started playing, and they all took their seats.


Robert Ludwig led the service that morning. As always, there were traditional hymns and relevant scripture readings. With the elections only forty-eight hours away, one of the readings was 1 Timothy 2:1-4, praying for leaders, and for truth. The other was Isaiah 33:22, "For the Lord is our judge, the Lord is our lawgiver, the Lord is our king; it is he who will save us."

As he began his message, Ludwig noted that he was continuing their series on Spiritual Warfare, this week emphasizing the Sword of the Spirit, the Word of God, which among all the equipment Paul mentions in his famous passage in Ephesians 6, is the only offensive weapon, along with prayer.

"Today I hope to use that sword of truth to cut through the lies that are so easy to hear all around us, and I want to credit my friend, Gary Thornton, sitting here in the fourth row, for providing me with some of the details I'm going to use."

Ludwig went on to give a powerful message on how Isaiah 33 was the Biblical foundation for our nation's three branches of government, specifying that the Lord was judge, lawgiver and executive. He cited quotes from the Founders acknowledging their reliance on this foundation, pointing out how important it was that each branch should be an equal and viable check on the power of the others.

And then he explained how the Constitution, the first of its kind in the world, was consciously written to enshrine those principles in a system which would be difficult to change on a whim, meaning that change could come, but organically, and with consensus across a broad spectrum. Not at the stroke of an executive's pen.

He repeated words that Tom had heard recently from the Speaker, that our only real protection, besides God, was not the police, the military, or technology, but the Constitution. And he quoted Benjamin Franklin that "They who can give up essential liberty to obtain a little temporary safety deserve neither liberty nor safety."

His final words encouraged everyone to go to the polls on Tuesday and to vote for the truths proclaimed in God's Word.

As Ludwig finished his message, it occurred to Tom that the pastor had delivered a powerful attack on the State of Emergency's restrictions without ever mentioning any current events—*well done*. And that Tom had now heard almost the same words from several different gifted believers in just the last few days—something Callie had encouraged him to watch out for as important.

The final hymn was "O God Our Help in Ages Past," and as they finished singing Tom moved slightly to look towards his mother. Above her and in the very back of the church, he thought he saw Erin MacNeil turn and leave. *How could that be?*

Everyone in their group began to chat, and Alexei shook Tom's hand again from the row behind him. "Thank you for last night," Alexei said. "I imagine you'll have to report my question, and that's OK. I really have nothing to hide, now that it's clear that I do more than run an internet provider on Cyprus. I'm actually just trying to ensure that what we're hearing is true."

Tom started to reply but Gary Thornton suggested they all have lunch together.

Tom, still next to Callie, turned to her, and said in a low voice. "I don't think I should."

She frowned. He could see his mother circling closer and said, "Listen. It's not like before. It's not that I'm afraid for myself to be seen with this group anymore—just the opposite. It's suddenly that I need to pull away for a good reason. I'm not sure, but I know that a photo of all of us together today is not what I'm supposed to do."

"OK. OK," she said, and quickly hugged him. "Go. I'll say that you have a meeting."

"Thanks. I'll call you." Tom gave a quick wave to everyone, turned, and walked out through a side door.

As Erin MacNeil turned the corner in the next block she glanced back and saw Tom coming out a door of the church. She hoped he hadn't seen her, and she traversed the next block even more quickly before turning again and calling for a ride.

*All those people—young people—singing hymns and praying. And that Pastor Ludwig who called me—he gave quite a message. Why did I come? To see these people for myself. I have to admit, it was powerful. Real. And there were Tom and that Callie woman. She wants this baby. Why?!?*

Erin was finally far enough from the spiritual heat of the church for Nenav to get close enough to restart the voices which had been silenced by the worship service, but now there were so many answered prayers of light and believers' voices landing on and around her that he couldn't risk it.

Soon the car arrived and she got in for the ride home, with the dialogue inside her still raging, but without the lies of Nenav's voices which a week ago would have overcome all other thoughts.

Tom was halfway back to his home when his Core Group phone buzzed.

"Emily, how are you?"

"OK. But have you seen the interview with your mother and Speaker Welch?"

"No, not yet, but I record all those shows."

"Then watch it. They blast everything about our Administration, from our Progressive policies 'creating more government dependence' to the State of Emergency 'destroying our freedoms'. They tell everyone to vote against Progressive candidates on Tuesday."

"I...uh...had no idea."

"So she's violated your latest Emergency rule. But the worst thing is a video they somehow smuggled out of the Detention Center with your father. Taken with a cell phone, apparently. There's a link to a longer video of him with a group of rabbis, imams and preachers sitting around and debating the true nature of God. At the end your father looks at the camera and says something about 'This isn't hate speech. It's free speech. Make your own decision about God. But don't kill our American freedom to respectfully speak our minds whenever we want, even in a Detention Center'. Can you believe that? Your parents are crazy! We're working with our Tech partners and the FBI to take down the video, but it keeps popping up again. I'm heading into the office early for our final Election Prep this afternoon, and I think you better come early, too. The president will be livid, I'm sure."

"Uh, OK. I'll be there. Let me watch the interview when I get home, then I'll come in."

"Where are you?"

"I'll see you this afternoon."

"And I suggest you have a plan."

Ablet Sabri and Kahar Bosakov were driving back into D.C. that afternoon following the older cousin's meeting in Towson with a man who had texted him with a code he had not seen since the end of their training in Afghanistan. They met in a crowded restaurant over lunch. Ablet instructed Kahar to remain in the car to watch for anyone suspicious, which also meant that he could not identify the contact if there were a problem later.

Ablet learned that their mission was still on—the leaders had decided to delay during the heightened vigilance during the State of Emergency—and that new instructions would soon include their roles in simultaneous attacks on several Chinese-national churches, daycare centers, university cultural centers and even restaurants, all across the nation on November 12$^{th}$, the anniversary of the Uyghurs' 1931 revolt against China and the formation of the first East Turkestan Republic. The man instructed Ablet to continue to pray and to be prepared to act in the coming weeks.

After Ablet returned to the car and told Kahar what he had learned, they drove in silence for ten minutes. Finally, Kahar, in the passenger seat, said, "What if our attacks on ordinary Chinese worshipers, teachers and nannies actually turn people against us, as Ahmad Rashid has predicted? What will we have accomplished?"

Ablet replied, "Revenge. Showing the Chinese that there is a blood price for their genocide against our people—we will kill ordinary Chinese, just as they are killing ordinary Uyghurs. It will be perfectly understood."

"But what if the demonstrations that these Americans are planning in D.C., New York, and the other cities might actually focus attention on our situation and force the government to change?"

"A demonstration connecting us with the Jews in Germany decades ago? Planned by American Jews and Christians? What good will that do?"

"Maybe a lot. And there are non-Uyghur Muslims involved, too, like those at our mosque."

"So Jews, Christians and other Muslims all protesting how the Chinese government is treating Uyghurs? Why would they do that? We're not members of their groups. Why would they care about us?"

"I'm not sure. But it seems to be what at least some Americans do—they stand up for a principle, no matter the group. These people know what's happening to us, and they want to help us."

"So these non-Uyghur, non-Muslim Americans want to help *us*?"

"I guess they believe it's the right thing to do—that we're all equal, so helping one helps all."

"No one will come, cousin. They don't really care." Ablet's voice changed and he looked over. "Are you getting cold feet about what we swore to do here?"

"No, of course not. But what if American pressure might actually be able to make our people's lives better in China?"

"You're dreaming. Better to just kill the Chinese bastards."

Callie, Grace and Kristen returned home after having lunch with their church-attending friends. When Callie opened the door to their ground-floor apartment, she found a large envelope that had apparently been dropped through the mail slot.

After putting Grace down for a rest, Callie opened the envelope. Inside was a picture of her with Grace as they came out of their home that morning, and a typed, unsigned letter, which read:

"You self-righteous bitch. We obviously know where you and your too-cute daughter live. You and the other bigots at your church should stop telling the rest of us how to live. You are the worst. Your white privilege and hetero-superiority scream at us, even when you don't speak. We've won, and we won't allow you to dictate to us anymore. Stop talking, writing and even praying like you're superior to the rest of us, or there will be consequences which you and your daughter won't like. We mean it."


After he arrived home Tom watched the recorded interview with his mother and Speaker Welch. What they said seemed rational and normal to Tom, though also clearly political, in that they wanted the president's party to lose seats in Tuesday's election. And they were highly critical of the State of Emergency, saying on air what both of them had said to him in private earlier. He grimaced, knowing that their words violated the orders his team had drafted only days before.

*Will the president want me to renounce my mother, like I did my father?*

Instead of that thought upsetting him, like it would have done a week ago, he actually smiled and felt at peace. *I won't. I wish she and the Speaker had obeyed the rules, but I think the rules are wrong. I know now that I overreached. We all did. We just need to get to the end of this and go back to the way it was, and live under The Constitution.*

After throwing a few balls for Beau in the backyard, he was cleaning up to go to the office for their afternoon meetings when he got a text from Callie asking him to come over as soon as possible.

Twenty minutes later she opened her door for him. He could see the concern on her face. "Come in. Thanks. Grace's upstairs with Kristen." As soon as she closed the door, she said, "Have a seat, and take a look at this."

He moved to a chair, then read the note and looked at the picture.

She took the sofa across from him. "That's from *this* morning. Someone was across the street and took that picture."

Tom studied the words again and shook his head. "*That's* hate speech."

"If it were just me, I wouldn't care. The problem is I can't stop being white, heterosexual, or someone who prays, so I obviously can't meet their demands. It occurred to me to put a sign in our window that says, 'Let's Talk.' But I can't do anything to risk Grace."

"Maybe you should take a short vacation."

"Do you really think they'll do something?"

"I hope not. But the last two months have shown what some people are capable of."

Callie nodded. "I just don't know. Hopefully after the election things will calm down. I called my parents, and we could go there—no problem. For now, Kristen and I talked, and we're going to tag team for a few days. Grace and I will move up and sleep in her guest room, and I'll keep Grace home from school. Hopefully it'll all blow over."

"I'll ask the FBI to take a look."

She smiled. "Thanks. It's all so crazy."


Forty-five minutes later President Bradshaw was sitting at the Resolute Desk in the Oval Office going over his latest stump speech remarks about the coming Progressive Revolution when vice president Reynolds, Emily Schofield and Tom Sullivan came in together and stood in front of him. He smiled and they greeted each other.

"We're almost there," he said.

Emily spoke. "Our final election meeting starts in five minutes in the Cabinet Room; then you both take off for the last twenty-four hours of campaigning. This time I'll join Patricia. But first and quickly, we have to deal with the latest issues with Tom's parents, who've both violated the State of Emergency today. Tom, do you have any suggestions?"

"I'm obviously embarrassed by what they've done, but..."

The president interrupted him. "Tom, it's OK." He smiled. "You can't control your parents. They're obviously misguided, but it doesn't matter. Despite them and everyone else who has no vision for our future, we're going to win big on Tuesday and start a new chapter in American, even world, history. Then in the future we'll watch people like them more closely, to prevent hate and interference."

When the three of them were silent, he stood and said, "Come on, let's go plan the last forty-eight hours."

"But Mr. President," Emily said, "even our internal polls show that the last minute swing appears to be against us. Independents are breaking against the State of Emergency—and in that context the Sullivans' public attacks are damaging."

As he walked around the desk, Bradshaw smiled again. "Emily, the polls must be wrong. Trust me, we're going to win, and win big. I can feel it. How about it, Patricia?"

"Uh, yes, it feels that way to me, too, Mr. President."

"So, Tom, I'm sorry your parents are stuck in their mistakes, but they'll have to find their way in a new world come Wednesday. Maybe you can help them adjust! Now, if you'll excuse me, I'm going to detour by the facilities before our meeting starts."


Tom stood aside as Patricia and Emily exited the Oval Office for The Cabinet Room. As Emily went by, he said, "I need to show you something that Callie found in her apartment today."

They stopped in the hallway. "OK."

He took out his phone and showed Emily the pictures he'd taken of the note and the photo from Callie's apartment.

"That's terrible," Emily said, returning the phone to him.

"I'm meeting with Tanya Prescott tomorrow, and I'm going to turn them over to her."

"Why?"

"Hate speech. Of the worst kind."

Emily paused and looked at Tom for a moment. "Not necessarily, Tom. There's hate speech, and then there's reality. Callie is a white, heterosexual Christian who wears her faith on her sleeve and readily attacks others with her claims of going-to-heaven superiority. You've said yourself that the rest of us get tired of it. Maybe she should be put back a step or two."

"With attacks on her daughter? And whether she's tiresome or not—which I don't think she is—that's no reason to threaten her."

"OK. Tell Tanya if you want. But I assure you that Director Toomey knows the FBI has more important, real, far right, white supremacist groups to go after than a few oppressed people of color, or gays, who are happy to finally be in control of their lives."

"You think that's what this is?"

"Sure. And, remember, at least they're telling Callie the truth. She, like your parents, needs to rethink her obvious white privilege and Christian prejudices. President Bradshaw is right—the world is moving on, and they, like the rest of us, need to get onboard."


As Air Force One sped to Dayton late that afternoon, President Bradshaw was alone at his desk, making a personal list of issues that he expected to address with the leaders of China and Russia when they divided the world into three spheres of national truths, after the election, and after he had input from a small group of Tech experts whom Drew was putting together for that purpose, along with their new White House senior team, which he expected to announce later in the week.

But he actually was not alone. Balzor and five other demons had free range of the aircraft. Other than a few crew members and a couple of reporters, there were no believers on this trip. And the prayers for the president had almost stopped completely—Balzor was thankful that most believers had given up on the president, so there was no spiritual light or heat to deter or concern their forces.

So Balzor settled in, read what the president was writing, and ramped up the voices they wanted inside the most powerful person on earth, including one about Tom Sullivan.

*I meant to ask Tom about that Uyghur thing.*

*Tom...*

*With parents like that, can we really trust him? What does he really believe, and will he be OK with what we have planned once we've won?*

*Tom was already in the White House and was a great resource during the emergency—and he had some good ideas—but is he really the best team player for the future?*

*I bet Drew knows some good candidates for National Security Advisor—someone who'll be open to working for world integration and peace...without any possible family baggage!*

He pushed a button on the desk.

"Yes, sir?" came a voice through a small speaker.

"Rob, please come here for a minute. The list you've almost finished with our new senior team for after the election—I want to add another position."

Erin MacNeil had called her friend Tracy and offered to fix a simple dinner if she would come over to talk. They were seated at the table in her small but tastefully decorated fourth floor apartment. Tracy was a few years older, also from Erin's hometown, and had helped her find the apartment when she moved to D.C. And she had driven Erin to the abortion clinic.

"I didn't call you earlier," Erin said, as she took a fork full of salad, "because I didn't know if I'd be eating. I had my first experience with morning sickness today, and I wasn't feeling well."

"I'm sorry," Tracy said. "I didn't get that far."

"Hmm. Well, after it got better and I'd texted you, for some reason I wanted to go to that church where Tom, and that Callie woman, and

Pastor Ludwig, the one who called me, all go. I'm not sure if I thought I'd tell them to stuff it, or what, but when I got there it was full of people our age—and they were really nice. So I sat down in the back row for what I thought would be five minutes, but I stayed for the whole service and just missed running into Tom."

"What was it like?"

"I..I couldn't believe the singing—the hymns. And Pastor Ludwig actually preached a sermon I could understand, not like some back home."

"So you liked it?"

"I'm not sure 'like' is the right word. But I understood it. And it was real."

"So...what are you thinking?"

"I...it's weird. The morning sickness is weird. You'd think it would put me off, and it isn't fun. But in a strange way it makes the pregnancy real. Like it's a bigger deal than I thought. It's real and it's impacting my body."

"What are you saying?"

Erin put her fork down. "I don't know. I'm not sure. There's Tom and Callie and the pastor and now my own body—all bugging me. What did I do to get into all this?"

Tracy almost laughed. "Girl, like me, I guess you slept with a man you're not married to."

For the first time that day Erin smiled and nodded her head. "Yes. Like they mentioned once or twice in our middle school Health class. You'd think I'd be smarter than that."

"Welcome to the club."

"I guess the question now is, what do I do next?"

"Yes. That *is* the question."

# 23

*The philosophy of the school room in one generation will be the philosophy of government in the next.*

Abraham Lincoln

Monday, November 2

Given the hectic schedule expected for the rest of election week, the president and Rob Thompson scheduled their regular weekly Emergency Council for early Monday morning in the Situation Room. The White House members, plus James Toomey and Tanya Prescott from the FBI, joined in person the now-familiar group on large video screens to discuss any developments over the weekend and to assess any upcoming threats. Tom was seated at the center of the table, facing the video screens.

And as had now become maddeningly routine, Agent Prescott, leading off the reports, could not offer any actionable intelligence that connected anyone in the WhiteStorm group with any of the earlier attacks, though there were many indirect connections that were still being investigated. Nor was there any chatter about imminent violent activity.

When she finished, the room was momentarily silent. Looking around the room, Tom asked a question. "Is it possible that there is no connection between all the attacks, starting with Air Force One, almost two months ago, to Chapel Hill? Are they all simply the result of individuals and small groups acting out their own misguided hate?"

From his chair at the end of the table President Bradshaw placed both hands on the surface and leaned forward. "Tom, you yourself have said many times that it's impossible. There have been too many, and they are too effective. I suspect we have no leads because they've gone deeper underground, thanks to all the measures we've enacted—many of them your ideas—to find them. I still think this WhiteStorm group is going to be the key to breaking it all wide open—they're clearly our prime suspects, and they hate our democracy. General Price or Director Toomey, could they be using a form of communication that defies our technology to intercept them?"

From the center video screen the general said, "Unlikely, but not impossible."

"Exactly. Look, we're regrettably going to have to end the State of Emergency in a week, but I want each of you to report on the specific measures, perhaps slightly modified, that you believe we can keep in place to help find these people. Or at least keep a lid on them. Give your report to Tom by the end of the week, but I want to read a copy myself. We need new ideas—new approaches. And, general, we also need a fast, joint study by your NSA, the FBI and, say, Juggle, working together, to explore every conceivable way they could be doing this, no matter how far-fetched it seems."

"Yes, sir, we will."

"Now, let's turn to the elections. Are they secure?"

Tom put down one folder and picked up another. "As we know, the federal oversight of the nation's many diverse Election Management Systems, and the centralization of the reporting process, enacted two years ago by Congress, brought upgrades and improvements to every aspect of the process. We should see the benefits of that hard work tomorrow, when there should be much less chaos than before, even though states are still free to use different equipment, so long as it adheres to the new federal standards.

"The relevant agencies—FBI, Homeland Security, Cyber Command, NSA—have been focused on the system for the past month, and we've given the FBI special access to the communication process to watch carefully tomorrow as the polls close. Director Toomey?"

"Yes, we've confirmed that within the last forty-eight hours the correct candidates and ballot issues have been manually loaded via flash drives into every voting machine in every precinct—without connecting any voting machine to the internet. So they're secure from tampering. And we've monitored and tested the reporting system as recently as this morning. Every part of the new federal process is in good working order, ready to receive, tabulate, and confirm the results."

The president spoke. "Thank you both—and all of you—for this extra effort. After the mistakes and questions in the past, it's critical that the American people have complete faith in our election process. It shows the value of concentration under one federal law. I look forward to a smooth process tomorrow." Turning back to Tom, he asked, "What about foreign interference?"

Tom glanced up at General Price, who said, "It's unusual—contrary to what we've seen in the past, but there appear to be almost no hacking probes or social media scams from the main actors—China and Russia. They're remarkably quiet. And the others we can handle."

"Good. Good," President Bradshaw said. He looked around the table. "Then we should hold the first election in quite a while where no one will have grounds for a complaint or a recount. Well done. Tom, Director Toomey and General Price, keep a close eye on everything, and, if all goes well, please be prepared to give your assessment to the nation once the election is finished."

"We will, sir," Tom said.

"Excellent. Then if there's nothing else for now, we've got some final campaigning to do. Emily?" He stood up and the others followed. She nodded, and together with Rob Thompson, the three of them left the room.

As the others began some small talk, Tom motioned to Agent Prescott.

"Can we talk for a minute?"

She smiled. "Sure."

They took adjoining seats at the Situation Room table. "Thanks. I've got two personal issues I want your input on, because they're also 'official business.'"

"Your father and mother?"

He paused. "No, although they're obviously important to me. What are your thoughts on them?"

"Your father violated the rules of his detention, so I'm afraid the wheels will just start turning, and he may wind up somewhere else, and for longer. Not sure. I'm sorry. On your mother, since she was with the Speaker and was asked a question, I've already told anyone who's upset to just get over it—there's an election."

"Thank you. I wish I'd never heard the term 'hate speech.'"

"Or tried to define it."

"Yes...Now about the two issues I'd like to tell you about...". He described whom he understood Alexei Nobikov to be, their mutual acquaintances, and how they'd met in a seemingly random way six weeks earlier, then kept running into each other.

"Saturday night at dinner Alexei told me that he 'occasionally' does social media work for the Russian government, and he asked me to opine on whether an initiative, supposedly from some private American, acting as a messenger from President Bradshaw to the Russian government on furthering world peace, was credible and official. I told him I knew nothing about it, which is true. But I want you to know about him contacting me in this way, and ask you to do whatever you do to find out more about him and the internet company he runs on Cyprus, just to be safe."

"OK." She had been taking notes while he spoke. "We assume that all Russian journalists and some of their businesspeople are connected in one way or another to the Kremlin. But thanks for tagging this one for sure. We'll look into it, and I'll get back to you."

"Good. Now, the other thing." Tom described the threat that had been made against Callie and Grace, and showed her the photo of the message.

Tanya frowned as she read the note on his phone. "Not good. And there doesn't seem to be much to go on. But send me that photo and we'll analyze it and compare it to others."

"Thanks. Any other suggestions?"

"She should install one of those video-recording doorbells, put serious locks on her doors and windows, and maybe take a trip for a while. I'll ask the D.C. police to put her address—and the child's school—on their patrol watch-list."

"Good. Thanks. I'll send them to you today." She nodded and he continued. "And, this is a bit awkward, but do you—or the FBI in general—treat any threats differently, depending on the possible political implications, or the views, of the threatened person?"

Tanya sat back and paused for a moment. "Tom, I can't tell you what others have done or may do—there are bad apples in every organization. I suspect that those at or close to the top may sometimes be motivated by those factors. But for me, personally, the bad guys are the bad guys, and I'm sworn to protect *all* Americans. Particularly a mother and her child, for goodness sake."

Tom nodded ever so slightly. "Thank you. Yes, I thought that about you. I've really enjoyed working with you on all this—you're a real professional."

She reached for her pad. "Just doing my job. Remember, my mother was originally from The Soviet Union and got out when it wasn't easy. I like to protect people from tyrants—of any size or shape...I'll get back to you on both of these as soon as I can."

They stood. "Thank you." Tom's Core Group phone buzzed with a text that the president wanted to see him. "Let's walk upstairs."


Two minutes later Tom was shown into the Oval Office. The president was standing and talking with Patricia Reynolds and Emily Schofield. They were holding computer bags and were obviously about to leave for their campaign swings. Rob Thompson was writing a note in a nearby chair.

"Tom," the president said, and waved him over. As Tom approached them, President Bradshaw said, "I've been meaning to ask you, but I forgot again this morning. I've heard there's some sort of big anti-Chinese demonstration planned for right after the election."

"Probably the one in support of the Uyghurs, whom the Chinese are persecuting." He glanced at Emily, whose expression never changed. "They're calling it genocide."

The president frowned. "Who is? Turkish Muslims in the middle of nowhere? I think it's totally bogus. No other Muslim nation, not even the Turks, is complaining. Can we stop it? It's pure hate speech."

Tom waited a moment. "Why would we do that? The State of Emergency will be over. How could we stop Americans from protesting what they believe—true or not—to be an ongoing genocide? I think they even plan to link it to what the Nazis did to the Jews." He again glanced at Emily, who did not move.

"What? That's preposterous! Please, Tom, figure out a way to stop those protests. The State of Emergency may have to end, but we should be able to keep people from telling lies. Why, the Uyghurs have done all sorts of terrorist things in China and elsewhere. Please get some of them designated as terrorist organizations. Then no American can support them. Thanks. Now, we've got to go."

Tom started to disagree, but the president turned to leave, and the two women followed.

He glanced back at Tom. "Tomorrow will be crazy, but I'll see you at the party tomorrow night. Thanks!"

At Reagan National Airport that morning, Erin MacNeil settled into her window seat for the long flight to Los Angeles and two days of business meetings. *No upgrade this time, but at least I've got a window seat. Looks like a full flight.*

A few minutes before the door closed a young woman with long, dark hair and a rucksack arrived at Erin's row, carrying a very young and very tiny baby. The flight attendant volunteered to hold the baby while she removed her backpack and settled into the middle seat next to Erin. She took the baby back, and when she turned toward Erin, the baby opened his eyes. Erin looked at them and smiled but thought *I hope he doesn't scream for six hours.*

"Hi. I'm Lori. And this is Henry."

"Hi, Henry."

"He's only three weeks old."

"Wow. Your first?"

"Yes, and obviously our first flight. I hope he doesn't bother you."

"I doubt it, though I do have some work to do. As a teenager I used to do a lot of babysitting."

Lori smiled as she moved Henry to her other shoulder. "Good. Maybe you can give me some pointers. I'm new at this. I'm leaving my parents to fly home to San Diego. First hours on my own with him. We're both learning!"

"So you have to change in L.A.?"

"Yeah. My husband's in the Navy, and his ship gets in tomorrow. I want to get Henry settled in our apartment."

"Your husband hasn't met him yet?"

"No, they've been gone six months. I had a problem and had to do bed rest for the last two months, so I stayed with my parents in Maryland. Now it's back to David."

"Two months of bed rest?"

"Yeah. It was pretty tough. But look, now he's here. Isn't he amazing? A miracle."

Erin nodded again, and Henry squirmed on Lori's shoulder.


From his office just before lunch Tom dialed on his Core Group phone.

"General Price, hey. It's Tom. Do you have time for a quick question?"

"Sure."

"Do you know of any Uyghur organizations that are engaged in terrorist activities?"

"Hm. Off the top of my head—at least against us—no. As you would imagine, given how the Chinese government has repressed those people, some incidents have happened, and the Chinese label them as terrorists. But it's pretty small potatoes, and their government has pretty well crushed them, along with all other dissent. Most Uyghurs in the U.S. live, I think, here in the D.C. area, and they keep a pretty low profile, out of fear of what the Chinese might do to their families back home. So the Chinese have designated some Uyghur groups as terrorists to justify their repression of what amounts to a whole nation."

"That's what I thought, but if you find anything different, please let me know."

"Will do. And I'm sure we'll be talking tomorrow about the elections."

Three hours into the flight, with Henry asleep on her shoulder, Lori turned slightly toward Erin, who was focused on her laptop.

"I know this is asking a lot, but could you hold him for a minute while I go to the restroom? I've got this burp cloth to protect your nice suit."

"Uh, sure. Just a second." Erin closed her laptop, leaned it against the bulkhead, and closed the table. "Let me have him."

Lori gave her the towel, which she draped over her right shoulder. Then she handed her Henry, who was still asleep.

"Thank you," Lori said. The man on the aisle unbuckled and stood. "I'll be right back."

Henry had not been on Erin's shoulder long when he moved around and rubbed one fist in a closed eye. Erin moved him slightly. He opened his eyes, looked at her, and smiled. She knew he was too young to smile for recognition, but, still, it gave her a strange feeling.

*OK. I don't think there's another baby on this plane. If this is You trying to get my attention, like all these people keep saying happened to them, I get it.*

Late that afternoon Tom finished the last meeting with his staff, including an update on the Trusted Citizen program, which Emily wanted to roll out immediately after the election. He closed that folder and looked out the window. The offices were unusually quiet—the president, vice president, and most of their staffs were immersed in the last hours of their Midterm Election campaigns. Balzor and the demons who were responsible for the president's key people were out of the city with them. Nepravel had stayed behind. Balzor had commanded him to deal with whatever pain the growing spiritual light and heat around Tom Sullivan might inflict, but find out what he was thinking and planning. Prince Proklor wanted to know, tonight.

So Nepravel had stationed himself in the empty Oval Office and over the afternoon made several forays down the hall into Tom's office, staying as long as he could before the pain was too much and he had to retreat.

By doing so he'd learned about the Trusted Citizen initiative, which sounded very promising for them to exploit, and about Tom's concern for the Uyghur demonstration. He had just recovered enough from the intense heat of his last visit to attempt another.

Tom stood, went out to his assistant and told everyone to knock off for the day. Then, after closing his door, he returned to his desk. He took out his L-pad and turned to a new page. He said a prayer for guidance and wisdom.

Nepravel left the Oval Office and moved down the hall towards Tom's office, always looking for people and information he could use. But almost no one was there, and something didn't feel right. There was too much spiritual light in front of him. As he rounded the last corner, he found that same radiant angel standing in front of Tom's closed door. Nepravel would not be visiting Tom again today, and he knew that Balzor and, worse, Prince Proklor, would be very unhappy.

Tom sat at his desk, his L-pad and pen in front of him. All day his mind had been ricocheting between the security incidents they were following, like WhiteStorm, to future initiatives, to safeguarding the elections, to his personal issues. Thinking there would be a "new beginning" after the elections and the end of the State of Emergency, he decided to make a To Do List, his long-standing habit to get ideas out of his mind and on to paper, hoping for clarity and wisdom.

But the first word he wrote at the top of the page was "Truth". *From now on I'm only going to speak and accept the truth. If I'm really going to be a follower of Jesus, I remember his famous statement to Pontius Pilate, "The reason I was born and came into the world is to testify to the truth. Everyone on the side of truth listens to me."*

Then he was a little surprised to find himself writing, "My Messes," though those same words had been weighing on him for days. He wrote:

"I pushed Erin, an intelligent and very capable woman, and a lot of other women, for sex, and now she's pregnant.

"A baby is going to be killed because of me.

"I publicly disowned my father, who has loved me and stuck by me, out of fear for what others will think of me. And fear of losing my job.

"I came up with the State of Emergency, and the idea to punish people for 'hate speech', which I can't define now. I have severely damaged our long-term freedoms out of fear that we might be attacked again.

"The president wants me to do more to ensure safety over freedom, which I now know is backwards. Will I do what he wants?

"If I quit, what will happen? Will the nation be better off, or worse? What should I do?"

He dropped down a line and wrote: "From now on, speak and act only the truth. God will do the rest."

*Wow. Where did all that come from?*

Immediately he heard again what Alexei had said at dinner about believers. *It's amazing how the Holy Spirit can speak so clearly to us when he lives in us, and other voices aren't drowning him out.* Tom shivered.

He decided to add the other categories of items later. Looking at what he'd already written, he slipped to his knees and prayed earnestly about each one, seeking guidance.

And he asked repeatedly that he would not rush in with his own quick conclusions, but would wait and listen to those whom he trusted.

Thirty minutes later, after deciding some difficult but important first steps, he sat again at his desk and wrote them down on his L-pad.

Then he dialed his mother's cell phone.

She answered. "Hey, dear, how are you?"

"I'm fine, Mom. Actually, really good. Are you available for dinner tonight at my place?"

Janet paused. "That's unexpected. And I wish I were, but I'm taping several interviews—the election."

"Is Seth one of them?"

"I offered him first, but he never called back."

"Let me see what I can do. How about getting together later to talk?"

"Sure. That would be wonderful. Aren't you concerned about being seen with me?"

"The night before the election I don't expect photographers to be massed outside my row house. Call me when you finish."

"I will. See you tonight."

Callie tucked Grace into bed upstairs in Kristen's apartment. An installer was due the next day to put video-camera ringers on both their front doors, plus a camera in back.

When Callie emerged from the bedroom, Kristen handed her a mug of herbal tea, and they settled on the sofa in Kristen's living room.

"Who would have thought, all those years ago, when I was having an affair with Tom's father, that we would be here tonight, forgiven and redeemed, praying for both these men, and for our nation?"

Callie looked down at the mug in her lap. "Or that you would for some reason take interest in a lost, pregnant young woman in the porn industry..." She looked up at her friend and mentor. "Isn't God's power to transform amazing?"

They were both silent for a long moment. "Yes. Yes, it is. And He is. Thank you, Lord. Where would we be without You? And now let's get down to tonight's business."

Each of them took out the three pages of notes and prayer requests that Kristen's network had emailed to thousands of prayer warriors across the nation—and actually around the world—and the two women added their voices to the chorus of praises and requests being lifted up that evening to the Throne of Grace.


At 9:30 Tom opened his front door and gave his mother a hug. He took her coat and offered her a drink, which she accepted, and they sat down together in his living room.

"It's been a wild few days, as you know," Janet said, settling into the sofa. "Thank you." She took a sip and smiled. "We came up here to attend a conference on unity, and now your father's in jail. I'm giving interviews with the Speaker on how this Administration is destroying our freedoms, and you're the one running the State of Emergency! Who'd have thought?" She took another sip.

Tom nodded. "Yes. It's pretty bad. I'm sorry. Particularly for my part. That's why I wanted to meet with you tonight. There's a lot to tell you."

"Go on."

He put his drink on the coffee table and leaned forward, his elbows on his knees. "It's hard to know where to start. The first bad news is that Dad has been moved to a different facility after that video he put out—not sure what that will mean. And the second is that I'm the father of a baby who will be aborted on Friday."

Janet put down her drink and sat up.

"The better news," Tom continued, "is that God has been working hard to get my attention—through Callie, her friends, Robert Ludwig, you, Dad, and even Patrick Tomlinson, if you can believe that—and a few days ago I realized what a mess I've made of so many things, and that I would continue to do so without His help. So I prayed for His forgiveness and guidance, and since Dad can't be here, I want to ask for your forgiveness for all the madness I've created, and I'd also like to ask for your wisdom as well."

Janet was silent for several moments, looking at her son. Then she smiled. "Of course, Tom. You're no worse than all the rest of us."

She stood and took a step to him. He stood, and she hugged him. "Welcome home. Now, before anything else, tell me more about my grandchild."

He told her how he'd met Erin, then Callie, and with the attacks he'd lost touch with Erin until she'd called with her news about being pregnant.

"She's a nice person—one of the crazy things is that I don't know her all that well, but I do like her. She's smart, funny, and good looking. Meanwhile, between Callie, Kristen, Grace, how I met Patrick Tomlinson, and a lot of other people, including a Russian Cypriot whom I think you met at the conference, who talked his sister out of an abortion, I'm sure that abortion is murder, and I don't want Erin to abort our baby. God intervened, I'm convinced, a week ago, to save her—I think she's a girl—and Callie offered to adopt the baby, which is incredible, but Erin's scheduled again for Friday."

Janet stood facing Tom. "Wow, that's a lot. Sit down, and let's talk about it."

Twenty minutes of talking later, including prayers by both mother and son, Tom told her what he planned to do, and they shifted to all the other issues on Tom's plate.

When he came to the end of the list, she mentioned that she'd had a nice conversation in her hotel lobby with Alexei Nobikov, who'd given them his card as they were being thrown out of the vice president's conference.

"He seems like a good man—he certainly knows a lot about America. And I think he has a strong faith, as best I can tell. Seems unusual for a Russian, even if he does now live on Cyprus."

"Yes. An unusual man for sure. Did he tell you how we met?"

"He did. Patrick Tomlinson's girlfriend is his niece. Patrick is next on my list. I can't wait to see him again."

Tom was up, fixing them a second round, when his doorbell rang. He walked to the door.

"Seth. Glad you could make it."

The Network producer walked in and smiled at Janet. "Mrs. Sullivan—so great to see you."

"What a surprise, Seth. This week is full of them!" She laughed.

Everyone greeted, took seats, and began catching up on their personal lives, starting with Janet's question to Seth about Natalie. When he finished describing Natalie's faith and their new relationship, which he found to be unexpectedly good, Janet said, "I had no idea that God was moving so much in all your lives. But I don't know why I'm surprised—it's what we've been praying for. And He does answer prayers."

They all smiled, then continued to talk for almost an hour, and Janet told Seth all the things she would have said in an interview, had The Network permitted it, about the current Administration's gross overreach into everyone's private lives.

As they talked, Tom shared a few key points he'd learned from his conversations with Gary Thornton which had convinced him that the government was simply too big and—combined with the Tech and Media giants—too powerful, controlling virtually every aspect of everyone's private lives. "Trust me—it is. And it's not how America was intended to be," he concluded.

Seth listened and occasionally rebutted one of their arguments, which generally drew a quick answer from Janet.

"Seth, I know you're a Progressive—I've known that for years, and I love you. We'll disagree on a lot of policies and programs. But what Tom and I are talking about is the truth, and our fundamental right to have those disagreements. Many Progressives, including our president, I think, choose not to acknowledge the truth, even when it's obvious, and have gone way beyond winning arguments to shutting down those arguments all together. All they care about is winning and being in control, no matter the cost to the rest of us."

"Hmm. Like not interviewing you."

"Exactly."

Tom said, "And here's the latest, which neither of you can mention to anyone. Seth, do you agree?" His friend nodded. "The president wants to stop the demonstrations you're planning against the Chinese suppression of the Uygurs next week."

"Why?" Seth asked. "We're bringing Muslims, Christians and Jews together on the anniversary of Kristallnacht to call out the Chinese government for suppression and genocide. Why would the president oppose that?"

"I don't know. To me it's irrational. Like claiming that the border is secure when tens of thousands cross it every day, or offering everyone extra free money to combat inflation. In all these cases the truth is obvious, but we act as if it's not."

Janet added, "Thanks to you connecting us, Seth, Natalie and I have reached out to the Chinese Christian Church here in D.C. to encourage them to join us, and they've tentatively agreed. What courage that will take, with family back home—Chinese Christians in America supporting Uyghur Muslims in China. If that's not our country at her best, I don't know what is."

Tom shook his head. "I'm not sure why he brought it up—he just mentioned it to me today. But he's serious. He said the Uyghurs are terrorists."

Seth put his drink on the table. "Crap. You and I have a lot of friends helping with this, including Logan and Ahmad, who I thought would never get together on anything."

"I know. I'll try to sort it out. Meanwhile, don't mention it to anyone."

"Except to God in prayer," Janet said. "If you're praying these days, Seth."

"You know, Mrs. Sullivan, it's still a little unnatural for me, but, yes, I'm praying. Can you believe that?" He smiled. "Watching Natalie—and others—these past weeks has impressed me that there really must be spiritual power. Power that can drastically change people—for the good. I've seen it. I haven't figured it all out, yet, but something or someone is definitely out there."

"And He'd love to hear from you," Janet said.

"I know. I know. Maybe, some day."

An hour later, as Janet took a car to her hotel and Seth walked to his home, the demonic leaders assembled again in the Oval Office. There was a huge horde of lesser demons summoned from all over the country while their charges mostly slept, acting to protect Prince Proklor and his generals by bending with their large, dark mass the shafts of answered prayers and the vocal supplications of believers which rained down on them.

In his decades in America, Proklor had never seen so many prayers directed against his forces, while simultaneously lifting up the nation's human leaders. He had planned to encourage his generals at their meeting, but now he was just angry. As he began to speak, a bolt of spiritual light actually landed right next to him, and a believer's voice commanded him to be gone.

"Idiots!" he yelled. He looked around at his inner circle, who were leaning in, close to the Resolute Desk. "They will shut up when they lose tomorrow. They always eventually get discouraged or angry, and stop praying. We don't need to meet tonight. Everything is in motion. Send your forces back to their posts so they can oversee all that we've prepared. We'll gather again tomorrow to celebrate our victory."

The demonic horde left the White House to fan out across the country, ready to ramp up the voices they needed to ensure that the right people would soon be totally in charge.

# Tuesday, November 3

Early on Tuesday morning, while voters lined up to express their choices in the midterm elections, Emily Schofield was at her desk in the White House. The day would be long, full of photo ops and press interaction, and hopefully a late victory celebration, but for now she had to concentrate on the president's bold plans for the next two weeks.

All the polls, even their own internal ones, showed that the nation was tired of the State of Emergency and wanted a change—which would not be good for their candidates, who had pushed Protection, Patriotism and a Progressive future.

But she was willing to concede that President Bradshaw and Vice President Reynolds were more experienced and could perhaps sense a victory not evident in the polls. So Emily followed her boss's instructions and prepared for the new day he assured her was coming.

She dialed Seth's number on her Core Phone and caught him on the sidewalk as he was about to walk into The Network's DC Headquarters. He turned and walked down the block.

"Seth, how are you on this election day?"

"Glad it's finally here, and busy. You?"

"The same. Listen, the president asked me whether you would like to do the first in-depth interview with him after the election.

Seth smiled. "Yes, of course. When?"

"Maybe just a few days after the election, like early next week. Should be a big audience. We see you chairing a panel. Maybe even two nights—domestic and international."

"Yeah. Sure. I'll check with Rachel, but, yes, thanks."

"Great. And we'd like to ask you then to do something for us. We need to start laying the groundwork for identifying the Uyghurs in China as terrorists. They actually are, and we want Americans to start to realize it."

Seth paused. "Emily, come on. Logan and I and a bunch of our friends—your friends—are planning a demonstration calling out the Chinese for genocide against the Uyghurs next week. We've got Muslims and Jews and Christians and even Atheists all united to show what the Chinese are doing—and have done for years—to suppress and destroy these people. It's terrible."

"That may be. But the Uyghurs have been doing terrorist acts against their government."

"They have? Perhaps a few. But recently? And that government you're talking about is the Chinese Communist Party, which hates the Uyghurs' natural independence, along with anyone's independence. If there are some Uyghur terrorists in Xinjiang, then which came first, the repression or the terrorists? I'm sure Patrick Henry was a terrorist to the British."

"Seth, sometimes we have to bend a bit so the broader program gets through. There's a lot at stake here that you'll one hundred percent agree with, and the president needs cover to declare the Uyghurs as terrorists."

"But it's not true."

"Seth, are you sure? Did you hear me? There are bigger issues at stake than some Muslim nomads in the middle of Chinese nowhere. We've always had your help—and you've had ours. As we've done for the last many years, your Network and our policies need to help each other. That's how we not only survive, but thrive."

Seth paused again as he started to walk back to the building. "OK. I'll tell Rachel about the interview. And I'll get back to you on the Uyghurs."

"Good. As always, we really appreciate your help."


An hour later Tom was also in his office, starting through his normal routine of briefings and meetings as he coordinated the best National Security advice he could give the president.

He knew it would be a long day but hoped that the new national election guidelines would speed up the reporting and certification of all the Congressional and Senate elections, so that it wouldn't be an all-nighter. And he knew that Special Agent Prescott, General Price, and their teams were monitoring every aspect of the process to ensure that accurate figures were reported.

He also noticed a certain inner peace. After talking with his mother and Seth last night, he found himself less worried, despite immediate issues like more arrests for Hate Speech, and the Uyghurs. He had finally given it all to God, and awaited His timing.

For the moment Tom felt no compulsion to rush into anything—just to wait, watch and listen. Which was a pleasant change. With one exception: he texted Erin about meeting on Thursday.

Kristen kept Grace upstairs that morning while Callie voted, and then Grace worked on math while Callie had an online interview with three key leaders at the Truth Action Forum. At the end of their hour, they told Callie that they'd already done the usual checks, and they'd like her to join them immediately as their Director of Communications. They were thrilled to hear about her close ties to many of those who were planning the demonstration in defense of the Uyghurs the following week.

Kahar Bosakov and his cousin spent the morning in a coffee house in downtown D.C. across the street from a small but well maintained dark-redbrick church. In the planting areas on each side of the central double doors were tasteful bushes and flowers, and a circular sign proclaimed the Chinese Fellowship Christian Church. Several times they walked around the area, noting the church's corner location that must have provided extra light into the sanctuary, and the narrow walkways along the two sides not facing on the streets.

This was the church which they would storm and take over on the morning of November 12$^{th}$.

While they didn't expect much resistance to four armed men with AR-15s, they knew it would be best to understand the church's weekday routine, including what appeared to be its active daycare program, and the drop-off patterns of the parents.

And so they watched, without being obvious. Kahar noted that while the majority of families they could see appeared to be of Chinese ancestry, quite a few did not. Perhaps there was also a Mandarin-immersion program for children.

They noted the sign inviting everyone to their Wednesday night dinner and Bible Study, so they planned to attend and to check out as much of the interior as possible.

Assuming the Chinese government would not give in to the demands which their group's leaders would broadcast after ten churches, schools, and daycares were taken hostage across the U.S., Kahar knew that his role would be to kill everyone inside, then himself.


Erin started that morning in L.A. by arriving for a 9am meeting with an entertainment software company CEO. At 9:30 she was still sitting in the firm's upper floor reception area, admiring the view and using her smartphone, but worried about her day's schedule. A woman just slightly older than her burst through the entrance door and hurried over. Erin stood and they shook hands.

"Erin, I'm so sorry to be late. Please forgive me. Here, come to our multimedia room—I know the others are waiting."

Erin smiled. "Thanks. I hope everything's OK."

As she opened the inner door for Erin and they walked inside, she laughed. "OK? They're great! My husband and I have been trying to adopt a baby for three years, and he came on Friday. Can you believe it? He's absolutely beautiful. My mother and sister-in-law have been helping, but we still didn't quite get it all together this morning. I'm still trying to figure out Maternity Leave."

"I see."

They arrived at the meeting room door. "Do you have children? Aren't babies incredible?"

Late that afternoon from his office Tom checked in with Special Agent Prescott and General Price. Although no polls had yet closed, their new Federal Election Integrity systems were ready to monitor the reporting paths from every one of the nation's many Election Management Systems, once each precinct's results had been loaded from flash drives into the tabulators, and they would continue to do so until every county's totals had been reported from across the nation.

Then he went home to change into a suit and to let Beau out before heading to a downtown hotel where the main ballroom was set up for a large party. Several huge screens on the walls showed different networks. But Tom was actually headed first to a special reception room on the penthouse level, from where the president, his Core Group, the Phoenix Team, and important friends and donors would watch the returns from the Eastern states in the early hours of the evening.

When he arrived in the high-ceilinged room with tall windows and terraces, it was already half full with officials, dignitaries and the leaders of the Progressive election efforts in the House and Senate. Conversation groups were gathered at the buffet table, the two bars, and next to the windows. As he headed to the closest bar, Tom thought he knew most of the people, but there were also a few new faces.

When he turned away from the bar with his drink, Emily was walking up in a light blue cocktail dress.

"For someone who gets around a lot, you also clean up pretty nice," Tom said, tipping his drink in her direction.

"A lot of practice." She smiled. "Boy, I thought I was busy before this election, but right now he's running me crazy."

"How does it look?"

"Our internal exit polls say it's going to be very, very close. And maybe not so good."

"Hmm. I know he'd be very disappointed if the other side wins after all this."

"Yes, he certainly will be. But, hey, have you designated the Uyghurs as terrorists yet?"

He shook his head. "Not yet. Still looking at it. Not a lot of data."

"Well, figure something out. He's really upset about the demonstrations, and Seth is going to do a piece on the East Turkestan Independence Movement."

"He is?"

"Yeah, we talked this morning."

"What about Logan? He's been helping to organize it."

"Not since Drew asked him to stop two days ago. Said it would be terrible for Juggle's business in China—and elsewhere."

"Oh."

She looked across the room and waved. "Gotta go. See you later, downstairs."

Tom tried to process Emily's news about Seth and Logan, but then spent another thirty minutes meeting and greeting others as the attendee numbers swelled. When he started toward the buffet table, Drew Boswell intercepted him and smiled.

"Tom, how are you? Should be a great night, don't you think?"

Tom almost asked Drew about Juggle and the Uyghurs, but instead said, "I certainly hope so. Is the president here?"

"We just came in from the White House. He's pumped."

"Good. Emily just..."

Drew interrupted. "Listen, I've been meaning to ask you. Have you thought about what you want to do after this gig at the White House is up?"

"...Uh, not really. I guess I always imagined doing similar work for a large bank."

"Look, you're young, and you've done an incredible job with this emergency. People said you were too inexperienced to be the National Security Advisor, but you've done amazingly well protecting the nation. It may be a good idea to cash in your government chips while all is well and move on. Coming off this post there's no limit to what you can do. Not just CIO or something, but I'm talking about COO, Board memberships...who knows? People want your advice. You can write your own ticket. And you can start with me—several of my friends in Big Tech have asked for an introduction to you. They want you. Should be a large salary and bonus. Would you mind if I put them in touch? You could even meet a couple tonight."

Tom looked at the older man, who waited expectantly. "Sure, I guess. That would be fine. Yes, I'll be glad to meet them."

"Good, good. Come with me, then. Zack Pruiett with FaceGram is right over here."

Three hours, several drinks, and many conversations later, Tom had adjourned with the others to the large ballroom downstairs. The polls in the Lower Forty-Eight states were now closed, and they had watched and cheered as state after state had reported a sweeping blue tide of Progressive victories from East to West.

Tom, Emily and Logan were standing together beneath the monitor on The Network, where Seth was engaged on a panel in the studio, when the president and First Lady, with a crowd around them, came close by.

President Bradshaw looked over and changed course to the threesome. Beaming, he gave Emily a long hug, then pulled back and said loud enough for his group to hear, "This is the brilliant lady who communicates our message to the world, and," shaking Tom's hand, "this is the man who's kept us all safe for the last two months. Thanks to you both."

"Thank you for your leadership," Emily said.

Tom nodded. "Yes, thank you."

"Now we've got a lot to do. The mandate we've been given tonight means we have to shift into high gear. Logan, that'll involve your company as well. So we'll hit the ground running tomorrow, but for now, tonight, please celebrate. You've certainly earned it."

All three shook the First Lady's hand as the president looked quickly around the room, and a moment later their group was off to the next stop.

Just before midnight Prince Proklor, his generals and key sector leaders were packed into the Oval Office. They had no need for extra spirits to help bend the light and heat from incoming prayers, because there were almost no prayers. As the prince had predicted, when believers realized the magnitude of the Progressive win, they became angry and discouraged, and stopped praying.

Temno began, "Despite it being an election day, we topped 3,000 in both abortions and divorces today. Well done. And you've all heard the election results, which you had so much to do with."

He turned to the prince, who spoke. "Thank you, my friend. Thank you all. Very well done. The stage is set. Stay close to your charges while we coordinate with our forces in China and Russia. Keep all the voices strong as we maneuver America, about to be under our total control."

# 24

*He who is void of virtuous attachments in private life is, or very soon will be, void of all regard for his country. There is seldom an instance of a man guilty of betraying his country, who had not before lost the feeling of moral obligations in his private connections.*

Samuel Adams

Wednesday, November 4

Tom arrived home a little after 1am. While riding in the backseat of the rideshare car he'd checked in on his Core Group phone with both Tanya and General Price—they'd seen no irregularities in the reporting feeds from the many county and state Election Management Systems to the new Federal Tabulation and Reporting Center, and they were prepared to say so at a press conference. It felt like the new Federally controlled election process had gone well on its first use, and the president's candidates had, in fact, won. He thanked them for a job well done. *Thank goodness that's behind us.*

Beau was more than waiting for him. As he tossed the ball for the lab in the backyard, Tom replayed several of the conversations he'd had that evening. As best he could tell, without trying, he had his pick of at least three very prestigious, high-paying, C-Suite jobs in the Big Tech private sector, starting whenever he wanted. One CEO suggested next month.

*Maybe Drew is right: I should leave government service on the "up" of this successful election and start to build my brand on the corporate side.*

Upstairs a few minutes later, as he brushed his teeth, he recalled that he'd have to figure out what to do about the Uyghurs. The truth is the truth, he heard.

Nearing his bed, he thought to pray about all of the day's events, the opportunities, and his upcoming coffee with Erin on Thursday. So he knelt beside the bed. As he began to pray, he suddenly realized that his mind had been racing all evening with him in the driver's seat, just as it used to do.

*Forgive me, Lord. Slow me down. Help me give it to You. To trust You. Listen to You. Ask for Your wisdom and guidance. Don't rush in. This is Your world, not mine. And none of this compares to killing our baby...*

He rose from his prayers with a different perspective. *Wow. It's easy to fall back into the old me...Forgive me, Lord, and stay close. Please. I so need You.*

As he slipped into bed and reached for the light, he thought, *I wonder what happened in those twenty-seven races we checked on?*

It was 2 am as the four couples settled into the comfortable chairs in the White House West Sitting Hall. The president and First Lady were joined by Sally and Drew Boswell, Patricia and Mark Reynolds, and Emily and Logan Schofield. The men's ties were loosened, and everyone had a fresh drink in hand.

"What a great day," President Bradshaw said, raising his glass.

"Yes," Drew agreed, as they all then sipped.

"Our Progressive pioneers, going back over a hundred years to Woodrow Wilson, could only dream about the magnitude of this victory, and about what our new programs will mean for the nation. It's taken decades of communicating our truths to the American people, but now they've given us a clear mandate, so we'll act."

"Do you plan a breather, and ramp up again in January?" Sally Boswell asked.

The president leaned forward and smiled. "Hell no. We won! Let's get going. Starting with nominating your husband for the Secretary of State position that Thomas McCord is about to vacate. Emily and her team have been working overtime on our full new program—some of which we mentioned in the election campaigns—some of which we didn't..." He looked around, smiled again, and took another sip. "...and Patricia and I now plan to roll out the details in front of these 'Christian conservatives' so they can see what the future holds for our nation while they're still here in D.C. Sort of a slow roast."

Emily nodded. "We're ready to go."

"In fact, for the past week our team has been organizing the final arguments for why, given this landslide, it makes perfect sense that we should implement our policies immediately, using Executive Orders, which everyone now accepts, anyway. There's no reason to wait several months or more to write and pass legislation when so much is at stake, from basic protection to social justice."

Patricia agreed. "I think it's a great strategy—come out of the gates next week with real change. I frankly didn't believe it possible, but you were right, Henry. With sixty-two Senators and at least a twenty-vote margin in the House, it'll be clear that we can do whatever we want in January. So, to help those who have suffered so much lately, I agree we should just go ahead now with our plans. Court challenges will take until January anyway, so we'll be good. And, God forbid, if there's another attack, people will be clamoring for us to take charge and move fast."

Bradshaw nodded and turned to Drew Boswell. "And we have a Peace Initiative on the way that Drew and I have worked on that'll save billions of dollars and thousands of lives. Woodrow Wilson would've given anything to have what we'll soon put in place."

"I'm so proud of all of you," the First Lady said. "A great day."


Callie and Kristen had stayed up late to watch the returns, and though the trend was depressing, they'd gone to bed before all the results were in.

Coming out of Kristen's guest room to get coffee that morning, Callie found her friend and her daughter, the latter still in her pajamas, side by side on the sofa, watching the TV with the volume turned down.

"They won everything," Kristen said.

"How bad?"

Kristen turned her head as Callie walked by to the kitchen. "At least a twenty-vote majority in the House, and, for the first time in decades, sixty-one or more in the Senate. A rout. They can do whatever they want."

Callie returned with her coffee and stood behind the sofa as Seth came on from the White House lawn saying, "...an historic legislative mandate for the president's team to implement their full Progressive agenda in January. We understand the White House will be outlining their program in more detail over the next few days, and we expect to interview the president on new domestic and foreign policy initiatives later this week. A great victory, indeed."

"Indeed," Callie repeated. "Wonderful."

Kristen looked at Grace sitting next to her and said, "We need to keep praying."

"Yeah, but it's not easy when our prayers seem to go unanswered," Callie said as she walked to her room to get dressed.

Thirty minutes later Callie descended the outside steps and put the key in the door to her apartment. Stepping inside, she found an envelope on the floor with her name and Grace's on the outside.

She hesitated, but then picked it up. In it was an unfired bullet and a single sheet of paper on which was typed, "We won. Stop your hate speech and publicly denounce your white privilege, or there will be consequences. We are watching, bitch."

By unspoken custom everyone arrived at their offices in the White House a little later that morning. Tom noticed more staffers in the halls than usual, sipping coffee, smiling and telling stories. Everyone appeared to be very happy.

After putting down his computer bag, Tom swiveled in his chair to his small wall safe, opened it, and took out the printed report and the USB drive about possible election hacking that he'd assembled for the president. With a quick copy and paste he deleted the details of equipment and protocols and made a new list with just the names of the key races, added twenty more to camouflage his focus, called his assistant, and asked her to give him the details on these races.

When Seth returned to The Network's DCNet headquarters after his piece on the White House lawn, he noted the air of triumphal victory in their offices. People were looking at the election results, smiling and laughing.

He checked in briefly with Rachel to start the formal process for their potential presidential interview, then he asked two interns to research any Uyghur initiated terrorist activities in China or elsewhere.

Clayton and Ahmad shared duty that morning in the Pentagon, ready to respond to any threats. After the DEA bombing and their follow-up on the WhiteStorm incident, there had not been a lot of action, except occasional violations of hate speech and "normal" crimes. They and their colleagues hoped nothing would derail their expected shift back to foreign-only threats with the end of the State of Emergency after one more week.

After logging in at their adjoining consoles, Clayton turned to Ahmad. "Tom called me on the way in this morning. He wants to know if either of us knows which came first: Chinese suppression of the Uyghurs, or Uyghur terrorist activities."

Ahmad frowned, then said, "That's easy. Chinese suppression. The CCP can't stand any type of independent thinking or action—look at Hong Kong, all religions, businesses, schools—and the Uyghurs represent to them the double-threat of an independent religious region within their own country. The suppression started early and has been brutal. Calling it counter-terrorism is like taking a sledgehammer to a tack. But I guess it gives cover for some Muslim countries on the Chinese dole to look the other way while our brothers and sisters suffer. Terrible."

"That's pretty much what I told him, but I thought I'd check with you. How's the demonstration looking next week?"

Ahmad turned away for a moment, then looked back to his friend. "Great. Several churches, synagogues and mosques have really gotten behind it, here and in the other cities. Your introduction to Natalie led to your friend Tom's mother, the former Congresswoman, who has been a huge help. She's no sluggard! She's been encouraging the Chinese church, the same way we've encouraged our mosque. People will be taking real risks to participate, but it might just happen. I think they see us coming together in the week the State of Emergency ends as a way to both call out the Chinese government and to celebrate the return of our own rights."

"Makes sense. I plan to be there, and Andrea, too, baby permitting."

"Good. But I just got a voicemail from Logan Schofield, saying he has a conflict and can't participate. Odd. And then there's the young Uyghur at our mosque who seems really interested in what we're doing, but is also afraid to be involved, which is understandable. I've been drilling down into what we have on the situation in Xinjiang today, to try to better understand and help them."

Right after lunch Tom's assistant caught him in the hall between meetings and handed him a folder. "Here are those results you wanted."

A few minutes later, alone at his desk, he prayed again about Erin and then opened the folder. He knew the key races the president had flagged almost by heart, but after a quick look he had to get out his boss's original handwritten list and go down it, one by one.

In every one of those races the Progressive candidate had won, and with an unexpectedly large margin. Every one out of all twenty-seven. *Is that likely?*

"Jacob?"

"Hi, Janet," the Speaker said on his phone as his Capitol Office meeting broke up. "Not a great day."

"No. We lost big. Even places that used to believe in our values. Was it the lockdown?"

He sighed. "Not sure. It really doesn't matter—they'll have the power in January to pass anything they want, to transform the nation in ways that'll be hard to come back from, if we ever even get another chance."

"Pretty depressing. How can so many good people be so deluded?"

"We've just been talking about that, looking at the high level numbers. Of course we'll drill down in the coming days. They simply trounced us. What does your son say?"

"I expect we'll talk soon—I try not to interrupt him. And I don't know where Richard is. I plan to stay here 'till they release him."

"I hope they do, after that video he made. Anyway, let's get together in a day or two for a drink or a prayer or both."

"You're on."

Daylight Savings Time had ended the previous Sunday, and so it was dark in the late afternoon as Tom prepared to leave his office. And it was raining.

He knew they would be back to full schedule the next day, and the president wanted an answer at their regular security briefing on classifying several Uyghur groups as terrorists. Tom had found only a few very thin examples from earlier years, and he knew that moving forward would jeopardize or limit the demonstrations that were now planned for the following Thursday. He had expected Emily's help in trying to slim down the president's request, but when he asked her that afternoon, she had begged off, saying she was too busy with the Progressive Program Rollout coming up.

Callie had texted that she wanted to see him, which was fine with him because he also wanted to talk with her about his lunch with Erin the next day, so he planned to take a car to her home.

Just before leaving he called Tanya Prescott to find out if she had any news about his father's "Video Six"—she did not, but would inquire in the morning. As they were about to hang up, he asked about the elections, and she responded that the FBI had monitored all the communications between every Election Management System and the new Federal Tabulation and Reporting Center. Everything seemed to be correct and without issue.

"I think the results are accurate, and with the wide margins involved, there won't be any recounts, even in the few places that still keep a paper ballot back-up. Congratulations! Director Toomey has already called it a very clean election, and I think I agree."

He thanked her, picked up his computer bag, and went to wait for his ride.

Five minutes later, as the driver navigated the wet streets of D.C., Tom called his mother and was surprised by the note of weariness and defeat in her voice. It was so unlike her. Between the unknown of her husband's fate, the repudiation by the American electorate at the polls of everything she believed to be important, and the imminent abortion of her grandchild, Janet Sullivan sounded, for the first time in a long time, "down".

Tom tried to encourage her and asked her to pray for Erin.

When they hung up, it struck Tom that he had helped create everything that now caused his mother such palpable distress. He said a silent prayer for forgiveness.

Callie had sent him a text telling him to ring the bell at Kristen's front door, which he did, while under an umbrella. Kristen opened the door and hurried him inside, where he hung his coat by the door and greeted the three ladies with as much positive spirit as he could muster, helped by the wonderful smell of good food.

"We're having homemade chili," Kristen said. "Would you like some? And maybe a beer?"

He stooped to pick up Grace for a hug and said, "Yes. Both sound great. Thank you."

Twenty minutes later, after discussing the devastating election results, Callie's research for her new job, Kristen's take on the D.C. office market, and Grace's history homework, they enjoyed some chili in bowls on their laps.

As Callie walked their empty bowls back to the kitchen, she suggested to Grace that she needed to finish her homework, and the adults were left sitting around the coffee table in the living room.

Callie showed Tom the envelope with the bullet.

"I can't believe this," he said, taking pictures with his phone. "I'll contact my friend at the FBI again tomorrow. Surely this is just some over-exuberant young person flaunting the election victory."

"With, apparently, a gun," Kristen noted. Tom nodded.

"We're not afraid for ourselves," Callie added. "But I have to think about Grace."

"Of course. Do what you think is best. I've shown I'm not very good at providing wise advice. Maybe you should take Alexei up on his offer to visit Cyprus!" he concluded, trying to be positive.

Callie shrugged and smiled. "Not a bad idea. Grace has a passport from our trip to Canada." She looked at Kristen. "We could take an all-girl-post-election-unwind-trip to the Mediterranean."

Kristen nodded. "Why not? And I think a trip to Israel—where I've always wanted to go—is just a short flight from there."

Tom said, "Seriously, I'll bring this up to Tanya Prescott at the FBI tomorrow. Hopefully she'll have more advice. But surely all of this will calm down in the next few days."

"Or get worse," Kristen said. "These people are deceived by the real enemy, and like their deceiver, they don't just want to win. They want to win and then humble us—even destroy us—for having the audacity to hold a different opinion. Like they went after the bakery shops a few years ago. They want to be *seen* to be in control, to flaunt it. And they want us to acknowledge their superiority. So it actually could get worse now that they have this victory."

Tom nodded and took a sip of his beer. "Which, I must say, sort of bugs me. All the experts say the results are correct and true, but the overwhelming Progressive victory in every closely contested race just seems impossible."

Callie pointed her beer bottle at him. "You work for the president and were in charge of making sure it was all OK. And you're telling us that *you're* not sure?"

He raised his hand. "I know. The safeguards were all in place. No voting machine was ever connected to the internet. You'd have to tamper with thousands of machines all over the country to get this outcome. But it just doesn't seem logical."

They were silent for a few moments. "Then if you keep hearing that voice, pray about it," Kristen said.

He looked at both of them and nodded. "Speaking of prayer, let me tell you about the most important thing, which is my meeting with Erin tomorrow for lunch and what I'm going to tell her. Then I hope we can pray for her, and for wisdom and the right words for me."


That midnight in the Oval Office there was again no need for extra forces to bend incoming prayer vectors away from the demonic leadership gathered around the Resolute Desk. The believers' prayers had almost completely stopped.

Prince Proklor and his generals—and many of the D.C. sector leaders like Balzor—congratulated each other on their coming control of all the levers of power in the world's "greatest and freest nation".

"Well done. Well done, my friends," the prince said from above the desk. "Look around! As we knew, once they lost, they gave up and stopped praying. We're free from all that interference and can again focus on silencing any mention of Him or his Son. Anywhere. Any time.

"When the men we controlled won the parliamentary elections in Germany in '33, we had no idea where that nation would wind up, but Adolf started ruling by decree just a month later, after the Reichstag fire, and it just got better and better every year. We can expect the same thing for America in the coming years—with maybe just a bit more window dressing, but the same powerful result. And this time there is no other country to undo what America will become, like happened to Germany, because the world will be divided into thirds, and *our* truth—not His—will reign in all three. What a glorious victory!"

# Thursday, November 5

Tom slept fitfully for only a few hours and was up at 4 am. After turning on the coffee pot before its appointed time, he first knelt in his living room, dark except for the streetlamp on a pole outside, then lay face down on the hardwood floor and implored God for wisdom and guidance for all the day's upcoming meetings and decisions.

*Will Erin listen to me? What will the president say when I tell him the truth about the Uyghurs? I hope I can deliver that message in private. And my father? The election results?* All the others...He prayed more, but the peace he sought would not come.

He was in his office by seven, reviewed the usual overnight traffic from around the globe, and a little before eight arrived in The Situation Room for the Presidential Daily Briefing. He sat at the table between Emily and Tanya, with the president in the end seat.

As the briefer from the CIA reviewed both old and new threats, Tom noticed in the interchanges that the president was unusually animated and engaged, and seemingly in a hurry to get on with his day, as he moved the briefer along.

After the CIA brief, Rob, as usual, asked if others around the table had input. Tanya reported that there was nothing new from the WhiteStorm leads in Germany, nor from their interrogations of the earlier attackers. When there was silence, the president stood, as did everyone, and just before turning to leave he looked at Tom, smiled and said, "Don't worry about that Uyghur thing. We took care of it. Emily can brief you. Everyone have a great day! Finally, we're about to be in full control, and there's a lot to do."

Tanya hurried out to another meeting; Tom turned to Emily and waited.

"In an hour we'll be announcing that Thomas McCord will be stepping down as Secretary of State, and then he'll announce later that he's running for the Senate in North Carolina. Drew Boswell will be the president's nominee to replace him. Secretary McCord will be putting three Uyghur organizations on our Terrorist Watch List today, and Seth's going to do a piece on them, which we hope will discourage anyone from taking their side in any protests."

For a moment Tom was speechless. "Why would McCord do that?"

Emily shrugged. "Maybe with this week's election he's seen which way our party and the nation are headed and wants to be in the good graces of the president and his Progressive wing." She smiled. "But you'd have to ask him."

"And Seth? I thought he was organizing the demonstrations as a human rights issue, and that Logan was helping."

"I guess they finally realized the truth."

"Emily, the truth is that those Uyghur organizations, if they've done one or two small incidents, are nothing compared to the suppression and genocide they've suffered from their own government. You've heard it all."

"Well, that's not the truth as I now understand it. And I can assure you it's not what the president believes. Much better just to get onboard and go with the flow when the issue is a bunch of third-class nomads on the other side of the world."

He paused. "No. I prefer the truth, whatever it is or whatever it means. And I thought Progressives cared about *all* people."

Her smile broadened. "Wow, that's a new Tom Sullivan. Be careful, that might get you in trouble! The Uyghurs are no big deal. But I gotta go. The president acts like he's, like, twenty years younger and full of energy and ideas—but I have to keep them all together. And we have some more changes at the top to announce later. Plus your Trusted Citizen Program. All good. See ya."


An hour later Tom was at his desk when Tanya Prescott knocked on the open door, holding a cup of coffee. "Got a minute?"

"Sure. Come in."

She walked to his desk, and he invited her to a chair.

"I have some not great news about your father and the other men in that video. The authorities at the detention center were apparently really embarrassed, and they're throwing the book at them for violating rules and laws that exist outside the State of Emergency. I'm afraid he's been transferred to a minimum security but very real prison in Maryland, and they're preparing charges against him which, if proven, could result in five or more years behind bars."

"My father, the non-violent attorney who just wanted clarity about truth from a bishop?"

"I'm afraid so."

"That's insane. What can you or we do about it?"

"At least for now, and as a friend, I suggest nothing. It would not look good for us to intervene in what's an internal matter within the prison system. Hopefully calmer heads will prevail."

"I wonder if that's what people said in Berlin in 1934."

"What?"

"Sorry...between this news and classifying the Uyghurs as terrorists and another threat of violence to my friend Callie and her daughter, I'm beginning to really fear what we've unleashed on our country."

"You couldn't have known."

"But I guess that's the point. That's why we have our rights protected in the Constitution—so we don't ever find out what actually lies just outside those guardrails."

They were silent for a few moments.

Tom continued. "Let me know when you learn more about Dad. But, listen, I'm still concerned about Tuesday's election results. The wins and the majorities just seem so out of whack. Is there no way someone could have interfered?"

"Your boss won. And you'd either have to physically tamper with most of the voting machines in a county or a state, or with the Election Management System tabulation machines that the voting machines feed into through physical thumb drives. The first would be a logistics impossibility, and we carefully monitored everything that was put into the EMS reporting system, from every county. It was all correct. And my boss has clearly opined on that fact."

He thought for a few moments. "Could someone on your team drill down further? Look with a fresh pair of eyes?"

Tanya moved in her seat and pursed her lips. "I guess someone could. But not the FBI. Just the fact that we were doing that would be leaked and cause a big ruckus that I couldn't explain, particularly to the Director. You said the president wanted an election that was clean *and* looked clean. The FBI starting an investigation for no cause would not exactly fit that outcome."

"You're right, of course. But, what if we asked an outside party to quietly look into it? You could give me the information, or tapes, or links, or whatever they would need to check on it, for, say, one or two sample county EMS tabulation machines, and I would pass it along. No one in government would be doing it. And they would report to you and me. Could that work?"

She moved again, thinking. "I guess so. But vote tampering just seems so impossible. Who would do the checking?"

"I'll have to think about it. I have several friends in that business who are pretty good. Would anything involved be classified?"

"No. The election is over, and all the passwords and codes will change before the next one. But I imagine it would take several experienced people and some sophisticated software to do a really deep dive."

"OK. Let me think and pray about it. Thank you. And, Tanya, do you pray about things like this?"

She smiled. "In my line of work, what do you think?"

"I thought so. Maybe pray for this. And start pulling together the info for just a couple of those machines. I'll let you know if I think we should do it."

She stood. "Fine. And I'll keep as close an eye on your father as I can."

"Thanks."

Tanya left, and Tom looked at his watch. Despite his prayers, his stomach was in revolt as he grabbed his coat and headed out.


For their lunch meeting Tom had chosen a white tablecloth seafood restaurant near Erin's office on Massachusetts Avenue. Nenav, uncertain of her destination, followed Erin on the sidewalk; she was wearing a beige coat against the brisk wind and cooler temperature.

But the spiritual temperature increased dramatically when she opened the door to the wood paneled foyer, and Tom greeted her. Nenav had to turn away from the blast of heat and light—both internal from Tom and as accompanying answered prayers for Erin from others—when Tom smiled and took her hand. With this intensity, Nenav knew he would be unable to stay with Erin and manage the voices within her—at best he would have to dip in and out.

The greeter led them to a table near the front window, and they ordered sparkling water. Erin smiled.

"How was your trip?" he asked.

"Fine. Busy, as always. But California is just the exactly wrong distance away. And congratulations on the president's team winning so big on Tuesday. That Senate race you had me look at turned out to be not even close."

"You noticed? I was going to ask you about it. I may—*may*—ask someone to take another look at those results, after the fact, on a deep dive, and I wonder if you might be interested? Completely off the grid. I think with your skills you'd be the perfect person to lead a small team."

"Now I'm both intrigued and confused. A team?"

"I'm not sure. Maybe. Here's why I'm interested." He took five minutes, interrupted while they ordered, to give her the background, the true scope of his original inquiry, and the seeming improbability of the results.

When he finished, she took a sip and said, "Yes, as you know, to really check that out, it would take quite a bit of computing power, looking through all the codes. You might get lucky, or it might take a while. And you probably won't find anything. But, look, thank you for asking, and let me know if you decide to do it. I'll be glad to help."

"Thank you." They chatted some more until their dishes arrived, and Tom asked if Erin would like some wine. She declined, and then he asked if he could say a blessing, to which she nodded, and so they bowed their heads for his short vocal prayer—and a longer silent one.

They took their first bites, and he said, "Erin, the election issue is important, and I'm really glad you're interested. It will be great to have someone running it who I know and trust. But of course the main reason we're here is our baby. Thank you for coming and being willing to listen to me. I know this is awkward, but I've got quite a bit to say—to get off my chest—so I hope you'll let me say it all before you respond."

She smiled. "Sure. In my condition, I always feel like eating. So go ahead."

He paused. "First, I know that I'm a jackass. Really. Since before I came to D.C. my focus has been solely on me—success, fun, the next great adventure, the next great conquest. I'm sorry you got caught up in my selfishness, and I hope—whatever else happens—that I haven't hurt you too badly, and that you'll forgive me."

Looking at him, she took another bite.

"Second, I'm not the same person you went to the beach with. For several reasons—our situation first among them—I've rediscovered the faith I had years ago. It's good, and it's powerful. And it's personal. I'm not talking about 'religion,' but about a growing relationship with the only one who can ultimately forgive me and make my story right—by making it part of His story. From now on I want Him to run my life and to lead me with every decision."

He paused to cut a piece of grilled swordfish, and she reached for the bread.

"Next, that faith tells me that the life inside you is a real baby, and that we—mostly me—are responsible. The baby is innocent and precious in God's sight, and we have no right to kill him or her. Legally, yes. Morally, and in God's eyes, it would be abhorrent.

"Finally, I like you a lot. You're smart, funny and attractive. I like being with you. I suspect, given some real time together, we will grow to love each other. So here's the new part: I'm asking you to marry me, and to have the baby together. I don't expect you to answer now, for all the obvious reasons. But I'm very serious.

"As you consider it, think, like I did, of all the people we know who got married because they were 'in love', when they were really 'in lust'. They'd been living together and just thought it must be right to get married. The guy probably felt guilty not to, after taking a year or more out of the girl's life. So they get married and realize not long after that there's really nothing holding them together, that it was just the easiest thing to do after living together.

"Then think about us, or at least me. I have a real reason to be committed to you—our child. And I certainly like you. And my faith says that marriage won't work unless we both let Him be the real head, which I'm prepared to do. It also says that a believer shouldn't marry a non-believer, but in this case I think raising our child together is at least as important, and maybe someday you'll embrace that faith as well.

"So here's what I'm proposing. Think, even pray, about marrying me. I will do my best to be the spiritual head of our family and to love you sacrificially. I mean that, with God's help and yours. If for any reason that's not possible, then have the baby with more support than you can imagine and either we'll raise her or him as single parents with my full support, or we can give the baby up for adoption. But, whatever you do, please don't kill our baby tomorrow. Or at least delay that irreversible act while you consider these alternatives, and, again, hopefully become my wife. And that means for the rest of our lives."

She had not taken a bite for quite a while, and now she stared at him. Finally she said, "OK."

"OK what?"

"OK, I won't have the abortion tomorrow. I'll postpone it and think about all you said."

He broke into a broad smile. "Erin, really? Great! Thank you. You can't imagine how happy this makes me."

"Actually, I think I can. And that's why I'm agreeing. What's next?"

He laughed. "I guess we should go on dates."

She grinned. "Yes, I guess we should. Who knows what might happen?"

"Thank you, Erin. And thank you, Lord."

"Yes."

Emily was in her office at the White House that afternoon and called Seth. "Hey, I'm confirming you're all set for the live Domestic interview on Monday night and the Foreign Policy interview on Tuesday, timed to be right before Veterans Day. Each night you'll be on with a panel of two other friendly journalists, but you'll be the anchor. OK?"

"Sounds good. Do you want to see our questions ahead of time?"

"Of course. And, listen, we'll have Patricia Reynolds with the president the first night, then Andrew Boswell on Tuesday, who'll be the new Secretary of State when this all rolls out. He has tremendous experience all over the world, and this will be a great venue to launch him in his new role."

"OK, great. We'll do some quick research."

"Last thing: Logan and I are having a celebration of the election this Saturday night at our place. We'd love for you and Natalie to come. We should have the usual crowd plus some more."

"I'll check, but sounds great. Thanks!"


From the back seat of the car returning to his office, Tom called Callie and gave her the news about Erin's decision.

"Tom, that's so good. Thank Him—and you. I'll let Kristen and the others know, and we'll shift gears with the prayers. And how did she react to your offer?"

Tom hesitated, visualizing the conversation he'd had the night before with Callie and Kristen when he told them about his decision to do what was right, and they had agreed. "She seemed open to at least consider marrying. I have no idea where we'll wind up, but for now the baby's safe."

"I know it was tough—and tough for someone else I know pretty well—but it was the right thing. We'll keep praying for God's guidance. Meanwhile, we're having a meeting of the congregation after Sunday's service because the church and several of us have received so many threats, telling us to stop our hate speech against Critical Race Theory, LGBTQ rights, BLM, and all the rest, or else there'll be 'consequences.'"

"Violent threats against hate speech? That's a twist."

"Yes."

"I wish I'd never heard that term. Or used it."

"Come to the service. And bring Erin."

"We'll see. Thanks."

They hung up. Tom looked out the car window. As much as he didn't want to think about it, the election results still bothered him. A voice pestered him to be sure—his responsibility. He dialed his phone again.

"Tanya, hey. I want to go ahead with that check of the results in at least two races... I know, but humor me, please. Can you get me the passwords you used to monitor the federal communications with two random EMS tabulators, and also the flash drives –or copies of their contents—for the results between the voting machines and the tabulators? Let's make it nearby and easy—one set from that Virginia race on the list and one from eastern Pennsylvania. By tomorrow? I have a good person to run it, and I'm thinking how to put together a team to help her."

"The communication passwords I can get. Not sure about the information on the flash drives, unless we open an actual investigation, which we really don't want to do. Tell you what, I live in that part of Virginia and know the guy who runs the elections pretty well—we have kids in the same school. I'll contact him and see if I can go over and make some copies. Not sure about the other one."

"Thanks, Tanya, for anything you can do to help me put this to bed. It's driving me crazy."

Nenav had only been able to hear snippets of Tom and Erin's lunch conversation, but the result, which he confirmed an hour later when he was alone with her and she called the Northeast Pregnancy Center to reschedule her abortion, was terrible.

General Bespor had just reported that outcome, which had been passed up the chain of command that evening, to Prince Proklor, who was livid, despite their huge victories only two days before.

Fuming with anger that another Sullivan appeared to be complicating their mission, he raged at Bespor to use whatever means necessary to get rid of Tom Sullivan permanently, and to remove him from the White House immediately, before he did any more damage.

# Friday, November 6

Tom awoke that morning and immediately thanked God that he was not again standing outside the abortion clinic—until yesterday he had thought he would be. And he would text Erin shortly and ask her to join him at the Election Celebration that Emily and Logan were planning for Saturday. He smiled and shook his head. *An actual date with the mother of our child...And she agreed to meet Mom.*

As he went downstairs for coffee, it occurred to him *What if Erin had been in town two months ago and I hadn't met Callie at Seth's party? Where would we all be?* He had a chill. *Thin threads.*

Erin was dressed and having yogurt and berries in her condo, with her phone on the breakfast table, talking to Tracy.

"So he didn't pressure me at all. In fact, there's an interesting forensic cyber-thing he wants me to help him with, and...he asked me to marry him."

"What?"

Erin laughed. "Yes. Of all the things he might have said, I wasn't expecting that one. I didn't know what to say, and he wants us to date before I answer...but he believes we can love each other and wants to try for the long term. Isn't that unbelievable?"

"Yes. Unbelievable."

"Starting with, he wants me to have dinner with his mother tonight. She's still in town because of that mess with his father."

"Can't wait to hear."

President Bradshaw and Drew Boswell were alone in the West Sitting Room, having coffee before their breakfast that morning with Patricia Reynolds, Nancy Cantrell, and Gerry Veazy.

"It all worked," the president said to his old friend. Then he smiled and took a sip.

"Yes, it did."

"And we're good?"

"Yes. Untraceable. But if it were, it would only be to a rogue cyber gang in China. And here?"

"We're good. The FBI and NSA have signed off on the process and the results. The margins are too great to trigger recounts, and with the impressive new federal reporting system, most places ditched expensive paper ballots anyway. And if anything ever did come up, Jim and Nathan will be ready with the usual fog at the Bureau and at NSA—they know what's at stake to be sure only good people stay in power. We can finally implement all the key policies so many before us could only dream about."

"The Chinese are ready to go, as you know. The call with the Premier on Sunday will be a great first step on the road to world peace. The Russians are still trying to figure out if our offer is real. I'm going over there after our TV panel, and when they hear how much business and wealth will flow from the peace we'll usher in, they'll jump on with us."

"Good, good. And, look, Drew. One more thing. Unfortunately our State of Emergency ends on Tuesday, so there will be a great clamoring to go back to the way we were before the attacks. No more surveillance or monitoring of domestic emails and speech."

Boswell sighed. The president continued, "But as we've discussed—and, by the way, I've had a similar conversation with Jim at the Bureau—we aren't going to stop immediately. Or completely. We'll stop publicly pre-censoring meetings and speeches—I get that—very public—but we'll take our time on rolling back the less obvious ways we have to find out what people are saying and thinking—it's still a very dangerous time. These past two months have shown the country the benefits from strong leadership and Progressive policies. That's what we'll continue to give our people, with or without a formal State of Emergency. And we'll act forcefully, when we have to. Our policies are too important to leave to the whims of future voters who don't understand."

"I completely agree. And remember I have reliable friends who can take any kind of 'action' that's needed, off the grid and without a trace, if that's ever necessary."

Bradshaw nodded. "I hope it never is, but it's good to know. So let's look at a short list of who we think will help with this—General Price should be one. But I don't think Tom will buy in. And I'm not sure about Tanya Prescott. I think those two will have to be replaced with people who understand how really important this all is."

"Yes. I have great candidates for both their positions. Good people who get it."

"Excellent. Let me meet them." Bradshaw picked up a folder from the table next to him. "In fact, let's go over the full list of who we want on our inside team working together from here on—in government, business and media—for the big push during the next two years."


Tanya Prescott tapped on the door at her county's Election Commission office thirty minutes before it was to open. A tall, middle-aged African American opened the door and smiled.

"Come in."

"Thank you, Bill, for meeting me on my way in." She stepped through the door and he locked it behind them.

"Sure. Glad to help my favorite FBI star. What's up? You want some coffee?"

"Thank you. Like I said last night, we've been asked to take some process samples to help improve the new federal reporting program for the next election. I thought I'd reach out to a friend to see if you can help us."

"Tanya, as long as you only copy stuff and leave all the originals here, in case there's some kind of crazy challenge during the next six months, that'll be fine." He motioned for her to follow him to the breakroom and then, coffees in hand, to a locked storeroom.

He pressed the code into the lock, opened the door, and switched on the light. There were two rows of floor to ceiling shelves full of small plastic boxes, arranged by precinct numbers.

"The machines themselves are back in our secure warehouse, but this is where we keep the USB flash drives from each voting machine for at least six months after every election, according to the new federal regulations. Each box contains the drives from all the voting machines in a single precinct. Before the election we load all the correct information—candidates and issues—onto each flash drive from a single-purpose computer run by special software approved by the federal government. The flash drives are then inserted into the machines, locked to each one with a seal, and the machines are taken out to the precincts. They are never connected to the internet. The results from each machine are recorded on the same flash drive and returned here under two-person control for tabulation. It's really secure."

Tanya nodded. "Looks like it. So...I guess I should copy contents from the flash drives from a couple of precincts to let the cyber folks see what they might do to improve the process."

"Fine, but I'll have to make the copies. For security, these are special flash drives which only fit into voting machines. But I have a separate device which allows me to one-way copy from a voting machine flash drive to a standard flash drive. Did you bring any?"

She held up a bag. "Lots."

"Good. Pick a couple of precincts and we'll get to work."

Tanya selected two of the boxes and handed them to her friend. He led her to a table with a small electronic device. It had two ports—an input side for the special drives, and an output for the standard drives like Tanya brought. He opened the first precinct.

"A large one. Nine voting machines. But we must have thought there were ten, because we loaded an extra flash drive. It was never put in a machine, but it's here, so I'll include it as a special bonus."

She smiled. "Thanks, Bill. You're a great friend."

Late that morning Tom was returning from a briefing in the Situation Room and his assistant handed him a folder. Tanya Prescott walked up as he read the first line: "State Department labels three American Uyghur organizations as terrorists and imposes sanctions on their activities."

He looked up. Tanya smiled and held up a cloth bag. "I got 'em."

"Come in."

He closed his office door behind them, and Tanya explained what she had and how she'd obtained them. "It's only two precincts in one of the races you asked about, but it's all I could do off the grid, without raising a lot of questions and turning it official. I got one copy and then made another of the USB drive from each voting machine in each precinct. And here," handing him a folded paper, "are the unique passwords used this cycle for how the new federal Election Integrity System communicated with the EMS in our county, both for downloading security updates and for uploading the final results the night of the election. And, again, we've monitored and checked that process regularly for the last two weeks."

"Thank you. It's probably not anything, anyway, and I don't want to raise any flags, but it's bugging me, and this should settle it. You have no one who could take a look at these?"

"Don't want to. We've already opined on the election, and I suspect that Director Toomey would not be pleased if I started something now on my own. If you're going to look into this, then be my guest, but do it with someone who has no reason to question why, or to leak what's going on—use someone far removed from anything official."

"I have a friend, Erin MacNeil, who's well versed in the skills we need, and she'll re-check all those communications to be sure no one interfered. But she doesn't have the computers on hand to look deeply into the flash drives. I have an idea about that, though. And I want to ask again, there's nothing secret or confidential on these, is there?"

"No. And after the post-election period, the protocol is to erase and reformat them before they're used again."

"Good. You keep one of the sets for safety as a back-up and give me one. I'll ask my team to make another copy this afternoon, without telling them any details. I know you think I'm crazy, but thank you

PARKER HUDSON

again for your help. Let's take a minute to call Erin together, so she can hear that you're at least unofficially involved, and I'll tell you what I'm thinking about for the deep dive. And let's keep all this just between us for now, since it's probably nothing. Then we can both get back to more important stuff, like getting my father out of custody when the State of Emergency ends on Tuesday."


Ahmad had the day off from Pentagon duty and was walking to his car after Friday Prayers at their mosque when Kahar Bosakov called from behind him. He stopped, smiled and waited for Kahar and his cousin, Ablet Sabri, to walk over. They all greeted and shook hands.

Mavlan, the demon who now stayed close to the two cousins, silently suggested to Ablet that he should be on guard for some sort of trap. Ablet took a pace back and, while the other two spoke, he regularly scanned the parking lot.

Kahar said, "Ahmad, have you seen this?" he asked, holding up his phone.

"I guess not. What?"

"It's on The Network. The government has just named three Uyghur organizations here in the U.S. as terrorist groups and forbidden Americans from associating with them. We know the groups. They raise money to help poor families, and they try to connect people here and there. Does that make them terrorists?"

Ahmad took the phone and scrolled quickly through the article. "I have no idea. It sounds crazy, But I'll make some calls this afternoon to find out."

Kahar was silent and glanced at Ablet before asking Ahmad, "With this, will the demonstrations at the Chinese embassy and consulates for our people still happen on Thursday?"

"As far as I know. Here, give me your number, and I'll text you when I know more."

Tanya Prescott had just unwrapped a sandwich at her desk at FBI Headquarters when her laptop signaled an incoming video call from Nathan Price at the NSA. She clicked. "General, hi. How are you?"

He was at Camp Meade at his desk. "I'm fine, thanks. Listen, quick question. A standard notice popped up from a county election office in Virginia saying the FBI asked them to make copies of USB flash drives from the election. I got it because the subject is flagged for High Priority, given that we're supposed to be reporting on the election together, and your name's mentioned. What's up?"

She put down her sandwich. "Uh, oh. Sorry. Not a big deal. Tom asked us to do a deeper review to see if we can improve the process in the future. So I contacted my friend in our county and he made a copy of two precincts' results for us. I haven't mentioned it to Director Toomey yet—it's no big deal."

"Tom asked? Neither your team nor ours saw any issues with the election. Why would Tom want you to look further?"

"I'm not sure, really. He said it's for the future. I haven't even assigned anyone to do the review yet. Probably won't for a while. Again, it's not an investigation. You know Tom—I think he just wants to improve the process next time around."

"OK. Let me know if you find anything. We'd like to help if we can."

"Will do. Thanks. Have a great weekend."

She hung up, forgot about her lunch, and started drafting a short note to her boss, hoping it would arrive before the general made a second call.


Clayton was at lunch in the Pentagon cafeteria with a teammate when Ahmad called.

"I know, I was going to call you in a few minutes. It's terrible. We can't participate in a demonstration supporting a designated terrorist group. We're specifically prohibited."

"That's what I thought, but I wanted to check. What now?"

"I don't know, but everyone in our group has bailed, or been forced to."

Ahmad paused. "Terrible. Our Uyghur friends will be angry and disappointed. I thought I was beginning to win them over to a different way of changing things."

"I'd like to see the research behind all this, but there's no time."

"I've actually been doing that for the past week, and our experts tell me the only terrorist training camp is small, and next door in Afghanistan."

"So there's some validity to the terrorist claim?"

"I guess. But get this—our guys believe the camp is paid for and protected by the Chinese Communists. They *want* there to be a small group of Uyghur Muslim terrorists for just this reason—to stir up hatred and to give them an excuse to overreact. Actually, a pretty smart policy on their part if you want people to hate each other."

"And you want to keep rounding them up for reeducation and sterilization."

"Exactly. Or blaming them for your problems."

"What can you do for your friends at the mosque?"

"I guess I'll have to tell'em that we'll try to sort it out and demonstrate later."

"Not good."

"Erin," Tom said on his phone, "I know it's short notice, but can we meet in the bar at the seafood restaurant around the corner from your office right after work, before we go to dinner with Mom? There's someone I want you to meet, and he's catching a plane this evening."

"Uh, sure. A little after five?"

"Great! I'll come by your office and we'll walk over. See you then."

That afternoon Emily knocked at Tom's open door. He smiled from his desk and waved her in.

"I need your words about the Trusted Citizen Program for the president's Domestic Program roll-out on Monday with Seth's panel. It's gonna be amazing—we have so much to announce."

He looked at his watch. "OK. I'm not crazy about it, but you'll have it in an hour."

"It's a great program. And I thought you suggested it."

"Not exactly—it was Patricia. But I'm on it. Is it domestic on Monday and international on Tuesday?"

"Yes, the president speaks to the nation, with Patricia on Monday and Drew on Tuesday, with a very patriotic theme before Veterans Day, and there'll be a panel of three interviewers to ask them questions. I think it'll be awesome—he's excited to be bringing in all these changes, particularly using Executive Orders, and he's really good with this sort of thing."

"And Seth will be one of the interviewers?"

She smiled. "Of course. The leader. He's almost part of the White House now."

"Great. Can't wait. I'll get it to you."

"And see you tomorrow night at our place. Are you bringing Erin?"

Tom smiled. "Yes. I hope you'll get to know her better."

"I'm sure we will. See 'ya."


After Tom and Erin's eyes adjusted to the dimmer light in the bar, Tom saw Alexei Nobikov seated at a four top on the left side. They walked over, Alexei stood and smiled, and Tom introduced them.

Pulling out a chair for Erin, Tom said, "This is going to take a little explaining, so I'll order our drinks and then be as brief as possible—I know you have a plane to catch, Alexei. While I hit the bar, maybe you could each tell the other your professional backgrounds, particularly related to cyber skills."

When Tom returned with their drinks Erin and Alexei were deep into a discussion on the pros and cons of relying on AI for stopping Zero

Day attacks. Tom distributed the drinks—a fizzy water with lime for Erin—and sat down.

"We've actually attended some of the same conferences," Alexei said. "Erin has quite a resume."

"And it sounds like Alexei is a man of many talents, to say the least," which was Erin's pre-arranged sign with Tom that her first impression of Alexei was good.

After a few more minutes of general discussion and sips of their drinks, Tom said, "Alexei, Erin is going to head up an unofficial, off-the-grid review of how the votes in our recent election were set up, recorded and tabulated in one precinct in one county in Virginia. It appears that everything across the nation went correctly, and both the FBI and the NSA have stated as such. We assume they're right, and this review will probably produce nothing new—or perhaps some suggestions for even more integrity in the future.

"Anyway, though the FBI knows what we're doing, and helped with supplying the raw materials for the study, this cannot be official. The deepest dive in a technical sense will be to review every coding detail on the flash drives used to load and then to register the votes on each machine. That will take some time, processing power, and luck. If we asked you to help us with that part, do you have the capacity, would you be willing to do it, and would you keep what you find just between us until we allow you to release it, which might be never?"

The Russian sat back, clearly not expecting this turn to the conversation. He thought for several moments. Finally he said, "Why would you ask me to do this? You know that I have close ties to the Russian effort to destabilize through social media."

Erin turned to look at Tom, who said, "You're right. It makes no sense. But it has to be done somewhere not open to all the domestic intercepts we're running. Off the grid and out of the country. Plus two women—my mother and Callie Sawyer—have told me they believe you're a good man who can be trusted—that means a lot. You're a believer who talks sincerely about the truth and your faith. And you seem to be concerned about many of the same things that worry me—in both our countries. Plus, officially, there's nothing classified on these drives, and no information that could be used against us. I ask for your promise of silence on the results simply because Erin and I will want to evaluate whatever you might find—which in all likelihood will be nothing. Yes, it's a bit of a gamble. So I'll simply ask you, as a believer, can we trust you?"

Alexei looked from Tom to Erin for several beats, appearing to be weighing a decision. "Well, if you're serious, and given all that's going on in my own country, of course I'll help. I may have to send a couple of the less flexible members of our team on a mission somewhere for a few days, but the rest of us should be able to do the analysis you need. Did you say flash drives?"

Tom nodded and took an envelope from his computer bag. "Yes. Ten. The precinct uses SecureVote20C machines. The dark web is full of its internal software, which is why the machines are never connected to the internet. Everything on each flash drive is issued by and checked through the Federal Election Integrity Commission, and all communications with the tabulation machines are sent through encrypted, monitored lines."

Alexei took the envelope. "Sounds pretty secure. But we'll take a look."

Erin handed Alexei her card. "Let's connect as soon as you get back to Cyprus, and we'll coordinate any final issues. I'll be double checking those communication protocols. Given the current situation here, we might do best to just use the phone."

Tom reached into his bag again and took out three identical sets of printed pads. "If you do think you've found something, Alexei, just say that to Erin on the phone, and we'll switch to these onetime encoding pads for email. They're simple but almost unbreakable in the short run. Use each page only once, in order."

Alexei smiled. "Wow. Do you have a PanAm Clipper waiting to fly me home?"

Erin looked confused. Tom smiled and said, "That's how spies flew to Europe just before World War II." Turning to Alexei, he added, "Thank you, but I hope your mission is a total failure."

"Me, too," Alexei said, then looked at his watch. "I better go. Erin, great to meet you, and I look forward to working with you. As they say, 'more to follow.'"


Kahar was reading in a chair in their small apartment when his phone's text buzzed; Ablet was preparing for one of his last nights experiencing America's worldly pleasures, before achieving the much more incredible eternal pleasures which were soon to be his.

The text for Kahar from Ahmad was crushing. Not only were peaceful Uyghur organizations now officially labeled by the US government as terrorists, but as a result the demonstrations planned to call attention to their plight were being scaled back or called off.

Kahar had started to imagine that he could convince Ablet to delay their attack, to see what effect the demonstrations might have on the Chinese Communist Party, particularly if Americans of all faiths participated. Now he was doubly angry because Ablet was right about this nation after all.

And Mavlan, sitting next to him, made sure his anger and resolve built on each other. Mavlan found it interesting that none of his Muslim charges training in Afghanistan had ever figured out, or even thought to question, that the Chinese government was ultimately in control of everything they did. The Communist Party allowed the camp to exist, funded it through Muslim organizations, and handsomely bribed the leaders to follow their commands while teaching Jihad and instilling hate for everyday Chinese.

Mavlan smiled—these guys believed a double lie: Islamic Fundamentalism and Revenge against China. They ultimately would be used by the Chinese Communist Party as unsuspecting foot soldiers to further the interests of the Chinese central government, and if that included taking out a few Chinese in the U.S., particularly Chinese Christians, then it was a small price to pay for the CCP to prove that the Uyghurs were terrorists, and that the world needed their culture to be destroyed.

Kahar rose and went into the bedroom, unbuttoning his shirt. "I think I'll join you tonight."

Mavlan smiled again. He looked forward to reporting at midnight that Uyghur attacks on Chinese people across the U.S. were right on schedule.

Tom dropped Erin off at her apartment after their dinner with his mother, and thirty minutes later she was on her bed in her pajamas, drinking some herbal tea and talking on the phone with her friend, Tracy.

"She's very nice, but it had to be one of the strangest potential mother and daughter-in-law first meetings ever, given why Tom's dad couldn't be there, and she knows about the baby."

"What did you talk about?"

"Everything. I'm actually working with Tom on an interesting review of the election, which we shared a bit with her. You know, she used to be a Congresswoman, and before that, a TV exec."

"I knew about Congress, but not about TV."

"Yeah, when Tom was a kid. So she's really smart and attractive and seems to want the best for us, as well as for the nation. A neat lady."

"And the baby?"

"Yes, and the baby...She wasn't pushy, but everyone knows she's as Pro Life as they come. So we had a good discussion."

"Really?"

Just then Nepravel pushed through the searing pain of the spiritual heat from the prayers landing on and around Erin.

"Yeah. She's pretty up to date on what a fetus is like at this point—a lot of new research with new equipment. Like, I didn't realize that all its major organs are already functioning, all four chambers of the heart and its valves are working, and it even breathes and exhales amniotic fluid. Can you believe that? Its eyes open and close. And it has fingernails and scratches its face."

"Sounds like she did her homework to talk to you."

Erin paused. "Yeah, I guess she did. I told you she's smart. And she clearly wants to hold her grandchild."

"Mmm...So what are you going to do?"

"I'm still not sure. But that thing you hear about God, or Tom, or someone getting my attention, I guess it might be working a little."

"I guess."

As they continued to talk, Nepravel tried to ramp up the voices of *My Body*, and *I'm Not Ready*, but neither gained any hold, and he finally had to give up and flee the light and the heat.

# 25

*Religion and good morals are the only solid foundation of public liberty and happiness. Neither the wisest constitution nor the wisest laws will secure the liberty and happiness of a people whose manners are universally corrupt. A general dissolution of principles and manners will more surely overthrow the liberties of America than the whole force of the common enemy. While the people are virtuous they cannot be subdued; but when once they lose their virtue then will be ready to surrender their liberties to the first external or internal invader.*

Samuel Adams

Saturday, November 7

Callie and Natalie had planned a full morning together. Natalie had joined Callie's volunteer group of women to meet with and mentor girls from the neighborhood around their church on two Saturdays a month. When that finished, Kristen joined them, bringing Grace, and the four of them walked through the Eastern Market, looking for items to help decorate Natalie's new apartment.

Now they were back at the apartment with their purchases, placing them and sharing fresh coffee. As Natalie arranged a vase of dried flowers, she said to Callie, "Do you realize it's been less than two months since I met you at Seth's birthday party? My life has been forever changed. What if you hadn't been there?"

Callie paused while hanging a landscape print with Kristen in the breakfast area. "You're right. You can thank Emily for inviting me." She smiled. "And I guess Tom for having me hang around a while."

"Thereby changing my life."

"That wasn't me. That was God."

Natalie shook her head. "You know Emily and Logan are having a big group over tonight to celebrate the election. I'm really sorry you won't be there."

Callie put the hammer on the table and nodded to Kristen. "Well, I'm not interested in celebrating those results, though I would like to see the people. But Tom's doing the right thing with Erin—I guess it's ironic that his re-found faith makes him much more attractive, but also pulls him away, for a good reason. I just want to keep that baby alive—then support Erin, or them, or however it works out."

"You're pretty amazing."

"No, I'm not."

There was a knock on the door and Natalie welcomed Seth with a peck on the cheek.

"Hi, ladies," he said, taking off his jacket, "if I can still use that term today." He smiled and handed Natalie a bag. "Here are the light bulbs, some pliers, and some WD-40. Every apartment needs WD-40."

Natalie took the bag and set it on the breakfast table. "If you say so. Want some coffee? What've you been doing?"

"Yeah, sure. This morning? I've been stuck doing research for the two panels I'm going to chair with the president.

Kristen asked, as she reached in a cabinet for a mug. "Grace, can you get the milk out of the fridge for Mr. Cohen?"

Callie took some bulbs out of the bag. "We need these in the bedroom. Seth, that's a big deal."

"Yeah. I'm feeling the responsibility."

Kristen walked over to Seth with the mug of coffee. "Did you hear that Callie's now working for the Truth Action Forum?"

"Callie, that's great. They're old-school investigative journalists. And pretty conservative. But thorough."

Callie turned on a lamp in the bedroom. "I'm glad you think so. I only know them by what I've read, and their video blog. The leadership says they're committed to simply finding the truth, wherever that leads, at whatever cost."

Seth took a sip and walked next to Natalie. "What a concept—truth in journalism."

Callie emerged again and said, "I'm curious. Will you have to clear your questions for the panel interview with the White House ahead of time?"

Seth paused for a moment. "Well, Emily and I have developed an understanding over the years on what works and what doesn't. So not every question. But most of them."

"And does 'what works' always lead you to the truth?"

He smiled. "Grace, your Mom's going to be tough. Unfortunately, here in D.C., truth is not always what journalism is about."

"What's it about, then?"

He took another sip. "I guess most of the time it's about getting ahead."

"Getting ahead?"

"Yeah. A program. A person. A career. An idea. Spend money. Get something to work. Win. You know. Progress. Get ahead. Together."

"At the cost of truth?"

He paused. "Yes, I guess sometimes at the cost of less truth."

Natalie turned to him. "Less truth? Isn't truth sort of black or white?"

"Not always. But, hey, I didn't say I'm proud of it. Or that I agree with it. But it's what we do at The Network. And so, like everyone else, I go along to get ahead."

Callie picked up another print to hang. "I guess that's the difference. The Truth Action Forum feels right for me because I'm a follower of the One who creates only truth, and that's what I want to 'get ahead'—not me, but truth."

Seth stood with his mug, nodding. "I understand. I get it. I've been thinking a lot about all this. About truth. About Natalie—and you. Maybe someday I'll be able to focus on the truth. For now my journalism works, as The Network expects, in a way that moves us all ahead together."

"To what?" Natalie asked.

"And if truth isn't there at the end," Callie added, "what will be? Lies?"

Seth thought for several moments. "I hope not. But it's certainly possible. It is what it is."

"Because we let it. What if you changed it?"

"I'd be out of a job."

"Is that so bad?" Callie asked. "And someone would hire you the next day. You have great skills and intuition, Seth. Just use those gifts for the truth, not for corporate success."

He smiled. "I hear you. We'll see. Now, do you want this one here?"

President Bradshaw, Emily Schofield, and members of their key policy teams were in the Residence working that Saturday to prepare for the upcoming domestic and foreign policy rollouts on Monday and Tuesday with the press panels. Of key importance was introducing the importance of initiating immediate changes by Executive Orders, which would precede the legislation itself, set to roll in a few months later with the new Congress.

With Patricia Reynolds they finished the domestic list, preparing for the expected questions that Emily had prepared. As they took sandwiches from the buffet they were joined by members of the international policy team, which would begin work after lunch.

The president sat in his usual chair in the West Sitting Hall with a sandwich and chips, Patricia on one side and Emily on the other. "That went really well. We're gonna knock their socks off. We're going to do so much good for so many people, and so quickly. America will never be the same, and will never look back. Who'll want the mush of legislative bickering when we can move so much more quickly with Executive Orders?"

Emily nodded. Drew Boswell came through the door and greeted everyone. Bradshaw waved with his sandwich hand. "Glad you're here. Grab some lunch and let's plan the future."

A few minutes later the next Secretary of State was seated at the same coffee table, and the conversation expanded to foreign initiatives, plus all the funds they planned to save on Defense, to plow back into more and larger domestic entitlements.

"It will indeed be a new day," Patricia offered. "I'm so glad we're all part of it."

They talked across a wide range of topics while eating. As they stood to put their plates on a tray before shifting to the foreign agenda, Drew asked Emily, "What's this Nathan Price told me about Tom reviewing the election results in Virginia?"

The president stopped and turned around. "What?"

Emily looked back and forth between them. "I don't know. I hadn't heard."

"Makes no sense," the president said, focusing on Boswell. "Tom said they were the cleanest elections in decades, after both the FBI and the NSA monitored every step." He turned to Emily. "What's Tom doing?"

Before she could answer, Drew added, "Nathan said something about even better elections in the future. I called Jim Toomey, but I haven't heard back yet."

"Well, I don't like it. Drew, doesn't one of your Juggle companies make those machines?"

"Yes. Both the machines and the software. Under federal controls and oversight."

Emily said, "I'll see Tom tonight and ask him."

"*Tell* him he doesn't have to check on anything. If he wants to improve anything, he knows exactly how to contact Drew, and Drew'll take care of it."

"Yes, sir."

"Tom has good ideas, but sometimes he's a loose cannon. I don't like his Lone Ranger approach. We're a team."

"I'll tell him. Now, let's shift gears to our foreign policy briefing. How much do you plan to say about the new approaches to China and Russia?"

The president looked at Drew, who said, "Not a lot yet. Just hint at what should be coming when all our new people are in place, people with a better understanding of how the world really works."

Balzor, who was spending the entire day ramping up voices in this group, was delighted with what he heard and looked forward to reporting their progress.

A year earlier Emily and Logan Schofield had "moved up" to a red brick Georgetown row house, and tonight they were hosting a party to celebrate Tuesday's election results. Each had invited a wide circle of government and business friends, including Emily's former apartment-mates.

A gathering of this size also included a swarm of the demons assigned to mislead these mostly young humans exercising generally oversized powers. Nepravel, Obman, Zloy and several others hung around their charges, gathering information and ramping up the usual voices of *Pride*, *One-Up*, and *We Know Best*.

When Tom and Erin arrived, the party was in full swing. The entrance hallway extended straight back, opening on the right to the living room and then to the dining room and kitchen. A stairwell on the left of the hall ascended and turned to a sitting room in the front and then a hallway to bedrooms in the rear. People were standing, drinking and talking in all of the major rooms, with a gracious buffet available in the dining room.

Taking off her coat, Erin looked around. "Wow. Nice place."

Tom took her coat to hang on an already full rack and smiled. "Yeah. The Government-Industrial Complex rewarding its own at full tilt. Not bad work, if you can get it. Come and meet my friends; they're here somewhere."

Before they could move, Emily emerged from the living room and hugged each of them. "Erin, so glad to see you again. Please make yourself at home. Sorry for the crowd—we'll do this again with less folks. The food and drinks are that way. But before you go, Tom, I've got a quick question."

"Sure."

"The president heard this morning from Drew that you're looking into the election results in Virginia. He was pretty upset and wanted me to ask you about it. He said that a Juggle subsidiary makes the machines and wrote the software, so if we want to improve things, we ought to work with them, through Drew, not conduct one-off investigations."

Tom smiled. "Wow. News does get around. I've asked an independent team to look into how we might improve the system in the future. As the National Security Advisor, that's not a big deal for me to do."

Emily frowned. "Well, he wants to move on and thought any possible election issues were behind us—and squeaky clean. So he wants you to stop, or to at least work with Juggle."

"I got it. I'll talk with him on Monday."

"Good. Good. Now, sorry for that bit of business, Erin. Please have a great time."

As Emily walked away, Erin said, "So the president doesn't like what you—we—are doing? Is that OK?"

He took her hand. "It's a little complicated, but it happens all the time. I guess he's more sensitive than I realized. Anyway, it's no big deal. We'll keep going, for now."

After thirty minutes of meeting and greeting others, including one of the Tech execs whom Tom had met Tuesday night and who again encouraged him to join their team near the top, the couple met up with Natalie and Seth in the second floor sitting room.

"I'm so glad to see you again," Natalie said. "Tom can't stop talking about you."

Erin smiled and glanced at Tom. "I bet. On several subjects. I'm glad to be here."

"When things calm down a bit," Tom said, "I hope the two of you can spend some time together—just don't share any stories about me! And the four of us should have dinner together."

Everyone nodded and took a drink.

"Are you gearing up for your big interviews?" Tom asked Seth.

He nodded. "I am. A lot to get ready for."

Just then Clayton Hunt joined them, drink in hand.

Tom introduced him to Erin. "Can't remember whether you met earlier, but Erin works at Information Initiatives and is really good at what she does."

Obman came in from hall to check on Seth but was instantly hit by the spiritual light and heat inside the three believers. He turned back.

"Great to meet you." Clayton looked at the group. "Andrea sends her best, but didn't feel like putting herself and our new son through the stress of a large gathering. She still gets pretty tired this time of day. We'll have you over soon."

"Must be tough on her," Seth said.

"But she says she wouldn't trade it for anything she's ever done."

They had just finished catching up on their latest news, including more about Seth's upcoming presidential interviews, when their hosts walked up.

"Is everything OK?" Logan asked.

"Wonderful," Natalie said. "Thank you."

"A great group of people," Seth added.

"Yes," Tom said. "But while you're both here, I understand you're backing out of the Uyghur demonstration on Thursday, and that The Network is doing a segment for the news on Uyghurs as terrorists?"

Seth glanced at Natalie and then Emily. "We are. Because I understand State labeled several of their U.S. organizations as terrorists, or at least influenced by terrorists."

Natalie turned to Seth. "But Tom's mother and I've met with the Chinese American Fellowship Church here, and they're ready to join us to support the human rights of Muslim Uyghurs in their home country. That's a *huge* leap for them. And at great risk to their families. We can't just drop them."

Seth started to respond when Logan said, "And Juggle doesn't want us, particularly managers, participating in public political acts. So they said I should step back."

Tom asked, "Have they ever asked you not to participate in an event before?"

"Well, no."

"And, Seth, I wouldn't have labeled them as terrorist groups."

"But that's the State Department's job, isn't it? They must have good reasons."

Tom looked at Emily a little too long.

Clayton said, "As active duty officers, Ahmad and I can't participate if they're terrorists."

"So with the stroke of a pen the State Department has stopped all these plans. What if the Uyghurs *aren't* terrorists?"

"They must be, if State labeled them," Seth said.

"Really? Maybe. But isn't that what journalists do—investigate what governments say and do—to ensure the truth?"

"To some extent. But often we have to start from what the government says, and go from there."

"To some extent? Isn't the truth either the truth, or not? Why would you want to report anything that isn't the truth? Isn't that your role? Isn't that why you're called the Fourth Estate—to keep the other three in line with the truth?"

Tom saw the others staring at him and took a breath. "OK. Sorry. This is your very nice party. I got worked up. Sorry, Seth. I guess I'm just tired of the truth being trodden on for some immediate short-term political gain, or other reason. The truth is simple, and usually pretty easy to find, if you just look. And I feel like that's your job. And all our jobs—not to act on the basis of half-truths or lies. Calling the Uyghur organizations terrorists is a lie. And I think you know it, Seth. And Emily and Logan."

Again there was silence from the circle of friends.

Emily smiled. "It's OK, Tom. We've all been under a lot of pressure with the elections, and you've had some extras. But that's why we're here tonight, to relax and celebrate our Progressive victory. So, please, enjoy."

Tom looked around the group. "Yes, please. Don't mind me. Sorry. Thanks again to you both."

Seth took Natalie's elbow. "You need a refill." He nudged her, and they walked away.

As the group broke up, Erin said quietly to Tom, "Wow. You were on fire. What's up? Are conversations with your friends always so intense?"

He turned to face her and nodded. "We've all known each other a long time, and been through a lot. So we don't sugarcoat much. Like I said, I've decided I just want the truth, wherever it leads. Pretty simple, but different from the Tom Sullivan they've known all these years. Could be tough. I guess I wish others felt the same."

"They seem like good people. Of course they will."

"We'll see. Hopefully. Now, do you need some more fizzy water?"

"Yes. And, by the way, you're pretty impressive when you're fired up."

"Great. Tell that to my Dad in jail and my Mom hunkered down in a hotel room."

As Seth and Natalie left the room for the bar, with Obman trailing just within hearing range, Seth said, "Two lectures on truth in journalism in one day. Am I that bad?"

"No. But think how much better you could be, if you focused on finding the truth."

"And how unemployed."

"Not for long. You would gain so much credibility."

He pointed her to the line. "Is this what you described as God trying to get your attention? I'm so dense I need several lessons on the same thing in one day?"

She smiled. "Maybe."

Obman was appalled and vowed to renew Seth's voices of *Skepticism* and *I'm Too Smart* as soon as he and the journalist were alone.

At the midnight meeting in the White House, though their plans for the coming weeks and months seemed to be in good shape, there were conflicting reports about the events of the day. The uncertainty revolved around Tom Sullivan and the party he attended. While a great horde of demons had enjoyed a free run of the Schofields' home to monitor their usual charges, whenever Tom and Natalie were together, their spiritual heat, plus the incoming prayers for Erin, were simply too much to bear, and no one was sure what they had discussed.

Prince Prolkor knew it was past time to rid themselves of the meddling by all the Sullivans and their friends, and he again instructed his generals to end their influence, once and for all.

# Sunday, November 8

Tom had taken Erin home after the party and said goodnight inside the foyer to her apartment building. They had kissed, and she smiled at him as she entered the elevator.

It was now a little after midnight and Tom was sitting in his most comfortable living room chair, sipping a cup of tea and scratching Beau's ear.

His thoughts were ricocheting between people and subjects. There was so much coming up in the next few days, he didn't know where to start. As he thought and prayed, he knew that his two principles would be to rely on God, not on himself or others, and to seek the truth in every situation. Starting with going to church that morning, no matter the consequences. He texted Erin, apologizing for the late hour, and asked her to join him.

"I know you've known Tom a long time," the president said to Emily late that morning as they walked together into the Oval Office to work with the Phoenix Team on his opening remarks for the next evening's press panel. "But there's just something that worries me about him. Maybe his parents." He stopped at the door and faced her. "Does he believe in the same things we believe?"

She straightened up. "Not as much. He comes from a different background. Right now he seems to be on a search for 'truth' and doesn't think the Uyghur organizations are terrorists."

"Truth?" Bradshaw turned red. "The truth? The truth is that people of color, women, and the disadvantaged—plus, of course, just regular people not making millions—will continue to be oppressed by white, male racists unless people like us stay in power so we can continue to help them, and we'll have much more to help them with if we're not wasting enormous amounts of money on aircraft carriers and other crap, and that transformation will happen with China's help. So we just won't care what happens to a few Uyghurs if it helps our people—particularly our oppressed people!"

Emily nodded. "I know. I get it. And I told him to stop looking into the election."

"What'd he say?"

"He said he'd talk with you tomorrow."

He paused. "I think it's time for him to go. We have a replacement ready—a friend of Drew's." She started to speak, but he interrupted. "Don't worry. We'll kick him upstairs to a great new job in Big Tech—if he agrees not to talk about his time here. Anyway, I'm going to tell him tomorrow. The sooner the better."

"I guess it's a natural time for transitions. I'm sure he'll get it."

"Exactly." He extended his hand toward the door. "Now, let's get ready for your other friend, Seth, tomorrow night."


Robert Ludwig had preached that morning on the persecution of the early church, and reminded the congregation of Jesus' words in Matthew 5:


*Blessed are those who are persecuted for righteousness' sake, for theirs is the kingdom of heaven.*

*Blessed are you when others revile you and persecute you and utter all kinds of evil against you falsely on my account. Rejoice and be glad, for your reward is great in heaven, for so they persecuted the prophets who were before you.*


He had concluded with the modern examples of early 20th century Russia and Germany, where civilized society disappeared after "good" people with policy differences that seemed important at the time pulled back and would no longer talk to each other, abandoning the public square to those who got their way not by argument, but with coercion and violence. Almost overnight there was no public square at all in either country. He prayed that the same would never happen in America. He prayed that believers would not pull back from debate or prayer, but would instead engage, always seeking God's wisdom and truth in every situation.

Immediately after the service ended most of the congregation stayed for a meeting. Tom thought how remarkable it was that he was sitting on the fifth row of a church he had hardly known about two months ago, next to or near Erin, Callie and Grace, Kristen, Natalie and Seth, Gary Thornton and his wife, Kate and Patrick, Clayton and Andrea with Clayton, Jr., and his mother.

And his earlier faith was rebuilding every day.

*How did this happen?*

Pastor Ludwig, along with five of the Senior Elders, all in chairs on the raised dais, led a discussion and asked for examples of threats or attacks on church members in the previous several weeks.

As people rose and spoke, Tom realized he was not prepared; he asked Erin for their copy of the church bulletin and started taking notes in the margin.

Callie spoke about the written threat to her, including the picture and the bullet. Two other members in her neighborhood recounted the same experience.

For thirty minutes people reported being called into their HR Departments for things said in conversations months or years earlier, supposedly indicating racist and homophobic oppression. One white man was reprimanded by his female boss for recommending a promotion for another white male. The headmaster at a private school declined admission for the younger brother of an attending student because he said their family did not fit in with the progressive future of the school.

As they spoke, it became clear that many of the threats and actions had begun ramping up on Wednesday, the day after the election. One woman, asked by her HR Head to remove or cover the cross hanging around her neck, was told that the nation was clearly on a new course in which "outward displays of oppressive religion will no longer be allowed to offend people."

When the congregation was finished, Pastor Ludwig rose and admonished them not to disengage, but to pray, "to be friendly and winsome as we push back, employing the rights guaranteed to us in the Constitution—except for the last two months," he added, with a quick glance at Tom.

"Of course if you have young children, older family members, or infirm people living with you or counting on you, take any precautions you feel are necessary. We have to be prepared for the fact that the situation will probably get worse before it gets better. And maybe quickly, given how some people are apparently feeling emboldened. But be assured that everything that happens is actually part of His plan for us."

Twenty minutes later their group was outside on the sidewalk. The Hunts were saying goodbye while the others chatted and made last minute lunch plans.

Erin sought Callie out and apologized for being so short when they'd first met at her office a week earlier..

Callie smiled and shrugged it off. "You have a lot going on. Please just let me know if I can ever help."

And Tom made a point to apologize to Seth for coming on so strongly the night before Seth smiled. "What are friends for?"

Tom's mother, Kristen and Grace joined them. Callie looked at her older mentor. "After listening to Robert, maybe I'll take you up on your offer to drive Grace to my parents' home, for her to stay for a couple of weeks. When everything cools down, I can go get her. I just have to be at my new job tomorrow."

Kristen looked down at her Goddaughter. "Of course. Road trip! Want to go see Papa and Nannie?"

"If Kristen's gone, Callie, you can't be by yourself. Where will you stay?" Tom asked.

"I've got a blow-up air mattress in my new digs," Natalie said. "Come join me."

Andrea added, "Our place is a little hectic at all hours, but you're welcome to join us."

Callie laughed. "Thank you. We'll see. For now," looking at Grace, "let's go call Nannie and arrange your trip."

"Before you go," Tom said to the half-circle of friends, "I just want to say," and he nodded towards his mother, "that listening to what's going on right now has driven home how wrong I've been. For two months I've led the charge to stop 'big hate speech' by giving the government special powers to silence people of its choosing, and that's clearly wrong. All we've done is empower another group—the side that now thinks it's in favor—to come down on their neighbors and to get their way, because no one can object. I see now that the Constitution only works if it *always* works."

The others stood in silence for a few moments. Finally Seth, who had mostly listened all morning, said, "Tom, you're never boring." He smiled. "I need to take you, Erin, Natalie—and you, Mrs. Sullivan—to lunch to hear more. And, also, I'm starving."


After lunch, Erin invited Tom up to have a cup of coffee in her modern, small, but stylish fourth-floor apartment just north of Chinatown. While Tom took in the view from her living room, she put the coffee on.

"I don't get a view like this from the old row house," he said, looking toward the Capitol.

"But there's not much D.C. charm here...It was nice of Seth to take us to lunch."

"Yeah. He's a good guy. He has two huge days coming up—I'm surprised he had time for us. But he and Mom have always enjoyed each other, though they don't agree on much. He'd be a great investigative reporter, but not at The Network."

"I'm glad I got to spend some more time with Natalie. She seems like the real thing."

"She always was, but her sincerity and resolve since the explosion are really remarkable. And another good thing about both Natalie and Seth—they're trying to figure out about her new faith and their relationship. I think God may actually be working on Seth."

Erin walked over and handed him a mug. They sat on the sofa. She smiled.

"Seems like I hear that a lot when I'm around you—that God's working on someone."

He shrugged. "I guess so. He certainly got my attention these last two months."

They sipped in silence. "Callie?"

He thought. "Yes. And others. The whole situation. All that's happened, from the attacks to our baby. I've finally realized that I'm not in control. He is."

"I was going to say I notice you seem unusually calm today. Church, lunch, and now coffee."

"I've decided to just seek the truth in all things, and to let Him guide me."

"How does He do that?"

Tom paused. "I think through his Word, prayer, and listening to people who I know have His wisdom."

She thought. "Maybe I'll try to do more of that."

"Do. Yes. But first give your life to Him."

"There you and God go again." He smiled and nodded. "In the meantime," she continued, "do you think Natalie and your mother are really going to demonstrate with the Chinese Church to support the Uyghurs on Thursday?"

"I think they've met with them a couple of times, and she's been very impressed by their courage to speak out for what's right, even with possible consequences. And Mom won't care what the State Department might say. When she feels strongly about doing what's right, don't get in her way."

"I'll remember that."


In the late afternoon Ablet and Kahar were sitting in their apartment and finishing their beers before going out again to enjoy one of their last nights of worldly pleasures.

Ablet took a long pull and leaned back in his chair, then turned to Kahar and used his beer bottle to emphasize his statement.

"You know, I was almost ready to delay our teams on Thursday—maybe just to the afternoon. Or even to Friday—to see what might come of the demonstrations you and Ahmad and the others at the mosque keep talking about.

"But now the American government says we're terrorists, and all these brave Americans are suddenly too scared to demonstrate? They're just like the Chinese. Sheep. They think we're terrorists? OK, we'll give them terrorists. Thursday morning. Allah be praised!"

Kahar thought for a moment. "Yes. Sheep. They're all afraid. We're not." He stood. "Want another beer?"

# Monday, November 9

Tom was in his office a little after six that morning, reviewing the incoming intelligence before the last Special Operations Briefing in the Situation Room under the State of Emergency, and then the Presidential Daily Briefing on more "normal" intelligence and security issues right after it in the Oval Office.

At the top of the stairs leading to the Situation Room he saw Tanya Prescott talking with Emily Schofield, balancing cups of coffee and their computer bags.

"Good morning. Last one of these."

"OK by me," Tanya said. "I just wish we had whoever is behind all this."

Emily nodded to Tom. "We will. The same teams on the ground will still be working after today. Just with fewer tools. The perps have to slip up some time."

"I hope," Tom said. "Let's go down."

"Meanwhile," Emily added, "one less meeting every day is OK with me. As you're about to see, the president's on fire to roll out our new Agenda, starting tonight with Seth's panel."

Twenty minutes later, after summary reports from each of the reporting Cabinet offices, the president addressed the group, including several on monitors, from his seat at the end of the table.

"I want to thank all of you and your teams for tackling this difficult assignment for the last two months. We'll scale back most of the State of Emergency requirements after today, including these daily get-togethers. But I know you'll stay focused on finding those responsible for so much death and destruction. Report through your normal chains of command, and we'll convene special response teams as necessary."

He looked around, and everyone nodded. "Tom, if you could stick around for a minute, everyone else is free to go. It's going to be a busy week."

When the room had cleared, Tom shifted in his seat next to his boss, who said, "You've had a great run and contributed an incredible amount to protecting the nation. I understand you don't believe these Uyghur organizations are terrorists, but I do. I know they are. So we're going to isolate them."

"Is there any proof?"

"Yes. At the State Department. But, look, going beyond that, I think it's time for you to consider your future. With the end to the State of Emergency, which was your good idea, and the election, and our new initiatives, you'll have a much brighter future in one of the Big Tech companies, which I know would love to have you. Hasn't Drew introduced you to some?"

"He has. But, frankly, for the next few months I'd like to continue serving as your National Security Advisor, 'til we find these guys."

Bradshaw paused, then leaned forward. "Well, Tom, that just won't be possible. You need to take one of those firms up on their offer right away—today would be great, so you can move on by the end of the week, and we'll name your replacement on one of the panels coming up."

"Today? You're firing me?"

He smiled. "No, not exactly. I—we—are holding open a door for your great personal advancement. You'll be set for life, Tom, if you're positive about your time here, and move on to any of the jobs Drew's found for you. Maybe some Board positions, too. You'll have incredible influence on important decisions for decades to come, because of what you've accomplished here—you'll impact people and policies that need your input—along with some wealth and power. Not a bad future."

"But today?"

"Yes. We're going to be putting in a new team with Drew and Patricia—foreign and domestic. They both have people they want to use. You'll go out at the top. And, so everything will be set right, if your father and mother will agree to stop fighting everything we do, I'll issue a presidential pardon for your father, and he'll be home this week."

Tom looked at President Bradshaw for a few moments. "If that's what you want, you're obviously the president. Getting my parents to be quiet may not be easy, but I know Mom will be glad to have Dad out."

"Good." The president leaned in, his finger tapping the table. "Now, one last thing. What's this I hear about you checking on the election results? These were the cleanest elections in years—you and the FBI and the NSA have all said so. The new Federal Election Integrity procedures worked as we hoped. What on earth are you doing?"

Tom noted the older man's anger for several beats.

"The results just seemed anomalous to me, so I thought we ought to check, in case we can make further improvements for the next time."

It was the president's turn to pause. "Anomalous? Does that mean irregular? We just ran a great, winning campaign, and you call it 'anomalous?' Stop. Right now. Don't do any more looking. The elections are finished, and they were *not* anomalous. If you have any specific issues, leave a note for your successor, and he or she will take it up with Drew's company, which built the system and understands the ins and outs perfectly. If any improvements are needed, Drew can make them. Understood?"

"Yes, sir. I understand."

"Good, then go finish up protecting the country, get ready for the transition, and leave the elections to those who understand them."


Clayton arrived at the Pentagon command center at noon to relieve Ahmad and to start his own eight-hour watch for incoming foreign and domestic threats. He sat and logged into the console next to Ahmad, who was focused on his screen while in a deep conversation over his mic. Finally Ahmad finished and turned to his friend.

"After I brief you and you take over, I'm going to stick around."

"What's going on?" Clayton asked, as he toggled into the flow of information.

"After all this talk about Uyghurs and terrorism, you wouldn't believe it, but we've got a Muslim cleric in Belgium telling a friend on a call that the Uyghurs are about to do something big here."

"Here? You mean, in D.C.? Why would they do that?"

"That's what I want to find out. I hope this doesn't turn personal. Mariam is planning to meet Andrea, Natalie and Tom's mother at the

Chinese Church on Thursday morning, to help lead their group down to the embassy."

"There may not be many joining them, and this news means the embassy may be dangerous. Maybe we should tell them not to go."

"I know, I know. I'd planned on being there myself, of course, but...And this intelligence isn't confirmed, so it's a mess."


A little before 1 pm Robert Ludwig's assistant led Tom into the pastor's office, where he had already been talking with Tom's mother, seated on a small sofa across from his desk. Ludwig stood and shook Tom's hand, and then the two men sat in chairs.

"Thank you both," Tom began. "I need some counsel, and with Dad still 'away', I thought I'd ask you." The two older people nodded.

Tom continued, "Before all this I would have just called you on the phone, and that may be OK again soon—on the way over I noticed the Restricted Zone being dismantled—but for now I'm still concerned about eavesdropping on phone calls."

"We, of all people, understand," Ludwig said. "Please."

Tom described to them how the president that morning had asked him to move on and offered to pardon his father if his parents would stop opposing his actions. He also described the very attractive positions which recently opened up for him in several high-tech firms, implying a long career of influencing decisions for the good, he would hope.

"And there are issues on my plate that need resolving, like this Uyghur mess. But it looks like others will now take over. By the way, are you still going to demonstrate on Thursday at the embassy?"


When Tom returned to the White House in the early afternoon, there was a note on his desk from the president's Secretary to stop by the Oval Office.

"I was right," the president said, when Tom came through the door. "Have you seen the latest from the NSA and FBI intercepts?"

Walking to the president's desk, Tom said, "No, I just got back."

"Looks like one or more groups of Uyghurs are planning to attack Chinese nationals at unspecified targets in the U.S., Tom. Soon. In the U.S.!" He stood and held out the paper to his National Security Advisor.

"Why would they do that?"

"Because they're terrorists, like I've been telling you."

"OK. Let me digest this, and then we should send out an alert."

"No way. That might divulge our methods and, besides, we want the American people to see how evil these Uyghurs really are, if they go through with it."

"That could cost a lot of damage and lives, sir."

Bradshaw waved his hand. "OK, we can alert law enforcement to quietly beef up general security around the Chinese embassy and consulates. If anyone gets hurt, it'll mostly be Chinese and Uyghurs. But it will give a strong message to our people about the wisdom of staying out of other people's arguments, and that's more important than a few foreigners' lives."

Tom just stood, reading the paper. Finally the president said, "Have you thought about which position to take when you leave here?"

"Right now I think I'll pass, even though the offers are really generous. I'll thank Mr. Boswell—Drew—for setting them up. You can announce my departure whenever you want, and my last day will be Friday, or whenever you think is best for a transition."

"OK. Seems like you're passing up a great steppingstone, but it's your decision. What about your parents and the pardon?"

Tom laid the paper back on the desk. "My Mom says she'll ask Dad on their weekly call tonight, but I doubt they'll do it."

"Stubborn. Really not smart—even if they are your parents." He smiled and picked up the paper. "Well, anyway, I tried to do the right thing. Not a word about this Uyghur thing to anyone, of course. And be sure to watch Patricia and me on Seth's interview tonight. Your Trusted Citizen Program will be one of the highlights. I'll talk to Drew about the transition timing."

"I hope it all goes well." Tom turned and left for his office, where he closed the door and prayed for several minutes.

Janet Sullivan was in her hotel room, talking with her husband, who was on a pay phone in the prison hallway, for their one, fifteen-minute call allowed each week.

"Of course we aren't going to be quiet," Richard said. "Even if they keep me here for a couple of years. I hate it, but we aren't going to cave into them."

Janet smiled. "I told Tom that would be our answer, but I wanted to hear you say it."

"Yes. This is terrible. But Jesus said he and his followers are always and only on the side of truth, no matter what. And that's where we are, as painful as it is right now."

"I agree. And, by the way, God's been working on Tom. His faith has returned, it's real, and he's struggling with sticking to the truth, just like we are. We must keep praying for him."

"Good. Then let's do so now."


Tom arrived home early to be ready for Seth's Presidential Interview on the Network. He was at his kitchen table, working on his L-pad to make his To Do List for his unexpected transition out of the White House. Beau brought him a ball. He opened the backdoor and they went outside in the twilight for some tosses. His phone vibrated. Erin.

"Look at the email from Alexei. I'll stay on the line."

He called Beau back inside and clicked on his email. An encoded message. Two months ago he would have asked Erin what it said, but that would defeat the whole point of the encryption, even on his special phone, since hers was not on the Core Group network.

"OK. Give me a few minutes. How are you?"

He found the one time pad in his computer bag, tore off the first page, and started decrypting the message.

"I'm fine. Thanks for coming over after lunch yesterday."

He worked in silence through the letters and symbols in Alexei's email. When he finished, it read, "May have found a breech. Complex. How can Erin and I talk? Ham radio? Can she come here?"

He thought for a few moments. "Interesting."

"To say the least. What should I do?"

"I'll make a few calls. You might pack a bag."


"I know it's late, dear," Alexei told his wife on the phone from his office, "but I might be sleeping on the couch here. There's a lot going on—maybe nothing, but maybe something—and I can't leave until we get to the bottom of it. I sent Sveta and her three buddies home for a break after the American elections finished, so we're short-handed.

He looked up. Denis was at his door. "Yuri wants you to see something." He nodded.

"OK. I gotta go. I gave my word that I'd take care of this, not let it go sideways, or wind up in the wrong hands. Please pray for us."


Universities compete by spending. The plush, cozy auditorium hosting the two Presidential Interviews was an example. A little before the 8 pm airtime it was filled with handpicked friends and supporters of the recent winning ticket, ready to hear the details of the coming Progressive Transformation of America.

President Bradshaw and Vice President Reynolds were to be seated in comfortable chairs facing the audience, with small tables on either side for their water bottles; Seth and two female journalists, African American and Hispanic, would be angled a little stage left in similar chairs, with Seth closest to the president. On the right side of the stage was a large monitor on which videos of citizens asking questions could be played.

Emily had designed the set to give the greatest possible impression of a free-for-all Q&A session, though in fact the two hours would be heavily scripted. The three journalists were all friends of the

Administration; their questions, as well as those recorded from others, were fully vetted and organized to ensure that all the president's new domestic programs would be given a full hearing, but from the proper perspective.

Just before 8 pm the auditorium was darkened, the three panelists took their seats, and Seth began. "Thank you for joining us tonight, less than a week after President Bradshaw's Progressive candidates won their historic mandate to implement sweeping improvements to almost every aspect of our lives. Tonight we've asked the president and vice president to lay out their domestic policy plans, and to answer your questions—and then tomorrow evening we'll do the same for foreign policy with the president and his newly nominated Secretary of State. So, let me introduce my fellow panelists, and then we'll welcome the president and vice president."

A few moments later the two Leaders of the Free World appeared in a shaft of light at the back of the dark stage, walked forward and stood together, waving and acknowledging the audience's loud applause, then took their seats. The applause continued.

Seth finally quieted the auditorium. "Welcome Mr. President and Ms. Vice President. We look forward to hearing your vision for the nation following the landslide victory for your policies in virtually every state last week. It must be exciting."

President Bradshaw smiled and nodded his head. "Yes, Seth, it's really gratifying to know that, after years of educating our nation on the benefits of Progressive policies for *all* our citizens, and despite the terrible challenges of the last two months, those truths have finally taken hold. We're here tonight to lay out for the American people what we plan to accomplish in the coming days and weeks in response to this mandate, and again in the first few months of next year, once the new Congress is in place, thanks to the voters' unprecedented support and a filibuster-proof Senate."

There followed a lively discussion and lots of questions leading to enthusiastic explanations on key subjects like Climate Change, Renewable Energy, Guaranteed Citizenship, Equity vs. Equality, Debt Forgiveness, Anti-Racism, Free Early Childcare, Free College Tuition,

Wealth Redistribution, Abortion Protection, Guaranteed Incomes, Slavery Reparations, Transgender Protection, Bank Oversight, Expanding the Supreme Court, and Corporate Liability.

Near the end of the evening, in answer to a question, the president said, "Yes, we're about to roll out a great new program to address that issue: the Trusted Citizen. I'm pleased to say it's the brainchild of Tom Sullivan, our National Security Advisor, who, with the end to the State of Emergency, is moving on to new challenges. We'll miss him, but we wish him well. The Trusted Citizen Program will let us reward those who sign on to help the nation by being patriotic and transparent with all their words and actions—it will really benefit a lot of people, and we'll be opening up the details and the website to apply for the first designations very soon."

He looked at the vice president, who smiled and nodded. "It's a very simple but powerful way to reward our citizens for their loyalty."

"Sounds exciting," Seth said. "But with that we're out of time tonight. Thank you both for your full and frank descriptions and answers. I'm sure the American people look forward to the upcoming Executive Orders in all of these areas with great excitement. And thanks to all of you at home for joining us. Come back tomorrow night for a similar discussion on foreign policy."

In between several calls on his Core Group Phone, Tom listened to The Network's panel interview. He was troubled, because he was starting to hear again the voice of God's Holy Spirit, quenched by his own choices for over a decade.

God's truth did not match what he heard from the president in so many areas, from abortion to a lack of personal responsibility in almost every area of life. *Have I just been asleep, or too focused on protecting the office, and not listening to the policies? And my "protection" focus has now led to the Trusted Citizen Program, which will make permanent almost all the excesses of the State of Emergency. God forgive me.*

Tom slipped to his knees and prayed, first for forgiveness, and then for guidance and wisdom.

# 26

*Truth is simple, and delights in simple statements. It expects to make its way by its own intrinsic force, and is willing to pass for what it is worth. Error is noisy and declamatory, and hopes to succeed by substituting sound for sense, and by such tones and arts as shall induce men to believe that what is said is true, when it is known by the speaker to be false.*

Albert Barnes

Tuesday, November 10

It was late Monday evening in D.C., but south of Greenland it was already Tuesday morning. Callie and Erin, both in jeans and sweaters, were sitting across from each other in plush tan seats on the Gulfstream G650 that Callie's new firm had chartered several hours earlier–the lamp over the writing table between them offering the only light.

Callie, facing forward, put down her book and took a sip from her coffee.

Erin smiled. "I can't believe Tom organized all this so quickly."

Callie nodded. "Or that my company would go along with its newest employee's expensive ask."

Erin looked around. "Yes, you do have good taste in aircraft."

"I hope something comes of this, or my job may be the shortest ever."

They flew on in silence for a few moments.

"How are you feeling?" Callie asked.

"Mostly OK. The mornings are better." More silence for almost a minute as Callie closed her eyes and prayed to herself. Erin continued, "I guess I'm trying to understand how it can be that you and I—the journalist and the cyber engineer—united only by Tom Sullivan—are on our way to Cyprus in a corporate jet to see what some Russians may have found about our election. Does that make any sense?"

Callie shook her head. "No."

"And I guess the eight hundred pounder in the cabin is this baby." She put her hand on her stomach."

"Hmm."

"I would never have imagined having a baby, but then Tom asked me to marry him. That changed everything. Like with this trip, my head is spinning." She paused. "Do you love Tom?"

Callie put her cup down and leaned forward a bit. "I...I like Tom. I stopped seeing him because he was so full of himself and his State of Emergency, and he had no faith. Now he seems to have changed on all of those, which makes him more attractive for sure. But a big reason for that change is you and your baby. And your potential life together. Tom and I never got to 'love', and I assure you we never will. I knew he was going to propose to you, and I completely endorsed it then, and now. The two of you are good together, and I think he'll make a great husband and father."

Erin thought. "I think you mean it....and it must be hard."

Callie smiled. "In some ways. But not important ones. I'll always support you—all three of you—and I hope you'll take him up on his offer so we can plan your wedding."

Erin smiled. "My head continues to spin."


Late that morning the chartered jet landed at the Paphos Airport on the western side of Cyprus, where a gray minivan picked up the two passengers. Forty minutes later they pulled under the porte cochere at the front of a modern, sand colored, five story office building, three blocks from the oceanfront near the center of Limassol.

Alexei Nobikov came outside to greet them and helped Erin step down from the van. He was wearing khaki pants and a blue shirt, with a day's growth on his face.

"Sorry I couldn't come to the airport, but we were busy all night."

Erin turned her face to the warm sun and stretched her legs, as Alexei reached to help Callie with her bag and a black satchel. When she descended, he smiled and they hugged. "Callie, I didn't realize it, but I'm certainly glad you're part of this team."

She smiled. "Hey, Alexei. Yeah, I guess I'm the scribe, to record what happens. And I'm also in charge of this." She picked up the satchel.

"Excellent. Glad you're here."

Erin said, "We didn't sleep much, either."

"We'll take you over to your hotel in a little while, but I thought we ought to get together here first. Please come in. We occupy the fifth floor."

In the lift lobby upstairs, large double glass doors and signage welcomed them to InternetOne, the island's premier internet service provider, but Alexei steered them left to an unmarked door and used the keypad to open it. They entered a small waiting area, then crossed a main hallway linking several offices to a large conference room with a spectacular view of the coast. There were two white boards with coding diagrams, several stacks of papers and books, and a trash can filled with paper plates and cups.

"Please put your bags down here. Sorry for the mess. There are usually twelve of us on this more discreet side of our office, but I've given several of them a few days off, including my second-in-command, Svetlana Pankratova, who might take issue with what we're doing. Five of us have been working non-stop on your project, including my top technical guy, Pavel Stepanov. Here he is now."

Everyone greeted each other. Pavel said, "Welcome. We just put on a fresh pot of coffee. Please freshen up if you need to, and let's meet in ten minutes. Did you bring the machine?"

Callie placed her satchel on the conference table. Erin opened it and said, "Yes. The electronic heart of the SecureVote20C voting machine, with a two-button switch connected by a cable. These are used to train poll watchers. And a single-purpose, government-built laptop like the ones that receive all updates with the candidate lists for the flash drives, to ensure the voting machines are never connected to the internet."

"Great. While you get coffee, we'll set them up and attach them to several monitors and recorders."

"Be sure to use 110 volts, or we won't have them for long."

Pavel smiled, "Yes, we will."

Fifteen minutes later the nine people gathered in Alexei's conference room had introduced themselves and nibbled at a delivered lunch. Now the locals were describing what they had tried and accomplished so far.

"So," Alexei concluded from one end of the table, "that's why we asked you to bring this equipment. We couldn't find anything suspicious or different in any of the used flash drives, and were about to give up, but then we took a look at the extra one that wasn't used to update or to load a machine. Our computers compared its content with the others, and there's some code on it that they don't have. So we made a copy, and now we want to use it, as if we were loading a real machine in...where?"

"Virginia," Erin answered.

Alexei moved toward the black box which their guests had brought over. "By the way, who makes these?"

Erin answered, "Juggle, under a design created by the government with the new Federal Election Integrity Law."

"Where?"

"I don't know."

"I can ask Tom if he knows." Callie reached for her purse to get the one time encryption pad for her text.

Alexei continued. "So, the machine is plugged into our monitoring equipment. One of our American guests, please take it from here." And, turning to his teammate who was video recording their meeting, he said, "Tom gave instructions to be sure to get in close to capture every detail of what's being done."

Erin took the flash drive. "I've watched this process as a volunteer several times, including at a precinct just last week. The content on the flash drive comes from the special laptop connected to the Federal Election Integrity Commission through an encrypted channel. Once loaded with the candidates, the flash drive goes into the machine and then when you push the Update button, it runs a final system security check and loads the candidates for the races in this specific precinct. The flash drive then stays in the voting machine throughout the day, secured by a wire and a seal."

The voting machine hardware came to life and ran for about thirty seconds, while Alexei's equipment monitored and recorded the code for every step.

Erin continued. "OK, now I'll press Start on the machine, and, using this toggle switch that inputs 'votes', mimicking the actual voting hardware normally giving input to the machine, we're going to vote for 100 Lefts and 100 Rights. I know it's a little crazy, but watch and count with me, and be sure to get this part on the video."

She began clicking the switch, left then right, and counting. When she reached 100 of each, she said, "Now I press Finish on the machine, and it will tabulate the votes and load the results onto the attached flash drive."

A minute later, when the machine stopped running, Erin removed the flash drive. "In the real world these flash drives are then transported to the County or Municipal Election Management Center under two-person control. They are then logged in and loaded one at a time into this same special laptop, which tabulates the totals and communicates the results to the centralized Federal Election Integrity Commission. And the FBI monitors all those channels to be sure that there are no intrusions. The flash drives are then stored for at least six months, in case there are any challenges."

As they watched, Erin turned on the laptop, inserted the flash drive, and pressed Tabulate, then Send.

On the laptop in front of Callie, simulating the FEIC monitor, the results were displayed in large figures:

Left: 107.

Right: 93.

Nenav, whose assignment was to keep the abortion voices spinning inside Erin, invisibly materialized behind her, but was immediately beset by the spiritual heat and light emanating from Callie, Alexei, Pavel, and two others, along with the prayers from Kristen's prayer warriors, alerted by Callie right before she and Erin had left. He backed away, the heat and light excruciating, but determined to return and learn what these people were doing.

Erin looked at Alexei, then Pavel, then Callie. "Did I just see what I think I saw?"

Callie nodded. "A huge spurious vote swing. At least I think so."

"Guys...you need to triple check everything we just did to run this test. There can't be any questions when we call Tom and report what we just saw."

Alexei looked first at his team, then back to the Americans. "Yes. We will. Why don't you go check-in at the hotel, and maybe walk on the beach, or try to take a nap? We'll regroup here in a couple of hours."

Callie nodded. "Good idea. Check everything, and then we'll figure out together what to tell Tom."


When they came together again in the conference room that afternoon, Erin said, "I took a cat nap and do feel better. And the views from the hotel are great. Thank you."

Pavel nodded, then passed around some papers. "We've confirmed that the code in the flash drive we just used has now changed by pre-design to look exactly like the other flash drives which we already have. Once the results were reported, the extra code simply disappeared."

"So if we hadn't had that one unused drive," Erin said, "we, or anyone checking, would never have seen that code, or known what it did."

"Exactly," Alexei said.

They all sat quietly for a few more moments.

Alexei, looking at Erin, then Pavel, said, "If all the flash drives used in the election were like this, this could be huge. You should check to see if there are any more preserved ones that are unused."

Erin said. "Is the video of what we did good, and do you have a copy of that flash drive, from before we used it?" Pavel nodded. "Then please make some more copies, and we need to report to Tom."

"Let's take a minute," Callie said, "to agree together on what we all think happened, and what we recommend. Then we'll report to Tom."

As Callie moved to the white board to start writing, Erin added, "Yes, conclusions first. Then, Alexei and Pavel, can you drill your team into the disappearing code and try to decipher exactly what it's doing?"

Alexei nodded.

Nenav had returned in time to hear the summary, and he knew he needed help.


Tom was at his desk in the White House and had almost finished his day, a little early, going through his files and trying to organize his thoughts with an L-pad To Do List for departing the Administration and turning over the current key issues to his successor, whomever that might be. It was quieter than usual, since the next day was Veterans Day, and most of the staff would enjoy the holiday.

A text from Erin arrived on his phone. He took out the one time pad. Three minutes later he read:

"Possible serious election tampering. Not sure by whom. In the machines and flash drives. We need to talk. Call me?"

He stared at the message for a minute and hesitated, then picked up his Core Phone and dialed. Since she didn't have a Core Phone, their call would not be encrypted. He hoped, with the State of Emergency winding down, the NSA was no longer monitoring calls from the US to overseas, but he was aware they might still be doing so.

The working group on Cyprus put him on speaker phone, and Tom asked that they not mention any specific names or locations while they tried to figure out what was going on. Erin, Callie and Alexei then described what they had found so far, and how they planned to keep studying the unexpected code on their copies of the unused flash drive. Everyone agreed that more unused flash drives needed to be found. And Pavel asked who wrote the code for the final security check on the flash drives, and where.

As they concluded, Tom told them, "Thank you. This was certainly not expected. Let me get some reinforcements and get back to you as soon as possible to watch that video."

He called Tanya Prescott, but she didn't answer.

Ninety minutes later, from his kitchen table at home, he tried Tanya again. This time she answered as she was arriving at her own home in Virginia.

As she took off her coat in their entrance hall and waved quickly to her two daughters, who were on their screens in the family room, she listened to Tom's description of the discovery made in Cyprus.

"That just seems impossible. What if it impacted every voting machine in every precinct in the nation?"

"Or just the key ones. Either way you'd have a landslide, like the landslide we just had."

"But who could be behind that? Who could hack into the final security update and content checker software sent by the Federal Government to every Election Management Center in the entire nation?"

Tom paused. "Are we sure it's a hacker? What if the original source—the government provider—coded it that way?"

She stood in silence for several moments. "That would be unbelievable."

"Yes."

"We need to see the video they made, and talk to them about the details."

"Yes. But how?" Tom asked.

"Didn't the State of Emergency end at midnight? So now we can go back to encrypting our emails and voice calls. Correct?"

"You're right. I almost forgot what that's like. It's late over there, but can you take a look in ten minutes, if we can set up a video call?"

"Make it fifteen so I can get our casserole in the oven. I'll get out my laptop. Send me the link, and let's see it."

Though it was after midnight on Cyprus, the coding experts were still hard at work, while Erin, Callie and Alexei refined their thoughts, based on what the team uncovered, ready to report when Tom got back to them. Finally, he did, and they opened an encrypted video call, with the Cyprus team gathered in the conference room, and the two U.S. participants on their laptops at their homes.

After introductions, Alexei's team played the video of the bogus vote tally which they had captured that afternoon.

In answer to Tanya's first question, Pavel said, "I guess it could have been a hack, of course, but the code is so perfectly written to create this outcome and then to disappear, and the firewalls around your new Federal election system are so strong, that it's just hard to imagine how it could be done."

"So it might have been an inside job, as we say?" Tom asked.

Erin nodded. "It looks that way to us."

"Then that means Juggle. Or their Chinese partners. Drew Boswell's team."

"The Secretary of State nominee," Erin added, for the Cypriots.

Silence. Finally Tom said, "Tanya, what do you recommend?"

She shook her head. "This has moved way above my pay grade."

"But we can't ignore it."

"I know. I know. The implications are almost too much to imagine. I think I need to tell my boss, Jim Toomey, and get his advice."

"OK. And I'll tell the president, who won't be pleased, either with this news or with me. But let's keep the Cyprus track working as well. It's too important."

"I agree. At least for now."

Alexei spoke up. "It would be great to have more of the original unused flash drives, if you can find any. Meanwhile, we'll keep drilling into this copy to learn all we can about who wrote it."

"Great work, everyone. Alexei, please remind your team not to speak about this to anyone while Tanya and I figure out the next steps. And thank you, Erin and Callie."

Erin smiled. "We had nothing else quite like this to do...We'll try to get some sleep, and we'll be in touch."

Callie, who had been quiet until now, said, "Tom, I'm troubled. What if this really does come from the top, and the president and Drew Boswell are somehow involved?"

Silence again. "That just seems impossible," Tom finally said.

"I don't know them—you do. I just think you—all of us—should be really careful with everything we do and say until we know more."

"That's good advice. But it may be easier to say than to do."

"Based on our own abilities, yes. We should pray for His wisdom and protection."

"Yes," Tom said. "Thank you. Of course. Please lead us off."

And they spent the next ten minutes praying for His guidance, and against the demonic forces in both places. When it seemed that everyone had prayed, Erin, for the first time out loud, voiced her plea to God for guidance and wisdom.

Fifteen minutes later the team on Cyprus agreed that the coding experts would continue in shifts through the night, while the rest would try to get some sleep. Alexei drove Erin and Callie to their hotel, where he said goodnight and headed home to his wife.

The two American women walked into the lobby, which was empty except for the young man behind the desk who greeted them. But there were a few people seated in the bar in an alcove at the back of the lobby.

Callie said, "I'm still pretty wired. Can I buy you a glass of wine? Oh, wait, I mean, a soda?"

Erin smiled. "I read somewhere that an occasional glass of wine isn't terrible for a baby—or at least a lot of them seem to have survived much worse over the last couple of thousand years."

Callie laughed, and five minutes later they were seated by themselves at the side of the bar, each with a glass of red wine, and a single candle lighting their table.

They reviewed the events of their long day and night.

"You know so much more about this than I ever will," Callie said. "What are the odds that a hacker was able to break in and put that code in the software that loaded the flash drive?"

Erin took a sip. "There's always more to learn, but from my experience and from what we've seen so far, it would be almost impossible."

"So somehow it must have come from the source—and that's Juggle and their contractors."

"And with the new federal system, unlike the old Hodge-Podge of state systems and procedures, there's really no telling where that centralized code may have wound up. Could it have been in every machine in the nation?"

Callie said, "Or maybe in just some key races?"

Erin nodded and they were silent for a few beats. Then she said, "I was struck by your take on the need to be careful—that we may be up against more than we know, and that we need to pray about it."

Callie nodded.

"Do you often get, I guess, leadings like that?"

"Not really. But this one was pretty specific." She smiled. "Loud, I guess you'd say."

"Hmm. I've never heard anyone talk like that. Or pray like you pray, though Tom's been trying to get me to. What is it about you—and Tom—that's so different? Is it just your faith?"

Callie thought, then took another sip and said, "I wouldn't say 'just' our faith. I'd say my faith is everything, in that it utterly transformed me from a pain-filled garbage heap to being loved by the perfect father. From death to life. My faith isn't like a folder on a shelf that I occasionally pull down to read. It inhabits everything I do, and so, I guess, it more easily finds its way into all my thoughts and actions. Like the warning for us to be careful."

Erin digested Callie's words, then said. "When we first met in that coffee shop, what, ten days ago? Wow, it seems like a year, doesn't it? Anyway, you told me about how you went from making porn movies to being a mom to where you are now. I must say, it's pretty impressive. Now that I know you, I understand how hard it must have been. I have to ask: How did you do it?"

Callie smiled. "I didn't. He did. It was all Him. After Kristen told me when I was in the middle of that mess how God had transformed her, I turned my life over to His Son, and He's faithful. He didn't let me down. I surrendered; He took over. It wasn't always easy, by any means. But He led me through it. And I'm at peace, whatever happens next."

"Yes! That's the word I've been looking for, for you—Peace."

"You can have it, too."

"How?"

Callie smiled, thinking of Kristen's words to her those years ago, and her own words to Natalie in the hospital. "I'll tell you."

After a dinner of leftovers and a walk around the neighborhood with Beau, including a check on Kristen and Callie's vacant row house, Tom remained troubled by what Callie had said. He texted her, Erin and Tanya, asking for another brief video chat, even though it was quite late in Europe.

Fifteen minutes later he was again on his laptop with them. "I wanted to have just us, without the Cypriots, to work through some 'what ifs,' like Callie was talking about, and like I've been thinking about ever since."

Tanya nodded. "Me, too."

The four of them strategized various possibilities and actions for almost thirty minutes, then prayed again.

Tom finally concluded the call. "Thanks to all of you. Get some sleep. I suspect we'll need our wits and our energy in the coming days."

The set-up for the second presidential interview was the same as Monday evening, with Seth and two panelists on the left of the stage, facing two chairs in the middle, and a large screen on the right.

This time the president and Drew Boswell entered in shafts of light from the back of the stage, taking their seats, as Seth introduced them and the panelists.

The president began by giving Drew's qualifications to be the new Secretary of State, then launched into a description of how, with their new mandate and a new team, his Administration was going to bring about true world peace and real solutions to climate change.

Tom watched on The Network while, during the hour, Drew Boswell and the president took turns answering questions and describing a new world in which order and prosperity would be guaranteed by "the key players working together in new and far more coordinated ways."

They would focus on reducing greenhouse gasses, increasing food production, wind farms, education, eliminating fossil fuels, reparations for earlier oppressions, curbing nuclear energy, reducing third world debt, integrating international markets, and raising minimum taxes on corporations worldwide.

When it was over, Tom realized there was no mention of human rights, women's rights, freedom, democracy, or the rule of law.

Nevertheless, he sent Seth a congratulatory text from his old phone.


The White House gathering that night included Proklor's generals and all the Sector Leaders. No incoming prayers bothered them—most believers seemed to have given up on praying. There was an air of expectant victory, and Temno's news that they again topped 3,000 in both divorces and abortions just added to their excitement. They'd all either attended or watched the domestic policy interview—the immediate adoption of so many changes meant more woke control for the government, which would quickly make their goal to stop the spread of God's truth so much easier.

Prince Proklor, smiling, spoke to his leaders. "Today was just like with Adolf in '33. It's amazing how, when we get the right people and fill them with our voices for years, working on the right projects, it can actually all happen so fast. And they don't even know it."

Legat said, "Our forces in China have prepared those leaders to join in the 'peace pact' as soon as the president announces it. We expect Russia to come into line any day now."

"And Thursday?" Proklor asked.

"All set," Temno confirmed. "It will be spectacular, and instantly give the president the reasons he needs to reestablish the State of Emergency for another month."

"And then another month, and another," Legat added.

"Good. And those damn Sullivans? What have you done about them?" Proklor asked.

The generals turned to Balzor, who was in the front row.

"We've lured the mother to the event on Thursday, so that will be the end of her, which should at least silence the father, if he ever gets out of prison. It's harder to track the son—the heat and light around him are intense. But we convinced the president, where we don't have that problem, to get rid of him, so he'll be out of the White House this week."

"Excellent," Proklor said. "Kill him as soon as you can, so he won't be here to meddle when we're finally in control."

# Wednesday, November 11

Tom slept five hours that night; his head was cloudy when he rose at 5:30, hoping to be in the White House to see the President as early as possible, before his boss became involved in his official Veterans Day events. Tom opened the back door for Beau, and as he poured his coffee, he checked for news from Cyprus—there was nothing new.

Thirty minutes later, as he was latching his front door to catch his rideshare, he got a text to come to the White House residence as soon as possible.

When he arrived upstairs in the West Sitting Hall, the president came out of his bedroom fully dressed in a dark blue suit with a red tie, carrying a file of papers. There was no offer of a handshake, nor of breakfast.

Visibly red, the president said, "What are you doing? Jim Toomey called me an hour ago. Have you lost your mind? I told you to stop investigating the election. We won. There are no issues—as our experts have all verified, including you."

"I know. But this new information indicates that someone added code to the final security check of the voting equipment, loaded on trusted flash drives, to distort the election results as they were recorded and reported."

"That's impossible."

"I thought so, too, until I saw a video with that result actually happening on a voting machine."

The president moved a step closer. "A video? Tom, what have you done? Who's been doing this investigation?"

"One of the experts who looked at election security for us, as you asked."

"One person?"

"And a small team of cyber experts on Cyprus working with her."

He came very close to Tom, almost in his face. "On Cyprus? Overseas? You have a foreign group looking at our election results?"

Tom stood, silent, and nodded. The president turned and walked over to the window, thinking. He turned to Tom.

"Who knows about all this?"

"The computer team who work at InternetOne on Cyprus, Agent Prescott, obviously her boss, and us."

President Bradshaw stared at him. Unseen by either of them, Nepravel came in through the outer wall, his hands blocking the intense spiritual light and heat which now emanated from Tom. The pain was excruciating. Luckily, the president had listened to the fallen angels' voices for several decades, so it would not take long. Nepravel quickly whispered in the ear of the president the instructions Balzor had given him. "Fire him. Right now. Gone." The message delivered, Nepravel, almost blinded by the light, retreated to the south lawn.

The president turned to his National Security Advisor. "Tom, we're moving your last day up from Friday to today. I don't have faith in you anymore. I'll start the process this morning. We'll brief-in your replacement ourselves. We don't need to make a big deal. We've already publicly mentioned it. We appreciate all that you did right after the attacks, and we wish you well. But you shouldn't be investigating something that doesn't need investigating, especially after I ordered you not to. If there's any follow up needed, Drew and Jim will handle it. Leave a complete file with us of who's involved in what you've been doing. And don't mention any of this to anyone, because it's not true."

Tom stood for several beats and silently prayed for help. "I understand, and I'm sorry you feel that way, Mr. President. I have only ever wanted the truth...and to help the nation. I'll be out of my office as soon as they can process the paperwork tomorrow morning."

He waited to see if the president would shake his hand. After an awkward moment, Tom turned and left.

The president was now alone in the West Sitting Hall, except for Nepravel, who had returned once Tom left. Looking out the window, Bradshaw could hear Margaret's blow dryer in their bedroom. With encouragement from a thought from Nepravel, which he heard clearly, he picked up his Core Phone.

"Drew?"

"Good morning. I'm in the office preparing for my meetings in Beijing and Moscow."

"You did a great job last night and I'm glad that Beijing is ready to join us. Hopefully Moscow after you meet with them. But, listen, we may have a problem that needs immediate attention."

"What?"

Bradshaw described what he knew about Tom's digging into the election results, focusing on the flash drives, including the call from Jim Toomey at the FBI.

Drew sounded incredulous. "So Tom told some people on Cyprus to dig into the code on our U.S. voting machines, even though you told him not to, and now that lead FBI agent has a glimpse of it as well?"

"That's right. I fired Tom this morning. He'll be gone tomorrow."

"Not good."

"Why?"

"I'd rather have him where we can see him, and try to control him. Who else knows about this?"

"I told Tom to leave a file on his desk with the list of who's involved. I think other than him and Agent Prescott, the others are at some internet company on Cyprus. InternetOne, I think."

There was a long pause as the president thought, and Nepravel helped him. "Drew, what are we going to do? We have to stop them. Even though no one could ever connect us to the vote swing we manufactured, we can't let them overturn the election results for any reason. This is the moment Progressives have worked for over a hundred years! Now, thanks to our actions, it's in our grasp, and we can't let it go again. The nation needs us too much. What if those idiots get back in power? They'd undo everything we've worked so hard for. Everything the nation so needs."

Drew paused. "I agree. And actually, Cyprus is a great location for staging all types of work in the Middle East. We have some friends there who might be able to help. Sounds like some computer technicians need to pay InternetOne a visit."

"Hmm."

"And Washington can be a very dangerous place, Mr. President. Traffic. Crime. Break-ins. Terrible things can happen to almost anyone, anytime."

"I see. Yes, you're right about this city."

"I'll make two calls. You call Jim and tell him to deal with that agent."

"I will. Thanks, Drew."

"As you said, it's too important. I'm sorry they wouldn't leave it alone, but now we'll just have to fix it."

They hung up, and the president went for more coffee. Nepravel left to find Balzor, with the expectation of good news to follow.

As Tom walked through the nearly empty West Wing, he noticed Emily's open door and saw her at her desk. He knocked and went inside. When she looked up, he smiled.

"You're working today? Which, by the way, is my last day. Or tomorrow morning, I guess, when I can sign the right papers."

She put down the file she was reading. "I thought your last day was Friday."

He shrugged. "I made him mad. He wants me gone."

She frowned.

"I wouldn't stop asking questions about the election results. In fact, Erin and Callie are looking into possible tampering right now."

"Erin and Callie? Together? That must be different. Election tampering?"

He nodded. "Yes. They actually may have found something."

"Erin and Callie? What?"

He paused. "I'd better not say. I don't want you to be in trouble, too."

"Seriously? The election last Tuesday?"

He nodded again. "I hope they're wrong, but if it ever does come up again, just remember that all I ever wanted was the truth. And that I didn't want to leave my job."

She stood and came around the desk, shaking her head in mock concern. "The truth. The truth. You're a broken record there."

He smiled. "Yes, I guess so. I wasn't so much before. But now it's really all there is."

"What will you do?"

"Not sure. Something will turn up. Anyway, if there's ever anything more about this election being tampered with, don't dismiss it out of hand. It may be true."

She reached out and hugged him. "OK. I got it. And we're still best friends. And are you guys going to be a threesome or something?"

He laughed. "Not hardly. I asked Erin to marry me, and I'm waiting for her answer."

"Wow. You're full of news. Let me know on that one, too. We'll have you over soon."

"That'll be great. Thanks for all you've done to get us through these difficult months."

"No, thank you. Most of the ideas were yours."

Tom turned and walked to his office, where he wrote short notes for his two assistants, thanking them and asking them to help with the upcoming transition. Then he went into his inner office and closed the door. Going to his safe, he removed a single sheet of paper and copied its two lines of content onto a sheet on his L-pad. Then he replaced the paper in the safe and locked it. He knew there were official procedures to follow for checking him out the next day, but he wanted to get a head start.

He called Tanya Prescott, but she didn't answer; he left her a voicemail. He agonized about the president's directive that he leave a list of everyone working on the election results. In the end, since he didn't know all the names of the team on Cyprus, he listed Tanya, Erin, Alexei and Callie.

Then he called Clayton Hunt, who was driving home from overnight duty at the Pentagon. Clayton agreed to see him at a late lunch, and suggested he come to their home, since it was a holiday.

Tom made a small pile on the conference table of his personal items—there weren't many—along with his books from the shelves.

He had just returned to his desk when Tanya Prescott unexpectedly arrived. She looked flustered, and he motioned for her to close the door. She sat across from him and took out her Core Group phone.

"Hey. A crazy Veterans Day morning. No holiday for us, I guess. Because I'm still on the distribution list for election issues from the Federal Election Integrity Commission, I just got a text from them reminding everyone, among other things, that with the elections now over, any flash drives with vote counts on them must be retained for six months, but—get this—'any flash drives that were loaded with local candidates but were then unused in the election must be wiped clean immediately and returned to the general inventory for future use.'"

Tom was about to speak, but Tanya held up her hand.

"And I'd just read that text when I got a call from Jim Toomey. Yes, himself, on a holiday. He thanked me for all my hard work with the White House team since the attacks, and he's promoting me to run our office in Denver. Friday's my last day here, and I'm supposed to report to Denver in ten days."

Tom said, "The President just moved up my departure to today—or officially tomorrow, I guess." They looked at each other for several beats. He signaled with a finger over his lips and then a circular motion that there might be mics in his office. Then he continued, taking out his own Core Group phone. "Here. Since I'm the one to whom others have turned in their phones when they left, I'm going to turn mine in to the FBI. To you. I'm turning it off now." He slid it across the desk to her. "I'll record that on my check-out form tomorrow. And I'd like to have lunch with you today. Are you available?"

"Uh, I guess so. Sure."

"Good." He took a paper out of his L-pad and wrote an address on it. "Let's meet here. And bring this paper with you. I'll add a few more addresses then."

They stood. Tanya put Tom's phone in her bag. "OK, see you in a little while."

Later that morning President Bradshaw, after calls with Jim Toomey and General Nathan Price, left the Oval Office and walked to the vice president's office, where Patricia Reynolds was working the holiday at her conference table with Rob Thompson, Emily Schofield, and two senior members of the Phoenix Team.

As he walked over to them, the vice president smiled. "We're using this morning to put the finishing touches on the ten key Executive Orders that we announced Monday evening, along with the Trusted Citizen Program, all of which you can sign tomorrow. Then we should have ten more next week."

The president nodded. "Good. Very good. Our programs should be well in place when the new Congress gets around to voting them in next year. Well done...But, listen, I'd like you to add two things. We're going to need a Declaration of a State of Emergency, patterned after our last one, ready to go except for filling in the details and the dates. I'm not sure when, but I suspect we'll be attacked again, and I want us ready to move quickly this time to take control—for the sake of the nation."

Emily said, "We already have it almost ready."

"Thank you. The other thing, Patricia, is that you and Drew need to settle on your final choice for National Security Advisor. Tom's leaving today, so we need to fill that position immediately."

She nodded. "You'll have it by tomorrow at the latest."


When Tom and Tanya left Clayton's home after lunch, Tom realized that he didn't have to go anywhere. Tomorrow he'd officially check-out of the White House, he had no job, and other people he trusted were following up on the election results. While waiting for them, he had nowhere he had to be.

So he accepted Tanya's offer for a ride back to the city.

"What are you doing here?" Ahmad asked later that afternoon, as Clayton sat down at the computer terminal next to him. "Didn't you have the midwatch last night?"

"Hey. Yes, I did. But then I had lunch with Tom and his FBI agent friend, and now I'm back to see if I can run down a few pretty crazy things. I'm headed over to our Comm Team in a minute. Anything new here?"

"It's been slow, so I've been drilling more into the China-Uyghur mess. It's really terrible—worse than we thought just a month ago. And it turns out the NSA has intercepted conversations with the Muslim Uyghur training camp leader in Afghanistan which confirm that the whole anti-Chinese extremist effort is secretly paid for by the Chinese government itself. It's awful. Mariam, Natalie, and Tom's mother are going to demonstrate at the Chinese Embassy at eleven tomorrow. They're meeting at the church beforehand to get ready. I really wish we could join them."

Clayton picked up his computer bag. "Me, too. Let me go see the Comm guys, and I'll check back with you."


Tom took Beau for a long walk around the neighborhood, and on the way home they stopped by Kristen's row house. Callie had shown Tom where she hid a key back when the threats to them first started, and he used it to go inside.

Mixed in with the mail below the door slot was a manilla envelope addressed to "The Christian Bitch." He opened it and found a picture of the home with a threat to burn it that night if Callie didn't immediately renounce her white privilege and gender bigotry on FaceGram.


As the sun set late that afternoon, Kahar Bosakov and Ablet Sabri closed the blinds in their apartment, moved some furniture, and hung the Turkic Islamic Republic of East Turkestan flag on the blank wall.

Then, one at a time, each of them sat in front of the flag with an AR-15 rifle across his chest, while the other ran the video camera, and described why he was privileged to be a martyr to free his people from Chinese Communist tyranny.

Clayton, very tired, rejoined his colleague and friend at their secure post in the Pentagon.

Rashid said, "I told you I've been checking regularly on Xinjiang, and in just the last two hours we have satellite images of Chinese troops mobilizing and fanning out all across the region. I guess they also know tomorrow's a significant anniversary in Uyghur history."

"I hope there's no bloodshed."

Just then Clayton's internal message system buzzed. "It's the Comm guys."

A little after nine that evening, Clayton and Tanya, who had already been talking on a video call for several minutes, called Tom with their joint report.

When they finished, Tom texted Seth, who called back from his home thirty minutes later. There was then a second video call with the four of them.

In the physically dark but spiritually alive Oval Office late that night, Prince Proklor listened to reports from Generals Temno and Bespor, and from Sector Leader Balzor, along with an emissary from their counterparts in China, all pointing to human plans which they had planted with ever-increasing urgency over the last two months, and which now their charges appeared ready to launch the next morning.

When they finished, Proklor looked around at the assembled Evil and nodded. "Excellent, excellent. How fitting that on the anniversary of Kristallnacht we should now take down the main fortress of the Light. Well done. Let's gather here tomorrow and watch the American leaders whom we've lied to for decades seize control for us."

# 27

*We ought to be no less persuaded that the propitious smiles of Heaven can never be expected on a nation that disregards the eternal rules of order and right which Heaven itself has ordained.*

George Washington
Thursday, November 12

It was 3am when two men in black military gear, wearing night-vision goggles, dropped over the fence and into the backyard of Tom's darkened row house.

A few moments later they were standing on the landing outside the backdoor.

The operation had been put together hastily. The two ex-Special Ops soldiers were told to expect no alarm, a dog, and a single male, probably unarmed, in the front upstairs bedroom. They would make the murder look like a break-in gone bad.

It only took a minute to pick quietly through the lock on Tom's backdoor. One man crept into the living room, while the other stayed at the kitchen door, listening. They expected the dog to bark and for their target to come down the stairs. They raised their night-vision goggles, in case he turned on a light, and readied their suppressed handguns.

On Cyprus, the full team gathered again in the conference room for coffee, fruit and yogurt. Callie, with Erin's help, had written a script for a short video to show and explain what they had discovered, and now they were discussing the details before attempting a first take with Erin as the narrator.

Richard Sullivan, troubled and unable to sleep, slipped out of his bunk in the detention cell and dropped to his knees. He silently prayed for the nation, for his family, and against the forces of darkness.

After waiting several minutes on the ground floor of Tom's row house for a response from the second floor, the two men moved to the stairs and began climbing. Using hand signals they approached the front bedroom door, then flung it open. They wanted Tom to stand so that their shots would penetrate his front torso.

But there was no one in the bed, and no dog. Within a minute they confirmed that the home was empty, and they left the way they had entered.

Tom had expected to sleep on Callie's sofa to ward off any attack on Kristen's townhome. But after Clayton's call, he'd been up for several hours in her apartment, Beau at his feet, video conferencing with his former apartment mate, plus Rashid and the military experts Clayton had injected into the mix. He fell asleep just before 3am.

As the eastern sky started to lighten for what promised to be a beautiful if chilly fall day, Tom awoke, called Seth, and got up to fix some coffee. When he put his phone down he noticed that the camera in his kitchen had tripped, and he watched the replay. He immediately called Tanya Prescott, then sent her the video clip.

Twenty minutes later he and Beau headed over to Seth's home with a travel mug of coffee and Tom's computer bag.

Ninety minutes later, as Tanya Prescott was driving to a quickly called meeting with Tom and Seth that morning she got a call from her friend at the county election management headquarters. She answered on her hands-free.

"Tanya, hey, it's Bill."

"Hey. Thanks again for your help with the flash drives."

"No problem. And, look, that's why I'm calling. We got a directive yesterday to erase any unused drives from this past election, and I found three of them in the boxes for other precincts. I thought I'd ask if you'd like copies of those as well, before we reformat them."

"Bill, you're an angel. Thank you. Yes. And in fact, I'm not far from you right now. Can I stop by and pick them up in a little while?"

"Sure. And would it help if I made calls to a few of my friends in other counties, to see if they have any?"

"Bill, that would be great. Thank you."

As the president tied his tie and the First Lady worked at her dressing table in their bedroom that morning, he said, "Yesterday's wreath laying ceremony at Arlington was really moving. I just hope with our initiatives that there will be far fewer Unknown Soldiers in the years ahead."

"I'm sure you're right, dear. And you've worked hard to get us here."

He turned to her. "It's finally all come together. The right people with the right ideas, ready to act. Now the election mandate. And, as tragic as they were, the attacks in September opened the door for us to make more laws by Executive Order, which is so much more efficient."

She stood and straightened his tie, smiling. "The nation is lucky to have you."

Balzor, stationed just behind her, could not have agreed more.

A little past 8:30 Janet Sullivan, wearing a dark blue suit and a warm coat, waited on the corner near the front entrance to the Chinese Fellowship Christian Church. She expected people—mostly women—from Robert Ludwig's church and several others, plus Mariam Rashid and several Muslims from her mosque, to meet and to go inside.

As she waited, she noted the coming and going of parents dropping off young children for the Mandarin-immersion daycare which met at the church. And the many students attending the grade school, all of whom entered through the front door of the adjoining Administration Building.

As 9 am approached, Robert Ludwig, Natalie and Mariam arrived and joined Janet. They went inside through the sanctuary entrance and were greeted by the Chinese American pastor, who led them to the Fellowship Hall on the ground floor of the Administration Building, accessed through a connecting door in the common wall. There they found a group of ten men and women who appeared to be of Chinese descent—sipping coffee and chatting near tables on the side of the room. Everyone greeted them, and the newcomers got coffee.

Three younger people were working at a nearby table, making signs, some denouncing the suppression of Uyghurs, others the persecution of People of Faith.

The pastor asked everyone to gather around. He said they would leave at 9:30 and rendezvous outside the Chinese Embassy with groups coming from several synagogues, mosques, and other churches.

Robert Ludwig thanked the pastor and everyone for coming, introduced former Congresswoman Janet Sullivan, noting that her husband was still in jail, and mentioned the serendipity that November

9$^{th}$ through 12th held such significance for the repression of both Muslims in China and of Jews in Germany.

"While the crimes against Jews are thankfully mostly history, we particularly want to recognize and thank our Chinese American friends for stepping out in faith to demonstrate publicly against today's abuse of basic human rights in China. We imagine that in some cases there could be reprisals. And we also mourn the constant weakening of the rights guaranteed here in America—as witnessed by those incarcerated with Richard Sullivan for exercising their right of free speech.

"So we celebrate that people of faith—Jews, Muslims and Christians—and also people of no faith—are gathering in America today to speak out about abuses in China. But we do so with the sober caution that those rights here, like everywhere, are under attack from those who want to control every aspect of our lives, including our thoughts."

As the president was about to enter the Oval Office for a photo op with several donors to recent Progressive campaigns, his secretary signaled from her desk.

"I took the Sign-out folder with the documents to Tom's office, but he's not there, and his assistant said he texted her a note that he might come in this afternoon, but that he'd turned in his Core Group Phone to the FBI, and she gave me the list you asked him for."

"Uh, OK. Thanks. Listen, that reminds me—please get General Price on the phone this morning."

Kahar Bosakov and Ablet Sabri, dressed in jeans and hoodies and carrying backpacks, arrived across from the Chinese Fellowship Christian Church a little after nine, where they met their two teammates, who had been watching the church for an hour.

Kahar listened as one of them reported to Ablet, their leader, "Seems like more adults than usual went inside, maybe for a meeting, but otherwise it's been normal. The schoolkids are all in there."

Ablet responded, "OK. Allah be praised. We must be in place when the demands go out on the internet at nine thirty. When we get inside, Kahar and I will go upstairs to get the children and teachers. You two control the adults. Shoot anyone who resists. May Allah be merciful."

The four young men walked across the street and Ablet motioned for Kahar, who had the best English, to ring the bell for the door to the Admin Building.

A Chinese man with a white collar came to the door, opened it, and smiled. "Are you here for the demonstration?"

"Uh, yes," Kahar answered, starting to move inside.

"And, pardon me asking, but are you by chance Uyghurs?"

Kahar was immediately defensive. "Yes."

As they all moved into the foyer, the Chinese pastor appeared to be pleased. "Wonderful. Come through and join the others." He turned to lead the way, but instead of following him, the two cousins walked quickly toward the stairs. "No, that's not the way."

Each of the other two men extracted a rifle from their partner's backpack. The taller one pointed his rifle at the pastor, who backed up. "Show us!" he said.

On the street, a Network mobile broadcast truck pulled up and parked in a commercial space. Two men prepared the communication antenna, and the reporter read her notes for the interview which Seth had organized with the two pastors after Natalie told him about their plans to join the demonstration, despite the government's recent determination of Uyghur terrorism.

Nepravel and Mavlan, who, along with six other demons, had ensured that the gunmen arrived on time that morning, could not go into the church, or even remain near it. The spiritual heat and light from all the believers inside, and from the prayers arriving for them, was too much for them to bear. Nepravel circled in the streets, remaining about a block away, and cursing.

Janet Sullivan had just finished her coffee and was headed for the restroom before departing for the embassy when through the door from the main building came the church pastor followed by two young men with assault rifles. The second one waved his rifle and yelled, "Everyone against the wall, and no one will get hurt!"

Robert Ludwig started toward them, and the closer one fired his rifle just over the pastor's head, striking the wall and making a very loud noise.

That provoked screams from upstairs, and two more rifle shots from the upper floors. Then more screams.

"I said get against the wall. Now!"

Janet grabbed Ludwig's shirt sleeve and pulled him back. She looked for Natalie and Mariam who were by the table. "Come on, Robert," she whispered.

"No talking!" the shorter one shouted, and pointed his rifle at her.

Slowly, all of them moved to the far wall. Above, they could hear more young men yelling, teachers trying to control children, some screams, and footsteps coming down the stairs.

The Network reporter, who had served in Iraq, yelled to her technicians, "Those were rifle shots! Call 911 and HQ. Get us on the air!"

Everyone on the sidewalks had frozen, or were moving away from the church, after the screams and gunshots. A single police officer ran up to the Admin Building door, but it was locked. He called in on his radio.

While one gunman trained his rifle on the line of adults standing against the wall, the other pulled out those who appeared to be of Chinese ancestry and grouped them on the left side—everyone else on the right, where Janet, Mariam, Natalie and Pastor Ludwig were joined by three others.

From the hallway outside the Fellowship Hall they could hear footsteps descending the stairs, children crying and talking, and men yelling "Quiet!"

Janet, who was silently praying and holding Natalie's hand, saw the first teacher come through the door, leading a line of children. Behind them a young man was standing with a rifle, herding them from the hallway into the Fellowship Hall. One of the first pair of gunmen instructed the teachers to have the children sit on the floor and to be quiet.

When the last student and teacher entered the hall, the fourth gunmen came inside and stood next to the double doors. He nodded to the one who had been ahead of him. "That's all."

"Kahar!" Mariam quietly gasped.

The gunman closest to the adults turned to her. "What did you say?"

"Nothing," she whispered.

But now Kahar looked at her, and it was obvious that they knew each other. He looked momentarily flustered, while the other gunman pulled Mariam forward to stand alone.

Kahar appeared to regroup. "What are you doing here?"

"I...We're going to protest the treatment of your people at the Chinese Embassy."

"From here? A Chinese church? You're Muslim."

"Yes."

Ablet, standing next to the children, intervened. "Enough! Get back in line and be quiet."

As she stepped back, he addressed all of them. "We're here as part of a glorious movement to free our Uyghur homeland and people from oppression and torture at the hands of the gangster Chinese government. Our demands will soon be posted on the internet. Their government will have three hours to agree. If they do, you will all be released unharmed."

Janet knew what all the adults around her were thinking, and she momentarily locked eyes with Robert Ludwig, but no one spoke.

A young girl on the floor started to cry for her mommy. Ablet fired a shot into the ceiling and yelled, "Shut up!"

He looked at the Chinese pastor and pointed with his rifle towards a table near the door. "Does that television work? Turn on The Network. And if any of you starts to think you're a hero, and rush us, we'll shoot the children first, then you. So if you don't want to kill children, do as we say."

The president and Drew Boswell were meeting in the Cabinet Room with Gerald Veazy and other members of their party's Senate leadership on expediting the confirmation of the new Secretary of State. As that meeting broke up, the two men planned to spend some time finishing their timetable for bringing China and Russia into their world-sharing alliance with as little fanfare as possible.

The president's secretary entered the room as the last Senator left. "Director Toomey says he must speak to you," and she pointed to the phone next to him, which then buzzed.

At DCNet, the headquarters for The Network in the capital, Rachel Shaw looked up from her desk at the live feed on her monitor, watched it for a minute, and then walked quickly to a small studio at the back of their space where several people were gathered around a table, talking and pointing to monitors on the wall. She came in, picked up the remote, and clicked to their live news feed.

"Seth, I think you all should see this."

It only took Seth ten seconds to turn to Tom Sullivan, sitting next to him. "I think that's where Natalie went this morning."

"And my mother," Tom added. "And Clayton's Muslim friend, Mariam."

They all watched the reporter on the street and clearly heard a gunshot.

"Damn," Seth said, standing up.

They watched another minute. Tom touched Seth's arm and said, "We can't do anything there, at least right now. But we can here. Since Rachel's here, let's show her."

As they began, Tanya Prescott stood and picked up her phone. "I need to check in."

Ten minutes later the president and Drew Boswell, joined by Patricia Reynolds, Rob Thompson and Emily Schofield were downstairs in the Situation Room with the rotating on-site team, and with Jim Toomey and General Price connected on video screens.

From the end of the table, President Bradshaw addressed one of the screens on the wall at the other end.

"All right, Jim, what do we know?"

The FBI Director responded, "In D.C. and in each of five U.S. cities with a Chinese consulate, a group identifying themselves as 'Uyghurs for Freedom' have seized a soft target full of mostly Chinese and Chinese American children and have issued a list of demands on the internet. If the Chinese government does not agree to meet these demands in three hours, they threaten to kill everyone inside each location."

"What are their demands?"

"What you would expect. No more persecution, internment or re-education of Uyghurs in China. No more forced sterilization. The freedom to practice their Muslim faith. The freedom to travel within and outside China. Freedom of information on the internet. Dismantling of the extra security cameras and restrictions in Xinjiang Province. And several more."

"Hmm. Not likely to happen. At least not in three hours, for sure. How many hostages do they have, and where in D.C.?"

"Overall, probably over a hundred children. Here they've taken over the Chinese Fellowship Christian Church, which runs an elementary school and daycare center."

"Bastards. I've been warning everyone that these people are terrorists, just like our friends in China have been telling us."

There was silence around the table.

A third screen on the wall came to life, and they saw the Network's reporter standing near the church with her microphone, as police tried to move everyone back.

After watching the confusion for a few moments, the president continued, "Jim, make every preparation to storm that church—and the other locations—before their deadline, if this plays out like I expect it will.

"And, Jim, I doubt many people will show up at the Chinese Embassy to protest in favor of terrorists, so let's have a huge law enforcement presence there, federal and local, and arrest every one of them. We want our partners to see that we know how to deal with dissent.

"Drew, you're now our acting Secretary of State, and you've got the best contacts in Beijing. Get on your phone, tell them what we're doing, and see what their leadership is thinking. While you guys set those steps in motion, the rest of us will adjourn to the Oval Office. And Nathan, I'm going to call you in a minute."

Drew, staying in his seat, looked at the FBI Director on the monitor. "Jim, I'm told we've got a State Department office building right next to the embassy off Van Ness, if you need a place to park some reserves, or to use for detentions."

"Thanks. I'll let the Scene Commander know."

It had been almost an hour since the gunmen had entered the Fellowship Hall. The children were sitting on the floor in groups with their teachers. Janet and the adults were in chairs, lined up along the wall. No one spoke, but a few children were crying.

All their phones had been turned off and piled in the far corner.

The television was tuned to The Network. The police had moved everyone more than a block away when they cordoned off the area, but the church was still visible at the intersection over the reporter's shoulder as she interviewed parents and church members, and switched to her colleagues in the other five cities with similar hostage takeovers.

While the two men previously unknown to Kahar watched the front and back doors, Ablet stood guard near the adults, and Kahar was stationed between the television and the internal door leading to the sanctuary.

A little girl of about four, crying, said, "I have to go to the bathroom." Her teacher took her hand and looked back and forth between Ablet and Kahar.

Ablet looked at Kahar and nodded. "One at a time, a teacher can take a child to the bathroom in the hall. Kahar will watch from the door. If anyone tries to escape, we'll shoot one child from each class. So do as we say!"

As their group came up the stairs from the White House basement, the president called General Price on his Core Group phone and talked while he walked.

"Nathan. Yes, this is terrible. But, listen, Tom Sullivan left us as Security Advisor...Yes, I know...He turned in his Core Phone to the FBI. But don't I remember that you and he had some code or something set up that first night at Fort Meade that made our special phone system work?"

"Yes, sir. The key. A very long series of numbers and symbols. Only he and I have it."

"Well, I'm not sure how all that works, but with him gone, I think you should change it, or whatever."

"Good thought, sir. Yes, I will."

"OK, good. Now help Jim come down on these damn Uyghurs, and hard."

"Yes, sir. We will."

When the president, his closest advisors, and the vice president met in the Oval Office, they sat on the two sofas by the coffee table. Unseen to them, Prince Proklor and his key generals were against the walls, watching, while Balzor and two others whispered continuously to their charges.

The president took out his Core Group phone, called Nancy Cantrell, put it on speaker, and placed the phone on the table.

"How is the next Speaker of the House this morning?"

"I was fine 'til we got the news about the Uyghurs and the hostages. Have you seen it?"

"Yes, yes, of course. But it's really not bad news. I'm here with Patricia, Drew, Rob and Emily. Are you alone?"

"Yes."

"OK. Good. Then let's make a quick plan how to use this crisis to get back our emergency powers and to introduce the new world alignment. Drew, after last night's TV panel, I think everyone's ready for us to work with our key international partners, especially at a time when one's being attacked by terrorists. Emily, can you get us time on all the networks today to denounce Uyghur terrorism, to support China, and to reinstate our State of Emergency for another month?"

"Yes. About eleven thirty?"

"Correct. Before the deadline. We need them to hear our resolve in a strong message before we send in the FBI and the SWAT Team."

"Got it."

Rob said, "If we move too quickly, a lot of children could be hurt. And there are reports of some other adults who were meeting at the church before the demonstration at the Chinese Embassy."

The president clenched his fists. "If we *don't* move early, it could be even worse. And we told Americans not to join those anti-Chinese, terrorist demonstrations."

"OK. And we'll get the updated Declaration of a State of Emergency ready."

"Good. Patricia, just like we planned, you should now be the go-to face for all internal security measures, while Drew handles international.

Both of you should join me on today's televised message to the nation as we battle this threat. Any questions? Let's make the most of this. Nancy, thanks for helping. I'll call Jim at the Bureau and be sure they're ready to go in at the church before the deadline."

Fifteen minutes later, after several teachers and children had gone to the restroom, Janet raised her hand and indicated to Ablet that she had the same need. He motioned with his rifle toward Kahar at the door.

Janet rose and walked directly past the younger gunman, then turned right down the hall while he watched, and into the restroom.

In the stall she sat and touched her new watch, which allowed her to text. She quickly wrote to her son: "4 men. Rifles. Fellowship Hall. Mariam knows one. Kahar? Watching The Network. Do not reply."

Then she flushed the toilet and returned to her chair.

"Kahar is one of the gunmen?" Rashid asked remotely from a video monitor on the wall of the darkened DCNet studio, where he had been working with Tom and the others.

Tom, seated at the table with Seth while Tanya paced on the other side of the room, said, "That's what my mother just texted from inside the church. There are four of them. Tanya's relaying that info to the SWAT Team. And the president wants national airtime at eleven-thirty, in forty minutes."

"OK. Give me ten minutes and either Clayton or I will get back to you."

Tom turned to another monitor, showing the dining room in Alexei's home on Cyprus, with the team from his office, including Erin and Callie, talking together and working on their laptops.

"Are you guys OK?" Tom asked.

Alexei looked up from talking with Erin. "Yes, we're fine. Thanks to that earlier head's up, we moved to my home."

"We'll try to stay on the schedule we planned, but obviously this hostage situation now has to be the focus here. It looks bad."

Erin spoke as Callie walked over. "Clayton and Rashid have been incredible with their help. We should be up to speed soon."

Callie looked at the camera. "Tom, what's happening there is terrible. We're going to stop in a minute and pray for the children, your Mom, Natalie, Mariam, Pastor Ludwig and all the others."

"Thank you. Then let us know when you're ready."

Nepravel, who had circled the church, trying in vain to battle the spiritual light and heat to see what was going on, finally decided to go to DCNet, where he expected to find no spiritual interference, and where he could at least keep up with events, if not influence them.

He came in through the front wall of The Network office/studio and was immediately relieved to see the nearly total spiritual darkness around him. He made his way through the area, searching for Seth or other familiar humans. As he came through the wall of the small studio in the back, he was shocked to find Tom Sullivan, whose inner spiritual light shone brightly, but was dimmed and held back by the weight of all the surrounding darkness. Nepravel could tolerate the diminished discomfort, so he watched and listened.

The president and Drew Boswell were alone in the Oval Office, editing Emily's draft of the president's upcoming message.

From the sofa, Drew said, "I've added some language for China. We want them to see us holding up our end of the new order."

At the Resolute Desk, sitting with Prince Proklor directly behind him, the president asked, "Did I hear you tell Jim that State has an office building next to the Chinese Embassy?"

"Yes. The Office of Foreign Missions. A lot of other embassies are in the immediate area, and there's a good-sized park with lots of trees across a narrow street from both buildings."

"Drew, that sounds like a place where some violence might break out in the middle of a rag-tag, unlawful demonstration. Maybe some shots fired. Who knows what might happen or who might get hurt? It would be terrible. Probably a lot of people arrested. After children being shot at a church, that kind of major street violence might require very stern measures from the government to protect the nation."

Drew thought for a few moments. "Yes, that would be terrible. Let me make a call."

The president nodded. "Any news on Tom or the others?"

Boswell silently shook his head. "Nothing's been reported."

"I haven't seen Agent Prescott today."

"Jim promoted her and moved her to Denver. Maybe she's on her way."

"I'll check with him when this is over."

Kristen Holloway had arrived back to D.C. that morning from driving Grace to her grandparents' home. In her living room with her laptop and phone, she simultaneously watched events on The Network and talked with Callie on Cyprus, elders at her church, and, briefly, with Tom.

Within twenty minutes she became a one-woman prayer hub, sending out emails and texts to the leaders of prayer chains all over the nation, who then forwarded them to their own prayer warriors.

As a result, there were now thousands of prayers arching up to Heaven, creating the bright spiritual lights of thousands of answered prayers raining down on every person and place under attack by those doing the work of the Prince of Lies.

A little after eleven, Ahmad Rashid, sitting at his console next to Clayton in the Pentagon, spoke to Tom and the others on a joint video feed.

"I have Kahar's cell phone number, but he won't answer."

In the studio, Tanya put her hand over her cell phone's mouthpiece and said, "The FBI's SWAT Team has assembled in a park between here and the church. I'm going over there now to meet with the team leader."

"If they go in now there'll be carnage," Seth said, "including lots of children, Natalie, Mariam and Tom's mother."

Clayton added, "It looks from the satellite images that under the cover of night the Chinese are massing a large force just outside the capital in Xinjiang. They seem to be readying for a sweep into the city when the sun comes up."

Seth stood. "Natalie's in that meeting hall with those children. And Mariam. And Mrs. Sullivan. I gotta talk to Rachel. I'll be back for the president's address."

At 11:30, all the networks aired the president's address from the Oval Office.

"My fellow Americans," President Bradshaw began from his desk, with Patricia Reynolds and Drew Boswell standing behind him, while a host of demons filled the space. "We are once again under attack, only this time we know exactly who the perpetrators are.

"Only three days after letting down the important protections in our State of Emergency, following the heinous murder of President Rhodes and so many others, our new weakness was exploited by Uyghur terrorists who simultaneously attacked both us and our friends in China, threatening to murder innocent children. The terrorists' tired demands have been proven time and again to be based on lies and subterfuge. We cannot let this stand. We will respond.

"These cowards who attack children have given a deadline only one hour from now for the Chinese government to agree to their impossible demands. In response, we now give them this deadline—come out of these sites without harming anyone no later than noon, or suffer the consequences. Neither the American nor Chinese people will give in to threats of violence, particularly against children.

"And to further protect our people, I am today reinstituting our State of Emergency for one more month, to give us again the tools we need to safeguard our freedoms while we implement the historic progressive mandates which you, the people, gave us in last week's election.

"We *will* improve your lives. We *will* protect you. And we will *not* be bullied.

"Our watchwords remain the same: Protection. Patriotism. Progress. May God bless America."

Three men dressed in jeans and nondescript gray hoodies parked their unmarked van in the parking lot next to Alexei's office building on Cyprus. The sun had already set, and in the growing darkness they could see that the lights on the fifth floor shone brightly behind the closed blinds.

The driver turned back to his colleague, who was monitoring a piece of equipment in his lap. "They're still up there," he said, having confirmed that the cell phones for Alexei, Erin and Callie were all pinging off the tower a block away.

"Then let's go," the driver said.

They exited the van and walked toward the lobby door, each carrying a zippered bag marked "ComputerGeeks."

When The Network's telecast of the president's address ended, Janet Sullivan, in the Fellowship Hall, felt a chill. The gunman on her side of the room, the one who appeared to be in charge, said something which sounded like an expletive and walked quickly over to the one whom Mariam had called Kahar. They stood closely together in animated and agitated conversation. Then they appeared to argue.

Janet took the hands of Natalie and Mariam, bowed her head, and prayed.

Rob Thompson, who, along with Emily Schofield, had watched the president's address from the other side of the camera, came forward as their boss was shaking hands with Patricia and Drew. Rob placed a document on the desk.

"Here's the Executive Order for reinstating the State of Emergency for another month. We'll put it out to the press within the hour."

"Good." Out of habit the president paused and looked up, as Emily moved two photographers into their positions.

"Protection. Patriotism. Progress," the president said, as he signed the document.

All around him, the demons smiled and congratulated each other.

"Why did he do that?" Clayton asked from a video monitor on the wall in the DCNet studio. "That will just move up their timeline. They'll act before being taken."

"I'm not sure," Tom said from his chair at the table.

Clayton shook his head. "It's almost like they want a disaster."

Ablat and Kahar stood face to face in the wide doorway between the Fellowship Hall and the sanctuary, arguing in Uyghur.

"We'll start killing them just after noon," Ablat said.

Kahar shook his head. "No. We said twelve-thirty. The Chinese haven't responded."

"They won't, and the Americans will storm this place. Either way, many will die, but it's important that *we* are in charge of their deaths, and of ours. Not them!"

Kahar said nothing.

One of the Chinese American adults sitting against the wall whispered just loud enough for the others to hear, "They're going to start killing us in thirty minutes."

Rachel Shaw opened the door to the DCNet studio and walked over to Seth. Tom and the others, both in the studio and on the two video monitors, waited.

"I just got off the phone with Agent Prescott, who's with the team on site. You're cleared. Go ahead."

From the closest monitor, Rashid said, "Give me five minutes to finish my notes while Clayton gets the feeds. We'll be ready."

Nepravel, on the far wall, was worried. He left the studio momentarily to tell one of the lesser demons at DCNet to go find Balzor.

The three men in jeans and hoodies went past the lifts in the Cypriot office building's lobby and climbed the stairs. On the third floor landing they opened their bags and took out their assault rifles, pistols, and spare magazines. Then they continued upward.

When the first two gunmen reached the fifth-floor landing, the third man paused one floor below.

As the leader reached for the door, it flew open from the interior, as did the one below, flash grenades landed in the stairwell, and the doors were slammed shut.

The resulting light, noise and force stunned the gunmen, and two seconds later the doors reopened. A voice with a loudhailer yelled, "Police. Throw down your weapons. Now!"

Ten minutes later the three men were in cuffs in the back of a police van, on the way to interrogation.

In the Fellowship Hall, Kahar stood between the wall-mounted television and the door into the hall leading to the sanctuary, looking at the children on the floor as they sat around their teachers. He knew that in a few minutes he was going to start shooting them, after first killing all the adults. This would exact revenge on their Chinese tormenters, and secure his place in paradise. He started to perspire as his finger touched on and off the trigger of his assault rifle.

The Network was showing a map of the five other cities where hostages were being held when it went blank for a moment and then there was a close-up of Ahmad Rashid, sitting at a desk in his Army uniform. Kahar was stunned, and he looked across at Ablat, who quickly focused on the screen.

"My name is Major Ahmad Rashid," he began, "and I'm speaking from the Pentagon with the approval of the FBI Senior Agent in Charge of Counterterrorism.

"I'm a first-generation Muslim-American who is proud of our American heritage. I've served on the front lines in Afghanistan and Iraq.

"Right now I'm speaking specifically to all the Uyghur gunmen who have taken adults and children hostage in six of our cities, and particularly to Kahar Bosakov and Ablet Sabri here in D.C., whom I know from our mosque.

"Ablet and Kahar, you have been deceived and lied to. The training camp in Afghanistan you attended [a map and then a satellite image of the camp appeared on the screen as he spoke] was created by and is today funded by the Chinese Communist Party."

Balzor arrived and joined Nepravel in the studio half-way through Ahmad's news, glad that the intense spiritual darkness inside was able to bend many of the prayers that seemed to be increasing at a rapid pace, so that only a few got through to cause problems.

But he was appalled to see Tom Sullivan sitting at the table, and was even more distressed as he watched and listened to the Muslim Army officer.

The president was having an early lunch with Patricia Reynolds and Drew Boswell in the Oval Office when Emily Schofield knocked and quickly entered.

"You should see this." She reached for the remote on the coffee table and turned on the television.

"You are being duped by the Chinese Communists into fulfilling their stereotype for Uyghurs as terrorists, creating an excuse for them to crack down even harder on your people, and giving other nations the best reason possible not to demand that they change."

"Who and what the hell is this?" President Bradshaw said, putting down his sandwich. "Who authorized that man to speak?"

"Here's a picture of the training camp leader meeting with Chinese officials in a village near the camp. It's grainy, but I'm sure you recognize him. And here's a copy of a payment wired to a bank account in Dubai which I assure you belongs to him."

Kahar looked again at Ablet, who started to walk towards the television.

The live picture came back to Ahmad. "You and your fellow men are being used right now by the Chinese government, who hope to make the lives of your families and your people even more horrific if you follow their directions. The Chinese *want* you to pull those triggers. They *want* you to kill those children. They helped plan for it. Here's a live satellite image using infrared showing their forces massing around Urumqi. They want you to kill those innocent people so they can then slaughter or imprison hundreds or thousands more of your people, all in the name of stopping terrorism."

Ablet reached to take the remote control from the table, but Kahar took his arm. "Let him finish."

"Don't do it. Don't be duped by the very people you want to stop. They've paid all the bills to get you here, hoping you'll murder innocent people as they, the Chinese, have trained you. The Americans in that church are ready to demonstrate peacefully outside the Chinese Embassy to protest all of this, and to shine the light of truth on what the Chinese government is doing. After all that has happened today, that light will be very bright, and irrefutable to the whole world.

"Don't harm anyone. Don't give anyone here the reason to kill you, and don't give your enemies the tool they want to destroy your people. Put down your weapons now, while any charges against you are minor, and we will all do our best to ensure that any court takes all of this into account. As Muslim men, do the right thing to protect your people. Let the truth, with your help, speak louder than any gun ever could."

The picture of the Uyghur camp leader meeting with Chinese officials came back to the screen.

"Those are all lies!" the president fumed. "Emily, get me Jim and Nathan. What the hell is going on? The SWAT Team has got to go in, *now*. Get those guys!"

"Those are all lies!" Ablet said to Kahar in Uyghur, a few inches from his face, his right hand pointing to the screen.

"I don't think so," Kahar replied, just as forcefully. "It actually makes terrible sense. Look at that picture."

"A fake. All lies. We're going to start our revenge now!"

Ablet turned back toward the people in the room, his hand moving to his rifle. The Chinese-American man yelled "They're going to shoot!"

Robert Ludwig stood up, grabbed his chair and ran toward them.

As Ablet raised his rifle and the children screamed, Kahar took his own rifle and smashed its butt into the back of Ablet's head. Ablet crumbled, but a single shot split the chair and struck Ludwig in the left arm. Kahar then wrapped his arms around Ablet, pulling him down.

Janet, Natalie and two men piled on the pair, dropping them to the floor. Natalie pulled the rifle from Ablet's hands and flung it to the side.

Mariam ran through the sanctuary to the front door and told the gunman to put down his rifle, that it was over, and that he had been tricked. He pushed her aside and took off for the Fellowship Hall, so Mariam opened the front door, waved, yelled, and motioned to the SWAT Team a block away.

When the lead SWAT members came into the Fellowship Hall, after checking for terrorists in the sanctuary and working through a sea of running, screaming children, they found the four Uyghur gunmen sitting on the ground, surrounded by the adults who had been their hostages, each one holding a rifle or a handgun. Janet and two others were on the ground ten feet away, tending to Robert Ludwig's wound.

Janet raised her hands and told the rest to do the same. The police surrounded them. As the police confiscated the weapons, Janet pointed to Kahar, and said, "That man saved our lives."

"Nathan, how the hell did this happen?" the president, standing in the Oval Office, almost yelled into his Core Phone.

General Price replied, "We've known about the origins of that camp for a while, Mr. President."

"But, then...when? Why didn't you tell me?"

"The State Department asked us to confirm that there are Uyghur terrorist groups, and there are. They didn't ask about the training camp."

"Bloody hell." He looked up again to The Network, where it was being reported that the hostages in all the cities had been released unharmed, and all the gunmen taken into custody. "Drew, you better get on the phone to Beijing—they won't be happy about what that Army guy just said. And this friggin' training camp. Those Uyghurs will talk. Jim needs to use the State of Emergency to slow this down."

He was about to hang up when General Price said, "Mr. President, about changing the code that we talked about earlier."

"Yes?"

"We've tried, but it won't go through."

"Why?"

"We're not sure. We'll keep on it."

"But the phones obviously work. Are we still encrypted and locked down?"

"Yes."

"OK. Just keep it that way. And you and Jim need to get people over here fast to brief me on this training camp crap, so I won't look like a complete idiot when we go back to the nation to celebrate this great victory."

"Yes, sir. Will do."

Proklor and his generals, watching from the periphery of the Oval Office, were not sure what had happened, but they knew that no one had yet been killed, because no souls had passed, and that worried them. The prince sent for news from his minions at the church.

"It's my mother!" Tom said to those in the studio with him and on the two monitors. He touched his cell phone and put it to his ear. A moment later, he said, "Thank God. Let me put you on speaker—there are lots of people here who'll want to hear you." He put the phone in the center of the table.

"Of course. Yes, we're OK. Only Robert Ludwig was shot—in the arm—it's bad, but we stopped the bleeding and the paramedics just arrived. I'm still in the hall, and we're hugging and crying. The police are everywhere. The kids are outside. If you're with Seth, tell him Natalie's fine—she'll call him in a minute, after answering some questions. If you know how to get in touch with that Army officer, tell him he was great, and his wife is right here with me. I think she's calling him now."

They looked at the feed from the Pentagon, as Ahmad answered his phone.

"What now, Mom?" Tom asked. "Should I come over there?"

"No need. We're still going to the Chinese Embassy. This just made us even more determined. Seth, if you're listening, tell the world what the Chinese have done today—to us and to these Uyghurs—and encourage people to join us. We're driving up there as soon as the police finish with us."

"We will, Mrs. Sullivan. We will. And some other stuff—some truth." Seth glanced at Rachel Shaw, standing to the side, who nodded. "And if I come to the church right now, will you do an interview with me, so we can get the truth out about the manipulation of these Uyghur men, along with all that they're doing to the Uyghurs back home?"

"Yes, of course, Seth. Come on."

"It's not far, and our satellite truck is already there. Find it when you get out, and I'll meet you there."

"You're on. And I'll of course bring Natalie—and maybe some others."

As Seth put his gear into his computer bag, Balzor moved next to Rachel and whispered in her ear. She said, "Tom, maybe you should join your mother at the embassy."

Tom looked at Seth, but before he could respond, his mother said over the cell phone, "Someone named Tanya just asked me to tell you that she'll be heading to the White House in a little while."

"Thanks, Mom. We need to finish up what we're doing here, and then I'll see you at the embassy. Be careful. I love you."

"I love you, too."

President Bradshaw cancelled the rest of his afternoon schedule and had Emily book another block of all-networks time for 4 o'clock so that he could thank the Intelligence Corps and First Responders for the defeat of yet another terrorist attack on the nation.

A little after one, he, Drew, Patricia, Rob, Emily and several other staff members were back in the Situation Room with Jim Toomey from the FBI, and with General Price from the NSA on a monitor.

From the end of the table, the president said, "Thank you all for coming. We've just had a great victory over hardened terrorists, and I want to not only thank those who risked their lives, but also underline how important are the measures in the State of Emergency for protecting us. Now, please, give us your input so the writers can start writing what we'll tell the nation in two hours."

Jim Toomey looked up from his seat on the left side of the table at Nathan Price on the monitor. After some silence, he said, "Well, from what we now know—and it's early—the extra measures in the State of Emergency had little to do with it. These guys were in the U.S. for months without our intercepts or emergency measures picking them up, and it was apparently a personal contact at the church this morning who made the connection to talk one of them down from the cliff. Seems totally random, and very lucky."

"Damn it, Jim, that's not what we or the nation want to hear," the president exclaimed. "There *must* be some connection to show the value of what we're doing. Nathan, you learned about those training camps through our extra intercepts, right?"

"Actually, we've known about them for years, and we confirmed a while ago that the Chinese funded them—with regular intercepts, not any special State of Emergency measures."

"Well, the two of you need to figure out something we can say in less than two hours to bolster why the State of Emergency is so important—which it is—and don't leave 'til you do."

He got up, and before anyone else could stand, he left the room.

Ahmad Rashid, after talking with his wife and then with Tanya Prescott, left the Pentagon to meet the FBI/Police task force which would be booking the four Uyghur hostage takers. He wanted to help them, and especially Kahar, as early in the process as possible.

Callie walked into the living room in Alexei's comfortable home, located up the slope from the beach in Limassol, with a great view from almost every window. Erin was waking up from a nap on the couch. "Are you feeling better?"

Erin lifted her head onto a pillow, as Callie sat in an adjacent chair, and smiled. "Yes. It's just that this baby-making business wears you down after a long day."

Callie handed her a glass of water. "I understand."

"Any more news from the police about the men at Alexei's office?"

"Not that we've heard. But there are two vans-full of police outside the house here."

She took a sip. "Good...And I'm so glad Tom's mom is OK. She's a great lady."

"She has a lot of wisdom, and courage...The hostage taking over there threw our schedule off, but I think we're even better prepared, thanks to all your hard work."

Erin smiled again. "Our work. You're quite a writer."

"We'll see. Rest for now and take care of that baby."

"Yes."

The two men who had broken into Tom's row house very early that morning awoke in their extended stay hotel on the outskirts of D.C. While fixing sandwiches and commiserating over their lost success fee, they received a text directing them to the area around the Chinese Embassy, where about a hundred protestors were expected. Along with extra instructions, the text added that their earlier target might be there as well. They Juggled the embassy's address in the northwest of the city, repacked their equipment bags, and headed out.

Standing together with the church in the background, Seth interviewed former Congresswoman Janet Sullivan, along with the church's pastor. They recounted what they and the children had been through, thanked the Uyghur gunman who actually helped stop the attack, and encouraged everyone to join them outside the Chinese Embassy—and outside the consulates in the other five cities—to peacefully protest the Chinese government's genocide of the Uyghurs, their funding of a terrorist training camp to encourage attacks on their own people, and their manipulation of literally everyone within their grasp, inside and outside the country, for the sake of their own power.

"The authoritarian actions of the Chinese government, leading to violence right here in America, like the earlier tyranny of Nazi Germany and the Soviet Union, must be condemned by free people. Peaceful protest is what we're guaranteed in America—all of us—and free speech. They're fundamental to who we are. Without interference, surveillance, or reprisal, as happens every day in China. So join us in protesting all forms of totalitarian tyranny, starting with China. If you're in D.C., come to the Chinese Embassy right now, so that your voice will be heard," Janet concluded, standing next to Seth with the Chinese pastor and Natalie.

When they finished, everyone hugged. "Are you coming to the embassy, Seth?" Janet asked.

"No, we've got something important back at DCNet headquarters that I've got to get ready for. I think you'll want to see it. But we have a satellite truck already at the embassy, so we'll be able to cover the protest."

Janet smiled. "We'll try to make a ruckus with our small group."

"Good." He looked at Natalie. "Be careful. And keep your phones handy for our streaming content."

She nodded. "We will." Then the leaders and their group boarded vans and headed toward the embassy.

Tom, in the DCNet studio, finished with the technicians and the team on Cyprus. "I'm going up to the Chinese Embassy," he told everyone, "but I'll be back for the president's address at four."

He connected with a rideshare driver and headed north to the embassy. As often happened when he was alone in the midst of all the turbulence, he thought about Erin and their baby. They'd obviously put the marriage and childbirth discussion on hold when Erin suddenly left for Cyprus. But Tom thought about her in most quiet moments, impressed with her talents and intelligence. He just hoped that the current assignment was not asking too much of her, especially while pregnant. He just wanted her to be happy, and for them to be together.

So he bowed his head in the back of the car and prayed for Erin, their baby, his parents, Callie, and Alexei.

The Chinese Embassy's main entrance was on a short street which bisected a semi-circle that looped south from, and then back to, Van

Ness, in the northern part of the District, two blocks from the Van Ness-UDC Metro stop. Several other embassies occupied the outside of the semicircular loop, and in its elevated center was a park filled with trees and shrubs.

In accordance with the permit issued for up to two hundred demonstrators, several DC police were stationed at each end of the short street connecting the embassy's entrance to the loop street. They blocked vehicular access and checked the bags of the few demonstrators who had already arrived, allowing them to gather outside the gate to the embassy's entrance, where more police were stationed.

A Network satellite truck was parked just inside one of the two police checkpoints.

When the two gunmen turned off Van Ness onto the loop road, they drove past the police and continued as if they were going to one of the other embassies, but then parked on the far side of the wooded park, which blocked their view from the Chinese Embassy.

A few minutes later, after walking around the area outside the checkpoints, they sat on a park bench and enjoyed the warm afternoon.

Prince Proklor, his lead generals, and their key D.C. sector leaders, who had assembled earlier in the Oval Office to witness the final transition from Light to Dark through murder, mayhem and martial law, could not believe the reports from the D.C. church, or from the other hostage sites.

Proklor fumed at Balzor, who cowered beneath his glare. "Are you saying that no one was killed, no one even harmed, and all the gunmen gave up? How?!?"

"I don't know, my liege, but I will find out."

Turning to General Temno, he almost screamed, "We're supposed to be in control today!"

Fifteen minutes later the three vans carrying Janet, Mariam, Natalie and members of the Chinese American Fellowship Church were on Connecticut Avenue near the Cleveland Park Metro Station, one stop south of Van Ness-UDC, when they ran into very heavy traffic. They inched along for several minutes, but finally Natalie, looking at the map on her phone, said that walking would be faster. So they left the vans and continued on foot, mixing with a lot of other people on the sidewalks, heading north.

Given the earlier events, four DC policemen accompanied their group, and as they neared the intersection of Connecticut Avenue and Van Ness, the officers had to open a path for them to continue through the crowd. It became easier when those around them, learning who they were, began to clap and thank them for their bravery.

Finally, at about 2pm, Janet, the pastor, and the others made it through the gathering throng to the podium set up in front of the embassy's gates. They unfurled the signs which they'd made, and, using portable speakers and a microphone, the pastor introduced himself as an American of Chinese descent, and a Christian, who was calling out the Chinese government for persecuting Uyghur Muslims, and others, for no reason except their desire for personal freedoms—the same freedoms which Americans had until recently taken for granted, but which were now also in peril.

Callie was in a chair in the bedroom which Anna had given her, using her laptop on a video call with Kristen.

"I just did a call with Grace at Mom's house," Callie said. "She seems fine—very chatty."

Kristen smiled. "Yes. I check in on them every day. And I'm actually over at Andrea's now—we got another threat through the mailbox yesterday—but it hasn't stopped us from praying. In fact, Andrea and I have teamed up to watch The Network, talk to any of you who can share anything, and then send out Prayer Bulletins pretty much every hour."

"How many are you sending?"

"We're up to eleven thousand on our email server, and many of those are forwarded to others."

"That's fantastic, Kristen. I can't talk about what we hope to do later today, but we really need His help, wisdom and intervention. Please keep praying for us."

"We will. And for Clayton, Ahmad, Mariam...and of course for Tom and the president. How's Erin?"

"She's fine. Tired, like we all are, but more so, of course. She's an amazing woman. Great skills and personality. I hope she and Tom get together—they'll be so strong. And she asked me about faith in Jesus the same way I asked you years ago, in that motel room in California. She listened, but hasn't yet taken the step."

"Then we really have a lot to pray about."

"As always! Let's start." They bowed their heads and Callie began praying out loud.

Erin, who had been coming to see Callie and stopped to listen outside her bedroom door, walked quietly into the room and knelt next to her friend. Callie stopped praying and looked at her.

As they knelt side by side, Erin took Callie's hand. "I'm ready. I've watched you, and I want what you have. I can't keep doing this myself."

Callie nodded and smiled. "Then pray with me. 'Father, I confess that I'm a sinner, separated from you for eternity by my sins. Forgive me. I believe that by surrendering my life to your Son Jesus, who willingly died in my place, I can once again be your true daughter—forever. Please accept my prayer and fill me with your Holy Spirit, that every day I may be more like your Son in all that I say and do. Empty me of me, and fill me with Your truth. In Jesus' name I pray.'".

The demons in that part of Cyprus, who already could not go near Alexei's house because of the spiritual heat and light, now cowered behind buildings in terror as the deafening roar of God's Holy Spirit Himself moved across the island, stopped briefly, and took up residence inside Erin.

Tom was in the back seat of the rideshare car, still many blocks from the embassy. He'd called Jacob Welch, the Speaker of the House, and invited him to come to DCNet headquarters to hear and comment on the president's second talk, expected at four that afternoon. Tom persisted, and the Speaker said he would try.

Now, as Tom looked from the stopped car to the road ahead filled with unmoving traffic, he noted the time, thanked the driver, and walked to the Woodley Park Metro station.

President Bradshaw and his advisors were sitting on the sofas around the coffee table in the Oval Office, taking notes for his talk in just under an hour. The Network was on the monitor, muted.

From her seat Patricia Reynolds glanced at the monitor and said, "Look at that."

They turned to see what appeared to be a huge gathering outside the gates of the Chinese Embassy. As the elevated camera panned around 360 degrees, all the streets were full of people—it looked like many thousands, all standing together and listening to a woman with a microphone amplified by large, portable speakers.

Emily picked up the remote, and they heard Janet Sullivan say "...and those same freedoms are being attacked today here in our own country by the overreaching, power grabbing Administration in the White House. Just today they have re-instituted martial law, and they rule by Executive Order. That's what dictators do, like in Nazi Germany, the Soviet Union and Communist China, which we are protesting today. We must..."

"Holy crap!" the President exclaimed. "Who is that?"

"Janet Sullivan," replied the vice president.

"Damn!"

"Look at all those people," Emily said. "I thought we expected less than a hundred."

"That was before this morning," Rob said, "and the revelations about the Chinese government's involvement."

"Drew, how can we go on television and congratulate this result? The Chinese will go crazy."

A drone view came on the screen, showing the streets in the area jammed with all those trying to get to the embassy on foot, most watching on their phones as Janet continued her speech, attacking the excesses of the Administration, and the people around her cheered.

"Not good, Mr. President," Drew said quietly. "We better look again at our message."

Bradshaw thought for a moment. "We'll just ignore them. We have the power and the media. We'll stick with our message, repeat it, and in a day or two of friendly coverage no one will remember this little Uyghur blip."

They looked at each other and nodded. The president continued, "Emily, as soon as our broadcast is over, work up some talking points for the next few days, and talk with Seth. Drew will handle Beijing. Patricia and our domestic team will move ahead with the benefits of the Trusted Citizen Program, and everyone will forget about this Chinese pastor and a has-been Congresswoman."

The two gunmen had intended to use the cover of the park in the middle of the circular loop to fire several shots, as instructed, hitting a speaker if possible, creating mayhem in the small crowd, and escaping in the ensuing chaos as the authorities blamed Uyghur terrorists.

But now they found themselves surrounded by thousands of people, including those standing shoulder to shoulder in the park and listening to the speakers in front of the embassy—any possible escape routes were completely blocked.

They looked at each other and simply shook their heads.

The last speaker at the podium in front of the embassy was to be Mariam Rashid, wearing a scarf to cover her head. Janet handed her the mic, and she began.

"I had not intended to speak today, but after seeing the heroism of so many ordinary people this morning, from this Chinese Christian pastor to the young Uyghur who both called out the Chinese government's genocide and helped prevent violence here, I have to speak. And my message is to Muslim governments and people everywhere—so long as the Chinese government persecutes its own people for what they believe, Muslims cannot continue 'business as usual' with this regime, no matter how attractive the offers. Particularly for us as American Muslims, we must stand up for the most basic human rights, which this country has always defended and championed, at home and around the globe."

Janet took the mic, the two women hugged, and then Janet thanked everyone for coming. "Please continue to put pressure on this repressive regime to stop the persecution of the Uyghurs—and of others who simply want freedoms—by sending emails and by posting in social media. And continue to demonstrate peacefully against the growing repression of our own freedoms here in America, in the name of 'protecting' us. Our greatest protection has always been to keep our freedoms strong."

The crowd nearest to the embassy clapped and cheered, and then people started moving toward Connecticut Avenue and the Metro Station.

Fifteen minutes later, at four o'clock, all the networks and streaming services again interrupted their Thursday schedule and cut to the president sitting at the Resolute Desk, with Patricia Reynolds and Drew Boswell standing next to his chair.

"My fellow Americans," President Bradshaw began, "we are delighted to speak to you again today to thank our intelligence community, law enforcement officers, and first responders for their heroic work in stopping a group of determined Uyghur terrorists from committing unspeakable acts of murder and mayhem in six cities across our nation.

"Vice President Reynolds, Acting Secretary of State Boswell and I are going to describe how the enhanced protections in our State of Emergency made this victory possible, and how we're going to make our nation even safer with new peace initiatives, as well as our new Trusted Citizen Program..."

As he continued, everyone watching on The Network or its streaming services suddenly saw Seth and Tom at opposite ends of a studio news desk, with a large monitor positioned between them. The president's address from the Oval Office shrank to the bottom left third of the screen, on mute, but with closed captioning showing his words.

"Network viewers, I'm Seth Cohen, and we're pre-empting the president's second message today to bring you even more important news about last week's election. I'm joined here on the set by Tom Sullivan, until earlier today the President's National Security Advisor, and on this monitor by a team of forensic programmers, whom you'll meet in a minute.

"But first, I have a personal confession to make, and it's been approved by the corporate decision makers here at The Network, as has the following report in full.

"You've had every right to think of me as an investigative journalist, searching out and bringing you only the truth on every subject I report to you on. But that has not been the case. I, and many others here and in our profession, have been mouthpieces for those in power, skewing the truth, or even ignoring it, to help those in power stay in power. Because that meant that we would continue our special access and favors—in effect, that we would also stay in power. I want you to know that I am guilty of this bias, this devaluing of the truth in favor of power, but I've decided that from today, whatever the personal consequences, I will report only the truth, starting with the story you are about to see—a piece of incredible investigative journalism which demands all of our attention."

Natalie, Janet and the others had begun walking with the crowd from the embassy back to where the vans were waiting. Natalie, looking at her phone, said, "Seth texted me to watch at four, and this looks pretty interesting. Janet, do you have their streaming feed? I'll turn it up."

The camera tightened on Seth. "First, you're about to see irrefutable proof that the results of last week's midterm elections were illegally stolen by secret internal programming to insure the landslide election of the president's choices. That's right, the elections were stolen, and we will show you exactly how it was done. Second, we'll tell you, again with irrefutable proof, who ordered and organized this theft, and why. Needless to say, from here on we at The Network won't be expecting any special access or favors from the White House, but it actually feels good. Let me start by introducing Tom Sullivan, who until today worked on National Security in The White House, and whom I've known personally for two decades."

From his desk the president had just finished describing on the other networks the reasons why keeping one more month of Emergency Powers was so important, and was starting to introduce the Trusted Citizen Program, when the teleprompter stopped and Emily briefly appeared on camera to hand him a note, which he quickly read.

He thought for a moment and then looked at the camera. "My staff has just alerted me that we may be under attack again by terrorists, and we must take action. There is no cause yet for general alarm, and we will report back to you as soon as possible. For now, regrettably, we must address the threat. Thank you."

The feed from the White House ended and the extra lights were turned off.

The president stood and asked Emily, "Tom and Seth are on The Network now, about our election? What the hell?"

Emily turned on the monitor against the wall. They all stood and watched.

"Thank you, Seth," Tom said as the camera focused on him. "Our purpose today is to show you exactly how the election was subverted, and by whom. Behind what you are about to see are outstanding people with different skills, including individuals from the FBI and the Pentagon. Who they are, and all the specific details they have uncovered will be published later today. For now, let's start with what happened, and for that I want to introduce Callie Sawyer, a journalist, and Erin MacNeil, a cyber security expert."

The two women came up on the monitor, sitting together at a conference table with bookshelves and a white board behind them.

Callie smiled briefly and began. "Thank you, Tom, and Seth. What happened last Tuesday would not have been possible—or not as easily possible—just a few years ago when our national elections were actually a hodge-podge of different state and local election rules and processes. Some thought that was archaic and inefficient, and subject to abuse. So Congress passed the National Election Integrity Act, which centralized the process under a national structure, with a mandatory, standardized process for tabulating and reporting all election results from around the country into a single federal repository.

"The design for that standardized process was defined by several federal agencies over several months' work, but then the implementation was left to one company with the resources and the skills to be the low bidder for this massive project—Juggle. And Juggle in turn employed internal teams from its offices around the world, including China, to write the necessary code.

"The result is a system in which, as we have often heard, no voting machine is ever connected to the internet, to prevent outside hacking...and in which security checks, candidate loading, and final reporting are all done via tightly controlled flash drives, also secure from outside hacking. But not secure from internal tampering. Erin?"

"Thank you." Erin held up one of the flash drives. "This is a specially designed flash drive which is only used in these particular election machines. Just before election day, it is loaded at the local Election Management Office with information sent to the office over an encrypted connection from the Federal Election Center, and then each drive is attached to an election machine with a seal. After voting, the process is reversed to report the results, and the flash drives are always under two-person control. It sounds very secure, and it is. Unless the last download from the Federal Election Center itself contains malware—an inside job, so to speak. We have proof that this was actually the case in last Tuesday's election, with significant incorrect votes being reported. Let me show you what happened."

Erin then narrated the video of their simulated voting test, showing how the actual 100/100 vote turned into an officially reported vote of 107/93.

"For this test we used certified copies of flash drives from a "Battleground" Virginia voting precinct. The bad code was written so that once its work was done, it completely disappeared from the used drives, destined to be stored in case of any contested votes. The only reason we uncovered the theft is because we also had one flash drive which had not been used during the election, and the bad code was still resident, though very hard to detect.

"We believe that a nearly invisible and then disappearing code such as this could not have been pulled off by an outside hacker. It had to have been added during the final Security Check/Candidate Loading process—that is, it must have come over the encrypted line from the trusted software provider, Juggle."

In the White House, standing next to the president, Drew Boswell whispered, "Crap."

The president turned to his inner team. "Yes, crap. Impossible. Emily, listen—Seth and Tom are *your* friends. *You* brought them inside with us. What the hell are they doing? These are all lies."

"I, uh...I'm not sure. I'll try to call Seth." She took out her phone.

The Network view shifted out to the news desk. Seth, on the left, said, "So that's what happened in at least one key battleground precinct.

We cannot imagine that so much work was done for just one precinct, so we are asking those in charge of voting machines and flash drives across the nation to maintain them as is, with no erasing or resetting, until they can all be checked.

"At this point, given the overwhelming and frankly unexpected landslide victories for Progressives in every important voting district, we believe that last Tuesday's election was rigged in this way to guarantee this false result, no matter how the people actually voted."

He looked down. "Hold on, another friend, Emily Schofield, who works in the White House, is calling. Hello, Emily."

There was a moment of feedback noise as Seth held the phone near his mic, but it cleared up. "Seth, what are you doing? No one rigged the election. You know that."

He smiled. "I wish that were true, Emily. But as I said, I'm now only seeking and reporting the truth. However, your call is the perfect introduction to the key information Tom Sullivan's investigation has uncovered about who stole the election, and why."

The camera tightened on Tom. "Throughout the State of Emergency, while every citizen's personal and business emails and phone calls were being intercepted and reviewed by government agencies like the NSA, a select group at the top of your government had—and still have today—a special, highly secure and encrypted phone system which is immune from intercept and impossible to decrypt, even if its transmissions could be recorded. I helped set up this phone system on the day after President Rhodes was killed, when we had no idea whom to trust. It is incredibly secure, a way for those in power to communicate secretly when no one else could. But like all man-made systems, it has structure, and a key.

"Two days ago, through a trusted FBI agent, I gave that key—a long code and a daily algorthm—to a special team in the Pentagon which deciphers communications, along with the special phone I had been using. These experts, led by someone I've known for years, were then able to access all the servers housing all the encrypted calls beginning from that first day, and, working backwards, they used Artificial Intelligence algorithms looking for keywords to search through all the calls. Here, now, are a few of them."

In the White House, the president said, "Damn him."

Back on The Network set, conversations were heard while the monitor showed a picture of the person talking, with the words spoken visible in closed captions below the picture.

*"Drew, what are we going to do? We have to stop them. Even though no one could ever connect us to the vote swing we manufactured, we can't let them overturn the election results. This is the moment Progressives have worked for over a hundred years! Now, thanks to our actions, it's in our grasp, and we can't let it go again."*

*"I just confirmed again that our friends in China are ready to go on the post-election order. And on the extra help we discussed, the head of our Juggle coding team over there, someone I've known for years, farmed out the work to a couple of groups, so no one has the whole picture. He's run tests with the finished product, and we're all set. The updates will be sent to our U.S. team today to load on Monday."*

*"Excellent."*

The view came back to the set, where Tom and Seth had been joined at the desk by Jacob Welch, the Speaker of the House. Before Seth could speak, Emily's voice came over the open line from the phone in her hand.

"Is that true? Did you rig the election?"

"Hang up that phone!"

The three men at the desk, and the two women on the monitor, paused. After a few moments, Seth said, "We'd like to welcome the Honorable Jacob Welch, the Speaker of the House of Representatives, who has been in our studio, listening to these same conversations. Mr. Speaker, thank you for joining us."

"Thank you for calling me this morning. I had no idea."

"None of us understood what had really happened until the experts at The Pentagon were able, in a matter of hours, to search the massive collection of phone calls made within this special group, finding the ones you heard, and many more, which clearly point to collusion by at least the president and Andrew Boswell, the CEO of Juggle and the president's nominee to be the next Secretary of State, plus unknown groups in China, to steal the election by the means we've just laid out."

Welch replied, "Yes, it's deplorable. We have to wonder who else was involved?"

In the Oval Office, the president fumed as he walked to his desk. "I can't believe Tom gave them that damn key. Drew, in case you're wondering, we now know where Tom is!"

"Uh, yes, Mr. president."

He pushed a button on his desk phone. "Get me Nathan Price or Jim Toomey, whichever is..."

The door opened and Tanya Prescott entered, followed by five agents, who fanned out around the room. She nodded, "Mr. President."

"What the hell is this?"

"This, sir, is the arrest of Mr. Andrew Boswell on several charges enumerated in this warrant, including attempting to subvert an election and conspiring to commit murder. There is some murkiness surrounding the legality of arresting a sitting president, so others will have to tackle that one, or otherwise we would also be arresting you on the same charges."

Three of the agents moved over to Drew, who had been standing with Patricia, Emily and Rob. One agent recited the Miranda Rights, while the others cuffed his hands behind his back.

The president looked at Tanya and around at the others. "You can't do this. Stop. Jim Toomey will have all your asses."

In a calm voice, Tanya responded from the other side of his desk. "As of ninety minutes ago, when we played the same conversations you heard on The Network for Mr. Toomey and his senior staff, the Director thought it best, after agreeing with the arrest of Mr. Boswell, to put himself on administrative leave while the rest of the conversations are sorted out. Haeden Chalmers is the new Acting FBI Director, and I'm sure she's looking forward to speaking with you very soon about all this. And the rest of you here might consider following Jim Toomey's example, depending on what you think you may have done, or said on your phones, over the last two months."

With a smile and a nod, Agent Prescott and her team left the Oval Office with Drew Boswell between them.

When they were gone, Emily asked, "Can they just listen to our calls like that?"

"It's allowed in the State of Emergency," Patricia said. "We just always thought we had a way around it...Until now." She glanced at the muted monitor. "Jacob Welch is with Tom on The Network. Let's hear what they're saying."

Emily turned up the volume. The Speaker was talking. "...never in a situation like this before. Clearly we have to invoke the 25$^{th}$ Amendment to remove a criminal president, but then what about the vice president? Did she also participate? And can we legally call for another round of midterm elections? We have to clean up this mess and also govern at the same time. There's no precedent, but it has to be done quickly, and correctly."

"Mr. Speaker," Tom said, "we appreciate that you suddenly have a lot to do. Thank you for joining us. We'll turn over the results of our investigation to the FBI, and continue to help them if asked."

"Thank you. We need to act right away." Welch looked up. "Madame vice president, if you're watching, let's meet in your office in the Executive Office Building as soon as we both can get there."

The president looked at the vice president. "What's he talking about? You're not really going to meet with him, are you? This is all absurd. Rob, Emily, we need a plan to counter these lies."

The vice president asked, "Are they lies, Henry?"

"The truth is that our policies are too important to allow us to lose an election. You know that, Patricia. The nation needs our policies and our leadership. If we stick together, this will blow over. It always has and it always will."

"So you *did* rig the election, with help from Drew and his Chinese code writers?"

"We still would have won. Just maybe not by such a majority."

"Henry, you subverted the election for our party to win."

"Only for the good of the nation! You all know that as well as I do. Without our leadership, the nation won't make it. Democracy will be crushed."

The four of them stood in silence for a moment. Finally, Patricia said, "Emily, Rob, did you know anything about this?"

They silently shook their heads.

"Then I think you better come with me to talk with Jacob Welch. This isn't going to be easy. Good day, Henry."

In the studio Tom and Seth shook hands with Speaker Welch, and all three thanked Erin, Callie and the Cyprus team on the monitor.

"Tom, can you come with me to meet with Patricia, and then with—I'm not sure who. It will depend on what she says. On the way over I'll ask my staff to put the leadership from the House and Senate on standby, and frankly we'll need experts in the Constitution to help us."

"Yes, of course. Gary Thornton could help there."

"Good idea. And where's your mother? I'd like her to join us. Common sense and wisdom."

"I'll call her and ask her to come to the Executive Office Building. Before we go, Mr. Speaker, I have one favor to ask for the team on Cyprus who actually discovered the bad code."

"Of course. Let's walk and talk. And you better ask them to be available for several more hours. We may need their expertise. Seth, thank you, and your team, again. Well done."

President Bradshaw sat alone at his desk in the Oval Office, looking out the window, while Prince Proklor and the prince's leaders circled around him.

"Tell him to do something!" Proklor yelled at Balzor, who had moved as far from the prince as he could. "He's the President of the United States! He has all the power."

In a low voice, Balzor, looking away, replied, "He's been caught in lies, my liege, about the elections, the Chinese, the State of Emergency. People don't like being lied to by their leaders."

"We lie to these people every day and every night about everything. And they repeat our lies. Especially about Him. And act on them! They don't believe He exists! They don't think eternity is real! They think we're just Halloween characters, when we actually change their eternity! Lying is what we do, and they believe us, or most of them do. Are you saying you botched the lies you planted? That you made them too obvious? That this mess is your fault?" All the spiritual eyes in the room turned to Balzor, fearing what might happen next.

"No! No. They're excellent lies, protected by layers of the best technology and cut-outs. It's just that Tom Sullivan wouldn't stop digging, and the people around him have exceptional skills, which we could never have foreseen. No one should have ever discovered any of this!"

"Tom Sullivan did."

"Yes. But maybe He...," Balzor paused. "Maybe He brought these people together, here, and now, specifically to stop us."

Prokor's anger raged. "That's impossible! We were—*are*—angels. This is *our* world." He turned to Temno and the generals. "If He was meddling in our plans, you should have seen it, and countered. Go do something to put Bradshaw back in power, before all our work here is lost forever!"

Proklor, standing invisibly in front of the president, screamed at him, "Get up, you turd! Call your agency friends and have these people arrested for treason. You're the president. *You* give the orders. They're traitors!"

He turned to Balzor and Temno, hovering nearby, while the rest of the generals stayed close to the far wall. "Balzor, speak into him. He must act. Adolf would never have put up with this! The nation is ours if he'll just take it. Now!"

The president, unaware of the argument raging around him, but feeling an unusual oppression, picked up his desk phone and buzzed his assistant. "Would you please call Margaret and ask her to come down?"


Twenty minutes after leaving DCNet, Tom and Speaker Welch entered the Eisenhower Executive Office Building next to the White House, and then passed through to a large, portrait-lined office with a long conference table and beautiful chandeliers, designated as the vice president's Ceremonial Office. They shook hands with the vice president, Emily, and Rob, who had been sitting and talking at one end of the table.

"Jacob, thank you for suggesting we meet here. Most of my staff is still available, and Gerald Veazy should be here in a few minutes. Please, have a seat."

Sitting down, he said, "I called Gerry, too."

"Good. It's important right now that we're all on the same page."

"Yes. So, Patricia, for me that means this: did you participate in the election fraud, or know about it?"

She put her hand on the table. "No, Jacob. I couldn't believe what I saw and heard on Seth's show"—she nodded to Tom—"and I completely oppose it."

Tom and Emily exchanged quick glances. The Speaker seemed to visibly relax a bit, but leaned in. Before he could speak, she said, looking to Emily and Rob, "And Henry all but confessed to us this afternoon that they did it, albeit for 'the good of the country.'"

They all paused. Gerald Veazy opened a door and came in. They greeted, he joined them at the table, and Tom summarized their discussion so far, ending with, "I think there could not be a clearer case for invoking the 25$^{th}$ Amendment. I reread it yesterday, and we need a short letter from you, Madame vice president, to the Speaker and to the President Pro-Tem, signed by a majority of the Executive Officers in the Cabinet, to have you immediately replace President Bradshaw."

She took a deep breath. "We were already talking about it. Given the circumstances, I think it's important for the nation to see that I—we—as members of the party who benefitted from the fraud, are faithful first to The Constitution, not to any party or group."

The others nodded and waited.

"So I and my staff, which now I think includes Rob and Emily, will reach out immediately to the Cabinet members to get them here this evening to sign the letter, which I expect someone from your office, Jacob, could help Rob draft."

"Of course."

"Then, even though I was not party to any of whatever they did to rig the election, I *was* here. Many voters will rightly question what I really knew. So, to help get a clean start, my third order of business as president, after canceling the State of Emergency and pardoning anyone still in detention, will be to resign, which, Jacob, should make you the president."

"Patricia, that's above and beyond, and...."

She put her hand on his. "No, it's not. It's clearly the right thing. We have our political differences, but our basic freedoms, like honest voting and free speech, are way above those."

"Thank you. But what if Bradshaw protests with a letter, as provided in the Amendment, and demands to have his office back?"

After another long pause, Emily looked at Tom and said, "He won't. I'll make certain of that."

Before anyone could respond, Tom said, "And we're going to need a lot of bi-partisan support either to figure out who really won Tuesday's races, or to hold new elections in a matter of weeks. Neither of those will be easy."

Patricia raised her hand. "Yes, but first things first. I suggest we use this old room as our staging area to get the 25$^{th}$ Amendment letter written and signed by the Cabinet tonight. Hopefully by tomorrow morning, Jacob, you'll have a fresh start as the new President. May God bless, protect and provide for you in that office."

A door opened and Janet Sullivan, still wearing her coat, walked quickly over to the table. "Sorry I'm late," she said, as she shook the Speaker's hand. "It's crazy out there. No one knows who or what to believe, or to do. The sun's going down, and the streets are filling up with unhappy people."

"Hmm," Welch said. "We need to let the nation know what we're doing, and quickly. Emily? And, Rob, can you write that letter now, on a legal pad if you have to—the wording's in the Amendment—and let's get the Cabinet members here asap?"

Turning to Janet, Welch said, "Would you like to be the next vice president?"

During the late afternoon Seth worked with Rachel Shaw and the team at The Network to cover all the demonstrations that erupted across the country after the Network's expose' on the election, and the speeches at the Chinese Embassy. Politicians of every stripe were standing in front of mics, claiming that their side had been maligned by what was revealed, and that the election had been stolen from them.

Angry crowds began to face off against each other around Federal buildings in many major cities, including D.C.

Seth was on the air a lot as other reporters asked him about the revelations and the process. He did his best to calm emotions, assuring viewers that the Constitution provided for a process which he was sure, based on knowing several of the people involved, was being followed, and that the outcome would be both correct and transparent.

During a break he spoke with Rachel at the back of the studio. "I wish I actually felt as positive about the next few days as I've been saying on the air."

"You're doing great. It's a tough day. Your original show with Tom and the people in Cyprus was amazing."

He nodded. "Thanks. And, listen, let me tell you an idea I have for a new show."

"Shoot."

For the next two hours in the vice president's Ceremonial Office and in adjoining spaces in the Eisenhower Executive Office Building, several small groups worked together, hoping to move the government back within its Constitutional guardrails.

At one end of the room the vice president and her team managed the process to get Cabinet Members to come by to sign the necessary letter certifying the president's unfitness to serve. Two refused even to consider doing so, citing the need to continue the Progressive agenda at any cost. Three who came needed to spend time in a small office down the hall, interacting on a video call with the team on Cyprus, hearing in detail again all that was said and done by the president.

At the other end of the large room Jacob Welch and his own executive team, along with Janet Sullivan, worked around another table to make lists of their first steps, and of those whom they wanted for key leadership roles.

At a third table Emily, Rob, and the Speaker's Communications Director crafted the Interim President's executive orders, along with a draft communication to the nation.

Tom circulated between the three working groups, giving his input to each one. He told the Speaker that he should consider Diane Marsh for a Chief of Staff position, following her immediate release from prison, and following Tom's own apology to her. And he spent ten minutes on a video call with Erin, Callie and Alexei in Cyprus.

As the sun set The First Lady sat on a sofa in the Oval Office, looking out at the darkening sky, and sipping her drink while the president paced with his. The White House was eerily quiet—the president had sent the few remaining staff home.

"I guess there'll be a trumped-up trial, or impeachment, or something," he said, then took a sip. "The bastards. They'll make up lies about how we only want power, but what we really want is to make the nation better, more just, more progressive. Stop the oppression. We need social justice and equity for all. Only we can do it. We're so right, and they're so wrong, so small-minded and so full of hate."

"I know, dear."

"I won't go to prison for trying to make the nation better. I'll lay it all out. They'll see."

She smiled. "I hope so."

He stopped in front of her. "Margaret, here's a short list of things I need from the Residence, including that small satchel I keep in the bedside table. Please get these for me, and when you come back, bring a coat. We'll be going over to the Press Room."

A little before 7pm the vice president gathered Gerald Veazy, Emily and Rob, and they walked to the table where Speaker Welch and his team were at work.

While a staff person video recorded them, the vice president began, standing by the table, "Mr. Speaker and Mr. President Pro-Tem, in accordance with the requirements of the 25$^{th}$ Amendment to the United States Constitution, I give you this letter signed by me as vice president, along with fifteen of our twenty-five Cabinet members, affirming that

Henry Bradshaw is no longer fit to serve as President of the United States."

The speaker stood, and the vice president handed the letter to him. Several on the periphery of the group took videos.

Veazy spoke. "Then you, Patricia, are now the President of the United States. I asked the Chief Justice to be available, and she will swear you in."

Patricia Reynolds raised her right hand, and a minute later she was sworn in.

"It is with extreme sadness, not joy, that I take on this duty, and only briefly. I have a couple of Executive Orders to sign, and then I ask you all to join us in the West Wing Press Room in an hour for the more important ceremony. Thank you all for your help at this difficult time."

As those gathered started to turn away, the new president asked Emily, "Let's shared this video with the press now, and are the networks lined up for eight?" Emily nodded. "Thank you. It's been a tough day. But I think the president—uh, Henry Bradshaw—needs this letter delivered to him."

Tom and Emily motioned and said simultaneously, "I'll do it."

"Great. Both of you take it over to him. And get a picture of the delivery." She handed the copy to Emily.

As he turned to go, Tom's mother pulled him off to the side. "Your father and I are so proud of what you've done. Without your intervention, the nation would be in the midst of a terrible disaster from which it might not ever recover. Rule by decree forever."

Tom shook his head. "It may look like I intervened, but we both know who really did."

She smiled. "Well, you listened. And you acted."

"Thanks, Mom." They hugged. "It'll be great to have Dad home."

"Yes, it will. And, oh, Jacob asked me to ask you to stay on—or to come back—as his National Security Advisor. After all this, he thinks you're more than qualified."

He paused. "OK. We'll see. Sounds interesting. I suspect there'll be a lot to do."

She nodded.

"But right now Emily and I have a letter to deliver."

"See you at eight."

It was a short walk to the West Wing, and as they crossed West Executive Avenue they could hear the raised voices and shouts from the large crowds which had gathered in the streets outside the White House compound.

Emily said to Tom, "Hopefully the press release and photo of President Reynolds will calm some of them, but I'm not sure."

"Jacob Welch should restore confidence in an hour. He's a great speaker."

Emily walked on in silence for several steps, then said, "All the years of getting our Progressive Agenda in place thrown away by two old white men who had to go for broke and rig the election. They've cost us everything."

Tom stopped. Emily took another step and then turned back to him. "Wait. As best I can tell, the voters intended to vote against that agenda, and the only way to prevent that outcome was to rig the results—but they got caught. Either way, there would be no Progressive Agenda, now or in January."

Her voice rising, Emily said, "Come on, Tom. Of course there'd be. We'd just have to claim irregularities, show examples of how our defeat crushes people of color, lower incomes, and old age, and gear up to win in two years. Our agenda would still be very much alive in universities, schools, corporations, the media—just like it has been for years, and growing all the time. But now these two have called everything we do into question by reaching for too much. Some people will back away completely. Hell, I think Seth may even be on the ropes."

Tom shook his head. "So Progressives are now victims of their own leaders' mistakes?"

"Yes, exactly. Stupid old white men. They can screw up anything."

He started walking again. "Wow. I hadn't thought of that."

In the dining room on Cyprus Erin closed her laptop after a final video conference with a Cabinet member in D.C., as Alexei and his wife brought glasses of champagne out of the kitchen to the team members there and in the living room.

"He says he's going to sign the letter, too, even though they have more than enough."

"Great," Callie said from across the table, accepting a glass from Anna.

Erin stood and stretched, but declined a glass. "It's been a long day, now that it's really tomorrow morning."

When everyone had been served, Alexei stood between the two rooms. "Who would have imagined a week ago that our little group on Cyprus would have such an impact on American politics? Maybe even on world history?

"In a minute I'm going to offer a toast to Erin and Callie, for coming all the way over here to help unravel this mystery, but first I want to offer a prayer to the One who knew about all this before the world began, and who protected us from the evil that others intended."

They all bowed their heads, and Alexei lifted up a heartfelt thanksgiving. His words joined with tens of thousands of others, all arriving at the Throne Room of God, thanking Him and praying for His continued guidance for America's future.

Tom and Emily had expected to find the president's assistant still at her desk outside the Oval Office—instead they noticed the door to the office cracked open and, when they looked inside, Bradshaw was sitting alone at the Resolute Desk, writing on a note pad.

Unseen to any of them, the Oval Office was filled with the nation's demonic leadership, including Prince Proklor, who watched while Balzor spoke with his familiar voice into Bradshaw's mind, encouraging him to act against his enemies.

He looked up. "It's you. Margaret'll be back in a minute. What do you want? You disobeyed and betrayed me. This whole mess is because of you."

They walked over to the desk. Tom handed him the letter, while Emily took a picture and Bradshaw frowned. "President Reynolds asked us to give you this letter. Under the provisions of the 25<sup>th</sup> Amendment, you are no longer the President of the United States."

He stood. "Damn if I'm not! I'll fight you on this, starting tonight."

Emily said quietly, "No you won't, Henry. Not unless you want the world, including Margaret, to know about the summer I interned with you."

"What? Are you with them now, Emily?"

"You're damaged goods, Henry. You went too far. Progressives are reeling. We've got to do damage control, starting with blaming it all on you. Then find the usual faults with these Right Wing bigots, and build up again for victory in two years."

"But I was just making notes on how everything we—I—did was for the good of the country. Especially to help oppressed victims like, like your people, Emily."

"Just give us what oppressed people always need, Henry—money and power. Don't rig an election."

"But Drew said it was foolproof."

"Then Drew was wrong, and we're all paying for it. I guess that makes you a victim, too, in a way. But you've got to go."

Tom, who had watched in silence as they argued, said, "You know, I came to this job two months ago to defend all of us from attack. Not some of us. All of us. But I bought the lie that to do so, in these difficult times, we had to ignore the Constitution—even temporarily get rid of its key provisions. That was my big mistake.

"Because since then I've been challenged to go back and read what those old white men wrote, and, you won't believe it, but they knew *exactly* about this difficult time. They knew that without checks and balances, with our God-given rights to defend those checks guaranteed at all times, *some* group—well-meaning or otherwise—would gain power and claim that those checks and those rights were good enough for some other times or some other people, but not for these times.

"I understand now, because I've been praying for God to show me His truth, that once I helped dismantle those protections in the name of 'national safety,' whoever was in power at the time would use that vacuum to advance their power and priorities over the rest of us. The Founding Fathers predicted exactly that and tried to protect us with the Constitution.

"If the attacks had occurred at some other time, with someone else in power, we might just as well have wound up with an imposed right-wing theocracy. As it was, you, Henry, and your Progressives, were placed in power by the attacks, and your mantra was perfect—victims need protection. But not just physical protection. Because no one could check you, you naturally added on the Progressive shopping list of protection from feeling bad, from 'hate speech', from bad personal decisions, from bad luck, from previous 'oppression', from oppressor groups—all in the name of 'social justice' and 'equity'.

"And the unchecked power to do those things, as our Founders predicted, led you to use even more power—more arrests, more controls, and, finally, rigging the election.

"What really sank Progressives, Emily, was not just rigging the election, but having no questioning press, no dissenting voices, no other views. In that vacuum, why not rig an election?

"The Founders never talked about victims or oppressors, except for the nation as a whole, under British rule. And those white men wrote words of truth into the Declaration and the Constitution that resulted in women and people of color attaining those same rights—not because their group suddenly came into power and pushed it through, but because the Constitution mandated it.

"So, yes, the Founders knew that what just happened will happen again, unless we enforce the Constitution at all times, particularly in difficult times, to protect our God-given, not man-given, rights and responsibilities."

"Aren't you the philosopher?" Bradshaw sneered.

"Not really. Just common sense. And I learned most of it from a young man who was supposed to be aborted twenty years ago. How's that for coincidence, or for God's planning?"

Bradshaw rose on the balls of his feet, his face turning red. "God. God! What the hell does he have to do with any of this? He doesn't exist!"

Proklor and Temno exchanged glances, then nodded to Balzor.

"Get out, both of you!"

At eight that evening the West Wing Press Room was filled with everyone who had a permanent pass, or who could get a temporary one. Seth was in the front row. The event was being broadcast live.

A group filed in from behind the podium: Patricia Reynolds, Jacob Welch, Gerald Veazy all stood on the dais. Tom, Emily, Rob and the Speaker's key team members stood to the left. Patricia stepped forward to the lectern.

"Thank you for coming on short notice to help us conclude what must certainly be one of the most fateful and tumultuous days in our nation's history, with no previous script to follow. My role tonight will be brief.

"After the revelations earlier today that President Bradshaw and others conspired to steal last week's midterm elections, and his admission to me that this was in fact the case, those of us entrusted with protecting the Constitution took the specific steps provided for in the 25th Amendment to remove Henry Bradshaw from his office. As of an hour ago, I am now the President of the United States.

"I have taken two Executive Actions. We have canceled the State of Emergency and all the extra domestic surveillance measures implemented over the last two months, and we have ordered the immediate pardon and release of everyone detained under those special provisions, but not including anyone who committed, or is suspected of committing, an act of violence, who will receive swift due process under our laws.

"I want to thank all those who had the courage and the determination to find and to document the terrible act of stealing a national election, a crime that strikes at the very foundations of our way of life.

"In order to remove any thought that I or any additional Cabinet members had anything to do with this crime, or knew anything about it, I am now going to resign my office. Under the Constitution, with no sitting vice president, the next in line for the Presidency is the Speaker of the House of Representatives, Jacob Welch, whom I have known for years, and in whom our nation can have real hope for both good government and reconciliation.

"Jacob, here is my Letter of Resignation. May God bless you and our nation."

The Speaker stepped forward, they hugged, and Chief Justice Warner emerged from those standing nearby. The Speaker's wife followed her, holding a Bible. With his hand on the Bible, Jacob Welch was sworn in as the President of the United States. As the others moved to the side, the new president addressed the nation.

"Fellow citizens, there is so much to say and to do, but most of that we will tackle in the coming days. Tonight, let me give you some broad outlines of our governing philosophy, and of what must quickly be accomplished, with your help.

"It was exactly two months ago that on the same night individuals killed President Rhodes, Vice President Carpenter, and Speaker Gordon. While those terrible events may have been related, our best experts have been unable to connect them. The timing may have just been a tragic coincidence, but they, along with the next attacks, threw our nation into a state of fear and of government repression previously unknown here.

"I want to be clear that our Administration, with God's wisdom and help, will not abrogate nor circumvent the Constitution or the Laws of this land to defend our nation against any further attacks. But we *will* defend our nation.

"To move forward we need a duly elected Congress in January, and that means that we have to sort out the results from last week's election. The early indications are that the malignant code was only deployed in thirty-one key races, and experts from the Pentagon and the NSA believe that in a few days they can reverse the effects and produce the correct original vote totals.

"We will pursue this remedy with complete transparency, including members from both parties in every impacted race, along with the media. Ultimately, according to the Constitution, it will be up to the state legislatures to certify the results, and if one or more determines that a new election is required in their state, we will honor that decision.

"And that, in general, will be our governing philosophy—less top-down directives, and more state, local and individual determination, which we believe has always been the strength of our nation.

"It will take a few days, at least, to assemble our Administration, but we're already hard at work, starting with nominating former Congresswoman Janet Sullivan, a person of great wisdom, common sense, and character, to be the next vice president."

He glanced to his right toward Janet, who acknowledged him with a nod of her head.

"And, by the way," he continued, "we're working to get her husband out of jail tonight or tomorrow." There was a smattering of laughter.

"Rather than ram through Executive Orders based on our own principles, we will wait until the final make-up of the new Congress is determined, and then we will work with members of both parties to enact laws which we hope—based on those principles—will mean a smaller federal government, less spending, less regulatory interference in everyday life, less naming of victims, and more emphasis on creating the environment in which individuals and companies can flourish and add to the general wealth and to the general welfare, as the Founders intended.

"That will be our approach, along with reliance on faith and prayer in all that we do.

"If that makes sense to you, or you are at least willing to give it a try after decades of bigger government and more personal restrictions, I invite you to come out at noon on Saturday in your city or hometown, to gather peacefully in your parks and squares, not to engage in name-calling or diatribe—but rather, if you feel like it, bring a lunch and find people with whom you may agree or disagree on different issues, and just talk about them. Or do the same in restaurants, or even online, if outdoors doesn't work. We'll call it a Day of National Discussion. Who knows what we might learn from and about each other?

"Finally for tonight, if you feel so led, please pray for our nation, for this new Administration, and for our enemies, that through men and women of good will, God's truth and wisdom will again guide all our actions. Thank you. We understand and will do our best to live up to your trust. There will be more tomorrow. May God bless our nation.

And let me say to the press that in general I enjoy answering all of your questions, but tonight there is just too much to do in too little time. We'll reconvene for questions and answers in a day or two—I promise! Thank you."

The new president and his former team, along with the vice president nominee, left through the door behind the podium.

Tom, Emily and Patricia Reynolds stepped down to talk with Seth.

Patricia shook Seth's hand. "I bet my record for the shortest Presidency lasts a long time."

He smiled. "I suspect you're right. Listen, does anyone know where Henry Bradshaw is?"

"We last saw him in the Oval Office," Tom said. "But I imagine the new president is headed there now. Presumably Bradshaw'll spend tonight in the Residence, then leave tomorrow. There's so much to do in a transition, even when there's the normal time. But like with us two months ago, this one may be a bit unorthodox."

"Given all that's happened, you know it must be hard on them," Patricia added, "particularly if Henry goes to jail." Emily nodded, but said nothing.

"Listen, Patricia," Seth said, "I've been thinking. You're suddenly out of a job, and I want to try something new. The last few days have really convicted me that journalists must find and report only the truth and all the truth, not what we think will advance some cause. Otherwise, we put everyone at risk." He glanced at Emily, who crossed her arms. "And you seem like a pretty reasonable person, willing to listen and to consider all sides of an issue. What if we teamed up with a new investigative show on The Network, and interviewed people like Emily and Tom in government and business, with no agenda other than what research and fact-checking will uncover?"

She smiled. "Seth, I just quit! But it might be interesting. Can we talk in a day or two? I told Janet I'd help her adjust to her new role."

"Sure, sure. I just want to do a show that's so good and so well thought of for its commitment to the truth that politicians and CEOs seek us out, rather than the other way around."

"Seth, are you OK?" Tom quipped.

"I think so. Being around you Sullivans and your friends has finally gotten through to me, at least on this subject. I guess I'm a slow learner."

"Patricia, as you talk with the new team," Emily said, "tell them I'll be happy to help them as well, though I doubt we'll share much on content." She turned to Seth. "And, Seth, I'm sticking with the same 'truth' that I knew when we first met. Nothing has changed. Except the rich are even richer and the oppressed are more victimized."

Seth paused. "You'll be a great first interview, Emily. And I mean that."

As President Welch, Janet Sullivan and six members of Welch's team made the short walk to the Oval Office they were met in the hall by a three-person Secret Service detail.

"Mr. President, I'm Senior Agent Clark Talbot."

They shook hands. "Glad to meet you."

"Yes, sir. There's been some confusion. We got word that the vice president would likely become the president, so we reduced our resources around President Bradshaw and began deploying to upgrade her status. But then that changed a few minutes ago, so we're pulling those officers back, and we should be correctly deployed around you and your family within the hour."

Welch smiled. "I completely understand. It's an unusual moment—'confusion' is an accurate summary. I'm sure we'll all be fine with you in charge."

"Thank you, sir.

The Oval Office was packed with demonic forces. For his decades in Washington, Prince Proklor had loved the symbolism of meeting there, but he and his generals had just learned from a lowly street leader in an obscure House office—no demon could stand the spiritual heat and light from those gathered in the Press Room—that Jacob Welch was now the president.

"What?" Proklor started to fume, but the Oval Office walls began to glow and the temperature rose dramatically as Welch, Janet and the rest came close and stopped in the hallway outside. Suddenly the demons were bombarded with incoming prayers for the new President and the nation, and even their massed spiritual darkness could not deflect them all. As they jostled to avoid the pain, Proklor was hit several times, and he heard the voices of believers from all over the nation demanding that he leave.

"Damn! The Residence. He'll have to go there, and we'll wait for him."

The new president and his team had been working from the sofas in the Oval Office for twenty minutes when Tom joined them.

"Whether I stay on as National Security Advisor or not, may I give you my two cents on what to do and what not to do, given that we just went through this?"

The president smiled. "By all means. Here, have a seat."

It was almost midnight. Prince Proklor and his forces had filled the Residence, waiting for President Bradshaw to return. The lesser demons floated through the space, awed to be in the private rooms of the most powerful human leader on Earth.

Standing with the other generals by the window in the West Sitting Room, Temno repeated to his Prince, "He wrote out a plan, and we'll be ready to help him enforce it. With our help, he'll regain power."

"Yes. That's..."

Suddenly they felt a spiritual cleaving beneath them and heard the sound of an approaching tempest. A chasm opened beneath them, and several terrible princes—Proklor's equal or worse—emerged from the pit and moved the lesser spirits back.

With a loud thunderclap the Prince of Lies himself rose and towered over the group; Proklor was directly in front of him, unable to move back.

Satan addressed them with rising anger. "What have you done? I sent you here to take over this nation, not to rekindle His believers! Instead of extinguishing His flame, the strongest believer in decades is now the president, and Janet Sullivan—*Janet Sullivan*—is in line to be vice president! Her son, an advisor. Secular Progressives are discredited and pulling back. The damn Founding Fathers quoted again as experts. Television people and celebrities are looking for the 'truth,' and are ready to give Him credit. People are actually talking about Him again, in public! What have you done?"

"I...we...My liege, our lies have worked better and better every year...Most believe them. Their schools. Their corporations. Even their military. We're very close. Bradshaw just got greedy—he believed our lies so well that he tried to take it all. And a small group of damn believers wouldn't let up. They kept praying and digging. I don't know why..."

"You failed! Most of those believers didn't even know each other two months ago, but they beat you."

"His Truth...It's powerful. It changes people. They..."

"That's why you have to keep them quiet and the public confused. Instead, this new President is going to be talking about Him and the Founding Fathers all the time, and the public will know how this all happened!"

"I...The plan is good. But these demons you gave me..."

"*You* failed, Proklor. Millions of wretched humans will be saved from eternity with us because of you, so you can spend eternity in the Abyss, starting now."

"No, I..."

Prince Proklor exploded and disappeared in a burst of flame.

Satan slowly looked around at the others, who pushed back as far as they could.

"Temno, talk among yourselves. Give me your best ideas. I'll be back tomorrow at the same time. Starting now, I will take on America myself."

As the demons watched, a black cavern opened beneath him, and they could clearly hear screams and cries from those below. Their master descended, followed by his lieutenants, and with a loud clap of thunder the cavern closed behind them.

Temno looked at the other generals. It was a long time before anyone spoke.

The FBI and D.C. Police thought, given all the publicity, that Tom was no longer a murder target, but they wanted to stake out his townhouse that night. So after spending two hours with the new president's team, Tom and Beau went back to Callie's apartment, where he found a bottle of wine and a note from Kristen, inviting him up for coffee in the morning.

He couldn't believe that he'd been on the same couch the previous evening—it seemed like a month ago. After a quick shower he collapsed under two blankets and slept well, Beau on the floor next to him.

# 28

*I am sure that never was a people, who had more reason to acknowledge a Divine interposition in their affairs, than those of the United States; and I should be pained to believe that they have forgotten that agency, which was so often manifested during our Revolution, or that they failed to consider the omnipotence of that God who is alone able to protect them.*

George Washington

Friday, November 13

"Dad's supposed to get to D.C. about eleven," Tom said, as he picked up a second croissant at Kristen's breakfast room table. "Mom volunteered me to keep helping with the transition, so I guess we'll meet at The White House."

"That's great." She walked over and refilled his cup.

"Thanks. Why don't you join us?"

"No, no," she smiled. "Your parents have been miraculously gracious to me, but that's family time for you guys. And I've got to figure out how to get Grace home. Is your sister Susan coming up?"

"Yes, I think mom mentioned that last night—it's a bit of a blur. She wants to meet Patrick Tomlinson."

"I bet. And maybe Erin?"

Tom shrugged. "I don't know. I hope so."

"When are they due in?"

"I think about three. The president sent a transport plane to the RAF Base at Akrotiri on Cyprus to pick them up. Along with Alexei, his team, and all their family members who want to come."

"That's good."

"Yeah, given all that's happened, the threats, and their earlier connection to the Kremlin, I asked the president to give them asylum here. He agreed. And, look, speaking of asking, thank you for all your prayers for so many people and so many issues over the last days and weeks. I know now that prayer makes all the difference, and you were one of the leaders."

She smiled. "Just following my orders: 'Pray without ceasing.'"

President Welch, the new First Lady, and Janet Sullivan spent the night across Pennsylvania Avenue from the White House at Blair House, the government's official guest residence. They had agreed to continue their meetings in the Cabinet Room, where they would be joined by their growing staff, along with possible Cabinet Members.

A little before eight they walked across to the White House with a Secret Service detail. The First Lady left them for her first look at the Residence. Standing outside the Oval Office was Senior Agent Talbot.

"Good morning, Agent Talbot," the president said. "Everything seems to be working smoothly this morning."

Talbot shook his head. "Not really."

"Why?"

"The Residence staff prepared breakfast this morning as usual, but when neither the president—uh, former President—or the First Lady came out to get a plate, the senior person finally knocked on their bedroom door. No one was inside, and the bed looked unslept in. All of their clothes are in their closets, but they're not here."

"Where can they be?" Janet asked.

"In the last twenty minutes we searched the building and went back through the security tapes. I've just learned that both of them were captured on tape a little after eight last night at the exit door from the tunnel connecting the East Wing to The Treasury Building, while you were speaking, and we were dealing with the confusion. I'm afraid we don't know where they are. We've alerted the FBI, and they will of course start a search."

The main transition team was meeting in the Cabinet Room, with sub-groups spread around other White House offices. The new president's assistant came in and whispered to Tom, "Someone outside wants to see you." Then to the whole group she said, "The buses should arrive in about thirty minutes."

Tom followed her out to the small conference room next to the Oval Office, where Diane Marsh was sitting, wearing a gray suit. She stood, expressionless, when he came in. She started to speak, but he raised his hand.

"Diane, I'm so glad you're here, and I hope you got my text. You had the right wisdom and correct judgment, and I made a huge mistake—one of many, I'm afraid. I'm so sorry that largely because of me, we put you through what must have been a very unpleasant two months, and I sincerely ask your forgiveness."

She looked at him for a few beats. "I've thought about it a lot, and I can imagine the position you suddenly found yourself in, largely responsible for defending the nation against unexplained attacks. I should have come to you and the others, not the press, with my concerns, so I'm willing to say that we both made mistakes." A small smile crossed her face.

He stepped towards her. "Thank you, but yours were nothing compared to mine." He extended his hand. "Welcome back. I hope you're here to help, because this group really needs your experience."

She shook his hand. "Yes. It'll be an honor to work with Jacob Welch—and your mother. When will I start?"

He stepped aside and motioned to the door. "How about right now?"

Twenty minutes later Tom was back in his office on a three-way video call.

"Logan, this is Special Agent Tanya Prescott. She knows that you and I go way back, and that you're married to Emily, who helped us get through yesterday, despite her long relationship with President Bradshaw."

Logan, from the desk in his Juggle office, nodded. "We talked about it last night. It's called 'do the right thing.'"

"Yes. Agent Prescott is on the way to Juggle now with a lead team of people who have a huge challenge ahead of them, from investigating a crime to trying to figure out how to correct—or redo—the election results. The nation needs the latter, in particular, to be done quickly, and we think that will only happen if Juggle and her task force work together."

"How can I help? This place went crazy after Boswell was arrested, and we all got word not to destroy any emails or documents. I think the Board is meeting now,"

"Tanya needs someone to talk to whom she can trust to give her team the true lay of the land, to identify the right people to get to the bottom of what actually happened, and where, and what, the options are to fix it."

"I'm not an expert on technology, but of course I'll help. All of us want this mess behind us as soon as possible."

"Thank you, Mr. Schofield," Prescott said. "We should be there in about ten minutes, and I look forward to meeting you."

When the first large bus pulled up in the West Wing driveway, the president and his team were waiting, along with several members of the press.

The door opened and one by one the Executive Order detainees came down the steps. The president greeted each one with a handshake and an apology. They were mostly men, and from their dress it was clear that they came from different ethnic backgrounds.

After meeting the president, each one was given a large envelope with further travel details and shown into the Press Briefing Room, where, as soon as the second bus arrived, the president wanted to say a few words to all of them, and then send them home to their families.

Richard Sullivan was the tenth detainee to exit the bus. With a huge smile he heartily shook his friend's hand, and then he and Janet embraced for a long kiss and a longer hug. Finally he turned to Tom, and there was another hug.

"Thanks for sprigin' me, though I didn't know you'd have to upend the whole government to do it."

Tom laughed. "Anything for you, Dad."

Richard turned to Janet. "How is Robert?"

"They think they've saved his arm, though he'll probably lose some function. He wants to see you—us."

"Yes. I'm free this afternoon. You?"


With guidance from Diane and Tom, the president's transition team grew and split into more sub-groups, and by that afternoon they had drafts of 100 Day Priorities and key Cabinet members circulating.

Tom left them at about two and took an official car with a driver out to Joint Base Andrews. He was on the tarmac when the C-17 taxied up.

The forward door opened and the internal stairs extended. Callie waved from inside but then stepped aside so that Erin could be the first off.

Tom, not sure exactly what to expect, smiled broadly and took her hand on the stairs. She immediately hugged him tightly and said into his ear, "I'm so glad I'm home. Would life with you always be this crazy?"

He pulled back, smiling. "I'm not sure. Yes, probably."

Callie was next down the stairs. He helped her. They embraced. "You guys did a great job," Tom said.

"No, all these folks did." She turned as Alexei, his wife, and their team members descended and joined them on the tarmac.

The two men shook hands and then embraced. "Thank you, Alexei, for everything. They're ready inside to begin processing the forms you'll need, and you have reservations at a hotel in D.C. Tonight we have something special planned."

"We're in your hands."

"I'll take you ladies into town," Tom said.

"No, you and Erin go ahead," Callie replied. "I'll be sure Alexei's group gets going, and then I'll try to find my new office again to tell them about the last few days."

Tom nodded, picked up Erin's bag, and soon the two of them were in the back seat of the car, headed to Erin's apartment.

Sitting together, Tom reached for Erin's hand, and they turned toward each other.

"Monday night seems like about half my life ago," Erin said. "What a trip, and what great people."

"Your experience and insights made it possible."

She shook her head and smiled. "No. Callie and Alexei did the hard work."

Now he smiled. "You all did. But you were our American-in-charge on the technical side who could verify and explain what Alexei's team found. Without your confirmation, Seth and The Network would never have run with it. I'm so proud of you—OK, all of you."

They rode on in silence for a few moments. "Tom, the most important thing—and I don't fully understand it, yet—is that yesterday, with Callie's help, I asked God to forgive me for all I've done, and for Jesus to be my Savior. Forever." She almost laughed. "It's crazy—whatever you and she and Alexei have, I wanted it. And now I do—Him. Peace. Joy. Callie's amazing, and she says she has lots of other believer friends who'll help me. I have *so* much more to figure out and to understand, but I know now that He's in charge of that, too. And that's why, no, we're not going to kill this baby and, yes, if you'll still have me, we're getting married. Hopefully soon."

Tom was almost speechless. Finally he said, "Erin, that's incredible. I've been thinking about and praying for you and our baby the whole time you've been gone. What a wonderful answer! I just hope I'll be a decent husband and father."

She leaned over, and they kissed. "I think you'll probably do all right. And I suspect that God and I will let you know."

What began as a plan for the two of them to meet Tom's father soon grew, partly because of Janet's new Secret Service requirements, into a special request to cordon off the back of the Carpathian Restaurant for a private gathering.

After his father arrived that morning, Tom had asked Patrick Tomlinson for help, and emailed him a list. The result was an exceptional turnout of friends to welcome Richard and the Cypriot Team to D.C.

By design, Tom, Erin and his parents arrived thirty minutes early.

"Dad, meet Erin. I'm very happy to tell you and Mom that she's agreed to marry me!"

They all hugged, asked questions, and began to talk about Pastor Ludwig, whom Richard and Janet had just visited, Richard's detention, Cyprus, and the new Administration, when others started arriving.

Gary Thornton, his wife, Patrick and Katherine, Susan and her husband, Callie, Kristen, Robert Ludwig's wife, Seth and Natalie, Tanya Prescott and her husband, Clayton and Andrea, Ahmad and Mariam were all there, standing and talking around their tables, when Alexei and his team arrived. The Americans clapped and offered them a warm welcome.

Two hours later the food, drink and conversation threatened to run late, and Janet said to Tom and Erin, "This is absolutely wonderful. But we have so much to do, starting early at the White House. Enjoy yourselves, and we hope to see you there."

"Thank you for coming—it means so much to everyone. You know, I invited Emily and Logan, and I wish they'd come."

"Maybe someday, dear. I hope so. I'll reach out to her. Thank you again. Good night for now."


The Oval Office was, as usual, almost dark before midnight. The new president and First Lady had decided to stay one more night at Blair House, so that the staff could complete the personal transition. But it was not just physically dark.

When the generals and key sector leaders cautiously approached through the walls, they found Satan himself, surrounded by six huge, menacing princes, hovering above the Resolute Desk.

"Come in," he ordered. "I have much to tell you."

Balzor, Bespor and Nepravel did their best to remain near the back, out of Satan's sightline, fearful of what he might do to those who had failed.

"The Council and I have listened today to reports from Generals Temno, Legat and others on Prince Proklor's plan to control this nation and stop virtually any mention of Him throughout the world.

"We've determined that his plan failed because it relied too much on the government, for imposing controls when the people were not ready. Proklor and Bradshaw were correct that the end is close—but they moved too soon.

"Instead of imposing controls on these people, we must make the people long for the controls themselves! After decades of work in this nation's education, entertainment, media, and, yes, even some churches and many laws, we are close. His name, truth and power are almost never publicly proclaimed, much less revered.

"But some families continue to teach their children about Him, and some people still tell others, mostly in private. When all that stops, the majority, who will never have heard of Him, will beg for controls to silence the very few.

"And we now have the power to do this, thanks, as always, to their technology—their screens. Social media. And their new Artificial Intelligence. Just like we did in education and entertainment decades ago, we must now be sure that only humans who listen to us make decisions about what is included in 'intelligence'.

"None of them can tell now whether a human or a machine is speaking to them. If we control the content on all the machines, and always portray Him and His followers as irrational, hateful and privileged, soon no human will want anything to do with Him. And, most importantly, no human will be able to change what everyone agrees is 'intelligent,' because there will be only one 'true intelligence'—ours!"

"So, keep up your work in all our home areas, but also turn your focus to every use they make of Artificial Intelligence, particularly in their communication. If we control the decision makers, it won't be artificial—it will be purposeful!

"This shouldn't take long. Businesses and the military will follow what everyone agrees is the intelligent approach to any issue. 'Don't question the Science!' And *we* will define that intelligence.

"Let the others control the government for a few years. It won't matter. When we control what everyone believes to be true, the government will have no choice but to do what the people will soon demand. No one will have to steal an election. They will *demand* that their government silence *His* 'lies'. What a day that will be!

"Prince Temno, are you willing to lead what should be the final chapter for this nation, or should we look elsewhere?"

The prince was surprised, but he recovered. "Yes, yes my Liege. I will lead our forces."

"Then bring the other generals and come with us to The Council. The rest of you, be ready. Tomorrow you will have new orders."

The area under the Resolute Desk opened, and within a loud, dark vortex The Prince of Lies and his key leaders descended.

When they were gone, Balzor looked at Bespor and Nepravel, who were clearly relieved. He nodded. "We're still here. And the new plan sounds good."

"We have some studying to do, to be ready," Nepravel said. "I can think of several of my charges in technology who need immediate promotions."

# Saturday, November 14

Tom walked Erin up to her apartment a little after midnight. They stood outside her door.

"What a wonderful night," she said. "Your father is amazing, and I really like your sister Susan. It's so crazy to think that without them, Patrick wouldn't be here. And then, I guess, we wouldn't be standing here."

He smiled. "Yes. Very thin threads, but threads which He wove together. In the coming years, when we're tempted to worry about anything, we've got to remind each other about this week, and this night."

She came close. "We will. I promise."

They kissed.

"I'm supposed to be back at The White House early to keep planning. Try to get there about eleven."

"See you then."

They kissed again, and Tom left to let Beau out.


The two couples were exhausted by the events of the last few days and the long flight, but they'd been able to get some sleep on Drew Boswell's personal Gulfstream. Now they sat across from each other in comfortable chairs, sipping flutes of champagne, as the plane circled to land on the Boswells' private island in The Maldives.

Drew raised his glass. "Here's to the judge who thought $1 million was an extraordinary amount for bail, not just a cost of doing business."

The former president smiled. "Yes, and to friends with houses in safe places."

"Not just a house," Sally Boswell corrected. "An island. Margaret, you're going to enjoy decorating the wing where you'll be staying, along with the three new cottages."

Henry Bradshaw sighed. "Yes, we could be here quite a while."

Drew tapped his knee, not seeing Nenav between them. "But probably not. The right-wing nut jobs have won a round, and they'll think they're in charge for a year or two. But we've spent decades filling the government, the media and big corporations with smart, progressive people who won't go along with their stupid, oppressive ideas. They'll push back. And we've got all that data, and Artificial Intelligence. We'll confuse the hell out of them."

"Thanks, Drew. Our son started the process of wiring funds from all the dummy corporations you set up for us years ago to accept the offshore money. It'll take a few days." He smiled. "What a great idea that was, my friend. All that money's just been sitting there, bidin' it's time until we needed it."

Drew nodded. "After another election there'll be a new president, new 'facts' uncovered, and certainly a pardon. Henry, you needed a break anyway to write your book about your vision for America, and with the communications set-up we've got here, you can stay in touch with everyone, just like I will. Think of it as an all-expenses-paid vacation."

Henry looked at Margaret and smiled. "Sounds good, Drew. Really good."

Drew took another sip, put his flute down, and looked at his friend. "So long as all the power is concentrated in D.C., where the best people like us can know, help and support each other, no matter what—-social justice will ultimately prevail. What can stop us?"


Everyone from the previous evening's party and many more were invited to be the guests of the new president at the White House that morning.

It was a beautiful, clear day, and at eleven-thirty they assembled on the South Portico, facing the Ellipse and the Washington Monument on the Mall. Tom, Erin, and his family were gathered by the railing and watched the large number of people entering the park and The Mall, many carrying blankets and lunch baskets.

The president spoke briefly about the focus of his Administration on individual liberty and responsibility, smaller government, and weaving

God's truth into every aspect of daily life, believing that the right laws would then follow.

"God says His Word will not return to Him void, but it's our responsibility to speak His Word to our family, friends, colleagues and neighbors. I hope you'll join me in practicing that now at our Day of Discussion on the Mall. We need healing, not division. We need discussion, not name calling. We need empowerment, not victimization. I invite you to go out, find people you don't know, listen and engage them with His truth. Who knows what friends we might make, and what seeds we might plant."

He prayed, and then he, the First Lady, his team, and their guests went downstairs and out of the White House in all directions, fanning out in pairs to join what were now many thousands, all gathered to mark the new beginning.

While the press focused on the president, the rest of them walked on. Tom and Erin went south to the Mall, which was full of blankets, lawn chairs, and people. They immediately came across a young man and woman carrying a homemade sign which read, "It's My Body—I'll decide!"

Tom smiled and put out his hand. "Hi. I'm Tom Sullivan, and this is my fiancée, Erin MacNeil..."

# Afterword to Four Novels

At almost age seventy-six, I hope you will indulge me in a slightly expanded Afterword for *Nation On The Edge*, since, if it takes me several years to write each novel, God might reassign me before I finish the next one!

In 1992 I was forty-five and had, by the grace of God, been a believer for eight years. That summer I prayed regularly for guidance and wisdom for what He wanted me to do with what I imagined to be the last half of my time on Earth.

My wife told me I should write a book, which seemed far-fetched for a real estate guy. Then that fall, when I got the general idea for a family in trouble without God's leadership and started typing the story forming in my head, I doubted I would ever finish. But *On The Edge* poured out of me over four months, and, with no agent or introduction, Thomas Nelson in Nashville, the nation's largest Christian publisher, published it!

While not being autobiographical, I wanted the book to capture the spiritual conflict for each individual's soul in that family, and apparently my totally amateur style somehow deeply touched quite a few readers. One wrote that he would not be alive but for reading the book. Another read it straight through overnight and broke up with his "other woman" the next morning. Another said she hated it so much that she threw it up against the wall, and that felt so good, she picked it up and threw it against the wall again!

In those days it took a year to publish a new novel, so in early 1993 my wife told me I should next write "a book about the government." Across two years of writing came *The President*, which Multnomah published. I tried to tackle the biggest issues of the day by weaving them around a story which would keep the reader's interest. I was shocked a few years later that several people had copied the State of the Union Address as a stand-alone on the internet, and that a church in Texas had written a Bible Study based on the novel! Even today, I have to say that parts of *The President* still read like today's newspaper, which is not about me, but about Him.

Of course I wasn't writing in a vacuum—I still today have a career in commercial real estate, and we raised five wonderful children who thankfully mostly take after their mother. We've been active at Church of the Apostles (www.apostles.org[1]) in Atlanta for over three decades, and much of my real estate work at various times took place in Russia. So writing was not always easy.

In the early 2000's I turned to short stories, each with a pointed message. Those became *Ten Lies and Ten Truths,* which, with the help of our graphic designer son, we published ourselves in 2005.

At that same time I began to worry about the increasingly dangerous impact big government and big tech corporations, working together, could have on all our lives and freedoms. Particularly if a large tech enterprise was secretly the front for a CEO-jihadist, bent on destroying our country. Unlike the first two novels, *Enemy In The Room* took six years to finish, and we published it in 2013.

In 2010 I started a blog at the intersection of faith, economics and policy, and it's still going strong. www.parkerhudson.com/blog[2]. I've enjoyed the discipline of writing a monthly nonfiction article about a current topic across those years.

All of this is a long introduction to how I came to write *Nation On The Edge.*

First, in the intervening years I continued to read, study and pray about spiritual warfare. I read all the Biblical passages on the subject, as well as several excellent books. The best and most relevant books are ***Conquer***[3] by Dr. Michael Youssef (www.ltw.org[4]) and ***Sense & Nonsense About Angels & Demons***[5] by Ken Boa and Robert Bowman, Jr. (www.kenboa.org). I strongly recommend both books.

---

1.      http://www.apostles.org/

2.      http://www.parkerhudson.com/blog

3.      *https://store.ltw.org/p-148-conquer-your-battle-plan-for-spiritual-victory-book.aspx*

4.      http://www.ltw.org/

5.      *https://kenboa.org/product/sense-and-nonsense-about-angels-and-demons/*

My key conclusion is that we are not passive observers of a spiritual battle between demons and angels. Nor are we the passive victims of all-powerful demonic forces. *We are the actual combatants*—the war is waged by believers against the lies of the demons for the souls of our families and friends. For their eternities. God gives all of us free will. We are to choose. As believers, it is our incredibly important role to do all we can to ensure that those whom we know and love choose God's Truth.

So I wanted to revisit a story which included angels and demons visible to the reader, as they were in *On The Edge*, but with a deeper understanding of the demons' hate for us, and of their methods for deceiving so many of us. Along with the power of prayer and believers' witnessing to overcome those lies.

It seemed natural to consider an update to *On The Edge*, moving Tommy Sullivan and the other characters ahead by twenty or so years, to see where they might have wound up.

Second, while studying the craft of fiction writing, I learned that authors today need one or more "series," because readers like to return to books in a series. Oops. No one mentioned that in the 90's, and I had three stand-alone novels, not a series.

But I also had several characters across the three stories who, with a little twisting here and there, I thought could bring their backgrounds to this new story, without the earlier novels being a requirement for understanding. So Callie Sawyer, the young woman in *Enemy In The Room*, became one of the female leads here. And of course Kristen Holloway, the other woman in *On The Edge*, continues to radiate the joy of Christian forgiveness and redemption.

The theme for the new story would expand on the last two novels to show, with supercharged demonic intervention, the ever-increasing power of our ever-increasing government to turn us away from the core foundations of our faith and our freedoms.

And so in 2015 I imagined a story in which the government clamps down "temporarily" on our freedoms in order to protect us from attacks. I started doing research on high-tech, large-scale surveillance and security. But, as always, I needed interesting human story threads to weave around the truths which I hoped to make clear. And I needed characters and a setting to provide the framework for the story itself.

One of our sons had moved to Washington, D.C., and when we visited him it struck me that so many relatively young people appear to have so much power and influence, primarily because they are everywhere and in everything. Compared to burned out or skeptical 40-year-olds, the younger crowd is generally super-confident, progressive and hard working. So I imagined Tom Sullivan with an important position in that world, and the human story lines developed from there.

Except for *On The Edge*, I am clearly a slow writer. In an industry where some authors turn out four or more novels a year, I've managed to write four in thirty years. And I'm not an Outliner—I'm a Discovery Writer. While at times frustrating, this slower, more organic approach allows me to listen to other voices—hopefully His—to figure out what should happen next, how, and to whom.

From that early research with several experts in 2015-2016, as I began writing, the stories and characters for conveying the truths took shape over the next couple of years.

But then Covid-19 hit, and I am so thankful that I had not just published this novel, because it would have instantly been out of date. Actions I had imagined earlier which the government might take suddenly became common, and so I had to re-imagine even stricter measures.

As I write this in the early summer of 2023, the work of discovering what He wants written in this novel appears to be finished, though the war depicted continues to rage, and the issues which impact us become ever crazier, as some in power regularly hold up an orange and swear to us that it's an apple. And if we don't agree that it's an apple, we must be silenced—cancelled—before we harm others with our "phobic" truths.

So the war is really eternal, and we are right now privileged to speak Truth to those in our generation. Hopefully each of us will answer His call to do so.

Over these eight years of writing *Nation On The Edge* I have been helped by many, many good people, in large and small ways. Two main groups added a lot at the beginning—experts in technical issues, and those working in various government positions. Denis Gushcha, Kevin Sandlin, Jim Hudson, Tim Turner and Kayli Westling each contributed to my understanding. Many others, perhaps for obvious reasons, did not want to be named, but I thank them just as sincerely. Of course none of them is responsible for my mistakes or misunderstandings.

Most of the historic quotes at the beginning of each chapter come from the curated research at a wonderful Christian resource—WallBuilders, and, specifically, from their book *Original Intent* by David Barton. I have recommended their splendid work for several decades. www.wallbuilders.com[6].

I am blessed with a great group of Beta Readers who volunteered to read earlier versions of the manuscript and then gave really helpful input for increased clarity. I want to thank Zanese Duncan, Kathy Paparelli, Bick Cardwell, Scot Sinnen, Bill Honaker, Carla Smith, Denetra Mitchell, Janis Chapman, Stan Carder, and Margot and Currell Berry for giving so many hours to help in this way.

The editing team at Adriel Wiggins Author Services and Consulting had great ideas to improve the story's flow and to enhance the characters. www.adrielwiggins.com[7]. A deep thanks to you all.

And it was a joy to work again with our son Marshall on the cover—he has now redone all our covers to give them a coordinated and current look. www.marshallhudson.com[8].

I would be remiss if I did not also thank three Brits who have had an incredibly positive impact over many years on all of us who imagine that we are, or might someday be, authors. They are Joanna Penn of www.thecreativepenn.com[9]. And Mark Dawson and James Blatch of www.selfpublishingformula.com[10]. If you have the urge to write—fiction or nonfiction, and in any genre—check out these gifted and unselfish experts.

---

6.    http://www.wallbuilders.com/

7.    http://www.adrielwiggins.com/

8.    http://www.marshallhudson.com

9.    http://www.thecreativepenn.com

10.    http://www.selfpublishingformula.com

So if this is *the* eternal war for the souls of our nearest and dearest family and friends, and if you and I are followers of Jesus, then are we in the battle, or are we merely observers? Specifically, what gifts has He given each of us which He wants us to bring to the fight?

If you're not sure, I suggest two questions. What are you good at? And what do you enjoy? If He wants you to be a plumber, he'll give you a wrench, not a hammer. What gifts has He given you? He gave these to you for a purpose. His purpose.

I'm a clear example of Him combining a very imperfect man with His gift of writing to touch many hearts and minds for His purpose.

But there are as many gifts as there are unique people.

What is your gift? Hospitality? Service? Parenting? Teaching? Protecting? Comforting? Encouraging? Mentoring? Fundraising? Constructing? Coaching?

What are you good at? And what do you enjoy?

He uses us all the time for His purpose. Sometimes He raises the curtain just a bit so we get a glimpse of what He's up to. That happened to me in the first year after *On The Edge* came out, when I was working for a time in Moscow. I heard from a friend that American missionaries in Eastern Russia were encouraged by reading my book and were using it in their outreach!

It occurred to me that only God could use an illiterate servant in an Egyptian household seventy years ago to instill the scripture in a boy who had been scheduled for abortion, but who instead miraculously wound up in Atlanta as a young pastor at a church, preaching God's Word to a large congregation, one of whom was a real estate guy who was so touched by the preaching that he wrote a book about how God had transformed him, and that book wound up encouraging missionaries in Siberia!

When you see those kinds of dots connected, you know that it has not very much to do with you, and everything to do with Him.

Satan's forces continue to lie and to deceive people all around us, to lead them to an eternity without God. What are we doing with the gifts He's given us to counter those lies and to save our loved ones?

What are you good at? What do you enjoy? Use those questions to find your gift(s), and then join the battle.

# ALSO BY PARKER HUDSON

On The Edge
ISBN 978-0-9666614-0-8
Edge Press, LLC

As I read the last chapter of *On The Edge*, I found my heart so full of the Holy Spirit that I thought I would explode. When I closed the book for the last time, I realized that I was crying....I cannot tell you how this book has changed my life and my husband's.

Lori Wells

I finished your book *On The Edge* a few months ago and reflect on its content often. I can honestly say that no novel has ever had as much real and emotional effect on me. I find myself praying more....The final few pages put me in the presence of God...I finished those pages overcome with emotion and sobbing with joy.

Jim Ezell

Available at ParkerHudson.com[1]

---

1. http://www.ParkerHudson.com/

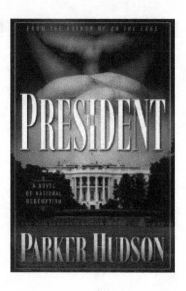

The President
ISBN 978-0-9968665-4-5
Edge Press, LLC

If I had a vote, *The President* would immediately move to the top of the best seller list.

Earle B. May, Jr.

I just finished *The President* after being unable to put it down for the past six days. It is a great book!

Phyllis Trail

Having just completed your second novel, *The President*, I can truly say that it is a masterpiece thematic presentation of the relationship between God, mankind and the force of evil in our lives. Like Grisham, it opens with a Wow and keeps on building.

John M. Stone

It is a riveting novel which was faith-building, historically factual, eye opening and challenging to me as a Christian.

Eric Hofer

...*The President* really overwhelmed me. It is possibly the most powerful book I've ever read.

Lee A. Catts

Of hundreds of books read in my life this is the first time I have ever written to an author to say, 'Well done and Amen!'

Sylvia Westrom

Available at ParkerHudson.com[2]

---

2. http://www.ParkerHudson.com/

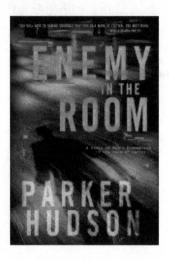

Enemy In The Room
ISBN 978-0-9666614-3-9
Edge Press, LLC

"Having read *The President* and *On the Edge*, I was really looking forward to *Enemy in the Room*. I was not disappointed. In fact, I could not put the book down. Many of the situations and characters could have been plucked from the front pages of our newspapers. The story, while complex, is believable and thought-provoking. I found the moral lessons in the book very insightful and truthful. In my opinion, considering the struggles we now face as a nation, this book is both timely and crucial. It is a 'must read.'"

Trudy Coble

"I could relate to every element of the story. The book gets five stars. I loved the conversations. The ending is exciting. I recommend this book to everyone."

Kathy Paparelli

Available at ParkerHudson.com[3]

3. http://www.ParkerHudson.com/

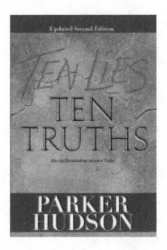

Ten Lies and Ten Truths
ISBN 978-0-9968665-0-7
Edge Press, LLC

"My sense is—most people today don't want to be challenged to think. If that describes you, don't read this book! But if you enjoy being confronted with new perspectives, and truly desire to know the truth—this book is for you."

Jim Reimann

"The book shows the power of fiction to draw the reader into a topic by touching the heart as well as the mind. Hudson's purpose is to break up the concrete around "truths" that people believe without thinking, or without considering the consequences, and he succeeds in a way that keeps the reader turning pages. 'Parable' may be too strong a comparison, but Hudson certainly confirms that fiction can teach truth in a powerful and memorable way."

Dr. Ted Baehr

Available at ParkerHudson.com[4]

---

4. http://www.ParkerHudson.com/

[1] The "Golden Triangle of Freedom," from Os Guinness, *A Free People's Suicide*.

[2] Ephesians 6:10-17. New International Version

[3] [Paul David Tripp. *New Morning Mercies*. November 30th

9 780996 866569